# THE CHILDREN'S
# TREASURE HOUSE
# OF STORIES

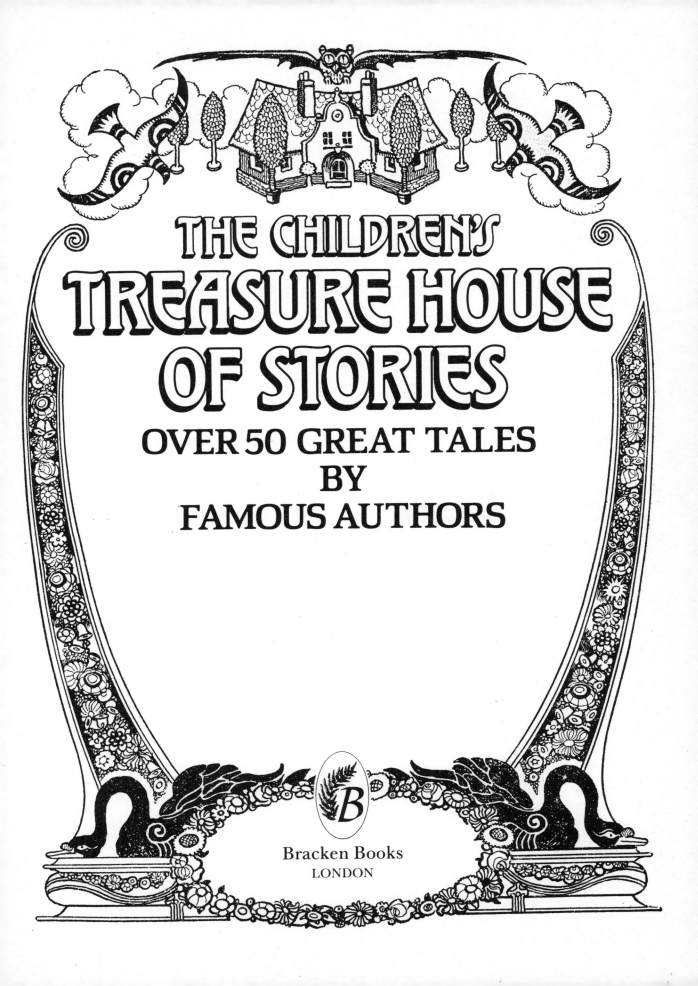

# THE CHILDREN'S TREASURE HOUSE OF STORIES

## OVER 50 GREAT TALES
## BY
## FAMOUS AUTHORS

Bracken Books
LONDON

*First published 1937.*

*This edition is published by Bracken Books,*
*a division of Bestseller Publications Ltd,*
*Brent House, 24–28 Friern Park,*
*North Finchley, London N12 9DA in 1986.*

*ISBN 1 85170 036 6*

*Printed and bound by Kultura, Hungary.*

# CONTENTS

# COLOUR ILLUSTRATIONS

# INTRODUCTION

When I was a small boy I used to go and stay with my grandmother who lived in the Lake District. There was a small hill at the back of her house which you could climb in about ten minutes. We always used to walk up this hill because when you reached the top you had the most marvellous view. In the north you could see the great mountains, Scafell, Helvellyn, Langdale Pikes; to the south-east you could see the Pennine ridge which runs like a backbone down the centre of England and at your feet there was the great expanse of Morecambe Bay stretching out to the sea with the winding silver threads of the rivers slowly entering at its head.

I don't know if you have ever been to the top of a hill like that but if you have you will know what I am talking about. This book is rather like that hill. You need only take a short walk, a few minutes to read a few pages and you will find many wonderful things inside. If you want to settle down for a good hour then there are some fine stories for you. They are the great hills of the book. *Lorna Doone* is one of them, it is a lovely, stirring tale: *The Boyhood of David Copperfield* is another. *David Copperfield*, is by the famous Victorian novelist, Charles Dickens. It is a wonderful book but it is very, very long. Only the first part has been included and it has been shortened and retold to make it easier for you to read. It is very sad in places but it ends happily and is full of characters. Another exciting adventure is *The Great Stone Face* by the famous American writer Nathaniel Hawthorne. He wrote many fine stories and this is one of his best. You will also find extracts written by many of the greatest names in English literature: George Borrow, Henry Longfellow, Mrs Gaskell, Oliver Goldsmith, Charles Kingsley, Sir Walter Scott and Charlotte Bronte. Don't think that because they wrote 'classics' they are boring writers. They aren't. I hope that you enjoy the short pieces in this book and you can then go on to read some of the longer books they wrote.

But there are many, many more modern writers and many, many types of story for you to find. You can read some of Aesop's *Fables*, written over two thousand years ago; you can read some of the famous fairy tales written by Hans Christian Andersen and The Brothers Grimm; there are stories for the very young and some for those of you who are a bit older. All in all this book contains nearly 450 pages and over 200,000 words. I can't tell you the *exact* number because I haven't counted every single one but it is certainly a lot of words. If you want to know how to work out the number of words in a book very quickly then write and ask me and I'll tell you how it is done. I will also suggest one or two other books that you might like to read.

Good reading

YOUR EDITOR

# THE BOYHOOD OF
# DAVID COPPERFIELD

### *by* CHARLES DICKENS

*Retold by Stuart Campbell*

## CHAPTER I

### A CHANGE IN MY LIFE

I NEVER knew my father, after whom I was named David Copperfield. He died some months before I was born.

Thus, my earliest recollections are filled by my widowed mother and her devoted maid, Clara Peggotty. Peggotty we always called her, because her Christian name was the same as my mother's.

While life lasts, a picture of my mother will ever be printed on my memory. She was so small and slender, and had such pretty fair hair, that she seemed more of a fairy than a mortal when standing beside Peggotty. For Peggotty was stout and strong, and had a big red face from which sparkled two bright eyes as dark as those of a gipsy.

We lived in a rambling old house called the Rookery, in the Suffolk village of Blunderstone. In the summer I spent most of my time in the big garden, helping to pick fruit or to feed the chickens, or else chasing the butterflies which fluttered over the flowers.

Perhaps my happiest memories, though, are of the long winter evenings when we sat by the fire in our cosy parlour. Peggotty, who was treated more as one of the family than a servant, would busy herself with her sewing, while my mother patiently taught me to read and write, and to do my sums. During these lessons, I fear that my glance often wandered to the tiny box, shaped like a thatched cottage, in which Peggotty kept her yard measure. Or to her workbox, the sliding lid of which was adorned with a picture of St. Paul's Cathedral, complete with a pink dome.

I was about eight years old when the first cloud came, which I recall, to shadow my happiness. My mother began to go out a good deal alone, seldom returning until quite late. I missed her so much that I would beg Peggotty to let me sit up until she came home, but many times I fell asleep over the book I was reading, and had to be carried to bed.

Then, one evening, my mother came back quite early, accompanied by a gentleman with hair and whiskers of the jettest black.

" My dear," said my mother, stooping to kiss me, " this is Mr. Murdstone, who has come to see you."

" And this is Davy, eh ? " remarked Mr. Murdstone, in the deepest voice I had ever heard. " How do you do, old fellow ? "

I stood and stared at him dumbly, for at first sight I had taken a strange but instant dislike to our visitor.

" Come along, Davy, won't you be friends ? " he laughed. " Let us shake hands as a start."

My right hand was holding my mother's, so I offered the other.

" Why, that's the wrong hand, Davy," objected Mr. Murdstone.

My mother tried to push my right hand forward, but I stubbornly held it back, so that in the end Mr. Murdstone had to take the left one. He was still smiling, but in his eyes I caught an expression which made me shrink.

After that day, Mr. Murdstone was constantly visiting our house, so that in time I became used to his presence. My first dislike of him persisted, however, and I felt certain that Peggotty shared my feelings. For although she never spoke a word against him to me, I saw how she kept out of his way.

Things seemed so different that I almost jumped for joy when Peggotty asked me if I would care to go with her to Yarmouth, for a fortnight's holiday. I had never been to the seaside, and I thought that here was a chance to escape from Mr. Murdstone for a while.

" But we can't leave mother here alone, Peggotty," I protested.

" Bless you, boy, but she won't be here," Peggotty replied. " Didn't she tell you she was going away herself for a fortnight ? "

That being so, I had no objection to going with Peggotty.

A few days later, we climbed into the carrier's cart which was to carry us to Yarmouth, and I waved my handkerchief until I could no longer see my mother standing at our gate.

We stayed with Peggotty's brother, who was a fisherman. His house was to me as wonderful as an Aladdin's palace, for it consisted of a boat the size of a barge, and it stood on the shore high beyond reach of the sea. A tall iron chimney rose above it, while a door had been cut in the side. Within, the rooms were small but clean and cosy.

With Mr. Peggotty lived a little niece of almost my own age, whose father had been drowned at sea. Emily and I played all day on the sands or paddled in the water ; then at night, Mr. Peggotty would spin yarns of his life as a sailor. But when bedtime came, and I climbed into the bunk in my own little cabin, my thoughts would go to my mother. More and more I longed to see her again, so that I was really glad when Peggotty and I at last set out on our homeward journey.

How slow that journey seemed. Our horse must have been the laziest in the world, the way he shuffled along with his head down. And instead of whipping him to a smarter pace, Mr. Barkis, the carrier, just whistled or appeared to doze.

At length, however, I began to recognise familiar landmarks, and knew we were getting near home. Excited though I was, I now became aware that Peggotty kept shooting strange glances towards me.

I was puzzling over her manner when our house came into view, its red walls and latticed windows half-hidden by the elm trees in front.

My impatience would hardly allow me to wait for Peggotty to climb from the cart and collect her numerous parcels. I ran on before her to knock at the door.

When the door opened, I was taken aback. Instead of my mother, it was a strange servant who faced me.

" Hasn't my mother come home yet ? " I quavered, turning to Peggotty.

" Yes, of course she is home," replied Peggotty. " Wait a bit, Master Davy, and I'll—I'll tell you some news."

Her obvious uneasiness frightened me.

" What is the matter, Peggotty ? " I asked, as she took me by the hand and led me through to the kitchen.

" Nothing is the matter, Master Davy, bless you," she answered, trying to laugh, but looking more like tears.

" But why didn't mother greet us at the door ? " I persisted. " She— she isn't dead, is she ? "

" Bless me, of course she's not ! " Peggotty said. " You see, Master Davy, I should have explained things before, but I haven't been able to bring myself to do it."

" What do you mean, Peggotty ? " I demanded.

" I ought to have told you, Master Davy, that you've got a father," she said, untying her bonnet with fingers that shook.

" But my father is dead ! " I replied.

" This—this is a new father," Peggotty explained. " Come along and see him, Master Davy."

" I don't want to see him," I said, feeling dazed at the news.

" But you want to see your mother, don't you ? " asked Peggotty.

At that I took her hand, and she took me to the best parlour. On one side of the fire sat my mother, on the other—Mr. Murdstone.

I came to a sudden halt as I realised the truth. My new father was the man I had disliked and feared the first moment I saw him.

## CHAPTER II

### MY STEPFATHER

At sight of me, my mother dropped a book and rose hurriedly, but a little timidly as I thought.

" Now, Clara, my dear," said Mr. Murdstone gruffly, " recollect my advice. Control yourself, always control yourself. Well, Davy, how do you do ? "

I gave him my hand, then, after a moment of suspense, went and kissed my mother. She kissed me, patted me gently on the shoulder, then sat down again with her book.

I could not look at my mother, nor at Mr. Murdstone, because I knew he was watching us both. I turned to the window and stood looking out. Everything looked cold and grim under the lowering grey sky.

As soon as I could I crept upstairs, only to find that I had been moved out of my own little bedroom, into another that seemed bleak and cheerless. Feeling utterly miserable, I curled myself up in the counterpane, and cried myself to sleep.

I was awakened by somebody saying, " Here he is ! "

Opening my eyes, I saw my mother and Peggotty bending over me.

" What is the matter, Davy ? " asked my mother.

" Nothing," I answered, but my trembling lips betrayed me.

" Davy," my mother cried. " Davy, my child ! "

*I knew he was watching us both.*

I could not speak, but turned my back on her to hide my tears. Upon which my mother turned and stamped her foot at Peggotty.

" This is your doing, Peggotty," she cried. " You have poisoned my boy's mind against me and the man I have wed."

" I have done nothing of the sort, Mrs. Copperfield," replied Peggotty sharply. " Whatever opinion of your new husband I may hold, I have never discussed him with Master Davy. And surely I would never say a word to turn the boy against his own mother."

Before my mother could say more, Mr. Murdstone entered the room. He walked straight to the bed and gripped my arm, so that I was forced to slip to the floor.

" Clara, have you forgotten my instructions ? " he said sternly. " Firmness is what you need, my dear, firmness."

" I am sorry, Edward," faltered my mother. " I meant to act as you advised, but—but I was upset."

"Indeed!" Mr. Murdstone ejaculated. "That is a bad beginning, Clara."

He drew her to him and whispered in her ear, then kissed her. My mother's head bowed on his shoulder, and I knew from that moment that he could bend her to his will, whatever he chose to do or say.

"Now go downstairs, my dear," said Mr. Murdstone, pushing her towards the door. "Davy and I will follow presently."

As soon as my mother had gone, he turned upon Peggotty.

"As for you, my friend," he snapped, "do you know your mistress's name?"

"I ought to, sir," retorted Peggotty, undaunted by his scowl. "She has been my mistress a long time."

"As I came upstairs," said Mr. Murdstone, "I thought I heard you address her by a name that is no longer hers. She is now Mrs. Murdstone, remember. Do not forget again."

Peggotty went out of the room without replying, but not without an uneasy glance at me.

When we were alone, my stepfather shut the door, and holding me before him, gazed steadily at me. I was compelled to meet his eyes, and could feel my heart beating from sudden fear of him.

"Davy," he said harshly, "if I have an obstinate horse or dog to deal with, what do you think I do?"

"I don't know," I whispered.

"I beat him," he told me. "I make him smart until he behaves as I wish him to. Remember that, and you may save yourself a lot of trouble. Now just wash your face and hands, then come with me."

Had I disobeyed him, I am sure that he would have knocked me down with his clenched fist. When I had washed, he gripped me firmly once more and led me down to my mother in the parlour.

"I don't think that this young man will upset you any more, Clara," he announced. "A few lessons will improve his behaviour immensely."

A kind word then from either him or my mother might have altered the whole of my life. But my mother looked too scared to speak to me, while my stepfather's glance remained cold and severe.

We three dined alone, for Peggotty was now banished to the kitchen with the new maid. During the meal I was hardly spoken to, but I learnt that an elder sister of Mr. Murdstone's was coming to stay with us, and that she was expected to arrive that evening.

Barely had Peggotty cleared the table than we heard a coach pull up at the front gate, and my stepfather went out to welcome his sister. As I followed with my mother, she halted in the dimly lit hall and gave me a quick embrace.

"I want you to love your new father, and to be obedient to him, Davy," she breathed, before letting go of me in great haste, as if she feared being caught displaying such tenderness.

Miss Murdstone was a gloomy-looking lady. She was dark like her brother, whom she much resembled in face and voice, and she had thick black eyebrows which almost met above her big nose. She had brought with her two black boxes, which had her initials on their lids in brass-headed nails. When she paid the coachman, she took the money from a steel purse, which she replaced in a very jail of a bag that hung from her arm by a heavy chain, and which shut with a snap like the closing of a trap. Everything about Miss Murdstone was hard and metallic, as I was to find her character to be.

After greeting my mother, she fixed her hard gaze upon me.

" Is this your boy, sister-in-law ? " she asked.

My mother nodded.

" Generally speaking," said Miss Murdstone, " I don't like boys. How d'ye do, my boy ? "

After so discouraging a greeting I could only mumble a reply, and Miss Murdstone turned from me with a sniff.

" His manners need attention," she declared.

Fortunately she soon asked to be shown her room, being tired after the long journey she had come. But to my dismay, Peggotty told me that her visit was not a temporary one. Miss Murdstone had come to stay, and to help my mother with the mangement of the house.

## CHAPTER III

### I FALL INTO DISGRACE

ON the very first morning after her arrival, Miss Murdstone was up at dawn, and prowling about as if to see that the servants did their work to her satisfaction. And breakfast over, she swooped down upon my mother.

" Clara, my dear," she said, " I am sure that you will make my brother an excellent wife in many ways. But I am equally sure that you lack the firmness to run a household as it should be done. As I am here to help you all I can, you will be good enough to let me have the keys to the cupboards and storeroom, so that I can attend to the ordering of everything in future."

My mother meekly obeyed, and the keys were placed in Miss Murdstone's jail of a bag, which she kept on her arm even at meals. Indeed, I wondered whether she wore it there when asleep.

After that, my mother had very little say in the running of her home. Miss Murdstone used to plan things with her brother as if my mother did not exist.

On the one occasion that she protested at not being consulted, both Miss Murdstone and her brother seemed astounded.

" Clara, I am surprised at you," said my stepfather sternly. " Can you not trust us to attend to affairs on your behalf ? "

" It is very hard that I should have no say in the running of my own house," protested my mother.

" Your own house ? " said Mr. Murdstone, frowning.

" Our own house, I should have said," replied my mother, tears in her eyes. " But I think I should have a voice in the planning of things. Peggotty will tell you that I managed very well previously."

Miss Murdstone rose from her chair.

" Edward," she said stiffly, " it is obvious that your wife has no gratitude for my efforts to make things easier for her. I can see that I am not wanted here, and I shall leave to-morrow."

*A long, vicious-looking cane it was.*

"Sit down, Jane Murdstone," said my stepfather. "As for you, Clara, I am surprised at you. When my sister puts herself out to the extent of coming here to assist you, you reward her with base ingratitude."

That was the end of my poor mother's resistance to the rule of Jane Murdstone and her brother.

Both of them were gloomy and unsmiling, both made firmness their rule of life. Neither of them knew the meaning of love or kindness, and neither had any thought for the feelings of others.

Before long they were discussing the need of sending me to a boarding-school, taking my mother's consent for granted. While the matter was being debated, my mother continued my lessons at home.

Once I had enjoyed those lessons, but it was different now. For Mr. and Mrs. Murdstone always sat in the room when I was at work, eager to jump upon every mistake that I made, and to insist upon my mother setting harder and ever harder tasks for me to do.

Their very presence seemed to cast a spell upon me, making me so nervous that I could do nothing right in the end.

Then one morning, when I marched into the parlour with my books, my mother met me with an anxious look. Beyond her I saw Miss Murdstone, frowning grimly, while my stepfather was busy binding the end of a cane. A long, vicious-looking cane it was, with which he swished the air as he saw me watching.

"I tell you, Clara," he said, "I have often been flogged myself."

"To be sure," nodded his sister.

"But—but do you think flogging does any good, Edward?" faltered my mother.

"Do you think it did me any harm, Clara?" Mr. Murdstone inquired sternly.

"Do you?" echoed his sister.

To this my mother could make no answer.

While I waited apprehensively, Mr. Murdstone stared coldly at me.

"Now, David," he said, swishing the cane again, "you had better try a little harder with your work to-day."

I had, as I thought, prepared my lessons better than usual for that morning, but Mr. Murdstone's cane seemed to have wiped away every word I had learnt. I could remember almost nothing of my history, nor of my geography, and went steadily from bad to worse.

At last we came to the test in mental arithmetic with which Mr. Murdstone himself always wound up the morning's work.

Usually it was cheeses of which I had to work out the price, but this time the sum dealt with canes. Before I could begin to work out an answer, my mother suddenly burst into tears.

"Clara!" snapped Miss Murdstone, warningly.

"I—I can't help it, Jane," sobbed my mother. "I am not well."

I saw my stepfather nod solemnly to his sister as he gripped his cane and stood up.

"We can hardly expect you to feel yourself, Clara," he said, "when this boy's laziness is such a trial to you. Perhaps a little firmness will work wonders with him. David, you will come upstairs with me."

As he led me towards the door, my mother jumped up as if to interfere. But Miss Murdstone caught her arm and held her back.

"Clara! Are you a perfect stupid?" she rapped.

I could hear my mother crying as we went up the stairs. Mr. Murdstone paraded very, very slowly towards my room, as if I give me longer to think of the punishment that lay before me.

Once in my bedroom, he twisted my head under his arm.

"Don't, Mr. Murdstone!" I cried. "Pray don't beat me! I've tried my best to learn, but I can't do my lessons when you and Miss Murdstone are standing over me."

"You can't, eh?" he grated. "Then you will have to learn!"

At the first merciless cut of the cane I went frantic with pain and anger. The hand by which he held my shoulder was only an inch from my mouth, and I buried my teeth in its flesh.

After that he was like a madman, and I almost believe he would have beaten me to death had not my cries reached those below. I heard the voices of my mother and of Peggotty on the stairs.

My stepfather flung me on the floor and left the room, turning the key after him.

It must have been an hour later before I crawled to my feet and saw my face in a mirror, all red and swollen from crying. It was a torture to move, because of the weals made by the cane, and I was possessed with dread when I remembered biting Mr. Murdstone. He would never forgive me, I realised, and I wondered what punishment would befall me for my act.

The house seemed dead quiet, and no one came near my room. Darkness had fallen before Miss Murdstone appeared with some food and milk, which she placed on a table without uttering a word. Then, after glaring at me once, she went out and locked the door again.

For five days I was kept a prisoner in my room, apart from being allowed to walk in the garden for half an hour each morning. During that time, the only person I saw was Miss Murdstone, who kept a grim watch upon me while I took my short spell of exercise. I felt like a condemned prisoner, and all the time my mind was tortured by imaginations of the fate which Mr. Murdstone had in store for me.

On the fifth night I was asleep in bed when I awoke with a start. I thought I had heard a voice call my name.

"Is that you, Peggotty?" I asked sitting up with a jerk.

"It is," came a muffled whisper. "Come to the door, Davy, so that we can speak through the keyhole. I don't want him or his sister to hear us talking."

"How is my mother, Peggotty?" I asked. "Is she very angry with me for biting Mr. Murdstone?"

"I don't think she is, Davy," Peggotty replied.

"What are they going to do with me?" I whispered.

"You are to be sent to a school near London, I think it is," came the answer. "You are going away to-morrow."

"Shan't I see mother before I go?" I anxiously inquired.

"Oh, yes, Master Davy," Peggotty assured me. "You'll see her in the morning."

There was a moment's pause, then Peggotty spoke again.

"Davy," she said, "I haven't been seeing so much of you since those Murdstones came to the house. It's not because I love you any less, Davy, but because I feared it might make things worse for you. If I had said anything those people didn't like, they'd have taken out their spite on you or your mother. But now you're going away from home, don't you ever forget old Peggotty. Write and let me know how you get on, and I'll write back to you."

"I'll never forget you, Peggotty," I promised.

Then I heard a stair creak as she went away.


## CHAPTER IV

### I LEAVE HOME

PEGGOTTY proved correct, for when Miss Murdstone brought my breakfast next morning she told me that I was to leave for school that day.

A little later, I was told to follow her downstairs, where I found my mother waiting in the parlour. She was very pale, and her red eyes told me she had been crying.

"Oh, Davy!" she cried, as I ran to her arms. "How could you hurt one whom I love? You must pray to be cured of your evil temper, Davy. I forgive you for what you did to your father, but I grieve to think you guilty of such a vicious act."

It was easy to see that my stepfather and his sister had persuaded her that all the fault lay upon my side, and that I was a wicked boy. So that she was grieving over my sin, rather than sorrowing at my going away. This knowledge hurt me almost as much as Mr. Murdstone's cane had done, and I crept to a chair to await the coming of the carrier.

It was a relief when at last I saw the van at the gate.

"Master Copperfield's box, please," called Miss Murdstone, who had been watching my mother and me all this while in silence.

I expected Peggotty to bring the box, but it was the new maid who appeared, and who gave the box to Mr. Barkis, the carrier.

Tears came to my mother's eyes afresh as I stood up to go, but Miss Murdstone was watchful still.

"Clara!" she warned. "Remember to control yourself. Be firm, both to yourself and others."

"I will, Jane," replied my mother meekly. "Good-bye, Davy. You are going away for your own good. When you come home for your holidays, I am sure that we shall find you a better boy."

I think she would have kissed me again, had not Miss Murdstone coughed meaningly at her back. Mr. Murdstone did not show himself, but his sister led me to the gate, where she expressed the hope that I would repent before I came to a bad end.

As the cart moved off I looked back, but Miss Murdstone had already gone into the house and shut the door. There was no sign of my mother at the parlour window, no Peggotty to wave me farewell, and I felt miserable enough to wish myself dead.

We had gone about half a mile when the carrier suddenly reined-up, and I saw Peggotty's stout figure squeezing through a gap in the hedge.

Climbing into the cart, she put her two big red arms about me, and gave me such a squeeze that I could hardly breathe. Then she dived into her deep pocket and brought out some paper bags full of cakes, which she placed beside me. Finally, after thrusting a small purse into my hand, she squeezed me tightly once more, climbed out of the cart, then ran off back along the road.

Not a word had Peggotty spoken the whole time, and I believe that she had burst nearly every button from her dress in hugging me so hard. Anyway, there were several lying on the floor of the cart, and I picked one up to carry as a keepsake of the dear old soul.

Mr. Barkis looked at me, as if to inquire whether Peggotty was coming back. I shook my head, and the carrier nodded, to save himself the trouble of speaking.

"Come up!" he grunted to his lazy horse, and we moved on.

Seeing Peggotty had cheered me immensely, and I now examined the little purse. It was a stiff new leather one, and it contained three bright shillings. But its most precious contents were two half-crowns, folded together in a small piece of paper. On the paper was written: "For Davy. With my love."

This sign of affection from my mother made my eyes misty again, but I felt it would be unmanly to cry in front of Mr. Barkis.

After we had jogged along for some time, I asked the carrier if he was taking me all the way.

"All the way where?" he inquired.

"To my school near London," I said.

"Why, young sir," he said, "that horse o' mine would be dead 'fore he covered half that distance. I be just going to Yarmouth, where I'm to put you down at the place where you'll catch the stage-coach."

Beginning to feel hungry, I opened one of Peggotty's bags of cakes. Out of politeness, I offered the bag to Mr. Barkis.

"Did she make them cakes?" he asked presently.

"Peggotty, do you mean?" I inquired.

"Ay, her," he replied.

"Yes, Peggotty made them," I said. "She makes all our pastry, and does all our cooking."

"Do she though?" he grunted.

He sat looking at his horse's ears as we crawled along.

"Nobody walks out with her?" he asked presently.

*"When you're writin' to her, young sir, p'r'aps you'd recollect to say that Barkis is willin'. Would you, now"?*

"With Peggotty?" I asked, not very sure of whom he was speaking.

"Ay, her," he said.

"Oh, no," I assured him. "Peggotty has never had a sweetheart."

"Hasn't she, though?" Mr. Barkis commented. "Well, now, I'll tell you what, young sir. Mebbe you'll be writing to her?"

"I certainly shall," I replied.

"Ah," he grunted. "Then when you're writin' to her, young sir, p'r'aps you'd recollect to say that Barkis is willin'. Would you, now?"

"That Barkis is willing," I repeated blankly. "Is that all?"

"Ye-es," he said, considering. "That's all. Barkis is willin'."

I could not understand the meaning of his message, but I repeated my promised to give it to Peggotty when I wrote.

It was afternoon when we reached Yarmouth, where Barkis turned into the courtyard of the coaching inn. The coach was already standing in the yard, shining in its new paint, but there were some hours to wait before the journey to London was due to start.

Barkis put my box down beside the coach, and handed me over to a lady who seemed to know all about me and my destination.

Orders had been given to provide me with a meal, and after I had eaten, I remembered about writing to Peggotty. The waiter got me pen and paper, for which I gave him one of my new shillings in payment. As he had been telling me that travelling gentlemen usually gave him a handsome tip, I told him he could keep any change there might be and felt myself to be quite a man.

My note was very short, but I did not forget Mr. Barkis's message.

"MY DEAR PEGGOTTY,—I have got here safe. Barkis is willing.
My love to mother.
"Yours affectionately, DAVY.

"P.S.—He particularly wants you to know—Barkis is willing."

My letter finished and sealed, I spent my time staring at the maps which lined the walls of the coffee room in place of pictures. At last I heard the clatter of horses' hoofs on the cobblestones of the yard, and soon afterwards there sounded the notes of a post-horn, to summon intending passengers to the London coach.

I ran out in such haste that I completely forgot to take with me the remainder of Peggotty's cakes.


# CHAPTER V

## I REACH LONDON

THE guard helped me to climb the steep back of the coach to my seat on the roof, where I found myself wedged between two stout gentlemen. Barely had I settled myself than the guard gave a blast on his horn, the driver cracked his whip, and we swung out of the yard.

It was late afternoon when we left Yarmouth, and we reached London at eight next morning. I was unable to sleep a wink all night, and hunger made me mourn for the bag of cakes I had forgotten.

When we reached the inn in Whitechapel which was our destination, the guard's eye lighted on me as he was getting down, and he went to the door of the booking-office.

"Is there anybody here for a youngster from Blunderstone, in Suffolk?" I heard him shout. "He's booked in the name o' Murdstone, to be left till called for."

Apparently nobody answered, for the guard scratched his head.

"Try the name of Copperfield, if you please," I suggested.

But there was no one to meet me under that name, either, so I went into the booking-office. Here the clerk invited me to go behind the counter and sit on the scales used for weighing parcels.

Presently a man came in and spoke to the clerk, who lifted me from the scales and pushed me across the counter to him, just as if I had been a parcel waiting to be called for.

The stranger was gaunt and sallow, and had dry, rusty hair. He was dressed in rusty black clothes, which looked rather short for him in both arms and legs.

" You're the new boy ? " he asked.

" Yes, sir," I answered, presuming him to be from the school for which I was intended.

" I'm one of the masters from Salem House," he told me.

He told the clerk that a carrier would call for my box, after which he took my hand and led me into the street.

" If you please, sir," I said when we had walked some way, " is it far to the school ? "

" Down near Blackheath," he replied.

" How far is that, sir ? " I inquired.

" About six miles," he said, " but we will ride most of the way."

I felt so tired, and was so faint with hunger, that the thought of the journey appalled me. I mustered up courage to tell him that I had not eaten since noon yesterday, and begged him to let me buy some food.

" Certainly, my boy," he said. After a little consideration, he went on, " I want to call on an old woman living near here. If you buy some provisions, no doubt she would cook them for you."

For a few coppers I bought a small loaf, a rasher of bacon, and an egg, then we walked on over a bridge across the Thames. It was a row of small alms-houses to which my guide took me, and we entered one, to find an old woman using a pair of bellows on a small fire.

" My Charley ! " the old woman cried, upon seeing the master from Salem House.

But seeing me at his heels, she looked confused and gave a curtsey. I learnt that the master's name was Mr. Mell, and at his request the old woman fried my egg and bacon, and gave me some milk to drink.

Never do I recall enjoying a meal so much. While I ate, Mr. Mell produced a flute. It seemed very dismal music that he played, but the old woman sat and listened as if she greatly appreciated it.

Having eaten, I fell into a doze. Every now and then I would wake, to hear Mr. Mell playing his flute, or talking with the old woman.

Once I heard him address her as mother, which solved the mystery of a certain likeness I had seen between them. I wondered drowsily how it came that a schoolmaster's mother should live in such humble circumstances, particularly the mother of a master at a school with so imposing a name as Salem House. But as both had been so kind to me, I resolved to ask no questions. We must have been there nearly two hours when the scrape of a chair made me open my eyes.

" It is time we were going, Copperfield," Mr. Mell said.

Luckily we had not far to go to catch our coach, inside which I soon fell asleep again.

When I awoke, we were proceeding at a walking-pace up a steep hill, which was lined with green trees instead of the houses of London. At the top we stopped, and Mr. Mell told me to alight.

A short walk brought us to a building enclosed by a high brick wall. The place looked dull and uninviting, but over a door in the wall I saw a board, upon which was the name

SALEM HOUSE.

We had arrived at my school.

## CHAPTER VI

### AT SALEM HOUSE

MR. MELL pulled the handle of a bell, and after a short wait the door in the wall was opened. I found myself being surveyed by a stout, bull-necked man with a wooden leg.

" This is the new boy," said Mr. Mell as we entered.

The other said nothing, but locked the gate behind us.

Mr. Mell was leading me towards the big house, which stood among some dark trees, when a shout made us look back. The one-legged man was standing in the doorway of a little lodge.

" Hey ! The cobbler's been while you were out, Mr. Mell," he cried. " He says he can't mend your boots any more, as there ain't enough o' the original boots left. He says you ought not to expect miracles of him ! "

So saying, he threw a pair of boots towards Mr. Mell, who went back to pick them up. As he looked disconsolately at them, I noticed for the first time that the boots he was wearing were much worn, and that there were countless darns in his stockings. I was greatly surprised at such signs of poverty, since I had always believed his profession to be well-paid. Salem House I found to be a square brick building, with a bare and unfurnished appearance.

Everything seemed so quiet that I remarked upon it to Mr. Mell.

" I suppose the boys are all out at present." I said.

" They are on their holidays," he replied. " Mr. Creakle, the owner of the school, is also away at the seaside, with his wife and

*Over a door in the wall was the name Salem House.*

daughter. I understand that special arrangements were made for you to come here in holiday-time, as punishment for your conduct at home."

First he took me into the schoolroom, which was the most desolate place I had ever seen. It was a long room, with three long rows of desks, with rows of forms on either side. The walls bristled with pegs for hats and slates to hang upon, and scraps of paper and old copy-books littered the dirty floor.

Two miserable little white mice, left behind by their owner, ran up and down a cage; while in another a bird hopped up and down from a perch never attempting to sing or even chirp.

Ink was splashed everywhere, and the air was foul and stuffy, every window being shut tight.

Mr. Mell left me there while he took his unmendable boots away, so I walked up the room. Suddenly I came to where a square of cardboard was lying on a desk. On it was written the warning :

" Beware ! He bites."

Thinking the warning referred to some ferocious dog, I peered nervously about me, and was still doing so when Mr. Mell returned.

" What are you looking for, Copperfield ? " he asked.

" The dog, sir," I replied.

" What dog ? " he inquired.

" Why, sir, the one this notice refers to," I answered, pointing to the card.

" That doesn't refer to a dog, Copperfield," he said gravely. " It refers to a boy. My instructions, Copperfield, are to fasten this placard on your back. I am sorry, but I must obey my orders."

Turning me round, he tied the placard securely to my shoulders, and forbade me on any account to remove it.

" If you do so, Copperfield," he warned me, " it would be very much the worse for you when Mr. Creakle returns."

Nobody can imagine what I suffered through wearing that card. I always felt that somebody was reading it, whether people were about or not. Tungay, the wooden-legged janitor, took a delight in aggravating my sufferings. If ever he saw me leaning my back against a wall or a tree, he would point at me and roar :

" Hullo, there ! You, Copperfield ! Show that placard plainly, else I'll report you ! "

There was a gravelled playground in front of the school, and Tungay commanded that I should walk to and fro there each morning, so that tradesmen might see me and my label when they called with goods.

My existence as the solitary pupil in the empty school was a dreary one. For several hours each day, I was occupied with tasks set by Mr. Mell, who would sit at a desk near me making out the bills which were to be sent to the boys' parents when the school reassembled. Although the lessons were hard, I found myself able to get through them without disgrace, now that I was free from the watchful eyes of Mr. Murdstone and his sister.

I felt loneliest at night, when I lay in bed in a barn-like dormitory, among a grove of empty iron bedsteads. It was then that my thoughts flew back to my mother as she used to be, or to dear old Peggotty.

In the playground was an old door, upon which many of my future schoolmates had carved their names. Sometimes, when I was free from lessons and could evade the hated Tungay, I would stand in front of this door, and try to guess the character of the boys from their names.

I tried to imagine, also, how they would treat me when they read the placard I was condemned to wear on my back. Fear of what they might say, and do, made me dread the day of their return.

## CHAPTER VII

### MY FIRST TERM AT SCHOOL

ABOUT a month had passed when the wooden-legged Tungay began to stump about with a mop and a bucket of water, from which I inferred that preparations were being made for the start of the new term.

Then Mr. Mell informed me that the owner of the school, Mr. Creakle, was expected home that evening. After tea, I heard that he had arrived. And before bedtime, Tungay came to take me in to him.

I had heard so much about Mr. Creakle that I was trembling as Tungay led me into his part of the house, which was a great deal more comfortable-looking than the school side.

Mrs. and Miss Creakle were sitting in his study, but I had only eyes for the headmaster himself.

Mr. Creakle was a stout man, with a big watch-chain across his middle. His face was a fiery red, his eyes small and deep-set. He was almost bald, and had a small nose and a massive chin.

What impressed me most, however, was his voice. He could only speak in a wheezy whisper, and even this was such an effort that it made his face go redder still.

" So this is the young gentleman whose teeth are to be filed," he whispered, glowering at me. " Turn him round, Tungay."

The wooden-legged janitor swung me round to exhibit the placard on my back, then after an interval swung me to the front once more.

" What's the report on this boy ? " Mr. Creakle demanded in his whisper.

" There's nothing against him yet," replied Tungay. " Of course, he's had little opportunity so far."

I thought Mr. Creakle looked disappointed. But snatching my first glance at his wife and daughter, who were thin, quiet-looking ladies, I thought they seemed relieved.

" Come here, sir," whispered Mr. Creakle, beckoning to me.

" Come here ! " echoed Tungay loudly, and repeating the gesture.

When I was near enough, Mr. Creakle took me by the ear.

" I have the pleasure of knowing your stepfather well," he whispered. " He is a worthy man, and one of strong character. I know him, and he knows me. Now do you know me ? Hey ? "

As he asked the question he pinched my ear.

" I don't know you yet, sir," I said, flinching with pain.

" Not yet, hey ? " repeated Mr. Creakle. " But you will know me soon, hey ? "

" You will soon, hey ? " bellowed Tungay.

I afterwards found that the bull-voiced Tungay generally passed on Mr. Creakle's words to the boys, since the master had such difficulty in making himself heard.

I was very much frightened of the pair of them as they glared at me, and said I hoped I should know Mr. Creakle very soon. As I said it, my ear felt as if it was ablaze, he pinched it so hard.

" I'll tell you what I am," whispered Mr. Creakle, giving my ear a final screw that brought water to my eyes. " I'm a Tartar, I am."

" A Tartar," echoed Tungay loudly.

" When I say I'll do a thing, I do it," said Mr. Creakle. " And when I say I want a thing done, I'll have it done."

" I will have it done," Tungay repeated.

" Well," Mr. Creakle concluded, " you have begun to know me, my young friend. Now you may go."

I was glad to get this order, but I had something on my mind.

" If you please, sir," I began.

Before I could say more, Mr. Creakle leant forward in his chair.

" What's this ?  What's this ? " he wheezed.

" If you please, sir," I faltered, " I am very sorry indeed for what I did to my stepfather, and would never do such a thing again.  Do you think, sir, I might be allowed to remove this placard from my back before the other boys return, and——"

Mr. Creakle sprang from his chair with such a fierce expression that I turned and fled in a panic. I did not stop until I reached the dormitory, where I sat quaking until it was time for bed.

The first of the boys to appear was Tommy Traddles, a good-natured youth whose hair stood up stiffly all over his head, like the bristles of a hedge-hog. We were soon good friends, for, instead of mocking me for the warning on my back, he sympathised with me as a victim of Mr. Creakle's hateful methods.

Thanks to his introduction, most of the boys treated me in the same way, and only a few of them pretended to treat me as a dangerous dog.

I was not considered to be formally accepted by the boys, however, until I had met Steerforth, the head boy. When he arrived, I was escorted before him as if he had been a magistrate sitting on the bench.

Steerforth was a good deal older than any other boy in the school. He was very good-looking and was well-dressed, and Traddles had told me that he was very clever at his work.

Fortunately I was well received by Steerforth, who declared it was a jolly shame that I should have to wear my placard.

" I see that you have been put into my dormitory, young Copperfield," he said, as we walked round the playground together afterwards.  " It is the usual thing, you know, for a new boy to stand a dormitory feed. How are you off for money ? "

For answer, I turned the remaining seven shillings out of my purse, being careful to retain the scrap of paper bearing my mother's message

"Do you want to keep any of it for yourself?" Steerforth asked.

"No, thank you," I answered politely.

"Then I'll get the prog for you, if you like," he offered. "How about spending a couple of shillings on a bottle of currant wine? And what d'you say to an almond cake, and some biscuits? And perhaps some fruit?"

Delighted to be consulted by so great a personage, I at once agreed.

"That's all right, then." he remarked. "You can trust me to get the best feed possible with the money, young Copperfield."

As he walked off with all my precious money in his pocket, I felt a little uneasy. But I felt very proud of myself that evening, when Steerforth presided over the feast I had paid for. Sitting on the floor and talking in whispers, we devoured the cake and biscuits and fruit which he had smuggled in. When it came to drinking the currant wine, we had only one wineglass between us, and that was without a stem. Still, we took it in turns to use it, and all the boys drank my health, while I drank that of Steerforth.

During the feast, I learned a good many things about my new school and its masters.

Mr. Creakle, I was told, was incapable of taking a class, having had no education himself. He had been a hop-merchant until he went bankrupt, when he had used his wife's money to start the school. But all agreed that he had correctly described himself as a Tartar. Every boy in the school went in fear of him except Steerforth, whom he had never been known to punish.

"If he dared to touch me, I should brain him with that big bottle of ink in the classroom," put in Steerforth quietly without a trace of bragging.

As regards the under masters, Mr. Sharp and Mr. Mell, I was told that they were quite decent fellows, but were poorly paid, and were afraid to stand up to Mr. Creakle.

We talked for some time after our feast was finished, until Steerforth said we had better get to bed.

"Good-night, young Copperfield," called Steerforth as he pulled the blankets over him. "I'll take care of you at Salem House."

I thought my seven shillings was well spent to have made such a friend, for to me Steerforth was already a hero fit to count with the best of those I had read about in our books at home.


## CHAPTER VIII

### MR. MELL RESIGNS HIS POST

SCHOOL began in earnest next day.

I shall always remember how the uproar in the schoolroom changed to a sudden, deathly silence when Mr. Creakle entered, and stood in the doorway like a story-book giant surveying his captives.

Tungay was at Mr. Creakle's elbow, and quite unnecessarily bellowed, "Silence!"

*" So you're the boy famous for biting, hey ? "* he whispered, *flourishing a thick cane under my nose as he spoke.*

Mr. Creakle's lips moved, but I could not hear a word he said. Tungay, however, repeated his speech.

" Now, boys, this is a new term. Be careful how you behave. Face your lessons with fresh vigour, I advise you, for I have plenty of fresh vigour with which to punish you. I shan't hesitate to do so, either. And it will be no good rubbing yourselves afterwards, for you won't be able to rub out the marks I shall make. Now get to work ! "

After this grim address, Tungay stumped from the room. To my dismay, I saw Mr. Creakle making straight towards me.

" So you're the boy famous for biting, hey ? " he whispered. " Well, I'm famous for biting, too. What d'you think of this for a tooth, hey ? "

He flourished a thick cane under my nose as he spoke.

" Is that a sharp tooth, hey ? " he wheezed. " A double tooth, hey ? Does it bite, hey ? Does it ? Does it ? "

With every question he gave me a cut that made me writhe.

But if I thought I was to be picked out as a special victim for Mr. Creakle's cane, I speedily found myself mistaken. No sooner had he turned away from me than he was thrashing into another boy.

From one to another he went, so that half the boys were crying and wriggling before the first lesson was properly begun.

All this was but a sample of Mr. Creakle's method of ruling his school. He was an ignorant brute, who delighted in cowing and tormenting the unfortunate boys at his mercy.

When we were being taught by the under-masters, Mr. Creakle would sit at a desk from which he could watch the whole classroom. Every few minutes he would declare that some poor wretch was not paying proper attention, and would call him up for a caning. Or he would walk behind us when we were bent over our books, and deal out cuts as the whim suited him.

Fear of Mr. Creakle and his cane haunted us every moment of the day. Even when we were at play after school, we kept our eyes lifting to the window of his private room, knowing that he was always likely to be watching for an excuse to drop upon one of us. If his face appeared, every game stopped and all became silent.

Once Tommy Traddles was unlucky enough to break the window of Mr. Creakle's dining-room with a ball. When we heard the smash of glass and saw what had happened, we all stood as though turned to stone, so terrified were we of the consequences.

Traddles was a happy-go-lucky boy in many ways, but he had very strict ideas about we boys standing by each other. No sooner had he seen what he had done, than he resolved to own up, knowing that otherwise Mr. Creakle would behave like a madman, and cane everybody within reach.

I can still picture Traddles, dressed in a tight, sky-blue suit, and with his bristly hair more erect than usual, walking forward to confess, as Mr. Creakle's scarlet face showed at the broken window.

Traddles was accustomed to canings—he had at least one a day—but on that occasion it was hours before he could begin to draw skeletons round the margins of his lesson book, which was his peculiar way of solacing himself after a beating.

There was only one small crumb of satisfaction that Mr. Creakle's severity brought to me. One day, finding that my placard protected me from his cane, he tore it off, and I never had to wear it again.

The continued friendship of the mighty Steerforth was the happiest thing in my life at Salem House. Steerforth found that I had read many books, so suggested that at bedtime each night I should tell him what I remembered of them.

"I can't get to sleep as a rule, young Copperfield," he said, "and it would pass the time if you told me a story. We'll go through the books you've read one after another, and make a regular Arabian Nights affair of it."

Often of a night I was so tired that I felt I could not face the task, but my desire to please Steerforth would compel me to struggle through. And I had my reward in the envy of the other boys, when they saw him take my arm and walk round the playground at my side.

One thing I did not quite like about my hero, however. This was the way in which he treated Mr. Mell, who always showed himself a good friend to me, and who always took a special interest in my learning. Steerforth seemed to dislike him, and never lost a chance to be cheeky to Mr. Mell, or to egg on smaller boys to ignore his orders.

In the end, something happened which pained me a good deal.

We had a half-holiday on Saturday afternoons, when we usually played games or went for a walk with the masters. On this occasion it rained, so that we had to keep in the classroom. And because Mr. Creakle was confined to his room with a slight chill, we were bidden to read instead of playing games, which might disturb our tyrant.

Mr. Mell was left in charge of us that day.

Things were quiet at first, but believing Mr. Creakle and his cane to be safely out of the way for once, boys soon began to give way to their feelings of relief.  Mr. Mell pretended to ignore the talking and fidgeting as he went from boy to boy, seeing how each was getting on with his work.  Then, suddenly, everybody seemed to go mad.

Some boys started whistling, others singing or shouting, or stamping their feet, while about a dozen began playing leapfrog.

Mr. Mell had been sitting beside me on the form, and for a few moments he appeared too stunned by the clamour to act.  Then he sprang up, and struck the desk with a book.

" Silence ! " he cried.  " What does this mean ?  Silence, at once ! "

His sharp tone startled the majority of the boys, who had never heard him speak sternly before.  Most of them became quiet, but Steerforth was lounging against the wall, whistling.

" Silence, please, Mr. Steerforth ! " said Mr. Mell.

" Silence yourself," replied Steerforth, turning red.  " To whom d'you think you are talking ? "

" Be quiet and sit down," commanded Mr. Mell.

" Sit down yourself," retorted Steerforth, " and mind your own business, too."

There was a titter and a few cheers for Steerforth's boldness.  But Mr. Mell was so white that the noise quickly died away.

" You may think, Steerforth, that I did not notice you urging on the smaller boys to create that uproar just now," the master said.

" I should never trouble to think about you at all," Steerforth replied.

" Possibly not," said Mr. Mell, his lip trembling.  " It is well known that you are treated with favouritism in this school, and now you take advantage of your position to insult a gentlman."

" A gentleman ? " sneered Steerforth.  " Where is he, pray ? "

" Shame, Steerforth ! " cried Traddles, red with indignation.

" Hold your tongue, Traddles, please," commanded Mr. Mell, then turned to Steerforth again.  " When you insult one in a less fortunate position in life than yourself, Steerforth, you prove that you are not a gentleman yourself.  Now, Copperfield, continue with your translation."

As I took up my book, however, Steerforth strode up the room.

" Wait a bit, young Copperfield ! " he cried.  " I've something to say to Mr. Mell.  I'll not take impudence from a beggar ! "

It looked as if they might come to blows, but suddenly I noticed all the boys go rigid.  Mr. Creakle was in the room, his face less red than usual, but wrath in his eyes.  Tungay was at his side, and in the doorway stood Mrs. and Miss Creakle, looking frightened.

Mr. Mell sank on to a form, and buried his face in his hands.

" Mr. Mell," whispered Mr. Creakle, shaking him by the arm.  " You have not forgotten yourself, I hope ? "

When the master did not answer, Mr. Creakle turned to Steerforth.

" Perhaps, sir, you'll tell me what this is all about ? " he wheezed.

" I objected to Mr. Mell saying that I was treated with favouritism," Steerforth replied.

" Favouritism ! " repeated Mr. Creakle, the veins in his forehead swelling.
" Did you suggest that I permitted favouritism in my school, Mr. Mell ? "

" I did, sir," answered Mr. Mell in a low voice. " And I said that no pupil had a right to use such favouritism to treat me with disrespect."

" Disrespect, hey ? " wheezed Mr. Creakle. " My stars ! But allow me to ask you, Mr. What's-your-name, whether you showed proper respect to me, when you talk about favouritism. To me, sir, the principal of this establishment, and your employer."

" It was not wise, sir, I admit," said Mr. Mell. " I should not have said it had I been calm."

" He also said I was not a gentleman, sir," put in Steerforth. " In return, I called him a beggar. I should hardly have done so had I not been in a temper, sir, but I am ready to take the consequences for it."

Mr. Creakle nodded approvingly.

" *I mean that Mr. Mell's mother lives on charity in an alms-house,*"
*Steerforth said.*

" Your confession does you credit, Steerforth," he whispered. " But I am surprised, greatly surprised, that you should attach such an epithet as beggar to any person employed at Salem House."

Steerforth laughed shortly.

" If the name doesn't apply to Mr. Mell, it does to somebody closely related to him," he sneered.

He glanced at me as he spoke, and I felt my face flush. It was I who had confided to him the story of my visit to the alms-house with Mr. Mell, and of how I had learnt that the old woman was his mother. To nobody else had I told the secret, and I was hurt that Steerforth should make such use of his knowledge.

As if he understood my feelings, Mr. Mell placed his hand gently on my shoulder.

" What is it you mean, Mr. Steerforth ? " wheezed Mr. Creakle.

"I mean that Mr. Mell's mother lives on charity in an alms-house," Steerforth said.

Mr. Creakle turned to his assistant, who continued to pat my shoulder.

"You have heard what this gentleman said, Mr. Mell," said Mr. Creakle with a frown. "I hope you are in a position to deny his statement?"

"I fear he has only spoken the plain truth, sir," answered Mr. Mell, in the midst of dead silence.

"Then you have no business to hold a position in my establishment," Mr. Creakle declared, his veins swelling bigger than ever. "Having the reputation of Salem House to keep up, I'd be glad to part from you at the earliest moment."

"As there is no time like the present, I will leave now," answered Mr. Mell quietly. "As for you, Steerforth, I can only hope that one day you will have the decency to feel ashamed for what you have done."

With a final pat on my shoulder he went to his desk, and collected his beloved flute and some books of his own. Tucking the latter under his arm, he walked out of the room.

I never met him again, but some years later I learned that he went to Australia, where he did very well with a school of his own.


CHAPTER IX

HOME FOR THE HOLIDAYS

ALTHOUGH I never had the same unquestioning faith in Steerforth after Mr. Mell was forced to leave, it was hard to resist his fascination. I continued my story-telling for his benefit, and I shared with him a hamper which I received from Peggotty.

Apart from the ever-present terror of Mr. Creakle and his cane, there is little more to recall of my first term at Salem House.

At last the holidays grew near again, and the boys began to get excited at the idea of escape from the school we all hated so deeply. As regards myself, I had fears that Mr. Murdstone would arrange for me to stay where I was; but to my great relief, Steerforth brought me word that I was to go home.

Even when I was actually in the Yarmouth coach, I could hardly believe that I was free, and that I should not feel the lash of Mr. Creakle's cane at any moment.

Having an inside seat this time, I was able to get snatches of sleep on the journey. It was still early morning when we reached Yarmouth, but there was hot tea and a roaring fire in the coffee-room of the Dolphin Inn.

At nine o'clock I was called for by the carrier, Mr. Barkis. His was the first familiar face I had seen, but if I had expected a warm welcome after my long absence I was mistaken. He just looked at me with the same wooden expression as if I had merely left his van a moment to change a sixpence.

As soon as my box and I were in the cart, the horse was off at his old lazy pace.

" You look very well, Mr. Barkis," I said, trying to be friendly.

Mr. Barkis rubbed his ear, but made no response, so I tried again.

" I gave your message to Peggotty when I wrote to her," I said.

" Ah," replied Mr. Barkis gruffly.

" Wasn't it all right ? " I asked.

" What ? " he growled.

" The message," I said.

" The message was right enough, mebbe," answered Mr. Barkis, " but it come to an end there."

Not understanding what he meant, I repeated, " It came to an end, Mr. Barkis ? "

" Nothing came of it," he explained, looking at me sideways. " There were no answer."

" Oh, there was an answer expected, was there ? " I exclaimed.

" O' course," replied Mr. Barkis. " When a man says he's willin', it's as much as to say that man's waitin' for an answer. I've been waitin' for her answer all this time."

" But you must see Peggotty in Blunderstone nearly every day," I said in surprise. " Why don't you tell her you're waiting a reply ? "

Mr. Barkis slowly shook his head.

" No," he growled, " I ain't got no call to go an' tell her, not havin' spoken six words to her in me life. It ain't for me to tell her."

" Would you like me to do it ? " I inquired doubtfully.

" Ay, you might tell her, if you would," he agreed. " Tell her that Barkis is waitin' for an answer. Mebbe she'll say, ' An answer to what ? ' Then you'll say, ' To the message I gave you, that Barkis is willin',' says you."

This suggestion Mr. Barkis accompanied by a nudge of his elbow.

After that, he became silent again, his gaze fixed on his horse's ears.

My feelings were mixed as we drew near to Blunderstone. I longed to see my mother and Peggotty, but I dreaded meeting my stepfather and his sister.

At last I sighted the bare tops of the elm trees in front of our house.

Mr. Barkis put me and my box down at the front gate, and drove on without a word. As I walked up the front path, I glanced fearfully at the windows, expecting to see Mr. or Miss Murdstone glowering at me. But I saw nobody look out, and I timidly let myself in at the front door, which was seldom locked in the daytime.

As I stood in the hall, the first thing I heard was my mother singing in a low voice. It was a song I seemed to faintly remember her singing to me years ago. Peeping in at the parlour door, I saw her sitting by the fire, a baby in her arms. Otherwise the room was empty.

Some slight noise I made must have made her look up.

" Why, Davy, my own boy ! " she cried. " Come and talk to your little brother, Davy."

I think I was jealous of the baby for a few moments. But when my mother drew me to my knees at her side, and put his tiny hand in mine, my jealousy vanished.

Soon Peggotty entered, to embrace me so fiercely that she burst off a shower of buttons that went rolling over the floor.

It appeared that I had not been expected so soon, the carrier being much before his usual time. And to my joy, I found that the Murdstones had gone visiting, and would not be back until late that night.

It really seemed like the old days, the three of us gathered in the parlour with no one to shadow our happiness. We dined together at the fireside, my mother insisting that Peggotty should eat with us, as she used to do.

While we were at table, I remembered the promise I had made to speak to Peggotty on Mr. Barkis's behalf. Before I could finish my message, however, Peggotty began to laugh, and covered her face with her apron.

" Whatever is the matter, Peggotty ? " asked my mother.

It was some time before Peggotty could reply, she laughed so much.

" Why, drat the man ! " she gasped at last. " Mr. Barkis wants to marry me."

I gaped at this revelation of what Mr. Barkis's message had meant.

" It would be a very good match for you," said my mother seriously. " He is a steady fellow, and he does well with his business."

" I wouldn't marry him if he was made of gold, nor anybody else, either," declared Peggotty.

" Then why don't you tell him so, poor man ? " my mother asked.

" Tell him so ? " retorted Peggotty. " Why, he has never dared ask me, himself. He knows better, for if he was so bold as to say a word I would box his ears."

But a second later she broke into another fit of laughing, as if greatly amused at Mr. Barkis's queer way of proposing to her.

Looking from her big red face to my mother's, I noticed for the first time how white and worn the latter seemed. She looked years older than when I left for school, and as if some illness troubled her.

Presently she rested her hand on Peggotty's arm.

" And you are really not going to get married, yet ? " she asked.

" Me, ma'am ? Bless you, no ! " replied Peggotty vigorously.

" I'm glad of that, Peggotty," said my mother. " I should like you to stay with me. Perhaps it won't be so very long I shall keep you."

" Now don't you talk that way ! " cried Peggotty, while I found my own eyes grow misty as I put my arm round my mother's waist, and rested my cheek against hers.

" You'll be keeping me until I get so old and useless you won't want to keep me any more," went on Peggotty. " When I get to that stage, I'll go to my Davy and ask him to find a corner for me."

" And I'd make you as welcome as any queen, Peggotty," I replied.

After she had cleared the table, Peggotty brought her sewing and sat with us. There was the work-box I knew so well, with the picture of St. Paul's Cathedral on its lid ; and the little thatched cottage which held her yard-measure.

I had to tell of my school, and my account of Mr. Creakle and his cane made Peggotty stop her sewing, while my mother hugged me the tighter. I also told them of Steerforth and Traddles.

Afterwards there was a silence, while we sat and stared at the fire, in the glowing coals of which I was beginning to trace pictures when Peggotty spoke again.

" I wonder how Davy's great-aunt is faring ? " she said.

" Whatever made you think of her, Peggotty ? " inquired my mother. " Were you hoping for another visit from her ? "

" Heaven forbid ! " replied Peggotty firmly.

I had heard them talk of Betsey Trotwood before. She was my father's aunt, and lived in a cottage by the sea—at Dover, or Folkestone, I believe it was. Apparently she was a mannish, self-willed lady, who had overawed even Peggotty on the one occasion she had visited the Rookery. That had been about the time I was born, and Aunt Betsey had been so annoyed to find that I was a boy, instead of the girl she had wished for, that she had flounced off and never returned. Indeed, she had never even written a line to my mother since that day.

" Aunt Betsey was certainly a very plain-spoken woman," my mother sighed. " Still, she is the only real relative that Davy would have, if anything happened to me."

" And outspoken though she was, it's my opinion she was much better than another person I could name," remarked Peggotty meaningly.

" There you go again, Peggotty," complained my mother. " You can never say a good word for Miss Murdstone. But we mustn't quarrel about her again, Peggotty, especially now that our Davy is at home."

We sat talking until it was close on ten o'clock, when the sound of wheels brought Peggotty to her feet. " That will be the Murdstones," she cried, hastily picking up her sewing things ready to retreat to the kitchen.

" You had better run off to bed quickly, Davy," said my mother. " Mr. Murdstone would not approve of you being up so late."

*I had to tell of my school, and my account of Mr. Creakle and his cane made*
*Peggotty stop her sewing.*

She lit a candle for me, and I was upstairs before my stepfather entered the house. But I heard the front door open to admit him and his sister, and it seemed that with them came a cold blast which blew away the happiness that had crept back into my heart.

# CHAPTER X

### I RETURN TO SCHOOL

IT was with reluctance that I went down to breakfast next morning, as I dreaded my meeting with Mr. Murdstone. I had not set eyes upon him since that day when I bit him.

However, after hesitating some time, and making one or two false starts, I found the courage to go down and enter the parlour.

My stepfather was standing with his back to the fire, while his sister was making the tea.

Mr. Murdstone looked at me stonily as I entered, but made no sign of recognition. After a moment's confusion, I forced myself to walk up to him.

" I want to beg your pardon, sir," I said. " I am very sorry for what I did, and I hope you will forgive me."

" I am glad to hear you are sorry, Davy," he replied coldly.

The hand he gave me was the one I had bitten. As I took it, I saw a red mark where my teeth had entered ; but it was not so red as my face became, when I looked up to catch the sinister expression in his face. It was only too evident to me that he would neither forgive nor forget what I had done.

" How do you do, ma'am ? " I greeted Miss Murdstone politely.

" Oh, dear me ! " sighed Miss Murdstone, giving me the tips of her fingers. " How long a holiday have you ? "

" A month, ma'am," I told her.

" Counting from when ? " she asked.

" From to-day," I answered.

" Ah ! " she said. " Then there is one day we can knock off."

So saying, she went straight away to score off that day's date from the calendar which hung on the wall. This she did every day, becoming steadily more agreeable as the time came nearer for my return to school.

As neither Mr. Murdstone nor his sister appeared to welcome my company I tried to please them by keeping out of their way as much as possible. I would tramp the muddy lanes on the fine days, and on the wet ones I would sit in my bleak bedroom alone, wrapped in an old overcoat for warmth and with my nose in a book. Of an evening, I would steal down to the kitchen to be with Peggotty.

But even by acting thus, I did not please my stepfather.

One day after dinner, when I was going to steal off as usual, he called me back.

" David," he said, " I am sorry to see that you have a sullen nature."

" He's as sulky as a bear," agreed his sister.

I stood still, and hung my head.

" Of all evil tempers," went on Mr. Murdstone, " a sullen, obstinate one is the worst."

" And there never was a more sullen and obstinate boy than this one," added Miss Murdstone spitefully. " Even you, my dear Clara, must have noticed that."

" I beg your pardon, Jane," said my mother timidly, " but are you quite sure that you understand Davy ? "

" I should be ashamed of myself if I could not understand him, Clara," replied Miss Murdstone sharply. " The boy's character is plain enough for any one to read, more's the pity. But I am afraid we are interrupting what my brother had to say."

Mr. Murdstone frowned, and addressed himself to me again.

" I was remarking on your sullen nature, David," he said sternly. " I warn you that I will not suffer such behaviour from you. You must improve your ways, or I shall improve them for you."

" I beg your pardon, sir," I faltered. " I have never meant to be sullen since I came home."

" Don't take refuge in a lie, sir ! " he shouted, so fiercely that my mother tremblingly put out her hand, as if to intervene. " You have spent most of your time sulking in your own room. From now onwards, I require you to be with us here. Don't you dare to disobey me ! If you do, you will know what to expect."

Miss Murdstone gave a grim chuckle of approval. But her brother had not finished with me yet.

" One thing more," he said. " I notice that you are fond of low company, and I will not have it. You are not to associate with servants, who will not improve you as you need improving. I will say nothing of the woman who encourages you to visit the kitchen, since her long service has caused your mother to feel a certain regard for her."

" An attachment of which I entirely disapprove," put in Miss Murdstone sourly.

" I will only say," concluded Mr. Murdstone, " that you are to keep from seeking Peggotty's company. Now, David, you have heard my commands, and you know what will happen if you fail to obey them."

From that time, I was forced to mope in the parlour every day, under the menacing watch of the Murdstones.

Mostly I had to sit still in a chair with nothing to do, and with Mr. Murdstone or his sister immediately glaring at me whenever I made the slightest movement. While if my mother so much as spoke to me, they would frown at her so severely that she would at once become silent again.

So the days dragged by, until at last Miss Murdstone was able to draw a line through the date that marked the end of my holiday.

Despite the thought of Mr. Creakle and his cane waiting for me at Salem House, I was glad to go. I should at least have the company of Steerforth and Traddles, to compensate for my beatings.

Once more Mr. Barkis pulled up at our gate, and once more Miss Murdstone's warning voice called " Clara ! " as my mother bent to kiss me farewell.

I was in the carrier's cart when I heard my mother calling to me.

Looking out, I saw her standing at the garden-gate, holding my baby brother up for me to see. It was a cold, still day, and not a hair of her head nor a fold of her dress was stirred, while her eyes rested unblinkingly upon me with a yearning intentness.

That was the picture of her that I carried away with me.

## CHAPTER XI

### AN UNHAPPY BIRTHDAY

BACK at school, things went on much as before. Steerforth and Traddles welcomed me heartily, and I at once had to begin my nightly duty of entertaining the former with my stories. We had a new assistant master in place of Mr. Mell, but Mr. Sharp was still with us. Of course, Mr. Creakle still used his cane as ferociously as ever, while Tungay trailed at his elbow to repeat whatever he whispered.

Two months had crept by, and my birthday arrived.

How distinctly I recollect that March day. I can still smell the fog that hung about the place; I can see the frost that whitened the trees outside, making them appear ghostly and unreal. I can imagine myself back in the chilly classroom, with the candles sputtering here and there to light the foggy morning, and the boys' breath visible as they try to blow a little warmth into their frozen fingers.

Having only just come in from breakfast, we had not started our first lesson when Mr. Sharp entered the room.

" David Copperfield is to go into the parlour," he called.

Anticipating that a birthday hamper had arrived from Peggotty, my face brightened. Some of my neighbours must have jumped to the same conclusion for several whispered that they hoped I would let them share in the good things.

I was hurrying eagerly from the room when Mr. Sharp spoke again.

" Don't hurry, David," he said. " There's plenty of time."

I might have been surprised by the kindly tone of his voice, but I gave it no thought until afterwards.

I hastened to Mr. Creakle's side of the house, where I tapped at the parlour door and entered.

Mr. Creakle was still at breakfast, with his cane and a newspaper beside his plate. Mrs. Creakle sat on the other side of the table, an opened letter in her hand. But of a hamper there was no sign.

I looked inquiringly at Mr. Creakle, but he shook his head, his mouth full of buttered toast. Mrs. Creakle rose and led me to a sofa, where she sat down beside me.

" David Copperfield," she said gently, " I want to speak to you very particularly. I have something to tell you, my child."

There was a pause before she continued.

" You are too young to realise how the world changes every day," she went on " and to know how the people in it pass away. But we all have **to** learn it, David. Some of us when we are young, some of us when we are old and some of us at all times of our lives."

I looked at her earnestly, wondering what was coming next.

" When you left home at the end of your holiday, did you leave everybody well ? " she asked. " Was your mama well ? "

I trembled without knowing why, still staring at her fixedly.

" I asked," she said, " because I hear this morning that she is ill."

A mist seemed to come between Mrs. Creakle and myself. Beyond it I heard her say, " I grieve to tell you that she is dangerously ill."

I knew all too plainly what was to come next.

*" Your mama is dead, David," added Mrs. Creakle softly.*

" Your mama is dead, David," added Mrs. Creakle softly, but I had burst into tears before she could say it.

Mrs. Creakle was very kind to me, and kept me with her all day, comforting me as best as she could. I wondered how my little brother would fare, robbed of his mother at so tender an age, but Mrs. Creakle told me that he, too, was very ill, and was not expected to survive.

I was to go home to-morrow night, so I had to spend another night in the dormitory before I went. There was no story-telling that evening, and Traddles did his best to show his sympathy by insisting I should borrow his pillow to make my bed more comfortable.

It was Traddles, also, who gave me a sheet of paper covered with skeletons he had drawn, as something to amuse me during my journey.

When I left Salem House next afternoon, I little thought that I should never return there again.

The first thing I was told upon reaching home was that my little brother had also died. But by then I was so dazed from mourning my mother that the news seemed to cause no pain.

Of the events of the next few days, I can only clearly recall that final scene in the churchyard, which lay in full view of our house. The grave in which my father was buried had been reopened, and into it was lowered the coffin containing the remains of my mother and my baby brother.

As soon as we got back to the Rookery, I fled to my bedroom. I had seen little of Peggotty since I had been home, but now she stole up to join me, and to tell me of my mother's illness.

"Ever since she married again, she was never well," said Peggotty. "And from that fatal day, she was seldom happy. The only time I saw her like her old self was the day when you came home from school, and when the Murdstones were out of the way. After she had seen you start off back at the end of your holiday, she came and told me she would never see her Davy again."

It was not until I was older that Peggotty told me that she was sure that it was the cold harshness of Mr. Murdstone and his sister that had broken my mother's gentle heart.

## CHAPTER XII

### PEGGOTTY GETS HER NOTICE

ON the very next day after the funeral, Miss Murdstone gave Peggotty a month's notice. Had it not been for me, it would no doubt have been Peggotty who gave notice first, for she would have been glad enough to get away from the Murdstones. But she had resolved to stay on, if allowed to do so, for my sake.

I feel certain that the Murdstones would have been happy could they have dismissed me with a month's notice. As it was, no word was said of my future.

Once I mustered the courage to ask Miss Murdstone when I was to go back to school, and she answered sourly that she believed I should not be going back at all.

I was very anxious to know what was going to be done with me, and so was Peggotty. But neither of us could discover anything.

Of one thing I was glad. I was no longer compelled to sit like a prisoner in the parlour, watched over by my stepfather and his sister. Indeed, Miss Murdstone would nod her head towards the door when she saw me there. I had fears that she or her brother would take up my education again, but they made no move to do so.

Shut out from the parlour, I got into the habit again of seeking Peggotty in the kitchen, and Mr. Murdstone said nothing against my doing so. In fact, so long as I kept out of his way, he seemed little interested in what I did.

"Peggotty," I said one evening, as I sat warming my hands at the kitchen fire, "I believe that my stepfather hates me more than he used to. He never liked me at any time, but now it seems he cannot even bear to see me about the house."

"Perhaps it is because of his sorrow at your mother's death, Davy," she replied.

"No, it isn't, Peggotty," I declared. "There's a difference between sadness and anger, and Mr. Murdstone always looks angry as soon as he sees me."

Peggotty said no more for a while.

" Davy," she said at length, " I have tried my best to get another situation here in Blunderstone, so as to be near in case you wanted me at any time. But there is no place to be got."

" Then what will you do, Peggotty ? " I asked wistfully. " Does that mean you will have to go right away ? "

" I expect I shall have to go to Yarmouth," she answered.

" Well, that's not so bad," I remarked, brightening. " It's not so very far, and I shall be able to come and see you sometimes."

" And as long as you are here, Davy," she promised, " I'll come over one day a week to see you. As long as I live, I'll do that."

I felt greatly cheered by this pledge, but Peggotty had not finished.

" When I leave, Davy," she said, " I mean first of all to stay for a fortnight with my brother. I've been thinking that p'r'aps they would let you come along with me for that time."

My heart leaped with joy as I remembered the previous holiday I had spent with Peggotty at Yarmouth, in a house that was really a stranded ship. I saw myself running on the wet sands again with little Emily, Mr. Peggotty's niece.

My hopes fell, however, when I wondered what chance there was of Miss Murdstone consenting to the plan.

When Miss Murdstone came out to the kitchen a little later, Peggotty boldly made her suggestion.

" The boy would be idle there, and idleness is the root of all evil," replied Miss Murdstone sourly. " Still, David would be idle here, or anywhere else for that matter."

Peggotty looked as if she would have liked to make an angry retort, but kept silent while Miss Murdstone considered the matter.

" It is more important than anything," she finally said, " that my brother should be free from anything or any one to disturb him. Therefore, I suppose I had better say yes."

I thanked her, but was careful not to appear too pleased in case she changed her mind.

When the month ended, I was ready to go with Peggotty.

The carrier's cart stopped outside, and to my surprise Mr. Barkis came into the house for Peggotty's boxes. Never before had I known him to come inside the front gate. As he shouldered the biggest box, he gave me what I took for a meaning look.

Peggotty was naturally upset at leaving the house that had been her home for so many years, and when she first took her seat she kept her handkerchief to her eyes. While she did so, Mr. Barkis sat looking a picture of woe. But when she began to look about and talk to me, he became more cheerful and even grinned at me several times.

" It's a beautiful day, Mr. Barkis," I said politely.

" It ain't bad," he answered, with a cautious look at the sky.

" Peggotty feels better now," I remarked, to reassure him.

" Does she, though ? " he commented.

After reflecting about it, Mr. Barkis looked at Peggotty.

" Are you quite comfortable ? " he inquired.

Peggotty smiled and nodded.

Presently Mr. Barkis edged up closer to her, making remarks at wide intervals in his queer way, and apparently well pleased with himself. And with our journey about half-covered, he pulled up at an inn and insisted that we should both dine at his expense.

When we reached Yarmouth, Mr. Peggotty and a nephew of his were waiting to carry Peggotty's luggage to the ship-house. As they began to walk off with the boxes, Mr. Barkis beckoned to me.

" I say," he confided hoarsely, " it was all right."

" Oh," I answered, not knowing for a moment what he meant, but trying to look wise.

Mr. Barkis nodded knowingly.

" It didn't come to an end there," he whispered. " It was all right."

" Ah," I said blankly.

" You know who was willin'," he went on. " It was Barkis, and Barkis only."

I nodded assent, and Mr. Barkis shook my hand solemnly.

" It's all right," he repeated. " I'm a friend o' your'n. It was you that made it all right in the first place, like. It's all right."

In his attempt to make the matter clear, Mr. Barkis was so mysterious that I hadn't the least idea what he was talking about. I might have stood gaping at him for an hour had not Peggotty called to me.

" What was he saying to you, Davy ? " she asked when I joined her.

" He kept telling me it was all right," I replied.

*As he shouldered the biggest box he gave me a meaning look.*

" Like his impudence ! " she declared. " But still, I don't mind. Listen, Davy. What should you say if I thought of getting married ? "

" Would you like me as much then, Peggotty ? " I asked, after a little consideration.

" Of course, I should, Davy," she answered, with a hug to prove it. " But tell me what you would say ? "

" If you were thinking of getting married to Mr. Barkis ? " I said, light breaking suddenly upon me.

" Yes," Peggotty answered.

" I should think it would be a very good thing," I declared. " For one thing, Peggotty, you would always have the horse and cart to bring you over to see me. And it would cost you nothing for your fare."

" There's sense in that, bless you," Peggotty laughed. " It's what I've been thinking the past month. And I don't know that I could settle down in service to anybody else, after being with your precious mother so long. But I wouldn't have given marriage a thought if you'd been against it, Davy."

" I'm really glad about it, Peggotty," I assured her earnestly.

Reaching Mr. Peggotty's strange house, I found that I should not have my playmate so much this time. Little Emily was away at school all day, and I found her grown shy and quiet.

But even if I had to amuse myself most of the day, I enjoyed my holiday and began to recover from the first shock of my mother's death.

Each evening Mr. Barkis used to call to see Peggotty. He would sit and look at her and smile, never speaking unless spoken to. Every time he would bring a bundle with him, which he would put down behind the door, and which, when he had gone, was always found to contain a present for Peggotty.

Such a queer assortment of presents he gave her, too ! The first time it was a bag of oranges ; others were a set of pigs' trotters, a huge pin-cushion, a half-bushel of apples, a pair of jet earrings, some Spanish onions, a box of dominoes, a canary in a cage, and a leg of pickled pork.

But for all his funny ways, Mr. Peggotty said that Mr. Barkis was a good, honest man.

He and Peggotty were quietly married at the end of my fortnight's holiday. Only the two of them went into the church, while Emily and I sat in the porch outside.

After the wedding, we went to Peggotty's new house, where she took me to a little room in the roof, which she said would always be mine as often as I chose to use it. The dear soul had even placed on the little table a book of hers, which I had read again and again when first I began to read.

I slept there the night, and next day I returned to Blunderstone with Mr. Barkis and herself. They left me at the gate, and it gave me an odd feeling to see the cart go on, taking Peggotty away.

## CHAPTER XIII

### I AM PROVIDED FOR

DURING the months that followed, my life was a strange one for a boy.

The Murdstones did not beat or ill-treat me in any way. They simply ignored me, and allowed me to drift along as I willed. I moped about the house or wandered the lanes alone, with never a soul to take the least interest in what I did. Except for Peggotty, of course, who kept her promise to come to Blunderstone once a week to see me.

Sometimes she came to the house, but mostly we met somewhere nearby, to picnic from the well-filled basket she always brought. I begged several times to be allowed to go and stay with Peggotty, but only rarely would Miss Murdstone permit me to go, and then my stay was to be only a brief one.

The loneliness and idleness came to irk me so much that I would gladly have gone to a school, even had it been in charge of a tyrant ten times worse than Mr. Creakle.

At length my stepfather was visited by a friend, a Mr. Quinion. I took my breakfast with them, and was about to leave the room when Mr. Murdstone called me back.

"David," he said, "to the young this is a world for action. Not one in which to mope and idle."

"As you do yourself, Edward," put in his sister tartly.

"Do not interrupt me, please, Jane," he replied shortly. "I was saying, David, that this is a world for action. Idling will not do, especially for a boy of your disposition. Nothing would so quickly bend your stubborn will as to go out into the working world."

"We want no more of his stubbornness here," Miss Murdstone joined in. "He wants that crushed out of him."

My stepfather gave her a glance that was half-annoyance, half-approval.

"I suppose you know, David," he continued, "that I am not rich. At any rate you know now that I have told you. Already you have received considerable education, which cost me a good deal of money. I cannot afford to give you more, and even if I were able to, I don't think you would benefit by continuing at school. You will have to fight your own way in the world, and the sooner you begin, the better."

He paused for this to sink in, then went on.

"You may have heard, David, that I am connected with the wine trade in London?"

"I think I have heard some talk of it, sir," I answered, with a vague memory of hearing him discussing business matters with his sister.

"I am a partner in the firm of Murdstone and Grinby," he explained, "and Mr. Quinion is the manager of our business. We employ a number of boys, and Mr. Quinion suggests that a place could be found for you among them, on the same terms as the others."

"He having no other prospect, Murdstone," interposed Mr. Quinion in a low voice.

My stepfather dismissed the interruption with an impatient gesture.

"You will be paid enough to provide you in food and pocket-money," he said. "Your lodging, for which I have arranged, will be paid for by me. So will your washing."

"Which must cost no more than my estimate," snapped his sister.

"I shall also attend to the matter of your clothes, as you will be unable to buy them yourself yet awhile," my stepfather told me. "You are to go to London with Mr. Quinion to-morrow, David, to begin to earn your own living."

"In short, you are provided for," Miss Murdstone observed. "The rest will depend on yourself."

I quite understood that the arrangement was a plan to get me off their hands. In a way I was pleased to get away from them, but at the same time it was a little frightening to be turned out into the world at such short warning.

Next morning, attired in a black coat and waistcoat, and a pair of hard, stiff corduroy trousers which Miss Murdstone considered most suited for hard wear, I departed with Mr. Quinion. My only luggage was a very small trunk.

We rode into Yarmouth by the post-chaise which connected with the London coach, so that I found no opportunity of calling upon Peggotty to tell her of the new life I was entering upon. But I resolved that my first duty in London would be to send a letter to her.

## CHAPTER XIV

### I START TO EARN MY LIVING

I WAS ten years old when I made my start in the working world, at the warehouse of Murdstone and Grinby.

The warehouse was at the riverside, close to Blackfriars, and had a wharf of its own that overhung the water at high tide, and the black mud when the tide was low. It was a crazy old building, overrun with rats, its walls grimed with dirt, and its floors rotten with age.

If I thought I was to be employed in the counting-house, where my schooling might have been made use of, I was sadly mistaken.

I was conducted to a corner of the warehouse, where three or four boys were busy washing dirty bottles, which they afterwards examined for cracks or flaws. Other boys were busy fitting new corks to bottles freshly filled with wine, after which they had to seal the bottles, stick new labels on them, and carefully pack them in crates or barrels.

My place, I learned, was to be among these boys.

The oldest of the regular boys was told to show me my duties. His name was Mick Walker, and he wore a ragged apron and a paper cap. Mick informed me that his father was a bargeman, and that he walked in the Lord Mayor's Show, wearing a black velvet head-dress. He also introduced another boy to me, by the name of Mealy Potatoes. I found, however, that this was not the name by which the youth had been christened, but had been given him in the warehouse on account of the paleness of his face.

*The warehouse was a crazy old building, overrun with rats.*

By day, Mealy's father was a waterman. At night he acted as fireman at a theatre, where Mealy's little sister had also appeared as an imp in a pantomime.

Mick, Mealy, and the other boys in the warehouse seemed decent enough youngsters; but when I noted the raggedness of their clothes, their starved look, and the uncouthness of their speech, I felt horrified to think that I was to labour among them at such work as they were doing. What chance was there, I asked myself, of rising to such a position in the world as my father must have held? How could I ever hope to find myself again the equal of Steerforth, Traddles, and the other boys whom I had known at Salem House?

All that morning I was busy washing bottles, and holding them up to the light to see they were free from flaws, while the deepest misery filled me.

Mick had told me that we stopped for dinner at half-past twelve, and the clock was just on this time when Mr. Quinion tapped on the counting-house window, and beckoned to me.

Going in, I found there a stoutish, middle-aged man. He wore a brown coat drawn in tightly at the waist, tight black trousers and shoes. There was not a single hair upon his head, nor upon the big, round face which he turned towards me. His clothes were shabby, but his chin was buried in an imposing white collar, while he carried a jaunty-looking stick ornamented by a couple of rusty tassels. From his neck a quizzing-glass hung by a ribbon; this also was for adornment, I afterwards found, for he very seldom looked through it, and couldn't see anything when he did.

"This is he," said Mr. Quinion, nodding to myself.

The stranger looked at me hard.

" So this," he said, with a condescending roll in his voice, and with a genteel air that impressed me very much, " this is Master Copperfield. I hope I see you well, sir ? "

" Yes, thank you, sir," I replied, thinking it useless to tell him of my great unhappiness. " I trust you are the same, sir," I added politely.

" I am grateful to say that I am quite well," he assured me. " I have received a letter from Mr. Murdstone. In it, he desires that you should be received into a rear apartment of my house, which is at present unoccupied —in short," he went on, in a burst of confidence, " he wishes me to let an empty bedroom to the young beginner whom I have the pleasure to address."

The stranger smiled genially, waved his hand in a careless gesture, and settled his chin deeper into his collar.

" This is Mr. Micawber," explained Mr. Quinion to me. " He brings us orders on commission, when he can get any. He knows Mr. Murdstone, with whom he has arranged to take you as a lodger."

" My address," said Mr. Micawber, " is Windsor Terrace, City Road. As possibly your peregrinations in the metropolis have not been extensive, so that you might have difficulty in penetrating our Modern Babylon success-fully in the direction of City Road—in short," he added with another burst of confidence, " as you might lose yourself, I shall be pleased to call for you this evening, and to show you the nearest way to my house."

" Thank you very much, sir," I replied gratefully.

" At what hour shall I call ? " Mr. Micawber asked.

" At about eight," Mr. Quinion told him.

" Very good, sir," said Mr. Micawber. " I will intrude no longer."

He put on his hat at a jaunty angle, tucked his stick under his arm, and went out humming a tune.

Mr. Quinion told me that my wages were to be six shillings a week, and he paid me my first week's money in advance.

Out of my six shillings, I gave Mealy sixpence to get my trunk carried to Windsor Terrace. Small though it was, it was too heavy for me.

Then I went out to buy my first dinner. Another sixpence bought me a meat pie, which I washed down by a drink at a neighbouring pump. After a brief walk in the crowded city streets, I returned to my bottle-washing.

At the appointed time in the evening, Mr. Micawber reappeared. I had washed myself carefully to do honour to his gentility, and was quite ready to accompany him. Our progress was rather slow, for Mr. Micawber kept stopping to impress upon me the names of the streets that we passed, and the looks of the corner houses, so that I might be able to find my own way to the warehouse in the morning.

We arrived at last at his house in Windsor Terrace, which I noticed to be somewhat shabby like himself ; but also, like himself, it seemed trying to make the best show it could. The first-floor blinds were down, as I afterwards discovered, in order to conceal the fact that there was no furniture in the rooms.

Entering, I was presented to Mrs. Micawber, a thin and faded lady. With her were a pair of twin babies, a boy of about four and a girl of about three. There was also a sallow complexioned young woman with a habit of snorting, whom I found to be a servant secured from a near-by workhouse.

My room was at the top of the house, at the back. It was small and stuffy, and its walls were covered with a design which I took to represent blue muffins. Its furniture was very scanty.

Mrs. Micawber had conducted me upstairs, one of the twins in her arms, and she sat down to recover her breath.

"I never thought," she said, "when I lived with my papa and mama before my marriage, that I should ever find it necessary to take a lodger. But. Mr. Micawber being in financial difficulties, all considerations of private feelings must give way."

"Quite, ma'am," I agreed sympathetically.

*I was presented to Mrs. Micawber, a thin and faded lady.*

"Mr. Micawber's difficulties are almost overwhelming just at present," continued Mrs. Micawber, "and whether it is possible to bring him through them I don't know."

She went on to tell me a good deal about Mr. Micawber, of which I fear that I grasped but little. I have a hazy idea that she said he had been an officer in the Marines at one time. Now his occupation was to try to get orders for a variety of tradespeople, but he made little or nothing at it, from what I gleaned.

"If Mr. Micawber's creditors will not give him time," Mrs. Micawber declared, "they will have to take the consequences. Blood cannot be obtained from a stone, nor can any money be obtained at present from Mr. Micawber."

I could not understand at the time why Mrs. Micawber confided such family troubles to a boy of my age. But thinking it over in later years, I concluded that the matter was so much on her mind that she must often have discussed it with the baby twins, just to relieve her feelings.

It was not long before I became acquainted with some of the people who were seeking from Mr. Micawber the money he owed them.

At seven o'clock next morning, a dirty-faced man put his head in at the front door.

" Come on, Micawber, pay up, will you ? " he yelled. " Don't hide your face, but pay my bill. Come on ! "

Getting no answer, he began to call Mr. Micawber a robber and a swindler. He was, I discovered, a boot-maker, and he always came and shouted into the house at the same time each morning.

When he had gone away, Mrs. Micawber sat with a handkerchief to her eyes, while Mr. Micawber strode the room and waved his arms in gestures of despair. He frightened me by threatening suicide, in such a tragic manner that I expected him to do something desperate at any moment.

To my surprise, however, by the time I was ready to set off to work, Mr. Micawber was polishing his shoes and humming a lively tune as if he hadn't a care in the world.

I was to find that Mrs. Micawber regained her spirits in just the same way. At three o'clock one day, the receipt of a tax notice sent her into a fainting fit. Yet at four she was able to make a hearty meal, which had been bought by pawning a couple of teaspoons.

Living in their house, I was a good deal concerned over the financial troubles of the Micawbers, haunted as they were by a host of people demanding their money, some of them very fierce and insulting.

But at the same time, I had my own problems of making both ends meet, as I had to keep myself in food all the week on my six shillings.

For breakfast, I usually bought myself a penny loaf and a pennyworth of milk. In the cupboard in my room I kept another small loaf and a scrap of cheese, which provided me with supper.

Sometimes I had a meat pie for my dinner. But often, when on my way to work of a morning, I would spend precious pennies on the stale pastries offered at half-price in a baker's shop. This would leave no money for meat at dinner-time, so I had to make do with a roll or a slice of pudding.

I remember two pudding-shops between which I divided my custom. At one, the pudding was very full of currants, but it cost twopence for a smallish slice. The other shop only charged a penny for a bigger portion, but the pudding was pale and flabby, and its raisins were few and far between. Many a day I was glad to get it, however.

When I dined well, I had a saveloy and a roll sometimes. Or a four-penny plate of underdone beef, with now and then bread and cheese as a change.

We had half an hour off for tea in the afternoons. When I could afford it, I would have bread and butter and a mug of coffee. But more often I had to satisfy myself with a walk along Fleet Street, where I would look at all the good things in the cooking-house windows, and wish I had money enough to buy just one good meal.

At work I soon grew as adept as the other boys at cleaning bottles, and at sealing and labelling them when filled, though my distaste for such work increased day by day. With the boys I got on quite well, but could not make a friend of any of them.

Thus my spare time was mainly spent in wandering about London alone. Soon I had seen all the chief sights, but I still delighted particularly in exploring the fruit market at Covent Garden, or in watching the floating traffic that passed up and down the Thames.

In my loneliness I became quite attached to the Micawbers, who always treated me as if I was a friend of their own age. Even their troubles gave me something to think about, and when I was at home on Sundays they would tell me all the latest news as to Mr. Micawber's financial position.

At the beginning of such talks, Mr. Micawber would be sobbing despondently. But an hour later, he would be singing some cheerful ditty of the sea, while Mrs. Micawber entertained me with stories of her life at home, with her papa and mama.

## CHAPTER XV

### I LOSE MY LODGINGS

AT last Mr. Micawber's difficulties reached the crisis which his wife had so often declared to be at hand. He was arrested, and carried off to the debtors' prison in the Borough.

Before leaving home, Mr. Micawber left an invitation that I should dine with him the following Sunday. For apart from having to stay in the prison until their debts were somehow settled, debtors in those days had many privileges.

Accordingly, I presented myself at the prison gate on the Sunday morning. When the turnkey opened the gate, Mr. Micawber was waiting for me inside, and he conducted me to his room high up in the lofty prison.

As was his custom, Mr. Micawber began by bursting into tears at being in such a position.

" Take warning from my fate, Master Copperfield," he sobbed. " Make sure you never spend more than you receive, my boy. If a man earns twenty pounds a year, and spends nineteen pounds, nineteen shillings and sixpence, he will be happy. But if he spends twenty pounds and one shilling, he is steering straight to disaster and misery."

After that he borrowed a shilling from me with which to send out for some porter, and gave me a written order to Mrs. Micawber to repay that amount. Then he put away his handkerchief and cheered up immensely.

For dinner we had a loin of mutton, shared with another debtor. I had to hunt round and borrow a knife and fork before I could eat.

I was afterwards introduced to several other inmates of the prison, with whom Mr. Micawber was already on terms of great friendliness. Indeed, he was talking of forming a social club, of which he was to be president, secretary and treasurer.

When I finally left, I was charged with affectionate messages to be given to Mrs. Micawber and the children.

The next day most of the remaining furniture was seized to help pay the bills, so Mrs. Micawber decided that it would be better for her to take the children and join Mr. Micawber in prison. But before going, she was considerate enough to fix up a new lodging for me on the south side of the river.

My new abode was near enough to the prison for me to visit the Micawbers of an evening. I used to walk up and down the yard with Mr. Micawber, or else play cards with his wife and listen to her stories of her papa and mama.

These worthy parents had apparently rescued Mr. Micawber from jail on three or four occasions, but were now dead. I was glad to learn, however, that some of Mrs. Micawber's other relatives were now coming to the rescue, so that there was a hope of him regaining his liberty shortly.

I reached the prison one evening to find that he was actually to be released next day.

To celebrate the occasion, Mr. Micawber was being entertained to a farewell supper by the members of the club he had formed. As the gathering seemed rather noisy, I joined Mrs. Micawber in the midst of her sleeping family.

"May I ask, ma'am," I inquired, "what you and Mr. Micawber intend to do, now that he is out of his difficulties."

"My family," replied Mrs. Micawber, who always uttered the two words with a lofty air, "my family are of the opinion that Mr. Micawber should quit London, and exert his talents in the country. You know, Master Copperfield, that Mr. Micawber is a man of great talent."

"I am sure of it," I murmured politely.

"Of great talent," Mrs. Micawber repeated. "My family are of opinion that, with a little influence, a man of his ability might be found an opening in the Custom House. The influence that my family possesses being a local one, it is their wish that Mr. Micawber should travel down to Plymouth. They think it necessary that he should be on the spot."

"So that he will be ready if an opening occurs," I suggested.

"Exactly," agreed Mrs. Micawber. "He must be on the spot in case anything turns up."

"And do you go too, ma'am?" I asked.

The question was an unfortunate one. Mrs. Micawber had been sorely tried of late, and the mere thought of being left behind caused her to work herself up into a state of hysterics.

"I will never desert Mr. Micawber," she sobbed. "He has his faults, I do not deny. I'll not deny that he is improvident. But I'll never desert him! No! No! No!"

Her voice rose to a perfect scream, which frightened me so much that I ran off to the clubroom. Mr. Micawber was just leading a rollicking chorus when I appeared, but he broke off to rush to his wife, his waistcoat full of the heads and tails of shrimps, of which he had been eating. To my relief, he soon succeeded in pacifying Mrs. Micawber, and I stayed with them until the ringing of the bell which ordered visitors to leave the prison.

The Micawbers lodged at the house where I was staying, until the end of the week, when they were leaving for Plymouth. On the final day, Mrs. Micawber called at the warehouse, to tell Mr. Quinion that he was going, and to suggest that I had better be found a more suitable lodging.

Mr. Quinion said that I could stay with one of the carmen, a decent fellow named Tipp. But as the room would not be free for another week, I was to stay in my present place for the time being.

Before they left, the Micawbers entertained me to dinner. I took a

*Before they left, the Micawbers entertained me to dinner, and my hosts kept expressing their regret at our parting.*

spotted wooden horse for the boy, Wilkins Micawber, and a doll for his sister Emma. The twins I considered hardly old enough yet to appreciate a toy. We had a loin of pork and apple sauce, followed by a pudding, and my hosts kept expressing their regret at our parting.

" Never, Master Copperfield," observed Mrs. Micawber, " never shall I recall the period when Mr. Micawber was in difficulties, without at the same time thinking of you. Your conduct has always been of the most helpful description. I refer especially to the occasions when you have obliged me by taking various articles to the pawnshop, for the purpose of raising money to provide food and drink for my offspring. You have not been a lodger, but a friend."

Before my blushes could subside, Mr. Micawber was paying me his tribute.

" My dear," he beamed, " Copperfield has a heart to feel for the distress of his fellow creatures, and a head to plan, and a hand to—in short, he has shown a real ability to get the best price possible for such property as we could spare."

I thanked him for this praise, and said I was very sorry we were to lose each other.

" My dear young friend," Mr. Micawber replied with much feeling, " I am older than you, and have had some experience of life and—in short, I know what it is to be in financial difficulties. At present, and until something turns up—as I hourly expect it to do—I have nothing to give you but advice. Still, my advice is worth taking, although I have never taken it myself. Had I done so, I might not have been the miserable wretch you now behold."

He had been smiling happily until he came to the last words, when he suddenly remembered himself and frowned gloomily.

"You have heard my advice before, Copperfield," he said, "but I'll repeat it so that you will never forget. Briefly it is this. Annual income twenty pounds, annual spending nineteen pounds, nineteen and six, result happiness.   Annual income twenty pounds, annual spending twenty pounds and sixpence, result misery. The blossom is blighted, the leaf is withered, the—in short, you are for ever floored. As I am!"

Mr. Micawber sighed deeply, but another glass of punch restored his smile, and soon he was whistling a hornpipe.

Next morning I was at the coach-office to see them off, and handed their parcels up to them as they took their seats at the back of the coach.

"Farewell, Copperfield," cried Mr. Micawber with glistening eyes. "I wish you every happiness and prosperity. In case of anything turning up —of which I am very confident—it would give me great pleasure if it should be in my power to improve your own prospects."

As I stood looking wistfully up at them, I think that Mrs. Micawber suddenly saw for the first time what a little chap I really was. For she beckoned me to climb up, put her arm round my neck with a new and motherly expression on her face, and gave me such a kiss as she might have given her own boy.

A moment later the coach started, and I stood watching it recede until I could no longer see the handkerchiefs of the Micawber family waving at the back.


## CHAPTER XVI

### I MAKE A GREAT RESOLVE

IT was early morning when the Micawbers left London, and after seeing them off I went to begin my weary day at Murdstone and Grinby's warehouse. But as I walked towards there, a great resolve was in my mind. Rather than continue at such a hopeless occupation, I had determined to run away.

Lately I had been thinking of the aunt who was my only living relation; at least, I supposed her to be still alive, having heard nothing to the contrary.

According to Peggotty, Aunt Betsey Trotwood was a dread and awful personage. But my mother had believed there might be a spot of gentleness in her, after all, for on one occasion she had found her leaning over my cot, with a soft smile on her face.

In any case, Aunt Betsey was of my own flesh and blood, and I could at least introduce myself to her. If she would have nothing to do with me, I should be little worse off than at present.

Not knowing Aunt Betsey's address, I wrote a long letter to Peggotty, and asked her if she could tell me it. The question I put in a roundabout way, giving no hint of my intention to seek my aunt. In the letter I also said that I specially needed half a guinea, and that if Peggotty could lend it to me, I would repay her at the first chance.

Peggotty's answer soon arrived, and was as affectionate as ever. She enclosed the half-guinea, and told me that Aunt Betsey lived near Dover. But whether at Dover itself, or at Hythe, Sandgate, or Folkestone, she could not say.

One of the men at the factory was a native of those parts, however, and he told me that all these places were quite close together. I therefore decided to set out in search of my aunt at the end of that week.

I had not forgotten that I had been receiving my wages in advance since starting work, and at the same time I was determined not to owe Murdstone and Grinby a penny when I left their employ. It was for this reason I had borrowed the half-guinea from Peggotty, so that I should have funds for my journey.

*I slipped away, leaving my next week's money unclaimed.*

Saturday came, when I was to have moved to my new lodging with Tipp, the carman. In the evening, when the men were filing into the counting-house to get their wages, I asked Mick Walker to tell Mr. Quinion that I had gone to get my box shifted to Tipp's. Then I slipped away, leaving my next week's money unclaimed, so that I thus finished all-square with the firm.

While at work, I had written a label to be fixed to my box. It read, " Master David, to be left till called for, at the Coach Office, Dover."

I intended to fasten this label to my box, after I had got it from my old lodging. On the way there, I kept my eyes open for some one who would help me carry it to the nearest booking-office.

Near the Obelisk, in the Blackfriars Road, I saw a long-legged young man with an empty donkey-cart. He was a surly-looking fellow, but I asked him if he wanted a job.

" What job ? " he growled.

" To move a box for me," I said. " Will you take it to the Dover coach-office for sixpence ? "

"A tanner it is," he replied, getting on his cart and whipping up his donkey, so that I had difficulty in keeping pace with him.

There was a brazen manner about the young man that I did not much like, but as the bargain was made I took him up to my room and showed him the box. I did not want to put the label on the box until clear of the house, in case my landlord guessed that I was running away, and tried to detain me. So I asked the young man to wait for me down the road.

He drove off so rapidly that I was out of breath when I caught up to him. In my haste to get the card from my pocket, I jerked my half-guinea out also, and put it between my teeth while I tied the label.

As I finished the task, I received a violent chuck under the chin from the long-legged young man, and saw my half-guinea fly out of my mouth into his hand.

"Hallo!" he cried, seizing my collar with a frightful grin. "This looks like a police case to me! Been pinchin' money, 'ave you? Now I s'pose you're tryin' to bolt, but you're not a-goin' to. You come along with me to the police, you young warmint! Come along, now!"

"You give me my money back, if you please," I said, very much frightened. "And let go of me."

"You come with me to the police," he replied, "then you can prove the money is yourn."

*All the money I now owned was three-half-pence of my last week's wages.*

"Give me my money and my box," I pleaded, bursting into tears.

"I'll take 'em to the police along o' you," he retorted, dragging me towards the cart.

Suddenly, however, he seemed to change his mind, for he let go of me and jumped into the cart himself, then lashed at his donkey.

"I'm going straight to the police now," he yelled over his shoulder as the cart rattled away over the cobblestones.

I ran after him as fast as I could, until I was too out of breath to run any farther, and could only stand and watch him race out of sight.

But I did not stand still for long. I was struck by the fear that half London's police would be hunting for me soon, so turned and began to run in the opposite direction. This was towards Greenwich, which I had been told to be my road to Dover.

Having run a mile or so, I sat down to rest on a doorstep in the Kent Road, and was able to think things over clearly.

I realised now that it was most unlikely that the long-legged young man would go to the police, as his whole object must have been to steal my box and my half-guinea.

It was the loss of the half-guinea that worried me most, for I had relied on the money to feed and lodge me on my tramp in search of Aunt Betsey. All the money I now owned was three-halfpence, left over from my last week's wages.

But black though my position was, I determined not to go back to Murdstone and Grinby's, and the life I loathed.

A church clock struck ten as I rose and went on, miserable at heart but walking as fast as I could.

## CHAPTER XVII

### I TRAVEL A LONG ROAD

BEFORE long I came to a row of shops, one of which showed a notice saying that left-off clothes were bought, and that best prices were given for rags, bottles, and bones. I had often done business at such establishments on behalf of the Micawbers, and I came to an abrupt halt as I saw that here I might be able to raise a little money.

I went into a side street, took off my waistcoat and rolled it neatly under my arm, and walked back towards the shop. The owner of the shop was sitting at the door in his shirt sleeves, smoking. Behind him I saw coats and pairs of trousers dangling from the low ceiling, looking for all the world like men the shopkeeper had hanged out of sheer spite.

" If you please, sir," I said, " I am to sell this for a fair price."

He took the waistcoat into the shop, where he spread it on the counter and examined it closely.

" What d'you call a price, now, for this little weskit ? " he asked.

" Oh, you know best, sir," I answered modestly.

" I can't be buyer and seller, too, can I ? " he replied impatiently. " Put a price on the weskit, now."

" Would eighteenpence be about right ? " I hinted, after some hesitation.

The man rolled the waistcoat up again and gave it me back.

" I should be robbin' my family if I was to offer ninepence for it," he retorted.

I didn't want to rob the shopkeeper's family, but I considered my own need was great, so I said I would take the ninepence. He gave me the money, but not without grumbling a good deal to himself.

Luckily it was a warm summer's night, so I did not miss my waistcoat when I buttoned my jacket about me. But I reflected soberly that I should probably have to part with my coat also before I got to Dover, for tenpence-halfpenny would not carry me far.

I could not afford to pay for a night's lodging, but already I had planned where to sleep.

After a long day in the warehouse, I was beginning to feel very weary, but I trudged on up the hill to Blackheath. Here I hunted for Salem House, where I had been at school. Just against one of the school's walls I knew there to be a haystack, against which I should be able to lie snugly.

Before lying down, though, I looked through the gate at the house. All was dark and silent within, as I gazed at the windows and thought of the boys who would be sleeping there.

Steerforth was no longer there, for he was to have left soon after I was called away. But probably Traddles was still a pupil, and the majority of the boys I had known. How I wished I could have crept into the dormitory and shared a bed amongst them!

Never shall I forget the lonely sensation of my first lying down with no roof over my head. Still, sleep soon came upon me, as it must that night have come upon many other outcasts.

Once I woke with a start, to look up wildly at the stars glistening above me. And remembering where I was at that desolate hour, a feeling stole over me that made me get up and walk about, afraid of I don't know what.

Presently my fear passed, and I lay down again and slept. Nor did I stir until awakened by the once-familiar ringing of the getting-up bell at Salem House, to find the sun shining warmly upon me.

Not wishing to meet any of my old schoolfellows in my present state, I stole away while they were still dressing, and was soon treading the dust of the Dover Road.

There is no need for me to tell of all that I endured on that dreadful journey; of my nights spent shivering in the open, of the pawning of my jacket in Chatham where an old second-hand clothes dealer frightened the life out of me with his insults and threats before finally giving me one shilling and fourpence for the jacket. With the aid of this money, on the sixth day I reached the downs near Dover, and prayed I might find Aunt Betsey here and not at Folkestone or one of the other places Peggotty had named.

## CHAPTER XVIII

### I FIND A RELATIVE

I ARRIVED in the streets of Dover a dusty, sunburnt, half-clothed urchin, with my toes peeping out of one of my shoes. I had not a halfpenny in my pocket, and I had eaten nothing since yesterday. After spending more than half the day in inquiring for my aunt, I was no nearer than at the beginning, for nobody seemed to know her.

Too hungry and despondent to try further, I was sitting on the step of an empty shop when a horsecloth fell from the driver's seat of a passing fly. I picked it up, and carried it to the driver.

As he thanked me, I was struck by the good-natured expression of his face, and plucked up courage to ask my question once again.

" If you please," I said politely, " do you know of a Miss Trotwood living in the neighbourhood ? "

" Trotwood ? " he said. " Let me see, I seem to know the name. Old lady, is she ? "

" Yes," I replied hopefully, " she would be rather old."

" Is she pretty stiff in the back ? " he asked, drawing himself upright to make his question clear.

This sounded very much like Peggotty's description of Aunt Betsey, and I nodded eagerly, too excited to speak.

" Carries a bag, doesn't she ? " he went on. " A bag with a lot of room in it. A gruffish old lady, and comes down on you pretty sharp ? "

My heart sank at this, for it agreed with Peggotty's impression at the time of my aunt's visit to the Rookery. By now I had hoped she would have softened a good deal.

" That would be the lady, I feel sure," I declared to the fly-driver.

" Why, then, I'll tell you where to find her," he said. " If you follow the road I'm pointing to, you'll come to some houses facing the sea. She lives in one of those. But I warn you, my boy, the old party ain't like to hand out anything, so here's a penny for you."

I accepted the gift gratefully, and bought a loaf to devour before testing my fate with Aunt Betsey.

Following the road he had indicated, it was some time before I came to the houses mentioned. At length I saw them, and close at hand a small general shop. This I entered, and asked the young man behind the counter if he would kindly tell me where Miss Trotwood lived.

He had been serving a young woman, and it was she who turned to answer my question.

" What do you want with my mistress ? " she asked.

" I wish to speak to her, if you please," I replied.

" To beg of her, you mean ? " she retorted.

" No, indeed," I answered, but felt my face burn when it suddenly struck me that I really had come to throw myself on to my aunt's hands.

When she had been served, my aunt's maid—as I presumed the young woman to be—told me that I could follow her, if I wished to find where Miss Trotwood lived.

I needed no second invitation, though by this time I was in such a state of agitation that my legs shook under me.

I followed my guide to a very neat little cottage with cheerful bow-windows. In front was a small garden full of flowers, carefully tended and smelling deliciously.

" This is Miss Trotwood's," said the young woman, and hurried into the house, as if to shake off all responsibility for my presence.

As I stood at the gate, hardly knowing what to do next, the extreme tidiness of the cottage and its garden made me all the more aware of my own disreputable appearance. Even my hair had not been combed for a week, and I felt to be caked all over with the dust of the roads.

Presently a grey-headed, pleasant-looking gentleman looked out of an upstairs window. Seeing me, he screwed up one eye and nodded to me several times, then shook his head, laughed, and went away.

I had felt uneasy before, but the gentleman's strange behaviour made me more so.

I was actually on the point of slinking off to think things over, when out of the house came a lady with a handkerchief tied over her cap. She was wearing gardening gloves, and carried a pruning-knife in her hand. I knew her at once to be Aunt Betsey, for she came stalking from the house exactly as my poor mother had described her as stalking up our garden at the Rookery.

" Go away ! " she snapped upon seeing me. " Get along with you ! No boys allowed here."

With my heart in my mouth I watched her march to a corner of her garden, where she stooped to pull up an intruding weed. Then, my desperation giving me courage, I followed her.

" If you please, ma'am," I faltered.

She started, and looked up.

" If you please, aunt," I began again.

" Eh ? " she cried, in a tone of blank amazement.

" If you please, aunt, I am your nephew," I announced timidly.

" Good gracious ! " gasped my aunt, and sat down on the path.

" I am David Copperfield, from Blunderstone," I went on hastily. " You came there and saw me when I was a baby. Since my mother died, I have been very unhappy. I have been neglected and taught nothing, then I was sent out to earn my own living at work which I hated. I ran away to find you, being my only relative. I was robbed when I first set out, and have walked all the way from London, never sleeping in a bed since I started."

At this point I broke down, and fell into a passion of crying.

My aunt had sat staring at me from the path until I began to sob. Then she jumped up in a great hurry, took my arm and led me into the parlour. Here she put me on the sofa, with a shawl under my head and a handkerchief under my feet, as if to prevent me from dirtying the cover.

Until I was able to check my tears, my aunt stalked up and down the room with her hands behind her back. At regular intervals she would exclaim, " Mercy on us ! "

After a time she rang the bell, and her maid appeared.

" Janet," said my aunt, " go and give my compliments to Mr. Dick, and say I wish to speak to him."

Janet looked a little surprised to see my lying stiffly on the sofa, but she went off on her errand.

A minute or so later, there entered the gentleman who had acted so queerly at the window above. He was still laughing to himself.

" Mr. Dick," said my aunt, " please be serious, for nobody can be wiser than you when you choose. We all know that."

The gentleman ceased laughing, and gazed gravely at me.

" You have heard me mention David Copperfield, Mr. Dick ! " my aunt continued. " Now don't pretend to have forgotten, for you and I know better."

" David Copperfield ? " murmured Mr. Dick, who did not appear to recall the name. " Ah, David Copperfield. To be sure, David."

" Well," said my aunt, " this boy is his son. He would be the living likeness of his father when a boy, if he had not some of his mother's looks also."

*" Go away ! Get along with you ! No boys allowed here."*

" His son, eh ? " murmured Mr. Dick. " David's son, indeed ? "

" Yes," replied my aunt, " and he has done a pretty piece of business. He has run away. His sister Betsey, if he had had one, would never have run away."

My aunt shook her head, as if still regretting that I had not been born a girl instead of a boy.

" You think that his sister wouldn't have run away ? " Mr. Dick inquired earnestly.

" Bless and save the man ! " cried my aunt sharply. " How he talks ! Of course David's sister wouldn't have run away, if he had had one. She would have come and lived with her aunt in the first place, and would have been perfectly happy. Where, in the name of wonder, would his sister have run away from, or to ? "

" Nowhere," said Mr. Dick helplessly.

" Well, then," returned my aunt, " how can you pretend to be wool-gathering, Mr. Dick, when you are really as sharp as a surgeon's lancet ? Now here is young David Copperfield, and the question I ask is this. What shall I do with him ? "

" What shall you do with him ? " murmured Mr. Dick, feebly scratching his head. " Oh ! What shall you do with him ? "

" Yes," my aunt nodded, holding up a finger to emphasise her words. " Come, I want some sound advice."

" Why, if I was you," began Mr. Dick slowly, and staring vacantly at me, " if I was you, I should——"

A sudden idea seemed to strike him, and his eyes brightened.

" I should wash him," he concluded briskly.

My aunt turned to her maid with an air of triumph.

" Janet," she said, " Mr. Dick sets us all right. Heat the bath at once."

While this talk had been going on, I had been taking closer observation of my aunt.

There was a strong will shown in her face, her voice, her stride, and her carriage, which explained why she had so much overawed my gentle mother and Peggotty. But her features were handsome, though stern. I particularly noticed that she had a quick, bright eye. She wore a lavender-coloured dress that had nothing frilly nor ornamental about it, and a little lace cap on her head. At her waist hung a gentleman's gold watch.

I had also been puzzling over Mr. Dick. His eyes had a kind of watery brightness, which in combination with his vacant manner made me suspect him of being a little mad. Though if he were so, I could not understand how he came to be in my aunt's house, instead of an asylum. He was dressed like any normal gentleman in a grey morning coat and waistcoat, with white trousers, in the pockets of which he rattled some money, as if proud to possess it.

Janet had only been gone a minute or two when I was amazed to see my aunt suddenly grow rigid with indignation.

" Janet ! " she cried. " Donkeys ! "

I heard Janet's feet race along a passage, while at the same time my aunt rushed from the room. Peering from the window to see what the commotion was about, I saw a strange sight.

Three donkeys had appeared on the piece of grass in front of the house, two of them ridden by ladies, the other by a child. Darting out of the gate, Janet warned the ladies that they had no business riding on that patch of green, while my aunt seized the boy in charge of the donkeys, and boxed his ears for allowing the animals to trespass.

I could never learn whether my aunt had any real claim to own that strip of grass, but in her own mind she had decided it was hers, and she would never allow a donkey to step on it. She was in a state of constant warfare against the donkey-boys and their charges, and would stop anything she was doing if one of her hated enemies came in sight.

There were even pots of water kept in secret places, all ready to throw over offending boys ; and sticks with which to belabour the donkeys themselves.

Three times my aunt and Janet had sallied forth before my bath was ready.

The hot bath seemed to soothe all the aches out of my weary body, and after it I dressed myself in a shirt and some trousers belonging to Mr. Dick. I must have looked a strange sight in the garments, which were big enough to hold two or three boys of my size, but I was too drowsy to think about the matter.

I lay upon the sofa, covered in shawls, and was asleep almost as soon as my head touched the cushion my aunt had arranged. Yet I seem to recall my aunt softly stroking my head before I dozed away.

# CHAPTER XIX

### I TELL MY STORY

IT was evening when I awoke, to find the table prepared for a late dinner. We had roast fowl and a pudding, and how good it all tasted after having had little but plain bread for a week.

While I ate, I was deeply anxious to know what my aunt was going to do with me. But she dined in a profound silence, except when she fixed her eyes on me sitting opposite, and muttered to herself, " Mercy upon us ! " Which did not in the least relieve my anxiety.

When the cloth was removed, my aunt sent up for Mr. Dick to join us. He tried to look wise when she told him to listen to my story.

I began my narration from the time when Mr. Murdstone first came on the scene, and faithfully recounted all the chief things I could remember to have happened since. I told of how the Murdstones had treated me, of my life at Mr. Creakle's school, of my mother's death and of Peggotty's getting wed to Mr. Barkis, and of the subsequent way I was neglected at home. I went on to tell of my work at the warehouse, of my stay with the Micawbers, and finally of my adventures when I had decided to run away in search of my aunt.

During my recital, Aunt Betsey had kept her eyes firmly on Mr. Dick, who I believe would otherwise have gone to sleep. Whenever he lapsed into a smile, her frown made him become solemn again.

" Well," exclaimed my aunt, when I finished, " your mother was always young and rather helpless, to my mind, but why she must go and get married again I can't conceive."

" Perhaps she fell in love with her second husband," Mr. Dick suggested.

" Fell in love ! " cried my aunt. " What do you mean ? And what business had she to do so ? "

" Perhaps she did it for pleasure," murmured Mr. Dick.

" Pleasure, indeed ! " my aunt snapped. " Much pleasure the poor child gained through fixing her faith in a brute of a man, certain to ill-use her. What did she think to gain, I should like to know ? She had this boy, and what more did she want ? "

Mr. Dick shook his head, as if the question was beyond him.

" I knew David's wife had little judgment, when she must have a baby boy instead of a girl," continued Aunt Betsey, as if she could not forget her old grievance against my mother. " But I never imagined she would bring trouble on her boy by marrying this Murderer—or whatever the man's name is. And now, on top of it all, that woman Peggotty must go and marry. I only hope that she has found a bully of a husband, who will beat her well at least once a week ! "

I had to interfere at that, for I could not bear to hear my dear old Peggotty decried.

" You mustn't say that, aunt," I cried indignantly. " Peggotty was the best and truest friend that my mother and I ever had, and she deserves the greatest happiness in the world.  Why, my mother died in her arms, and—and——"

I wanted to tell her what Peggotty had meant to me since my mother's death, but the words became choked by tears, and I could only lay my face in my hands upon the table.

"Well, well," said my aunt in a milder tone, "the boy is right to stand up for his friends."

She laid her hand on my shoulder, and in another instant I feel sure that I should have flung my arms about her, and have begged her to take me into her protection.  Had I done so, we might have come to understand each other.

*"Now, Mr. Dick," she said, "What would you do with him?"*
*"Oh! I think I should—Yes! I should put him to bed."*

At that moment, however, my aunt stiffened as her glance fell upon something outside.

"Janet! Donkeys!" she called, and went flying out to assail a new bunch of long-eared trespassers.

When Aunt Betsey returned, she seemed to have forgotten my troubles, and instead began to talk about taking legal action against the combined donkey-owners of Dover.

It was when Janet had lit the candles and drawn the blinds that Aunt Betsey turned abruptly to Mr. Dick.

"Now, Mr. Dick," she said, holding up one finger as before to ensure attention, "I am going to ask you another question.  Look at this child."

"At David's son?" inquired Mr. Dick, with a puzzled face.

"Exactly," returned my aunt.  "What would you do with him?"

"Do with David's son?" murmured Mr. Dick.

"Yes," replied my aunt, "with David's son."

"Oh!" Mr. Dick said thoughtfully. "I think I should—— Yes! I should put him to bed!"

"Janet!" cried my aunt, with the same complacent triumph that I had noticed before. "Mr. Dick sets us all right. If the bed is ready, we'll take David up to it."

Janet reporting that the bed was quite ready, I was escorted upstairs as if I were either a royal guest or a prisoner. My aunt went in front, and Janet brought up the rear. A little taper was burning in my room, and Aunt Betsey warned me it would last only five minutes.

When my aunt left me, I heard her lock the door on the outside. From which I supposed that she feared it was a habit of mine to run away, and that she wished to be certain I was in safe keeping.

My room was a pleasant one, at the top of the house. It overlooked the sea, on which the moon was shining brilliantly.

After I had said my prayers, and the taper had gone out, I sat looking at the moonlight on the water, as if I could hope to read my fortune in it. Or as if I hoped to see my mother with my baby brother in her arms, coming from Heaven along that shining path, to look at me as she had looked when I last saw her sweet face.

I remember the solemn feeling with which I at last turned away from that magic view, to nestle between the snow-white sheets of my bed. I remember how I thought of all the solitary places under the night sky where I had slept, and how I prayed that I might never be homeless again, and might never forget those who had no home.

## CHAPTER XX

### MY FATE IS IN THE BALANCE

ON going down in the morning, I found my aunt musing so deeply at the breakfast table that she was allowing the hot water from the urn to overflow the teapot. When my entrance brought her out of her thoughts, half the table was flooded.

I felt sure that Aunt Betsey had been thinking about me, but dared not ask her what she had decided to do about my fate.

Every now and then I snatched a glance at her while we breakfasted, and each time found her looking at me with a faraway expression.

Presently she pushed away her plate, folded her arms, and stared at me fixedly. I tried to get on with my breakfast as if undisturbed by her gaze, but managed to drop first my knife, then my fork, and finally nearly choked myself with my tea.

"David," said my aunt at last.

I looked up, and met her sharp, bright glance respectfully.

"I have written to him," she said.

"To whom?" I asked.

"To your stepfather," she replied. "I have sent him a letter that he will attend to without delay, else he and I will fall out!"

"Does he know where I am, aunt?" I inquired, alarmed.

My aunt nodded.

"Shall I be given up to him?" I faltered.

"I don't know," my aunt replied. "We shall see."

"Oh!" I cried wildly. "I can't think what I should do if I had to go back with Mr. Murdstone!"

"It's no use talking about it yet," answered my aunt.

My spirits sank at the mere idea of returning to the charge of the Murdstones, and I had no heart for any more breakfast.

My aunt, appearing not to notice my depression, put on a coarse apron and cleared the table, then proceeded to dust and tidy the room. Afterwards she sat down with some needlework.

"I wish you would go upstairs," she said, as she threaded a needle, "and give my compliments to Mr. Dick. Tell him I should be glad to know how he is getting on with his Memorial."

I rose with eagerness, glad of something to do to take my mind off the Murdstones. But my aunt stayed me with a gesture.

"I suppose," she said, "that you think Mr. Dick is a very short name."

"I thought so when I first heard it, yesterday," I confessed.

"Don't think that he hasn't a longer name to use if he chooses," explained my aunt, with a slightly lofty air. "His true name is Babley, Mr. Richard Babley."

"Would it not be more respectful if I called him by his proper name, aunt?" I suggested modestly.

"Under no circumstances must you do so," my aunt declared sharply. "He can't bear his own name. That's a peculiarity of his. Mr. Dick is his name here, and everywhere else, now. Not that he ever goes anywhere else, except in my company. So take care, child, that you call him Mr. Dick, and nothing else."

I promised to obey, and went upstairs with my message.

Through the open door, I saw Mr. Dick sitting at a table, with his head almost resting on a large sheet of paper. There was a long pen in his hand.

He was so intent on his work that I had plenty of time to survey his room. There was a huge paper kite in one corner, bundles of manuscripts scattered everywhere, and pens all over the place.

Suddenly Mr. Dick became aware of my presence.

"Ha, Phœbus!" he cried, laying down his pen. "How does the world go? I'll tell you what," he added, in a lower tone, "I shouldn't like you to mention it to any one else, but this is a mad world. Mad as Bedlam, my boy!"

He took a pinch of snuff from a box as he said it, and laughed heartily.

Politeness compelled me to laugh also, although I could not quite see the joke. Then I delivered my message.

"Well," replied Mr. Dick, "my compliments to Miss Trotwood, and you may tell her I believe I have made a start with my Memorial," casting an anything but confident look at his manuscript.

Then, before I could think of a remark to make, he took me confidentially by the arm.

"Have you been to school?" he asked.

THE BOYHOOD OF DAVID COPPERFIELD

The guard helped me to climb the steep back of the coach
to my seat on the roof. (Page 20)

**SPRING SONG**

Spring is coming, Spring is coming.
All around is fair. (Page 87)

" Yes, sir," I answered. " For a short time."

" Ah," said Mr. Dick, looking at me and taking up his pen. " Do you recollect the date when King Charles the First was beheaded ? "

" I believe it was in the year 1649," I replied.

" That's what the books say," Mr. Dick said doubtfully, " but I don't see how it can be right. Because if it happened so long ago, how did they manage to put some of the trouble out of his head into mine, after his was cut off ? "

I was much surprised by the question, and at the same time my suspicions of him were confirmed. Harmless though he seemed, there could be no doubt that Mr. Dick was a little mad.

*I saw Mr. Dick sitting at a table, his head almost resting on a large sheet of paper and a long pen in his hand.*

" It is very strange," murmured Mr. Dick despondently, " that I can never get that matter quite right, about King Charles's head and my own. But no matter, no matter," he cried cheerfully, " there's time enough to work it out. My compliments to Miss Trotwood, and tell her I am getting on very well indeed."

But before I could go away, he called my attention to the kite.

" What do you think of that ? " he asked proudly.

" It's a beauty," I answered, for it must have been seven feet high.

" I made it," he told me. " We'll go and fly it, you and I."

I saw that the kite was covered with very close, neat writing. As I glanced along the lines, I thought I saw some references to King Charles's head in places.

" You see, I have written on it all about King Charles and myself," explained Mr. Dick. " There's plenty of string, and when it flies high, the kite takes all those facts a long way."

I stared at him afresh, but he looked so normal and pleasant that I wondered if I had been wrong after all in thinking him mad. It occurred to me that he was joking at my expense, so I again laughed politely, and he did the same, and we parted the best of friends.

" Well, child," said my aunt. " And how is Mr. Dick getting on ? "

I repeated his message that he was getting on very well indeed.

" And what do you think of Mr. Dick ? " she asked me bluntly.

" I—er—he seems a very nice gentleman," I stammered evasively.

But my aunt was not to be put off.

" Come, speak what is in your mind, child," she commanded. " I want a direct and honest answer."

" Is he—is Mr. Dick at all out of his mind ? " I stammered.

" Not a morsel," replied my aunt.

" Oh," I observed faintly.

" No," declared my aunt, with great decision, " if there is one thing that Mr. Dick is not, it is mad."

" Oh, indeed," I rejoined.

" He has been called mad, certainly," admitted Aunt Betsey. " But for that, I should not have had the pleasure of his society for the past ten years. Actually, he is only a little eccentric, having convinced himself that somebody took the troubles out of King Charles's head when it was chopped off, and placed them in his own. Apart from that one delusion, Mr. Dick is a wise and clever man."

She went on to explain that a well-to-do brother had wished to place Mr. Dick in an asylum. But my aunt had intervened, offering to look after Mr. Dick and to see that he came to no harm. He had a small income of his own, enough to keep him well fed and clothed.

" What is this Memorial he is writing, aunt ? " I inquired. " Is it a history of his own life ? "

" I understand it to be a petition concerning his affairs," she replied, rubbing the side of her nose uncertainly. " His intention is to forward it, when finished, to the Lord Chancellor, or some such personage whose duty it is to read and consider Memorials. So far, however, Mr. Dick has not been able to complete the document to his satisfaction. No matter how he tries, some mention of King Charles's head will creep into his writing, and he has to start all over again."

I found out afterwards that Mr. Dick had been trying to keep King Charles the First out of his Memorial for upwards of ten years, but without success.

After learning how my aunt had taken poor, harmless Mr. Dick into her care, I felt more hopeful concerning my own future.

At length a letter from Mr. Murdstone came. Aunt Betsey informed me that my stepfather was coming to see her in person next day.

# CHAPTER XXI

## MY AUNT DECIDES

NEXT day I was in such an inward fever that I had not a word for any one.

Still bundled up in my borrowed clothing, I sat with my gaze wandering to and fro between the clock and the garden gate. Every moment I expected to be startled by the sight of that gloomy face that had so often filled me with terror.

My aunt was a little more imperious and stern than usual, but I saw no other sign that she was expecting a visitor out of the ordinary. As I watched her calmly sewing, I wished that I could regard Mr. Murdstone's coming with so little concern.

My aunt had ordered Janet to postpone dinner until my stepfather should arrive. But afternoon came without his appearing, and at last Aunt Betsey told Janet to wait no longer.

It was just then that I saw a lady, mounted on a donkey, ride deliberately on to the forbidden strip of green. To my horror I recognised it to be Miss Murdstone.

I was too dismayed to say anything for the moment.

Meanwhile, my aunt had seen the trespasser, who had stopped the donkey and was looking about her. Aunt Betsey put her head out of the window, and shook her fist.

"Go along with you!" she shouted. "You have no business there! How dare you trespass like that? Go along, you bold-faced thing!"

As Janet went rushing out to expostulate with the invader at closer quarters, I managed to recover my speech.

"That is Miss Murdstone, aunt," I warned her. "And there is Mr. Murdstone coming up the hill behind her."

"I don't care who it is!" retorted my aunt, still shaking her fist. "I won't be trespassed upon. I won't allow it. Will you go away, ma'am? Turn that donkey round, Janet, and lead him off!"

From the window, I was the witness of a regular battle. The donkey spread his feet and stood firm, objecting to go anywhere. Janet tried to pull him sideways off the green, while Mr. Murdstone also gripped the reins and tried to urge him onwards. As for Miss Murdstone, she was striking at Janet with her parasol to make her leave go. Finally, to add to the confusion, a small crowd of boys stood round and cheered.

Aunt Betsey could not witness such a struggle without wishing to take part, especially as she recognised one of the boys to be the donkey's guardian, and an old enemy of hers.

"Go and fetch a constable, Janet!" she cried. "I'll have this young scoundrel sent to prison, for I've had enough of his trespassing."

But her captive suddenly wriggled loose, and fled across the flower-beds, in which he left deep impressions of his hob-nailed boots.

Miss Murdstone having by now dismounted, the boy squeezed **through** a gap in the hedge, clutched his donkey's bridle, and ran off.

*Mr. and Miss Murdstone entered.*

Mr. Murdstone and his sister entered the gate, but my aunt, a little ruffled by the combat, turned her back on them with much dignity and marched into the house. Janet followed to announce the visitors' names.

"Shall I go away, aunt?" I asked, trembling.

"Certainly not," snapped my aunt.

She pushed me into a corner near her, and fenced me in with a chair, so that I felt like a prisoner in the dock at a court of justice.

Aunt Betsey rose from her chair as Mr. and Miss Murdstone entered.

"I was not aware to whose presence it was I had the pleasure of objecting," my aunt greeted them. "But I don't allow anybody to ride over that turf. I make no exceptions, nobody must do it."

"Your regulation is rather awkward to strangers," said Miss Murdstone, in the acid tone I knew so well.

"Is it?" my aunt replied coldly.

Mr. Murdstone hastened to interpose.

"Miss Trotwood," he began.

My aunt turned to him quickly, with a keen look.

"I presume," she said, "that you are the Mr. Murdstone who married the widow of my nephew, David Copperfield?"

"I am," replied Mr. Murdstone.

My aunt rang the bell.

"Janet," she said when the maid appeared, "my compliments to Mr. Dick, and beg him to come downstairs."

Until he came, my aunt sat stiffly erect, frowning at the wall. Mr. Dick came in looking rather foolish, and biting a forefinger.

"This is Mr. Dick," my aunt announced. "He is an old and close friend, upon whose judgment I always rely."

My aunt bent her head for Mr. Murdstone to speak.

"On receipt of your letter, Miss Trotwood," my stepfather began pompously, "I considered it an act of greater justice to myself, and perhaps of respect to you——"

"Thank you," interrupted my aunt sharply, "but you need not worry about me."

"I considered it," pursued Mr. Murdstone, with a frown, "much better to answer your letter in person, however inconvenient the journey might be. In a written reply it would have been difficult to tell you all about this boy, who has run away from his friends and his occupation——"

"And whose appearance," broke in his sister, glaring at me in my borrowed garments, "is perfectly scandalous and disgraceful."

"Jane Murdstone," said her brother, "please do not interrupt me. As I was about to say, Miss Trotwood, this unhappy boy has been the cause of much trouble and worry, both during the lifetime of my late wife, and since. He has a sullen, rebellious spirit and a violent temper. Both my sister and I have tried to correct his faults, but without success."

"It is hardly necessary that I should add anything to what my brother has said," Miss Murdstone remarked. "Yet I cannot help saying that this is the worst boy in the world."

"That's rather strong," observed my aunt.

"But not at all too strong for the facts," Miss Murdstone declared.

"H'm," grunted Aunt Betsey. "Well, sir, and what more?"

She and Mr. Murdstone had been regarding each other closely, and I had been noticing his face grow darker and darker.

"I have had my own opinions," he continued, "as to the best way of bringing the boy up, and of trying to cure his wicked ways. My methods have been founded partly on my experience of him, and partly on the means at my disposal. I thought it best to place the boy in a respectable business, where he would be under the eye of a friend of mine. But that did not please him. He must run away from his work, make himself a common vagabond running about the country, and finally come here, in rags, to appeal to you, Miss Trotwood. I should like to warn you of the consequences if you abet him in his appeal."

"We won't consider consequences just yet," replied my aunt coldly. "First of all, what about this respectable business you speak about? Is it one to which you would have put your own boy, if you had one?"

"If he had been my brother's own boy," broke in Miss Murdstone, "he would have been of a totally different character."

"And what if the boy's mother had been alive?" persisted Aunt Betsey. "Would he have gone in the same business then?"

"I do not believe," replied Mr. Murdstone, "that Clara would have objected to any plan which my sister and I agreed was for the best."

"Humph!" my aunt muttered. "Poor Clara!"

Both the Murdstones scowled at my aunt's meaning comment, but she had turned to shake her head at Mr. Dick. He had been rattling the money in his pockets very loudly, but he now stopped.

"And what of my poor niece's annuity?" my aunt asked. "Did that die with her?"

"It did," my stepfather answered.

"Then what about the house they lived in, the Rookery?" my aunt went on. "Did not Clara leave that to her boy?"

"My late wife loved her second husband devotedly, ma'am," replied Mr. Murdstone loftily. "She also trusted him implicitly."

"Which means, in short," retorted my aunt, "that you persuaded my niece not to make a will. Thus, you inherit the house, and her boy gets nothing. I'm afraid, sir, that your late wife was a most unhappy, most unfortunate innocent, whom you found it easy to dupe. And now, what have you to say next?"

"Merely this, Miss Trotwood," he returned, his face black with fury. "I am here to take David back and to deal with him as I think proper. I am not here to give any promise as to what I will do with him. You may possibly have some idea, Miss Trotwood, of backing him in his action of running away. You may think of backing him in any complaints he has made against me. Your manner has been unfriendly towards my sister and me.

"Now I must caution you," he continued in his firmest manner, "that if you abet the boy once, you abet him for always. I will not be trifled with, Miss Trotwood, and you must make your choice now. I am here, for the first and last time, to take him away. Is he ready to go? If he is not ready, or if you are not willing to let him return with me unconditionally, my doors are finally closed to him. In that case, I take it that you will make yourself responsible for him?"

To this address, my aunt had listened with the closest attention, sitting perfectly upright with her hands folded in front of her, and looking grimly at the speaker. When he had finished, she turned her eyes on Miss Murdstone, without moving any other part of herself a fraction.

"Well, ma'am," she said coldly, "have you anything to remark?"

"Indeed, Miss Trotwood," replied Miss Murdstone, "all that I could say has been so well said by my brother that I have nothing to add. Except to thank you for your politeness," she added, with an irony that had no more effect on my aunt than it would have had on the cannon I slept beside at Chatham.

"And what does the boy say?" inquired my aunt. "Are you ready to go with Mr. Murdstone, David?"

"No, aunt, no!" I cried passionately. "Please don't let them take me away! They have never liked me, never been kind to me. They made my mother unhappy, the way they treated me. Oh, please, aunt, for my father's sake do not let me go back with them!"

My aunt gave no sign of hearing me, but turned to Mr. Dick.

"Mr. Dick," she said, "this is a matter for your wisdom to decide. What shall I do with this boy?"

Mr. Dick considered for a time, then brightened suddenly.

"Have him measured for a suit of clothes, at once," he said.

My aunt beamed triumphantly.

"There!" she exclaimed. "Mr. Dick, your common sense is invaluable. Give me your hand!"

Having shaken Mr. Dick's hand with great cordiality, my aunt reached out and pulled me to her side.

" Sir," she said to Mr. Murdstone, " you can go as soon as you like, but David stays with me. I'll take my chance with him. If he's as bad as you say he is, I can at least do as much with him as you have done. But I don't believe a word of what you have said about him."

Mr. Murdstone shrugged his shoulders as he rose.

" If you were a gentleman, Miss Trotwood," he began.

" Bah ! Stuff and nonsense ! " interrupted Aunt Betsey. " Don't talk to me ! "

" How exquisitely polite ! " sneered Miss Murdstone.

" *Sir, you can go as soon as you like, but David stays with me.*"

But turning a deaf ear to her, my aunt continued to address my step-father.

" Do you think I don't realise," she said, " what a life you must have led my poor niece ? Do you think I don't realise what a woeful day it was for that poor, sweet, gentle creature when you first came into her way ? "

" I never heard any one so insulting ! " cried Miss Murdstone.

" I can see it all as plainly as if I had been there," pursued my aunt. " I can see you being so smooth and silky at first, to deceive that poor innocent. You would pretend to dote on her boy, and promise to be all that a loving father should be to him. All this to persuade that soft, trusting Clara to marry you. Ugh ! "

" I never met such a rude person in all my life ! " Miss Murdstone gasped, while her brother stood speechless.

" And when you had made sure of her," went on my aunt, " I can guess how you would gradually break her will. But you did more than that ! You kept on until you broke her heart, also, through the way you ill-treated the boy she loved."

" This is unbearable ! " exclaimed Miss Murdstone, in a perfect agony at not being able to draw my aunt's attack to herself.

But still stone-deaf to the interrupting voice, Aunt Betsey concluded her fiery indictment of my stepfather.

" Perhaps nobody has ever had the courage to speak so plainly to you before," she said, " but you know it's the truth ! "

Mr. Murdstone had been standing by the door, his black eyes fixed upon my aunt.  There was a smile on his lips, but a frown on his brow.

" I'll bid good-day to you, sir," my aunt said coldly, " and good-bye. Good-bye to you also, ma'am," she added, turning abruptly to Miss Murdstone.  " And if ever I see you ride a donkey over my green again, as sure as you've a head on your shoulders, I'll knock your bonnet off and trample on it ! "

I shall never forget the look on my aunt's face as she fired off this unexpected threat, nor the expression on Miss Murdstone's face.

But my aunt's bearing, no less than her speech, was so fierce that Miss Murdstone made no attempt to answer.  Instead, she took her brother's arm, and walked haughtily out of the cottage.

My aunt stood at the window, ready, as I believed, to make good her threat if the donkey reappeared.  No attempt at defiance being made, however, her face gradually relaxed, and she turned to me with a smile of unbelievable gentleness.

She said nothing, but just opened her arms, and gladly I threw myself into her embrace.

# THE GIRL WHO TROD ON THE LOAF

### *by* HANS ANDERSEN

THE story of the girl who trod on the loaf to avoid soiling her shoes, and of the misfortune that befell this girl, is well known. It has been written, and even printed.

The girl's name was Ingé : she was a poor child, but proud and presumptuous ; there was a bad foundation in her, as the saying is. When she was quite a little child, it was her delight to catch flies, and tear off their wings, so as to convert them into creeping things. Grown older, she would take cockchafers and beetles, and spit them on pins. Then she pushed a green leaf or a little scrap of paper towards their feet, and the poor creatures seized it, and held it fast, and turned it over and over struggling to get free from the pin.

"The cockchafer is reading," Ingé would say. " See how he turns the leaf round and round ! "

With years she grew worse rather than better ; but she was pretty, and that was her misfortune ; otherwise she would have been more sharply reproved than she was.

"Your headstrong will requires something strong to break it ! " her own mother often said. " As a little child, you used to trample on my apron ; but I fear you will one day trample on my heart."

And that is what she really did.

She was sent into the country, in service in the house of rich people, who kept her as their own child, and dressed her in corresponding style. She looked well, and her presumption increased.

When she had been there about a year, her mistress said to her, " You ought once to visit your parents, Ingé."

73

And Ingé set out to visit her parents, but it was only to show herself in her native place, and that the people there might see how grand she had become ; but when she came to the entrance of the village, and the young husbandmen and maids stood there chatting, and her own mother appeared among them, sitting on a stone to rest, and with a faggot of sticks before her that she had picked up in the wood, then Ingé turned back, for she felt ashamed that she, who was so finely dressed, should have for a mother a ragged woman who picked up wood in the forest. She did not turn back out of pity for her mother's poverty, she was only angry.

And another half-year went by, and her mistress said again, " You ought to go to your home, and visit your old parents, Ingé. I'll make you a present of a great wheaten loaf that you may give to them : they will certainly be glad to see you again."

And Ingé put on her best clothes, and her new shoes, and drew her skirts around her, and set out, stepping very carefully, that she might be clean and neat about the feet ; and there was no harm in that. But when she came to the place where the footway led across the moor, and where there was mud and puddles, she threw the loaf into the mud, and trod upon it to pass over without wetting her feet. But as she stood there with one foot upon the loaf and the other uplifted to step farther, the loaf sank with her, deeper and deeper, till she disappeared altogether, and only a great puddle, from which the bubbles rose, remained where she had been.

And that's the story.

But whither did Ingé go ? She sank into the moor ground, and went down to the Moor Woman, who is always brewing there. The Moor Woman is cousin to the Elf Maidens, who are well enough known, of whom songs are sung, and whose pictures are painted ; but concerning the Moor Woman it is only known that when the meadows steam in summer-time, it is because she is brewing. Into the Moor Woman's brewery did Ingé sink down ; and no one can endure that place long. A box of mud is a palace compared with the Moor Woman's brewery. Every barrel there has an odour that almost takes away one's senses ; and the barrels stand close to each other ; and wherever there is a little opening among them, through which one might push one's way, the passage becomes impracticable from the number of damp toads and fat snakes who sit out their time there. Among this company did Ingé fall ; and all the horrible mass of living creeping things was so icy cold, that she shuddered in all her limbs, and became stark and stiff. She continued fastened to the loaf, and the loaf drew her down as an amber button draws a fragment of straw.

The Moor Woman was at home, and on that day there were visitors in the brewery. These visitors were Old Bogey and his grandmother, who came to inspect it ; and Bogey's grandmother is a venomous old woman who is never idle : she never rides out to pay a visit without taking her work with her ; and accordingly she had brought it on the day in question. She sewed biting-leather to be worked into men's shoes, and which makes them wander about, unable to settle anywhere. She wove webs of lies, and strung together hastily-spoken words that had fallen to the ground ; and all this was done for the injury and ruin of mankind. Yes, she knew how to sew, to weave, and to string, this old grandmother !

Catching sight of Ingé she put up her double eyeglass, and took another look at the girl.

"That's a girl who has ability!" she observed, "and I beg you will give me the little one as a memento of my visit here. She'll make a capital statue to stand in my grandson's antechamber."

And Ingé was given up to her, and this is how Ingé came into Bogey's domain. People don't always go there by the direct path, but they can get there by roundabout routes if they have a tendency in that direction.

That was a never-ending antechamber. The visitor became giddy who looked forward, and doubly giddy when he looked back, and saw a whole

*She put up her eyeglass and took another look at the girl.*

crowd of people, almost utterly exhausted, waiting till the gate of mercy should be opened to them—they had to wait a long time! Great fat waddling spiders spun webs of a thousand years over their feet, and these webs cut like wire, and bound them like bronze fetters; and moreover, there was an eternal unrest working in every heart—a miserable unrest. The miser stood there, and had forgotten the key of his strong box, and he knew the key was sticking in the lock. It would take too long to describe the various sorts of torture that were found there together. Ingé felt a terrible pain while she had to stand there as a statue, for she was tied fast to the loaf.

"That's the fruit of wishing to keep one's feet neat and tidy," she said to herself. "Just look how they're all staring at me!"

Yes, certainly, the eyes of all were fixed upon her, and their evil thoughts gleamed forth from their eyes, and they spoke to one another, moving their lips, from which no sound whatever came forth: they were very horrible to behold.

" It must be a great pleasure to look at me ! " thought Ingé, " and indeed I have a pretty face and fine clothes." And she turned her eyes, for she could not turn her head, her neck was too stiff for that. But she had not considered how her clothes had been soiled in the Moor Woman's brewhouse. Her garments were covered with mud ; a snake had fastened in her hair, and dangling down her back ; and out of each fold of her frock a great toad looked forth, croaking like an asthmatic poodle. That was very disconcerting. " But all the rest of them down here look horrible," she observed to herself, and derived consolation from the thought.

The worst of all was the terrible hunger that tormented her. But could she not stoop and break off a piece of the loaf on which she stood ? No, her back was too stiff, her hands and arms were benumbed, and her whole body was like a pillar of stone ; only she was able to turn her eyes in her head, to turn them quite round, so that she could see backwards : it was an ugly sight. And then the flies came up, and crept to and fro over her eyes, and she blinked her eyes, but the flies would not go away, for they could not fly : their wings had been pulled out, so that they were converted into creeping insects : it was horrible torment added to the hunger, for she felt empty, quite, entirely empty.

" If this lasts much longer," she said, " I shall not be able to bear it."

But she had to bear it, and it lasted on and on.

Then a hot tear fell down upon her head, rolled over her face and neck, down on to the loaf on which she stood ; and then another tear rolled down, followed by many more. Who might be weeping for Ingé ? Had she not still a mother in the world ? The tears of sorrow which a mother weeps for her child always make their way to the child ; but they do not relieve it, they only increase its torment. And now to bear this unendurable hunger, and yet not to be able to touch the loaf on which she stood ! She felt as if she had been feeding on herself, and had become like a thin hollow reed that takes in every sound, for she heard everything that was said of her up in the world, and all that she heard was hard and evil. Her mother, indeed, wept much and sorrowed for her, but for all that she said, " A haughty spirit goes before a fall. That was thy ruin, Ingé. Thou hast sorely grieved thy mother."

Her mother and all on earth knew of the sin she had committed ; knew that she had trodden upon the loaf, and had sunk and disappeared ; for the cowherd had seen it from the hill beside the moor.

" Greatly hast thou grieved thy mother, Ingé," said the mother ; " yes, yes, I thought it would be thus."

" Oh that I had never been born ! " thought Ingé ; " it would have been far better. But what use is my mother's weeping now ? "

And she heard how her master and mistress, who had kept and cherished her like kind parents, now said she was a sinful child, and did not value the gifts of God, but trampled them under her feet, and that the gates of mercy would only open slowly to her.

" They should have punished me," thought Ingé, " and have driven out the whims I had in my head."

She heard how a complete song was made about her, a song of the proud girl who trod upon the loaf to keep her shoes clean, and she heard how the song was sung everywhere.

" That I should have to bear so much evil for that ! " thought Ingé ; " the others ought to be punished, too, for their sins. Yes, then there would be plenty of punishing to do. Ah, how I'm being tortured ! "

And her heart became harder than her outward form.

" Here in this company one can't even become better," she said, " and I don't want to become better ! Look how they're all staring at me ! " And her heart was full of anger and malice against all men. " Now they've something to talk about at last up yonder. Ah, how I'm being tortured ! "

And then she heard how her story was told to the little children, and the little ones called her the godless Ingé, and said that she was so haughty and ugly that she must be well punished.

Thus even the children's mouths spoke hard words of her.

But one day, while grief and hunger gnawed her hollow frame, and she heard her name mentioned and her story told to an innocent child, a little girl, she became aware that the little one burst into tears at the tale of the haughty, vain Ingé.

" But will Ingé never come up here again ? " asked the little girl.

And the reply was " She will never come up again."

" But if she were to say she was sorry, and to beg pardon, and say she would never do so again ? "

" Yes, then she might come ; but she would not beg pardon," was the reply.

" I should be so glad if she would," said the little girl ; and she appeared to be quite inconsolable. " I'll give my doll and all my playthings if she may only come up. It's too dreadful—poor Ingé ! "

And these words penetrated to Ingé's inmost heart, and seemed to do her good. It was the first time any one had said, " Poor Ingé," without adding anything about her faults : a little innocent child was weeping and praying for her. It made her feel quite strangely, and she herself would gladly have wept, but she could not weep, and that was a torment in itself.

While years were passing above her, for where she was there was no change, she heard herself spoken of more and more seldom. At last one day a sigh struck on her ear : " Ingé, Ingé, how you have grieved me ! I said how it would be ! " It was the last sigh of her dying mother.

Occasionally she heard her name spoken by her former employers, and they were pleasant words when the woman said, " Shall I ever see thee again, Ingé ? One knows not what may happen."

But Ingé knew right well that her good mistress would never come to the place where she was.

And again time went on— a long, bitter time. Then Ingé heard her name pronounced once more, and saw two bright stars that seemed gleaming above her. They were two gentle eyes closing upon earth. So many years had gone by since the little girl had been inconsolable and wept about " poor Ingé," that the child had become an old woman, and was now to be called home to heaven ; and in the last hour of existence, when the events of the whole life stand at once before us, the old woman remembered how as a child she had cried heartily at the story of Ingé.

And the eyes of the old woman closed, and the eye of her soul was opened to look upon the hidden things. She, in whose last thoughts Ingé had been

*The peasant set up a pole with ears of corn bound to the top.*

present so vividly, saw how deeply the poor girl had sunk, and burst into tears at the sight; in heaven she stood like a child, and wept for poor Ingé. And her tears and prayers sounded like an echo in the dark empty space that surrounded the tormented captive soul, and the unhoped-for love from above conquered her, for an angel was weeping for her. Why was this vouchsafed to her? The tormented soul seemed to gather in her thoughts every deed she had done on earth, and she, Ingé, trembled and wept such tears as she had never yet wept. She was filled with sorrow about herself: it seemed as though the gate of mercy could never open to her; and while in deep penitence she acknowledged this, a beam of light shot radiantly down into the depths to her, with a greater force than that of the sunbeam which melts the snowman the boys have built up; and quicker than the snowflake melts, the stony form of Ingé was changed to mist, and a little bird soared with the speed of lightning upward into the world of men.

But the bird was timid and shy towards all things around; he was ashamed of himself, ashamed to encounter any living thing, and hurriedly sought to conceal himself in a dark hole in an old crumbling wall; there he sat cowering, trembling through his whole frame, and unable to utter a sound, for he had no voice. Long he sat there before he could rightly see all the beauty around him; for it was beautiful. The air was fresh and mild, the moon cast its mild radiance over the earth; trees and bushes exhaled fragrance, and it was right pleasant where he sat, and his coat of feathers was clean and pure. How all creation seemed to speak of beneficence and love! The bird wanted to sing of the thoughts that stirred in his breast, but he could not; gladly would he have sung as the cuckoo and the nightingale sang in the spring-time. But Heaven, that hears the mute song of praise of the worm, could hear the notes of praise which now trembled in the breast of the bird, as David's psalms were heard before they had fashioned themselves into words and song.

For weeks these toneless songs stirred within the bird ; at last the holy Christmas-tide approached. The peasant who dwelt near set up a pole by the old wall, with some ears of corn bound to the top, that the birds of heaven might have a good meal, and rejoice in the happy, blessed time.

And on Christmas morning the sun arose and shone upon the ears of corn, which were surrounded by a number of twittering birds. Then out of the hole in the wall streamed forth the voice of another bird, and it soared forth from his hiding-place ; and in heaven it was well known what bird this was.

It was a hard winter. The ponds were covered with ice, and the beasts of the field and the birds of the air were stinted for food. Our little bird soared away over the high road, and in the ruts of the sledges he found here and there a grain of corn, and at the halting-places some crumbs. Of these he ate only a few, but he called all the other hungry sparrows around him, that they, too, might have some food. He flew into the towns, and looked round about ; and wherever a kind hand had strewn bread on the window-sill for the birds, he only ate a single crumb himself, and gave all the rest to the other birds.

In the course of the winter, the bird had collected so many bread-crumbs, and given them to the other birds, that they equalled the weight of the loaf on which Ingé had trod to keep her shoes clean ; and when the last bread-crumb had been found and given, the gray wings of the bird became white, and spread far out.

" Yonder is a sea-swallow, flying away across the water," said the children, when they saw the white bird. Now it dived into the sea, and now it rose again into the clear sunlight. It gleamed white ; but no one could tell whither it went, though some asserted that it flew straight into the sun.

---

## SPRING SONG

### ANON.

SPRING is coming, spring is coming,
   Birdies, build your nest ;
Weave together straw and feather,
   Doing each your best.

Spring is coming, spring is coming,
   Flowers are coming too,
Pansies, lilies, daffodillies
   Now are coming through.

Spring is coming, spring is coming,
   All around is fair,
Shimmer and quiver on the river,
   Joy is everywhere.

# THE GREAT STONE FACE

## *by* NATHANIEL HAWTHORNE

ONE afternoon, when the sun was going down, a mother and her little boy sat at the door of their cottage, talking about the Great Stone Face. They had but to lift their eyes, and there it was plainly to be seen, though miles away, with the sunshine brightening all its features.

And what was the Great Stone Face?

Embosomed among a family of lofty mountains, there was a valley so spacious that it contained many thousand inhabitants. Some of these good people dwelt in log-huts, with the black forests all around them on the steep and difficult hillsides. Others had their homes in comfortable farmhouses, and cultivated the rich soil on the gentle slopes or level surfaces of the valley. Others, again, were congregated into populous villages, where some wild, highland rivulet, tumbling down from its birthplace in the upper mountain region, had been caught and tamed by human cunning, and compelled to turn the machinery of cotton factories. The inhabitants of this valley, in short, were numerous, and of many modes of life. But all of them, grown people and children, had a kind of familiarity with the Great Stone Face, although some possessed the gift of distinguishing this grand natural phenomenon more perfectly than many of their neighbours.

The Great Stone Face, then, was a work of Nature in her mood of majestic playfulness, formed on the perpendicular side of a mountain by some immense rocks, which had been thrown together in such a position as, when viewed at a proper distance, precisely to resemble the features of the human countenance. It seemed as if an enormous giant, or a Titan, had sculptured his own likeness on the precipice. There was the broad arch of the forehead, a hundred feet in height; the nose, with its long bridge; and the vast lips,

### THE FLYING TRUNK

She was lying asleep on the sofa. She was so beautiful
that the merchant's son could not help kneeling down to
kiss her hand. (Page 98)

**WHAT THE MOON SAW**

"I saw a little girl weeping", said the Moon.
"She was weeping over the depravity of the world." (Page 145)

which, if they could have spoken, would have rolled their thunder accents from one end of the valley to the other. True it is, that if the spectator approached too near he lost the outline of the gigantic visage, and could discern only a heap of ponderous and gigantic rocks, piled in chaotic ruin one upon another. Retracing his steps, however, the wondrous features would again be seen ; and the farther he withdrew from them, the more like a human face, with all its original divinity intact, did they appear ; until, as it grew dim in the distance, with the clouds and glorified vapour of the mountains clustering about it, the Great Stone Face seemed positively to be alive.

It was a happy lot for children to grow up to manhood or womanhood with the Great Stone Face before their eyes, for all the features were noble, and the expression was at once grand and sweet, as if it were the glow of a vast, warm heart, that embraced all mankind in its affections, and had room for more. It was an education only to look at it. According to the belief of many people, the valley owed much of its fertility to this benign aspect that was continually beaming over it, illuminating the clouds, and infusing its tenderness into the sunshine.

As we began with saying, a mother and her little boy sat at their cottage door, gazing at the Great Stone Face, and talking about it. The child's name was Ernest.

" Mother," said he, while the Titanic visage smiled on him, " I wish that it could speak, for it looks so very kindly that its voice must needs be pleasant. If I were to see a man with such a face, I should love him dearly."

" If an old prophecy should come to pass," answered his mother, " we may see a man, some time or other, with exactly such a face as that."

" What prophecy do you mean, dear mother ? " eagerly inquired Ernest. " Pray tell me all about it ! "

So his mother told him a story that her own mother had told to her, when she herself was younger than little Ernest ; a story, not of things that were past, but of what was yet to come ; a story, nevertheless, so very old that even the Indians, who formerly inhabited this valley, had heard it from their forefathers, to whom, as they affirmed, it had been murmured by the mountain streams, and whispered by the wind among the tree-tops. The purport was that, at some future day, a child should be born hereabouts who was destined to become the greatest and noblest personage of his time, and whose countenance, in manhood, should bear an exact resemblance to the Great Stone Face. Not a few old-fashioned people, and young ones likewise, in the ardour of their hopes, still cherished an enduring faith in this old prophecy. But others, who had seen more of the world, had watched and waited till they were weary, and had beheld no man with such a face, nor any man that proved to be much greater or nobler than his neighbours, concluded it to be nothing but an idle tale. At all events, the great man of the prophecy had not yet appeared.

" Oh, mother, dear mother ! " cried Ernest, clapping his hands above his head, " I do hope that I shall live to see him ! "

His mother was an affectionate and thoughtful woman, and felt that it was wisest not to discourage the generous hopes of her little boy. So she only said to him, " Perhaps you may."

And Ernest never forgot the story that his mother told him. It was always in his mind, whenever he looked upon the Great Stone Face. He spent his childhood in the log-cottage where he was born, and was dutiful to his mother, and helpful to her in many things, assisting her much with his little hands, and more with his loving heart. In this manner, from a happy yet often pensive child, he grew up to be a mild, quiet, unobtrusive boy, and sun-browned with labour in the fields, but with more intelligence brightening his aspect than is seen in many lads who have been taught at famous schools. Yet Ernest had had no teacher, save only that the Great Stone Face became one to him. When the toil of the day was over, he would gaze at it for hours, until he began to imagine that those vast features recognised

*When the toil of the day was over Ernest would gaze at it for hours.*

him and gave him a smile of kindness and encouragement, responsive to his own look of veneration. We must not take upon us to affirm that this was a mistake, although the Face may have looked no more kindly at Ernest than at all the world besides. But the secret was that the boy's tender and confiding simplicity discerned what other people could not see; and thus the love, which was meant for all, became his peculiar portion.

About this time there went a rumour throughout the valley that the great man, foretold from ages long ago, who was to bear a resemblance to the Great Stone Face had appeared at last. It seems that, many years before, a young man had migrated from the valley and settled at a distant seaport, where, after getting together a little money, he had set up as a shopkeeper. His name—but I could never learn whether it was his real one, or a nickname that had grown out of his habits and success in life—was Gathergold. Being shrewd and active, and endowed by Providence with that inscrutable faculty which develops itself in what the world calls luck, he became an exceedingly rich merchant, and owner of a whole fleet of bulky-bottomed ships. All the countries of the globe appeared to join hands for the mere purpose of adding heap after heap to the mountainous accumulation of this one man's wealth. The cold regions of the north, almost within the gloom and shadow of the Arctic Circle, sent him their tribute in the shape of furs; hot Africa sifted for him the golden sands of her rivers, and gathered up the ivory tusks of her great elephants out of the forests; the East came bringing him the rich shawls, and spices, and teas, and the effulgence of diamonds, and the gleaming purity of large pearls. The ocean, not to be behindhand with the earth, yielded up her mighty whales, that Mr. Gathergold might sell their oil, and make a profit on it.

Be the original commodity what it might, it was gold within his grasp. It might be said of him, as of Midas in the fable, that whatever he touched with his finger immediately glistened, and grew yellow, and was changed at once into sterling metal, or, which suited him still better, into piles of coin. And when Mr. Gathergold had become so very rich that it would have taken him a hundred years only to count his wealth, he bethought himself of his native valley, and resolved to go back thither, and end his days where he was born. With this purpose in view, he sent a skilful architect to build him a palace fit for a man of his vast wealth to live in.

As I have said above, it had already been rumoured in the valley that Mr. Gathergold had turned out to be the prophetic personage so long and vainly looked for, and that his visage was the perfect and undeniable similitude of the Great Stone Face. People were the more ready to believe that this must needs be the fact when they beheld the splendid edifice that rose, as if by enchantment, on the site of his father's old weather-beaten farmhouse.

The exterior was of marble, so dazzlingly white that it seemed as though the whole structure might melt away in the sunshine, like those humbler ones which Mr. Gathergold, in his young play-days, before his fingers were gifted with the touch of transmutation, had been accustomed to build of snow. It had a richly ornamental portico, supported by tall pillars, beneath which was a lofty door, studded with silver knobs, and made of a kind of variegated wood that had been brought from beyond the sea. The windows, from the floor to the ceiling of each stately apartment, were composed, respectively, of but one enormous pane of glass, so transparently pure that it was said to be a finer medium than even the vacant atmosphere. Hardly anybody had been permitted to see the interior of this palace; but it was reported, and with good semblance of truth, to be far more gorgeous than the outside, insomuch that whatever was iron or brass in other houses was silver or gold in this; and Mr. Gathergold's bedchamber, especially, made such a glittering appearance that no ordinary man would have been able to close his eyes there. But, on the other hand, Mr. Gathergold was now so inured to wealth that perhaps he could not have closed his eyes unless where the gleam of it was certain to find its way beneath his eyelids.

In due time the mansion was finished; next came the upholsterers, with magnificent furniture; then, a whole troop of black and white servants, the harbingers of Mr. Gathergold, who, in his own majestic person, was expected to arrive at sunset. Our friend Ernest, meanwhile, had been deeply stirred by the idea that the great man, the noble man, the man of prophecy, after so many ages of delay, was at length to be made manifest to his native valley. He knew, boy as he was, that there were a thousand ways in which Mr. Gathergold, with his vast wealth, might transform himself into an angel of beneficence, and assume a control over human affairs as wide and benignant as the smile of the Great Stone Face. Full of faith and hope, Ernest doubted not that what the people said was true, and that now he was to behold the living likeness of those wondrous features on the mountain-side. While the boy was still gazing up the valley, and fancying, as he always did, that the Great Stone Face returned his gaze and looked kindly at him, the rumbling of wheels was heard, approaching swiftly along the winding road.

"Here he comes!" cried a group of people who were assembled to witness the arrival. "Here comes the great Mr. Gathergold!"

A carriage, drawn by four horses, dashed round the turn of the road. Within it, thrust partly out of the window, appeared the physiognomy of the old man, with a skin as yellow as if his own Midas hand had transmuted it. He had a low forehead, small, sharp eyes, puckered about with innumerable wrinkles, and very thin lips, which he made still thinner by pressing them forcibly together.

"The very image of the Great Stone Face!" shouted the people. "Sure enough, the old prophecy is true; and here we have the great man come at last!"

And, what greatly perplexed Ernest, they seemed actually to believe that here was the likeness which they spoke of. By the roadside there chanced to be an old beggar-woman and two little beggar-children, stragglers from some far-off region, who, as the carriage rolled onward, held out their hands and lifted up their doleful voices, most piteously beseeching charity. A yellow claw—the very same that had clawed together so much wealth—poked itself out of the coach-window, and dropped some copper coins upon the ground; so that, though the great man's name seems to have been Gathergold, he might just as suitably have been nicknamed Scattercopper. Still, nevertheless, with an earnest shout, and evidently with as much good faith as ever, the people bellowed:

"He is the very image of the Great Stone Face!"

But Ernest turned sadly from the wrinkled shrewdness of that sordid visage, and gazed up the valley, where, amid a gathering mist, gilded by the last sunbeams, he could still distinguish those glorious features which had impressed themselves into his soul. Their aspect cheered him. What did the benign lips seem to say?

"He will come! Fear not, Ernest; the man will come!"

The years went on, and Ernest ceased to be a boy. He had grown to be a young man now. He attracted little notice from the other inhabitants of the valley; for they saw nothing remarkable in his way of life, save that, when the labour of the day was over, he still loved to go apart and gaze and meditate upon the Great Stone Face. According to their idea of the matter, it was a folly, indeed, but pardonable, inasmuch as Ernest was industrious, kind, and neighbourly, and neglected no duty for the sake of indulging this idle habit. They knew not that the Great Stone Face had become a teacher to him and that the sentiment which was expressed in it would enlarge the young man's heart, and fill it with wider and deeper sympathies than other hearts. They knew not that thence would come a better wisdom than could be learned from books, and a better life than could be moulded on the defaced example of other human lives. Neither did Ernest know that the thoughts and affections which came to him so naturally, in the fields and at the fireside, and wherever he communed with himself, were of a higher tone than those which all men shared with him. A simple soul—simple as when his mother first taught him the old prophecy—he beheld the marvellous features beaming adown the valley, and still wondered that their human counterpart was so long in making his appearance.

By this time poor Mr. Gathergold was dead and buried ; and the oddest part of the matter was, that his wealth, which was the body and spirit of his existence, had disappeared before his death, leaving nothing of him but a living skeleton, covered over with a wrinkled, yellow skin. Since the melting away of his gold, it had been very generally conceded that there was no such striking resemblance, after all, betwixt the ignoble features of the ruined merchant and that majestic face upon the mountain-side. So the people ceased to honour him during his lifetime, and quietly consigned him to forgetfulness after his decease. Once in a while, it is true, his memory was brought up in connection with the magnificent palace which he had built, and which had long ago been turned into an hotel for the accommodation of strangers, multitudes of whom came, every summer, to visit that famous natural curiosity, the Great Stone Face. Thus, Mr. Gathergold being discredited and thrown into the shade, the man of prophecy was yet to come.

It so happened that a native-born son of the valley, many years before, had enlisted as a soldier, and, after a great deal of hard fighting, had now become an illustrious commander. Whatever he may be called in history, he was known in camps and on the battlefield under the nickname of Old Blood-and-Thunder. The war-worn veteran, being now infirm with age and wounds, and weary of the turmoil of a military life, and of the roll of the drum and the clangour of the trumpet, that had so long been ringing in his ears, had lately signified a purpose of returning to his native valley, hoping to find repose where he remembered to have left it.

The inhabitants, his old neighbours, were resolved to welcome the renowned warrior with a salute of cannon and a public dinner ; and all the more enthusiastically, it being affirmed that now, at last, the likeness of the Great Stone Face had actually appeared. An aide-de-camp of Old Blood-and-Thunder, travelling through the valley, was said to have been struck with the resemblance. Moreover, the schoolmates and early acquaintances of the general were ready to testify, on oath, that, to the best of their re-collection, the aforesaid general had been exceedingly like the majestic image, even when a boy, only that the idea had never occurred to them at that period. Great, therefore, was the excitement throughout the valley ; and many people, who had never once thought of glancing at the Great Stone Face for years before, now spent their time in gazing at it, for the sake of knowing exactly how General Blood-and-Thunder looked.

On the day of the great festival, Ernest, with all the other people of the valley, left their work, and proceeded to the spot where the sylvan banquet was prepared. As he approached, the loud voice of the Rev. Dr. Battleblast was heard, beseeching a blessing on the good things set before them, and on

*The Rev. Dr. Battleblast besought a blessing on the good things and on the distinguished friend of peace in whose honour they were assembled.*

the distinguished friend of peace in whose honour they were assembled. The tables were arranged in a cleared space of the woods, shut in by the surrounding trees, except where a vista opened eastward, and afforded a distant view of the Great Stone Face. Over the general's chair, which was a relic from the home of Washington, there was an arch of verdant boughs, with the laurel profusely intermixed, and surmounted by his country's banner, beneath which he had won his victories.

Our friend Ernest raised himself on his tiptoes, in hopes to get a glimpse of the celebrated guest ; but there was a mighty crowd about the tables anxious to hear the toasts and speeches, and to catch any word that might fall from the general in reply ; and a volunteer company, doing duty as a guard, pricked ruthlessly with their bayonets at any particularly quiet person among the throng. So Ernest was thrust quite into the background, where he could see no more of Old Blood-and-Thunder's physiognomy than if it had been still blazing on the battlefield. To console himself, he turned towards the Great Stone Face, which, like a faithful and long-remembered friend, looked back and smiled upon him through the vista of the forest. Meantime, however, he could overhear the remarks of various individuals, who were comparing the features of the hero with the face on the distant mountain-side.

" 'Tis the same face, to a hair ! " cried one man, cutting a caper for joy.

" Wonderfully like, that's a fact ! " responded another.

" Like ! why, I call it Old Blood-and-Thunder himself, in a monstrous looking-glass ! " cried a third. " And why not ? He's the greatest man of this or any other age, beyond a doubt."

And then all three of the speakers gave a great shout, which communicated electricity to the crowd, and called forth a roar from a thousand voices that went reverberating for miles among the mountains, until you might have supposed that the Great Stone Face had poured its thunder-breath into the cry. All these comments, and this vast enthusiasm, served the more to interest our friend ; nor did he think of questioning that now, at length, the mountain-visage had found its human counterpart. It is true, Ernest had imagined that his long-looked-for personage would appear in the character of a man of peace, uttering wisdom, and doing good, and making people happy. But, taking an habitual breadth of view, with all his simplicity, he contended that Providence should choose its own method of blessing mankind, and could conceive that this great end might be effected even by a warrior and a bloody sword, should inscrutable wisdom see fit to order matters so.

" The general ! the general ! " was now the cry. " Hush ! silence ! Old Blood-and-Thunder's going to make a speech."

Even so ; for, the cloth being removed, the general's health had been drunk amid shouts of applause, and he now stood upon his feet to thank the company. Ernest saw him. There he was, over the shoulders of the crowd, from the two glittering epaulets and embroidered collar upward, beneath the arch of green boughs with intertwined laurel, and the banner drooping as if to shade his brow ! And there, too, visible in the same glance, through the vista of the forest, appeared the Great Stone Face ! And was there, indeed, such a resemblance as the crowd had testified ? Alas, Ernest could not recognise it ! He beheld a war-worn and weather-beaten countenance, full of energy, and expressive of an iron will ; but the gentle wisdom, the deep, broad, tender sympathies were altogether wanting in Old Blood-and-Thunder's visage ; and even if the Great Stone Face had assumed his look of stern command, the milder traits would still have tempered it.

" This is not the man of prophecy," sighed Ernest to himself, as he made his way out of the throng. " And must the world wait longer yet ? "

The mists had congregated about the distant mountain-side, and there were seen the grand and awful features of the Great Stone Face, awful but benignant, as if a mighty angel were sitting among the hills, and enrobing himself in a cloud-vesture of gold and purple. As he looked, Ernest could hardly believe but that a smile beamed over the whole visage, with a radiance still brightening, although without motion of the lips. It was probably the effect of the western sunshine, melting through the thinly diffused vapours that had swept between him and the object that he gazed at. But—as it always did—the aspect of his marvellous friend made Ernest as hopeful as if he had never hoped in vain.

" Fear not, Ernest," said his heart, even as if the Great Face were whispering to him—" Fear not, Ernest ; he will come."

More years sped swiftly and tranquilly away. Ernest still dwelt in his native valley, and was now a man of middle age. By imperceptible degrees he had become known among the people. Now, as heretofore, he laboured for his bread, and was the same simple-hearted man that he had always been. But he had thought and felt so much, he had given so many of the best hours of his life to unworldly hopes for some great good to mankind, that it seemed as though he had been talking with the angels, and had imbibed a portion of their wisdom unawares. It was visible in the calm and well-considered beneficence of his daily life, the quiet stream of which had made a wide green margin all along its course. Not a day passed by that the world was not the better because this man, humble as he was, had lived. He never stepped aside from his own path, yet would always reach a blessing to his neighbour. Almost involuntarily, too, he had become a preacher. The pure and high simplicity of his thought, which, as one of its manifestations, took shape in the good deeds that dropped silently from his hand, flowed also forth in speech. He uttered truths that wrought upon and moulded the lives of those who heard him. His auditors, it may be, never suspected that Ernest, their own neighbour and familiar friend, was more than an ordinary man ; least of all did Ernest himself suspect it ; but, inevitably as the murmur of a rivulet, came thoughts out of his mouth that no other human lips had spoken.

When the people's minds had had a little time to cool, they were ready enough to acknowledge their mistake in imagining a similarity between General Blood-and-Thunder's truculent physiognomy and the benign visage on the mountain-side. But now, again, there were reports and many paragraphs in the newspapers, affirming that the likeness of the Great Stone Face had appeared upon the broad shoulders of a certain eminent statesman. He, like Mr. Gathergold and Old Blood-and-Thunder, was a native of the valley, but had left it in his early days, and taken up the trades of law and politics. Instead of the rich man's wealth and the warrior's sword, he had but a tongue, and it was mightier than both together. So wonderfully eloquent was he that whatever he might choose to say, his auditors had no choice but to believe him ; wrong looked like right, and right like wrong ; for when it pleased him he could make a kind of illuminated fog with his mere breath and obscure the natural daylight with it. His tongue, indeed, was a magic instrument : sometimes it rumbled like the thunder ; sometimes it warbled like the sweetest music. It was the blast of war—the song of peace ; and it seemed to have a heart in it, when there was no such matter.

In good truth, he was a wondrous man ; and when his tongue had acquired him all other imaginable success—when it had been heard in halls of state, and in the courts of princes and potentates—after it had made him known all over the world, even as a voice crying from shore to shore—it finally persuaded his countrymen to select him for the Presidency. Before this time—indeed, as soon as he began to grow celebrated—his admirers had found out the resemblance between him and the Great Stone Face ; and so much were they struck by it that throughout the country this distinguished gentleman was known by the name of Old Stony Phiz. The phrase was considered as giving a highly favourable aspect to his political prospects ; for, as is likewise the case with the Popedom, nobody ever becomes President without taking a name other than his own.

While his friends were doing their best to make him President, Old Stony Phiz, as he was called, set out on a visit to the valley where he was born. Of course, he had no other object than to shake hands with his fellow-citizens and neither thought nor cared about any effect which his progress through the country might have upon the election. Magnificent preparations were made to receive the illustrious statesman ; a cavalcade of horsemen set forth to meet him at the boundary line of the State, and all the people left their business and gathered along the wayside to see him pass. Among these was Ernest. Though more than once disappointed, as we have seen, he had such a hopeful and confiding nature that he was always ready to believe in whatever seemed beautiful and good. He kept his heart continually open, and thus was sure to catch the blessing from on high when it should come. So now again, as buoyantly as ever, he went forth to behold the likeness of the Great Stone Face.

The cavalcade came prancing along the road, with a great clattering of hoofs and a mighty cloud of dust, which rose up so dense and high that the visage of the mountain-side was completely hidden from Ernest's eyes. All the great men of the neighbourhood were there on horseback; militia officers in uniform; the member of Congress; the sheriff of the county; the editors of newspapers; and many a farmer, too, had mounted his patient steed, with his Sunday coat upon his back. It really was a very brilliant spectacle, especially as there were numerous banners flaunting over the cavalcade, on some of which were gorgeous portraits of the illustrious statesman and the Great Stone Face, smiling familiarly at one another, like two brothers. If the pictures were to be trusted, the mutual resemblance, it must be confessed, was marvellous. We must not forget to mention that there was a band of music, which made the echoes of the mountains ring and reverberate with the loud triumph of its strains; so that airy and soul-thrilling melodies broke out among all the heights and hollows, as if every nook of his native valley had found a voice to welcome the distinguished guest. But the grandest effect was when the far-off mountain precipice flung back the music; for then the Great Stone Face itself seemed to be swelling the triumphant chorus, in acknowledgment that, at length, the man of prophecy was come.

All this while the people were throwing up their hats and shouting, with enthusiasm so contagious that the heart of Ernest kindled up, and he likewise threw up his hat, and shouted, as loudly as the loudest, " Huzza for the great man! Huzza for Old Stony Phiz! " But as yet he had not seen him.

" Here he is, now! " cried those who stood near Ernest. " There! There! Look at Old Stony Phiz and then at the Old Man of the Mountain, and see if they are not as like as two twin-brothers! "

In the midst of all this gallant array came an open barouche, drawn by four white horses; and in the barouche, with his massive head uncovered, sat the illustrious statesman, Old Stony Phiz himself.

" Confess it," said one of Ernest's neighbours to him, " the Great Stone Face has met its match at last! "

Now, it must be owned that, at his first glimpse of the countenance which was bowing and smiling from the barouche, Ernest did fancy that there was a resemblance between it and the old familiar face upon the mountain-side. The brow, with its massive depth and loftiness, and all the other features, indeed, were boldly and strongly hewn as if in emulation of a more than heroic, of a Titanic, model. But the sublimity and stateliness, the grand expression of a divine sympathy, that illuminated the mountain visage and etherealised its ponderous granite substance into spirit, might here be sought in vain. Something had been originally left out, or had departed. And therefore the marvellously gifted statesman had always a weary gloom in the deep caverns of his eyes, as of a child that has outgrown its playthings or a man of mighty faculties and little aims, whose life, with all its high performances, was vague and empty, because no high purpose had endowed it with reality.

Still Ernest's neighbour was thrusting his elbow into his side, and pressing him for an answer.

" Confess ! confess ! Is not he the very picture of your Old Man of the Mountain ? "

" No ! " said Ernestly bluntly, " I see little or no likeness."

" Then so much the worse for the Great Stone Face ! " answered his neighbour ; and again he set up a shout for Old Stony Phiz.

But Ernest turned away, melancholy, and almost despondent : for this was the saddest of his disappointments, to behold a man who might have

*All the great men of the neighbourhood were there on horseback.*

fulfilled the prophecy and had not willed to do so. Meantime, the cavalcade, the banners, the music, and the barouches swept past him, with the vociferous crowd in the rear, leaving the dust to settle down, and the Great Stone Face to be revealed again, with the grandeur that it had worn for untold centuries.

" Lo, here I am, Ernest ! " the benign lips seemed to say. " I have waited longer than thou, and am not yet weary. Fear not ; the man will come."

The years hurried onward, treading in their haste on one another's heels. And now they began to bring white hairs, and scatter them over the head of Ernest ; they made reverend wrinkles across his forehead and furrows in his cheeks. He was an aged man. But not in vain had he grown old : more than the white hairs on his head were the sage thoughts in his mind ; his wrinkles and furrows were inscriptions that Time had graved, and in which he had written legends of wisdom that had been tested by the tenor of a life. And Ernest had ceased to be obscure. Unsought for, undesired, had come the fame which so many seek, and made him known in the great world, beyond the limits of the valley in which he had dwelt so quietly. College professors, and even the active men of cities, came from afar to see and converse with Ernest ; for the report had gone abroad that this simple husbandman had ideas unlike those of other men, not gained from books, but of a higher tone—a tranquil and familiar majesty, as if he had been talking with the angels as his daily friends. Whether it were sage, statesman, or philanthropist, Ernest received these visitors with the gentle sincerity that had characterised him from boyhood, and spoke freely with them of whatever came uppermost, or lay deepest in his heart or their own. While they talked together, his face would kindle, unawares, and shine upon them, as with a mild evening light. Pensive with the fullness of such discourse, his guests took leave and went their way ; and passing up the valley, paused to look at the Great Stone Face, imagining that they had seen its likeness in a human countenance, but could not remember where.

While Ernest had been growing up and growing old, a bountiful Providence had granted a new poet to this earth. He, likewise, was a native of the valley, but had spent the greater part of his life at a distance from that romantic region, pouring out his sweet music amid the bustle and din of cities. Often, however, did the mountains which had been familiar to him in his childhood lift their snowy peaks into the clear atmosphere of his poetry. Neither was the Great Stone Face forgotten, for the poet had celebrated it in an ode, which was grand enough to have been uttered by its own majestic lips. This man of genius, we may say, had come down from heaven with wonderful endowments. If he sang of a mountain, the eyes of all mankind beheld a mightier grandeur reposing on its breast, or soaring to its summit, than had before been seen there  If his theme were a lovely lake, a celestial smile had now been thrown over it, to gleam for ever on its surface. If it were the vast old sea, even the deep immensity of its dread bosom seemed to swell the higher, as if moved by the emotions of the song. Thus the world assumed another and a better aspect from the hour that the poet blessed it with his happy eyes. The Creator had bestowed him, as the last best touch to His own handiwork. Creation was not finished till the poet came to interpret, and so complete it.

The effect was no less high and beautiful when his human brethren were the subject of his verse. The man or woman, sordid with the common dust of life, who crossed his daily path, and the little child who played in it, were glorified if he beheld them in his mood of poetic faith. He showed the golden links of the great chain that intertwined them with an angelic kindred ; he brought out the hidden traits of a celestial birth that made them worthy of such kin. Some, indeed, there were who thought to show the soundness of their judgment by affirming that all the beauty and dignity of the natural world existed only in the poet's fancy. Let such men speak for themselves, who undoubtedly appear to have been spawned forth by Nature with a contemptuous bitterness ; she having plastered them up out of her refuse stuff, after all the swine were made. As respects all things else, the poet's ideal was the truest truth.

The songs of this poet found their way to Ernest. He read them after his customary toil, seated on the bench before his cottage door, where for such a length of time he had filled his repose with thought by gazing at the Great Stone Face. And now as he read stanzas that caused the soul to thrill within him, he lifted his eyes to the vast countenance beaming on him so benignantly.

" Oh, majestic friend," he murmured, addressing the Great Stone Face, " is not this man worthy to resemble thee ? "

The Face seemed to smile, but answered not a word.

Now it happened that the poet, though he dwelt so far away, had not only heard of Ernest, but had meditated much upon his character, until he deemed nothing so desirable as to meet this man, whose untaught wisdom walked hand in hand with the noble simplicity of his life. One summer morning, therefore, he took passage by the railroad, and, in the decline of the afternoon, alighted from the cars at no great distance from Ernest's cottage. The great hotel, which had formerly been the palace of Mr. Gathergold, was close at hand, but the poet, with his carpet-bag on his arm, inquired at once where Ernest dwelt, and was resolved to be accepted as his guest.

Approaching the door, he there found the good old man, holding a volume in his hand, which alternately he read, and then, with a finger between the leaves, looked lovingly at the Great Stone Face.

" Good-evening," said the poet. " Can you give a traveller a night's lodging ? "

" Willingly," answered Ernest ; and then he added, smiling, " Methinks I never saw the Great Face look so hospitably at a stranger."

The poet sat down on the bench beside him, and he and Ernest talked together. Often had the poet held intercourse with the wittiest and the wisest, but never before with a man like Ernest, whose thoughts and feelings gushed up with such a natural freedom, and who made great truths so familiar by his simple utterance of them. Angels, as had been so often said, seemed to have wrought with him at his labour in the fields ; angels seemed to have sat with him by the fireside ; and, dwelling with angels as friend with friends, he had imbibed the sublimity of their ideas, and imbued it with the sweet and lowly charm of household words. So thought the poet. And Ernest, on the other hand, was moved and agitated by the living images which the poet flung out of his mind, and which peopled all the air about the cottage door with shapes of beauty, both gay and pensive. The sympathies of these two men instructed them with a profounder sense than either could have attained alone. Their minds accorded into one strain, and made delightful music which neither of them could have claimed as all his own, nor distinguished his own share from the other's. They led one another, as it were, into a high pavilion of their thoughts, so remote, and hitherto so dim, that they had never entered it before, and so beautiful that they desired to be there always.

As Ernest listened to the poet, he imagined that the Great Stone Face was bending forward to listen too. He gazed earnestly into the poet's glowing eyes.

" Who are you, my strangely gifted guest ? " he said.

The poet laid his finger on the volume that Ernest had been reading.

" You have read these poems," said he. " You know me, then—for I wrote them."

Again, and still more earnestly than before, Ernest examined the poet's features ; then turned toward the Great Stone Face ; then back, with an uncertain aspect to his guest. But his countenance fell ; he shook his head and sighed.

" Wherefore are you sad ? " inquired the poet.

" Because," replied Ernest, " all through life I have awaited the fulfilment of a prophecy ; and, when I read these poems, I hoped that it might be fulfilled in you."

" You hoped," answered the poet, faintly smiling, " to find in me the likeness of the Great Stone Face. And you are disappointed, as formerly with Mr. Gathergold, and Old Blood-and-Thunder, and Old Stony Phiz. Yes, Ernest, it is my doom. You must add my name to the illustrious three, and record another failure of your hopes. For—in shame and sadness do I speak it, Ernest—I am not worthy to be typified by yonder benign and majestic image."

" And why ? " asked Ernest. He pointed to the volume. " Are not those thoughts divine ? "

" They have a strain of the Divinity," replied the poet. " You can hear in them the far-off echo of a heavenly song. But my life, dear Ernest, has not corresponded with my thought. I have had grand dreams, but they have been only dreams, because I have lived—and that, too, by my own choice—among poor and mean realities. Sometimes even—shall I dare to say it ?—I lack faith in the grandeur, the beauty and the goodness, which my own works are said to have made more evident in Nature and in human life. Why, then, pure seeker of the good and true, shouldst thou hope to find me in yonder image of the divine ? "

The poet spoke sadly, and his eyes were dim with tears. So, likewise, were those of Ernest.

At the hour of sunset, as had long been his frequent custom, Ernest was to discourse to an assemblage of the neighbouring inhabitants in the open air. He and the poet, arm in arm, still talking together as they went along, proceeded to the spot. It was a small nook among the hills, with a grey precipice behind, the stern front of which was relieved by the pleasant foliage of many creeping plants that made a tapestry for the naked rock, by hanging their festoons from all its rugged angles. At a small elevation above the ground, set in a rich framework of verdure, there appeared a niche, spacious enough to admit a human figure, with freedom for such gestures as spontaneously accompany earnest thought and genuine emotion. Into this natural pulpit Ernest ascended, and threw a look of familiar kindness around upon his audience.

They stood, or sat, or reclined upon the grass, as seemed good to each, with the departing sunshine falling obliquely over them, and mingling its subdued cheerfulness with the solemnity of a grove of ancient trees, beneath and amid the boughs of which the golden rays were constrained to pass. In another direction was seen the Great Stone Face, with the same cheer, combined with the same solemnity, in its benignant aspect.

Ernest began to speak, giving to the people of what was in his heart and mind. His words had power, because they accorded with his thoughts ; and his thoughts had reality and depth, because they harmonised with the life which he had always lived.  It was not mere breath that this preacher uttered ; they were the words of life, because a life of good deeds and holy love was melted into them.  Pearls, pure and rich, had been dissolved into this precious draught.

The poet, as he listened, felt that the being and character of Ernest were a nobler strain of poetry than he had ever written.  His eyes glistening with tears, he gazed reverentially at the venerable man, and said within himself that never was there an aspect so worthy of a prophet and a sage as that mild, sweet, thoughtful countenance, with the glory of white hair diffused about it.  At a distance, but distinctly to be seen, high up in the golden light of the setting sun, appeared the Great Stone Face, with hoary mists around it, like the white hairs around the brow of Ernest.  Its look of grand beneficence seemed to embrace the world.

At that moment, in sympathy with a thought which he was about to utter, the face of Ernest assumed a grandeur of expression so imbued with benevolence that the poet, by an irresistible impulse, threw his arms aloft, and shouted :

"Behold !  Behold !  Ernest is himself the likeness of the Great Stone Face ! "

Then all the people looked, and saw that what the deep-sighted poet said was true.  The prophecy was fulfilled.  But Ernest, having finished what he had to say, took the poet's arm, and walked slowly homeward, still hoping that some wiser and better man than himself would by and by appear, bearing a resemblance to the GREAT STONE FACE.

*" Behold !  Ernest is himself the likeness of the Great Stone Face ! "*

# THE CAMEL'S HUMP

*by* RUDYARD KIPLING

THE camel's hump is an ugly hump
　　Which well you may see at the Zoo;
But uglier yet is the hump we get
　　From having too little to do.

Kiddies and grown-ups too-oo-oo,
If we haven't enough to do-oo-oo,
　　　We get the hump—
　　　Cameelious hump—
The hump that is black and blue!

We climb out of bed with a frouzly head
　　And a snarly-yarly voice;
We shiver and scowl, and we grunt and we
　　　growl
　　At our bath and our boots and our toys;

And there ought to be a corner for me
(An' I know there is one for you)
    When we get the hump—
    Cameelious hump—
The hump that is black and blue !

The cure for this ill is not to sit still,
    Or frowst with a book by the fire ;
But to take a large hoe and a shovel also,
    And dig till you gently perspire ;

And then you will find that the sun and the
        wind,
And the Djinn of the Garden, too,
    Have lifted the hump—
    The horrible hump—
The hump that is black and blue !

I get it as well as you-oo-oo
If I haven't enough to do-oo-oo,
    We all get hump—
    Cameelious hump—
Kiddies and grown-ups, too !

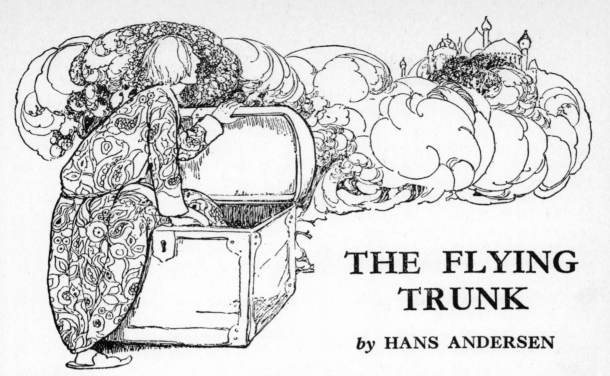

# THE FLYING TRUNK

## by HANS ANDERSEN

HERE was once a merchant, who was so rich that he might have paved the whole street of the town where he lived, and an alley besides, with pieces of silver, but this he did not do; he knew another way of using his money, and whenever he laid out a shilling he gained a crown in return. A merchant he lived, and a merchant he died.

All his money then went to his son. But the son lived merrily, and spent all his time in pleasures—went to balls every evening, made bank-notes into paper kites, and played at ducks and drakes in the pond with gold pieces instead of stones.

In this manner his money soon vanished, until at last he had only a few pennies left, and his wardrobe was reduced to a pair of slippers and an old dressing-gown. His friends cared no more about him, now that they could no longer walk abroad with him; one of them, however, more good-natured than the rest, sent him an old trunk, with this advice, " Pack up, and be off ! " This was all very fine, but he had nothing that he could pack up; so he put himself into the trunk.

It was a droll trunk : when the lock was pressed close it could fly. The merchant's son did press the lock, and lo ! up flew the trunk with him through the chimney, high into the clouds, on and on, higher and higher. The lower part cracked, which rather frightened him, for if it had broken in two, a pretty fall he would have had.

However, it descended safely, and he found himself in Turkey. He hid the trunk under a heap of dry leaves in a wood, and walked into the next town. He could do so very well, for among the Turks everybody goes about clad as he was, in dressing-gown and slippers. He met a nurse carrying a little child in her arms. " Hark ye, Turkish nurse," quoth he ; " what palace is that with the high windows close by the town ? "

" The King's daughter dwells there," replied the nurse. " It has been told of her that she shall be made very unhappy by a lover, and therefore no one may visit her, except when the King and Queen are with her."

" Thank you," said the merchant's son, and he immediately went back into the wood, sat down in his trunk, flew up to the roof of the palace, and crept through the window into the Princess's apartment.

She was lying asleep on the sofa. She was so beautiful that the merchant's son could not help kneeling down to kiss her hand, whereupon she awoke, and was not a little frightened at the sight of this unexpected visitor. But he told her, however, that he was the Turkish prophet, and had come down from the sky on purpose to woo her, and on hearing this she was well pleased.

So they sat down side by side, and he talked to her about her eyes, how they were beautiful dark-blue seas, and that thoughts and feelings floated like mermaidens therein ; and he spoke of her brow, how it was a fair snowy mountain, with splendid halls and pictures, and many other such-like things he told her.

Oh, these were charming stories ; and thus he wooed the Princess, and she immediately said " Yes."

" But you must come here on Saturday," said she ; " the King and Queen have promised to drink tea with me that evening ; they will be so proud and so pleased when they hear that I am to marry the Turkish prophet ! And mind you tell them a very pretty story, for they are exceedingly fond of stories. My mother likes them to be very moral and high-class, and my father likes them to be merry, so as to make him laugh."

" Yes, I shall bring no other bridal present than a tale," replied the merchant's son ; and here they parted, but not before the Princess had given her lover a sword all covered with gold. He knew excellently well what use to make of this present.

So he flew away, bought a new dressing-gown, and then sat down in the wood to compose the tale which was to be ready by Saturday, and certainly, he found composition not the easiest thing in the world.

At last he was ready, and at last Saturday came.

The King, the Queen, and the whole Court were waiting tea for him at the Princess's palace. The suitor was received with much ceremony.

" Will you not tell us a story ? " asked the Queen ; " a story that is instructive and full of deep meaning."

" But let it make us laugh," said the King.

" With pleasure," replied the merchant's son ; and now you must hear his story.

" There was once a bundle of matches, who were all extremely proud of their high descent, for their genealogical tree—that is to say, the tall fir-tree from which each of them was a splinter—had been a tree of great antiquity, and distinguished by his height from all the other trees of the forest. The matches were now lying on the mantelpiece, between a tinder-box and an old iron saucepan, and to these two they often talked about their youth.

" ' Ah, when we were upon the green branches," said they ; " when we really lived upon green branches—that was a happy time ! Every morning and evening we had diamond-tea " (that is dew) ; " the whole day long we had sunshine, at least whenever the sun shone, and all the little birds used to tell stories to us. It might easily be seen, too, that we were rich, for the other trees were clothed with leaves only during the summer, whereas our family could afford to wear green clothes both summer and winter.

" ' But at last came the woodcutters : then was the great revolution, and our family was dispersed. The paternal trunk obtained a situation as mainmast to a magnificent ship, which could sail round the world if it chose ; the boughs were transported to various places, and our work was henceforth to kindle lights for low, common people. Now you will understand how it comes to pass that persons of such high descent as we are should be living in a kitchen.'

" ' To be sure, mine is a very different history,' remarked the iron saucepan, near which the matches were lying. ' From the moment I came into the world until now, I have been rubbed and scrubbed, and boiled over and over again—oh, how many times ! I love to have to do with what is solidly good, and am really of the first importance in this house.

" ' My only pleasure is to stand clean and bright upon this mantelpiece after dinner, and hold some rational conversation with my companions. However, excepting the water-pail, who now and then goes out into the court, we all of us lead a very quiet domestic life here. Our only newsmonger is the turf-basket, but he talks in such a democratic way about " government " and the " people "—why, I assure you, not long ago, there was an old jar standing here who was so much shocked by what he heard said that he fell down from the mantelpiece and broke into a thousand pieces ! That turf-basket is a Liberal, that's the fact.'

" ' Now, you talk too much,' interrupted the tinder-box ; and the steel struck the flint, so that the sparks flew out. ' Why should we not spend a pleasant evening ? '

" ' Yes, let us settle who is of highest rank among us ! ' proposed the matches.

" ' Oh, no ; for my part I would rather not speak of myself,' objected the earthenware pitcher. ' Suppose we have an intellectual entertainment ? I will begin ; I will relate something of everyday life, such as we have all experienced ; one can easily transport oneself into it, and that is so interesting ! Near the Baltic, among the Danish beech-groves——'

" ' That is a capital beginning ! ' cried all the plates at once ; ' it will certainly be just the sort of story for us ! '

" ' Yes, there I spent my youth in a very quiet family ; the furniture was rubbed, the floors were washed, clean curtains were hung up every fortnight.'

" ' How very interesting. What a charming way you have of describing things ! ' said the hair-broom. ' Any one might guess immediately that it is a lady who is speaking ; the tale breathes such a spirit of cleanliness ! '

" ' Very true ; so it does ! ' exclaimed the water-pail ; and in his delight he gave a little jump, so that some of the water splashed upon the floor.

" And the pitcher went on with her tale, and the end proved as good as the beginning.

" All the plates clattered applause, and the hair-broom took some green parsley out of the sandhole and crowned the pitcher, for he knew that this would vex the others ; and, thought he, ' If I crown her to-day, she will crown me to-morrow.'

" ' Now I will dance,' said the fire-tongs, and accordingly she did dance, and oh ! it was wonderful to see how high she threw one of her legs up into the air ; the old chair-cover in the corner tore with horror at seeing her. ' Am not I to be crowned too ? ' asked the tongs ; and she was crowned forthwith.

" ' These are the vulgar rabble ! ' thought the matches.

" The tea-urn was now called upon to sing, but she had a cold ; she said she could only sing when she was boiling ; however, this was all her pride and affectation. The fact was she never cared to sing except when she was standing on the parlour table before company.

" On the window-ledge lay an old quill pen, with which the maids used to write ; there was nothing remarkable about her, except that she had been dipped too low in the ink ; however, she was proud of that. ' If the tea-urn does not choose to sing,' quoth she, ' she may let it alone ; there is a nightingale in the cage hung just outside, he can sing. To be sure, he had never learned the notes ; never mind—we will not speak evil of any one this evening ! '

" *Now I will dance,*" *said the firetongs, and accordingly she did dance.*

" ' I think it highly absurd,' observed the tea-kettle, who was the vocalist of the kitchen, and a half-brother of the tea-urn's, ' that a foreign bird should be listened to. Is it patriotic ? I appeal to the turf-basket.'

" ' I am only vexed,' said the turf-basket ; ' I am vexed from my inmost soul that such things are thought of at all. Is it a becoming way of spending the evening ? Would it not be much more rational to reform the whole house, and establish a totally new order of things, rather more according to nature ? Then every one would get into his right place, and I would undertake to direct the revolution. What say you to it ? That would be something worth the doing ! '

" ' Oh, yes ; we will make a grand commotion ! ' cried they all. Just then the door opened—it was the servant-maid. They all stood perfectly still, not one dared stir ; yet there was not a single kitchen-utensil among them all who was not thinking about the great things he could have done, and how great was his superiority over the others.

" ' Ah, if I had chosen it,' thought each of them, ' what a merry evening we might have had ! '

" The maid took the matches and struck a light—oh, how they spluttered and blazed up !

" ' Now every one may see,' thought they, ' that we are of highest rank. What a splendid, dazzling light we give—how glorious ! ' And in another moment they were burned out.

" That is a capital story," said the Queen ; " I quite felt myself transported into the kitchen. Yes, thou shalt have our daughter ! "

" With all my heart," said the King ; " on Monday thou shalt marry our daughter." They said " thou " to him now, since he was so soon to become one of the family.

The wedding was a settled thing ; and on the evening before, the whole city was illuminated ; cakes, buns, and sugar-plums were thrown out among the people ; all the little boys in the streets stood upon tiptoes, shouting " Hurrah ! " and whistling through their fingers—it was famous !

" Well, I suppose I ought to do my part, too," thought the merchant's son ; so he went and brought sky-rockets, squibs, Catherine-wheels, Roman-candles, and all kinds of fireworks ; put them all into his trunk, and flew up into the air, letting them off as he flew.

Hurrah ! what a glorious sky-rocket was that !

All the Turks jumped up to look so hastily that their slippers flew about their ears ; such a meteor they had never seen before. Now they might be sure that it was indeed the prophet who was to marry their Princess.

As soon as the merchant's son had returned in his trunk to the wood, he said to himself, " I will now go into the city and hear what people say about me, and what sort of figure I made in the air ; " and, certainly, this was a very natural idea.

Oh, what strange accounts were given ! Every one to whom he spoke had beheld the bright vision in a way peculiar to himself, but all agreed that it was marvellously beautiful.

" I saw the great prophet with my own eyes," declared one ; " he had eyes like sparkling stars, and a beard like foaming water."

" He flew enveloped in a mantle of fire," said another, " the prettiest little cherubs were peeping forth from under its folds."

Yes ; he heard of many beautiful things, and the morrow was to be his wedding-day.

He now went back to the wood, intending to get into his trunk again, but where was it ?

Alas ! the trunk was burned. One spark from the fireworks had been left in it, and set it on fire ; the trunk now lay in ashes. The poor merchant's son could never fly again—could never again visit his bride.

She sat the livelong day upon the roof of her palace expecting him ; she expects him still. He, meantime, goes about the world telling stories, but none of his stories now are so pleasant as that one which he related in the Princess's palace about the Brimstone Matches.

# THE KING OF THE VIPERS

## *by* GEORGE BORROW

AND a strange place it was, this Norman Cross, and, at the time of which I am speaking, a sad cross to many a Norman, being what was then styled a French prison, that is, a receptacle for captives made in the French war. It consisted, if I remember right, of some five or six casernes, very long, and immensely high; each standing isolated from the rest, upon a spot of ground which might average ten acres, and which was fenced round with lofty palisades, the whole being compassed about by a towering wall, beneath which, at intervals, on both sides, sentinels were stationed, whilst outside, upon the field, stood commodious wooden barracks, capable of containing two regiments of infantry, intended to serve as guards upon the captives. Such was the station or prison at Norman Cross, where some six thousand French and other foreigners, followers of the grand Corsican, were now immured.

What a strange appearance had those mighty casernes, with their blank blind walls, without windows or grating, and their slanting roofs, out of which through orifices where the tiles had been removed, would be protruded dozens of grim heads, feasting their prison-sick eyes on the wide expanse of country unfolded from that airy height. Ah! there was much misery in those casernes; and from those roofs, doubtless, many a wistful look was turned in the direction of lovely France. Much had the poor inmates to endure and much to complain of, to the disgrace of England be it said—of England, in general so kind and bountiful. Rations of carrion meat, and bread from which I have seen the very hounds occasionally turn away, were unworthy entertainment even for the most ruffian enemy, when helpless and a captive; and such, alas! was the fare in those casernes.

And then, those visits, or rather ruthless inroads, called in the slang of the place "straw-plait hunts," when in pursuit of a contraband article, which the prisoners, in order to procure themselves a few of the necessaries and comforts of existence, were in the habit of making, red-coated battalions were marched into the prisons, who, with the bayonet's point, carried havoc and ruin into every poor convenience which ingenious wretchedness had been endeavouring to raise around it ; and then the triumphant exit with the miserable booty ; and, worst of all, the accursed bonfire, on the barrack parade, of the plait contraband, beneath the view of the glaring eyeballs from those lofty roofs, amidst the hurrahs of the troops, frequently drowned in the curses poured down from above like a tempest shower, or in the terrific war-whoop of "*Vive l'Empereur !*"

It was midsummer when we arrived at this place, and the weather, which had for a long time been wet and gloomy, now became bright and glorious. I was subjected to but little control, and passed my time pleasantly enough, principally in wandering about the neighbouring country. It was flat and somewhat fenny, a district more of pasture than agriculture, and not very thickly inhabited. I soon became well acquainted with it.

At the distance of two miles from the station was a large lake, styled in the dialect of the country ' a mere,' about whose borders tall reeds were growing in abundance. This was a frequent haunt of mine ; but my favourite place of resort was a wild sequestered spot at a somewhat greater distance. Here, surrounded with woods and thick groves, was the seat of some ancient family, deserted by the proprietor, and only inhabited by a rustic servant or two. A place more solitary and wild could scarcely be imagined ; the gardens and walks were overgrown with weeds and briers, and the unpruned woods were so tangled as to be almost impervious.

About this domain I would wander till overtaken by fatigue, and then I would sit down with my back against some beech, elm, or stately alder tree, and, taking out my book, would pass hours in a state of unmixed enjoyment, my eyes now fixed on the wondrous pages, now glancing at the sylvan scene around ; and sometimes I would drop the book and listen to the voices of the rooks and wild pigeons, and not infrequently to the croaking of multitudes of frogs from the neighbouring swamps and fens.

In going to and from this place I frequently passed a tall, elderly individual, dressed in rather a quaint fashion, with a skin cap on his head and stout gaiters on his legs ; on his shoulders hung a moderate-sized leathern sack ; he seemed fond of loitering near sunny banks, and of groping amidst furze and low scrubby bramble bushes, of which there were plenty in the neighbourhood of Norman Cross. Once I saw him standing in the middle of a dusty road, looking intently at a large mark which seemed to have been drawn across it, as if by a walking-stick.

"He must have been a large one," the old man muttered half to himself, "or he would not have left such a trail, I wonder if he is near ; he seems to have moved this way."

He then went behind some bushes which grew on the right side of the road, and appeared to be in quest of something, moving behind the bushes with his head downwards, and occasionally striking their roots with his foot : at length he exclaimed, "Here he is !" and forthwith I saw him dart amongst the bushes. There was a kind of scuffling noise, the rustling of branches, and the crackling of dry sticks. "I have him !" said the man at last "I have got him !" and presently he made his appearance about twenty yards down the road, holding a large viper in his hand. "What do you think of that, my boy ? " said he, as I went up to him ; " what do you think of catching such a thing as that with the naked hand ? "

" What do I think ? " said I. " Why, that I could do as much myself."

" You do," said the man, " do you ? Lord ! how the young people in these days are given to conceit ; it did not use to be so in my time : when I was a child, childer knew how to behave themselves ; but the childer of these days are full of conceit, full of froth, like the mouth of this viper ; " and with his forefinger and thumb he squeezed a considerable quantity of foam from the jaws of the viper down upon the road. " The childer of these days are a generation of—God forgive me, what was I about to say ! " said the old man ; and opening his bag he thrust the reptile into it, which appeared far from empty. I passed on. As I was returning, towards the evening, I overtook the old man, who was wending in the same direction.

" Good-evening to you, sir," said I, taking off a cap which I wore on my head.

" Good-evening," said the old man ; and then, looking at me, " How's this ? " said he, " you ar'n't, sure, the child I met in the morning ? "

" Yes," said I, " I am ; what makes you doubt it ? "

" Why, you were then all froth and conceit," said the old man, " and now you take off your cap to me."

" I beg your pardon," said I, " if I was frothy and conceited, it ill becomes a child like me to be so "

*" What do you think of that, my boy ? What do you think of catching such a thing as that with the naked hand ? "*

"That's true, dear," said the old man; "well, as you have begged my pardon, I truly forgive you."

"Thank you," said I; "have you caught any more of those things?"

"Only four or five," said the old man; "they are getting scarce, though this used to be a great neighbourhood for them."

"And what do you do with them?" said I; "do you carry them home and play with them!"

"I sometimes play with one or two that I tame," said the old man; "but I hunt them mostly for the fat which they contain, out of which I make unguents which are good for various sore troubles, especially for the rheumatism."

"And do you get your living by hunting these creatures?" I demanded.

"Not altogether," said the old man; "besides being a viper-hunter, I am what they call a herbalist, one who knows the virtue of particular herbs; I gather them at the proper season, to make medicines with for the sick."

"And do you live in the neighbourhood?" I demanded.

"You seem very fond of asking questions, child. No, I do not live in this neighbourhood in particular. I travel about; I have not been in this neighbourhood till lately for some years."

From this time the old man and myself formed an acquaintance; I often accompanied him in his wanderings about the neighbourhood, and on two or three occasions assisted him in catching the reptiles which he hunted. He generally carried a viper with him which he had made quite tame, and from which he had extracted the poisonous fangs; it would dance and perform various kinds of tricks. He was fond of telling me anecdotes connected with his adventures with the reptile species.

"But," said he one day, sighing, "I must shortly give up this business, I am no longer the man I was, I am become timid, and when a person is timid in viper-hunting he had better leave off, as it is quite clear his virtue is leaving him. I got a fright some years ago, which I am quite sure I shall never get the better of; my hand has been shaky more or less ever since."

"What frightened you?" said I.

"I had better not tell you," said the old man, "or you may be frightened too, lose your virtue, and be no longer good for the business."

"I don't care," said I; "I don't intend to follow the business: I daresay I shall be an officer, like my father."

"Well," said the old man, "I once saw the king of the vipers, and since then——"

"The king of the vipers!" said I, interrupting him; "have the vipers a king?"

"As sure as we have," said the old man, "as sure as we have King George to rule over us, have these reptiles a king to rule over them."

"And where did you see him?" said I.

"I will tell you," said the old man, "though I don't like talking about the matter. It may be about seven years ago that I happened to be far down yonder to the west, on the other side of England, nearly two hundred miles from here, following my business. It was a very sultry day, I remember, and I had been out several hours catching creatures. It might be about three o'clock in the afternoon, when I found myself on some heathy land near the sea, on the ridge of a hill, the side of which, nearly as far down as the sea, was heath; but on the top there was arable ground, which had been planted and from which the harvest had been gathered—oats or barley, I know not which—but I remember that the ground was covered with stubble.

"Well, about three o'clock, as I told you before, what with the heat of the day and from having walked about for hours in a lazy way, I felt very tired; so I determined to have a sleep, and I laid myself down, my head just on the ridge of the hill, towards the field, and my body over the side down amongst the heath; my bag, which was nearly filled with creatures, lay at a little distance from my face; the creatures were struggling in it, I remember, and I thought to myself, how much more comfortably off I was than they; I was taking my ease on the nice open hill, cooled with the breezes, whilst they were in the nasty close bag, coiling about one another, and breaking their very hearts all to no purpose: and I felt quite comfortable and happy in the thought, and little by little closed my eyes, and fell into the sweetest snooze that ever I was in in all my life; and there I lay over the hill's side, with my head half in the field, I don't know how long, all dead asleep.

"At last it seemed to me that I heard a noise in my sleep, something like a thing moving, very faint, however, far away; then it died, and then it came again upon my ear as I slept, and now it appeared almost as if I heard crackle, crackle; then it died again, or I became yet more dead asleep than before, I know not which, but I certainly lay some time without hearing it. All of a sudden I became awake, and there was I, on the ridge of the hill, with my cheek on the ground towards the stubble, with a noise in my ear like that of something moving towards me, among the stubble on the field; well, I lay a moment or two listening to the noise, and then I became frightened for I did not like the noise at all, it sounded so odd; so I rolled myself on my belly, and looked towards the stubble.

"Mercy upon us! there was a huge snake, or rather a dreadful viper, for it was all yellow and gold, moving towards me, bearing its head about a foot and a half above the ground, the dry stubble crackling beneath its outrageous belly. It might be about five yards off when I first saw it, making straight towards me, child, as if it would devour me. I lay quite still, for I was stupefied with horror whilst the creature came still nearer; and now it was nearly upon me, when it suddenly drew back a little, and then—what do you think? it lifted its head and chest high in the air, and high over my face as I looked up, flickering at me with its tongue as if it would fly at my face.

"Child, what I felt at that moment I can scarcely say, but it was a sufficient punishment for all the sins I ever committed; and there we two were, I looking up at the viper, and the viper looking down upon me, flickering at me with its tongue. It was only the kindness of God that saved me: all at once there was a loud noise, the report of a gun, for a fowler was shooting at a covey of birds, a little way off in the stubble. Whereupon the viper sunk its head and immediately made off over the ridge of the hill, down in the direction of the sea.

"As it passed by me, however—and it passed close by me—it hesitated a moment, as if it was doubtful whether it should not seize me; it did not, however, but made off down the hill. It has often struck me that he was angry with me, and came upon me unawares for presuming to meddle with his people, as I have always been in the habit of doing."

" But," said I, " how do you know that it was the king of the vipers ? "

" How do I know ? " said the old man. " Who else should it be ? There was as much difference between it and other reptiles as between King George and other people."

" Is King George, then, different from other people ? " I demanded.

" Of course," said the old man ; " I have never seen him myself, but I have heard people say that he is a ten times greater man than other folks ; indeed, it stands to reason that he must be different from the rest, else people would not be so eager to see him. Do you think, child, that people would be fools enough to run a matter of twenty or thirty miles to see the king, provided King George——"

" Haven't the French a king ? " I demanded.

" Yes," said the old man, " or something much the same, and a queer one he is ; not quite so big as King George, they say, but quite as terrible a fellow. What of him ? "

" Suppose he should come to Norman Cross ! "

" What should he do at Norman Cross, child ? "

" Why, you were talking about the vipers in your bag breaking their hearts, and their king coming to help them. Now, suppose the French king should hear of his people being in trouble at Norman Cross, and——"

" He can't come, child," said the old man, rubbing his hands, " the water lies between. The French don't like the water ; neither vipers nor Frenchmen take kindly to the water, child."

When the old man left the country, which he did a few days after the conversation which I have just related, he left me the reptile which he had tamed and rendered quite harmless by removing the fangs. I was in the habit of feeding it with milk, and frequently carried it abroad with me in my walk.

---

# YELLOW SANDS

*by* WILLIAM SHAKESPEARE

COME unto these yellow sands,
    And then take hands :
Court'sied when you have, and kissed,—
    The wild waves whist,—
Foot it featly here and there ;
And, sweet sprites, the burthen bear.
Hark, hark !
    Bow, wow,
The watch-dogs bark :
    Bow, wow.
Hark, hark ! I hear
The strain of strutting chanticleer
    Cry, Cock-a-diddle-dow !

# THE BOTTLE-NECK

## *by* HANS ANDERSEN

IN a narrow crooked street, among other abodes of poverty, stood an especially narrow and tall house built of timber which time had knocked about in such a fashion that it seemed to be out of joint in every direction. The house was inhabited by poor people, and the deepest poverty was apparent in the garret lodging in the gable, where, in front of the only window, hung an old bent bird-cage, which had not even a proper water-glass, but only a Bottle-neck reversed, with a cork stuck in the mouth, to do duty for one. An old maid stood by the window: she had hung the cage with green chickweed; and a little chaffinch hopped from perch to perch, and sang and twittered merrily enough.

"Yes, it's all very well for you to sing," said the Bottle-neck; that is to say, it did not pronounce the words as we can speak them, for a bottle-neck can't speak; but that's what he thought to himself in his own mind, like when we people talk quietly to ourselves. "Yes, it's all very well for you to sing, you that have all your limbs uninjured. You ought to feel what it's like to lose one's body, and to have only mouth and neck left, and to be hampered with work into the bargain, as in my case; and then I'm sure you would not sing. But after all it is well that there should be somebody at least who is merry. I've no reason to sing, and, moreover, I can't sing. Yes, when I was a whole bottle, I sang out well if they rubbed me with a cork. They used to call me a perfect lark, a magnificent lark! Ah, when I was out a picnic with the tanner's family, and his daughter was betrothed! Yes, I remember it as if it had happened only yesterday. I have gone through a great deal, when I come to recollect. I've been in the fire and the water, have been deep in the black earth and have mounted higher than most of the others; and now I'm hanging here, outside the bird-cage, in the air and the sunshine! Oh, it would be quite worth while to hear my history; but I don't speak aloud of it, because I can't."

And now the Bottle-neck told its story, which was sufficiently remarkable. It told the story to itself, or only thought it in its own mind; and the little bird sang his song merrily, and down in the street there was driving and hurrying, and every one thought of his own affairs, or perhaps of nothing at all; and only the Bottle-neck thought. It thought of the flaming furnace in the manufactory, where it had been blown into life; it still remembered that it had been quite warm, that it had glanced into the hissing furnace, the home of its origin, and had felt a great desire to leap directly back again; but that gradually it had become cooler, and had been very comfortable in the place to which it was taken. It had stood in a rank with a whole regiment of brothers and sisters, all out of the same furnace; some of them had certainly been blown into champagne bottles, and others into beer bottles, and that makes a difference. Later, out in the world, it may well happen that a beer bottle may contain the most precious wine, and a champagne bottle be filled with blacking; but even in decay there is always something left by which people can see what one has been—nobility is nobility, even when filled with blacking.

All the bottles were packed up, and our bottle was among them. At that time it did not think to finish its career as a bottle-neck, or that it should work its way up to be a bird's glass, which is always an honourable thing, for one is of some consequence, after all. The bottle did not again behold the light of day till it was unpacked with the other bottles in the cellar of the wine merchant, and rinsed out for the first time; and that was a strange sensation. There it lay, empty and without a cork, and felt strangely unwell, as if it wanted something, it could not tell what. At last it was filled with good, costly wine, and it was provided with a cork, and sealed down. A ticket was placed on it marked "first quality"; and it felt as if it had carried off the first prize at an examination; for, you see, the wine was good and the bottle was good. When one is young, that's the time for poetry! There was a singing and sounding within it, of things which it could not understand—of green sunny mountains, whereon the grape grows, where many vine-dressers, men and women, sing and dance and rejoice. "Ah, how beautiful is life!" There was a singing and sounding of all this in the bottle, as in a young poet's brain; and many a young poet does not understand the meaning of the song that is within him.

One morning the bottle was bought, for the tanner's apprentice was dispatched for a bottle of wine—"of the best." And now it was put in the provision basket, with ham and cheese and sausages; the finest butter and the best bread were put in the basket too—the tanner's daughter herself packed it. She was young and very pretty; her brown eyes laughed, and round her mouth played a smile as elegant as that in her eyes. She had delicate hands, beautifully white, and her neck was whiter still; you saw at once that she was one of the most beautiful girls in the town: and still she was not engaged.

The provision basket was in the lap of the young girl when the family drove out into the forest. The Bottle-neck looked out from the folds of the white napkin. There was red wax upon the cork, and the bottle looked straight into the girl's face. It also looked at the young sailor who sat next to the girl.

He was a friend of old days, the son of the portrait painter. Quite lately he had passed with honour through his examination as mate, and to-morrow he was to sail away in a ship, far off to a distant land. There had been much talk of this while the basket was being packed; and certainly the eyes and mouth of the tanner's pretty daughter did not wear a very joyous expression just then.

The young people sauntered through the green wood, and talked to one another. What were they talking of? No, the bottle could not hear that, for it was in the provision basket. A long time passed before it was drawn forth; but when that happened, there had been pleasant things going on, for all were laughing, and the tanner's daughter laughed too; but she spoke less than before, and her cheeks glowed like two roses.

*The tanner's daughter herself packed the basket.*

The father took the full bottle and the corkscrew in his hand. Yes, it's a strange thing to be drawn thus, the first time! The Bottle-neck could never afterwards forget that impressive moment; and indeed there was quite a convulsion within him when the cork flew out, and a great throbbing as the wine poured forth into the glasses.

"Health to the betrothed pair!" cried the papa. And every glass was emptied to the dregs, and the young mate kissed his beautiful bride.

"Happiness and blessing!" said the two old people, the father and mother. And the young man filled the glasses again.

"Safe return, and a wedding this day next year!" he cried; and when the glasses were emptied, he took the bottle, raised it on high, and said, "Thou hast been present at the happiest day of my life, thou shalt never serve another!"

And so saying, he hurled it high into the air. The tanner's daughter did not then think that she should see the bottle fly again ; and yet it was to be so. It then fell into the thick reeds on the margin of a little woodland lake : and the Bottle-neck could remember quite plainly how it lay there for some time.

"I gave them wine, and they gave me marsh-water," he said ; "but it was all meant for the best."

He could no longer see the betrothed couple and the cheerful old people ; but for a long time he could hear them rejoicing and singing. Then at last came two peasant boys, and looked into the reeds ; they spied out the bottle, and took it up ; and now it was provided for.

At their home, in the wooden cottage, the oldest of three brothers, who was a sailor, and about to start on a long voyage, had been the day before to take leave. The mother was just engaged in packing up various things he was to take with him upon his journey, and which the father was going to carry into the town that evening to see his son once more, to give him a farewell greeting from the lad's mother and himself, and a little bottle of medicated brandy had already been wrapped up in a parcel, when the boys came in with the larger and stronger bottle which they had found. This bottle would hold more than the little one, and they pronounced that the brandy would be capital for a bad digestion, inasmuch as it was mixed with medicinal herbs. The draught that was now poured into the bottle was not so good as the red wine with which it had once been filled ; these were bitter drops, but even these are sometimes good. The new big bottle was to go, and not the little one ; and so the bottle went travelling again. It was taken on board for Peter Jensen, in the very same ship in which the young mate sailed. But he did not see the bottle ; and, indeed, he would not have known it, or thought it was the same one out of which they had drunk a health to the betrothed pair and to his own happy return.

Certainly it had no longer wine to give, but still it contained something that was just as good. Accordingly, whenever Peter Jensen brought it out, it was dubbed by his messmates "The Apothecary." It contained the best medicine, medicine that strengthened the weak, and it gave liberally so long as it had a drop left. That was a pleasant time, and the bottle sang when it was rubbed with the cork ; and it was called the Great Lark, "Peter Jensen's Lark."

Long days and months rolled on, and the bottle already stood empty in a corner, when it happened—whether on the passage out or home the bottle could not tell, for it had never been ashore—that a storm arose ; great waves came careering along, darkly and heavily, and lifted and tossed the ship to and fro. The mainmast was shivered, and a wave started one of the planks, and the pumps became useless. It was black night. The ship sank ; but at the last moment the young mate wrote on a leaf of paper, "God's will be done ! We are sinking !" He wrote the name of his betrothed, and his own name, and that of the ship, and put the leaf in an empty bottle that happened to be at hand : he corked it firmly down, and threw it out into the foaming sea. He knew not that it was the very bottle from which the goblet of joy and hope had once been filled for him : and now it was tossing on the waves with his last greeting and the message of death.

The ship sank, and the crew sank with her. The bottle sped on like a bird, for it bore a heart, a loving letter within itself. And the sun rose and set; and the bottle felt as at the time when it first came into being in the red gleaming oven—it felt a strong desire to leap back into the light.

It experienced calms and fresh storms; but it was hurled against no rock, and was devoured by no shark; and thus it drifted on for a year and a day, sometimes towards the north, sometimes towards the south, just as the current carried it. Beyond this it was its own master, but one may grow tired even of that.

The written page, the last farewell of the bridegroom to his betrothed, would only bring sorrow if it came into her hands; but where were the hands so white and delicate, which had once spread the cloth on the fresh grass in the green wood, on the betrothal day? Where was the tanner's daughter? Yes, where was the land, and which land might be nearest to her dwelling? The bottle knew not; it drove onward and onward, and was at last tired of wandering, because that was not in its way; but yet it had to travel until at last it came to land—to a strange land. It understood not a word of what was spoken here, for this was not the language it had heard spoken before; and one loses a good deal if one does not understand the language.

The bottle was fished out and examined on all sides. The leaf of paper within it was discovered, and taken out, and turned over and over, but the people did not understand what was written thereon. They saw that the bottle must have been thrown overboard, and that something about this was written on the paper, but what were the words? That question remained unanswered, and the paper was put back into the bottle, and the latter was deposited in a great cupboard in a great room in a great house.

Whenever strangers came, the paper was brought out and turned over and over, so that the inscription, which was only written in pencil, became more and more illegible, so that at last no one could see that there were letters on it. And for a whole year more the bottle remained standing in the cupboard; and then it was put into the loft, where it became covered with dust and cobwebs. Ah, how often it thought of the better days, the times when it had poured forth red wine in the green wood, when it had rocked on the waves of the sea, and when it had carried a secret, a letter, a parting sigh, safely enclosed in its bosom.

For full twenty years it stood up in the loft; and it might have remained there longer, but that the house was to be rebuilt. The roof was taken off, and then the bottle was noticed, and they spoke about it, but it did not understand their language; for one cannot learn a language by being shut up in a loft, even if one stays there twenty years.

" If I had been down in the room," thought the Bottle, " I might have learned it."

It was now washed and rinsed, and indeed this was requisite. It felt quite transparent and fresh, and as if its youth had been renewed in this its old age; but the paper it had carried so faithfully had been destroyed in the washing.

The bottle was filled with seeds, though it scarcely knew what they were. It was corked and well wrapped up. No light nor lantern was it vouchsafed to behold, much less the sun or the moon; and yet, it thought, when one goes on a journey one ought to see something; but though it saw nothing, it did what was most important—it travelled to the place of its destination, and was there unpacked.

"What trouble they have taken over yonder with that bottle!" it heard people say; "and yet it is most likely broken." But it was not broken.

The bottle understood every word that was now said; this was the language it had heard at the furnace, and at the wine merchant's, and in the forest, and in the ship, the only good old language it understood: it had come back home, and the language was as a salutation of welcome to it. For very joy it felt ready to jump out of people's hands; hardly did it notice that its cork had been drawn, and that it had been emptied and carried into the cellar

*In the garden flaming lamps hung like garlands, and among the leaves of the hedges stood bottles with a light in each.*

to be placed there and forgotten. There's no place like home, even if it's in the cellar! It never occurred to the bottle to think how long it would lie there, for it felt comfortable, and accordingly lay there for years. At last people came down into the cellar to carry off all the bottles, and ours among the rest.

Out in the garden there was a great festival. Flaming lamps hung like garlands, and paper lamps shone transparent, like great tulips. The evening was lovely, the weather still and clear, the stars twinkled; it was the time of the new moon, but in reality the whole moon could be seen as a bluish-gray disc with a golden rim round half its surface, which was a very beautiful sight for those who had good eyes.

The illumination extended, even to the most retired of the garden walks; at least so much of it, that one could find one's way there. Among the leaves of the hedges stood bottles, with a light in each, and among them was also the bottle we know, and which was destined one day to finish its career as a bottle-neck, a bird's drinking-glass. Everything here appeared lovely to our bottle, for it was once more in the green wood, amid joy and feasting, and heard song and music, and the noise and murmur of a crowd, especially in that part of the garden where the lamps blazed and the paper lanterns displayed their many colours. Thus it stood, in a distant walk certainly, but that made it the more important : for it bore its light, and was at once ornamental and useful, and that is as it should be : in such an hour one forgets twenty years spent in a loft, and it is right one should do so.

There passed close to it a pair, like the pair who had walked together so long ago in the wood, the sailor and the tanner's daughter ; the bottle seemed to experience all that over again. In the garden were walking not only the guests, but other people who were allowed to view all the splendour ; and among these latter came an old maid who seemed to stand alone in the world. She was just thinking, like the bottle, of the green wood, and of a young be-trothed pair—of a pair which concerned her very nearly, a pair in which she had an interest, and of which she had been a part in that happiest hour of her life—the hour one never forgets, if one should become ever so old a maid. But she did not know our bottle, nor did the bottle recognise the old maid : it is thus we pass each other in the world, meeting again and again, as these two met, now that they were together again in the same town.

From the garden the bottle was despatched once more to the wine mer-chant's, where it was filled with wine, and sold to the aeronaut, who was to make an ascent in his balloon on the following Sunday. A great crowd had been assembled to witness the sight ; military music had been provided, and many other preparations had been made. The bottle saw everything from a basket in which it lay next to a live rabbit, which latter was quite bewildered because he knew he was to be taken up into the air, and let down again in a parachute ; but the bottle knew nothing of the " up " or the " down " ; it only saw the balloon swelling up bigger and bigger, and at last, when it could swell no more, beginning to rise, and to grow more and more restless. The ropes that held it were cut, and the huge machine floated aloft with the aeronaut and the basket containing the bottle and the rabbit, and the music sounded, and all the people cried, " Hurrah ! "

" This is a wonderful passage, up into the air ! " thought the bottle ; " this is a new way of sailing : at any rate, up here we cannot strike upon anything."

Thousands of people gazed up at the balloon, and the old maid looked up at it also ; she stood at the open window of the garret, in which hung the cage with the little chaffinch, who had no water-glass as yet, but was obliged to be content with an old cup. In the window stood a myrtle in a pot ; and it had been put a little aside that it might not fall out, for the old maid was leaning out of the window to look, and she distinctly saw the aeronaut in the balloon, and how he let down the rabbit in the parachute, and then drank to the health of all the spectators, and at length hurled the bottle high in the air ; she never thought that this was the identical bottle which she had already once seen thrown aloft in honour of her and of her friend on the day of rejoicing in the green wood, in the time of her youth.

The bottle had no respite for thought, for it was quite startled at thus suddenly reaching the highest point in its career. Steeples and roofs lay far, far beneath, and the people looked like mites.

But now it began to descend with a much more rapid fall than that of the rabbit; the bottle threw somersaults in the air, and felt quite young, and quite free and unfettered; and yet it was half full of wine, though it did not remain so long. What a journey! The sun shone on the bottle, all the people were looking at it; the balloon was already far away, and soon the bottle was far away too, for it fell upon a roof and broke; but the pieces had got such an impetus that they could not stop themselves, but went jumping and rolling on till they came down into the courtyard and lay there in smaller pieces yet: the Bottle-neck only managed to keep whole, and that was cut off as clean as if it had been done with a diamond.

"That would do capitally for a bird-glass," said the cellarmen; but they had neither a bird nor a cage; and to expect them to provide both because they had found a bottle-neck that might be made available for a glass, would have been expecting too much; but the old maid in the garret, perhaps it might be useful to her; and now the Bottle-neck was taken up to her, and was provided with a cork. The part that had been uppermost was now turned downwards, as often happens when changes take place; fresh water was poured into it, and it was fastened to the cage of the little bird, which sang and twittered right merrily.

"Yes, it's very well for you to sing," said the Bottle-neck.

And it was considered remarkable for having been in the balloon—for that was all they knew of its history. Now it hung there as a bird-glass, and heard the murmuring and noise of the people in the street below, and also the words of the old maid in the room within. An old friend had just come to visit her, and they talked—not about the Bottle-neck, but about the myrtle in the window.

"No, you certainly must not spend a dollar for your daughter's bridal wreath," said the old maid. "You shall have a beautiful little nosegay from me, full of blossoms. Do you see how splendid that tree has come on? yes, that has been raised from a spray of the myrtle you gave me on the day after my betrothal, and from which I was to have made my own wreath when the year was past; but that day never came! The eyes closed that were to have been my joy and delight through life. In the depths of the sea he sleeps sweetly, my dear one! The myrtle has become an old tree, and I become a yet older woman; and when it faded at last, I took the last green shoot, and planted it in the ground, and it has become a great tree; and now at length the myrtle will serve at the wedding—as a wreath for your daughter."

There were tears in the eyes of the old maid. She spoke of the beloved of her youth, of their betrothal in the wood; many thoughts came to her, but the thought never came, that quite close to her, before the very window, was a remembrance of those times—the neck of the bottle which had shouted for joy when the cork flew out with a bang on the betrothal day. But the Bottle-neck did not recognise her, for he was not listening to what this old maid said—and still that was because he was thinking of her.

# CHRISTMAS BELLS

*by* HENRY WADSWORTH LONGFELLOW

I HEARD the bells on Christmas Day
Their old, familiar carols play,
    And wild and sweet
    The words repeat
Of peace on earth, good-will to men !

And thought how, as the day had come
The belfries of all Christendom
    Had rolled along
    The unbroken song
Of peace on earth, good-will to men !

Till, ringing, singing on its way,
The world revolved from night to day,
    A voice, a chime,
    A chant sublime
Of peace on earth, good-will to men !

Then from each black, accursed mouth
The cannon thundered in the South,
    And with the sound
    The carols drowned
Of peace on earth, good-will to men !

It was as if an earthquake rent
The hearth-stones of a continent,
    And made forlorn
    The households born
Of peace on earth, good-will to men !

And in despair I bowed my head ;
" There is no peace on earth," I said,
    " For hate is strong,
    And mocks the song
Of peace on earth, good-will to men ! "

Then pealed the bells more loud and deep :
" God is not dead, nor doth He sleep !
    The Wrong shall fail,
    The Right prevail,
With peace on earth, good-will to men ! "

# THE PANIC

### by MRS. GASKELL

I THINK a series of circumstances dated from Signor Brunoni's visit to Cranford, which seemed at the time connected in our minds with him, though I don't know that he had anything really to do with them. All at once all sorts of uncomfortable rumours got afloat in the town. There were one or two robberies—real *bona fide* robberies; men had been up before the magistrates and committed for trial—and that seemed to make us all afraid of being robbed; and for a long time at Miss Matty's, I know, we used to make a regular expedition all round the kitchens and cellars every night, Miss Matty leading the way, armed with the poker, I following with the hearth brush, and Martha carrying the shovel and fire-irons with which to sound the alarm; and by the accidental hitting together of them she often frightened us so much that we bolted ourselves up, all three together, in the back kitchen, or storeroom, or wherever we happened to be, till, when our affright was over, we recollected ourselves, and set out afresh with double valiance, By day we heard strange stories from the shopkeepers and cottagers, of carts that went about in the dead of night, drawn by horses shod with felt, and guarded by men in dark clothes, going round the town, no doubt in search of some unwatched house or some unfastened door.

Miss Pole, who affected great bravery herself, was the principal person to collect and arrange these reports so as to make them assume their most fearful aspect. But we discovered that she had begged one of Mr. Hoggins's worn-out hats to hang up in her lobby, and we (at least I) had doubts as to whether she really would enjoy the little adventure of having her house broken into, as she protested she should. Miss Matty made no secret of being an arrant coward, but she went regularly through her housekeeper's duty of inspection—only the hour for this became earlier and earlier, till at last we went the rounds at half-past six, and Miss Matty adjourned to bed soon after seven, " in order to get the night over the sooner."

Cranford had so long piqued itself on being an honest and moral town that it had grown to fancy itself too genteel and well-bred to be otherwise, and felt the stain upon its character at this time doubly. But we comforted ourselves with the assurance which we gave to each other that the robberies could never have been committed by any Cranford person ; it must have been a stranger, or strangers, who brought this disgrace upon the town, and occasioned as many precautions as if we were living among the Red Indians or the French.

This last comparison of our nightly state of defence and fortification was made by Mrs. Forrester, whose father had served under General Burgoyne in the American war, and whose husband had fought the French in Spain. She, indeed, inclined to the idea that, in some way, the French were connected with the small thefts, which were ascertained facts, and the burglaries and highway robberies, which were rumours. She had been deeply impressed with the idea of French spies at some time in her life ; and the notion could never be fairly eradicated, but sprang up again from time to time. And now her theory was this : The Cranford people respected themselves too much, and were too grateful to the aristocracy who were so kind as to live near the town, ever to disgrace their bringing up by being dishonest or immoral ; therefore, we must believe that the robbers were strangers—if strangers, why not foreigners ?—if foreigners, who so likely as the French ? Signor Brunoni spoke broken English like a Frenchman ; and, though he wore a turban like a Turk, Mrs. Forrester had seen a print of Madame de Staël with a turban on, and another of Mr. Denon in just such a dress as that in which the conjurer had made his appearance, showing clearly that the French, as well as the Turks, wore turbans. There could be no doubt Signor Brunoni was a Frenchman—a French spy come to discover the weak and un-defended places of England, and doubtless he had his accomplices.

For her part, she had always had her own opinion of Miss Pole's adventure at the George Inn, seeing two men where only one was believed to be. French people had ways and means which, she was thankful to say, the English knew nothing about ; and she had never felt quite easy in her mind about going to see that conjurer ; it was rather too much like a forbidden thing, though the rector was there. In short, Mrs. Forrester grew more excited than we had ever known her before, and, being an officer's daughter and widow, we looked up to her opinion, of course.

Really I do not know how much was true or false in the reports which flew about like wildfire just at this time ; but it seemed to me then that there was every reason to believe that at Mardon (a small town about eight miles from Cranford) houses and shops were entered by holes made in the walls, the bricks being silently carried away in the dead of the night, and all done so quietly that no sound was heard either in or out of the house. Miss Matty gave it up in despair when she heard of this. " What was the use," said she, " of locks and bolts, and bells to the windows, and going round the house every night ? That last trick was fit for a conjurer. Now she did believe that Signor Brunoni was at the bottom of it."

One afternoon, about five o'clock, we were startled by a hasty knock at the door. Miss Matty bade me run and tell Martha on no account to open the door till she (Miss Matty) had reconnoitred through the window; and she armed herself with a footstool to drop down on the head of the visitor in case he should show a face covered with black crepe, as he looked up in answer to her inquiry of who was there. But it was nobody but Miss Pole and Betty. The former came upstairs, carrying a little hand-basket, and she was evidently in a state of great agitation.

"Take care of that!" said she to me, as I offered to relieve her of her basket. "It's my plate. I am sure there is a plan to rob my house to-night. I am come to throw myself on your hospitality, Miss Matty. Betty is going to sleep with her cousin at the George. I can sit up here all night if you will allow me; but my house is so far from any neighbours, and I don't believe we could be heard if we screamed ever so!"

"But," said Miss Matty, "what has alarmed you so much? Have you seen any men lurking about the house?"

"Oh, yes!" answered Miss Pole. "Two very bad-looking men have gone three times past the house very slowly; and an Irish beggar-woman came not half an hour ago, and all but forced herself in past Betty, saying her children were starving, and she must speak to the mistress. You see, she said 'mistress,' though there was a hat hanging up in the hall, and it would have been more natural to have said 'master.' But Betty shut the door in her face, and came up to me, and we got the spoons together, and sat in the parlour window watching till we saw Thomas Jones going from his work, when we called to him and asked him to take care of us into the town."

*"Take care of that!" said she, as I offered to relieve her of her basket.*

We might have triumphed over Miss Pole, who had professed such bravery until she was frightened ; but we were too glad to perceive that she shared in the weaknesses of humanity to exult over her ; and I gave up my room to her very willingly, and shared Miss Matty's bed for the night. But before we retired, the two ladies rummaged up, out of the recesses of their memory, such horrid stories of robbery and murder that I quite quaked in my shoes. Miss Pole was evidently anxious to prove that such terrible events had occurred within her experience that she was justified in her sudden panic ; and Miss Matty did not like to be outdone, and capped every story with one yet more horrible, till it reminded me, oddly enough, of an old story I had read somewhere of a nightingale and a musician who strove one against the other which could produce the most admirable music, till poor Philomel dropped down dead.

One of the stories that haunted me for a long time afterwards was of a girl who was left in charge of a great house in Cumberland on some particular fair-day, when the other servants all went off to the gaieties. The family were away in London, and a pedlar came by, and asked to leave his large and heavy pack in the kitchen, saying he would call for it again at night ; and the girl (a gamekeeper's daughter) roaming about in search of amusement, chanced to hit upon a gun hanging up in the hall, and took it down to look at the chasing ; and it went off through the open kitchen door, hit the pack, and a slow dark thread of blood came oozing out. (How Miss Pole enjoyed this part of the story, dwelling on each word as if she loved it !) She rather hurried over the further account of the girl's bravery, and I have but a confused idea that somehow she baffled the robbers with Italian irons, heated red-hot, and then restored to blackness by being dipped in grease.

We parted for the night with an awe-stricken wonder as to what we should hear of in the morning ; and, on my part, with a vehement desire for the night to be over and gone—I was so afraid lest the robbers should have seen, from some dark lurking-place, that Miss Pole had carried off her plate, and thus have a double motive for attacking our house.

But until Lady Glenmire came to call next day we heard of nothing unusual. The kitchen fire-irons were in exactly the same position against the back-door as when Martha and I had skilfully piled them up, like spillikins, ready to fall with an awful clatter if only a cat had touched the outside panels. I had wondered what we should all do if thus awakened and alarmed, and had proposed to Miss Matty that we should cover up our faces under the bed-clothes, so that there should be no danger of the robbers thinking that we could identify them ; but Miss Matty, who was trembling very much, scouted this idea, and said we owed it to society to apprehend them, and that she should certainly do her best to lay hold of them and lock them up in the garret till morning.

When Lady Glenmire came we almost felt jealous of her. Mrs. Jamieson's house had really been attacked ; at least there were men's footsteps to be seen on the flower borders underneath the kitchen windows, " where nae men should be " ; and Carlo had barked all through the night as if strangers were abroad. Mrs. Jamieson had been awakened by Lady Glenmire, and they had rung the bell which communicated with Mr. Mulliner's room in the third storey, and when his nightcapped head had appeared over the banisters, in answer to the summons, they had told him of their alarm, and the reasons for it ; whereupon he retreated into his bedroom and locked the door (for fear of draughts, as he informed them in the morning), and opened the window, and called out valiantly to say, if the supposed robbers would come to him he would fight them ; but, as Lady Glenmire observed, that was but poor comfort, since they would have to pass by Mrs. Jamieson's room and her own before they could reach him, and must be a very pugnacious disposition indeed if they neglected the opportunities of robbery presented by the unguarded lower storeys, to go up to a garret, and there force a door in order to get at the champion of the house. Lady Glenmire, after waiting and listening for some time in the drawing-room, had proposed to Mrs. Jamieson that they should go to bed ; but that lady said she should not feel comfortable unless she sat up and watched ; and, accordingly, she packed herself warmly up on the sofa, where she was found by the housemaid when she came into the room at six o'clock, fast asleep ; but Lady Glenmire went to bed, and kept awake all night.

When Miss Pole heard of this, she nodded her head in great satisfaction. She had been sure we should hear of something happening in Cranford that night ; and we had heard. It was clear enough they had first proposed to attack her house ; but when they saw that she and Betty were on their guard, and had carried off the plate, they had changed their tactics and gone to Mrs. Jamieson's, and no one knew what might have happened if Carlo had not barked, like a good dog that he was !

Poor Carlo ! his barking days were nearly over. Whether the gang who infested the neighbourhood were afraid of him ; or whether they were revengeful enough—for the way in which he had baffled them on the night in question—to poison him ; or whether, as some among the more uneducated people thought, he died of apoplexy, brought on by too much feeding and too little exercise ; at any rate, it is certain that, two days after this eventful night, Carlo was found dead, with his poor little legs stretched out stiff in the attitude of running, as if by such unusual exertion he could escape the sure pursuer, Death.

We were all sorry for Carlo, the old familiar friend who had snapped at us for so many years ; and the mysterious mode of his death made us very uncomfortable. Could Signor Brunoni be at the bottom of this ? He had apparently killed a canary with only a word of command ; his will seemed of deadly force ; who knew but what he might yet be lingering in the neighbourhood willing all sorts of awful things !

We whispered these fancies among ourselves in the evenings ; but in the mornings our courage came back with the daylight, and in a week's time we had got over the shock of Carlo's death ; all but Mrs. Jamieson. She, poor thing, felt it as she had felt no event since her husband's death ; indeed, Miss Pole said, that as the Honourable Mr. Jamieson drank a good deal, and occasioned her much uneasiness, it was possible that Carlo's death might be the greater affliction. But there was always a tinge of cynicism in Miss Pole's remarks. However, one thing was clear and certain—it was necessary for Mrs. Jamieson to have some change of scene ; and Mr. Mulliner was very impressive on this point, shaking his head whenever we inquired after his mistress, and speaking of her loss of appetite and bad nights very ominously ;

and with justice, too, for if she had two characteristics in her natural state of health they were a facility of eating and sleeping. If she could neither eat nor sleep, she must be indeed out of spirits and out of health.

Lady Glenmire (who had evidently taken very kindly to Cranford) did not like the idea of Mrs. Jamieson's going to Cheltenham, and more than once insinuated pretty plainly that it was Mr. Mulliner's doing, who had been much alarmed on the occasion of the house being attacked, and since had said, more than once, that he felt it a very responsible charge to have to defend so many women. Be that as it might, Mrs. Jamieson went to Cheltenham, escorted by Mr. Mulliner; and Lady Glenmire remained in possession of the house, her ostensible office being to take care that the maid-servants did not pick up followers. She made a very pleasant-looking dragon; and, as soon as it was arranged for her to stay in Cranford, she found out that Mrs. Jamieson's visit to Cheltenham was just the best thing in the world. She had let her house in Edinburgh, and was for the time houseless, so the charge of her sister-in-law's comfortable abode was very convenient and acceptable.

Miss Pole was very much inclined to install herself as a heroine, because of the decided steps she had taken in flying from the two men and one woman, whom she entitled " that murderous gang." She described their appearance in glowing colours, and I noticed that every time she went over the story some fresh trait of villainy was added to their appearance. One was tall—he grew to be gigantic in height before we had done with him; he, of course, had black hair—and by and by it hung in elf-locks over his forehead and down his back. The other was short and broad—and a hump sprouted out on his shoulder before we heard the last of him; he had red hair—which deepened into carroty; and she was almost sure he had a cast in the eye—a decided squint. As for the woman, her eyes glared, and she was masculine looking —a perfect virago; most probably a man dressed in woman's clothes : afterwards we heard of a beard on her chin, and a manly voice and a stride.

If Miss Pole was delighted to recount the events of that afternoon to all inquirers, others were not so proud of their adventures in the robbery line. Mr. Hoggins, the surgeon, had been attacked at his own door by two ruffians, who were concealed in the shadow of the porch, and so effectually silenced him that he was robbed in the interval between ringing his bell and the servant's answering it. Miss Pole was sure it would turn out that this robbery had been committed by " her men," and went the very day she heard the report to have her teeth examined, and to question Mr. Hoggins. She came to us afterwards; so we heard what she had heard, straight and direct from the source, while we were yet in the excitement and flutter of the agitation caused by the first intelligence; for the event had only occurred the night before.

" Well ! " said Miss Pole, sitting down with the decision of a person who has made up her mind as to the nature of life and the world (and such people never tread lightly, or seat themselves without a bump), " well, Miss Matty ! men will be men. Every mother's son of them wishes to be considered Samson and Solomon rolled into one—too strong ever to be beaten or discomfited—too wise ever to be outwitted. If you will notice, they have always foreseen events, though they never tell one for one's warning before the events happen. My father was a man, and I know the sex pretty well."

She had talked herself out of breath, and we should have been very glad to fill up the necessary pause as chorus, but we did not exactly know what to say, or which man had suggested this diatribe against the sex; so we only joined in generally, with a grave shake of the head, and a soft murmur of, "They are very incomprehensible, certainly!"

"Now, only think," said she. "There I have undergone the risk of having one of my remaining teeth drawn (for one is terribly at the mercy of any surgeon-dentist; and I, for one, always speak them fair till I have got my mouth out of their clutches), and, after all, Mr. Hoggins is too much of a man to own that he was robbed last night."

"Not robbed!" exclaimed the chorus.

"*Don't tell me!*" *Miss Pole exclaimed.* "*I believe he was robbed.*"

"Don't tell me!" Miss Pole exclaimed, angry that we could be for a moment imposed upon. "I believe he was robbed, just as Betty told me, and he is ashamed to own it; and, to be sure, it was very silly of him to be robbed just at his own door; I dare say he feels that such a thing won't raise him in the eyes of Cranford society, and is anxious to conceal it—but he need not have tried to impose upon me, by saying I must have heard an exaggerated account of some petty theft of a neck of mutton, which, it seems, was stolen out of the safe in his yard last week; he had the impertinence to add, he believed that that was taken by the cat. I have no doubt, if I could get at the bottom of it, it was that Irishman dressed up in woman's clothes, who came spying about my house, with the story about the starving children."

After we had duly condemned the want of candour which Mr. Hoggins had evinced, and abused men in general, taking him for the representative and type, we got round to the subject about which we had been talking when Miss Pole came in; namely, how far, in the present disturbed state of the country, we could venture to accept an invitation which Miss Matty had just received from Mrs. Forrester, to come as usual and keep the anniversary of her wedding-day by drinking tea with her at five o'clock, and playing a quiet pool afterwards. Mrs. Forrester had said that she asked us with some diffidence, because the roads were, she feared, very unsafe. But she suggested that perhaps one of us would not object to take the sedan, and that the others, by walking briskly, might keep up with the long trot of the chairmen, and so we might all arrive safely at Over Place, a suburb of the town. (No; that is too large an expression: a small cluster of houses separated from Cranford by about two hundred yards of a dark and lonely lane.) There was no doubt but that a similar note was awaiting Miss Pole at home; so her call was a very fortunate affair, as it enabled us to consult together. . . . We would all much rather have declined this invitation; but we felt that it would not be quite kind to Mrs. Forrester, who would otherwise be left to a solitary retrospect of her not very happy or fortunate life. Miss Matty and Miss Pole had been visitors on this occasion for many years, and now they gallantly determined to nail their colours to the mast, and to go through Darkness Lane rather than fail in loyalty to their friend.

But when the evening came, Miss Matty (for it was she who was voted into the chair, as she had a cold), before being shut down in the sedan, like Jack-in-a-box, implored the chairman, whatever might befall, not to run away and leave her fastened up there, to be murdered; and even after they had promised, I saw her tighten her features into the stern determination of a martyr, and she gave me a melancholy and ominous shake of the head through the glass. However, we got there safely, only rather out of breath, for it was who could trot hardest through Darkness Lane, and I am afraid poor Miss Matty was sadly jolted.

Mrs. Forrester had made extra preparations, in acknowledgment of our exertion in coming to see her through such dangers. The usual forms of genteel ignorance as to what her servants might send up were all gone through; and harmony and preference seemed likely to be the order of the evening, but for an interesting conversation that began I don't know how, but which had relation, of course, to the robbers who infested the neighbourhood of Cranford.

Having braved the dangers of Darkness Lane, and thus having a little stock of reputation for courage to fall back upon; and also, I dare say, desirous of proving ourselves superior to men (*videlicet* Mr. Hoggins) in the article of candour, we began to relate our individual fears, and the private precautions we each of us took. I owned that my pet apprehension was eyes —eyes looking at me, and watching me, glittering out from some dull, flat, wooden surface; and that if I dared to go up to my looking-glass when I was panic-stricken, I should certainly turn it round, with its back towards me, for fear of seeing eyes behind me looking out of the darkness.

I saw Miss Matty nerving herself up for a confession; and at last out it came. She owned that, ever since she had been a girl, she had dreaded being caught by her last leg, just as she was getting into bed, by some one concealed under it. She said, when she was younger and more active, she used to take a flying leap, and so bring both her legs up safely into bed at once; but that this had always annoyed Deborah, who piqued herself upon getting into bed gracefully, and she had given it up in consequence. But now the old terror would often come over her, especially since Miss Pole's house had been attacked (we had got quite to believe in the fact of the attack having taken place), and yet it was very unpleasant to think of looking under a bed, and seeing a man concealed, with a great, fierce face staring out at you; so she had bethought herself of something—perhaps I had noticed that she had told Martha to buy her a penny ball, such as children play with—and now she rolled this ball under the bed every night: if it came out on the other side, well and good; if not, she always took care to have her hand on the bell-rope, and meant to call out John and Harry, just as if she expected men-servants to answer her ring.

We all applauded this ingenious contrivance, and Miss Matty sank back into satisfied silence, with a look at Mrs. Forrester as if to ask for *her* private weakness.

Mrs. Forrester looked askance at Miss Pole, and tried to change the subject a little by telling us that she had borrowed a boy from one of the neighbouring cottages and promised his parents a hundredweight of coals at Christmas, and his supper every evening, for the loan of him at nights. She had instructed him in his possible duties when he first came; and, finding him sensible, she had given him the major's sword (the major was her late husband), and desired him to put it very carefully behind his pillow at night, turning the edge towards the head of the pillow. He was a sharp lad, she was sure; for, spying out the major's cocked hat, he had said, if he might have that to wear, he was sure he could frighten two Englishmen, or four Frenchmen, any day. But she had impressed upon him anew that he was to lose no time in putting on hats or anything else; but, if he heard any noise, he was to run at it with his drawn sword. On my suggesting that some accident might occur from such slaughterous and indiscriminate directions, and that he might rush on Jenny getting up to wash, and have spitted her before he had discovered that she was not a Frenchman, Mrs. Forrester said she did not think that that was likely, for he was a very sound sleeper, and generally had to be well shaken or cold-pigged in a morning before they could rouse him. She sometimes thought such dead sleep must be owing to the hearty suppers the poor lad ate, for he was half-starved at home, and she told Jenny to see that he got a good meal at night.

Still this was not confession of Mrs. Forrester's peculiar timidity, and we urged her to tell us what she thought would frighten her more than anything. She paused, and stirred the fire, and snuffed the candles, and then she said in a sounding whisper :—

" Ghosts ! "

She looked at Miss Pole, as much as to say, she had declared it, and would stand by it. Such a look was a challenge in itself. Miss Pole came down upon her with indigestion, spectral illusions, optical delusions, and a great deal out of Dr. Ferrir and Dr. Hibbert besides. Miss Matty had rather a leaning to ghosts, as I have mentioned before, and what little she did say was all on Mrs. Forrester's side, who, emboldened by sympathy, protested that ghosts were a part of her religion; that surely she, the widow of a major in the army, knew what to be frightened at, and what not; in short, I never saw Mrs. Forrester so warm either before or since, for she was a gentle meek, enduring old lady in most things. Not all the elder-wine that ever was mulled could this night wash out the remembrance of this difference between Miss Pole and her hostess. Indeed, when the elder-wine was brought in, it gave rise to a new burst of discussion ; for Jenny, the little maiden who staggered under the tray, had to give evidence of having seen a ghost with her own eyes, not so many nights ago, in Darkness Lane, the very lane we were to go through on our way home.

In spite of the uncomfortable feeling which this last consideration gave me, I could not help being amused at Jenny's position, which was exceedingly like that of a witness being examined and cross-examined by two counsel who are not at all scrupulous about asking leading questions. The conclusion I arrived at was, that Jenny had certainly seen something beyond what a fit of indigestion would have caused. A lady all in white, and without her head, was what she deposed and adhered to, supported by a consciousness of the secret sympathy of her mistress under the withering scorn with which Miss Pole regarded her. And not only she, but many others, had seen this headless lady, who sat by the roadside wringing her hands as in deep grief. Mrs. Forrester looked at us from time to time with an air of conscious triumph ; but then she had not to pass through Darkness Lane before she could bury herself beneath her own familiar bedclothes.

We preserved a discreet silence as to the headless lady while we were putting on our things to go home, for there was no knowing how near the ghostly head and ears might be, or what spiritual connection they might be keeping up with the unhappy body in Darkness Lane ; and, therefore, even Miss Pole felt that it was as well not to speak lightly on such subjects, for fear of vexing or insulting that woebegone trunk. At least, so I conjecture ; for, instead of the busy clatter usual in the operation, we tied on our cloaks as sadly as mutes at a funeral. Miss Matty drew the curtains round the windows of the chair to shut out disagreeable sights, and the men (either because they were in spirits that their labours were so nearly ended, or because they were going down hill) set off at such a round and merry pace that it was all Miss Pole and I could do to keep up with them. She had breath for nothing beyond an imploring " Don't leave me ! " uttered as she clutched my arm so tightly that I could not have quitted her, ghost or no ghost. What a relief it was when the men, weary of their burden, and their quick trot, stopped just where Headingley Causeway branches off from Darkness Lane ! Miss Pole unloosed me and caught at one of the men.

" Could not you take Miss Matty round by Headingley Causeway ?—the pavement in Darkness Lane jolts so, and she is not very strong ? "

A smothered voice was heard from the inside of the chair—

" Oh ! pray go on ! What is the matter ? What is the matter ? I will give you sixpence more to go on very fast ; pray don't stop here."

" And I'll give you a shilling," said Miss Pole, with tremulous dignity, " if you'll go by Headingley Causeway."

The two men grunted acquiescence and took up the chair, and went along the causeway, which certainly answered Miss Pole's kind purpose of saving Miss Matty's bones ; for it was covered with soft, thick mud, and even a fall there would have been easy till the getting-up came, when there might have been some difficulty in extrication.

# WHAT THE MOON SAW

## by HANS ANDERSEN

### INTRODUCTION

IT is a strange thing, that when I feel most fervently and most deeply, my hands and my tongue seem alike tired, so that I cannot rightly describe or accurately portray the thoughts that are rising within me ; and yet I am a painter : my eye tells me as much as that, and all my friends who have seen my sketches and fancies say the same.

I am a poor lad, and live in one of the narrowest of lanes ; but I do not want for light, as my room is high up in the house, with an extensive prospect over the neighbouring roofs. During the first few days I went to live in the town, I felt low-spirited and solitary enough. Instead of the forest and the green hills of former days, I had here only a forest of chimney-pots to look out upon. And then I had not a single friend ; not one familiar face greeted me.

So one evening I sat at the window, in a desponding mood ; and presently I opened the casement and looked out. Oh, how my heart leaped up with joy ! Here was a well-known face at last—a round, friendly countenance, the face of a good friend I had known at home. In fact it was the MOON that looked in upon me. He was quite unchanged, the dear old Moon, and had the same face exactly that he used to show when he peered down upon me through the willow trees on the moor. I kissed my hand to him over and over again, as he shone far into my little room ; and he, for his part, promised me that every evening, when he came abroad, he would look in upon me for a few moments. This promise he has faithfully kept. It is a pity that he can only stay such a short time when he comes. Whenever he appears, he tells me of one thing or another that he has seen on the previous night or on that same evening.

" Just paint the scenes I describe to you "—that is what he said to me—
" and you will have a very pretty picture-book."

I have followed his injunction for many evenings. I could make up a new
" Thousand and One Nights," in my own way, out of these pictures, but the
number might be too great, after all. The pictures I have here given have
not been chosen at random, but follow in their proper order, just as they
were described to me. Some great gifted painter, or some poet or musician,
may make something more of them if he likes ; what I have given here are
only hasty sketches, hurriedly put upon the paper, with some of my own
thoughts interspersed ; for the Moon did not come to me every evening—
a cloud sometimes hid his face from me.

### FIRST EVENING

" Last night,"—I am quoting the Moon's own words—" last night I was
gliding through the cloudless Indian sky. My face was mirrored in the waters
of the Ganges, and my beams strove to pierce through the thick intertwining
boughs of the bananas, arching beneath me like the tortoise's shell. Forth
from the thicket tripped a Hindoo maid, light as a gazelle, beautiful as Eve.
Airy and ethereal as a vision, and yet sharply defined amid the surrounding
shadows, stood this daughter of Hindostan : I could read on her delicate
brow the thought that had brought her hither. The thorny creeping plants
tore her sandals, but for all that she came rapidly forward. The deer that had
come down to the river to quench her thirst, sprang by with a startled bound,
for in her hand the maiden bore a lighted lamp. I could see the blood in her
delicate finger-tips, as she spread them for a screen before the dancing
flame. She came down to the stream, and set the lamp upon the water, and
let it float away. The flame flickered to and fro, and seemed ready to expire ;
but still the lamp burned on, and the girl's black sparkling eyes, half-veiled
behind their long silken lashes, followed it with a gaze of earnest intensity.
She well knew that if the lamp continued to burn so long as she could keep
it in sight, her betrothed was still alive ; but if the lamp was suddenly extinguished, he was dead. And the lamp burned bravely on, and she fell on
her knees and prayed. Near her in the grass lay a speckled snake, but she
heeded it not—she thought only of Bramah and of her betrothed.

" ' He lives ! ' she shouted joyfully, ' he lives ! ' And from the mountains
the echoes came back upon her, ' he lives ! ' "

### SECOND EVENING

" Yesterday," said the Moon to me, " I looked down upon a small courtyard surrounded on all sides by houses. In the courtyard sat a clucking hen
with eleven chickens ; and a pretty little girl was running and jumping
around them. The hen was frightened, and screamed, and spread out her
wings over the little brood. Then the girl's father came out and scolded
her ; and I glided away and thought no more of the matter.

" But this evening, only a few minutes ago, I looked down into the same courtyard. Everything was quiet. But presently the little girl came forth again, crept quietly to the hen-house, pushed back the bolt, and slipped into the apartment of the hen and chickens. They cried out loudly, and came fluttering down from their perches, and ran about in dismay, and the little girl ran after them. I saw it quite plainly, for I looked through a hole in the hen-house wall. I was angry with the wilful child, and felt glad when her father came out and scolded her more violently than yesterday, holding her roughly by the arm : she held down her head, and her blue eyes were full of large tears. 'What are you about here?' he asked. She wept and said, 'I wanted to kiss the hen and beg her pardon for frightening her yesterday ; but I was afraid to tell you.'

" And the father kissed the innocent child's forehead, and I kissed her on the mouth and eyes."

### THIRD EVENING

" In the narrow street round the corner yonder—it is so narrow that my beams can only glide for a minute along the walls of the house, but in that minute I see enough to learn what the world is made of—in that narrow street I saw a woman. Sixteen years ago that woman was a child, playing in the garden of the old parsonage in the country. The hedges of rose bushes were old, and the flowers were faded. They straggled wild over the paths, and the ragged branches grew up among the boughs of the apple trees ; here and there were a few roses still in bloom—not so fair as the queen of flowers generally appears, but still they had colour and scent too. The clergyman's little daughter appeared to me a far lovelier rose, as she sat on her stool under the straggling hedge, hugging and caressing her doll with the battered pasteboard cheeks.

" Ten years afterwards I saw her again. I beheld her in a splendid ball-room : she was the beautiful bride of a rich merchant. I rejoiced at her happiness, and sought her on calm quiet evenings—ah, nobody thinks of my clear eye and silent glance ! Alas ! my rose ran wild, like the rose bushes in the garden of the parsonage. There are tragedies in everyday life, and to-night I saw the last act of one.

" She was lying in bed in a house in that narrow street ; she was sick unto death, and the cruel landlord came up, and tore away the thin coverlet, her only protection against the cold. 'Get up !' said he, 'your face is enough to frighten one. Get up and dress yourself. Give me money, or I'll turn you out into the street ! Quick—get up !' She answered, 'Alas ! death is gnawing at my heart. Let me rest.' But he forced her to get up and bathe her face, and he put a wreath of roses in her hair ; and he placed her in a chair at the window, with a candle burning beside her, and went away.

" I looked at her, and she was sitting motionless, with her hands in her lap. The wind caught the open window and shut it with a crash, so that a pane came clattering down in fragments ; but still she never moved. The curtain caught fire, and the flames played about her face ; and then I saw that she was dead. There at the window sat the dead woman, preaching a sermon against *sin*—my poor faded rose out of the parsonage garden ! "

### FOURTH EVENING

"This evening I saw a German play acted," said the Moon. "It was in a little town. A stable had been turned into a theatre; that is to say, the stable had been left standing, and had been turned into private boxes, and all the timber-work had been covered with coloured paper. A little iron chandelier hung beneath the ceiling, and that it might be made to disappear into the ceiling, as it does in great theatres, when the *ting-ting* of the prompter's bell is heard, a great inverted tub had been placed just above it.

"'*Ting-ting!*' and the little iron chandelier suddenly rose at least half a yard and disappeared in the tub; and that was the sign that the play was going to begin. A young nobleman and his lady, who happened to be passing through the little town, were present at the performance, and consequently the house was crowded. But under the chandelier was a vacant space like a little crater: not a single soul sat there, for the tallow was dropping, drip, drip! I saw everything, for it was so warm in there that every loop-hole had been opened. The male and female servants stood outside, peeping through the chinks, although a real policeman was inside, threatening them with a stick. Close by the orchestra could be seen the noble young couple in two old arm-chairs, which were usually occupied by his worship the mayor and his lady; but these latter were obliged to-day to content themselves with wooden forms, just as if they had been ordinary citizens; and the lady observed quietly to herself, 'One sees, now, that there is rank above rank;' and this incident gave an air of extra festivity to the whole proceedings. The chandelier gave little leaps, the crowd got their knuckles rapped, and I, the Moon, was present at the performance from beginning to end."

*Close by the orchestra was the noble young couple in two old arm-chairs.*

### FIFTH EVENING

" Yesterday," began the Moon, " I looked down upon the turmoil of Paris. My eye penetrated into an apartment of the Louvre. An old grandmother, poorly clad—she belonged to the working class—was following one of the underservants into the great empty throne-room, for this was the apartment she wanted to see—that she was resolved to see ; it had cost her many a little sacrifice and many a coaxing word to penetrate thus far. She folded her thin hands, and looked round with an air of reverence.

" ' Here it was ! ' she said, ' here ! ' And she approached the throne from which hung the rich velvet fringed with gold lace. ' There,' she exclaimed, ' there ! ' and she knelt and kissed the purple carpet. I think she was actually weeping.

" ' But it was not *this very* velvet ! ' observed the footman, and a smile played about his mouth.

" ' True, but it was this very place,' replied the woman, ' and it must have looked just like this.'

" ' It looked so, and yet it did not,' observed the man : ' the windows were beaten in, and the doors were off their hinges, and there was blood upon the floor.'

" ' But for all that you can say, my grandson died upon the throne of France. Died ! ' mournfully repeated the old woman.

" I do not think another word was spoken, and they soon quitted the hall. The evening twilight faded, and my light shone vividly upon the rich velvet that covered the throne of France.

" Now, who do you think this poor woman was ? Listen, I will tell you a story.

" It happened in the Revolution of July, on the evening of the most brilliantly victorious day, when every house was a fortress, every window a breastwork. The people stormed the Tuileries. Even women and children were found among the combatants. They penetrated into the apartments and halls of the palace. A poor half-grown boy in a ragged blouse fought among the older insurgents. Mortally wounded with several bayonet thrusts, he sank down. This happened in the throne-room.

They laid the bleeding youth upon the throne of France, and wrapped the velvet of imperial purple round his wounds. There was a picture ! —the splendid hall, the fighting groups ! A torn flag lay upon the ground, the tricolor was waving above the bayonets, and on the throne lay the poor lad with the pale glorified countenance, his eyes turned towards the sky, his limbs writhing in the death agony, his breast bare, and his poor, tattered clothing half-hidden by the rich velvet embroidered with silver lilies. At the boy's cradle a prophecy had been spoken : ' He will die on the throne of France ! ' The mother's heart had fondly imagined a second Napoleon.

" My beams have kissed the wreath of *immortelles* on his grave, and this night they kissed the forehead of the old grandam, while in a dream the picture floated before her which thou mayest draw—the poor boy on the throne of France."

## SIXTH EVENING

" I've been in Upsala," said the Moon : " I looked down upon the great plain covered with coarse grass, and upon the barren fields. I mirrored my face in the Tyris river, while the steamboat drove the fish into the rushes. Beneath me floated the waves, throwing long shadows on the so-called graves of Odin, Thor, and Friga. In the scanty turf that covers the hill side, names have been cut. There is no monument here, no memorial on which the traveller can have his name carved, no rocky wall on whose surface he can get it painted ; so visitors have the turf cut away for that purpose. The naked earth peers through in the form of great letters and names ; these form a network over the whole hill. Here is an immortality, which lasts till the fresh turf grows !

" Up on the hill stood a man, a poet. He emptied the mead horn with the broad silver rim, and murmured a name. He begged the winds not to betray him, but I heard the name. I knew it. A count's coronet sparkles above it, and therefore he did not speak it out. I smiled, for I knew that a poet's crown adorned his own name. The nobility of Eleanora d'Este is attached to the name of Tasso. And I also know where the Rose of Beauty blooms ! "

Thus spake the Moon, and a cloud came between us. May no cloud separate the poet from the rose !

## SEVENTH EVENING

" Along the margin of the shore stretches a forest of firs and beeches, and sweet, fresh, and fragrant is this wood ; hundreds of nightingales visit it every spring. Close beside it is the sea, the ever-changing sea, and between the two is placed the broad, high road. One carriage after another rolls over it ; but I did not follow them, for my eyes love best to rest upon one point. A Hun's Grave lies there, and the sloe and blackthorn grow luxuriantly among the stones. Here is true poetry in nature.

" And how do you think men appreciate this poetry ? I will tell you what I heard there last evening and during the night.

" First, two rich landed proprietors came driving by. ' Those are glorious trees ! ' said the first. ' Certainly ; there are ten loads of firewood in each,' observed the other : ' it will be a hard winter, and last year we got fourteen dollars a load '—and they were gone. ' The road here is wretched,' observed another man who drove past. ' That's the fault of those horrible trees,' replied his neighbour : ' there is no free current of air ; the wind can only come from the sea '—and they were gone. The stage coach went rattling past. All the passengers were asleep at this beautiful spot. The postillion blew his horn, but he only thought, ' I can play capitally. It sounds well here. I wonder if those in there like it ? '—and the stage coach vanished.

" Then two young fellows came galloping up on horseback. There's youth and spirit in the blood here ! thought I ; and, indeed, they looked with a smile at the moss-grown hill and thick forest. ' I should not dislike a walk here with the miller's Christine,' said one—and they flew past. The flowers scented the air ; every breath was hushed : it seemed as if the sea were a part of the sky that stretched above the deep valley.

"A carriage rolled by. Six people were sitting in it. Four of them were asleep; the fifth was thinking of his new summer coat, which would suit him admirably ; the sixth turned to the coachman and asked him if there were anything remarkable connected with yonder heap of stones. ' No,' replied the coachman, ' it's only a heap of stones ; but the trees are remarkable.' ' How so ? ' ' Why, I'll tell you how they are very remarkable. You see, in winter, when the snow lies very deep, and has hidden the whole road so that nothing is to be seen, those trees serve me for a landmark. I steer by them, so as not to drive into the sea ; and, you see, that is why the trees are remarkable.'

"Now came a painter. He spoke not a word, but his eyes sparkled. He began to whistle. At this the nightingales sang louder than ever. ' Hold your tongues ! ' he cried, testily ; and he made accurate notes of all the colours and transitions—blue, and lilac, and dark brown. ' That will make a beautiful picture,' he said. He took it in just as a mirror takes in a view ; and as he worked he whistled a march of Rossini. And last of all came a poor girl. She laid aside the burden she carried and sat down to rest upon the Hun's Grave. Her pale handsome face was bent in a listening attitude towards the forest. Her eyes brightened, she gazed earnestly at the sea and the sky, her hands were folded, and I think she prayed, ' Our Father.' She herself could not understand the feeling that swept through her, but I know that this minute, and the beautiful natural scene, will live within her memory for years, far more vividly and more truly than the painter could portray it with his colours on paper. My rays followed her till the morning dawn kissed her brow."

EIGHTH EVENING

Heavy clouds obscured the sky, and the Moon did not make his appearance at all. I stood in my little room more lonely than ever, and looked up at the sky where he ought to have shown himself. My thoughts flew far away, up to my great friend, who every evening told me such pretty tales, and showed me pictures. Yes, he has had an experience indeed. He glided over the waters of the Deluge, and smiled on Noah's ark as he lately glanced down upon me, and brought comfort and promise of a new world that was to spring forth from the old.

When the Children of Israel sat weeping by the waters of Babylon, he glanced mournfully upon the willows where hung the silent harps. When Romeo climbed the balcony, and the promise of true love fluttered like a cherub towards heaven, the round Moon hung, half-hidden among the dark cypresses, in the lucid air. He saw the captive giant at St. Helena, looking from the lonely rock across the wide ocean, while great thoughts swept through his soul. Ah ! what tales the Moon can tell. Human life is like a story to him. To-night I shall not see thee again, old friend. To-night I can draw no picture of the memories of thy visit. And, as I looked dreamily towards the clouds, the sky became bright. There was a glancing light, and a beam from the Moon fell upon me. It vanished again, and dark clouds flew past ; but still it was a greeting, a friendly good-night offered to me by the Moon.

### NINTH EVENING

The air was clear again. Several evenings had passed, and the Moon was in the first quarter. Again he gave me an outline for a sketch. Listen to what he told me.

"I have followed the polar bird and the swimming whale to the eastern coast of Greenland. Gaunt ice-covered rocks and dark clouds hung over a valley, where dwarf willows and barberry bushes stood clothed in green. The blooming lychnis exhaled sweet odours. My light was faint, my face pale as the water-lily that, torn from its stem, has been drifting for weeks with the tide. The crown-shaped Northern Light burned fiercely in the sky. Its ring was broad, and from its circumference, the rays shot like whirling shafts of fire across the whole sky, flashing in changing radiance from green to red. The inhabitants of that icy region were assembling for dance and festivity ; but accustomed to this glorious spectacle, they scarcely deigned to glance at it. 'Let us leave the souls of the dead to their ball-play with the heads of the walruses,' they thought in their superstition, and they turned their whole attention to the song and dance. In the midst of the circle, and divested of his furry cloak, stood a Greenlander, with a small pipe, and he played and sang a song about catching the seal, and the chorus around chimed in with ' *Eia, Eia, Ah.*' And in their white furs they danced about in the circle, till you might fancy it was a polar bear's ball.

"And now a Court of Judgment was opened. Those Greenlanders who had quarrelled stepped forward, and the offended person chanted forth the faults of his adversary in an extempore song, turning them sharply into ridicule, to the sound of the pipe and the measure of the dance. The defendant replied with satire as keen, while the audience laughed and gave their verdict.

"The rocks heaved, the glaciers melted, and great masses of ice and snow came crushing down, shivering to fragments as they fell : it was a glorious Greenland summer night. A hundred paces away, under the open tent of hides, lay a sick man. Life still flowed through his warm blood, but still he was to die ; he himself felt it, and all who stood round him knew it also ; therefore, his wife was already sewing round him the shroud of furs, that she might not afterwards be obliged to touch the dead body.

"And she asked, ' Wilt thou be buried on the rock, in the firm snow ? I will deck the spot with thy *kayak*, and thy arrows, and the *angekokk* shall dance over it. Or wouldst thou rather be buried in the sea ? ' ' In the sea,' he whispered. ' Yes, it is a pleasant summer tent, the sea,' observed the wife. ' Thousands of seals sport there, the walrus shall lie at thy feet, and the hunt will be safe and merry ? ' And the yelling children tore the outspread hide from the window-hole, that the dead man might be carried to the ocean, the billowy ocean, that had given him food in life, and that now, in death, was to afford him a place of rest. For his monument he had the floating, ever-changing icebergs, whereupon the seal sleeps, while the storm bird flies round their gleaming summits."

### TENTH EVENING

"I knew an old maid," said the Moon. "Every winter she wore a wrapper of yellow satin, and it always remained new, and was the only fashion she followed. In summer she always wore the same straw hat, and I verily believe the very same gray-blue dress.

"She never went out, except across the street to an old female friend; and in later years she did not even take this walk, for the old friend was dead. In her solitude my old maid was always busy at the window, which was adorned in summer with pretty flowers, and in winter with cress, grown upon

*My old maid was always busy at the window.*

felt. During the last months I saw her no more at the window, but she was still alive. I knew that, for I had not yet seen her begin the 'long journey,' of which she often spoke with her friend. 'Yes, yes,' she was in the habit of saying, 'when I come to die, I shall take a longer journey than I have made my whole life long. Our family vault is six miles from here. I shall be carried there, and shall sleep there among my family and relatives.'

Last night a van stopped at the house. A coffin was carried out, and I knew that she was dead. They placed straw round the coffin and the van drove away. There slept the quiet old lady, who had not gone out of her house once for the last year. The van rolled out through the town gate as briskly as if it were going for a pleasant excursion. On the high road the pace was quicker yet. The coachman looked nervously around every now and then—I fancy he half-expected to see her sitting on the coffin, in her yellow satin wrapper. And because he was startled, he foolishly lashed his horses, while he held the reins so tightly that the poor beasts were in a foam; they were young and fiery. A little hare jumped across the road and startled them, and they fairly ran away. The old sober maiden, who had for years and years moved quietly round and round in a dull circle, was now, in death, rattled over stock and stone on the public highway. The coffin in its covering of straw tumbled out of the van, and was left on the high road, while horses, coachman, and carriage flew past in wild career. The lark rose up carolling from the field, twittering her morning lay over the coffin, and presently perched upon it, picking with her beak at the straw covering, as though she would tear it up. The lark rose up again, singing gaily, and I withdrew behind the red morning clouds."

### ELEVENTH EVENING

" I will give you a picture of Pompeii," said the Moon. " I was in the suburb in the Street of Tombs, as they call it, where the fair monuments stand, in the spot where, ages ago the merry youths, their temples bound with rosy wreaths, danced with the fair sisters of Lais. Now the stillness of death reigned around. German mercenaries, in the Neapolitan service, kept guard, and played cards and diced ; and a troop of strangers from beyond the mountains came into the town, accompanied by a sentry. They wanted to see the city that had risen from the grave illumined by my beams ; and I showed them the wheel-ruts in the streets paved with broad lava slabs. I showed them the names on the doors, and the signs that hung there yet : they saw in the little courtyard the basins of the fountains, ornamented with shells ; but no jet of water gushed upwards, no songs sounded forth from the richly-painted chambers, where the bronze dog kept the door.

" It was the City of the Dead ; only Vesuvius thundered forth his ever-lasting hymn, each separate verse of which is called by men an eruption. We went to the temple of Venus, built of snow-white marble, with its high altar in front of the broad steps, and the weeping willows sprouting freshly forth among the pillars. The air was transparent and blue, and black Vesuvius formed the background, with fire ever shooting forth from it, like the stem of a pine tree. Above it stretched the smoky cloud in the silence of the night, like the crown of the pine, but in a blood-red illumination.

Among the company was a great lady singer. I have witnessed the homage paid to her in the greatest cities of Europe. When they came to the tragic theatre, they all sat down on the amphitheatre steps, and thus a small part of the house was occupied by an audience, as it had been many centuries ago. The stage still stood unchanged, and its walled side-scenes, and the two arches in the background, through which the beholders saw the same scene that had been exhibited in the old times—a scene painted by Nature herself, namely, the mountains between Sorrento and Amalfi. The singer gaily mounted the ancient stage, and sang. The place inspired her, and she reminded me of a wild Arab horse, that rushes headlong on with snorting nostrils and flying mane—her song was so light and yet so firm. Anon I thought of the mourning mother beneath the cross at Golgotha, so deep was the expression of pain. And, just as it had done thousands of years ago, the sound of applause and delight now filled the theatre. ' Happy, gifted creature ! ' all the hearers exclaimed. Five minutes more, and the stage was empty, the company had vanished, and not a sound more was heard —all were gone. But the ruins stood unchanged, as they will stand when centuries shall have gone by, and when none shall know of the momentary applause and of the triumph of the fair songstress.

## TWELFTH EVENING

" I looked through the windows of an editor's house," said the Moon. " It was somewhere in Germany. I saw handsome furniture, many books, and a chaos of newspapers. Several young men were present : the editor himself stood at his desk, and two little books, both by young authors, were to be noticed. ' This one has been sent to me,' said he. ' I have not read it yet ; what think *you* of the contents ? ' ' Oh,' said the person addressed—he was a poet himself—' it is good enough ; a little broad, certainly ; but, you see, the author is still young. The verses might be better, to be sure ; the thoughts are sound, though there is certainly a good deal of commonplace among them. But what will you have ? You can't be always getting something new. That he'll turn out anything great I don't believe, but you may safely praise him. He is well read, a remarkable Oriental scholar, and has a good judgment. It was he who wrote that nice review of my *Reflections on Domestic Life*. We must be lenient towards the young man.'

" ' But he is a complete hack ! ' objected another of the gentlemen. ' Nothing is worse in poetry than mediocrity, and he certainly does not go beyond that.'

" ' Poor fellow ! " observed a third, ' and his aunt is so happy about him. It was she, Mr. Editor, who got together so many subscribers for your last translation.'

" ' Ah, the good woman ! Well, I have noticed the book briefly. Undoubted talent—a welcome offering—a flower in the garden of poetry— prettily brought out, and so on. But this other book—I suppose the author expects me to purchase it ? I hear it is praised. He has genius, certainly : don't you think so ? '

" ' Yes, all the world declares as much,' replied the poet, ' but it has turned out rather wildly. The punctuation of the book, in particular, is very eccentric.'

" ' It will be good for him if we pull him to pieces, and anger him a little, otherwise he will get too good an opinion of himself.'

" ' But that would be unfair,' objected the fourth. ' Let us not carp at his faults, but rejoice over the real and abundant good that we find here : he surpasses all the rest.'

" ' Not so. If he be a true genius, he can bear the sharp voice of censure. There are people enough to praise him. Don't let us quite turn his head.'

" ' Decided talent,' wrote the editor, ' with the usual carelessness. That he can write incorrect verses may be seen in page 25, where there are two false quantities. We recommend him to study the ancients, etc.'

" I went away," continued the Moon, " and looked through the window in the aunt's house. There sat the bepraised poet, the *tame* one ; all the guests paid homage to him, and he was happy.

"I sought the other poet out, the *wild* one; him also I found in a great assembly at his patron's, where the tame poet's book was being discussed.

"'I shall read yours also,' said Mæcenas; 'but to speak honestly—you know I never hide my opinions from you—I don't expect much from it, for you are much too wild, too fantastic. But it must assuredly be allowed that, as a man, you are highly respectable.'

"A young girl sat in a corner; and she read in a book these words:

"'In the dust lies genius and glory,
    But ev'ry day talent will *pay*.
It's only the old, old story.
    But the piece is repeated each day.'"

### THIRTEENTH EVENING

The Moon said, "Beside the woodland path there are two small farmhouses. The doors are low, and some of the windows are placed quite high, and others close to the ground; and white horn and barberry bushes grow around them. The roof of each house is overgrown with moss and with yellow flowers and houseleek. Cabbage and potatoes are the only plants cultivated in the gardens, but out of the hedge there grows a willow tree, and under this willow tree sat a little girl, and she sat with her eyes fixed upon the old oak tree between the two huts.

"It was an old withered stem. It had been sawn off at the top, and a stork had built his nest upon it; and he stood in this nest clapping with his

*"I'm watching the stork," the little girl said.*

beak. A little boy came and stood by the girl's side : they were brother and sister.

" ' What are you looking at ? ' he asked.

" ' I'm watching the stork,' she replied : ' our neighbour told me that he would bring us a little brother or sister to-day ; let us watch to see it come ! ' "

" ' The stork brings no such things,' the boy declared, ' you may be sure of that. Our neighbour told me the same thing, but she laughed when she said it, and so I asked her if she could say " On my honour," and she could not ; and I know by that that the story about the storks is not true, and that they only tell it to us children for fun.'

" ' But where do the babies come from, then ? ' asked the girl.

" ' Why an angel from heaven brings them under his cloak, but no man can see him ; and that's why we never know when he brings them.'

" At that moment there was a rustling in the branches of the willow tree, and the children folded their hands and looked at one another : it was certainly the angel coming with the baby. They took each other's hand, and at that moment the door of one of the houses opened, and the neighbour appeared.

" ' Come in, you two,' she said. ' See what the stork has brought. It is a little brother.'

" And the children nodded gravely at one another, for they had felt quite sure already that the baby was come."

### FOURTEENTH EVENING

" I was gliding over the Lüneberg Heath," the Moon said. " A lonely hut stood by the wayside, a few scanty bushes grew near it, and a nightingale who had lost his way sang sweetly. He died in the coldness of the night : it was his farewell song that I heard.

" The morning dawn came glimmering red. I saw a caravan of emigrant peasant families who were bound to Hamburgh, there to take ship for America, where fancied prosperity would bloom for them. The mothers carried their little children at their backs, the elder ones tottered by their sides, and a poor starved horse tugged at a cart that bore their scanty effects. The cold wind whistled, and therefore the little girl nestled closer to the mother, who, looking up at my decreasing disc, thought of the bitter want at home, and spoke of the heavy taxes they had not been able to raise. The whole caravan thought of the same thing ; therefore the rising dawn seemed to them a message from the sun, of fortune that was to gleam brightly upon them.

" They heard the dying nightingale sing : it was no false prophet, but a harbinger of fortune. The wind whistled, so they did not understand that the nightingale sang, ' Far away over the sea ! Thou hast paid the long passage with all that was thine, and poor and helpless shalt thou enter Canaan. Thou must sell thy self, thy wife, and thy children. But your griefs shall not last long. Behind the broad fragrant leaves lurks the Goddess of Death, and her welcome kiss shall breathe fever into thy blood. Fare, away, fare away, over the heaving billows.' And the caravan listened well pleased to the song of the nightingale, which seemed to promise good fortune. The day broke through the light clouds ; country people went across the heath to church : the black-gowned women with their white head-dresses looked like ghosts that had stepped forth from the church pictures. All around lay a wide dead plain, covered with faded brown heath, and black charred spaces between the white sand hills. The women carried hymn books, and walked into the church. Oh, pray, pray for those who are wandering to find graves beyond the foaming billows."

## FIFTEENTH EVENING

" I know a Pulcinella," the Moon told me. " The public applaud vociferously directly they see him. Every one of his movements is comic, and is sure to throw the house into convulsions of laughter ; and yet there there is no art in it all—it is complete nature. When he was yet a little boy, playing with other boys, he was already Punch. Nature had intended him for it, and had provided him with a hump on his back, and another on his breast ; but his inward man, his mind, on the contrary, was richly furnished. No one could surpass him in depth of feeling or in readiness of intellect. The theatre was his ideal world. If he had possessed a slender well-shaped figure, he might have been the first tragedian on any stage : the heroic, the great, filled his soul ; and yet he had to become a Pulcinella. His very sorrow and melancholy did but increase the comic dryness of his sharply-cut features, and increased the laughter of the audience, who showered plaudits on their favourite. The lovely Columbine was indeed kind and cordial to him, but she preferred to marry the Harlequin. It would have been too ridiculous if beauty and ugliness had in reality paired together.

" When Pulcinella was in very bad spirits, she was the only one who could force a hearty burst of laughter, or even a smile from him : first she would be melancholy with him, then quieter, and at last quite cheerful and happy. ' I know very well what is the matter with you,' she said; ' yes, you're in love ! ' And he could not help laughing. ' I and Love ! ' he cried, ' that would have an absurd look. How the public would shout ! ' ' Certainly, you are in love,' she continued ; and added with a comic pathos, ' and I am the person you are in love with.' You see, such a thing may be said when it is quite out of the question—and, indeed, Pulcinella burst out laughing, and gave a leap into the air, and his melancholy was forgotten.

" And yet she had only spoken the truth. He *did* love her, love her adoringly, as he loved what was great and lofty in art. At her wedding he was the merriest among the guests, but in the stillness of night he wept : if the public had seen his distorted face then, they would have applauded rapturously.

" And a few days ago Columbine died. On the day of the funeral, Harlequin was not required to show himself on the boards, for he was a disconsolate widower. The director had to give a very merry piece, that the public might not too painfully miss the pretty Columbine and the agile Harlequin. Therefore Pulcinella had to be more boisterous and extravagant than ever ; and he danced and capered, with despair in his heart ; and the audience yelled, and shouted, ' *Bravo! bravissimo!* ' Pulcinella was actually called before the curtain. He was pronounced inimitable.

"But last night the hideous little fellow went out of the town, quite alone, to the deserted churchyard. The wreath of flowers on Columbine's grave was already faded, and he sat down there. It was a study for a painter. And he sat with his chin on his hands, his eyes turned up towards me, he looked like a grotesque monument—a Punch on a grave—very peculiar and whimsical. If the people could have seen their favourite, they would have cried, as usual, ' *Bravo, Pulcinella! bravo, bravissimo!* ' "

## SIXTEENTH EVENING

Hear what the Moon told me. " I have seen the cadet who had just been made an officer put on his handsome uniform for the first time ; I have seen the young bride in her wedding dress, and the Princess girl-wife happy in her gorgeous robes ; but never have I seen a felicity equal to that of a little girl of four years old, whom I watched this evening. She had received a new blue dress and a new pink hat ; the splendid attire had just been put on, and all were calling for a candle, for my rays, shining in through the windows of the room, were not bright enough for the occasion, and further illumination was required. There stood the little maid, stiff and upright as a doll, her arms stretched painfully straight out away from her dress, and her fingers apart ; and, oh, what happiness beamed from her eyes and from her whole countenance ! ' To-morrow you shall go out in your new clothes,' said her mother ; and the little one looked up at her hat and down at her frock, and smiled brightly. ' Mother,' she cried ' what will the little dogs think when they see me in these splendid new things.' "

## SEVENTEENTH EVENING

" I have spoken to you of Pompeii," said the Moon : " that corpse of a city, exposed in the view of living towns : I know another sight still more strange, and this is not the corpse, but the spectre of a city. Whenever the jetty fountains splash into the marble basins, they seem to me to be telling the story of the floating city. Yes, the spouting water may tell of her, the waves of the sea may sing of her fame ! On the surface of the ocean a mist often rests, and this is her widow's veil. The Bridegroom of the Sea is dead, his palace and his city are his mausoleum ! Do thou know this city ? She has never heard the rolling of wheels or the hoof-tread of horses in her streets, through which the fish swim, while the black gondola glides spectrally over the green water.

"I will show you the place," continued the Moon, "the largest square in it, and you will fancy yourself transported into the city of a fairy tale. The grass grows rank among the broad flagstones, and in the morning twilight thousands of tame pigeons flutter around the solitary lofty tower. On three sides you find yourself surrounded by cloistered walks. In these the silent Turk sits smoking his long pipe ; the handsome Greek leans against the pillar, and gazes at the upraised trophies and lofty masts, memorials of power that is gone. The flags hang down like mourning scarves. A girl rests there : she has put down her heavy pails filled with water, the yoke with which she has carried them rests on one of her shoulders, and she leans against the mast of victory. This is not a fair palace you see before you yonder, but a church : the gilded domes and shining orbs flash back my beams; the glorious bronze horses up yonder have made journeys, like the bronze horses in the fairy tale : they have come hither, and gone hence, and have returned again.

"Do you notice the variegated splendour of the walls and windows ? It looks as if Genius had followed the caprices of a child, in the adornment of these singular temples. Do you see the winged lion on the pillar ? The gold glitters still, but his wings are tied—the lion is dead, for the King of the Sea is dead ; the great halls stand desolate, and where gorgeous painting hung of yore, the naked wall now peeps through. The *lazzaroni* sleeps under the arcade, whose pavement in old times was to be trodden only by the feet of the high nobility. From the deep wells, and perhaps from the prisons by the Bridge of Sighs, rise the accents of woe, as at the time when the tambourine was heard in the gay gondalas, and the golden ring was cast from the Bucentaur to Adria, the Queen of the Seas. Adria ! shroud thyself in mist ; let the veil of thy widowhood shroud thy form, and clothe in the weeds of woe the mausoleum of thy bridegroom—the marble, spectral Venice ! "

### EIGHTEENTH EVENING

"I looked down upon a great theatre," said the Moon. "The house was crowded, for a new actor was to make his first appearance that night. My rays glided over a little window in the wall, and I saw a painted face with the forehead pressed against the panes. It was the hero of the evening. The knightly beard curled crisply about the chin ; but there were tears in the man's eyes, for he had been hissed off, and indeed with reason. The poor Incapable ! But Incapables cannot be admitted into the empire of Art. He had deep feelings, and loved his art enthusiastically, but the art loved not him. The prompter's bell sounded ; ' *the hero enters with a determined air,*' so ran the stage direction in his part, and he had to appear before an audience who turned him into ridicule.

"When the piece was over, I saw a form wrapped in a mantle creeping down the steps : it was the vanquished knight of the evening. The scene-shifters whispered to one another, and I followed the poor fellow home to his room. To hang oneself is to die a mean death, and poison is not always at hand, I know ; but he thought of both. I saw how he looked at his pale face in the glass, with eyes half-closed, to see if he should look well as a corpse. A man may be very unhappy, and not exceedingly affected. He thought of death, of suicide ; I believe he pitied himself, for he wept bitterly ; and when a man has had his cry out he doesn't kill himself.

"Since that time a year had rolled by. Again a play was to be acted, but in a little theatre, and by a poor strolling company. Again I saw the well-remembered face, with the painted cheeks and the crisp beard. He looked up at me and smiled ; and yet he had been hissed off only a minute before—

*The little maiden often sits there on her stool when the evening bells ring.*

hissed off from a wretched theatre by a miserable audience. And to-night a shabby hearse rolled out of the town gate. It was a suicide—our painted, despised hero. The driver of the hearse was the only person present, for no one followed except my beams. In a corner of the churchyard the corpse of the suicide was shovelled into the earth, and nettles will soon be rankly growing over his grave, and the sexton will throw thorns and weeds from the other graves upon it."

### NINETEENTH EVENING

" I come from Rome," said the Moon. " In the midst of the city, upon one of the seven hills, lie the ruins of the imperial palace. The wild fig tree grows in the clefts of the wall, and covers the nakedness thereof with its broad gray-green leaves ; trampling among heaps of rubbish, the ass treads upon green laurels, and rejoices over the rank thistles. From this spot, whence the eagles of Rome once flew abroad, whence they ' came, saw, and conquered,' one door leads into a little mean house, built of clay between two pillars ; the wild vine hangs like a mourning garland over the crooked window. An old woman and her little granddaughter live there : they rule now in the palace of the Cæsars, and show to strangers the remains of its past glories. Of the splendid throne-hall only a naked wall yet stands, and a black cypress throws its dark shadow on the spot where the throne once stood. The dust lies several feet deep on the broken pavement ; and the little maiden, now the daughter of the imperial palace, often sits there on her stool when the evening bells ring. The keyhole of the door close by she calls her turret-window ; through this she can see half Rome, as far as the mighty cupola of St. Peter's.

" On this evening, as usual, stillness reigned around ; and in the full beam of my light came the little granddaughter. On her head she carried an earthen pitcher of antique shape filled with water. Her feet were bare, her short frock and her white sleeves were torn. I kissed her pretty round shoulders, her dark eyes, and black shining hair. She mounted the stairs ; they were steep, having been made up of rough blocks of broken marble and the capital of a fallen pillar. The coloured lizards slipped away, startled, from before her feet, but she was not frightened at them. Already she lifted her hand to pull the door-bell—a hare's foot fastened to a string formed the bell-handle of the imperial palace. She paused for a moment—of what might she be thinking ? Perhaps of the beautiful Christ-child, dressed in gold and silver, which was down below in the chapel, where the silver candlesticks gleamed so bright, and where her little friends sang the hymns in which she also could join ? I know not. Presently she moved again—she stumbled ; the earthern vessel fell from her head, and broke on the marble steps. She burst into tears. The beautiful daughter of the imperial palace wept over the worthless broken pitcher ; with her bare feet she stood there, weeping, and dared not pull the string, the bell-rope of the imperial palace."

### TWENTIETH EVENING

It was more than a fortnight since the Moon had shone. Now he stood once more, round and bright, above the clouds, moving slowly onward Hear what the Moon told me.

" From a town in Fezzan I followed a caravan. On the margin of the sandy desert, in a salt plain, that shone like a frozen lake, and was only covered in spots with light drifting sand, a halt was made. The eldest of the company —the water-gourd hung at his girdle, and on his head was a little bag of unleavened bread—drew a square in the sand with his staff, and wrote in it a few words out of the Koran, and then the whole caravan passed over the consecrated spot. A young merchant, a child of the East, as I could tell by his eye and his figure, rode pensively forward on his white snorting steed. Was he thinking, perchance, of his fair young wife ? It was only two days ago that the camel, adorned with furs and with costly shawls, had carried her, the beauteous bride, round the walls of the city, while drums and cymbals had sounded, the women sang, and festive shots, of which the bridegroom fired the greatest number, resounded round the camel ; and now he was journeying with the caravan across the desert.

" For many nights I followed the train. I saw them rest by the well-side among the stunted palms ; they thrust the knife into the breast of the camel that had fallen, and roasted its flesh by the fire. My beams cooled the glowing sands, and showed them the black rocks, dead islands in the immense ocean of sand. No hostile tribes met them in their pathless route, no storms arose, no columns of sand whirled destruction over the journeying caravan. At home the beautiful wife prayed for her husband and her father. ' Are they dead ? ' she asked of my golden crescent ; ' Are they dead ? ' she cried to my full disc. Now the desert lies behind them. This evening they sit beneath the lofty palm trees, where the crane flutters round them with its long wings, and the pelican watches them from the branches of the mimosa. The luxuriant herbage is trampled down, crushed by the feet of elephants. A troop of negroes are returning from a market in the interior of the land ; the women, with copper buttons in their black train, and decked out in clothes dyed with indigo, drive the heavily-laden oxen, on whose backs slumber the naked black children. A negro leads a young lion, which he has bought, by a string. They approach the caravan ; the young merchant sits pensive and motionless, thinking of his beautiful wife, dreaming, in the land of the blacks, of his white fragrant lily beyond the desert. He raises his head, and——"

But at this moment a cloud passed before the Moon, and then another. I heard nothing more from him this evening.

### TWENTY-FIRST EVENING

" I looked down on Tyrol," said the Moon, " and my beams caused the dark pines to throw long shadows upon the rocks. I looked at the pictures of St. Christopher carrying the Infant Jesus that are painted there upon the walls of the houses, colossal figures reaching from the ground to the roof. St. Florian was represented pouring water in the burning house, and the Lord hung bleeding on the great cross by the wayside. To the present generations these are old pictures, but I saw when they were put up, and marked how one followed the other. On the brow of the mountain yonder is perched, like a swallow's nest, a lonely convent of nuns. Two of the sisters stood up in the tower tolling the bell ; they were both young, and therefore their glances flew over the mountain out into the world. A travelling coach passed by below, the postillion wound his horn, and the poor nuns looked after the carriage for a moment with a mournful glance, and a tear gleamed in the eyes of the younger one. And the horn sounded faintly and more faint, and the convent bell drowned its expiring echoes."

### TWENTY-SECOND EVENING

" I saw a little girl weeping," said the Moon : " she was weeping over the depravity of the world. She had received a most beautiful doll as a present. Oh, that was a glorious doll, so fair and delicate ! She did not seem created for the sorrows of this world. But the brothers of the little girl, those great naughty boys, had set the doll high up in the branches of a tree, and had run away.

" The little girl could not reach up to the doll, and could not help her down, and that is why she was crying. The doll must certainly have been crying too, for she stretched out her arms among the green branches, and looked quite mournful. Yes, these are the troubles of life of which the little girl had often heard tell. Alas, poor doll ! it began to grow dark already ; and suppose night were to come on completely ! Was she to be left sitting there alone on the bough all night long ? No, the little maid could not make up her mind to that. ' I'll stay with you,' she said, although she felt anything but happy in her mind. She could almost fancy she distinctly saw little gnomes, with their high-crowned hats, sitting in the bushes ; and farther back in the long walk, tall spectres appeared to be dancing. They came nearer and nearer, and stretched out their hands towards the tree on which the doll sat ; they laughed scornfully, and pointed at her with their fingers.

"Oh, how frightened the little maid was ! 'But if one has not done anything wrong,' she thought, 'nothing evil can harm one. I wonder if I have done anything wrong ?' And she considered. 'Oh, yes ! I laughed at the poor duck with the red rag on her leg ; she limped along so funnily, I could not help laughing ; but it's a sin to laugh at animals.' And she looked up at the doll. 'Did you laugh at the duck, too ?' she asked ; and it seemed as if the doll shook her head."

## TWENTY-THIRD EVENING

Hear what the Moon told me. "Some years ago, here in Copenhagen, I looked through the window of a mean little room. The father and mother slept, but the little son was not asleep. I saw the flowered cotton curtains of the bed move, and the child peep forth. At first, I thought he was looking at the great clock, which was gaily painted in red and green. At the top sat a cuckoo, below hung the heavy leaden weights, and the pendulum with the polished disc of metal went to and fro, and said 'tick, tick.' But no, he was not looking at the clock, but at his mother's spinning-wheel, that stood just underneath it. That was the boy's favourite piece of furniture, but he dared not touch it, for if he meddled with it he got a rap on the knuckles.

"For hours together, when his mother was spinning, he would sit quietly by her side, watching the murmuring spindle and the revolving wheel, and as he sat he thought of many things. Oh, if he might only turn the wheel himself ! Father and mother were asleep : he looked at them, and looked at the spinning-wheel, and presently a little naked foot peered out of the bed, and then a second foot, and then two little white legs.

"There he stood. He looked round once more to see if father and mother were still asleep—yes, they slept ; and now he crept *softly, softly,* in his short little nightgown, to the spinning-wheel, and began to spin. The thread flew from the wheel, and the wheel whirled faster and faster. I kissed his fair hair and his blue eyes, it was such a pretty picture.

"At that moment the mother awoke. The curtain shook ; she looked forth, and fancied she saw a gnome or some other kind of little spectre. 'In Heaven's name !' she cried, and aroused her husband in a frightened way.

"He opened his eyes, rubbed them with his hands, and looked at the brisk little lad. 'Why, that is Bertel,' said he. And my eye quitted the poor room, for I have so much to see. At the same moment I looked at the halls of the Vatican, where the marble gods are enthroned. I shone upon the group of the Laocoon : the stone seemed to sigh. I pressed a silent kiss on the lips of the Muses, and they seemed to stir and move. But my rays lingered longest about the Nile group with the colossal god. Leaning against the Sphinx, he lies there thoughtful and meditative, as if he were thinking on the rolling centuries; and little love-gods sport with him and with the crocodiles. In the horn of plenty sits with folded arms a little tiny love-god contemplating the great solemn river-god, a true picture of the boy at the spinning-wheel— the features were exactly the same. Charming and life-like stood the little marble form, and yet the wheel of the year has turned more than a thousand times since the time when it sprang from the stone. Just as often as the boy in the little room turned the spinning-wheel had the great wheel murmured, before the age could again call forth marble gods equal to those he afterwards formed.

*Bertel sat in his nightshirt by the spinning-wheel.*

"Years have passed since all this happened," the Moon went on to say. "Yesterday I looked upon a bay on the eastern coast of Denmark. Glorious woods are there, and high trees, an old knightly castle with red walls, swans floating in the ponds, and in the background appears, among orchards, a little town with a church.

"Many boats, the crew all furnished with torches, glided over the silent expanse—but these fires had not been kindled for catching fish, for everything had a festive look. Music sounded, a song was sung, and in one of the boats a man stood erect, to whom homage was paid by the rest, a tall, sturdy man, wrapped in a cloak. He had blue eyes and long white hair. I knew him, and thought of the Vatican, and of the group of the Nile, and the old marble gods. I thought of the simple little room where little Bertel sat in his nightshirt by the spinning-wheel. The wheel of time has turned, and new gods have come forth from the stone. From the boats there arose a shout: 'Hurrah! hurrah for Bertel Thorwaldsen!'"

## TWENTY-FOURTH EVENING

" I will now give you a picture from Frankfort," said the Moon. " I especially noticed one building there. It was not the house in which Goethe was born, nor the old council-house, through whose grated windows peered the horns of the oxen that were roasted and given to the people when the Emperors were crowned. No, it was a private house, plain in appearance, and painted green. It stood near the old Jews' Street. It was Rothschild's house.

" I looked through the open door. The staircase was brilliantly lighted : servants carrying wax candles in massive silver candlesticks stood there, and bowed low before an aged woman, who was being brought downstairs in a litter. The proprietor of the house stood bareheaded, and respectfully imprinted a kiss on the hand of the old woman. She was his mother. She nodded in a friendly manner to him and to the servants, and they carried her into the dark narrow street, into a little house, that was her dwelling. Here her children had been born, from hence the fortune of the family had arisen. If she deserted the despised street and the little house, fortune would also desert her children. That was her firm belief."

The Moon told me no more ; his visit this evening was far too short. But I thought of the old woman in the narrow despised street. It would have cost her but a word, and a brilliant house would have arisen for her on the banks of the Thames—a word, and a villa would have been prepared in the Bay of Naples.

" If I deserted the lowly house, where the fortunes of my sons first began to bloom, fortune would desert them ! " It was a superstition, but a superstition of such a class, that he who knows the story and has seen the picture, need have only two words placed under this picture to make him understand it ; and these two words are : " A mother."

## TWENTY-FIFTH EVENING

" It was yesterday, in the morning twilight "—these are the words the Moon told me—" in the great city no chimney was yet smoking—and it was just at the chimneys that I was looking. Suddenly a little head emerged from one of them, and then half a body, the arms resting on the rim of the chimney-pot. ' Ya-hip ! ' cried a voice. It was the little chimney-sweeper who had for the first time in his life crept through a chimney and stuck out his head at the top. ' Ya-hip ! ya-hip ! ' Yes, certainly that was a very different thing from creeping about in the dark narrow chimneys ! the air blows so fresh, and he could look over the whole city towards the green wood. The sun was just rising. It shone round and great, just in his face, that beamed with triumph, though it was very prettily blacked with soot.

" ' The whole town can see me now,' he exclaimed, ' and the moon can see me now, and the sun too. Ya-hip ! ya-hip ! ' And he flourished his broom in triumph."

## TWENTY-SIXTH EVENING

" Last night I looked down upon a town in China," said the Moon. " My beams irradiated the naked walls that form the streets there. Now and then, certainly, a door is seen, but it is locked, for what does the Chinaman care about the outer world ? Close wooden shutters covered the windows behind the walls of the houses ; but through the windows of the temple there was a faint light glimmering. I looked in, and saw the quaint decorations within.

"From the floor to the ceiling pictures are painted in the most glaring colours and richly gilt—pictures representing the deeds of the gods here on earth. In each nine statues are placed but they are almost entirely hidden by the coloured drapery and the banners that hang down. Before each idol (and they are all made of tin) stood a little altar of holy water, with flowers and burning wax lights on it.

"Above all the rest stood Fo, the chief deity, clad in a garment of yellow silk, for yellow is here the sacred colour. At the foot of the altar sat a living being, a young priest. He appeared to be praying, but in the midst of his prayer he seemed to fall into deep thought, and this must have been wrong, for his cheeks glowed and he held down his head. Poor Souihong ! Was he, perhaps, dreaming of working in the little flower garden behind the high street wall ? And did that occupation seem more agreeable to him than watching the wax lights in the temple ? Or did he wish to sit at the rich feast, wiping his mouth with silver paper between each course ? Or was his sin so great that, if he dared to utter it, the Celestial Empire would punish it with death ? Had his thoughts ventured to fly with the ships of the barbarians, to their homes in far-distant England ? No, his thoughts did not fly so far, and yet they were sinful, sinful as thoughts born of young hearts, sinful here in the temple, in the presence of Fo and the other holy gods.

"I know whither his thoughts had strayed. At the farther end of the city, on the flat roof paved with porcelain, on which stood the handsome vases covered with painted flowers, sat the beauteous Pu, of the little roguish eyes, of the full lips, and of the tiny feet. The tight shoe pained her, but her heart pained her still more. She lifted her graceful round arm, and her satin dress rustled. Before her stood a glass bowl containing four goldfish. She stirred the bowl carefully with a slender lacquered stick, very slowly, for she, too, was lost in thought.

"Was she thinking, perchance, how the fishes were richly clothed in gold, how they lived calmly and peacefully in their crystal world, how they were regularly fed, and yet how much happier they might be if they were free ? Yes, that she could well understand, the beautiful Pu. Her thoughts wandered away from her home, wandered to the temple, but not for the sake of holy things. Poor Pu ! Poor Soui-hong !

" Their earthly thoughts met, but my cold beam lay between the two like the sword of the cherub."

## TWENTY-SEVENTH EVENING

" The air was calm," said the Moon ; " the water was as transparent as the pure ether through which I was gliding, and deep below the surface I could see the strange plains that stretched up their long arms towards me like the gigantic trees of the forest. The fishes swam to and fro above their tops. High in the air a flight of wild swans were winging their way, one of which sank lower and lower, with wearied pinions, his eyes following the airy caravan, that melted farther and farther into the distance. With outspread wings he sank slowly, as a soap-bubble sinks in the still air, till he touched the water. At length his head lay back between his wings, and silently he lay there, like a white lotus flower upon the quiet lake. And a gentle wind arose, and crisped the quiet surface which gleamed like the clouds that poured along in great broad waves ; and the swan raised his head, and the glowing water splashed like blue fire over his breast and back. The morning dawn illuminated the red clouds, the swan rose strengthened, and flew towards the rising sun, towards the bluish coast whither the caravan had gone ; but he flew all alone, with a longing in his breast. Lonely he flew over the blue swelling billows."

## TWENTY-EIGHTH EVENING

" I will give you another picture of Sweden," said the Moon. " Among dark pine woods, near the melancholy banks of the Stoxen, lies the old convent church of Wreta. My rays glided through the grating into the roomy vaults, where Kings sleep tranquilly in great stone coffins. On the wall, above the grave of each, is placed the emblem of earthly grandeur, a kingly crown; but it is made only of wood, painted and gilt, and is hung on a wooden peg driven into the wall. The worms have gnawn the gilded wood, the spider has spun her web from the crown down to the sand, like a mourning banner, frail and transient as the grief of mortals. How quietly they sleep ! I can remember them quite plainly. I still see the bold smile on their lips, that so strongly and plainly expressed joy or grief. When the steamboat winds along like a magic snail over the lakes, a stranger often comes to the church, and visits the burial vault ; he asks the names of the Kings, and they have a dead and forgotten sound. He glances with a smile at the worm-eaten crowns, and if he happens to be a pious, thoughtful man, something of melancholy mingles with the smile. Slumber on, ye dead ones ! The Moon thinks of you, the Moon at night sends down her rays into your silent kingdom, over which hangs the crown of pine wood."

## TWENTY-NINTH EVENING

" Close by the high road," said the Moon, " is an inn, and opposite to it is a great wagon-shed, whose straw roof was just being re-thatched. I looked down between the bare rafters and through the open loft into the comfortless space below. The turkey-cock slept on the beam, and the saddle rested in the empty crib. In the middle of the shed stood a travelling carriage ; the proprietor was inside, fast asleep, while the horses were being watered. The coachman stretched himself, though I am very sure that he had been most comfortably asleep half the last stage. The door of the servants' room stood open, and the bed looked as if it had been turned over and over ; the candle stood on the floor, and had burned deep down into the socket. The wind blew cold through the shed : it was nearer to the dawn than to midnight. In the wooden frame on the ground slept a wandering family of musicians. The father and mother seemed to be dreaming of the burning liquor that remained in the bottle. The little pale daughter was dreaming too, for her eyes were wet with tears. The harp stood at their heads, and the dog lay stretched at their feet."

### THIRTIETH EVENING

" It was in a little provincial town," the Moon said ; " it certainly happened last year, but that has nothing to do with the matter. I saw it quite plainly. To-day I read about it in the papers, but there it is not half so clearly expressed. In the tap-room of the little inn sat the bear-leader, eating his supper ; the bear was tied up outside, behind the wood pile—poor Bruin, who did nobody any harm, though he looked grim enough. Up in the garret three little children were playing by the light of my beams ; the eldest was perhaps six years old, the youngest certainly not more than two. Tramp ! tramp !—somebody was coming upstairs : who might it be ? The door was thrust open—it was Bruin, the great, shaggy Bruin ! He had got tired of waiting down in the courtyard, and had found his way to the stairs. I saw

*The door was thrust open—it was Bruin, the great, shaggy Bruin !*

it all," said the Moon. " The children were very much frightened at first at the great shaggy animal : each of them crept into a corner, but he found them all out, and smelt at them, but did them no harm. ' This must be a great dog,' they said, and began to stroke him. He lay down upon the ground, the youngest boy clambered on his back, and bending down a little head of golden curls, playing at hiding in the beast's shaggy skin. Presently the eldest boy took his drum, and beat it till it rattled again : the bear rose up on its hind legs and began to dance. It was a charming sight to behold. Each boy now took his gun, and the bear was obliged to have one too, and he held it up quite properly. Here was a capital playmate they had found ! and they began marching—one, two ; one, two.

" Suddenly some one came to the door, which opened, and the mother of the children appeared. You should have seen her in her dumb terror, with her face as white as chalk, her mouth half-open, and her eyes fixed in a horrified stare. But the youngest boy nodded to her in great glee, and called out in his infantile prattle. ' We're playing at soldiers.' And then the bear-leader came running up."

### THIRTY-FIRST EVENING

The wind blew stormy and cold, the clouds flew hurriedly past ; only for a moment now and then did the Moon become visible. He said, " I looked down from the silent sky upon the driving clouds, and saw the great shadows chasing each other across the earth. I looked upon a prison. A closed carriage stood before it ; a prisoner was to be carried away. My rays pierced through the grated window towards the wall : the prisoner was scratching a few lines upon it, as a parting token ; but he did not write words, but a melody, the outpouring of his heart. The door was opened, and he was led forth, and fixed his eyes upon my round disc. Clouds passed between us, as if he were not to see my face, nor I his. He stepped into the carriage, the door was closed, the whip cracked, and the horses galloped off into the thick forest, whither my rays were not able to follow him ; but as I glanced through the grated window, my rays glided over the notes, his last farewell engraved on the prison wall—where words fail, sounds can often speak. My rays could only light up isolated notes, so the greater part of what was written there will ever remain dark to me. Was it the death-hymn he wrote there ? Were these the glad notes of joy ? Did he drive away to meet his death, or hasten to the embraces of his beloved ? The rays of the Moon do not read all that is written by mortals."

### THIRTY-SECOND EVENING

" I love the children," said the Moon, " especially the quiet little ones—they are so droll. Sometimes I peep into the room, between the curtain and the window frame, when they are not thinking of me. It gives me pleasure to see them dressing and undressing. First, the little round naked shoulder comes creeping out of the frock, then the arm ; or I see how the stocking is drawn off, and a plump little white leg makes its appearance, and a little white foot that is fit to be kissed, and I kiss it too.

"But about what I was going to tell you. This evening I looked through a window, before which no curtain was drawn, for nobody lives opposite. I saw a whole troop of little ones, all of one family, and among them was a little sister. She is only four years old, but can say her prayers as well as any of the rest. The mother sits by her bed every evening, and hears her say her prayers ; and then she has a kiss, and the mother sits by the bed till the little one has gone to sleep, which generally happens as soon as ever she can close her eyes.

"This evening the two elder children were a little boisterous. One of them hopped about on one leg in his long white nightgown, and the other stood on a chair surrounded by the clothes of all the children, and declared he was acting Grecian statues. The third and fourth laid the clean linen carefully in the box, for that is a thing that has to be done ; and the mother sat by the bed of the youngest, and announced to all the rest that they were to be quiet, for little sister was going to say her prayers.

"I looked in, over the lamp, into the little maiden's bed, where she lay under the neat white coverlet, her hands folded demurely and her little face quite grave and serious. She was praying the Lord's Prayer aloud. But her mother interrupted her in the middle of her prayer. 'How is it,' she asked, 'that when you have prayed for daily bread, you always add something I cannot understand ! You must tell me what that is.' The little one lay silent, and looked at her mother in embarrassment. 'What is it you say after *our daily bread?*' 'Dear mother, don't be angry : I only said, *and plenty of butter on it.*'"

---

# GRASSHOPPER GREEN

## ANON

GRASSHOPPER green is a comical chap ;
He lives on the best of fare.
Bright little trousers, jacket, and cap,
These are his summer wear.
Out in the meadows he loves to go,
Playing away in the sun ;
It's hopperty, skipperty, high and low,
Summer's the time for fun.

Grasshopper green has a quaint little house ;
It's under the hedge so gay.
Grandmother Spider, as still as a mouse,
Watches him over the way.
Gladly he's calling the children, I know,
Out in the beautiful sun ;
It's hopperty, skipperty, high and low,
Summer's the time for fun.

# THE VILLAGE SCHOOLMASTER

*by* OLIVER GOLDSMITH

BESIDE yon straggling fence that skirts the way,
With blossomed furze unprofitably gay,
There, in his noisy mansion, skilled to rule,
The village master taught his little school;
A man severe he was, and stern to view;
I knew him well, and every truant knew;
Well had the boding tremblers learned to trace
The day's disasters in his morning face;
Full well they laughed, with counterfeited glee,
At all his jokes, for many a joke had he;
Full well the busy whisper, circling round,
Conveyed the dismal tidings when he frowned;
Yet he was kind; or if severe in aught,
The love he bore to learning was in fault;
The village all declared how much he knew;
'Twas certain he could write, and cypher too;
Lands he could measure, terms and tides presage,
And e'en the story ran that he could gauge.
In arguing too, the parson owned his skill,
For e'en though vanquished, he could argue still;
While words of learned length and thundering sound
Amazed the gazing rustics ranged around,
And still they gazed, and still the wonder grew,
That one small head could carry all he knew.

# TEDDY BEAR'S BEE TREE

### *by* CHARLES G. D. ROBERTS

THEY were exploring the high slopes of the farther shore of Silverwater. It had been an unusually long trip for the Babe's short legs, and Uncle Andy had considerately called a halt, on the pretext that it was time for a smoke. He knew that the Babe would trudge on till he dropped in his tracks before acknowledging that he was tired.

A mossy boulder under the ethereal green shade of a silver birch offered the kind of resting-place—comfortable yet unkempt—which appealed to Uncle Andy's taste ; and there below, over a succession of three low wooden ridges, lay outspread the enchanting mirror of the lake. Uncle Andy's pipe never tasted so good to him as when he could smoke it to the accompaniment of a wide and eye-filling view.

The Babe, who had squatted himself cross-legged on the turf at the foot of the boulder, would have appreciated that superb view also, but that his eager eyes had detected a pair of brown rabbits peering out at him inquiringly from the fringes of a thicket of young firs.

" Perhaps," he thought to himself, " if we keep very still indeed, they'll come out and play."

He was about to whisper this suggestion to Uncle Andy when, from somewhere in the trees behind him, came a loud sound of scrambling of claws scratching on bark, followed by a thud, a grunt, and a whining, and then the crash of some heavy creature careering through the underbrush. It paused within twenty or thirty paces of them in its noisy flight, but the bushes were so thick that they could not catch a glimpse of it. The rabbits vanished. The Babe, startled, shrank closer to his uncle's knees, and stared up at him with round eyes of inquiry.

"He's in a hurry all right, and doesn't care who knows it!" chuckled Uncle Andy. But his shaggy brows were knit in perplexity.

"Who's *he*?" demanded the Babe.

"Well, now," protested Uncle Andy, as much as to say that the Babe ought to have known that without asking, "you know there's nothing in these woods big enough to make such a noise as that except a bear or a moose. And a moose can't go up a tree. You heard that fellow fall down out of a tree, didn't you?"

"Why did he fall down out of the tree?" asked the Babe, in a tone of great surprise.

"That's just what I——" began Uncle Andy. But he was interrupted.

"Oh! *Oh!* It's stung me!" cried the Babe shrilly, jumping to his feet and slapping at his ear. His eyes filled with injured tears.

Uncle Andy stared at him for a moment in grave reproof. Then he, too, sprang up as if the boulder had suddenly grown red-hot, and pawed at his hair with both hands, dropping his pipe.

"Gee! I see why he fell down!" he cried. The Babe gave another cry, clapped his hand to his leg where the stocking did not quite join the short breeches, and began hopping up and down on one foot. A heavy, pervasive hum was beginning to make itself heard.

"Come!" yelled Uncle Andy, striking at his cheek angrily and ducking his head as if he were going to butt something. He grabbed the Babe by one arm, and rushed him to the fir thicket where the rabbits had been.

"Duck!" he ordered. "Down with you—flat!" And together they crawled into the low-growing, dense-foliaged thicket, where they lay side by side, face downwards.

"They won't follow us in here," murmured Uncle Andy. "They don't like thick bushes."

"But I'm afraid we've brought some in with us, Uncle Andy," replied the Babe, trying very hard to keep the tears out of his voice. "I think I hear one buzzing in my hair. *Oh!*" And he clutched wildly at his leg.

"You're right!" said Uncle Andy, his voice suddenly growing very stern as a bee crawled over his collar and jabbed him with great earnestness in the neck. He sat up. Several other bees were creeping over him, seeking an effective spot to administer their fiery admonitions. But he paid them no heed. They stung him where they would—while he was quickly looking over the Babe's hair, jacket, sleeves, stockings, and loose little trousers. He killed half a dozen of the angry crawlers before they found a chance to do the Babe more damage. Then he pulled out three stings, and applied moist earth from under the moss to each red and anguished spot.

The Babe looked up at him with a resolute little laugh, and shook obstinately from the tip of his nose the tears which he would not acknowledge by the attentions of his handkerchief or his fist.

"Thank you *awfully*," he began politely. "But oh! Uncle Andy, your poor eye is just dreadful. Oh-h-h!"

"Yes, they *have* been getting after me a bit," agreed Uncle Andy, dealing firmly with his own assailants now that the Babe was all right. "But this jab under the eye is the only one that matters. Here, see if you can get hold of the sting."

The Babe's keen eyes and nimble little fingers captured it at once. Then Uncle Andy plastered the spot with a daub of wet, black earth, and peered over it solemnly at the Babe's swollen ear. He straightened his grizzled hair, and tried to look as if nothing out of the way had happened.

" I wish I'd brought my pipe along," he muttered. " It's over there by the rock. But I reckon it wouldn't be healthy for me to go and get it just yet ! "

" What's made them so awful mad, do you suppose ? " inquired the Babe, nursing his wounds and listening uneasily to the vicious hum which filled the air outside the thicket.

*He went sprawling and clawing down the face of a steep.*

" It's that fool bear ! " replied Uncle Andy. " He's struck a bee tree too tough for him to tear open, and he fooled at it just long enough to get the bees good and savage. Then he quit in a hurry. And we'll just have to stay here till the bees get cooled down."

" How long 'll that be ? " inquired the Babe dismally. It was hard to sit still in the hot fir thicket, with that burning, throbbing smart in his ear and two little points of fierce ache in his leg. Uncle Andy was far from happy himself; but he felt that the Babe, who had behaved very well, must have his mind diverted. He fished out a letter from his pocket, rolled himself, with his heavy pipe tobacco, a cigarette as thick as his finger, and fell to puffing such huge clouds as would discourage other bees from prying into the thicket. Then he remarked irrelevantly but consolingly :

" It isn't always, by any means, that the bees get the best of it this way. Mostly it's the other way about. *This* bear was a fool. But there was Teddy Bear, now, a cub over the foothills of Sugar Loaf Mountain, and *he* was *not* a fool. When he tackled his first bee tree—and he was nothing but a cub, mind you—he pulled off the affair in good shape. I wish it had been *these* bees that he cleaned out."

The Babe was so surprised that he left go of his leg for a moment.

" Why," he exclaimed, " how could a cub do what a big, strong, grown-up bear couldn't manage ? " He thought with a shudder how unequal *he* would be to such an undertaking.

" You just wait and see ! " admonished Uncle Andy, blowing furious clouds from his monstrous cigarette. " It was about the end of the blue-berry season when Teddy Bear lost his big, rusty-coated mother and small glossy black sister, and found himself completely alone in the world. They had all three come down together from the high blue-berry patches to the dark swamps to hunt for roots and fungi as a variation to their fruit diet. The mother and sister had got caught together in a deadfall—a dreadfal trap which crushed them both flat in an instant. Teddy Bear, some ten feet out of danger, had stared for two seconds in frozen horror, and then raced away like mad with his mother's warning screech hoarse in his ears. He knew by instinct that he would never see the victims any more ; and he was very unhappy and lonely. For a whole day he moped, roaming restlessly about the high slopes and refusing to eat, till at last he got so hungry that he just *had* to eat. Then he began to forget his grief a little, and devote himself to the business of finding a living. But from being the most sunny-tempered of cubs he became all at once as peppery as could be.

" As I have told you," continued Uncle Andy, peering at the Babe with strange solemnity over the mud patch beneath his swollen eye, " the blue-berries were just about done. And as Teddy would not go down to the lower lands again to hunt for other kinds of rations, he had to do a lot of hustling to find enough blue-berries for his healthy young appetite. Thus it came about that when one day, on an out-of-the-way corner of the mountain, he stumbled upon a patch of belated berries—large, plump, lapis-blue, and juicy—he fairly forgot himself in his greedy excitement. He whimpered, he grunted, he wallowed as he fed. He had no time to look where he was going. So, all of a sudden, he fell straight through a thick fringe of blue-berry bushes and went sprawling and clawing down the face of an almost perpendicular steep.

" The distance of his fall was not far short of thirty feet, and he brought up with a bump which left him not breath enough to squeal. The ground was soft however, with undergrowth and debris, and he had no bones broken. In a couple of minutes he was busy licking himself all over to make sure he was undamaged. Reassured on this point, he went prowling in exploration of the place he had dropped into.

" It was a sort of deep bowl, not more than forty feet across the bottom, and with its rocky sides so steep that Teddy Bear did not feel at all en-couraged to climb them. He went sniffing and peering around the edges in the hope of finding some easier way of escape. Disappointed in this, he lifted his black, alert little nose, and stared longingly upward, as if contemplating an effort to fly.

" He saw no help in that direction ; but his nostrils caught a savour which for the moment put all thought of escape out of his head. It was the warm, delectable smell of honey. Teddy Bear had never tasted honey ;

but he needed no one to tell him it was good. Instantly he knew that he was very hungry. And instead of wanting to find a way out of the hole, all he wanted was to find out where that wonderful smell came from. If he thought any more at all of the hole, it was only to be glad he had had the great luck to fall into it.

" From the deep soil at the bottom of the hole grew three big trees, together with a certain amount of underbrush. Two of those were fir trees, green and flourishing. The third was an old maple, with several of its branches broken away. It was quite dead all down one side, while on the other only a couple of branches put forth leaves. About a small hole near the top of this dilapidated old tree Teddy Bear caught sight of a lot of bees, coming and going. Then he knew where that adorable smell came from. For though, as I think I have said, his experience was extremely limited, his mother had managed to convey to him an astonishing lot of useful and varied information.

" Teddy Bear had an idea that bees, in spite of their altogether diminutive size, were capable of making themselves unpleasant, and also that they had a temper which was liable to go off at half-cock. Nevertheless, being a bear of great decision, he lost no time in wondering what he had better do. The moment he had convinced himself that the honey was up that tree, up that tree he went to get it."

" Oh ! " cried the Babe, in tones of shuddering sympathy, as he felt at his leg and his ear. " Oh ! why *didn't* he stop to think ? "

Uncle Andy did not seem to consider that this remark called for any reply. He ignored it. Stopping just at this critical point, he proceeded with exasperating deliberation to roll himself another fat and clumsy cigarette. Then he applied fresh earth to both the Babe's stings and his own. At last he went on.

" That tree must have been hollow a long way down, for almost as soon as Teddy Bear's claws began to rattle on the bark the bees suspected trouble and began to get excited. When he was not much more than half-way up, and hanging to the rough bark with all his claws, *biff* !—something sharp and very hot struck him on the nose. He grunted, and almost let go in his surprise. Naturally, he wanted to paw his nose—for *you* know how it smarted ! "

" I guess *so* ! " murmured the Babe in deepest sympathy, stroking the patch of mud on his ear.

" But that cub had naturally a level head. He knew that if he let go with even one paw he would fall to the ground, because the trunk of the tree at that point was so big he could not get a good hold upon it. So he just dug his smarting nose into the bark, and clawed himself around to the other side of the tree, where the branches that were still green sheltered him a bit, and there was a thick shadow from the nearest fir tree, whose boughs interwove with those of the maple. Here the bees didn't seem to notice him. He kept very still, listening to their angry buzz till it had somewhat quieted down. Then instead of going about it with a noisy dash, as he had done before, he worked his way up stealthily and slowly till he could crawl into the crotch of the first branch. You see, that bear could learn a lesson.

" Presently he stuck his nose around to see how near he was to the bees' hole. He had just time to locate it—about seven or eight feet above him— when again *biff* ! And he was stung on the lip. He drew in his head again quick, I can tell you—quick enough to catch that bee and smash it. He *ate* it indignantly. And then he lay curled up in the crotch for some minutes, gently pawing his sore little snout, and whimpering angrily.

" The warm, sweet smell of the honey was very strong up there. And moreover, Teddy Bear's temper was now thoroughly aroused. Most cubs, and some older bears, would have relinquished the adventure at this point, for, as a rule, it takes a wise old bear to handle a bee tree successfully. But Teddy Bear was no ordinary cub, let me tell you. He lay nursing his anger and his nose till he had made up his mind what to do. And then he set out to do it.

" Hauling himself up softly from branch to branch, he made no more noise than a shadow. As soon as he was right behind the bees' hole he reached around, dug his claws into the edge of it, and pulled with all his might. The edges were rotten, and a pawful of old wood came. So did the bees !

" They were on him in a second. He grunted furiously, screwed his eyes up tight, tucked his muzzle down under his left arm—which was busy holding on—and reached around blindly for another pull. This time he got a good grip, and he could feel something give. But the fiery torture was too much for him. He drew in his paw, crouched back into the crotch, and cuffed wildly at his own ears and face as well as at the air, now thick with his assailants. The terrific hum they made somewhat daunted him. For a few seconds he stood his ground, battling frantically. Then, with an agility that you would never have dreamed his chubby form to be capable of, he went swinging down from branch to branch, whining and coughing and spluttering and squealing all the way. From the lowest branch he slid down the trunk, his claws tearing the bark and just clinging enough to break his fall.

" Reaching the ground, he began to roll himself over and over in the dry leaves and twigs till he had crushed out all the bees that clung in his fur."

" But why didn't the rest of the bees follow him ? They followed this other bear to-day ! " protested the Babe feelingly.

" Well, they didn't ! " returned Uncle Andy quite shortly, with his customary objection to being interrupted. Then he thought better of it, and added amiably : " That's a sensible question—a very natural question ; and I'll give you the answer to it in half a minute. I've got to tell you my yarn in my own way, you know—you ought to know it by this time—but you'll see presently just why the bees acted so differently in the two cases.

" Well, as soon as Teddy Bear had got rid of his assailants he clawed down through the leaves and twigs and moss—like *I* did just now, you remember, till he came to the damp, cool earth. Ah, how he dug his smarting muzzle into it, and rooted in it, and rubbed it into his ears and on his eyelids ! till pretty soon—for the bee-stings do not poison a bear's blood as strongly as they poison us—he began to feel much easier. As for the rest of his body—well, *those* stings didn't amount to much, you know, because his fur and his hide were both so thick.

" At last he sat up on his haunches and looked around. You should have seen him ! "

" I'm glad I wasn't there, Uncle Andy," said the Babe, earnestly shaking his head. But Uncle Andy paid no attention to the remark.

" His muddy paws drooped over his breast, and his face was all stuck over with leaves and moss and mud——"

*Something sharp and very hot struck him on the nose.*

"*We* must look funny, too," suggested the Babe, staring hard at the black mud-poultice under his uncle's swollen eye. But his uncle refused to be diverted.

"And his glossy fur was in a state of which his mother would have strongly disapproved. But his twinkling little eyes burned with wrath and determination. He sniffed again that honey smell. He stared up at the bee tree, and noted that the opening was much larger than it had been before his visit. A big crack extended from it for nearly two feet down the trunk. Moreover, there did not seem to be so many bees buzzing about the hole."

The Babe's eyes grew so round with inquiry at this point that Uncle Andy felt bound to explain.

"You see, as soon as the bees got it into their cunning heads that their enemy was going to succeeed in breaking into their storehouse, they decided that it was more important to save their treasures than to fight the enemy. It's like when one's house is on fire. At first one fights to put the fire out. When that's no use, then one thinks only of saving the things. That's the principle the bees generally go upon. At first they attack the enemy, in the hope of driving him off. But if they find that he is going to succeed in breaking in and burglarising the place, then they fling themselves on the precious honey which they have taken so much pains to store, and begin to stuff their honey-sacks as full as possible. All they think of, then, is to carry away enough to keep them going while they are getting established in new quarters. The trouble with the fool bear who has got us into this mess to-day was that he tackled a bee tree where the outside wood was too strong for him to rip open. The bees knew he couldn't get in at them, so they all turned out after him, to give him a good lesson. When he got away through the underbrush so quickly they just turned on us, because they felt they must give a lesson to somebody."

" *We* didn't want to steal their old honey," muttered the Babe in an injured voice.

" Oh, I'm not so sure ! " said Uncle Andy. " I shouldn't wonder if Bill and I'd come over here some night and smoke the rascals out. But we can wait. That's the difference between us and Teddy Bear. He wouldn't even wait to clean the leaves off his face, he was so anxious for that honey, and his revenge.

" This time he went up the tree slowly and quietly, keeping out of sight all the way. When he was exactly on a level with the entrance he braced himself solidly, reached his right paw around the trunk like lightning, got a fine hold on the edge of the new crack, and wrenched with all his might.

" A big strip of half-rotten wood came away so suddenly that Teddy Bear nearly fell out of the tree.

" A lot of bees came with it ; and once more Teddy Bear's head was in a swarm of little darting piercing flames. But his blood was up. He held on to that chunk of bee tree. A big piece of comb, dripping with honey and crawling with bees, was sticking to it. Whimpering, and pawing at his face, he crunched a great mouthful of the comb, bees and all.

" Never had he tasted, never had he dreamed of, anything so delicious ! What was the pain of his smarting muzzle to that ecstatic mouthful ! He snatched another, which took all the rest of the comb. Then he flung the piece of wood to the ground.

" The bees, meanwhile—except those which had stung him and were now crawling, stingless and soon to die, in his fur—had suddenly left him. The whole interior of their hive was exposed to the glare of daylight, and their one thought now was to save all they could. Teddy Bear's one thought was to seize all he could. He clawed himself around boldly to the front of the tree, plunged one greedy paw straight into the heart of the hive, snatched forth a big, dripping, crawling comb, and fell to munching it up as fast as possible—honey, bees, brood-comb, bee-bread, all together indiscriminately. The distracted bees paid him no more attention. They were too busy filling their honey-sacks."

The Babe smacked his lips. He was beginning to get pretty hungry himself.

" Well," continued Uncle Andy, " Teddy Bear chewed and chewed, finally plunging his whole head into the sticky mess—getting a few stings, of course, but never thinking of them—till he was just so gorged that he couldn't hold another morsel. Then, very slowly and heavily, grunting all the time, he climbed down the bee tree. He felt that he wanted to go to sleep. When he reached the bottom he sat up on his haunches to look around for some sort of a snug corner. His eyelids were swollen with stings, but his little round stomach was swollen with honey, so he didn't care a cent. His face was all daubed with honey, and earth, and leaves and dead bees. His whole body was a sight. And his claws were so stuck up with honey and rotten wood and bark that he kept opening and shutting them like a baby who has got a feather stuck to its fingers and doesn't know what to do with it. But he was too sleepy to bother about his appearance. He just waddled over to a sort of nook between the roots of the next tree, curled up with his sticky nose between his sticky paws, and was soon snoring.

"And did he ever get out of that deep hole?" inquired the Babe, always impatient of the abrupt way in which Uncle Andy was wont to end his stories.

"Of course he got out. He climbed out," answered Uncle Andy. "Do you suppose a bear like that could be kept shut up long? And now I think *we* might be getting out, too! I don't hear any more humming outside, so I reckon the coast's about clear."

He peered forth cautiously.

"It's all right. Come along," he said. "And there's my pipe at the foot of the rock, just where I dropped it," he added, in a tone of great satisfaction. Then, with mud-patched, swollen faces, and crooked but cheerful smiles, the two refugees emerged into the golden light of the afternoon, and stretched themselves. But as Uncle Andy surveyed first the Babe and then himself in the unobstructed light, his smile faded.

"I'm afraid Bill's going to have the laugh on us when we get home!" said he.

---

# SHUT THE DOOR

## ANON.

GODREY Gordon Gustavus Gore—
No doubt you have heard the name before—
Was a boy who never would shut the door.

The wind might whistle, the wind might roar,
And teeth be aching, and throats be sore,
But still he never would shut the door.

His father would beg, his mother implore,
"Godfrey Gordon Gustavus Gore,
We really wish you would shut the door!"

They rigged out a shutter with sail and oar,
And threatened to pack off Gustavus Gore
On a voyage to far-away Singapore.

But he begged for mercy, and said, "No more!
Pray do not send me to Singapore
On a shutter, and then I will shut the door."

"You will?" said his parents; "then keep on shore;
But mind you do, for the plague is sore
Of a fellow that never will shut the door—
Godfrey Gordon Gustavus Gore!"

# SEVEN TIMES ONE

### by JEAN INGELOW

THERE'S no dew left on the daisies and clover,
  There's no rain left in heaven;
I've said my "seven times" over and over,
  Seven times one are seven.

I am old, so old, I can write a letter;
  My birthday lessons are done;
The lambs play always, they know no better;
  They are only one times one.

O moon! in the night I have seen you sailing
  And shining so round and low;
You were bright! ah, bright! but your light is failing—
  You are nothing now but a bow.

O velvet bee, you're a dusty fellow,
  You've powdered your legs with gold!
O brave marsh marybuds, rich and yellow,
  Give me your money to hold!

O columbine, open your folded wrapper,
  Where two twin turtle-doves dwell!
O cuckoopint, toll me the purple clapper
  That hangs in your clear green bell!

And show me your nest with the young ones in it
  I will not steal them away;
I am old! you may trust me, linnet, linnet—
  I am seven times one to-day.

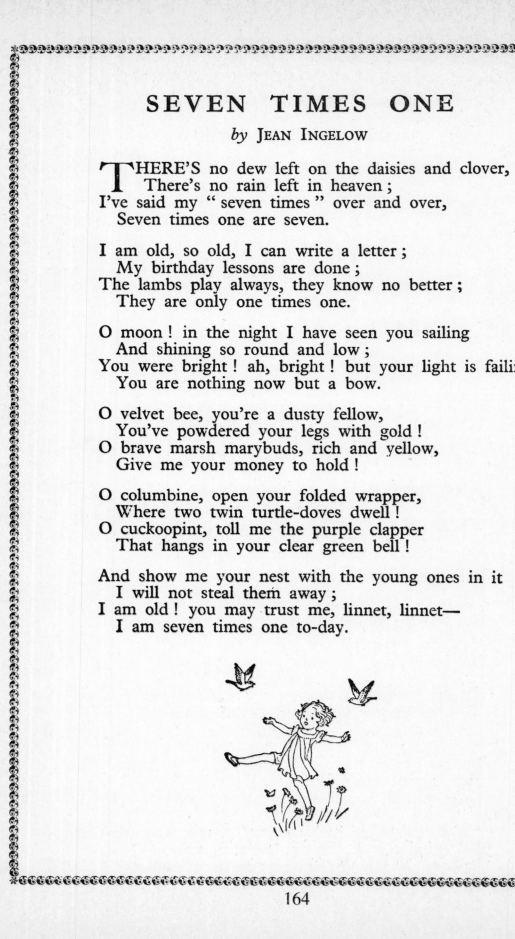

# THE ROSE ELF

## by HANS ANDERSEN

IN the midst of the garden grew a rose bush, which was quite covered with roses ; and in one of them, the most beautiful of all, there dwelt an elf. He was so tiny that no human eye could see him. Behind every leaf in the rose he had a bedroom. He was as well formed and beautiful as any child could be, and had wings that reached from his shoulders to his feet. Oh, what a fragrance there was in the rooms ! and how clear and bright were the walls ! They were made of the pale pink rose leaves.

The whole day he rejoiced in the warm sunshine, flew from flower to flower, danced on the wings of the flying butterfly, and measured how many steps he would have to take to pass along all the roads and cross-roads that are marked out on a single hidden leaf. What we call veins on the leaf were to him high and cross-roads. Yes, those were long roads for him ! Before he had finished his journey the sun went down, for he had begun too late !

It became very cold, the dew fell, and the wind blew : now the best thing to be done was to come home. He made what haste he could, but the rose had shut itself up, and he could not get in : not a single rose stood open. The poor little elf was very much frightened. He had never been out at night before ; he had always slumbered sweetly and comfortably behind the warm rose leaves. Oh, it certainly would be the death of him .

At the other end of the garden there was, he knew, an arbour of fine honeysuckle. The flowers looked like great painted horns, and he wished to go down into one of them to sleep till the next day.

He flew thither. Silence ! two people were in there—a handsome young man and a young girl. They sat side by side, and wished that they need never part. They loved each other better than a good child loves its father and mother.

165

" Yet we must part ! " said the young man. " Your brother does not like us, therefore he sends me away on an errand so far over mountains and seas. Farewell, my sweet bride, for that you shall be ! "

And they kissed each other, and the young girl wept, and gave him a rose. But, before she gave it him, she impressed a kiss so firmly and closely upon it that the flower opened. Then the little elf flew into it, and leaned his head against the delicate fragrant walls. Here he could plainly here them say, " Farewell ! farewell ! " and he felt that the rose was placed on the young man's heart. Oh, how that heart beat ! the little elf could not go to sleep, it thumped so.

But not long did the rose rest undisturbed on that breast. The man took it out, and as he went lonely through the wood, he kissed the flower so often and so fervently that the little elf was almost crushed. He could feel through the leaf how the man's lips burned, and the rose itself had opened, as if under the hottest noonday sun.

Then came another man, gloomy and wicked ; he was the bad brother of the pretty maiden. He drew out a sharp knife, and while the other kissed the rose, the bad man stabbed him to death, and then, cutting off his head, buried both head and body in the soft earth under the linden tree.

" Now he's forgotten and gone ! " thought the wicked brother ; " he will never come back again. He was to have taken a long journey over mountains and seas. One can easily lose one's life, and he has lost his. He cannot come back again, and my sister dare not ask news of him from me."

Then with his feet he shuffled dry leaves over the loose earth, and went home in the dark night. But he did not go alone, as he thought ; the little elf sat in a dry, rolled-up linden leaf that had fallen on the wicked man's hair as he dug. The hat was now placed over the leaf, and it was very dark in the hat, and the elf trembled with fear and with anger at the evil deed.

In the morning hour the bad man got home ; he took off his hat, and went into his sister's bedroom. There lay the beautiful, blooming girl, dreaming of him whom she loved from his heart, and of whom she now believed that he was going across the mountains and through the forests. And the wicked brother bent over her, and laughed hideously, as only a fiend can laugh.

Then the dry leaf fell out of his hair upon the coverlet ; but he did not remark it, and he went out to sleep a little himself in the morning hour. But the elf slipped forth from the withered leaf, placed himself in the ear of the sleeping girl, and told her, as in a dream, the dreadful history of the murder ; described to her the place where her brother had slain her lover and buried his corpse ; told her of the blooming linden tree close by it, and said, " That you may not think it is only a dream that I have told you, you will find on your bed a withered leaf."

And she found it when she awoke. Oh, what bitter tears she wept ! The window stood open the whole day : the little elf could easily get out to the roses and all the other flowers, but he could not find it in his heart to quit the afflicted maiden. In the window stood a plant, a monthly rose bush ; he seated himself in one of the flowers, and looked at the poor girl. Her brother often came into the room, and, in spite of his wicked deed, he always seemed cheerful, but she dared not say a word of the grief that was in her heart.

As soon as the night came, she crept out of the house, went to the wood, to the place where the linden tree stood, removed the leaves from the ground, turned up the earth, and immediately found him who had been slain. Oh, how she wept, and prayed that she might die also !

Gladly would she have taken the corpse home with her, but that she could not do. Then she took the pale head with the closed eyes, kissed the cold mouth, and shook the earth out of the beautiful hair. " That I will keep," she said. And when she had laid earth upon the dead body, she took the head, and a little sprig of the jasmine that bloomed in the wood where he was buried, home with her.

*Every morning he flew to the window of the poor girl.*

As soon as she came into her room, she brought the greatest flower-pot she could find : in this she laid the dead man's head, strewed earth upon it, and then planted the jasmine twig in the pot.

" Farewell ! farewell ! " whispered the little elf : he could endure it no longer to see all the pain, and therefore flew out to his rose in the garden. But the rose was faded ; only a few pale leaves clung to the wild bush.

" Alas ! how soon everything good and beautiful passes away ! " sighed the elf.

At last he found another rose, and this became his house ; behind its delicate fragrant leaves he could hide himself and dwell.

Every morning he flew to the window of the poor girl, and she was always standing weeping by the flower-pot. The bitter tears fell upon the jasmine spray, and every day, as the girl became paler and paler, the twig stood there fresher and greener, and one shoot after another sprouted forth, little white buds burst out, and these she kissed. But the bad brother scolded his sister, and asked if she had gone mad. He could not bear it, and could not imagine why she was always weeping over the flower-pot. He did not know what closed eyes were there, what red lips had there faded into earth. And she bowed her head upon the flower-pot, and the little elf of the rose bush found her slumbering there. Then he seated himself in her ear, told of the evening in the arbour, of the fragrance of the rose, and the love of the elves. And she dreamed a marvellously sweet dream, and while she dreamed, her life passed away. She had died a quiet death, and she was in heaven, with him whom she loved.

And the jasmine opened its great white bells. They smelt quite peculiarly sweet ; it could not weep in any other way over the dead one.

But the wicked brother looked at the beautiful blooming plant, and took it for himself as an inheritance, and put it in his sleeping-room, close by his bed, for it was glorious to look upon, and its fragrance was sweet and lovely. The little Rose-elf followed, and went from flower to flower—for in each dwelt a little soul—and told of the murdered young man, whose head was now earth beneath the earth, and told of the evil brother and of the poor sister.

"We know it !" said each soul in the flowers, "we know it ! have we not sprung from the eyes and lips of the murdered man ? We know it ! we know it !"

And then they nodded in a strange fashion with their heads.

The Rose-elf could not at all understand how they could be so quiet, and he flew out to the bees that were gathering honey, and told them the story of the wicked brother. And the bees told it to their Queen, and the Queen commanded that they should all kill the murderer next morning. But in the night—it was the first night that followed upon the sister's death—when the brother was sleeping in his bed, close to the fragrant jasmine, each flower opened, and invisible, but armed with poisonous spears, the flower-souls came out and seated themselves in his ear, and told him bad dreams, and then flew across his lips and pricked his tongue with the poisonous spears.

"Now we have avenged the dead man !" they said, and flew back into the jasmine's white bells.

When the morning came and the windows of the bed-chamber were opened, the Rose-elf and the Queen Bee and the whole swarm of bees rushed in to kill him.

But he was dead already. People stood around his bed, and said, "The scent of the jasmine has killed him !" Then the Rose-elf understood the revenge of the flowers, and told it to the Queen and to the bess, and the Queen hummed with the whole swarm around the flower-pot. The bees were not to be driven away. Then a man carried away the flower-pot, and one of the bees stung him in the hand, so that he let the pot fall, and it broke in picees.

Then they beheld the whitened skull, and knew that the dead man on the bed was a murderer.

And the Queen Bee hummed in the air, and sang of the revenge of the bees, and of the Rose-elf, and said that behind the smallest leaf there dwells ONE who can bring the evil to light, and repay it.

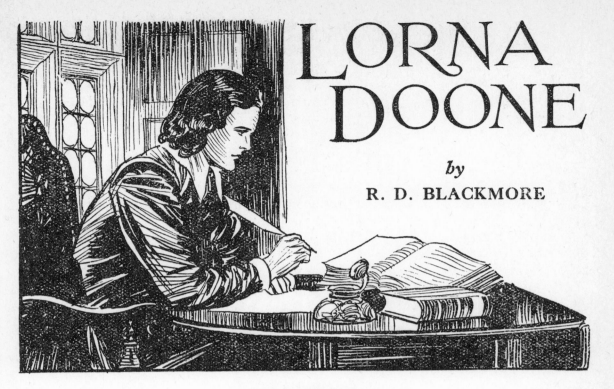

# LORNA DOONE

*by*

## R. D. BLACKMORE

## CHAPTER I

IF anybody cares to read a simple tale, I, John Ridd, of the parish of Oare, in the county of Somerset, yeoman and churchwarden, have had a share in some doings of this neighbourhood, which I will try to set down in order, God sparing my life and memory.

My father being of good substance, he, John Ridd, the elder, churchwarden and overseer, being a great admirer of learning, sent me, his only son, to be schooled at Tiverton, in the county of Devon, where, by the time I was twelve years old, I had risen into the upper school.

Now the cause of my leaving Tiverton school, and the way of it, were as follows : On the 29th day of November, in the year of our Lord 1673, the very day when I was twelve years old, we came out of school at five o'clock. According to custom, we drove the day-boys in brave rout down the causeway from the school-porch to the gate.

After these " charity-boys " were gone, we were leaning against the bars of the gate, some seven of us, and not conspicuous in the closing of the daylight. A boy leaning up against me would not allow me elbow room, and struck me very sadly in the stomach. This I felt so unkindly, that I smote him straightway in the face. Upon this he put his head down and presented it so vehemently at the middle of my waistcoat, that for a minute or more my breath seemed dropped, as it were, from my pockets. Before I came to myself again, there came round the post where the letters of our founder are, a small string of horses, and a red-faced man on the bigger nag.

" Plaise ye, worshipful masters," he said, " carn 'e tull whur our Jan Ridd be ? "

" Oh, John, John," I cried, " what's the use of your coming now ? The holidays don't begin till Wednesday fortnight, John." John Fry leaned forward in the saddle, and turned his eyes away from me.

169

"And father, oh, how is father?" I pushed the boys right and left as I said it.

"Vayther'll be at the crooked post, t'other zide o' telling-house."

He looked at the nag's ears as he said it; and, I knew that it was a lie. And my heart fell like lead, and I leaned back on the stay of the gate, and longed no more to fight anybody.

"Come up, Jack," said one of the boys, "he hit you, and you hit him, you know."

"Pay your debts before you go," said a monitor, striding up to me.

"Nay," I said, "I will not fight thee now, Robin Snell, but wait till I come back again."

"Take coward's blow, Jack Ridd, then," cried half a dozen boys, shoving Bob Snell forward to do it.

By this time the question of fighting was gone quite out of our own discretion; for sundry of the elder boys came running down the causeway, having heard that there had arisen "a snug little mill."

I felt upon me now a certain responsibility, a dutiful need to maintain, in the presence of John Fry, the manliness of the Ridd family, and the honour of Exmoor. Hitherto none had worsted me, and this success I owed partly to my native strength, and the Exmoor toughness in me. John Fry thought this was the first fight that had befallen me and says, "Doon't thee goo for to do it, for gude now." But I told him that now it was much too late to cry off; so he said, "The Lord be with thee, Jan."

It was not a large piece of ground in the angle of the causeways, but quite big enough to fight upon. The great boys stood in a circle around, being gifted with strong privilege, and the little boys had leave to lie flat and look through the legs of the great boys.

I marvel how Robin Snell felt. But I felt my heart go up and down as the boys came round to strip me; and greatly fearing to be beaten, I blew hot upon my knuckles. Then up to me came Robin Snell and he stood very square, and looked at me, and I lacked not long to look at him. He took me by the hand, and then smote me painfully in the face, ere I could get my fence up.

"Whutt be 'bout, lad?" cried John Fry; "hutt un again, Jan, wull 'e? Well done then, our Jan boy."

For I had replied to Robin now, and the strife began in a serious style, and the boys looking on were not cheated. All I know is, I came to my corner, when the round was over, with very hard pumps in my chest, and a great desire to fall away.

"Time is up," cried head monitor, ere ever I got my breath again. He began to count, one, two and three—but before the "three" was out of his mouth, I was facing my foe, with both hands up

"Finish him off, Bob," cried a big boy.

But I was not so to be finished off, though feeling in my knuckles now as if it were a blueness and a sense of chilblain. Nothing held except my legs, and they were good to help me.

Meanwhile John Fry was prowling about, asking whether I was like to be killed. But finding that I had foughten three-score fights already, he came up to me, and says in my ears :—

"Never thee knack under, Jan, or never coom naigh Hexmoor
no more."

At once I set both fists again, and my heart stuck to me like cobbler's
wax. Either Robin Snell should kill me, or I would conquer Robin Snell.
So I went and I gave him my right between his eyes, and he blinked, and
was not pleased with it. I feared him not, and spared him not, neither spared
myself. My breath came again, and my heart stood cool, and my eyes struck
fire no longer. How the rest of it was I know not; only that I had the end of
it, and helped to put Robin in bed.

We left the town very early in the morning, after lying one day to rest,
and it was high noon before we were got to Dulverton.

*Then up to me came Robin Snell and he stood very square, and looked at me.*

There we dined upon the rarest and choicest victuals that ever I did
taste. Hot mutton pasty was a thing I had often heard of from wealthy boys
and men, who made a dessert of dinner; and to hear them talk of it made
my lips smack, and my ribs come inwards.

When the mutton pasty was done, out I went to wash at the pump, being
a lover of soap and water, at all risk, except of my dinner. Then a lady's-
maid came out and I understood from her voice and manner that she was
not of this country, but a foreigner by extraction.

"How far you call it now to the bank of the sea at Wash—Wash—"
she asked.

"At Watchett, you mean, madam. Oh, a long way, and the roads as
soft as the road to Oare." Upon this, she retreated up the yard.

Now, up to the end of Dulverton town, we happened upon a great coach
and six horses labouring very heavily. John Fry rode on with his hat in his
hand; but I was amazed to that degree, that I left my cap on my head, and
drew bridle without knowing it. For in the front of the coach sate the foreign

lady, who had met me at the pump.  By her side was a little girl, dark-haired and very wonderful, and in the honourable place sate a handsome lady, very warmly dressed, and sweetly delicate of colour.  Close to her was a lively child, two or it may be three years old, staring at all and everybody.

I took off my cap to the beautiful lady, and she put up her hand and kissed it to me.  But now the foreign lady turned upon all this going-on, and looked me straight in the face.  I was about to salute her, but, strange to say, she stared at my eyes as if she had never seen me before, neither wished to see me again.  At this I was so startled that I startled Peggy also with the muscle of my legs, and she being fresh from stable broke away so suddenly, that I could do no more than turn round and lower my cap, to the beautiful lady.  Soon I overtook John Fry, and asked him all about them, but all that I could win out of him was that they were " murdering Papishers."


## CHAPTER II

MY father never came to meet us, at either side of the telling-house, although the dogs kept such a noise that he must have heard us.  I looked at the posts of the gate, and then at the door of the harness-room, where he used to smoke his pipe and sing.  And I felt in my pocket for the new pipe which I had brought him from Tiverton, and said to myself, " He shall not have it until to-morrow morning."

Woe is me!  I cannot tell.  How I knew I know not now—only that I slunk away, without a tear, or thought of weeping, and hid me in a saw-pit.

By and by, a noise came down, as of woman's weeping ;  and there my mother and sister were, choking and holding together.  Although they were my dearest loves, I could not bear to look at them, until they seemed to want my help, and put their hands before their eyes.

My dear father had been killed by the Doones of Bagworthy, while riding home from Porlock market, on the Saturday evening.  With him were six brother-farmers, all of them very sober.  The robbers had no grudge against him ;  for he had never flouted them, neither made over-much of outcry because they robbed other people.

These seven good farmers were jogging along, when suddenly a horseman stopped in the starlight full across them.  By dress and arms they knew him well, and by his size and stature ;  and though he seemed one man to seven, it was in truth one man to one.  Of the six there was not one but pulled out his money, and sang small beer to a Doone.

But father set his staff above his head, and rode at the Doone robber. With a trick of his horse, the wild man escaped the sudden onset.  But father, drawing at Smiler's head, to try to come back, was in the midst of a dozen men, who seemed to come out of a turf-rick, some on horse, and some a-foot.  Nevertheless, he smote lustily, and being of great size and strength, they had no easy job with him.  With the play of his wrist, he cracked three or four crowns, until the rest drew their horses away, and he thought that he was master.

But a man was crouching by the peat-stack, with a long gun set to his shoulder, and he got poor father against the sky, and I cannot tell the rest of it. Only they knew that Smiler came home, with blood upon his withers, and father was found in the morning dead on the moor, with his cudgel lying broken under him.

It was more of woe than wonder, being such days of violence, that mother knew herself a widow, and her children fatherless. I, John Ridd, was the eldest; next came sister Annie, with about two years between us; and then the little Eliza.

Now, before I got home and found my sad loss mother had done a most wondrous thing, which made all the neighbours say that she must be mad, at least. Upon the Monday morning, while her husband lay unburied, she set off on foot for the Doone gate.

In the early afternoon she came to the hollow and barren entrance. Two men led my mother down a steep and gliddery stairway and thence from the break of the falling water as far as the house of the captain. And there at the door they left her trembling, strung as she was, to speak her mind.

A tall old man, Sir Ensor Doone, came out with a bill-hook in his hand, and hedger's gloves going up his arms.

"Good woman, you are none of us. What has brought you hither?"

"Loth would I be," said mother, "loth indeed, Sir Ensor Doone, to accuse any one unfairly. But I have lost the very best husband God ever gave to a woman. Not that I would ever wish—oh, John, it seems too strange to me, and last week you were everything."

"This matter must be see to at once," the old man answered, moved a little in spite of all his knowledge. "Madam, if any wrong has been done, trust the honour of a Doone; I will redress it to my utmost. Come inside and rest yourself, while I ask about it. What was your good husband's name, and when and where fell this mishap?"

"Deary me," said mother. "My husband's name was John Ridd, sir; and there was not a better man in Somerset or Devon."

Counsellor Doone came in ere yet my mother was herself again; a square-built man of enormous strength.

"Here is a lady, Counsellor, who charges the Doones with having unjustly slain her husband——"

"Murdered him! Murdered him!" cried my mother; "if ever there was a murder. Oh, sir! you know it."

"Put the case," said the Counsellor.

"The case is this," replied Sir Ensor, holding one hand up to mother; "This lady's husband was slain, it seems, upon his return from the market at Porlock, no longer than last Saturday night."

"Cite his name," said the Counsellor.

"Master John Ridd, as I understand."

The square man with the long grey beard, quite unmoved by anything, drew back to the door and spoke.

"Four or five of our most peaceful gentlemen went to the market at Porlock with a lump of money. When they drew bridle to rest their horses, a robber of great size and strength rode into the midst of them, thinking to kill or terrify. He had smitten three of them senseless, for the power of his arm was terrible; whereupon the last man tried to ward his blow with a pistol. Carver, sir, it was, who saved the lives of his brethren and his own ; and glad enow they were to escape."

At this atrocious tale of lies mother was too much amazed to do any more than look at him, as if the earth must open.

" All the Doones are gentlemen," answered the old man gravely, " and we wish you clearly to conceive that we do not charge your poor husband with any set purpose of robbery." With that, she dried her tears in haste and went home.

Our good justiciaries feared to make ado, or hold any public inquiry about my dear father's death. So we buried him quietly in the sloping little church-yard of Oare, as meek a place as need be, with the Lynn brook down below it.

Then when I was turned fourteen it happened to me without choice to explore the Bagworthy water. And it came about in this wise.

Being resolved to catch some loaches, I set forth without a word to any one, in the forenoon of St. Valentine's day, 1675–6. I doffed my shoes and hose, and put them into a bag about my neck. Then I took a three-pronged fork firmly bound to a rod with cord, and a piece of canvas kerchief, with a lump of bread inside it ; and so went into the pebbly water. When I had travelled two miles or so, I found a good stream flowing softly into the body of our brook.

Hereupon I drew up, because the water was bitter cold, and my little toes were aching. So I rubbed them with a sprout of young sting-nettle, and having skipped about awhile, was inclined to eat a bit. As I ate more and more my spirit arose within me, and I thought of what my father had been, and how he had told me a hundred times never to be a coward. And then I grew warm, and said to myself, " Now if father looks, he shall see that I obey him." So I put the bag round my back again and buckled my breeches far up from the knee, expecting deeper water, and went stoutly up under the branches which hangs so dark on the Bagworthy river.

Here, although affrighted often by the deep, dark places, on the whole I had very comely sport of loaches, trout, and minnows. Now, if you have ever been fishing, you will not wonder that I was led on, forgetting all about danger, and taking no heed of the time, but shouting in a childish way when-ever I caught a " whacker." But in answer to all my shouts there never was any sound at all, and the place grew thicker and thicker, until I thought that the fishes might have a good chance of eating me, instead of my eating the fishes. And so, in a sorry plight, I came to an opening in the bushes, where a great black pool lay in front of me.

Skirting round one side, I came to a sudden sight and marvel. For, lo ! I stood at the foot of a long pale slide of water, coming smoothly to me, without any break or hindrance, for a hundred yards or more, and fenced on either side with cliff, sheer, and straight and shining.

The look of this place had a sad effect, scaring me very greatly, and making me feel that I would give something to be at home again.

Then says I to myself : " John Ridd, these trees, and pools, and lone-some rocks, are making a coward of thee. Shall I go back to my mother so and be called her fearless boy ? "

Nevertheless, I am free to own that it was not any fine sense of shame which settled my decision. But that which saved me from turning back was

*My elbow caught in a rock-hole; and so I managed to start again.*

a strange inquisitive desire to know what made the water come down like that, and what there was at the top of it.

Therefore, I bestowed my fish around my neck more tightly, and crawled along over the fork of rocks, where the water had scooped the stone out, and let my feet into the dip and rush of the torrent.

And here I had reckoned without my host; and it was much but that I went down into the great black pool, and had never been heard of more; and this must have been the end of me, except for my trusty loach-fork. But all in a moment, with a roar of water upon me my fork, praise God, stuck fast in the rock, and I was borne up upon it. I felt nothing except that here was another matter to begin upon; and it might be worth while, or again it might not, to have another fight for it.

I gathered my legs slowly back, as if they were fish to be landed. And in this manner I gained a footing, leaning well forward like a draught-horse, with the ashen stake set behind me. Then I said to myself, " John Ridd, the sooner you get yourself out by the way you came the better it will be for you." But to my great dismay and affright, I saw that no choice was left me now, except that I must climb somehow up that hill of water, or else be washed down into the pool and whirl around it till it drowned me.

Having said the Lord's Prayer, I grasped the good loach-stick under a knot, and steadied me with my left hand, and so with a sigh of despair began my course up the fearful torrent-way. I went carefully, step by step, but the greatest danger of all was just where I saw no jeopardy, when I ran up a patch of black ooze-weed, being now not far from the summit.

Here I fell very piteously, and was like to have broken my knee-cap, and the torrent got hold of my other leg while I was indulging the bruised one. And then a vile knotting of cramp disabled me, and for a while I could only roar, till my mouth was full of water, and all of my body was sliding. But the fright of that brought me to again, and my elbow caught in a rock-hole; and so I managed to start again, with the help of more humility.

At last the rush of forked water, where first it came over the lips of the fall, drove me into the middle, and I stuck awhile with my toe-balls on the slippery links of the pop-weed, and the world was green and gliddery, and I durst not look behind me. Then I made up my mind to die at last; only it did seem such a pity after fighting so long to give in, and the light was coming upon me, and again I fought towards it; then suddenly I felt fresh air, and fell into it headlong.

When I came to myself again, my hands were full of young grass and mould, and a little girl kneeling at my side was rubbing my forehead tenderly with a dock-leaf and a handkerchief.

"What is your name?" she said, as if she had every right to ask me; "and how did you come here, and what are these wet things in this great bag?"

"You had better let them alone," I said. "They are loaches for my mother. But I will give you some, if you like."

"Dear me, how much you think of them! Why, they are only fish. But how your feet are bleeding! Oh, I must tie them up for you."

"Oh, I don't think much of that," I replied. "I shall put some goose-grease to them. But how you are looking at me! I never saw any one like you before. My name is John Ridd. What is your name?"

"Lorna Doone," she answered, in a low voice, as if afraid of it. "If you please, my name is Lorna Doone. Why did you ever come here? Do you know what they would do to us if they found you here?"

"Beat us, I dare say, very hard; or me at least. They could never beat you."

"No. They would kill us both outright, and bury us here by the water."

"But what should they kill me for?"

"Because you have found the way up here, and they could never believe it. Now, please, go. They will kill us both in a moment. Yes, I like you very much"—for I was teasing her to say it—"very much indeed, and I will call you John Ridd, if you like; only please go, John. And when your feet are well, you know, you can come and tell me how they are."

"Hush!" A shout came down the valley; and all my heart was trembling, like water after sunset, and Lorna's face was altered from pleasant play to terror. She shrank to me, and looked up at me, with such a power of weakness, that I at once made up my mind to save her or to die with her.

"Come with me down the waterfall. I can carry you easily; and mother will take care of you."

"No, no," she cried, as I took her up; "I will tell you what to do. They are only looking for me."

"Stop," said I; "I see what to do. I must get into the water, and you must go to sleep."

Daring scarce to peep, I crept into the water, and lay down in it, with my head between two blocks of stone, and there seemed no chance at all but what the men must find me.

I caught a glimpse of the little maid. She was lying beneath a rock, feigning to be fast asleep.

Presently one of the great rough men came round a corner upon her, and caught her up in his arms.

## LORNA DOONE

A little girl kneeling at my side was rubbing my forehead
tenderly with a dock-leaf and a handkerchief. (Page 176)

**THUMBELINA**

Thumbelina bent down, put the feathers aside which covered
his head, and kissed him upon his closed eyes. (Page 235)

He set her dainty little form upon his great square shoulder, and going up that darkened glen, little Lorna turned and put up a hand to me, and I put up a hand to her, in the thick of the mist and the willows.

As daylight sank below the forget-me-not of stars, I knew that now must be my time to get away, if there were any.

Therefore, wringing my sodden breeches, I managed to crawl from the bank to a niche in the cliff which Lorna had shown me. Through the dusk I had trouble to see the mouth, and then I espied rough steps, made as if with a sledge-hammer.

How I climbed up, and across the clearing, and found my way home through the Bagworthy forest, is more than I can remember now, by reason of perfect weariness.

## CHAPTER III

Now a strange thing came to pass when I was twenty-one years old. Mr. Reuben Huckaback, whom many folk in Dulverton will remember long after my time, was my mother's uncle. He owned the best shop in the town, and did fine trade in soft ware. And we being now his only kindred (except indeed his granddaughter, little Ruth Huckaback), mother beheld it a Christian duty to keep as well as could be with him, both for love of a nice man, and for the sake of her children.

Now this old gentleman must needs come to spend the New Year-tide with us, and it was settled between us that we should expect him soon after noon on the last day of December.

Now when I came in, after seeing to the cattle, I fully expected to find Uncle Ben sitting in the fireplace, lifting one cover and then another, as his favourite manner was, for he loved our bacon rarely. But instead of my finding him with his quaint dry face pulled out at me—who should run out but the maid, Betty Muxworthy, and poke me with a saucepan-lid.

" Has Uncle Ben not arrived yet, Betty ? "

" Raived ! I knaws nout about that, whuther a hath or noo. Only I tell 'e, her baint coom. Rackon them Dooneses hath gat 'un."

" Oh, Johnny, Johnny," my mother cried, running out of the grand show-parlour, " I am so glad you are come at last. You are very sweet-tempered, I know, John Ridd, and perhaps a little too sweet at times, but what would you say if the people there "—she never would call them " Doones "—" had gotten your poor Uncle Reuben, horse, and Sunday coat, and all ? "

" Well, mother dear, I would be sorry. But let us have our dinner. After that I will go to seek for him in the thick of the fog, like a needle in a hayband."

So we made a very good dinner indeed, and then I set out with my gun to look for him. I followed the track on the side of the hill, from the farm-yard, and after that I went all along on the ridge of the rabbit-cleve, and then down to the Lynn stream, and leaped it, and so up the hill and the moor beyond.

Now when I came to an unknown place, where a stone was set up endwise, with a faint red cross upon it, I gathered my courage to stop and think, having sped on the way too hotly. Then a distant noise went by me, as of many horses galloping and in my fright I set my gun and said, " God send something to shoot at." Yet nothing came, and my gun fell back, without my will to lower it.

But presently, while I was thinking, "What a fool I am!" I heard a rough low sound very close in the fog, as of a hobbled sheep a-coughing. I listened, and feared, and yet listened again, though I wanted not to hear it. A dry sort of wheezing sound it was, barred with coughs and want of breath ; but thus I made the meaning of it.

"Lord have mercy upon me! An' if I cheated Sam Hicks last week, Lord knowest how well he deserved it. Oh, Lord, where be I a-going?"

*I set Uncle Ben astride the little horse, but he was too weak to stay so.*

I made towards the sound, and presently was met, point-blank, by the head of a mountain-pony. Upon its back lay a man bound down, with his feet on the neck and his head to the tail, and his arms falling down like stirrups.

"Good and worthy sir," I said to the man who was riding so roughly ; "fear nothing ; no harm shall come to thee."

"Help, good friend, whoever thou art," he gasped. "God hath sent thee, and not to rob me, because it is done already."

"What, Uncle Ben!" I cried, letting go the horse in amazement. "Dost thou not know me, thy dutiful nephew, John Ridd?"

Not to make a long story of it, I cut the thongs that bound him, and set him astride on the little horse ; but he was too weak to stay so. Therefore I mounted him on my back, turning the horse into horse-steps, and leading the pony by the cords which I fastened around his nose, set out for home.

Now as soon as ever I brought him in, we set him up in the chimney-corner, comfortable and handsome ; and he stamped about in the kitchen, until he was sure of his whereabouts, and then he fell asleep again until supper should be ready.

Of course, the Doones, and nobody else, had robbed good Uncle Reuben ; and then they grew sportive, and took his horse, and bound the master upon the wild one. For two or three hours they had fine fun chasing him through the fog, and making much sport of his groanings ; and then waxing hungry, they went their way, and left him.

Next day Master Huckaback demanded from my mother an escort into a dangerous part of the world. My mother made answer to this that he was welcome to take John Fry with him ; at which the good clothier laughed, and said that John was nothing like big enough ; but another John must serve his turn.

My mother found fifty reasons against my going, but I was quite resolved to see Uncle Reuben through with it. I soon persuaded mother to let me go and I was greatly vexed to find that this dangerous enterprise was nothing more than a visit to the Baron de Whichehalse, to lay an information, and sue a warrant against the Doones, and a posse to execute it.

We rode by way of Brendon town, Illford Bridge, and Babbrook, to avoid the great hill above Lynmouth. When we arrived at Ley Manor, we were shown very civilly into the hall, and refreshed with good ale and collared head, and the back of a Christmas pudding.

After that, we were called to the Justice-room, where the Baron himself was sitting with Colonel Harding, another Justiciary of the King's Peace, to help him.

Uncle Reuben made his best scrape, and then walked up to the table and addressed himself to De Whichehalse.

The baron smiled gently, and replied quite reasonably.

" A warrant against Sir Ensor Doone, and seven sons of Sir Ensor Doone, Christian names unknown. Sir Ensor himself was there, of course, as you have given evidence——"

" No, no, my lord, I never said that ; I never said——"

" If he can prove that he was not there, you may be indicted for perjury. But as for those seven sons of his, of course, you can swear that they were his sons, and not his nephews, or grandchildren, or even no Doones at all ? "

" My lord, I can swear that they were Doones."

" I am heartily glad to hear it," replied the Baron pleasantly ; " for it proves after all that this robbery (if robbery there has been) was not so very ruinous. Now, are you quite convinced, good sir, that these people (if there were any) stole, or took, or even borrowed anything at all from you ? "

" My lord, do you think I was drunk ? "

" Not for a moment, Master Huckaback. But how did you know that your visitors were of this particular family ? "

" Because it could be nobody else. Because, in spite of the fog——"

" Fog ! " said the Baron, with emphasis. " Ah, that explains the whole affair."

" Go back, my good fellow," said Colonel Harding ; " and if the day is clear enough, you will find all your things where you left them. I know what it is to be caught in an Exmoor fog."

"My lord, Sir Colonel, is this your justice! If I go to London myself for it, the King shall know how his commission—how a man may be robbed, and the justices prove that he ought to be hanged at the back of it; that in his good shire of Somerset——"

"Your pardon a moment, good sir," de Whichehalse interrupted him; "but I was about to mention the mal-feasance was laid in Somerset; but we are in the commission of his peace for the county of Devon only, and therefore could never deal with it."

All throughout the homeward road, Uncle Ben was very silent, but before he went to bed he said to me, "Nephew Jack, you have not behaved so badly as the rest to me. And I think that I may trust you. I have another card to play. You shall guide me to-morrow, without a word to any one, to a place where I may well descry the dwelling of these scoundrel Doones, and learn the best way to get at them, when the time shall come. Can you do this for me?"

I promised very readily to do my best to serve him.

Having reconnoitred thus the position of the enemy, Master Huckaback, on the homeward road, cross-examined me in a manner not at all desirable. He succeeded in making me promise to visit the place again, and to hold my own counsel about it.

## CHAPTER IV

NEXT day, I chose a seven-foot staff of ash, and fixed a loach-fork in it, to look as I had looked before; and leaving word upon matters of business, out of the back door I went, and so through the little orchard, and down the brawling Lynn brook. Not being now so much afraid, I struck across the thicket land between the meeting waters, and came upon the Bagworthy stream near the great black whirlpool. And still the great rocky slide was dark and difficult to climb; though the water, which once had taken my knees, was satisfied now with my ankles. After some labour, I reached the top; and halted to look about me well, before trusting to broad daylight.

While I was letting my thoughts go wild to sounds and sights of nature, a sweet song floated on the valley breeze at the quiet turn of sundown. I ventured to look forth where a bush was; and then I beheld the loveliest sight. By the side of the stream she was coming to me. The tremulous thrill of her song was hanging on her open lips; and she glanced around, as if the birds were accustomed to make answer. Scarcely knowing what I did, I came from the dark mouth of the chasm; and stood, afraid to look at her.

She was turning to fly, not knowing me, when I fell on the grass (as I fell before her seven years agone that day), and I just said, "Lorna Doone."

"Of, if you please, who are you, sir, and how do you know my name?"

"I am John Ridd," I answered, "the boy who gave you those beautiful fish, when you were only a little thing, seven years ago to-day."

"Oh, yes, I remember everything. But you seem not to remember, sir, how perilous this place is."

"Yes, I know enough of that; and I am frightened greatly, all the time, when I do not look at you."

Therefore without more ado, it struck me that I had better go, and have no more to say to her until next time of coming.

"Mistress Lorna, I will depart in fear of causing disquiet. Try to think of me now and then, and I will bring you some new-laid eggs."

"I thank you heartily," said Lorna; "you can put them in my little bower, where I am almost always—I mean whither daily I repair to read and to be away from them."

So I touched her white hand softly when she gave it to me, and for the rest of the homeward road, was mad with every man in the world who would dare to think of having her.

When the weather changed in earnest, and the frost was gone, and the south-west wind blew softly, it was more than I could do to keep from thought of Lorna, and as no Lorna came to me, except in dreams or fancy, forth I must again to find her. Therefore, without waiting longer for the moving of the spring, dressed I was in grand attire, and thinking my appearance good, round the corner of the woodstack went I very knowingly, and then I was sure of meeting none who would care or dare to speak to me.

I longed to take my gun, but when I came to remember the slippery nature of the waterslide, there seemed but little likelihood of keeping the powder dry. Therefore I was armed with nothing but a good stout holly staff, seasoned well for many a winter in our back-kitchen chimney.

I reached the top ere dark with more difficulty than danger, and sat in a place which comforted my back and legs so desirably, that I fell asleep.

Suddenly my sleep was broken by a shade cast over me; between me and the sunlight Lorna Doone was standing.

"Master Ridd, are you mad?" she said. "The Patrol will be here directly. Be quick, Master Ridd, let me hide thee."

"I will not stir a step," said I, "unless you call me 'John.'"

"Well, John, then—be quick, if you have any to care for you."

Without another word

*"Who are you, sir, and how do you know my name?"*

she led me to her little bower. The chamber was of unhewn rock, and gay with rich variety of fern, moss and lichen. Overhead there was no ceiling, but the sky itself, flaked with little clouds. The floor was made of soft low grass, mixed with moss and primroses; and in the midst a tiny spring arose.

While I was gazing at all these things, Lorna turned upon me lightly, and said :—

"Where are the new-laid eggs, Master Ridd?"

"Here be some," I answered, and I laid her out two dozen upon the moss of the rock-ledge. Lorna looked with growing wonder, and to my amazement burst into a flood of tears.

"What have I done?" I asked, "to vex you so?"

She answered very proudly, "You have been too kind; and I am not used to kindness."

Some sort of awkwardness was on me, at her words and weeping, therefore I abstained from speech. And as it happened, this was the way to make her tell me more about it. Although it wearied me no whit, it might be wearisome for folk who cannot look at Lorna, to hear the story all in speech, exactly as she told it; therefore, let me put it shortly to the best of my remembrance.

"I have no remembrance now of father or of mother; although they say that my father was the eldest son of Sir Ensor Doone, and the bravest and the best of them. And so they call me heiress to this little realm of violence. What I want to know is something none of them can tell me— what am I, and why set here, and when shall I be with them?

"Meantime, all around me is violence and robbery, coarse delight and savage pain, reckless joke and hopeless death. There is none to lead me forward, there is none to teach me right; young as I am, I live beneath a curse that lasts for ever."

Here Lorna broke down for a while, and cried so very piteously, that I went to wipe her eyes for her.

"Master Ridd," she began again, "it does not happen many times that I give way like this; more shame now to do so, when I ought to entertain you. But when I try to search the past, to get a sense of what befell me ere my own perception formed; to feel back for the lines of childhood, as a trace of gossamer, then I only know that nought lives longer than God wills it.

"We should not be so quiet here, and safe from interruption, but that I have begged one privilege rather than commanded it. This was that this narrowing of the valley might be looked upon as mine, except for purposes of guard. Therefore none beside the sentries ever trespass on me here, unless it be my grandfather, or the Counsellor or Carver.

"By your face, Master Ridd, I see that you have heard of Carver Doone. For strength and courage and resource he bears the first repute among us, as might well be expected from the son of the Counsellor."

"Among the riders there is none whose safe return I watch for, and indeed there seems no risk, all are now so feared of us. Neither of the old men is there whom I can revere or love (except alone my grandfather, whom I love with trembling); neither of the women any whom I like to deal with, unless it be Gwenny Carfax, a little maiden whom I saved from starving.

" Oftentimes I am vexed by things I cannot meddle with, yet which cannot be kept from me, so that I am at the point of flying from this dreadful valley, and risking all that can betide me in the unknown outer world. If it were not for my grandfather, I would have done so long ago ; but I cannot bear that he should die with no gentle hand to comfort him ; and I fear to think of the conflict that must ensue for the government, if there be a disputed succession.

" Of all this golden ease I hear, but never saw the like of it ; and haply, I shall never do so, being born to turbulence. Once, indeed, I had the offer of escape, and high place in the gay, bright world ; and yet I was not tempted much, or, at least, dared not to trust it." Here Lorna Doone could tell no more, being overcome with weeping.

After hearing that tale from Lorna, I went home in sorry spirits, having added fear for her, and misery about, to all my other ailments.

## CHAPTER V

ONE afternoon, when work was over, a man came riding up from the ford where the road goes through the Lynn stream. He stopped at our gate and hallooed as if he were somebody ; and all the time he was flourishing a white thing in the air.

" Service of the King ! " he saith ; " service of our lord the King ! Come hither, thou great yokel, at risk of fine and imprisonment."

Although not pleased, I went to him, as became a loyal man.

" Plover's Barrows farm ! " said he ; " God only know how tired I be. Is there anywhere in this cursed county a place called Plover's Barrows farm ? "

" Sir," I replied, " this is Plover's Barrows farm, and you are kindly welcome."

" Hungry I am, and sore of body ; yet may I not rest nor bite barley-bread until I have seen and touched John Ridd. God grant that he be not far away ! "

" Have no fear, good sir," I answered ; " you have seen and touched John Ridd. I am he."

" John Ridd, in the name of the King, His Majesty, Charles the Second, these presents ! "

He touched me with the white thing which I had first seen him waving, and which I now beheld to be sheepskin, such as they call parchment. It was tied across with cord, and fastened down with dabs of wax. By order of the messenger I broke the seals, and there I saw my name in large.

" Read, my son ; read, thou great fool if indeed thou canst read," said the officer to encourage me ; " there is nothing to kill thee, boy, and my supper will be spoiling."

" If you please, sir, what is your name ? " I asked.

" Jeremy Stickles is my name, lad, nothing more than a poor apparitor of the worshipful Court of King's Bench."

Then I read pretty nigh as follows : not that I give the whole of it, but only the gist and the emphasis :—

"To our good subject, John Ridd, etc., by these presents, greeting. These are to require thee, in the name of our lord the King, to appear in person before the Right Worshipful, the Justices of His Majesty's Bench at Westminster, laying aside all thine own business, and there to deliver such evidence as is within thy cognisance, touching certain matters whereby the peace of our said lord the King, and the well-being of this realm, is, are, or otherwise may be impeached, impugned, imperilled, or otherwise detrimented. As witness these presents." And then there were four seals, and then a signature I could not make out, only that it began with a J. Underneath was added in a different handwriting, "Charges will be borne. The matter is full urgent."

The messenger watched me, while I read so much as I could read of it ; and he seemed well pleased with my surprise, because he had expected it. Then, not knowing what else to do, I looked again at the cover, and on the top of it I saw, "Ride, Ride, Ride ! On his Gracious Majesty's business ; spur and spare not."

"Now, Master Stickles, when must we start ? " I asked him.

"My son Jack," replied Master Stickles, "never was I in such quarters yet ; and God forbid that I should be so unthankful to Him as to hurry away. And now I think on it, Friday is not a day upon which pious people love to commence an enterprise. I will choose the young pig to-morrow at noon, at which time they are wont to gambol ; and we will celebrate his birthday by carving him on Friday. After that we will gird our loins and set forth early on Saturday."

By dinner-time on Saturday we arrived at Porlock, and dined with my old friend, Master Pooke, now growing rich and portly. Thence we hired to Bridgwater, and from Bridgwater on to Bristowe, breaking the journey between the two. We never could have made our journey without either fight or running, but for the free pass which Annie had procured from her friend, Master Faggus the highwayman. And when I let it be known, by some hap, that I was the own cousin of Tom Faggus, there was not a house upon the road but was proud to entertain me, in spite of my fellow-traveller bearing the red badge of the King.

Now this being the year of our Lord 1683, more than nine years and a half since the death of my father, and the beginning of this history, all London was in a great ferment about the dispute between the Court of the King and the City. This seemed to occupy all the attention of the judges, and my case (which had appeared so urgent) was put off from time to time, while the Court and the City contended.

In Westminster Hall I found nobody ; not even the crowd of crawling varlets, who used to be craving evermore for employment or for payment. And before I had time to make up my mind what I should do the crier of the Court came out, and wanted to know who I was. I told him, as shortly as I could, that my business lay with His Majesty's bench, and was very confidential ; upon which he took me inside with warning, and showed me to an under-clerk, who showed me to a higher one, and the higher clerk to the head one.

When this gentleman understood all about my business he frowned at me very heavily, as if I had done him an injury.

"John Ridd," he asked me with a stern glance, "is it your deliberate desire to be brought into the presence of the Lord Chief Justice?"

*The messenger watched me while I read as much as I could of the manuscript.*

"Surely, sir, it has been my desire for the last two months."

"Now, if my lord cross-question you," the gentleman whispered to me, "answer him straight out truth at once, for he will have it out of thee. And mind, he loves not to be contradicted, neither can he bear a hang-dog look. Take little heed of the other two; but note every word of the middle one; and never make him speak twice."

I thanked him for his good advice, as he moved the curtain and thrust me in, but instead of entering withdrew, and left me to bear the brunt of it. There were only three men sitting here, one in the centre, and one on each side; and all three were done up wonderfully with fur, and robes of state, and curls of thick grey horsehair, crimped and gathered, and plaited down to their shoulders. Before I had time to look around twice, a stout man espied me, and shouted out with a flashing stare:—

"How now, countryman, who art thou?"

"May it please your worship," I answered him loudly, "I am John Ridd, of Oare Parish, in the shire of Somerset, brought to this London, some two months back by a special messenger, whose name is Jeremy Stickles; and then bound over to be at hand and ready, when called upon to give evidence, in a matter unknown to me. And now I desire to ask your worship, whether I may go home again?"

"Well done, John," replied his lordship, "I remember the matter well; and I myself will attend to it, although it arose before my time"—he was but newly Chief Justice—"but I cannot take it now, John. There is no fear of losing thee, John, any more than the Tower of London. I grieve for His Majesty's exchequer, after keeping thee two months or more."

"Nay, my lord, I crave your pardon. Not a groat have I received."

"Spank, is it so?" his lordship cried.

"My lord, my lord," whispered Mr. Spank, the chief-officer of evidence, "the thing has been overlooked, my lord, among such grave matters of treason."

"John Ridd," said the Lord Chief Justice, "thou hast been shamefully used, John Ridd. Answer me not, boy, not a word, but go to Master

Spank, and let me know how he behaves to thee; be thou here again to-morrow; and I will see justice done to thee. Now be off, boy; thy name is Ridd, and we are well rid of thee."

In the morning I met Mr. Spank waiting for me at the entrance, and very desirous to see me. He whispered:

"He is all alone this morning, John, and in rare good humour. John Ridd, my lord!" With that he swung up the curtain bravely; and according to special orders, I stood alone with Judge Jeffreys.

"May it please your worship," I said, "here I am according to order, awaiting your good pleasure."

"Hadst better answer me everything, lump. Now is there in thy neighbourhood a certain nest of robbers, miscreants, and outlaws, whom all men fear to handle?"

"Yes, my lord. At least, I believe some of them be robbers; and all of them are outlaws."

"What is the name of this pestilent race, and how many of them are there?"

"They are the Doones of Bagworthy forest, may it please your worship. And we reckon there be about forty of them, beside the women and children."

"Forty Doones, all forty thieves! and women and children! How long have they been there, then?"

"They may have been there thirty years, my lord; and indeed they may have been forty."

"Ay, long before thou wast born, John. There is a family called De Whichehalse living very nigh thee, John?"

"Yes, my lord, there is. At least, not so very far from us. Baron de Whichehalse, of Lay Manor."

"Now hast thou ever heard or thought that De Whichehalse is in league with the Doones of Bagworthy?"

Saying these words rather slowly, he skewered his great eyes into mine, so that it set my wits all wandering; and looking into me, he saw that I was groping for the truth.

"John Ridd, thine eyes are enough for me. I see thou hast never dreamed of it. Now hast thou ever seen a man whose name is Thomas Faggus?"

"Yes, sir, many a time. He is my own worthy cousin; and I fear he hath intentions——" Here I stopped, having no right to speak about our Annie.

"Tom Faggus is a good man," he said; and his great square face had a smile which showed me he had met my cousin; "Master Faggus hath made mistakes as to the title to property, as lawyers oftentimes may do; but take him all for all, he is a thoroughly straightforward man; presents his bill, and has it paid, and makes no charge for drawing it. Nevertheless, we must tax his costs, as of any other solicitor."

"To be sure, my lord!" was all that I could say, not understanding what all this meant.

"I fear he will come to the gallows," said the Lord Chief Justice, sinking his voice below the echoes; "tell him this from me, Jack.

"Now I have heard things in Taunton, and even nearer to you in Dulverton, and ever nigher still upon Exmoor; things which are of the pillory kind, and even more of the gallows. I see that you know naught of them. Nevertheless, it will not be long before all England hears of them. Now, John, I have taken a liking to thee; for never man told me the truth, without fear or favour, more thoroughly and truly than you hast done. Keep thou clear of this, my son. It will come to nothing; yet many shall swing high for it. Even I could not save thee, John Ridd, if thou were mixed in this affair. Keep from the Doones, keep from De Whichehalse, keep from everything which leads beyond the sight of thy knowledge. Now, get thee gone, Jack. I shall remember thee; and, I trow, thou wilt'st not forget me."

But though he had so far dismissed me, I was not yet quite free to go, in as much as I had not money enough to take me all the way to Oare, unless indeed I should go afoot, and beg my sustenance by the way, which seemed to go below me.

But I was saved in some degree from this lowering of my pride, for going to buy with my last crown-piece a little shot and powder, more needful on the road almost than even shoes or victuals, at the corner of the street I met my good friend Jeremy Stickles.

"Five pounds thou shalt have, Jack," said Jeremy Stickles; "five pounds, and I will take my chance of wringing it from that great rogue Spank. Put back your bits of paper, lad; I will have no acknowledgment. John Ridd, no nonsense with me!"

## CHAPTER VI

IT was the beginning of wheat-harvest, when I came to Dunster town, having walked all the way from London, and being somewhat footsore. For though five pounds was enough to keep me in food and lodging upon the road, it would have been nothing for horse-hire, as I knew too well by the prices Jeremy Stickles had paid upon our way to London. But being once there my troubles were gone, for mother's cousin, the worthy tanner, was in such indignation at the plight in which I came back to him, afoot, and weary, and almost shoeless, that he sent me forth on the very strongest nag he had.

But how shall I tell you the things I felt, and the swelling of my heart within me, as I drew nearer to the place of all I loved and owned—in a word, to home?

But it would take me all the afternoon to lay before you one-tenth of the things which came home to me in that one half-hour, as the sun was sinking. Mother, Annie, and little Eliza all declared how glad they were that I was home, and happier people could not be found than the whole of us were that evening.

Much as I longed to know more about Lorna, I could not leave them on the Sunday. So on the Monday morning what did I do but take my chance; reckless whether any one heeded me or not, only craving Lorna's heed, and time for ten words to her. Therefore I left the men of the farm as far away as might be, and strode right away, in good trust of my speed, without any more misgivings; but resolved to face the worst of it, and try to be home for supper.

And first I went to the crest of the broken highland, whence I had agreed to watch for any mark or signal. And, sure enough, at last I saw that the white stone had been covered over with a cloth or mantle—the sign that something had arisen to make Lorna want me. For a moment I stood amazed at my evil fortune; that I should be too late, in the very thing of all things on which my heart was set! Then after eyeing sorrowfully every crick and cranny to be sure that not a single flutter of my love was visible, off I set, with small respect either for my knees or neck, to make the round of the outer cliffs, and come up my old access.

At last a little figure came, in and out the wealth of trees, and liberty of the meadow. I know not whether my own Lorna was afraid of what I might say to her, or of her own thoughts of me; all I know is that she looked frightened, when I hoped for gladness.

*Tears of sorrow and reproach were lurking in her soft dark eyes.*

Therefore I went slowly towards her, and said all I could come to say with some distress in doing it.

"Mistress Lorna, I had hope that you were in need of me."

"Oh, yes; but that was long ago; two months ago, or more, sir." And saying this, she led me to her own rich bower.

"Then wanted me to promise, and even to swear a solemn oath, that I would wed my eldest cousin, this Carver Doone, who is twice as old as I am, being thirty-five and upwards. That was why I gave the token that I wished to see you, Master Ridd. And now I am watched, and spied, and followed, and half my little liberty seems to be taken from me. I could not be here speaking with you, even in my own nook and refuge, but for the aid of dear little Gwenny Carfax. She is now my chief reliance, and through her alone I hope to baffle all my enemies, since others have forsaken me."

Tears of sorrow and reproach were lurking in her soft dark eyes, until in fewest words I told her that my seeming negligence was nothing but my wretched absence far away; of which I had so vainly striven to give any tidings without danger to her. When she heard all this I raised her left hand, and before she could guess what I was up to, on her finger was my ring—sapphire for the veins of blue, and pearls to match the white fingers.

She drew my ring from off her finger and held it out to me; " John, I dare not take it now; else I should be cheating you. I will try to love you dearly, even as you deserve and wish. Keep it for me just till then."

Upon that she laughed at me in the sweetest manner, so that I knew—as in a glory—that Lorna Doone had now begun and would go on to love me.

## CHAPTER VII

ALTHOUGH I was under interdict for two months from my darling—lighter heart was not on Exmoor than I bore for half the time. For she was safe; I knew that daily by a mode of signals. Then the golden harvest came. All the parish was assembled in our upper courtyard; for we were to open the harvest that year. There must have been three-score of us, for the lane was full of people.

Parson Bowden read some verses from the parish Bible, then he laid the Bible down on the square head of the gate-post, and despite his gown and cassock, three good swipes he cut of corn.

When he had stowed the corn like that, mother entered, leaning on me, and we both said, " Thank the Lord for all His mercies, and these the first-fruits of His hand ! " And then the clerk gave out a psalm verse by verse, done very well. And when the psalm was sung, Parson took a stoop of cider and we all fell to at reaping.

Presently, I slipped away from the noise and went as far as my father's grave. I was surprised to see our Annie sitting there.

" What are you doing here, Annie ? " I inquired rather sternly.

" Oh, John, I will tell you everything, if you promise to forgive me. Oh, I am so miserable ! " and she laid her cheek against the tree, and sobbed till it was pitiful.

" Now will you stop ? " I said at last, harder than I meant it; for I knew that she would go on all night, if any one encouraged her.

" Yes, I will stop," said Annie, panting; " if somebody else had been taken so with a pain all round the heart, John, and no power of telling it, perhaps you would have coaxed, and made opportunity to be very loving."

" From your knowledge of these things, Annie, I demand to know this very moment who has taken such liberties."

" Cousins have a right to do things—and when they are one's god-father——" Here Annie stopped quite suddenly, having so betrayed herself; but met me in the full moonlight, being resolved to face it out.

" Alas, I feared it would come to this," I answered very sadly; " I knew he has been here many a time."

" You are not doing anything of that sort yourself, then, dear John ? "

" Only a common highwayman ! " I answered, without heeding her; " a man without an acre of his own, and liable to hang upon any common, and no other right of common over it——"

" John," said my sister, " are the Doones privileged not to be hanged upon common land ? "

At this I was thunderstruck, but soon discovered that she knew nothing, not even the name of my darling. Upon this I brought her back again to Tom Faggus and his doings.

"Now, Annie, don't talk nonsense so. I wish just to know the truth about you and Tom Faggus. Do you mean to marry him?"

"I to marry before my brother, and leave him with none to take care of him! Come home, dear, at once."

I allowed her to lead me home, where we found Uncle Ben with his granddaughter and heiress. My cousin Ruth arose, and made me a curtsey. And if ever any one looked unlike the heiress to great property, it was the little girl before me. Here mother came up to my rescue, as she always loved to do; and she said, "We have only been waiting for you, dear John, to have a little harvest dance, with the kitchen door thrown open."

There was no disobeying her, without rudeness; so I took little Ruth, and I spun her around, as the sound of the music came lively and ringing. Then Annie came sailing down the dance. She was blushing, with her fair cheeks red beneath her dear blue eyes, as she met my glance of surprise at the partner she was leaning on. It was Squire Marwood de Whichehalse. I would sooner have seen her with Tom Faggus, as indeed I had expected.

## CHAPTER VIII

I WAS up the very next morning before the sunrise, and away through the wild towards the Bagworthy water, at the foot of the long cascade. Much abashed with joy was I, when I saw my Lorna coming. Suddenly at sight of me, the bloom upon her cheeks was deepened, and the radiance of her eyes; and she came to meet me gladly.

"If you are come on purpose to ask anything, why do you delay so?" She turned away bravely, but I saw that her lips were trembling.

"I have waited long and long," I pursued, "and though I am so far below you, I can wait no longer; but must have my answer."

While I spoke, she glanced up shyly through her fluttering lashes, flung both her arms around my neck, and answered with her heart on mine,— "Darling, I am yours, for ever and for ever."

By this time I had taken one sweet hand and slipped my little ring upon the finger; and this time Lorna kept it.

I hurried home with deep exulting, yet some misgivings, for Lorna had made me promise now to tell my mother everything. Unluckily for my designs, who should be sitting down at breakfast with my mother and the rest but Squire Faggus, as everybody now began to entitle him. Being resolved to allow him fair field to himself, though with great displeasure that a man of such illegal repute should marry into our family, I carried my breakfast upon my back, and spent the whole day with the furrows.

When I returned, Squire Faggus was gone, and as I entered the house mother sent for me. I would regret to write down what mother said about Lorna, in her first surprise and tribulation; not only because I was grieved by the gross injustice of it, but rather because it is not well, when people repent of hasty speech, to enter it against them.

However, by the afternoon, our mother sat on the garden bench, scarcely knowing which of us she ought to make the most of, or which deserved most pity. Not that she had forgiven yet the rivals to her love—Tom Faggus, I mean, and Lorna—but that she was beginning to think a little better of them now.

Then my own affairs were thrown into disorder, for suddenly, without any warning, all my Lorna's signals ceased. Three times I went and waited at the bottom of the valley, but though I waited far into the night, all was lonely, drear, and drenched with sodden isolation.

Before I betook myself home at night, I resolved to penetrate Glen Doone from the upper end, and learn all about my Lorna.

The journey was a great deal longer to fetch around the Southern hills, and enter by the Doone-gate, than to cross the lower land and steal in by the water-slide. As the road approached the entrance, it became more straight and strong, like a channel cut from rock, with the water brawling darkly along the naked side of it. Not a tree or bush was left, to shelter a man from bullets ; all was stern, and stiff, and rugged.

And here I was particularly unlucky, for as I drew near the very entrance, the moon like an enemy broke upon me, filling all the open spaces with the play of wavering light. I shrank back into the shadowy quarter, on the right side of the road ; and gloomily employed myself to watch the triple entrance, on which the moonlight fell askew.

All across and before the three rude and beetling archways hung a felled oak overhead, black, and thick, and threatening. Behind this tree, the rocky mouth was spanned, as by a gallery, with brushwood and piled timber, all upon a ledge of stone, where thirty men might lurk unseen, and fire at any invader. And the access to this portcullis place was through certain rocky chambers known to the tenants only.

But the cleverest of their devices was that, instead of one mouth only, there were three to choose from, with nothing to betoken which was the proper access. I plunged into the middle way, holding a long ash staff before me, shodden at the end with iron.

Presently I was in black darkness, groping along the wall. Then I stumbled over something hard, and sharp, and very cold, and when I arose and felt it, and knew it to be a culverin, I was somewhat reassured thereby, inasmuch as it was not likely that they would plant this engine except in the real and true entrance.

Therefore I went on again, more painfully and wearily, and presently found it to be good that I had received that knock, for otherwise I might have blundered full upon the sentries, and been shot without more ado. There seemed to be only two of them, of size indeed and stature as all the Doones must be. They looked very happy, and were playing at push-pin or some trivial game of that sort. Each was smoking a long clay pipe, and would laugh from time to time.

" How long am I to stand crouching here ? " I asked of myself. And then, I needs must give them a startler—the whoop of an owl, done so exactly, as John Fry had taught me, and echoed by the roof so fearfully, that one of them dropped the tinder box ; and the other caught up his gun and cocked it, at least as I judged by the sounds.

*The sentries were playing at push-pin or some trivial game of that sort.*

"Curse it, Charlie, what was that? It scared me so, I have dropped my box."

"My pipe is out, Phelps, ever so long. Give me the lanthorn, and stay here."

"Well said, my boy, well said! Go straight to Carver's, and he will punch your head into a new wick for your lanthorn."

"Will he, though? Two can play at that!" And so after some rude jests, and laughter, and a few more oaths, I heard Charlie coming toward me, with a loose and not too sober footfall. So I let him reel on unharmed; and thereupon it occurred to me that I could have no better guide, passing as he would exactly where I wished to be; that is to say under Lorna's window.

Warm with this idea, I hurried after Charleworth Doone, being resolved not to harm him now, unless my own life required it. And while I watched from behind a tree, the door of the farthest house was opened; and sure enough it was Carver's self who stood bare-headed, and half-undressed in the doorway.

"Who wants me this time of night?" he grumbled, in a gruff voice.

"All I want is a light for my lanthorn and a glass of schnapps, if thou hast it."

"What is become of thy light, then? Good for thee I am not on duty."

"A great owl flew between me and Phelps, as we watched beside the culverin, and so scared was he at our fierce bright eyes that he fell and knocked the light out."

"Likely tale, or likely lie, Charles! We will have the truth to-morrow. Here, take thy light and be gone with thee." Then he slammed the door in the young man's face, having kindled his lanthorn by this time; and Charlie went up to the watchplace again.

THE FIR TREE

"A story! A story!" shouted the children; and they drew a little fat
man towards the Tree; and he sat down just beneath it. (Page 249)

**JOHNNY SCAN-THE-DUST**

He was dressed as richly as a prince, and drove in a
carriage drawn by ten cream horses. (Page 274)

My heart was in my mouth when I stood in the shade by Lorna's window, and whispered her name gently. I durst not speak aloud, because I saw another watchman posted on the western cliff, and commanding all the valley. And now this man espied me against the wall of the house, and advanced and challenged me. The nozzle of his gun was pointed full upon me, with the moonlight striking the barrel. Being almost desperate about it, I began to whistle, and as luck would have it my lips fell into a strange tune I had heard from Charlie. To my surprise the man fell back, dropped his gun, and saluted. That tune was Carver Doone's passport (as I heard long afterwards), which Charleworth Doone had imitated. The sentinel took me for that vile Carver, and withdrew himself to a good distance.

Meanwhile he had done me the kindest service; for Lorna came to the window at once, to see what the cause of the shout was.

"Oh, Lorna, don't you know me?" I whispered from the side, being afraid of startling her by appearing over suddenly.

"John!" she cried, yet with sense enough not to speak aloud. "Oh, you must be mad, John."

"Now tell me," I said; "what means all this? Why are you so pent up here? Are you in any danger?"

"My poor grandfather is very ill! I fear that he will not live long. The Counsellor and his son are now the masters of the valley; and I dare not venture forth, for fear of anything they might do to me. When I went forth, to signal for you, Carver tried to seize me; but I was too quick for him. You must watch this house, both night and day."

"How can I go without settling anything?" I asked, very sensibly. "How shall I know of your danger now?"

"I have been thinking long of something," Lorna answered rapidly. "You see that tree with the seven rooks' nests, bright against the cliffs there? Gwenny can climb like any cat. If you see but six rooks' nests I am in peril. If you see but five, I am carried off by Carver."

And then I stole below Carver's house, in the shadow from the eastern cliff; and knowing enough of the village now, betook myself to my well-known track in returning from the valley.

## CHAPTER IX

WHEN I went up one morning to look for my seven rooks' nests, behold there were but six to be seen; for the topmost of them all was gone, and the most conspicuous. For me to enter the valley now, during the broad daylight, could have brought no comfort, but only harm to the maiden, and certain death to myself.

When it grew towards dark, I was just beginning to prepare for my circuit around the hills, when suddenly I saw a short figure approaching on the left side of my hiding-place. It proved to be the little maid Gwenny Carfax.

"Young man," she said, "you must come with me. Old man be dying; he won't die without first considering thee."

"Considering me!" I cried. "What can Sir Ensor Doone want with considering me? Has Mistress Lorna told him?"

" All concerning thee, and thy doings ; when she knowed old man were so near his end."

Therefore I followed Gwenny. As we crossed towards the Captain's house, we met a couple of great Doones lounging by the waterside. Gwenny said something to them, and although they stared very hard at me, they let me pass without hindrance. It is not too much to say that when the little maid opened Sir Ensor's door, my heart thumped quite as much with terror as with hope of Lorna's presence.

She led me into a cold, dark room, rough and very gloomy, although with two candles burning. There was an old man, very stern and comely, with death upon his countenance ; not lying in his bed, but set upright in a chair. Only in his great black eyes, fixed upon me solemnly, all the power of his body dwelt, all his soul was burning.

" Ah," said the old man, " are you that great John Ridd ? "

" John Ridd is my name, your honour," was all that I could answer ; " and hope your worship is better."

" Child, have you sense enough to know what you do ? "

" Yes, I know right well," I answered, " that I have set mine eyes far above my rank."

" Are you ignorant that Lorna Doone is born of the oldest families remaining in North Europe ? "

" Sir," I answered, " the Ridds, of Oare, have been honest men twice as long as the Doones have been rogues."

He continued as if I had never spoken. " You will pledge your word in Lorna's presence never to see or to seek her again ; never even to think of her more. Now call her, for I am weary."

I found my love crying softly at a little window.

" Ye two fools ! " Sir Ensor said, with a depth of contempt which no words may express. " Ye two fools ! "

" May it please your worship," I answered softly. " Maybe we are not such fools as we look. But though we be, we are well content, so long as we may be two fools together."

" Fools you are ; be fools for ever," said Sir Ensor Doone, at last, while we feared to break his thoughts. " It is the best thing I can wish you ; boy and girl, be boy and girl, until you have grandchildren."

Partly in bitterness he spoke, partly in pure weariness, and then he turned so as not to see us ; and his white hair fell around him.

An hour or two ere the old man died, when only we two were with him, he looked at us very dimly and softly, and let his hand drop downward, and crooked one knotted finger.

" He wants something out of the bed, dear," Lorna whispered to me, " see what it is." I followed the bent of his poor shrunken hand, and sought among the pilings ; and there I felt something hard and sharp, and drew it forth and gave it to him.

" Why, it is my glass necklace ! " Lorna cried, in great surprise ; " the necklace which he always promised me. But grandfather kept it, because the children wanted to pull it from my neck. May I have it now, dear grandfather ? "

Darling Lorna wept again, because the old man could not tell her (except by one very feeble nod) that she was doing what he wished. Then she gave to me the trinket, for the sake of safety; and I stowed it in my breast. He seemed to me to follow this, and to be well content.

After all was over, I strode home across the moors very sadly, trying to keep the cold away by virtue of quick movement. In the bitter morning I arose, knowing the time from the force of habit, although the room was so dark and grey. I spread the lattice open, and saw at once that not a moment must be lost, to save our stock. All the earth was flat with snow, all the air was thick with snow; more than this no man could see, for all the world was snowing.

That night such a frost ensued as we had never dreamed of. The kettle by the fire froze, and the crock upon the hearth-cheeks; many men were killed, and cattle rigid in their head-ropes. This terrible weather kept Tom Faggus from coming near our house for weeks; at which, indeed, I was not vexed a quarter so much as Annie was; for I had never half-approved of him as a husband for my sister, in spite of his purchase from Squire Bassett and the grant of the Royal pardon. And this, I say, was the smallest thing; for it was far more serious that we were losing half our stock, do all we could to shelter them. I fell to at once, upon a hint from Lizzie, and built myself a pair of strong and light snow-shoes.

Upon the following day I started on my road across the hills and valleys to look into the Doone Glen. And now it struck me all at once that perhaps her ewer was frozen, and perhaps her window would not shut, any more than mine would; and perhaps she wanted blankets. This idea worked me up to such a chill of sympathy, that seeing no Doones now about, I resolved to slide the cliffs, and bravely go to Lorna.

The house was partly drifted up, though not so much as ours was. I examined all the windows; but these were coated so with ice, like ferns and flowers and dazzling stars, that no one could so much as guess what might be inside of them. I was forced, much against my will, to venture to the door and knock. Then I heard a pattering of feet and a whispering going on and then a shrill voice through the keyhole, asking, " Who's there ? "

" Only me, John Ridd," I answered; and the door was opened about a couple of inches, and the little voice went on :—

" Put thy finger in, young man, with the old ring on it. But mind thee, if it be the wrong one, thou shalt never draw it back again."

Laughing at Gwenny's mighty threat, I showed my finger in the opening; upon which she let me in, and barred the door again like lightning.

" What is the meaning of all this, Gwenny ? " I asked.

" Maning enough, and bad maning, too," the Cornish girl made answer. " Us be shut in here, and starving, and durstn't let anybody in upon us."

I was so frightened by her eyes, full of wolfish hunger, that I drew forth a large piece of bread, and placed it in her hands. She leaped at it, and ran away round the corner with it, no doubt for her young mistress. I meanwhile was occupied, to the best of my ability, in taking my snow-shoes off, yet wondering much within myself why Lorna did not come to me.

But presently I knew the cause, for Gwenny called me, and I ran, and found she had fainted away. When she had been brought round and eaten something, I begged to know the meaning of this.

" The meaning is sad enough," said Lorna ; " and I see no way out of it. We are both to be starved until I let them do what they like."

" That is to say until you choose to marry Carver Doone, and be slowly killed by him ? "

" Slowly ! No, John, quickly. I hate him so intensely, that less than a week would kill me."

Then I spoke with a strange tingle upon both sides of my heart, knowing that this undertaking was a serious one for all, and might burn our farm down.

" If I warrant to take you safe, Lorna, will you come with me ? "

" To be sure I will, dear," said my beauty, with a smile and a glance to follow it ; " I have small alternative, to starve, or go with you, John."

" Gwenny, have you courage for it ? Will you come with your young mistress ? "

" Will I stay behind ? " cried Gwenny, in a voice that settled it. And so we began to arrange about it ; and I was much excited.

" Come to this frozen window, John, and see them light the stack-fire. The Doones are firing Dunkery beacon, to celebrate their new captain."

Though Lorna took it so in joke, I looked upon it very gravely ; and then my second thoughts convinced me that I was a fool. For lo, what an opportunity ! All the Doones would be drunk, of course, in about three hours' time, and getting worse as the night went on. As for the fire, it must sink in about three hours or more, and only cast uncertain shadows friendly to my purpose.

" Sweetest, in two hours' time I shall be again with you. Keep the bar up, and have Gwenny ready to answer any one. You are safe while they are dining, dear, and drinking healths, and all that stuff ; and before they have done with that, I shall be again with you. I shall knock loud, and then wait a little ; and then knock twice, very softly."

With this I folded her in my arms, and took my leave.

I hastened home at my utmost speed, and told my mother to keep the house up till my return, and to have plenty of fire blazing, and plenty of water boiling, and food enough hot for a dozen people, and the best bed aired with the warming-pan. After this I took some brandy and provisions, and then I went to the upper linhay, and took out our new light pony-sled. Just as I was starting, out came Annie with a sealskin cloak. With that I drew my traces hard, and set my ashen staff into the snow, and struck out with my best foot foremost, and the sled came after me as lightly as a dog might follow. Daring not to risk my sled by any fall from the valley-cliffs, I dragged it very carefully up the steep incline of ice, through the narrow chasm, and so to the very brink and verge where first I had seen my Lorna, in the fishing days of boyhood.

The stack-fire was still burning strongly, but with more of heat than blaze ; and many of the younger Doones were playing on the verge of it. All these I passed, without the smallest risk or difficulty, and then I crossed to the door of Lorna's house, and made the sign, and listened, after taking my snow-shoes off.

But no one came, as I expected, neither could I espy a light. Then I knocked again more loudly, with a knocking at my heart ; and receiving no answer, set all my power at once against the door. In a moment it flew inwards, and I glided along the passage with my feet still slippery. There in Lorna's room I saw, by the moonlight flowing in, a sight which drove me beyond sense.

Lorna was behind a chair, crouching in the corner, with her hands up. In the middle of the room lay Gwenny Carfax, stupid, yet with one hand clutching the ankle of a struggling man. Another man stood above my Lorna, trying to draw the chair away. In a moment I had him round the waist, and he went out of the window with a mighty crash of glass. Then I took the other man by the neck; and he could not plead for mercy. I bore him out of the house as lightly as I would bear a baby, yet squeezing his throat a little more than I fain would do to an infant. By the bright moonlight I saw that I carried Marwood de Whichehalse. I cast him, like a skittle, from me into

*" If I warrant to take you safe, Lorna, will you come with me ? "*

a snowdrift, which closed over him. Then I looked for the other fellow, and found him lying stunned and bleeding, neither able to groan yet. Charleworth Doone, if his gushing blood did not much mislead me.

It was no time to linger now; I fastened my shoes in a moment, caught up Lorna, and telling Gwenny to follow me, I ran the whole distance to my sled, caring not who might follow me. Then by the time I had set up Lorna, with the sealskin cloak all over her, sturdy Gwenny came along, with two bags on her back. I set her in beside her mistress, to support her and keep warm; and then with one look back at the glen, I hung behind the sled, and launched it down the steep and dangerous way. With my staff from rock to rock, and my weight thrown backward, I broke the sled's too rapid way, and brought my grown love safely out, by the self-same road which first had led me to her girlish fancy, and my boyish slavery.

At my door were all our people; but I put the others by, and fetched my mother forward. "You shall see her first," I said. "Is she not your daughter? Hold the light there, Annie."

Dear mother's hands were quick and trembling, as she saw my Lorna sleeping, and she bent and kissed her forehead. And then she was taken with violent weeping, and I was forced to hold her. With this, they carried Lorna into the house, and I went and brought Gwenny in.

I asked her how she could have been such a fool as to let those two vile fellows enter the house where Lorna was; and she accounted for it so naturally, that I could only blame myself. For my agreement had been to give one loud knock and after that two little knocks. Well, these two drunken rogues had come; and one, being very drunk indeed, had given a great thump; and the other had followed his leader but feebly, and making two of it. Whereupon up jumped Lorna, and declared that her John was there.

All this Gwenny told me shortly, and then there came a message for me that my love was sensible, and was seeking me. So I went to see my dear. In the settle was my Lorna, propped with pillows round her, and her clear hands spread sometimes to the blazing fireplace. In her eyes no knowledge was of anything around her, neither in her neck the sense of leaning towards anything. Only both her lovely hands were entreating something, to spare her, or to love her; and the lines of supplication quivered in her sad white face.

"All go away, except my mother," I said very quietly. Then mother came to me alone; and she said, "The frost is in her brain; I have heard of this before, John."

"Mother, I will have it out," was all that I could answer her; "leave her to me altogether; only you sit there and watch." For I felt that Lorna knew me, and no other soul but me; and that if not interfered with, she would soon come home to me. Therefore I sat gently by her, leaving nature,

*Lorna went to mother's heart by the very nearest road.*

as it were, to her own good time and will. And presently the glance that watched me, as at distance and in doubt, began to flutter and to brighten, and to deepen into kindness, then to beam with trust and love. But the small entreating hands found their way, as if by instinct, to my great projecting palms, and rested there.

For a little while we lingered thus, then a little sob disturbed us, and mother tried to make believe that she was only coughing. But Lorna, guessing who she was, jumped up and ran to the old oak chair, where mother was by the clock-case, pretending to be knitting, and she took the work from mother's hands, and laid them both upon her head, kneeling, humbly, and looking up.

" God bless you, my fair mistress ! " said mother, bending nearer, and then as Lorna's gaze prevailed, " God bless you, my sweet child ! " And so she went to mother's heart by the very nearest road.


## CHAPTER X

JEREMY STICKLES was gone south, ere ever the frost set in, for the purpose of mustering forces to attack the Doone Glen. But, of course, this weather had put a stop to every kind of movement ; for even if men could have borne the cold, they could scarcely be brought to face the perils of the snow-drifts.

Although it was the longest winter ever known in our parts (never having ceased to freeze for a single night, and scarcely for a single day, from the middle of December till the second week in March), to me it was the very shortest and the most delicious ; and verily I do believe it was the same to Lorna. But when the Ides of March were come, lo, there were increasing signals of a change of weather. The fog, which had hung about, vanished, and the shrouded hills shone forth with brightness manifold. When the first of the rain began, and the old familiar softness spread upon the window glass, and ran a little way in channels, knowing at once the difference from the short sharp thud of snow, we all ran out, and filled our eyes and hearts with gazing.

In truth it was time for me to work ; for the rain was now coming down in earnest ; and all outlets being blocked with ice set up like tables, it threatened to flood everything. It was not long before I managed to drain off this threatening flood, by opening the old sluice-hole ; but I had much harder work to keep the stables, and the cowhouse, and the other sheds from flooding.

At first the rain made no impression on the bulk of snow, but ran from every sloping surface and froze on every flat one, through the coldness of the earth ; and so it became impossible for any man to keep his legs without the help of a shodden staff. After a good while, however, the air growing very much warmer, this state of things began to change, and a worse one to succeed it ; for now the snow came thundering down from roof, and rock, and ivied tree, and floods began to roar and foam in every trough and gulley.

It was now high time to work very hard, both to make up for the farm-work lost during the months of frost and snow, and also to be ready for a great and vicious attack from the Doones, who would burn us in our beds at the earliest opportunity.

Now in spite of the floods, and the state of the roads most perilous, Squire Faggus came at last, riding his famous strawberry mare. There was a great ado between him and Annie, as you may well suppose, after some four months of parting.

Tom Faggus had very good news to tell. He had taken up his purchase from old Sir Roger Bassett of a nice bit of land, to the south of the moors, and in the parish of Molland. When the lawyers knew thoroughly who he was, and how he had made his money, they behaved uncommonly well to him, and showed great sympathy with his pursuits. Now this farm of Squire Faggus was of the very finest pasture, when it got good store of rain. And Tom saw at once what it was fit for—the breeding of fine cattle. Then he pressed us both on another point, the time for his marriage to Annie ; and mother looked at me to say when, and I looked back at mother. However, knowing something of the world, and unable to make any further objection, by reason of his prosperity, I said that we must even do as the fashionable people did, and allow the maid herself to settle when she would leave home and all. But Tom paid little heed to this, and left the room to submit himself to Annie.

Upon this I went in search of Lorna, to tell her of our cousin's arrival, and to ask whether she would think fit to see him, or to dine by herself that day ; for she should do exactly as it pleased her in everything, while remaining still our guest. But Lorna had some curiosity to know what this famous man was like, and declared that she would by all means have the pleasure of dining with him, if he did not object to her company on the ground of the Doones' dishonesty.

Accordingly she turned away, with one of her very sweetest smiles, saying that she must not meet a man of such fashion and renown in her common gardening frock ; but must try to look as nice as she could, if only in honour of dear Annie. And truth to tell, when she came to dinner, everything about her was the neatest and prettiest that can possibly be imagined.

Two things caught Squire Faggus's eyes, and he kept his bright bold gaze first on one, and then on the other, until my darling was hot with blushes. The two objects were first, Lorna's face, and secondly, the ancient necklace restored to her by Sir Ensor Doone.

Now when the young maidens were gone—for we had quite a high dinner of fashion that day, with Betty Muxworthy waiting, and Gwenny Carfax at the gravy—Squire Faggus said quite suddenly, and perhaps on purpose to take us aback, in case of our hiding anything.

"What do you know of the history of that beautiful maiden, good mother ? "

" Not half so much as my son does," mother answered, with a soft smile at me ; " and when John does not choose to tell a thing, wild horses will not pull it out of him."

" Bravo, our John Ridd ! " he answered ; " fools will be fools till the end of the chapter ; and I might be as big a one, if I were in thy shoes, John. Nevertheless, in the name of God, don't let that helpless child go about with a thing worth half the county on her."

"She is worth all the country herself," said I; "but she has nothing worth half a rick of hay upon her."

"Tush," Tom Faggus cried, "the necklace, you great oaf, the necklace is worth all your farm put together, and your Uncle Ben's fortune to the back of it; ay, and all the town of Dulverton."

"What," said I, "that common glass thing, which she has had from her childhood!"

"Glass indeed! They are the finest brilliants ever I set eyes on."

"Surely," cried mother, now flushing as red as Tom's own cheeks, with excitement, "you must be wrong, or the young mistress would herself have known it."

"Trust me," answered Tom, "trust me, good mother, and simple John, for knowing brilliants when I see them. I would have stopped an eight-horse coach, with four carabined outriders, for such a booty."

"Master Faggus," began my mother, with a manner of some dignity, "you have won my daughter's heart somehow; and you have won my consent to the matter through your honest sorrow, and manly undertaking to lead a different life, and touch no property but your own. Annie is my eldest daughter, and the child of a most upright man. I love her best of all on earth, next to my boy John here, and I will not risk my Annie's life with a man who yearns for the highway."

Having made this very long speech (for her), mother came home upon my shoulder, and wept so that (but for heeding her) I would have taken Tom by the nose, and thrown him, and Winnie, his horse, over our farmyard gate. Now, as nothing very long abides, it cannot be expected that a woman's anger should last very long, if she be at all of the proper sort. And my mother being one of the very best, could not long retain her wrath against the Squire Faggus. And, as Annie put the case, Tom deserved the greater credit for vanquishing so nobly these yearnings of his nature; and it seemed very hard to upbraid him, considering how good his motives were. But how my mother contrived to know, that because she had been too hard upon Tom, he must be right about the necklace, is a point which I never could clearly perceive, though no doubt she could explain it.

To prove herself right in the conclusion, she went herself to fetch Lorna, that the trinket might be examined, before the day grew dark. She laid the glittering circlet in my mother's hands, and Tom Faggus took it eagerly, and bore it to the window.

"What will you take for it, Mistress Lorna? At a hazard, say now."

"I am not accustomed to sell things, sir," replied Lorna. "What is it worth, in your opinion?"

"There are twenty-five diamonds in it, and twenty-five large brilliants that cannot be matched in London. How say you, Mistress Lorna, to a hundred thousand pounds?"

My darling's eyes so flashed at this, brighter than any diamonds, and she took the necklace quietly from the hands of Squire Faggus, and went up to my mother with the sweetest smile I ever saw.

"Dear kind mother, I am so glad," she said in a whisper. "Now you will have it, won't you, dear? And I shall be so happy; for a thousandth part of your kindness no jewels in the world can match."

*Tom Faggus had gotten again the necklace which had such charms for him, and was delivering a dissertation on precious stones.*

Mother knew not what to say. Of course, she would never dream of taking such a gift as that ; and she called me to help her. But knowing that my eyes were full, I pretended not to hear my mother, but to see a wild cat in the dairy.

Therefore I cannot tell what mother said in reply to Lorna ; for when I came back, behold Tom Faggus had gotten again the necklace which had such charms for him, and was delivering all around a dissertation on precious stones, and his sentiments on those in his hand.

He said that the necklace was made in Amsterdam, two or three hundred years ago, and on the gold clasp he found some letters, done in some inverted way ; also a bearing of some kind, which he believed was a mountain-cat. We said no more about the necklace for a long time afterwards, and Tom Faggus took his departure the day after his arrival.


## CHAPTER XI

SCARCELY was he out of sight when in came Master Jeremy Stickles, splashed with mud from head to foot, and not in the very best of humours, though happy to get back again.

"Curse those fellows !" he cried, "a pretty plight you may call this, for His Majesty's Commissioner to return to his headquarters in ! Well, this is better than being chased over the moors for one's life, John. All the way from Landacre Bridge, I had ridden a race for my precious life, at the peril of my limbs and neck with three great Doones galloping after me."

The weather had been against him bitterly, closing all the roads around him. It had taken him eight days, he said, to get from Exeter to Plymouth ; whither he found that most of the troops had been drafted off from Exeter. When all were told, there was but a battalion of one of the King's horse regiments, and two companies of foot soldiers ; and their commanders had orders, later than the date of Jeremy's commission, on no account to quit the southern coast and march inland. Therefore, although they would gladly have come for a brush with the celebrated Doones, it was more than they durst attempt, in the face of their instructions.

Jeremy made no doubt he might manage, with the help of his own men, to force the stranghold of the enemy ; but the truth was that the officers, knowing how hard it would be to collect their men at that time of the year, and in that state of the weather, began with one accord to make every possible excuse. And so it came to pass that the King's Commissioner returned without any army whatever ; but with promise of two hundred men when the roads should be more passable. And meanwhile, what were we to do, abandoned as we were to the mercies of the Doones, with only our own hands to help us ? And herein I grieved at my own folly in having let Tom Faggus go, whose wit and courage would have been worth at least half a dozen men to us. Upon this matter I held council with my friend Stickles ; telling him all about Lorna's presence, and what I knew of her history. He agreed with me that we could not hope to escape an attack from the outlaws and recommended that a watch must be maintained at night. He thought it wise that I should go to Lynmouth and fetch every one of his mounted troopers who might now be quartered there.

Knowing how fiercely the floods were out, I resolved to travel the higher road, by Cosgate and through Countisbury ; therefore I swam my horse through the Lynn, and thence galloped up and along the hills. I could see all the inland valleys ribboned with broad waters ; and in every winding crook, the banks of snow that fed them ; while on my right the turbid sea was flaked with April showers.

I followed the bank of the flood to the beach, and there had the luck to see Will Watcombe on the opposite side, caulking an old boat. Though I could not make him hear a word, I got him to understand that I wanted to cross over. Upon this he fetched another man, and the two of them launched a boat and, paddling well out to sea, fetched round the mouth of the frantic river. The other man proved to be Stickles' chief mate ; and so he went back and fetched his comrades, bringing their weapons, but leaving their horses behind. There were but four of them, but I started again for my home, and the men would follow afoot, crossing our river high up on the moorland.

It was lucky that I came home so soon ; for I found the house in a great commotion, and all the women trembling. When I asked what the matter was, Lorna answered that it was all her fault. She had stolen out to the garden towards dusk, to watch some favourite hyacinths just pushing up, when she descried two glittering eyes glaring at her steadfastly, and then a calm, cruel face appeared ; and she knew it was the face of Carver Doone.

The maiden could neither shriek nor fly, but only gaze, as if bewitched. Then Carver Doone lifted his gun and pointed full at Lorna's heart. Then he lowered the muzzle. When it pointed to the ground, he pulled the trigger, and the bullet flung the mould all over her. While she leaned there, quite unable yet to save herself, Carver came to the brink of the flood.

"I have spared you this time," he said in his deep voice, "only because it suits my plans. But unless you come back to-morrow, and teach me to destroy that fool who has destroyed himself for you, your death is here, where it has long been waiting." Then he turned away and Lorna saw his giant figure striding across the meadowland.

Now expecting a sharp attack that night, we prepared a great quantity of food. For we would almost surrender rather than keep our garrison hungry. We sent all the women to bed quite early, except Gwenny Carfax and our old Betty. It was not likely that the Doones could bring more than eight or ten men against us, while their homes were in danger from flood, and to meet these we had eight good men, including Jeremy and myself, besides our three farm-servants and the parish-clerk and the shoemaker. I was not content to abide within the house, or go the rounds with the troopers ; but betook myself to the rick-yard, knowing that the Doones were likely to begin there.

The robbers rode into our yard as coolly as if they had been invited, having lifted the gate from the hinges first on account of its being fastened. I could see our troopers round the corner from where the Doones were, and expecting the order to fire. But Jeremy Stickles wisely kept them in readiness, until the enemy should advance upon them.

"Two of you lazy fellows go," it was the voice of Carver Doone, "and make us a light to cut their throats by. Only one thing, once again. If any man touches Lorna, I will stab him where he stands. Now for our rights. We have borne too long the insolence of these yokels. Kill man and child, and burn the cursed place down."

While I was hesitating a blaze of fire lit up the house and brown smoke hung around it. Six of our men had let go at the Doones, by Jeremy Stickles' order. Being unable any longer to contain myself, I came across the yard, and went up to Carver Doone, and took him by the beard and said, "Do you call yourself a man?"

And with that word, I laid him flat upon his back in our straw-yard. Seeing him down, the others ran, and some of them got their horses, before our men came up ; and some went away without them. And among these last was Captain Carver.

## CHAPTER XII

POSSIBLY I may have mentioned that little Ruth Huckaback had promised to spend her Christmas with us. I was begged over and over again to go and see Ruth, and make all things straight. So one beautiful spring morning, up the lane I stoutly rode, well armed and well provided.

When I came home my sister Eliza met me and said, "Don't go in there, John," pointing to mother's room, "until I have had a talk with you."

"In the name of Moses," I inquired, "what are you at now?"

"It is nothing we are at," she answered ; "neither may you make light of it. It is something very important about Lorna Doone."

" Let us have it at once," I cried.

" Do you know a man nearly as broad as he is long, and with a length of snow-white hair, and a thickness also, as the copses were last winter ? "

I was almost sure that the man who was come must be the Counsellor himself, of whom I felt much keener fear than of his son Carver. And knowing that his visit boded ill to me and Lorna, I went and sought her and led her to meet our dreadful visitor. Mother was standing by the door, listening to a long harangue delivered by the Counsellor.

Feeling that I must speak first, I took my darling round the waist and led her up to the Counsellor.

" Now, Sir Counsellor Doone," I said, " you know right well that Sir Ensor Doone gave approval."

" Approval of what, good rustic John ? "

" To the love betwixt me and Lorna, which your story shall not break, without more evidence than your word."

The Counsellor looked with great wrath in his eyes. " Young people of the present age," said he severely, " have no right feeling of any sort, upon the simplest matter. Lorna Doone, stand forth and state in your own voice whether you regard this as a pleasant trifle."

" You know without any words of mine," she answered softly, " that if John will have me I am his for ever."

This speech was too much for her, and the Counsellor beckoned to me to come away.

After breakfast the next morning, the Counsellor followed Annie into the dairy, to see how we managed the clotted cream, and thereupon they talked

*The Counsellor followed Annie to see how we made our clotted cream.*

a little; and Annie thought him a fine old gentleman, for he had nobly condemned the people who spoke against Tom Faggus.

"Have you ever heard," asked the Counsellor, "that if you pass across the top, without breaking the surface, a string of beads, the cream will set three times as solid, and in thrice the quantity?"

"No, sir, I have never heard that," said Annie. "I will get my coral necklace; it will not be witchcraft, will it, sir?"

"Certainly not," the old man replied; "but coral will not do, my child. The beads must be of plain common glass; but the brighter they are the better."

"Then I know the very thing," cried Annie; "dearest Lorna has a necklace of some old glass-beads."

"Bring it here, Annie, if you know where it is."

"To be sure I do," she answered.

Now as luck would have it Lorna had taken it into her head that I was far too valuable to be trusted with her necklace. So she had led me to give it up. Therefore Annie found it sparkling in the secret hole, near the head of Lorna's bed, which she herself had recommended for its safer custody; and without a word to any one she brought it down, and danced it in the air before the Counsellor, for him to admire its lustre.

"Now," he said, in a stern whisper, "not a word of this to a soul; neither must you nor any other enter this place for three hours. By that time the charm will have done its work. Put the bauble under this pannikin; which none must lift for a day and a night. Have no fear, not a breath of harm shall come to you, if you obey my orders."

"Oh, sir, that I will, if you will only tell me what to do."

"Go to your room, without so much as a single word to any one. Bolt yourself in, and for three hours read the Lord's Prayer backwards."

Poor Annie was only too glad to escape, upon these conditions. Meanwhile the Counsellor was gone. He bade our mother adieu, with so much dignity of bearing, and such high-bred courtesy of the old school, that when he had gone, dear mother fell back on the chair which he had used last night, as if it would teach her the graces.

"Oh, the wickedness of the world! Oh, the lies that are told of people because a man is better born, or has better manners! Oh, Lizzie, you have read me beautiful things about Sir Gallyhead, and the rest; but nothing to equal Sir Counsellor."

"You had better marry him, madam," said I, coming in very sternly; "he can repay your adoration. He has stolen a hundred thousand pounds."

"John," cried my mother, "you are mad!"

"Of course I am, mother. He has gone off with Lorna's necklace."

Hereupon ensued grim silence. Mother looked at me, to know; and as for me, I could have stamped almost on the heart of any one. It was not the value of the necklace; it was my fury at the breach of hospitality.

## CHAPTER XIII

BUT who shall tell of Annie's grief ? When we raised the pannikin, and there was nothing under it, poor Annie fell against the wall, which had been whitened lately ; and her face put all the white to scorn.

The same night Master Jeremy Stickles came back, with all equipment ready for the grand attack. " You know, my son," said Jeremy, " six months ago, I was riding one afternoon from Dulverton to Watchett. It was late in the afternoon, and I was growing weary. Watchett town was not to be seen, but close at hand and in the corner, as snug a little house blinked on me as ever I saw. I made the old horse draw hard, and we clomb above the spring-tide mark, and over a little piece of turf, and struck the door of the hostelry. Some one came and peeped at me through the lattice overhead, and then the bolt was drawn back, and a dark and foreign-looking woman met me very courteously.

" ' Can I rest here for the night ? ' I asked, with a lift of my hat to her.

" ' Yes, sir, you can rest and welcome.'

" I became desirous to know why a clever and handsome woman could have settled here in this lonely inn, and what was the meaning of the emblem set above her doorway, a very unattractive cat sitting in a ruined tree ?

" However, I had not long to strain my curiosity ; for when she found out who I was, and how I held the King's commission, her desire to tell me all was more than equal to mine of hearing it.

" By birth she was an Italian, and her Christian name was Benita. Being a quick and active girl, she found employment in a large inn ; and here she met a rich and noble English family. Some bitter feud had been among them ; Benita knew not what it was.

" But this Benita did know that they were all great people, rich and liberal ; so that when they offered to take her, to attend to the children, she was only too glad to go.

" At first all things went well. Then one day my lord rode on in front of his wife and friends, to catch the first of a famous view, on the French side of the Pyrenees hills. They waited for him, long and long ; but he never came again ; and within a week his mangled body lay in a little chapel-yard.

" At the end of October, the little English family went home towards their England. They landed somewhere on the Devonshire coast, and set out for Watchett in Somerset. Through the fog and through the muck the coach went on, as best it might ; but when they came to the pitch and slope of the sea-bank, leading on towards Watchett town, they saw a troop of horsemen, waiting under a rock hard by and ready to dash upon them. The postilions lashed towards the sea, and the drivers drove into the sea until the leading horses were swimming.

" But before the waves came into the coach, a score of fierce men were round it. They cut the traces and seized the wheel-horses. Then, while the carriage was heeling over, the lady exclaimed, " I know that man ! He is our ancient enemy." And Benita snatched a magnificent necklace of diamonds and cast it over the little girl's head, hoping to save it. Then the coach was thrown on its side, and the sea rushed in.

"When Benita recovered her senses, she found herself lying upon the sand, and her mistress was sitting upright on a little rock.

"Before the light of the morning came along, my lady died, and she lies in Watchett little churchyard."

"And what became of the little girl? And why did the woman stay there?" I asked.

"Well!" cried Jeremy Stickles, only too glad to be cheerful again. "Benita stayed in that blessed place because she could not get away from it. The Doones—if Doones indeed they were—took every stiver out of the carriage. She married a man who turned a wheel for making the blue Watchett ware."

"I understand all that, Jeremy, though you do tell things too quickly. Now for my second question. What became of the little maid?"

"You great oaf!" cried Jeremy Stickles. "As certain as I stand here, that little maid is Lorna Doone."

His tale moved me greatly. For when he described the heavy coach and the breaking down at Dulverton and the place of their destination, my mind replaced the pictures first of the foreign lady's-maid by the pump, and the beautiful dame, but most of all the little girl.

Jeremy was quite decided that not a word of all these things must be imparted to Lorna, or even to mother.

"Jeremy, you are right," I answered. "But supposing that we should both be shot in this attack, is Lorna to remain untold of that which changes all her life?"

"Both shot!" cried Jeremy Stickles. "My goodness, boy, talk not like that! Nay, nay, the yellows shall go in front; we attack on the Somerset side, I think. I from a hill will reconnoitre, and you shall stick behind a tree."

I laughed, for I knew his never-flinching courage.


## CHAPTER XIV

THE yellows and the reds together numbered a hundred and twenty men, and besides these we had fifteen troopers of the regular army. Jeremy Stickles gave orders to march. It had been arranged that either body of men should act in its own county only. So when we reached the top of the hill, the sons of Devon marched on, to attack with their culverin from the cliffs, and the yellow lads were to stay upon the eastern highland and keep their culverin in the woods.

The third culverin was entrusted to the fifteen troopers, who, with ten picked soldiers from either trained band, were to assault the Doone-gate itself; and with this force went Jeremy Stickles and myself. Now we five-and-thirty men lay back, in the hollow of the track which leads to the strong Doone-gate. Our culverin was loaded now to the muzzle. At last we heard the loud bang-bang, which proved that Devon and Somerset were pouring their indignation hot into the den of malefactors, or at least so we supposed; therefore we advanced round the bend of the cliff, hoping to find the gate

*On I leaped, like a madman, and pounced on one gunner.*

undefended, and to blow down all barriers with the fire of our cannon. We shouted a loud hurrah, as for an easy victory.

But while the sound of our cheer rang back, a shrill clear whistle cleft the air, and then a dozen carbines bellowed, and all among us flew murderous lead. " Now, my lads," cried Jeremy, " one dash and we are beyond them ! "

Our men with a brave shout leaped in under the feet of the foe, before they could load their guns again. But here an awful crash rang behind us, with the shrieks of men, and the din of metal, and the horrible screaming of horses. The trunk of the tree had been launched overhead, and crashed into the very midst of us. Our cannon was under it, so were two men, and a horse with his poor back broken,

Now I lost all presence of mind at this, and dashed headlong into the cavern. On I leaped, like a madman, and pounced on one gunner and hurled him across his culverin ; but the others had fled, and a heavy oak door fell to with a bang behind them. I hurried back to seek Jeremy, fearing that he must be smitten down. And so indeed I found him. The shot had taken him in the mouth ; about that no doubt could be, for two of his teeth were in his beard and one of his lips was wanting.

Finding nothing more to be done in the way of carrying on the war, we laid poor Master Stickles and two more of the wounded upon the carriage of bark and hurdles, and sadly wended homewards. Two of the Devonshire officers now took command of the men who were left and ordered all to go home again. So the Devonshire men went home, and our Somerset friends only stayed for two days more to backbite them.

Colonel Stickles' illness was a grievous thing to us, in that we had no one now to command the troopers. Be as it might, we knew that they once resolved to go, all our goods, ay, and our precious lives, would be at the mercy of the Doones. But yet another cause arose to prove the need of Stickles' aid, and calamity of his illness. For two men appeared at our gate one day, stripped to their shirts, void of horses, and looking very sorrowful.

These two fellows were come, for the public benefit, from the Court of Chancery. The Doones had welcomed the two apparitors and led them kindly down the valley, and told them then to serve their writ. Misliking the look of things, these poor men began to fumble among their clothes ; upon which the Doones stripped and lashed them out of the valley ; only bidding them come to us, if they wanted Lorna Doone.

We comforted and cheered them so considerably, that they showed their writs, to which they had stuck like leeches. And these were twofold ; one addressed to Mistress Lorna Doone, and bidding her keep in readiness to travel whenever called upon, and commit herself to nobody, except the accredited messengers of the right honourable Court ; while the other was addressed to all subjects of His Majesty, having custody of Lorna Doone, or any power over her. And now having Jeremy Stickles' leave, I laid bare to my mother as well what I knew concerning Lorna's parentage.

And then I said, " Now we are bound to tell Lorna, and to serve her citation upon her, which these good fellows have given us."

" Then go and do it thyself, my son," mother replied with a mournful smile. So I went to seek my darling.

" Now, Lorna," said I, " come and hear my moving story."

" I can bear anything."

" You are not a Doone, my Lorna, for that, at least, I can answer ; though I know not what your name is."

" And my father—what I mean is——"

" Your father was killed by an accident in the Pyrenean mountains, and your mother by the Doones—or at least they caused her death, and carried you away from her."

When my tale was done, she turned away and wept bitterly for the sad fate of her parents.

Now, instead of getting better, Colonel Stickles grew worse, and he roused himself up to a fever when he learned that Sergeant Bloxham had taken upon himself to send to London by the Chancery officers a full report of what had happened, together with an urgent prayer for a full battalion of King's troops.

Not knowing what might happen, I set forth one day for Watchett. When I knocked at the little door, a voice came through the keyhole,—

" Who is that wishes to enter ? "

" The boy who was at the pump," said I, " when the carriage broke down at Dulverton."

" Come in, you great leetle boy," she answered, while her dark eyes brightened.

Madam Benita Odam showed me into a little room and sat down and studied me steadfastly. Not wanting to talk about myself, I led her back to that fearful night of the day when first I had seen her.

" Would you know her again ? " I asked. " Would you know her as a full-grown maiden ? "

" I think I should," she answered. " It is not possible to say until one sees the person ; but from the eyes of the little girl, I think that I must know her."

At last I made her promise to come with me on the morrow, and set off for Watchett, to see the grave of Lorna's poor mother. And here I heard that Lorna's father was the Earl of Dugal. I gathered a little grass for Lorna and a sprig of the weeping-tree, and then returned to the Inn. We set out pretty early, and arrived before dusk of the summer's day safe at Plover's Barrows.

The first who came to meet us at the gate was Lorna. In her joy she ran straight up to the cart, and then stopped and gazed at Benita. At one glance her old nurse knew her. " Oh, the eyes, the eyes ! " she cried, and was over the rail of the cart in a moment.

This being so, there could be no doubt as to the power of proving Lady Lorna's birth, and rights, both by evidence and token.


## CHAPTER XV

WHEN at last the time for Annie's wedding came, Lorna came to me with appealing eyes.

" What is it ? " I asked.

" You don't think, John, that you could lend me any money ? "

" All I have got," I answered. " How much do you want, dear ? "

" I fear that I cannot do with less than ten pounds, John."

" Oh, dear, yes," I replied. " I understand. You want to give Annie a wedding present. And you shall do it, because it is so good of you."

" What can I get her good enough ? I am sure I do not know," she asked. " By the by, you seem to think, John, that I shall be rich some day."

" Of course you will. Would the Lord Chancellor trouble himself about you, if you were poor ? "

" Then perhaps you would lend me twenty pounds, dear John."

To this I agreed, upon condition that I should make the purchase myself. For this end I set off to Dulverton. Uncle Reuben was not at home, but Ruth was sure of his return in the afternoon, and persuaded me to wait for him. And by the time that I had finished all of my orders, the old gentleman rode into the yard, and was more surprised than pleased to see me.

" Once for all, John, I have resolved to let you know my secret ; and for two good reasons. Now, who do you suppose is at the bottom of all this Exmoor rebellion—not that I say there is none, mind—but who is at the bottom of it ? "

" Old Nick himself," said I.

" Nay, old Uncle Reuben ! " Saying this, Master Huckaback stood up and made the most of himself.

" Meet me," he answered. " Come alone, of course ; and meet me at the Wizard's Slough at ten to-morrow morning."

Knowing Master Huckaback to be a man of his word, I was careful to be in good time the next morning, by the side of the Wizard's Slough. Old

Master Huckaback beckoned me to come to him. Without any more ado, he led me to a great round shaft, bratticed up with timber. He signed to me to lift a heavy wooden corb with an iron loop across it, and sunk in a little pit of earth a yard or so from the mouth of the shaft. A very stout thick rope was fastened to the handle of the corb, and ran across a pulley hanging from the centre of the beam.

"I will first descend," he said. "Your weight is too great for safety. When the bucket comes up again follow me."

Then he whistled down, and clomb into the vehicle, and Uncle Ben went merrily down, and was out of sight, before I had time to think of him. At last up came the bucket; and with a short sad prayer I went into whatever might happen.

"Hail to the world of gold, John Ridd," said Master Huckaback, smiling in the old dry manner; "bigger coward never came down the shaft, now did he, Carfax?"

"They be all alike," said a short, square man, "fust time as they does it." With these words, Uncle Ben led the way along a narrow passage, roofed with rock, until we stopped at a great stone boulder.

"Thou great villain!" cried Uncle Ben, giving the boulder a little kick. "I believe thy time has come at last. Now, John, take the biggest of them sledge-hammers and crack this rogue in two for us."

*I took up the hammer, and with all my power delivered a crashing blow.*

"I will do my very best," said I, "but I fear he will prove too tough for me." I took up the hammer, and with all my power descending delivered the ponderous onset. Crashing and crushed, the great stone fell over, and threads of sparkling gold appeared in the jagged sides of the breakage.

"Thou hast done us a good turn, my lad," said Uncle Reuben. "Now, John, not a word about what you have learned."

Now I have not judged it in any way needful to enter into my wrestling adventures, or describe my progress. But a mighty giant had arisen in a part of Cornwall; and his backers sent me a haughty challenge, to meet him in the ring at Bodmin-town, on the first day of August, or else to return my champion's belt to them by the messenger.

It is no use to deny that I was greatly dashed and scared at first.

However, my mother would never believe that this man could beat me ; and Lorna being of the same mind, I resolved to go and try him, as they would pay all expenses and a hundred pounds, if I conquered him.

Now this story is too well known for me to go through it again. But trusting in my practice and study of the art, I resolved to try a back with him ; and when my arms were round him once, the giant was but a farthingale put into the vice of a blacksmith. The man had no bones ; his frame sank in, and I was afraid of crushing him.

Now this affair made a noise at the time, and redounded so much to my credit that I was deeply grieved at it. However, I got my hundred pounds.

Now coming into the kitchen with all my cash in my pocket, I found mother most heartily glad to see me safe.

" Where is Lorna ? " I asked at length. " I want her to come and see my money."

" The lady Lorna Dugal," said Lizzie, " is gone to London, brother John. But she left a letter in the cupboard, near her bed."

Without another word I rushed up to Lorna's room, and espied my treasure. Part of it ran as follows :—" Take it not amiss of me that, even without farewell, I go ; for I cannot persuade the men to wait, your return being doubtful. My uncle is appointed my guardian, and I must live beneath his care until I am twenty-one. I offered to abandon all if they would only let me stay where I was, but they only laughed, and said I must talk of that to the King's High Chancellor. Of one thing rest you well assured—I ever shall be, your own Lorna Dugal."

" No doubt it is all over," my mind said to me bitterly ; " trust me, all shall yet be right," my heart replied very sweetly.

This season, the harvest was a heavy one, even heavier than the year before, although of poorer quality. Therefore I was forced to work as hard as any horse could during all the daylight hours, and defer till night the brooding upon my misfortune. And now the house was so dull and lonesome, wanting Annie's pretty presence, and the light of Lorna's eyes, that a man had no temptation after supper-time even to sit and smoke a pipe.


## CHAPTER XVI

ALL our neighbourhood was surprised that the Doones had not ere now attacked, and made an end of us. For we lay almost at their mercy now, having only Sergeant Bloxham, and three men, to protect us, Captain Stickles having been ordered southwards with all his force.

Now the reason why the Doones did not attack us was that they were preparing to meet another and more powerful assault, when the sudden death of King Charles the Second threw all things into confusion.

We heard of it first in church, on Sunday, the eighth day of February, 1684–5, from a cousin of John Fry, who had ridden over on purpose from Porlock. Almost before we had put off the mourning, which as loyal subjects we kept for the King three months and a week, rumours of disturbances, of plottings, and of outbreak began to stir among us.

Nevertheless, in our part, things went on as usual, until the middle of June was nigh. We ploughed the ground, and sowed the corn, and tended the cattle as carefully as before ; and the only thing that moved us much was that Annie had a baby.

But when I was down at the blacksmith's forge by Brendon town, round the corner came a man upon a piebald horse. He made a flourish with his horse, and waved a blue flag, shouting with great glory,—

" Monmouth and the Protestant faith ! Monmouth, the good King's eldest son ! Down with the poisoning murderer ! "

" Why so, thou little varlet ? " I asked quietly, for the man was too small to quarrel with.

" Papist yourself, be you ? " said the fellow. " Then take this, and read it."

And he handed me a long rigmarole, which he called a " Declaration." I saw that it was but a heap of lies, and thrust it into the blacksmith's fire and blew the bellows thrice at it.

For the next fortnight we were troubled with conflicting rumours, each man relating what he desired, rather than what he had right, to believe. We longed for Captain Stickles, for then we should have trusty news, as well as good consideration. All the soldiers had been ordered away at full speed for Exeter, to join the Duke of Albemarle. As for us, we must take our chance of Doones, or any other enemies.

One day at the beginning of July, I came home from mowing about noon, to fetch some cider for all of us, and to eat a morsel of bacon. When I entered the kitchen, behold there was our Annie, with my godson in her arms, and looking pale and tear-begone.

" Don't cry, my darling sister," I said, as she dropped into the worn place of the settle. " Tell me what it is, my dear. Any grief of yours will vex me greatly ; but I will try to bear it."

" Then, John, it is just this. Tom has gone off with the rebels ; and you must, oh, you must go after him."

Moved as I was by Annie's tears, I yet declared that I could not go, and leave our house and homestead, far less my dear mother and Lizzie, at the mercy of the merciless Doones.

" Is that all your objection, John ? " asked Annie, in her quick way. " Would you go but for that, John ? "

" Now," I said, " be in no such hurry, there are many things to be thought about, and many ways of viewing it."

" Oh, you never can have loved Lorna, John, you can love nobody but your oat-ricks and your hay-ricks."

" Sister mine, because I rant not, neither rave of what I feel, can you be so shallow as to dream that I feel nothing ? "

" I am very sorry, John. What a shallow fool I am ! "

" I will go seek your husband," I said, to change the subject.

Right early in the morning, I was off. I took Kickums, and being well charged both with bacon and powder, forth I set on my wild-goose chase.

I reached Bridgwater on a Sunday night, and having sought vainly for Tom Faggus, I took to my hostel ; and went to bed, being as weary as weary can be.

Through the open window I heard the distant roll of musketry, and the beating of drums. Therefore I reviled my laziness; and up I arose, woke Kickums, and set out to see the worst of it.

I was guided mainly by the sound of guns and trumpets, in riding out of the narrow ways, and into the open marshes. At last my horse heard the neigh of a fellow-horse, and was only too glad to answer it; upon which the other, having lost its rider, came up and pricked his ears at us, and gazed through the fog very steadfastly.

I dismounted in haste, for there stood Winnie, looking at me with beseeching eyes. I went to her side, and patted her; but that was not what she wanted. She ran away toward the part of the field at which she had been glancing back, and then turned round, and shook her mane, entreating me to follow her.

I mounted my own horse again and, to Winnie's great delight, professed myself at her service. With her ringing silvery neigh she at once proclaimed her triumph, and told her master that she was bringing one who might be trusted.

The last scene of this piteous play was acting just as I rode up. The cavalry of the King dashed from either side upon the helpless mob of country-men. A few pikes feebly levelled met them; but they shot the pikemen, drew swords, and helter-skelter leaped into the shattered and scattering mass. How it must end was plain enough, and when Winnie led me away to the left, I was only too glad to follow her.

She stopped in front of a low black shed, such as we called a " lin-hay."

*There I found her sniffing gently at the body of Tom Faggus.*

And here she uttered a little greeting and entered; and I followed. There I found her sniffing gently at the body of Tom Faggus. I raised him up; and there was a wound, a savage one, gaping and welling in his right side. I bound it up with some of my linen, and gave him a little weak brandy and water.

After that he seemed better, and a little colour came into his cheeks. Then he managed to whisper, " Is Winnie hurt ? "

" As sound as a roach," I answered. " Then so am I," said he. " Put me upon her back, John; she and I die together."

While I was hesitating, a storm of horse at full gallop went by, bearing away all the country before them. " Now is the time," said my cousin Tom. " On their heels, I am safe, John, if I have only Winnie under me."

With a strong sash around his damaged waist, I set him upon Winnie's back, and placed his trembling feet in stirrups.

" God bless you, John. I am safe," he whispered. " Who can come near my Winnie mare ? Look out for yourself, John Ridd." He sucked his lips, and the mare went off, as easy and swift as a swallow.

And now my way was home again. Nobody could say but what I had done my duty, and rescued Tom.

But while thinking these things, I fell into a posse of soldiers, from which there was no exit. These met me, swaggering heartily, and with their barrels of cider set, like so many cannon, across the road, over against a small hostel.

" We have won the victory, my lord King, and we mean to enjoy it. Down from thy horse, and have a stoup of cider, thou big rebel."

" No rebel am I. My name is John Ridd. I belong to the side of the King and I want some breakfast."

These fellows were truly hospitable. So I made the rarest breakfast any man might hope for, and getting on with these fellows better than could be expected, when up came some more soldiers.

Now these men upset everything. My partners in breakfast swore that I was no prisoner, but the finest-hearted fellow they had ever the luck to meet with. Whereas the men from the linhay swore that I was a rebel and have me they would.

While this fight was going on, and the men were breaking each other's heads, a superior officer rode up, with his sword drawn and his face on fire.

" What, my lambs, my lambs ! " he cried. " Is this how you waste my time and my purse ? Who is this young fellow we have here ? Speak up, sirrah. What art thou, and how much will thy good mother pay for thee ? "

" My mother will pay naught for me," I answered. " So please your worship, I am no rebel, but an honest farmer."

" Ha, ha, a farmer art thou ? Those fellows always pay the best. Good farmer, come to yon barren tree; thou shall make it fruitful."

Colonel Kirke made a sign to his men and, before I could resist, stout new ropes were flung around me; and with three men on either side, I was led along very painfully. It is not in my power to tell half the thoughts that moved me when we came to the fatal tree and saw two men hanging there already. Though ordered by the Colonel to look steadfastly upon them, I could not bear to do so; upon which he called me a paltry coward, and promised my breeches to any man who would spit upon my countenance.

This vile thing one stepped forward to do for me, trusting no doubt to the rope I was led with. But, unluckily for him, my right arms was free for a moment, and I dealt him such a blow that he never spake again. At the sound and sight of that bitter stroke, Colonel Kirke gave orders to shoot me. The men raised their pieces and pointed at me, and a cold sweat broke all over me as the Colonel began slowly to say, " Fire."

But while he was yet dwelling on the " F," the hoofs of a horse dashed out on the road, and horse and horseman flung themselves betwixt me and the gun muzzles.

" How now, Captain Stickles ? " cried Kirke. " Dare you, sir, to come betwixt me and my lawful prisoner ? "

" Nay, hearken one moment, Colonel," replied my old friend Jeremy. " For your own sake, hearken." He looked so full of momentous tidings, that Colonel Kirke made a sign to his men not to shoot me till further orders, and then he went aside with Stickles.

" Then I leave him in your hands, Captain Stickles," said Kirke at last, so that all might hear him ; " and I shall hold you answerable for the custody of this prisoner."

" Colonel Kirke, I will answer for him," Master Stickles replied, with a grave bow. " John Ridd, you are my prisoner. Follow me."

Upon that, those precious lambs flocked away, leaving the rope still around me. I wrung the hand of Jeremy Stickles, and he almost wept as he answered, " Turn for turn, John."

## CHAPTER XVII

JEREMY STICKLES assured me, as we took the road to Bridgwater, that the only chance for my life was to obtain an order for my despatch to London, as a suspected person, believed to be under the patronage of the great Lord Jeffreys.

We were lucky enough to find in London Lord Churchill, who received us with great civility, and granted the order for my safe deliverance to the Court of King's bench at Westminster, and Stickles was empowered to convey me.

It happened that I abode in London betwixt a month and five weeks' time, ere ever I saw Lorna. Nevertheless I heard of her from a worthy furrier (whose name was Ramsack), who told me that the nobleman to whose charge Lady Lorna had been committed, by the Court of Chancery, was Earl Brandir of Lochawe, her mother's uncle. This noble had a house near the village of Kensington ; and here his niece dwelled with him when she was not in attendance on Her Majesty the Queen, who had taken a liking to her. Now since the King had begun to attend the celebration of mass, in the chapel at Whitehall, he had given order that the doors should be thrown open so that all who could get into the ante-chamber might see this form of worship. Master Ramsack told me that Lorna was there almost every Sunday ; and the worthy furrier, having influence with the doorkeepers, kindly obtained admittance for me, one Sunday, into the ante-chamber.

When the King and Queen crossed the threshold, a mighty flourish of trumpets arose, and a waving of banners. After all the men were gone, some to this side, some to that, a number of ladies, beautifully dressed, being of the Queen's retinue, began to enter, and were stared at three times as much as the men had been. And indeed they were worth looking at, but none was so well worth eye-service as my Lorna. Her dress was of the purest white, very sweet and simple, and her stately supple carriage showed at a distance of a hundred yards that she could be none but Lorna Doone.

By some strange chance she saw me. While with shy quick steps she passed, some one trod on the skirt of her dress, she looked up, and her eyes met mine. As I gazed upon her I was satisfied. Lorna had seen me, and had not even tried to " cut " me.

While I was storing this up, in my memory, a lean man with a yellow beard came up to me. With many sighs, because I was not of the proper faith, he took my reprobate hand, looked up at me, and winked with one eye. Although the skin of my palms was thick, I felt a little suggestion there, so I paid the man, and he went happy. Then I lifted up my little billet and read it. I will not expose it to every man who buys this book. Enough that my love told me, in her letter, just to come and see her.

When I came to Earl Brandir's house, my natural modesty forbade me to appear at the door for guests ; therefore I went to the entrance for servants and retainers. Here, to my great surprise, who should come and let me in but little Gwenny Carfax. I followed her to a little room, and there she ordered me to wait.

Almost ere I hoped the velvet hangings of the doorway parted, and Lorna stood before the crimson folds. The hand she offered me I took, and raised

*The hand she offered me I took, and raised it to my lips with fear.*

it to my lips with fear. " Is that all ? " she whispered ; and in another instant she was weeping on my breast.

" Master John Ridd, you shall tell the truth, the whole truth, and nothing but the truth. Now, why have you never, for more than a twelve-month, taken the smallest notice of your old friend, Mistress Lorna Doone ? "

" Simply for this cause," I answered, " that my old friend and true love took not the smallest heed of me. Nor knew I where to find her."

" What ! " cried Lorna. I told her that not a single syllable of any message from her had reached me, since the letter she left behind.

" Oh, you poor John ! " said Lorna. " And now for the head traitor. I have often suspected it ; but she looks me in the face, and wishes—fearful things, which I cannot repeat."

With these words, she moved an implement, which made a ringing noise at a distance. Before I had ceased wondering little Gwenny Carfax came, with a sullen face.

" Now, Gwenny," said Lorna, " if you thought it honest to keep the letters I sent to Mr. Ridd, was it honest to keep the money ? "

At this the Cornish maiden broke into a rage of honesty. " A putt the money by for 'ee. 'Ee shall have ever farden of it."

" What made you treat me so, little Gwenny ? " I asked, for Lorna would not ask lest the reply should vex me.

" Because 'ee be'est below her so. Her shanna' have a poor farmering chap, not even if her were a Carnishman. All her land, and all her birth—and who be you, I'd like to know ? "

" Gwenny, you may go," said Lorna, reddening with quiet anger.

After this, we spoke of many things, and when I left she gave me a sweet kiss.

## CHAPTER XVIII

THE good Earl Brandir kept his money in a handsome pewter box, with his coat of arms upon it, and a double lid and locks. Moreover, there was a heavy chain, fixed to a staple in the wall, so that none might carry off the pewter with the gold inside of it.

Now one evening towards September I espied a pair of villainous fellows watching a corner behind the Earl's dwelling. I resolved to wait and see what those two villains did, and save (if it were possible) the Earl of Brandir's pewter box. But inasmuch as those bad men were almost sure to have seen me leaving the house and looking back, and striking out on the London road, I marched along at a merry pace, until they could not discern me ; and then I fetched a compass round, and refreshed myself at an inn.

Here I remained until it was dark, and I thought it right to leave. I took up my position, two hours before midnight, among the shrubs at the eastern end of Lord Brandir's mansion.

When all was quiet, I heard a low whistle from a clump of trees close by, and then three figures passed between me and a whitewashed wall, and came to a window which opened into the servants' basement. This window was raised by some one inside the house, and all three men entered.

I crept along the wall, and entered very quietly after them. Keeping well away in the dark, I saw these fellows force open the door of the good Earl Brandir. When I came to the door of the room, I beheld two men trying to break open the pewter box, and the third with a pistol-muzzle laid to the night-cap of his lordship. With foul words, this man was demanding the key of the box.

The thief with the pistol began to count, as I crossed the floor very quietly, while the old Earl fearfully gazed at the muzzle, but clenched the tighter his wrinkled hand. The villain cried, " Three," and pulled the trigger ; but luckily I struck up the barrel with my staff, so that the shot pierced the tester, and then I brought the good holly down upon the rascal's head, in a manner which stretched him upon the floor.

Meanwhile the other two robbers had taken alarm and rushed at me, one with a pistol and one with a hanger. Fearing the pistol most, I flung the heavy velvet curtain of the bed across, that he might not see where to aim at me, and then I caught up the senseless robber and set him up for a shield and target ; whereupon he was shot immediately.

Now the other two were at my mercy. So I took these two rogues and bound them together ; and in the morning they were brought before the Justices of the Peace ; and now my wonderful luck appeared. These fellows were recognised as the very men against whom His Majesty the King bore the bitterest rancour, but whom he had hitherto failed to catch.

In the course of that same afternoon I was sent for by His Majesty. In great alarm and flurry I put on my best clothes, and forth I set, with my holly staff, wishing myself well out of it. I was shown at once into His Majesty's presence, and there I stood most humbly, and made the best bow I could think of.

" I have seen thee before, young man," he said. " Where was it ? Thou art most likely to know."

" May it please Your Most Gracious Majesty the King," I answered, " it was in the Royal Chapel."

" I am well pleased," said His Majesty, " to find that our subject is also a good Catholic."

" This is that great Johann Reed," said Her Majesty, coming forward, " for whom I have so much heard from the dear Lorna."

" Now, John Ridd," said the King, " thou hast done great service to the realm, and to religion. It was good to save Earl Brandir, but it was great service to catch two of the vilest bloodhounds ever laid on by heretics. Now ask anything in reason. What is thy chief ambition, lad ? "

" Well," said I, " my mother always used to think that, having been schooled at Tiverton, I was worthy of a coat of arms. And that is what she longs for."

" Thou shalt have a coat, my lad," said the King, smiling at his own humour ; " but it must be a large one to fit thee. And more than that shalt thou have, John Ridd, having done such service."

And while I wondered what he meant, he called to some of the people in waiting, and they brought him a little sword. Then he signified to me to kneel, and then he gave me a little tap on my shoulder before I knew what he was up to, and said, " Arise, Sir John Ridd ! "

This astonished and amazed me to such extent that I said to the King, without forms of speech :

" Sir, I am very much obliged. But what be I to do with it ? "

Beginning to be short of money, and growing anxious about the farm, longing also to show myself and my noble escutcheon to mother, I took advantage of Lady Lorna's interest with the Queen to obtain my acquittance and full discharge from even nominal custody. When the air of the autumn cleared its way to Ludgate Hill, such a yearning seized me for moory crag, and even the grunting of our sheep, that nothing but the new wisps of Samson could have held me in London town.

On my return home all the parishes round about united in a sumptuous dinner, to which I was invited. And if my health was no better next day, it was not from want of good wishes.

## CHAPTER XIX

As the winter passed, the Doones were not keeping themselves at home, and in spite of all the pledges given, they had ridden forth and carried away two maidens of our neighbourhood. Before we had finished meditating on this outrage, we had news of a thing far worse. Mistress Margery Badcock was nursing her child about six of the clock, and looking out for her husband, when by the light of the kitchen fire she saw six or seven armed men burst into the room upon her ; and she screamed so that the maid in the back-kitchen heard her, but was afraid to come to help. Two of the strongest and fiercest men at once seized Margery, tore the babe from her arms, and cast it on the floor. Then they bore her away to their horses, and rode off with their prize to the valley. And from the description of one of those two who carried off the poor woman, I knew beyond all doubt that it was Carver Doone himself.

The other Doones being left behind, set to with a will to scour the house, and to bring away all that was good to eat. And being a little vexed, for the Badcocks were not a rich couple, they came back to the kitchen, and there was the baby lying.

" Let us have a game of loriot with the baby ! Bye, bye, baby Bunting. Toss him up, and let me see if my wrist be steady."

The cruelty of this man is a thing it makes me sick to speak of ; enough that when the poor baby fell, the maid hiding in the back-kitchen heard them say as follows—

> " If any man asketh who killeth thee,
> Say 'twas the Doones of Bagworthy."

Now at last our gorge was risen, and our hearts in tumult.

The people came flocking all around me, and agreed that I was bound to take command and management. I was moved by the bitter wrongs of Margery, but now I felt this difficulty—the Doones had behaved very well to our farm, and all of us, while I was away in London. Therefore, would it not be mean for me to attack them now ?

Yet being pressed still harder, I agreed at last to this—that if the Doones, upon fair challenge, would not endeavour to make amends by giving up Mistress Margery, as well as the man who had slain the babe, then I would lead the expedition, and do my best to subdue them. All our men were content with this, being thoroughly well assured from experience that the haughty robbers would only shoot any man who durst approach them with such proposal.

And then arose a difficult question—who was to take the risk of making overtures so unpleasant? I waited for the rest to offer; and as none was ready, the burden fell on me.

It may have been three of the afternoon, when I appeared with our Lizzie's white handkerchief upon a stick, at the entrance of the robbers' dwelling. Two Doones appeared, and, hearing of my purpose, offered to go and fetch the Captain, if I would stop where I was.

At length a heavy step sounded along the stone roof of the way, and the great Carver Doone drew up.

"What is it you want, young man?" he asked, as if he had never seen me before.

I begged him to understand that a vile and inhuman wrong had been done, but that if he would make what amends he could by restoring the poor woman, and giving up that odious brute who had slain the harmless infant, we would take no further motion. He made me a bow of mock courtesy, and replied as follows:

"Sir John, your new honours have turned your head, as might have been expected. The insolence of your demand wellnigh outdoes the ingratitude. If there be a man upon Exmoor who has grossly ill-used us, kidnapped our young women, and slain half a dozen of our young men, you are that outrageous rogue, Sir John. We have laid no hand upon your farm, we have not carried off your women, we have even allowed you to take our Queen, by treachery; and we have given you leave of absence to help your cousin the highwayman, and to come home with a title. And now, how do you requite us? By inflaming the indignation at a little frolic of our men, and by coming with insolent demands, to yield to which would ruin us. Ah, you viper!"

And he turned away in sorrow from me, shaking his head at my badness.

Seeing no use in bandying words, I did my best to look calmly at him, and to say with a quiet voice, "Farewell, Carver Doone, this time our day of reckoning is nigh."

"Thou fool, it is come," he cried, leaping aside into the niche of rock by the doorway. "Fire."

Scarce was the word out of his mouth ere I was out of fire, by a single bound, behind the rocky pillar of the opening.

With one thing and another, I was so amazed that I turned and ran away from these vile fellows; and luckily for me they had not another charge to send after me. And thus by good fortune I escaped.

Without any further hesitation, I agreed to take command of the honest men who were burning to punish those outlaws. One condition, however, I made, namely, that the Counsellor should be spared if possible; for he seemed less violent. We arranged that all our men should come and fall into order with pike and musket, over against our dunghill. Several of the yeo-

*"What is it you want, young man?" he asked.*

manry from Barnstaple and from Tiverton were added to our numbers;
and inasmuch as these were armed with heavy swords and short carabines,
their appearance was truly formidable.

Tom Faggus also joined us heartily, being now quite healed of his wound,
and Uncle Ben came over to help us with his advice and presence, as well
as with a band of stout warehousemen, whom he brought from Dulverton.
For he had never forgiven the old outrage put upon him; and though it
had been to his interest to keep quiet during the last attack, for the sake of
his secret gold mine, yet now he was in a position to give full vent to his
feelings. For he and his partners had obtained from the Crown a licence to
adventure in search of minerals, by payment of a heavy fine and a yearly
royalty. Therefore they had now no longer any cause for secrecy, neither
for dread of the outlaws.

A clever thing was devised among us. It was known that the Doones
were fond of gold. Hence, what we devised was this—to delude from home
a part of the robbers and fall by surprise on the other part. We caused it to
be spread abroad that a large heap of gold was now collected at the mine
of the Wizard's Slough. And when this rumour must have reached them,
we sent Carfax to demand a secret interview with the Counsellor. Then he
was to set forth a list of imaginary grievances against the owners of the mine,
and to offer to betray into their hands, upon the Friday night, by far the greatest
weight of gold as yet sent up for refining. He was to have one quarter part,
and they to take the residue. But inasmuch as the convoy across the moors,
under his command, would be strong and strongly armed, the Doones must
be sure to send not less than a score of men, if possible. He himself,
at a place agreed upon, and fit for an ambuscade, would call a halt, and

contrive in the darkness to pour a little water into the priming of his company's guns.

It was settled that the yeoman should give account (with the miner's help), of as many Doones as might be despatched to plunder the pretended gold. And as soon as we knew that this party of robbers was out of hearing from the valley, we were to fall to, ostensibly at the Doone-gate rear, by means of my old water-slide.

## CHAPTER XX

THE moon was lifting well above the shoulder of the uplands, when we, the chosen band, set forth, having the short cut along the valleys to foot of the Bagworthy water ; and having allowed the rest an hour, we were not to begin our climb until we heard a musket fired from the heights on the left-hand side. John Fry was to fire his gun as soon as he heard the hurly-burly at the Doone-gate beginning ; which we, by reason of waterfall, could not hear down in the meadows here.

We waited a very long time, but suddenly the most awful noise that anything short of thunder could make, came down among the rocks and went and hung upon the corners.

" The signal, my lads," I cried. " Now hold on by the rope, and lay your quarter-staffs across, my lads, and keep your guns pointing to heaven, lest haply we shoot one another."

We stole up the meadows quietly, keeping in the watercourse. And the earliest notice the Counsellor had of our presence was the blazing of Carver's log-wood house. We took good care, however, to burn no innocent women or children in that most righteous destruction.

We laid our brands to three other houses, after calling the women forth, and in the smoke and rush and fire, they believed that we were a hundred ; and away they ran to the battle at the Doone-gate.

" All Doone-town is on fire, on fire ! " we heard them shrieking as they went. " A hundred soldiers are burning it, with a dreadful great man at the head of them ! "

Presently, just as I expected, back came the warriors of the Doones, leaving but two or three at the gate. Seeing how few there were of them, I was very loath to fire, thinking that we might take them prisoners. But my followers waited for no words. At a signal a dozen muskets were discharged, and half the Doones dropped lifeless. The rest fired wildly, not seeing us well among the hazel bushes ; and then they clubbed their muskets and furiously drove at us.

For a moment we fell back before their valorous fame, and the power of their onset. For my part, admiring their courage greatly, I withheld my hand awhile ; for I cared to meet none but Carver, and he was not among them. The reckoning was come that night ; and not a line we missed of it. Enough that ere the daylight broke upon that wan March morning, the only Doones still left alive were the Counsellor and Carver. And of all the dwellings of the Doones, not even one was left, but all made potash in the river.

# CHAPTER XXI

THE thing which next betided me was the return of Lorna. My mother sat in an ancient chair and wiped her cheeks and looked at her ; and even Lizzie's eyes must dance to the freshness and joy of her beauty. As for me, you might call me mad, for I ran out and flung my best hat on the barn.

Earl Brandir's ancient steward, in whose charge she had travelled, looked upon her as a lovely maniac. On the other hand, Lorna considered him a foolish old gentleman, to whom true happiness meant no more than money and high position.

These two last she had been ready to abandon wholly, and had in part escaped from them, as the enemies of her happiness. And she took advantage of the times in a clever manner. For that happened to be a time when everybody was only too glad to take money for doing anything. And the greatest money-taker in the kingdom was generally acknowledged to be the Lord Chief Justice Jeffreys.

Upon his return from the bloody assizes, he so pleased his Gracious Majesty that in his hand was placed the Great Seal of England.

So it came to pass that Lorna's destiny hung upon Lord Jeffreys ; for at this time Earl Brandir died. Now the Lady Lorna Dugal appeared to Lord Chancellor Jeffreys so exceeding wealthy a ward that the lock would pay for turning. Therefore he came to visit her, having heard that this wealthy maiden would not listen to any lord, having pledged her faith to the plain John Ridd.

Thereupon, our Lorna managed so to hold out golden hopes to the Lord High Chancellor, that, upon surety of a certain sum, he gave to his ward permission to marry that loyal knight, John Ridd, upon condition only that the King's consent should be obtained.

His Majesty, well disposed towards me for my precious service, consented without much hesitation.

Dear mother arranged all the ins and outs of the wedding, and Annie and Lizzie, and even Ruth Huckaback made such a sweeping of dresses that I scarcely knew where to place my feet. Then Lorna came out of a pew half-way, and took my left hand in her right, and I prayed God that it were done with.

Lorna's dress was of pure white, clouded with faint lavender (for the sake of the old Earl Brandir), and as simple as need be. I was afraid to look at her, as I said before, except when each of us said, " I will," and then each dwelled upon the other.

It is impossible for any one who have not loved as I have to conceive my joy and pride when, after all was done, Lorna turned to look at me with her glances of subtle fun subdued by this great act.

Her eyes told me such a depth of comfort, that I was almost amazed, thoroughly as I knew them. The sound of a shot rang through the church, and those eyes were filled with death.

Lorna fell across my knees ; a flood of blood came out upon the yellow wood of the altar steps, and at my feet lay Lorna. I lifted her up, and coaxed her, but it was no good ; the only sign of life remaining was a spirit of bright red blood.

I laid my wife in my mother's arms and went forth for my revenge. Of course, I knew who had done it. I leapt upon our best horse, with bridle but no saddle, and set the head of Kickums towards the course now pointed out to me. Weapon of no sort had I. With my vicious horse at a furious speed, I came upon Black Barrow Down. And there, about a furlong before me, rode a man on a great black horse, and I knew that man was Carver Doone.

Although he was so far before me, and riding as hard as ride he might, I saw that he had something on the horse in front of him, something which needed care, and stopped him from looking backward.

*I leapt upon our best horse and set forth at a furious speed.*

The man turned up the gulley leading from the moor to Cloven Rocks, but as he entered it, he turned round, and I saw that he was bearing his child, little Ensie, before him.

Carver Doone, with a vile oath, thrust spurs into his horse, and laid one hand on a pistol-stock. And a cry of triumph rose from the black depths of my heart. What cared I for pistols ? And I knew that the black steed in front, if he breasted the steep ascent, where the track divided, must be in our reach at once.

His rider knew this, and drew rein at the crossways sharply, and plunged into the black ravine leading to the Wizard's Slough.

I followed my enemy carefully, for I had him, as in a pitfall, whence no escape might be. He thought that I feared to approach him, for he knew not where he was ; and his low disdainful laugh came back.

Carver Doone turned the corner suddenly on the black and bottomless bog. With a start of fear he reined back his horse.

And then, wheeling, fired and rode at me.

His bullet struck me somewhere, but I took no heed of that. Fearing only his escape, I laid my horse across the way, and struck full on the forehead his charging steed. Ere the slash of the sword came nigh me, man and horse rolled over, and wellnigh bore my own horse down, with the power of their onset.

Carver Doone was somewhat stunned, and the little boy ran to me, and the terror of his eyes made me almost fear myself. "Ensie, dear," I said quite gently, grieving that he should see his father killed, "run up yonder and try to find a bunch of bluebells for the lady." The child obeyed me, while I prepared for business.

With a sullen, and black scowl, the Carver gathered his mighty limbs, and arose.

"I would not harm you, lad," he said with a sneer. "I have punished you enough for most of your impertinence. For the rest I forgive you, because you have been good and gracious to my little son."

For answer, I smote him on the cheek. I would not sully my tongue by speaking to a man like this.

There was a level space of sward between us and the slough and to this place I led him. I think that he felt that his time was come. At any rate a paleness came, an ashy paleness on his cheeks, and the calves of his legs bowed in, as if he were out of training.

Seeing this, I offered him first chance. I stretched forth my left hand, as I do to a weaker antagonist, and I let him have the hug of me. But in this I was too generous, having forgotten my pistol-wound, and the cracking of one of my short lower ribs. Carver Doone caught me round the waist, with such a grip as never yet had been laid upon me.

I heard my rib go. I grasped his arm and took him by the throat. In vain he tugged, and strained, and flung himself on me with gnashing jaws. Beneath the iron of my strength I had him helpless in two minutes, and his fiery eyes lolled out.

"I will not harm thee any more," I cried. "Carver Doone, thou art beaten. Own it, thank God for it, and go thy way."

It was all too late. The black bog had him by the feet ; the sucking of the ground drew on him, like the thirsty lips of death. In our fury, we had heeded neither wet nor dry, nor thought of earth beneath us. I myself might scarcely leap, with the last spring of o'er-laboured legs, from the engulfing grave of slime. He fell back and tossed his arms to heaven, and the glare of his eyes was ghastly. I could only gaze and pant ; for my strength was no more than an infant's. Scarcely could I turn away, while, joint by joint, he sank.

When the boy came back with the bluebells, the only sign of his father left was a brown bubble, upon a newly-formed patch of blackness. With pain, and shame at my own fury, I heavily mounted my horse again, and looked down at the innocent Ensie.

"Don"—for he never could say "John"—"Oh, Don, I am so glad that nasty, naughty man is gone away. Take me home."

When we came to the stable door, I rather fell from my horse than got off. Into the old farmhouse I tottered, like a child, with mother helping me along, yet fearing to look at me.

"I have killed him," was all I said, "even as he killed Lorna. Now let me see my wife, mother. She belongs to me still, though dead."

"You cannot see her now, dear John," said Ruth Huckaback, since no one else had the courage. "Annie is with her now."

"What has that to do with it? Let me see my dead one, and pray myself to die."

Ruth alone stood by me. Then one little hand of her stole into my great shaking palm, while she whispered gently:

"John, she is not your dead one. She may even be your living one yet, your wife, your home, and your happiness. But the sight of you, and in this sad plight, would be certain death to her. Now come first, and be healed yourself."

I obeyed her, like a child, whispering only as I went, "Almighty God will bless you, darling, for the good you are doing now."

If it had not been for this little maid, Lorna must have died at once. But the moment I left her Ruth came forward and took the command of every one. She made them bear her home at once upon the door of the pulpit, with the cushion under her dropping head. With her own hands she cut off the bridal dress, so steeped and stained, and with her dainty fingers she probed that vile wound in the side, and fetched the reeking bullet forth. All this while my darling lay insensible, and all the women around declared that she was dead.

But Ruth still sponged the poor side and forehead, and bade them fetch her Spanish wine. Then she parted the pearly teeth, and poured in wine from a spoon, and waited, and then poured in a little more.

For days she lay at the very edge of death, kept alive by nothing but the care, the skill and perpetual watchfulness of Ruth. The doctor had pronounced poor Lorna dead; wherefore Ruth refused most firmly to have aught to do with him. She took the whole case on herself; and with God's help she bore it through. Now whether it were the light and brightness of my Lorna's nature, or the freedom from anxiety—for she knew not of my hurt. But, anyhow, Lorna recovered long ere I did.

For the grief was on me still of having lost my love and lover at the moment she was mine. With the power of fate upon me, I had no faith in the tales they told. I believed that Lorna was in the churchyard, while these rogues were lying to me.

## CHAPTER XXII

ONE day when I was sitting in my bedroom, a knock sounded through my gloomy room, and supposing it to be the doctor, I tried to rise and make my bow. But to my surprise it was little Ruth, who had never once come to visit me, since I was placed under the doctor's hands.

"Can you receive visitors, Cousin Ridd?—why, they never told me of this!" she cried. "I knew that you were weak, dear John, but not that you were dying. Whatever is that basin for?"

"I have no intention of dying, Ruth. But that basin, if you must know, is for the doctor's purpose."

"What, do you mean bleeding you? You poor weak cousin! Is it possible that he does that still?"

"Twice a week for the last six weeks, dear. Nothing else has kept me alive."

"Nothing else has killed you, nearly. There!" And she set her little boot across the basin and crushed it. "Not another drop shall they have from you. Is Annie such a fool as that? Will you leave it to me, John? I have a little will of my own; and I am not afraid of doctors. I have saved your Lorna's life. And now I will save yours, which is a far easier business."

"You have saved Lorna's life! What do you mean by talking so?"

"Only what I say, Cousin John. Though perhaps I overprize my work. But at any rate she says so."

"I do not understand," I said, falling back with bewilderment. "All women are such liars."

"Have you ever known me tell a lie?" cried Ruth in great indignation; and if ever there was truth in the eyes of any woman, it was now in Ruth Huckaback's.

"I do not understand," was all I could say.

"Will you understand, if I show you Lorna? I have feared to do it for the sake of you both. But now Lorna is well enough, if you think that you are, Cousin John."

Following her, to the very utmost of my mind and heart, I felt that all she said was truth; and yet I could not make it out.

Before I had time to listen much for the approach of footsteps Ruth came back, and behind her Lorna. Ruth banged the door and ran away; and Lorna stood before me. But she did not stand for an instant, when she saw what I was like. At the risk of all thick bandages, and upsetting a dozen

*She managed to get into my arms, although they could not hold her.*

medicine bottles, and scattering leeches right and left, she managed to get into my arms, although they could not hold her.

I felt my life come back and warm ; I felt my trust in women flow ; I felt the joy of living now, and the power of doing it.

Little more have I to tell. The doctor was turned out at once ; and slowly came back my former strength, with a darling wife, and good victuals.

There is no need for my farming harder than becomes a man of weight. Lorna has great stores of money, though we never draw it out, except for some poor neighbour.

As for poor Tom Faggus, with a good wife and a wonderful horse, and all the country attached to him, he kept the law at a distance, until it became too much for its master ; and a new king arose. Upon this, Tom sued his pardon afresh ; and Jeremy Stickles was glad to help him in getting it. Thereafter the good and respectable Tom lived a godly life, and brought up his children to honesty.

My dear mother was as happy as possibly need be with us, having no cause for jealousy, as others arose around her. And everybody was well pleased, when Lizzie came in one day and tossed her bookshelf over, and declared that she would have Captain Bloxham, and nobody should prevent her.

I sent Ensie to Blundell's school, having changed his name, for fear of what any one might do to him.

Ruth Huckaback is not married yet, although on Uncle Reuben's death she came into all his property. I know a man ever worthy of her ; and though she is not very young, he loves her as I love Lorna. It is my firm conviction that in the end he will win her.

Of Lorna, my lifelong darling, my more loved wife, I will not talk ; for it is not seemly that a man should exalt his pride. Year by year her beauty grows, with the growth of goodness, kindness, and true happiness—above all with loving.

# THUMBELINA

## *by* HANS ANDERSEN

HERE was once a woman who wished for a very little child ; but she did not know where she should procure one. So she went to an old witch and said,

" I do so very much wish for a little child ! Can you not tell me where I can get one ? "

" Oh ! that could easily be managed," said the witch. " There you have a barleycorn : that is not of the kind which grows in the country-man's field, and which the chickens get to eat. Put that into a flower-pot, and you shall see what you shall see."

" Thank you," said the woman ; and she gave the witch twelve shillings, for that is what it cost.

Then she went home and planted the barleycorn, and immediately there grew up a great handsome flower, which looked like a tulip ; but the leaves were tightly closed, as though it were still a bud.

" That is a beautiful flower," said the woman ; and she kissed its yellow and red leaves. But just as she kissed it the flower opened with a *pop* ! It was a real tulip, as one could now see ; but in the middle of the flower there sat upon the green velvet stamens a little maiden, delicate and graceful to behold. She was scarcely half a thumb's length in height, and therefore she was called Thumbelina.

A neat polished walnut-shell served Thumbelina for a cradle, blue violet-leaves were her mattresses, with a rose-leaf for a coverlet. There she slept at night ; but in the day-time she played upon the table, where the woman had put a plate with a wreath of flowers around it, whose stalks stood in water ; on the water swam a great tulip-leaf, and on this the little maiden could sit, and row from one side of the plate to the other, with two white horse hairs for oars. That looked pretty indeed ! She could also sing, and, indeed, so delicately and sweetly, that the like had never been heard.

Once as she lay at night in her pretty bed, there came an old Toad creeping through the window, in which one pane was broken. The Toad was very ugly, big and damp : it hopped straight down upon the table, where Thumbelina lay sleeping under the rose-leaf.

" That would be a handsome wife for my son," said the Toad ; and she took the walnut-shell in which Thumbelina lay asleep, and hopped with it through the window down into the garden.

There ran a great broad brook ; but the margin was swampy and soft, and here the Toad dwelt with her son. Ugh ! he was ugly, and looked just like his mother. " Croak ! croak ! brek-kex-kex ! " that was all he could say when he saw the graceful little maiden in the walnut-shell.

" Don't speak so loud, or she will awake," said the old Toad. " She might run away from us, for she is as light as a bit of swan's-down. We will put her out in the brook upon one of the broad water-lily leaves. That will be just like an island for her, she is so small and light. Then she can't get away, while we put the state room under the marsh in order, where you are to live and keep house together."

Out in the brook grew many water-lilies with broad green leaves, which looked as if they were floating on the water. The leaf which lay farthest out was also the greatest of all, and to that the old Toad swam out and laid the walnut-shell upon it with Thumbelina. The little tiny Thumbelina woke early in the morning, and when she saw where she was she began to cry very bitterly ; for there was water on every side of the great green leaf, and she could not get to land at all. The old Toad sat down in the marsh decking out her room with rushes and yellow weed—it was to be made very pretty for the new daughter-in-law ; then she swam out, with her ugly son, to the leaf on which Thumbelina was. They wanted to take her pretty bed, which was to be put in the bridal chamber before she went in there herself. The old Toad bowed low before her in the water, and said :

" Here is my son ; he will be your husband, and you will live splendidly together in the marsh."

" Croak ! croak ! brek-kek-kex ! " was all the son could say.

Then they took the delicate little bed, and swam away with it ; but Thumbelina sat all alone upon the green leaf and wept, for she did not like to live at the nasty Toad's, and have her ugly son for a husband. The little fishes swimming in the water below had both seen the Toad, and had also heard what she said : therefore they stretched forth their heads, for they wanted to see the little girl. As soon as they saw her they considered her so pretty that they felt very sorry she should have to go down to the ugly Toad. No, that must never be ! They assembled together in the water around the green stalk which held the leaf on which the little maiden stood, and with their teeth they gnawed away the stalk, and so the leaf swam down the stream ; and away went Thumbelina far away, where the Toad could not get at her.

Thumbelina sailed by many cities, and the little birds which sat in the bushes saw her, and said, " What a lovely little girl ! " The leaf swam away with her, farther and farther ; so Thumbelina travelled out of the country.

A graceful little white butterfly always fluttered round her, and at last
alighted on the leaf. Thumbelina pleased him, and she was very glad of
this, for now the Toad could not reach them ; and it was so beautiful where
she was floating along—the sun shone upon the water, and the water glistened
like the most splendid gold. She took her girdle and bound one end of it
round the butterfly, fastening the other end of the ribbon to the leaf. The leaf
now glided onward much faster, and Thumbelina too, for she stood upon it.

There came a big Cockchafer flying up ; and he saw her, and immediately
clasped his claws round her slender waist, and flew with her up into a tree.
The green leaf was swimming down the brook, and the butterfly with it ;
for he was fastened to the leaf, and could not get away from it.

*There came a big Cockchafer flying up, and clasped his claws round her waist.*

Mercy ! how frightened poor little Thumbelina was when the Cockchafer
flew with her up into the tree ! But especially she was sorry for the fine
white butterfly whom she had bound fast to the leaf, for, if he could not free
himself from it, he would be obliged to starve. The Cockchafer, however,
did not trouble himself at all about this. He seated himself with her upon the
biggest green leaf of the tree, gave her the sweet part of the flowers to eat,
and declared that she was very pretty, though she did not in the least resemble
a Cockchafer. Afterwards came all the other Cockchafers who lived in the
tree to pay a visit : they looked at Thumbelina, and said,

"Why, she has not even more than two legs !—that has a wretched
appearance."

"She has not any feelers !" cried another.

"Her waist is quite slender——fie ! she looks like a human creature—
how ugly she is !" said all the lady Cockchafers.

And yet Thumbelina was very pretty. Even the Cockchafer who had carried her off saw that ; but when all the others declared she was ugly, he believed it at last, and would not have her at all—she might go whither she like. Then they flew down with her from the tree, and set her upon a daisy, and she wept, because she was so ugly that the Cockchafers would have nothing to say to her ; and yet she was the loveliest little being one could imagine, and as tender and delicate as a rose-leaf.

The whole summer through poor Thumbelina lived quite alone in the great wood. She wove herself a bed out of blades of grass, and hung it up under a shamrock, so that she was protected from the rain ; she plucked the honey out of the flowers for food, and drank of the dew which stood every morning upon the leaves. Thus summer and autumn passed away ; but now came winter, the cold long winter. All the birds who had sung so sweetly before her flew away ; trees and flowers shed their leaves ; the great shamrock under which she had lived shrivelled up, and there remained nothing of it but a yellow withered stalk ; and she was dreadfully cold, for her clothes were torn, and she herself was so frail and delicate—poor little Thumbelina ! she was nearly frozen. It began to snow, and every snow-flake that fell upon her was like a whole shovelful thrown upon one of us, for we are tall, and she was only an inch long. Then she wrapped herself in a dry leaf, and that tore in the middle, and would not warm her—she shivered with cold.

Close to the wood into which she had now come lay a great corn-field, but the corn was gone long ago ; only the naked dry stubble stood up out of the frozen ground. This was just like a great forest for her to wander through : and, oh ! how she trembled with cold. Then she arrived at the door of the Field Mouse. This Mouse had a little hole under the stubble. There the Field Mouse lived, warm and comfortable, and had a whole roomful of corn— a glorious kitchen and larder. Poor Thumbelina stood at the door just like a poor beggar girl, and begged for a little bit of barleycorn, for she had not had the smallest morsel to eat for the last two days.

" You poor little creature," said the Field Mouse—for after all she was a good Field Mouse—" come into my warm room and dine with me."

As she was pleased with Thumbelina, she said, " if you like you may stay with me through the winter, but you must keep my room clean and neat, and tell me little stories, for I am very fond of those."

And Thumbelina did as the kind old Field Mouse bade her.

" Now we shall soon have a visitor," said the Field Mouse. " My neighbour is in the habit of visiting me once a week. He is even better off than I am, has great rooms, and a beautiful black velvety fur. If you could only get him for your husband you would be well provided for. You must tell him the prettiest stories you know."

But Thumbelina did not care about this ; she thought nothing of the neighbour, for he was a Mole. He came and paid his visits in his black velvety coat. The Field Mouse told how rich and how learned he was, and how his house was more than twenty times larger than hers ; that he had learning, but that he did not like the sun and beautiful flowers, for he had never seen them.

Thumbelina had to sing, and she sang, " Cockchafer, fly away," and " When the parson goes afield." Then the Mole fell in love with her, because of her delicious voice ; but he said nothing, for he was a sedate Mole.

A short time before, he had dug a long passage through the earth from his own house to theirs ; and Thumbelina and the Field Mouse obtained leave to walk in this passage as much as they wished. But he begged them not to be afraid of the dead bird which was lying in the passage. It was an entire bird, with wings and beak. It certainly must have died only a short time before, and was now buried just where the Mole had made his passage.

The Mole took a bit of decayed wood in his mouth, and it glimmered like fire in the dark ; then he went first and lighted them through the long dark passage. When they came where the dead bird lay, the Mole thrust up his broad nose against the ceiling, so that a great hole was made, through which the daylight could shine down. In the middle of the floor lay a dead Swallow, his beautiful wings pressed close against his sides, and his head and feet drawn back under his feathers : the poor bird had certainly died of cold. Thumbelina was very sorry for this : she was very fond of all the little birds, who had sung and twittered so prettily before her through the summer ; but the Mole gave him a push with his crooked legs, and said, " Now he doesn't pipe any more. It must be miserable to be born a little bird. I'm thankful that none of my children can be that : such a bird has nothing but his ' tweet-tweet,' and has to starve in the winter ! "

" Yes, you may well say that, as a clever man," observed the Field Mouse. " Of what use is all this ' tweet-tweet ' to a bird when the winter comes ? He must starve and freeze. But they say that it's very aristocratic."

Thumbelina said nothing ; but when the two others turned their backs on the bird, she bent down, put the feathers aside which covered his head, and kissed him upon his closed eyes.

" Perhaps it was he who sang so prettily before me in the summer," she thought. " How much pleasure he gave me, the dear beautiful bird ! "

The Mole now closed up the hole through which the daylight shone in, and accompanied the ladies home. But at night Thumbelina could not sleep at all ; so she got up out of her bed, and wove a large beautiful carpet of hay, and carried it and spread it over the dead bird, and laid the thin stamens of of flowers, soft as cotton, and which she had found in the Field Mouse's room, at the bird's sides, so that he might lie soft in the ground.

" Farewell, you pretty little bird ! " said she. " Farewell ! and thanks to you for your beautiful song in the summer, when all the trees were green, and the sun shone down warmly upon us." And then she laid the bird's head upon her heart. But the bird was not dead ; he was only lying there torpid with cold ; and now he had been warmed, and came to life again.

In autumn all the swallows fly away to warm countries ; but if one happens to be belated, it becomes so cold that it falls down as if dead, and lies where it fell, and then the cold snow covers it.

Thumbelina fairly trembled, she was so startled ; for the bird was large, very large, compared with her, who was only an inch in height. But she took courage, laid the cotton closer round the poor bird, and brought a leaf that she had used as her own coverlet, and laid it over the bird's head.

The next night she crept out to him again—and now he was alive, but quite weak ; he could only open his eyes for a moment ; and look at Thumbelina, who stood before him with a bit of decayed wood in her hand, for she had not a lantern.

" I thank you, you pretty little child," said the sick Swallow ; " I have been famously warmed.  Soon I shall get my strength back again, and I shall be able to fly about in the warm sunshine."

" Oh ! " she said, " it is so cold without.  It snows and freezes.  Stay in your warm bed, and I will nurse you."

Then she brought the Swallow water in the petal of a flower ; and the Swallow drank, and told her how he had torn one of his wings in a thorn-bush, and thus he had not been able to fly so fast as the other swallows, who had sped away, far away, to the warm countries.  So at last he had fallen to the ground ; but he could remember nothing more, and did not know at all how he had come where she had found him.

The whole winter the Swallow remained there, and Tumbelina nursed and tended him heartily.  Neither the Field Mouse nor the Mole heard anything about it, for they did not like the poor Swallow.  As soon as the spring came, and the sun warmed the earth, the Swallow bade Thumbelina farewell, and she opened the hole which the Mole had made in the ceiling.  The sun shone in upon them gloriously, and the Swallow asked if Thumbelina would go with him ; she could sit upon his back, and they would fly away far into the green wood.  But Thumbelina knew that the old Field Mouse would be grieved if she left her.

" No, I cannot ! " said Thumbelina.

" Farewell, farewell, you good, pretty girl ! " said the Swallow ; and he flew out into the sunshine.  Thumbelina looked after him, and the tears came into her eyes, for she was heartily and sincerely fond of the poor Swallow.

" Tweet-tweet ! tweet-tweet ! " sang the bird, and flew into the green forest.  Thumbelina felt very sad.  She did not get permission to go out into the warm sunshine.  The corn which was sown in the field over the house of the Field Mouse grew up high into the air ; it was quite a thick wood for the poor girl, who was only an inch in height.

" You are betrothed now, Thumbelina," said the Field Mouse.  " My neighbour has proposed for you.  What great fortune for a poor child like you !  Now you must work at your outfit, woollen and linen clothes both ; for you must lack nothing when you have become the Mole's wife."

Thumbelina had to turn the spindle, and the Mole hired four spiders to weave for her day and night.  Every evening the Mole paid her a visit ; and he was always saying that when the summer should draw to a close, the sun would not shine nearly so hot, for that now it burned the earth almost as hard as a stone.  Yes, when the summer should have gone, then he would keep his wedding day with Thumbelina.  But she was not glad at all, for she did not like the tiresome Mole.  Every morning when the sun rose and every evening when it went down, she crept out at the door ; and when the wind blew the corn-ears apart, so that she could see the blue sky, she thought how bright and beautiful it was out here, and wished heartily to see her dear Swallow again.  But the Swallow did not come back ; he had doubtless flown far away, in the fair green forest.  When Autumn came on, Thumbelina had all her outfit ready.

" In four weeks you shall celebrate your wedding," said the Field Mouse.

But Thumbelina wept, and declared she would not have the tiresome Mole.

*Thumbelina wept, and declared she would not have the tiresome Mole.*

"Nonsense!" said the Field Mouse; "don't be obstinate, or I will bite you with my white teeth. He is a very fine man whom you will marry. The Queen herself has not such a black velvet fur; and his kitchen and cellar are full. Be thankful for your good fortune."

Now the wedding was to be held. The Mole had already come to fetch Thumbelina; she was to live with him, deep under the earth, and never to come out into the warm sunshine, for that he did not like. The poor little thing was very sorrowful; she was now to say farewell to the glorious sun, which, after all, she had been allowed by the Field Mouse to see from the threshold of the door.

"Farewell, thou bright sun!" she said, and stretched out her arms towards it, and walked a little way forth from the house of the Field Mouse, for now the corn had been reaped, and only the dry stubble stood in the fields. "Farewell!" she repeated, twining her arms round a little red flower which still bloomed there. "Greet the little Swallow from me, if you see him again."

"Tweet-weet! tweet-weet!" a voice suddenly sounded over her head. She looked up: it was the little Swallow, who was just flying by. When he saw Thumbelina he was very glad; and Thumbelina told him how loth she was to have the ugly Mole for her husband, and that she was to live deep under the earth, where the sun never shone. And she could not refrain from weeping.

"The cold winter is coming now," said the Swallow; "I am going to fly far away into the warm countries. Will you come with me! You can sit upon my back, then we shall fly from the ugly Mole and his dark room— away, far away, over the mountains, to the warm countries, where the sun shines warmer than here, where it is always summer, and there are lovely flowers. Only fly with me, you dear little Thumbelina, you who have saved my life when I lay frozen in the dark earthy passage."

"Yes, I will go with you!" said Thumbelina; and she seated herself on the bird's back, with her feet on his outspread wing, and bound her girdle fast to one of his strongest feathers; then the Swallow flew up into the air over forest and over sea, high up over the great mountains, where the snow always lies; and Thumbelina felt cold in the bleak air, but then she hid under the bird's warm feathers, and only put out her little head to admire all the beauties beneath her.

At last they came to the warm countries. There the sun shone far brighter than here; the sky seemed twice as high. But the Swallow flew still farther, and it became more and more beautiful. Under the more glorious green trees by the blue lake stood a palace of dazzling white marble, from the olden time. Vines clustered around the lofty pillars; at the top were many swallows' nests, and in one of these the Swallow lived who carried Thumbelina.

"That is my house," said the Swallow; "but it is not right that you should live there. It is not yet properly arranged by a great deal, and you will not be contented with it. Select for yourself one of the splendid flowers which grow down yonder, then I will put you into it, and you shall have everything as nice as you can wish."

"That is capital," cried she, and clapped her little hands.

A great marble pillar lay there, which had fallen to the ground and had been broken into three pieces; but between these pieces grew the most beautiful great white flowers. The Swallow flew down with Thumbelina, and set her upon one of the broad leaves. But what was the little maid's surprise? There sat a little man in the midst of the flower, as white and transparent as if he had been made of glass; he wore the neatest of gold crowns on his head, and the brightest wings on his shoulders; he himself was not bigger than Thumbelina. He was the angel of the flower. In each of the flowers dwelt such a little man or woman, but this one was their King.

"Heavens! how beautiful he is!" whispered Thumbelina to the Swallow.

The little Prince was very much frightened at the Swallow, for he was quite a gigantic bird to him, who was so small. But when he saw Thumbelina, he became very glad; she was the prettiest maiden he had ever seen. Therefore he took off his golden crown, and put it upon her, asked her name, and if she would be his wife, and then she should be Queen of all the flowers. Now this was truly a different kind of man to the son of the Toad, and the Mole with the black velvet fur. She therefore said "Yes" to the charming Prince. And out of every flower came a lady or a lord, so pretty to behold that it was a delight; each one brought Thumbelina a present; but the best gift was a pair of beautiful wings which had belonged to a great white fly; these were fastened to Thumbelina's back, and now she could fly from flower to flower. Then there was much rejoicing; and the little Swallow sat above them in the nest, and was to sing the marriage song, which he accordingly did as well as he could; but yet in his heart he was sad, for he was so fond, oh! so fond of Thumbelina, and would have liked never to part from her.

"You shall not be called Thumbelina," said the Flower Angel to her; "that is an ugly name, and you are too fair for it—we will call you Maia."

# WHAT THE BEES HEARD

### *by* VIOLET M. METHLEY

## CHAPTER I

ATCHING up her lilac-sprigged skirts on either side. Loveday ran quickly along the turfed path between the lavender bushes.

Her cheeks were pink with excitement under the lace border of the cap which almost hid her bright brown curls, her eyes shone like sunlit water, for this was the greatest morning she had known in her nearly seventeen years of days.

And because she was so happy, because what she had just heard was so important, there was something which Loveday felt must be done at once, without wasting an instant. Births or deaths or marriages, any news of great moment must be told at once to the bees—so old Tabby and the other servants had always taught her—or else the wise insects would be angry and ill luck would fall upon the house and family.

So that was why the girl hastened along the lavender-bordered path and through the walled kitchen garden to the strip of ground at the foot of the little hill which rose behind Loyalty House. Here the row of hives stood so that the bees might be close to their honey flowers, the heather and gorse and thyme which grew on the slopes up to the very feet of the three tall fir-trees on the crest of the rise. Beside the first hive where Loveday at last came to a standstill was a great bush of syringa, covered with sweet-scented white flowers. Bending till her head was close to the straw-thatched skep, the girl spoke aloud, softly, breathlessly.

"Bees—bees, do you hear what I am telling you—He is coming to-day."

As Loveday stood there a low murmur seemed to answer her from within the hive, the whirr of innumerable small wings, the buzzing of the bees. Yes, surely it was louder than usual, an almost angry-sounding humming. She went quickly from one hive to another, giving each the same message.

"Bees, He is coming to-day," until she reached the last of the row and stood upright, her face more rosy than ever, her eyes dancing, the sun turning

239

stray locks of her brown hair to gold, just as it was gilding the yellow lichen on the garden walls and on the roof of the hundred-years-old red brick house.

Loyalty House had been built by Loveday's great-grandfather in the days of the great Civil War. He had been one of the most faithful servants of King Charles ; that was why he had given the house that name, why on every pane of those latticed windows he had written " Loyauté " with the diamond in his ring. He had planted, too, the three fir trees on the hill, since in his days and later this was often used as a sign that in the house nearby servants of the king were always welcome.

These were the things which always made Loveday proud of her home and her family ; proud, too, to know that her father, Sir Romilly Preston, now travelling in France, was just as brave and loyal as his ancestors.

But it was not ancestors, or even of her father, that Loveday was thinking now as she stood there in the sunshine : some one else filled her mind. And then the warm stillness was suddenly broken, as a tall boy of nineteen strode out from behind the syringa-bush and spoke, almost fiercely.

" So you are expecting a ' he ' to-day, Mistress Loveday."

It was not only excited pleasure which made the girl's cheeks red now, as she cried angrily:

" How dare you spy on me like this, Phil ? "

" You can scarcely call it spying or eavesdropping, surely, if I have over-heard what you said to the *bees* ? " Phil Staveley pretended to laugh, but his dark brows were drawn together in a frown. " Fine secrets, indeed, which you tell *them*."

" I *do* call it spying when you hide behind bushes and hear what wasn't meant for you ! " Loveday flashed back.

" Oh—it is a secret then ? Well, I'd fain know the name of this man who's coming here to-day," Phil said.

" I shall not tell you ; 'tis no concern of yours," Loveday declared, tossing her head mutinously.

" Everything about you is my concern."

" Indeed ! " Loveday curtseyed mockingly. " Thank you for nothing, Philip. I can manage my own affairs."

" Is this man some one whom you love ? " Philip persisted. " Oh, yes, I can see he is by the way you blush."

" Yes, then—if you *will* have it ! " Loveday's chin was higher than ever, " I *do* love him. I would do anything for him—anything in the world."

Phil Staveley's face was very white and his fists clenched as he took a long stride nearer to Loveday.

" I *will* know his name ! " he said.

" You shall not."

" 'Tis not fair. You have deceived me, Loveday—you never told me that there was some one else you loved. You know that I have always . . . always—oh, 'tis hard to find you false like this."

" Phil, you've no right to speak so to me. You'll make me hate you."

" What does that matter if you love this other vile fellow ? "

" You must not—you shall not speak of him in that way ! "

" I'll speak of him as I choose, thief that he is. And if I find him, I'll say as much to his face," vowed Phil. " Does your father know of him ? "

" Yes—and loves him too," Loveday said defiantly, and stamped her foot in its black stuff shoe, tied with lilac ribbon. " And . . . and I *won't* be preached at by you, Phil, so please go away and . . . and don't come back till you're in a better temper."

" I'll go—and I won't come back," the boy declared furiously; and flung away up the slope and over the crest of the hill without once turning back.

Loveday stood looking after him until he was out of sight, and her eyes were bright with angry tears now instead of laughter. Far more slowly than she had come, she left the hives and walked soberly back through the garden, with the lavender-bushes brushing their sweet plumes against her skirts.

But by the time that she reached the house, Phil Staveley was almost forgotten; there was so much to do, so many things to make ready, since *He* was coming to-day. For Loveday was a notable little housekeeper and she had been mistress in her father's house since her mother died two years before, directing the maids, sewing, spinning,

*Loveday was a notable housekeeper.*

and 'stilling with her own hands, washing the best china and making the best pastry and puddings.

" I wonder if Deb hath saved enough cream for a tansy ? " she thought. " Or would raspberry tartlets be more fitting ? "

## CHAPTER II

ALTHOUGH Phil Staveley had vowed never to return to Loyalty House, he broke his word that same evening, for the boy felt that he must know who this " he " was for whom Loveday had flouted him.

Loveday and himself—why, they'd never had secrets from each other, ever since they'd played together as babies, for Philip was the son of Squire Staveley, of Staveley Hall, the Prestons' nearest neighbour.

" I'll see the fellow—aye, and have a word to say to him maybe," Phil thought fiercely, as he strode over the Downs between the two houses. " If I lie amongst the gorse-bushes on the top of the hill I can see all roads to Loyalty House and mark well when he comes."

It was very still and hot on the hillside; the scent of the gorse-bushes sweet and heavy as Phil crept amongst them. Grasshoppers scraped their fairy fiddles and from the hives came up a deep steady hum as though the bees were still discussing Loveday's news.

Phil looked round. The dusty hedge-bordered highway to the next town stretched in one direction, on the other a narrower road running down to the little bay, where a few fishing luggers rocked idly. The three tracks across the Downs he could see as well; no one could come to Loyalty House unobserved by him.

Suddenly the boy drew back his head, crouched lower behind the bushes. For some one was coming up the hill from the direction of Loyalty House, a some one who was Loveday herself.

She was wearing her best gown of rose taffeta and her cheeks were as pink as her skirts. There was a fichu of her mother's finest lace round her shoulders and a dainty lace cap under the broad-brimmed straw hat, with its rose-satin ribbons.

" She hath decked herself grandly for *him*," Phil thought, scowling. " All her best frills and furbelows forsooth ! "

Loveday paused quite close to his hiding-place and went on till she stood in the shade of the three firs. There she sat down on a thyme-covered hillock and waited, her mittened hands in her lap.

*Some one was coming from Loyalty House. It was Loveday herself.*

" He's to meet her there, then," the watcher thought. " Well, I'll be able to see him bravely ! "

Half an hour passed, hot and still, except for the buzzing of insects, and these insects were in great plenty about Phil's gorse-bush, teasing and stinging. The boy was glad enough when at last, along one of the Down paths, he saw a tall figure approaching, walking quickly towards the little hill.

It was too far away to see his face—and now he had descended into a dip and would not be visible again until, in some ten minutes or so, he arrived on the hill's crest by the fir-trees—and Loveday. Bad luck that he should have chosen that way, thought Phil, and waited eagerly—so eagerly that he saw nothing of what was happening about him, heard nothing of a strange, sinister sound which was drawing nearer.

Loveday, too, with her back towards Phil, was gazing towards the approaching stranger, seeing and hearing naught but him, her eyes wide and eager, her cheeks a deeper pink than ever.

But from behind those two who watched so eagerly a great multitude was coming up the hill—coming with the deep murmur of an angry and excited crowd. Nearer and near they came, throwing a dark shadow on the sunlit turf, that throng who had left one home to seek another—the huge swarm of bees from the hive below.

As they neared the hill-top they rose a little higher in the air and their excited buzzing grew louder as the hot smell of gorse reached them. They veered sideways towards the clump of bushes so thickly covered with golden flowers, the queen bee who led them seeking some place to settle, most of the swarm flying closely about her, scouts darting here and there around and before the main body.

They hovered close to the gorse-bushes now, but Phil was so breathlessly waiting for the head of the stranger to appear above the crest of the hill that he noticed nothing—until a dark cloud seemed to descend upon him, whirling round his head and face, dimming the sunlight.

Perhaps it was the knot of orange ribbons in Phil's hat which had tricked the queen bee into thinking it a flower.  She settled upon it—and at once the whole swarm followed, clustering thickly upon the brim and crown of the hat, a dark moving mass from which a kind of veil of bees darted backwards and forwards round Phil's face.

The boy stumbled to his feet, trying to beat them off, before he gathered together his wits enough to remember that he must not anger them more than could be helped, that his only wise plan was to remain as still as might be.  Already his face and neck and hands were smarting from stings.  If he would not fare worse he must mind that he did not further infuriate the excited insects.

But a kind of gasping cry escaped Phil, and reached Loveday where she stood under the fir trees, with another figure beside her, that of the stranger who had just reached the top of the hill, was just bending to kiss her hand, whilst the girl stammered in confusion :

" Nay—nay, that shouldn't be for me . . . oh, your——"

" Hush, none of that, little mistress—but what's to do here ? "  The newcomer broke off, staring towards the gorse-bushes.

Loveday turned to look, gave a cry of fear and surprise.

" Ah, 'tis Phil—and the bees !  Oh, what's to be done ?  They will sting him to death—I must go ! "

Even as she spoke, Loveday was running towards Phil.  Through his lashes, almost closed, for fear that the bees should reach his eyes, through the darting, whirling cloud of bees he saw her coming, and saw behind her, dimly, a man's tall figure.

But in spite of his own pain and danger at that moment the boy thought only of Loveday.

" Go away ! " he gasped.  " Don't come near me !  They may turn on you—sting you . . . ah, keep away, Loveday ! "

" I will not, then ! " Loveday declared.  " Stand still, Phil : don't move a finger if you can help it.  I understand what to do—I've taken swarms before, and the bees know me."

Her voice sounded clearly above the furious buzzing of the bees, and before Phil realised what was happening, she had seized his wide-leafed hat by the two sides of the brim and was lifting it, quietly and without haste, from his head.

Still moving very deliberately, with no jerks or flurry, she walked some yards away, the heavy mass of bees between her hands, stray insects in a cloud buzzing round her.  Then she set down hat and swarm upon a little bank of thyme-covered turf and moved away from it without hurry.

" See—they'll all gather about it now," Loveday said, with a little catch in her breath.  " But—oh, poor Phil, poor boy !  you must come and have your stings tended at once. Don't try to open your eyes—they're swollen already. See, I'll lead you down to the house—I've many healing washes and waters there, in the still-room."

Phil obeyed blindly. He felt Loveday's hand pushed through his arm and leading him down the hill, heard her voice speaking to that other dim figure.

" Do not come—stay out of sight : I'll be with you soon, sir."

Stumbling over the slippery turf, Phil let himself be guided down the hill. They went past the hives, along the garden-walk, where other bees buzzed in the lavender. They were in the cobbled yard behind the house, and Loveday called to a manservant.

" Peter ! There is a fine swarm on top of the hill—take an empty skep and hive them before they've time to fly away beyond our reach ! And you Phil, come this way into the house."

Out of the sunshine in the stone passages the air felt cool on Philip's burning, aching skin. Loveday led him into a room, curtained against the heat, sweet-scented with bowls of pot-pourri, where a wide dimity-covered couch stood by the open window.

" Sit down here," the girl said, " whilst I fetch a bowl and linen. Very soon the pain will be better, when I've bathed and anointed the stings."

His eyes and head throbbing, Phil leaned back against the soft cushions, whilst Loveday deftly bathed the swollen, reddened skin and removed the stings which the bees had left.

" There ! The fever will quickly go down," she said. " I've tended many stings before. But lie still and try to sleep a while ; I'll send Kate to you with a drink of lemon-water and soothing herbs, and later I'll come back."

She was gone, and Phil, the stings still throbbing and burning, lay back, eyes closed. He drank the cool, slightly bitter-tasting draught which the maidservant brought presently, and a little later, as the pain and heat grew less, fell asleep.

When he woke, a breeze was stirring the flowered chintz curtains and the room was filled with golden evening light pouring in from the long shadows from the poplar trees. And Loveday was there, sitting on the end of the couch, looking at him gravely.

" You're better now," she said.

" Aye," Phil muttered. " Much better—I must have been asleep for a long time."

" Yes, for hours," Loveday told him. " 'Twas the best thing for you. The swelling has gone down ; soon it will be well again."

" I can see again now," Phil said, and suddenly Loveday laughed softly.

" Yes, you can see—but, oh, Phil, 'twas very fortunate that you could not see up on the hill ! It was much better so, though it was a cruel way to blind you."

" I don't understand—but 'twas mean of me to spy upon you : I know that," Phil confessed shamefacedly. " I'm sorry, Loveday."

" 'Tis all well now ; he's away—half across the Channel to France by this time, and good fortune go with him ! " Loveday spoke softly, her cheeks flushed, her eyes bright. " Naught can harm him now."

" He ?  The man you met on the hill ? " Phil asked.  " The man you told me you loved ? "

" Yes, but only because 'tis my duty as a loyal subject, Phil," Loveday said demurely, " because it was . . . the son of the king."

" You mean, that 'twas the Pretender—Prince Charles Edward ? " Phil sat up staring.

" Yes, word came this morning that he was on his way here, he had been told how to guide himself by the three firs to this place, where a fishing smack would be ready to carry him oversea.  And since my father was away, there was only me to help him, Phil, to stand for the honour of Loyalty House. I could not tell you the truth . . . until he was safe.  All your family are for King George ;  it would have been almost your duty to speak, to betray the prince."

" So that was what you told the bees ? "

" Yes," Loveday confessed.  " It was foolish, maybe, but 'tis so old a custom.  And oh, Phil, I think it proved itself a good one !  For had you seen the prince, you must have known who he was at once, so close at hand. But you did not see him—the bees blinded you at the right moment for him and for yourself too—oh, those bees are wise insects !  I do believe they *knew* —that they did it on purpose because I told them first ! "

" Perhaps they did ;  'tis very strange," Philip said.  " And . . . you don't hate me now, Loveday ? "

" Of course not," Loveday told him earnestly.

" And perhaps some day—when you're older . . . old enough to wed . . . ? "

" When we're *much* older," Loveday nodded.  " Yes, Philip, I really believe I will ! "

*" You mean, that 'twas the Pretender—Prince Charles Edward ? "*

# THE FIR TREE

## *by* HANS ANDERSEN

UT in the forest stood a pretty little Fir Tree. It had a good place; it could have sunlight, air there was in plenty, and all around grew many larger comrades—pines as well as firs. But the little Fir Tree wished ardently to become greater. It did not care for the warm sun and the fresh air; it took no notice of the peasant children, who went about talking together, when they had come out to look for strawberries and raspberries. Often they came with a whole potful, or had strung berries on a straw; then they would sit down by the little Fir Tree and say, " How pretty and small that one is ! " and the Fir Tree did not like to hear that at all.

Next year he had grown a great joint, and the following year he was longer still, for in fir trees one can always tell by the number of rings they have how many years they have been growing.

" Oh, if I were only as great a tree as the other ! " sighed the little Fir, " then I would spread my branches far around, and look out from my crown into the wide world. The birds would then build nests in my boughs, and when the wind blew I could nod just as grandly as the others yonder."

It took no pleasure in the sunshine, in the birds, and in the red clouds that went sailing over him morning and evening.

When it was winter, and the snow lay all around, white and sparkling, a hare would often come jumping along, and spring right over the little Fir Tree. Oh ! this made him so angry. But two winters went by, and when the third came the little Tree had grown so tall that the hare was obliged to run round it.

" Oh ! to grow, to grow, and become old; that's the only fine thing in the world," thought the Tree.

246

In the autumn woodcutters always came and felled a few of the largest trees ; that was done this year too, and the little Fir Tree, that was now quite well grown, shuddered with fear, for the great stately trees fell to the ground with a crash, and their branches were cut off, so that the trees looked quite naked, long, and slender—they could hardly be recognised. But then they were laid upon waggons and horses dragged them away out of the wood. Where were they going ? What destiny awaited them ?

In the spring, when the Swallows and the Stork came, the Tree asked them, " Do you know where they were taken ? Did you not meet them ? "

The Swallows knew nothing about it, but the Stork looked thoughtful, nodded his head, and said,

" Yes, I think so. I met many new ships when I flew out of Egypt ; on the ships were stately masts ; I fancy these were the trees. They smelt like fir. I can assure you they're stately—very stately."

" Oh that I were only big enough to go over the sea ! What kind of thing is this sea, and how does it look ? "

" It would take too long to explain all that," said the Stork, and he went away.

" Rejoice in thy youth," said the Sunbeams ; " rejoice in thy fresh growth, and in the young life that is within thee."

And the wind kissed the Tree, and the dew wept tears upon it ; but the Fir Tree did not understand that.

When Christmas-time approached, quite young trees were felled, sometimes trees which were neither so old nor so large as this Fir Tree, that never rested, but always wanted to go away. These young trees, which were almost the most beautiful, kept all their branches ; they were put upon waggons, and horses dragged them away out of the wood.

" Where are they all going ? " asked the Fir Tree. " They are not greater than I—indeed, one of them was much smaller. Why do they keep all their branches ? Whither are they taken ? "

" We know that ! We know that ! " chirped the Sparrows. " Yonder in the town we looked in at the windows. We know where they go. Oh ! they are dressed up in the greatest pomp and splendour that can be imagined. We have looked in at the windows, and have perceived that they are planted in the middle of the warm room, and adorned with the most beautiful things— gilt apples, honey-cakes, playthings, and many hundreds of candles."

" And then ? " asked the Fir Tree, and trembled through all its branches. " And then ? What happens then ? "

" Why, we have not seen anything more. But it was incomparable."

" Perhaps I may be destined to tread this glorious path one day ! " cried the Fir Tree, rejoicingly. " That is even better than travelling across the sea. How painfully I long for it ! If it were only Christmas now ! Now I am great and grown up, like the rest who were led away last year. Oh, if I were only on the carriage ! If I were only in the warm room, among all the pomp and splendour ! And then ? Yes, then something even better will come, something far more charming, or else why should they adorn me so ? There must be something grander, something greater still to come ; but what ? Oh ! I'm suffering, I'm longing ! I don't know myself what is the matter with me ! "

" Rejoice in us," said Air and Sunshine. " Rejoice in thy fresh youth here in the woodland."

But the Fir Tree did not rejoice at all, but it grew and grew ; winter and summer it stood there, green, dark green. The people who saw it said, " That's a handsome tree ! " and at Christmas-time it was felled before any one of the others. The axe cut deep into its marrow, and the tree fell to the ground with a sigh : it felt a pain, a sensation of faintness, and could not think at all of happiness, for it was sad at parting from its home, from the place where it had grown up : it knew that it should never again see the dear old companions, the little bushes and flowers all around—perhaps not even the birds. The parting was not at all agreeable.

*The young ladies of the house decorated the Tree.*

The Tree only came to itself when it was unloaded in a yard, with other trees, and heard a man say, " This one is famous ; we only want this one ! "

Now two servants came in gay liveries, and carried the Fir Tree into a large, beautiful saloon. All around the walls hung pictures, and by the great stove stood large Chinese vases with lions on the covers ; there were rocking-chairs, silken sofas, great tables covered with picture-books, and toys worth a hundred times a hundred dollars, at least the children said so. And the Fir Tree was put into a great tub filled with sand ; but no one could see that it was a tub, for it was hung round with green cloth, and stood on a large many-coloured carpet. Oh, how the Tree trembled. What was to happen now ?

The servants, and the young ladies also, decked it out. On one branch they hung little nets, cut out of coloured paper ; every net was filled with sweetmeats ; golden apples and walnuts hung down as if they grew here, and more than a hundred little candles, red, white, and blue, were fastened to the different boughs. Dolls that looked exactly like real people—the Tree had never seen such before—swung among the foliage, and high on the summit of the Tree was fixed a tinsel star. It was splendid, particularly splendid.

"This evening," said all, "this evening it will shine."

"Oh," thought the Tree, "that it were evening already! Oh that the lights may be soon lit up! When may that be done? I wonder if trees will come out of the forest to look at me? Will the sparrows fly against the panes? Shall I grow fast here, and stand adorned in summer and winter?"

Yes, he did not guess badly. But he had a complete backache from mere longing, and the backache is just as bad for a Tree as the headache for a person.

At last the candles were lighted. What a brilliance, what splendour! The Tree trembled so in all its branches that one of the candles set fire to a green twig, and it was scorched.

"Heaven preserve us!" cried the young ladies; and they hastily put the fire out.

Now the Tree might not even tremble. Oh, that was terrible! It was so afraid of setting fire to some of its ornaments, and it was quite bewildered with all the brilliance. And now the folding doors were thrown open, and a number of children rushed in as if they would have overturned the whole Tree; the older people followed more deliberately. The little ones stood quite silent, but only for a minute; then they shouted till the room rang: they danced gleefully round the Tree, and one present after another was plucked from it.

"What are they about?" thought the Tree. "What's going to be done?"

And the candles burned down to the twigs, and as they burned down they were extinguished; and then the children received permission to plunder the Tree. Oh! they rushed in upon it, so that every branch cracked again: if it had not been fastened by the top and by the golden star to the ceiling, it would have fallen down.

The children danced about with their pretty toys. No one looked at the Tree except one old man, who came up and peeped among the branches, but only to see if a fig or an apple had not been forgotten.

"A story! a story!" shouted the children; and they drew a little fat man towards the Tree; and he sat down just beneath it,—"For then we shall be in the green wood," said he, "and the tree may have the advantage of listening to my tale. But I can only tell one. Will you hear the story of Ivede-Avede, or of Klumpey-Dumpey, who fell downstairs, and still was raised up to honour and married the Princess?"

"Ivede-Avede!" cried some, "Klumpey-Dumpey!" cried others, and there was a great crying and shouting. Only the Fir Tree was quite silent, and thought, "Shall I not be in it? shall I have nothing to do in it?" But he had been in the evening's amusement, and had done what was required of him.

And the fat man told about Klumpey-Dumpey who fell downstairs, and yet was raised to honour and married the Princess. And the children clapped their hands, and cried, "Tell another! tell another!" for they wanted to hear about Ivede-Avede; but they only got the story of Klumpey-Dumpey.

The Fir Tree stood quite silent and thoughtful ; never had the birds in the wood told such a story as that. Klumpey-Dumpey fell down stairs, and yet came to honour and married the Princess.

"Yes, so it happens in the world !" thought the Fir Tree, and believed it must be true, because that was such a nice man who told it. "Well, who can know ? Perhaps I shall fall downstairs too, and marry a Princess !" And it looked forward with pleasure to being adorned again, the next evening, with candles and toys, gold and fruit. "To-morrow I shall not tremble," it thought. "I will rejoice in all my splendour. To-morrow I shall hear the story of Klumpey-Dumpey again, and perhaps that of Ivede-Avede too."

And the Tree stood all night quiet and thoughtful.

In the morning the servants and the chambermaid came in.

"Now my splendour will begin afresh," thought the Tree. But they dragged him out of the room, and upstairs to the garret, and here they put him in a dark corner where no daylight shone.

"What's the meaning of this ?" thought the Tree. "What am I to do here ? What is to happen ?"

And he leaned against the wall, and thought, and thought. And he had time enough, for days and nights went by, and nobody came up ; and when at length some one came, it was only to put some great boxes in a corner. Now the Tree stood quite hidden away, and the supposition is that it was quite forgotten.

"Now it's winter outside," thought the Tree. "The earth is hard and covered with snow, and people cannot paint me ; therefore I suppose I'm to be sheltered here until spring comes. How considerate that is ! How good people are ! If it were only not so dark here, and so terribly solitary !—not even a little hare ! That was pretty out there in the wood, when the snow lay thick and the hare sprang past ; yes, even when he jumped over me ; but then I did not like it. It is terribly lonely up here !"

"Piep ! piep !" said a little Mouse, and crept forward, and then came another little one. They smelt at the Fir Tree, and then slipped among the branches.

"It's horribly cold," said the two little Mice, "or else it would be comfortable here. Don't you think so, you old Fir Tree ?"

"I'm not old at all," said the Fir Tree. "There are many much older than I."

"Where do you come from ?" asked the Mice. "And what do you know ?" They were dreadfully inquisitive. "Tell us about the most beautiful spot on earth. Have you been there ? Have you been in the store-room, where cheeses lie on the shelves, and hams hang from the ceiling, where one dances on tallow candles, and goes in thin and comes out fat ?"

"I don't know that," replied the Tree ; "but I know the wood, where the sun shines and the birds sing."

And then it told all about its youth.

And the little Mice had never heard anything of the kind ; and they listened and said :

"What a number of things you have seen ! How happy you must have been !"

"I ?" replied the Fir Tree ; and it thought about what it had told.

" Yes, those were really quite happy times." But then he told of the Christmas Eve, when he had been hung with sweetmeats and candles.

" Oh ! " said the little Mice, " how happy you have been, you old Fir Tree ! "

" I'm not old at all," said the Tree. " I only came out of the wood this winter. I'm only rather backward in my growth."

" What splendid stories you can tell ! " said the little Mice.

And next night they came with four other little Mice, to hear what the Tree had to relate ; and the more it said, the more clearly did it remember everything, and thought, " Those were quite merry days ! But they may come again. Klumpey-Dumpey fell downstairs, and yet he married the Princess. Perhaps I may marry a Princess too ! " And then the Fir Tree thought of a pretty little birch tree that grew out in the forest : for the Fir Tree, that birch was a real Princess.

" Who's Klumpey-Dumpey ? " asked the little Mice.

And then the Fir Tree told the whole story. It could remember every single word ; and the little Mice were ready to leap to the very top of the tree with pleasure. Next night a great many more Mice came, and on Sunday two Rats even appeared ; but these thought the story was not pretty, and the little Mice were sorry for that, for now they also did not like it so much as before.

" Do you only know one story ? " asked the Rats.

" Only that one," replied the Tree. " I heard that on the happiest evening of my life ; I did not think then how happy I was."

" That's a very miserable story. Don't you know any about bacon and tallow candles—a store-room story ? "

" No," said the Tree.

" Then we'd rather not hear you," said the Rats.

And they went back to their own people. The little Mice at last stayed away also ; and then the Tree sighed and said,

" It was very nice when they sat round me, the merry little Mice, and listened when I spoke to them. Now that's past too. But I shall remember to be pleased when they take me out."

But when did that happen ? Why, it was one morning that people came and rummaged in the garret : the boxes were put away, and the Tree brought out ; they certainly threw him rather roughly on the floor, but a servant dragged him away at once to the stairs, where the daylight shone.

" Now life is beginning again ! " thought the Tree.

It felt the fresh air and the first sunbeams, and now it was out in the courtyard. Everything passed so quickly that the Tree quite forgot to look at itself, there was so much to look at all round. The courtyard was close to a garden, and here everything was blooming ; the roses hung fresh and fragrant over the little paling, the linden trees were in blossom, and the swallows cried, " Quinze-wit ! quinze-wit ! my husband's come ! " But it was not the Fir Tree that they meant.

" Now I shall live ! " said the Tree, rejoicingly, and spread its branches far out ; but, alas ! they were all withered and yellow ; and it lay in the corner among nettles and weeds. The tinsel star was still upon it, and shone in the bright sunshine.

In the courtyard a couple of the merry children were playing, who had danced round the Tree at Christmas-time, and had rejoiced over it. One of the youngest ran up and tore off the golden star.

" Look what is sticking to the ugly old fir tree," said the child, and he trod upon the branches till they cracked again under his boots.

And the Tree looked at all the blooming flowers and the splendour of the garden, and then looked at itself, and wished it had remained in the dark corner of the garret; it thought of its fresh youth in the wood, of the merry Christmas Eve, and of the little Mice which had listened so pleasantly to the story of Klumpey-Dumpey.

" Past ! past ! " said the old Tree. " Had I but rejoiced when I could have done so ! Past ! past ! "

And the servant came and chopped the Tree into little pieces; a whole bundle lay there; it blazed brightly under the great brewing copper, and it sighed deeply, and each sigh was like a shot; and the children who were at play there ran up and seated themselves at the fire, looked into it, and cried, " Puff ! puff ! " But at each explosion, which was a deep sigh, the Tree thought of a summer day in the woods, or of a winter night there, when the stars beamed; he thought of Christmas Eve and of Klumpey-Dumpey, the only story he had ever heard or knew how to tell; and then the Tree was burned.

The boys played in the garden, and the youngest had on his breast a golden star, which the Tree had worn on its happiest evening. Now that was past, and the Tree's life was past, and the story is past too : past ! past ! —and that's the way with all stories.

*One of the youngest ran up and tore off the golden star.*

# THE YOUNG GIANT

## *by* THE BROTHERS GRIMM

NCE on a time a countryman had a son who was as big as a thumb, and did not become any bigger, and during several years did not grow one hair's breadth. Once when the father was going out to plough, the little one said, " Father, I will go out with you." " Thou wouldst go out with me ? " said the father. " Stay here, thou wilt be of no use out there, besides thou mightst get lost ! "

Then Thumbling began to cry, and for the sake of peace his father put him in his pocket, and took him with him. When he was outside in the field, he took him out again, and set him in a freshly-cut furrow. Whilst he was there, a great giant came over the hill. " Dost thou see that great bogie ? " said the father, for he wanted to frighten the little fellow to make him good ; " he is coming to fetch thee." The giant, however, had scarcely taken two steps with his long legs before he was in the furrow. He took up little Thumbling carefully with two fingers, examined him, and without saying one word went away with him. His father stood by, but could not utter a sound for terror, and he thought nothing else but that his child was lost, and that as long as he lived he should never set eyes on him again.

The giant, however, carried him home, and Thumbling grew and became tall and strong after the manner of giants. When two years had passed, the old giant took him into the forest, and said, " Pull up a stick for thyself." Then the boy was already so strong that he tore up a young tree out of the earth by the roots. But the giant thought, " We must do better than that," took him back again, and suckled him two years longer. When he tried him, his strength had increased so much that he could tear an old tree out of the ground.

That was still not enough for the giant, he again suckled him for two

253

years, and when he then went with him into the forest and said, " Now, just tear up a proper stick for me," the boy tore up the strongest oak-tree from the earth, so that it split, and that was a mere trifle to him. " Now that will do," said the giant, " thou art perfect," and took him back to the field from whence he had brought him. His father was there following the plough. The young giant went up to him, and said, " Does my father see what a fine man his son has grown into ? "

The farmer was alarmed, and said, " No, thou art not my son ; I don't want thee—leave me ! " " Truly I am your son ; allow me to do your work, I can plough as well as you, nay, better." " No, no, thou art not my son, and thou canst not plough—go away ! " However, as he was afraid of this great man, he left hold of the plough, stepped back and stood at one side of the piece of land. Then the youth took the plough, and just pressed it with one hand, but his grasp was so strong that the plough went deep into the earth. The farmer could not bear to see that, and called to him, " If thou art determined to plough, thou must not press so hard on it, that makes bad work." The youth, however, unharnessed the horses, and drew the plough himself, saying, " Just go home, father, and bid my mother make ready a large dish of food, and in the meantime I will go over the field."

Then the farmer went home, and told his wife to prepare the food ; but the youth ploughed the field which was two acres large, quite alone, and then he harnessed himself to the harrow, and harrowed the whole of the land, using two harrows at once. When he had done it, he went into the forest, and pulled up two oak-trees, laid them across his shoulders, and hung one harrow on them behind and one before, and also one horse behind and one before, and carried all as if it had been a bundle of straw, to his parents' house.

When he entered the yard, his mother did not recognise him, and asked, " Who is that horrible tall man ? " The farmer said, " That is our son." She said, " No, that cannot be our son, we never had such a tall one, ours was a little thing." She called to him, " Go away, we do not want thee ! "

The youth was silent, but led his horses to the stable, gave them oats and hay, and all that they wanted. When he had done this, he went into the parlour, sat down on the bench and said, " Mother, now I should like something to eat, will it soon be ready ? " Then she said, " Yes," and brought in two immense dishes full of food, which would have been enough to satisfy herself and her husband for a week. The youth, however, ate the whole of it himself, and asked if she had nothing more to set before him. " No," she replied, " that is all we have." " But that was only a taste, I must have more." She did not dare to oppose him, and went and put a huge cauldron full of food on the fire, and when it was ready, carried it in. " At length come a few crumbs," said he, and ate all there was, but it was still not sufficient to appease his hunger. Then said he, " Father, I see well that with you I shall never have food enough ; if you will get me an iron staff which is strong, and which I cannot break against my knees, I will go out into the world."

The farmer was glad, put his two horses in his cart, and fetched from the smith a staff so large and thick that the two horses could only just bring it away. The youth laid it across his knees, and snap ! he broke it in two in the middle like a bean-stick, and threw it away. The father then harnessed four horses, and brought a bar which was so long and thick, that the four horses could only just drag it. The son snapped this also in twain against his knees, threw it away, and said, " Father, this can be of no use to me, you must harness more horses, and bring a stronger staff." So the father harnessed eight horses, and brought one which was so long and thick, that the eight horses could only just carry it. When the son took it in his hand, he broke a bit from the top of it, also, and said, " Father, I see that you will not be able to procure me any such staff as I want, I will remain no longer with you."

So he went away, and gave out that he was a smith's apprentice. He arrived at a village, wherein lived a smith who was a greedy fellow, who never did a kindness to any one, but wanted everything for himself. The youth went into the smithy to him, and asked if he needed a journeyman.

" Yes," said the smith, and looked at him, and thought, " That is a strong fellow who will strike out well, and earn his bread." So he asked, " How much wages dost thou want ? " " I don't want any at all," he replied, " only every fortnight, when the other journeymen are paid, I will give thee two blows, and thou must bear them." The miser was heartily satisfied, and thought he would thus save much money. Next morning, the strange journeyman was to begin to work, but when the master brought the glowing bar, and the youth struck his first blow, the iron flew asunder, and the anvil sank so deep into the earth, that there was no bringing it out again. Then the miser grew angry, and said, " Oh, but I can't make any use of you, you strike far too powerfully ; what will you have for the one blow ? "

Then said he, " I will only give you quite a small blow, that's all. And

*The youth took the staff, broke it in two in the middle like a bean-stick, and threw it away.*

he raised his foot, and gave him such a kick that he flew away over four loads of hay. Then he sought out the thickest iron bar in the smithy for himself, took it as a stick in his hand, and went onwards.

When he had walked for some time, he came to a small farm, and asked the bailiff if he did not require a head-servant. "Yes," said the bailiff, "I can make use of one; you look a strong fellow who can do something, how much a year do you want as wages?" He again replied that he wanted no wages at all, but that every year he would give him three blows, which he must bear. Then the bailiff was satisfied, for he, too, was a covetous fellow. Next morning all the servants were to go into the wood, and the others were already up, but the head-servant was still in bed. Then one of them called to him, "Get up, it is time; we are going into the wood, and thou must go with us." "Ah," said he quite roughly and surlily, "you may just go, then; I shall be back again before any of you." Then the others went to the bailiff, and told him that the head-man was still lying in bed, and would not go into the wood with them. The bailiff said they were to awake him again, and tell him to harness the horses. The head-man, however, said as before, "Just go there, I shall be back again before any of you." And then he stayed in bed two hours longer.

At length he arose, got two bushels of peas from the loft, made himself some broth with them, ate it at his leisure, and when that was done, went and harnessed the horses, and drove into the wood. Not far from the wood was a ravine through which he had to pass, so he first drove the horses on, and then stopped them, and went behind the cart, took trees and brushwood, and made a great barricade, so that no horse could get through. When he was entering the wood, the others were just driving out of it with their loaded carts to go home; then said he to them, "Drive on, I will still get home before you do."

He did not drive far into the wood, but at once tore two of the very largest trees of all out of the earth, threw them on his cart, and turned round. When he came to the barricade, the others were still standing there, not able to get through. "Don't you see," said he, "that if you had stayed with me, you would have got home just as quickly, and would have had another hour's sleep?" He now wanted to drive on, but his horses could not work their way through, so he unharnessed them, laid them at the top of the cart, took the shafts in his own hands, and drew it over, and he did this just as easily as if it had been laden with feathers.

He said to the others, "There, you see, I have got over quicker than you," and drove on, and the others had to stay where they were. In the yard, however, he took a tree in his hand, showed it to the bailiff, and said, "Isn't that a fine bundle of wood?" Then said the bailiff to his wife, "The servant is a good one, if he does sleep long, he is still home before the others." So he served the bailiff a year, and when that was over, and the other servants were getting their wages, he said it was time for him to have his too. The bailiff, however, was afraid of the blows which he was to receive, and earnestly entreated him to excuse him from having them; for rather than that, he himself would be head-servant, and the youth should be bailiff. "No," said he, "I will not be a bailiff, I am head-servant, and will remain so, but I will administer that which we agreed on." The bailiff was willing to give him whatsoever he demanded, but it was of no use, the head-servant said no to everything. Then the bailiff did not know what to do, and begged for a fortnight's delay, for he wanted to find some way of escape. The head-servant consented to this delay. The bailiff summoned all his clerks together, and they were to think the matter over, and give him advice.

They pondered for a long time, but at last they said that no one was sure of his life with the head-servant, for he could kill a man as easily as a midge, and that the bailiff ought to make him get into the well and clean it, and when he was down below, they would roll up one of the mill-stones which was lying there, and throw it on his head; and then he would never return.

The advice pleased the bailiff, and the head-servant was quite willing to go down the well. When he was standing down below at the bottom, they rolled down the largest mill-stone and thought they had broken his skull, but he cried, " Chase away those hens from the well, they are scratching in the sand up there, and throwing the grains into my eyes, so that I can't see." So the bailiff cried, " Sh-sh,"—and pretended to frighten the hens away.

When the head-servant had finished his work, he climbed up and said, " Just look what a beautiful neck-tie I have on," and behold it was the mill-stone which he was wearing round his neck. The head-servant now wanted to take his reward, but the bailiff again begged for a fortnight's delay.

The clerks met together and advised him to send the head-servant to the haunted mill to grind corn by night, for from thence as yet no man had ever returned in the morning alive. The proposal pleased the bailiff, he called the head-servant that very evening, and ordered him to take eight bushels of corn to the mill, and grind it that night, for it was wanted. So the head-servant went to the loft, and put two bushels in his right pocket, and two in his left, and took four in a wallet, half on his back, and half on his breast, and thus laden went to the haunted mill. The miller told him that he could grind there very well by day, but not by night, for the mill was haunted, and that up to the present time whosoever had gone into it at night had been found in the morning, lying dead inside. He said, " I will manage it, just you go away to bed." Then he went into the mill, and poured out the corn.

About eleven o'clock he went into the miller's room, and sat down on the bench. When he had sat there a while, a door suddenly opened, and large table came in, and on the table, wine and roasted meats placed themselves, and much good food besides, but everything came of itself, for no one was there to carry it. After this the chairs pushed themselves up, but no people came, until all at once he beheld fingers, which handled knives and forks, and laid food on the plates, but with this exception he saw nothing.

As he was hungry, and saw the food. he, too, placed himself at the table, ate with those who were eating, and enjoyed it. When he had had enough, and the others also had quite emptied their dishes, he distinctly heard all the candles being suddenly snuffed out, and as it was now pitch dark, he felt something like a box on the ear. Then he said, " If anything of that kind comes again, I shall strike out in return." And when he had received a second box on the ear, he, too, struck out. And so it continued the whole night, he took nothing without returning it, but repaid everything with interest, and did not lay about him in vain. At daybreak, however, everything ceased.

When the miller had got up, he wanted to look after him, and wondered if he were still alive. Then the youth said, " I have eaten my fill, have received some boxes on the ear, but I have given some in return." The miller rejoiced, and said that the mill was now released from the spell, and wanted to give him much money as a reward. But he said, " Money I will not have, I have enough of it." So he took his meal on his back, went home, and told the bailiff that he had done what he had been told to do, and would now have the reward agreed on. When the bailiff heard that, he was seriously alarmed and quite beside himself ; he walked backwards and forwards in the room, and drops of perspiration ran down from his forehead. Then he opened the window to get some fresh air, but before he was aware the head-servant had given him such a kick that he flew through the window out into the air, and so far away that no one ever saw him again.

The head-servant said to the bailiff's wife, " If he does not come back, you must take the other blow." She cried, " No, no, I cannot bear it," and opened the other window, because drops of perspiration were running down her forehead. Then he gave her such a kick that she, too, flew out, and as she was lighter she went much higher than her husband. Her husband cried, " Do come to me," but she replied, " Come thou to me, I cannot come to thee." And they hovered about there in the air, and could not get to each other, and whether they are still hovering about, or not, I do not know, but the young giant took up his iron bar, and went on his way.

---

# BENDEMEER'S STREAM

## *by* T. MOORE

THERE'S a bower of roses by Bendemeer's stream,
    And the nightingale sings round it all the day long ;
In the time of my childhood 'twas like a sweet dream,
    To sit in the roses and hear the bird's song.
That bower and its music I never forget,
    But oft when alone, in the bloom of the year,
I think—Is the nightingale singing there yet ?
    Are the roses still bright by the calm Bendemeer ?

No, the roses soon withered that hung o'er the wave,
    But some blossoms were gathered while freshly they shone,
And a dew was distilled from their flowers, that gave
    All the fragrance of summer, when summer was gone.
Thus memory draws from delight, e'er it dies,
    An essence that breathes of it many a year ;
Thus bright to my soul, as 'twas then to my eyes,
    Is the bower on the banks of the calm Bendemeer !

# THE SHOEMAKER

### by CHARLES DICKENS

"OOD-DAY!" said Monsieur Defarge, looking down at the white head that bent low over the shoemaking.

It was raised for a moment, and a very faint voice responded to the salutation, as if it were at a distance—

"Good-day!"

"You are still hard at work, I see?"

After a long silence, the head was lifted for another moment, and the voice replied, "Yes—I am working." This time, a pair of haggard eyes had looked at the questioner, before the face had dropped again.

The faintness of the voice was pitiable and dreadful. It was not the faintness of physical weakness, though confinement and hard fare no doubt had their part in it. Its deplorable peculiarity was that it was the faintness of solitude and disuse. It was like the last feeble echo of a sound made long and long ago. So entirely had it lost the life and resonance of the human voice, that it affected the senses like a once beautiful colour faded away into a poor weak stain. So sunken and suppressed it was, that it was like a voice underground. So expressive it was, of a hopeless and lost creature, that a famished traveller, wearied out by lonely wandering in a wilderness, would have remembered home and friends in such a tone before lying down to die.

Some minutes of silent work had passed, and the haggard eyes had looked up again: not with any interest or curiosity, but with a dull mechanical perception, beforehand, that the spot where the only visitor they were aware of had stood, was not yet empty.

"I want," said Defarge, who had not removed his gaze from the shoemaker, "to let in a little more light here. You can bear a little more?"

259

The shoemaker stopped his work ; looked, with a vacant air of listening at the floor on one side of him ; then, similarly, at the floor on the other side of him ; then, upward at the speaker.

" What did you say ? "

" You can bear a little more light ? "

" I must bear it, if you let it in." (Laying the palest shadow of a stress upon the second word.)

The opened half-door was opened a little farther, and secured at that angle for the time. A broad ray of light fell into the garret, and showed the work-man with an unfinished shoe upon his lap, pausing in his labour. His few common tools and various scraps of leather were at his feet and on his bench. He had a white beard, raggedly cut, but not very long, a hollow face, and exceedingly bright eyes. The hollowness and thinness of his face would have caused them to look large, under his yet dark eyebrows and his confused white hair, though they had been really otherwise ; but they were naturally large, and looked unnaturally so. His yellow rag of shirt lay open at the throat, and showed his body to be withered and worn. He, and his old canvas frock, and his loose stockings, and all his poor tatters of clothes, had, in a long seclusion from direct light and air, faded down to such a dull uniformity of parchment yellow, that it would have been hard to say which was which.

He had put up a hand between his eyes and the light, and the very bones of it seemed transparent. So he sat, with a steadfastly vacant gaze, pausing in his work. He never looked at the figure before him, without first looking down on this side of himself, then on that, as if he had lost the habit of associating place with sound ; he never spoke, without first wandering in this manner, and forgetting to speak.

" Are you going to finish that pair of shoes to-day ? " asked Defarge, motioning to Mr. Lorry to come forward.

" What did you say ? "

" Do you mean to finish that pair of shoes to-day ? "

" I can't say that I mean to. I suppose so. I don't know."

But the question reminded him of his work, and he bent over it again.

Mr. Lorry came silently forward, leaving the daughter by the door. When he had stood, for a minute or two, by the side of Defarge, the shoemaker looked up. He showed no surprise at seeing another figure, but the unsteady fingers of one of his hands strayed to his lips as he looked at it (his lips and his nails were of the same pale lead colour), and then the hand dropped to his work, and he once more bent over the shoe. The look and the action had occupied but an instant.

" You have a visitor, you see," said Monsieur Defarge.

" What did you say ? "

" Here is a visitor."

The shoemaker looked up as before, but without removing a hand from his work.

" Come ! " said Defarge. " Here is monsieur who knows a well-made shoe when he sees one. Show him that shoe you are working at. Take it, monsieur."

Mr. Lorry took it in his hand.

" Tell monsieur what kind of shoe it is, and the maker's name."

There was a longer pause than usual, before the shoemaker replied—

" I forget what it was you asked me. What did you say ? "

" I said, couldn't you describe the kind of shoe, for monsieur's information ? "

" It is a lady's shoe. It is a young lady's walking shoe. It is in the present mode. I never saw the mode. I have had a pattern in my hand." He glanced at the shoe, with some little passing touch of pride.

" And the maker's name ? " said Defarge.

Now that he had no work to hold, he laid the knuckles of the right hand in the hollow of the left, and then the knuckles of the left hand in the hollow of the right, and then passed a hand across his bearded chin, and so on in regular

" *One Hundred and Five, North Tower.*"

changes, without a moment's intermission. The task of recalling him from the vacancy into which he always sank when he had spoken, was like recalling some very weak person from a swoon, or endeavouring, in the hope of some disclosure, to stay the spirit of a fast dying man.

" Did you ask me for my name ? "

" Assuredly I did."

" One Hundred and Five, North Tower."

" Is that all ? "

" One Hundred and Five, North Tower."

With a weary sound that was not a sigh, nor a groan, he bent to work again, until the silence was again broken.

" You are not a shoemaker by trade ? " said Mr. Lorry, looking steadfastly at him.

His haggard eyes turned to Defarge as if he would have transferred the question to him ; but as no help came from that quarter, they turned back on the questioner when they had sought the ground.

" I am not a shoemaker by trade ? No, I was not a shoemaker by trade. I—I learned it here. I taught myself. I asked leave to——"

He lapsed away, even for minutes, ringing those measured changes on his hands the whole time. His eyes came slowly back, at last, to the face from which they had wandered ; when they rested on it, he started, and resumed, in the manner of a sleeper that moment awake, reverting to a subject of last night.

" I asked leave to teach myself, and I got it with much difficulty after a long while, and I have made shoes ever since."

As he held out his hand for the shoe that had been taken from him, Mr. Lorry said, still looking steadfastly in his face—

" Monsieur Manette, do you remember nothing of me ? "

The shoe dropped to the ground, and he sat looking fixedly at the questioner.

" Monsieur Manette "—Mr. Lorry laid his hand upon Defarge's arm— " do you remember nothing of this man ? Look at him. Look at me. Is there no old banker, no old business, no old servant, no old time rising in your mind, Monsieur Manette ? "

As the captive of many years sat looking fixedly, by turns at Mr. Lorry and at Defarge, some long-obliterated marks of an actively intent intelligence in the middle of the forehead, gradually forced themselves through the black mist that had fallen on him. They were overclouded again, they were fainter, they were gone ; but they had been there. And so exactly was the expression repeated on the fair young face of her who had crept along the wall to a point where she could see him, and where she now stood looking at him, with hands which at first had been only raised in frightened compassion, if not even to keep him off and shut out the sight of him, but which were now extending towards him, trembling with eagerness to lay the spectral face upon her warm young breast, and love it back to life and hope—so exactly was the expression repeated (though in stronger characters) on her fair young face, that it looked as though it had passed, like a moving light, from him to her.

Darkness had fallen on him in its place. He looked at the two, less and less attentively, and his eyes in gloomy abstraction sought the ground and looked about him in the old way. Finally, with a deep, long sigh, he took the shoe up, and resumed his work.

" Have you recognised him, monsieur ? " asked Defarge, in a whisper.

" Yes ; for a moment. At first I thought it quite hopeless, but I have unquestionably seen, for a single moment, the face that I once knew well. Hush ! Let us draw farther back. Hush ! "

She had moved from the wall of the garret, very near to the bench on which he sat. There was something awful in his unconsciousness of the figure that could have put out its hand and touched him as he stooped over his labour.

Not a word was spoken, not a sound was made. She stood, like a spirit, beside him, and he bent over his work.

It happened, at length, that he had occasion to change the instrument in his hand for his shoemaker's knife. It lay on that side of him which was not the side on which she stood. He had taken it up, and was stooping to work again, when his eyes caught the skirt of her dress. He raised them, and saw her face. The two spectators started forward, but she stayed them with a motion of her hand. She had no fear of his striking at her with the knife, although they had.

He stared at her with a fearful look, and after a while his lips began to form some words, though no sound proceeded from them. By degrees, in the pauses of his quick and laboured breathing, he was heard to say—

" What is this ? "

With the tears streaming down her face, she put her two hands to her lips, and kissed them to him ; then clasped them on her breast, as if she laid his ruined head there.

" You are not the gaoler's daughter ? "

She sighed " No."

" Who are you ? "

Not yet trusting the tones of her voice, she sat down on the bench beside him. He recoiled, but she laid her hand upon his arm. A strange thrill struck him when she did so, and visibly passed over his frame ; he laid the knife down softly, as he sat staring at her.

Her golden hair, which she wore in long curls, had been hurriedly pushed aside, and fell down over her neck. Advancing his hand by little and little, he took it up, and looked at it. In the midst of the action he went astray, and, with another deep sigh, fell to work at his shoemaking.

But not for long. Releasing his arm, she laid her hand upon his shoulder. After looking doubtfully at it, two or three times, as if to be sure that it was really there, he laid down his work, put his hand to his neck, and took off a blackened string with a scrap of folded rag attached to it. He opened this carefully, on his knee, and it contained a very little quantity of hair : not more than one or two long golden hairs, which he had, in some old day, wound off upon his finger.

He took her hair into his hand again, and looked closely at it. " It is the same. How can it be ! When was it ! How was it ! "

As the concentrating expression returned to his forehead, he seemed to become conscious that it was in hers too. He turned her full to the light, and looked at her.

" She had laid her head upon my shoulder that night when I was summoned out—she had a fear of my going, though I had none—and when I was brought to the North Tower they found these upon my sleeve. ' You will leave me them ? They can never help me to escape in the body, though they may in the spirit.' Those were the words I said. I remember them very well."

He formed this speech with his lips many times before he could utter it. But when he did find spoken words for it, they came to him coherently, though slowly.

" How was this ? *Was it you ?* "

Once more, the two spectators started, as he turned upon her with a frightful suddenness. But she sat perfectly still in his grasp, and only said, in a low voice, " I entreat you, good gentlemen, do not come near us, do not speak, do not move ! "

"Hark!" he exclaimed. "Whose voice was that?"

His hands released her as he uttered this cry, and went up to his white hair, which they tore in a frenzy. It died out, as everything but his shoemaking did die out of him, and he refolded his little packet and tried to secure it in his breast; but he still looked at her, and gloomily shook his head.

"No, no, no; you are too young, too blooming. It can't be. See what the prisoner is. These are not the hands she knew, this is not the face she knew, this is not a voice she ever heard. No, no. She was—and he was—before the slow years of the North Tower—ages ago. What is your name, my gentle angel?"

Hailing his softened tone and manner, his daughter fell upon her knees before him, with her appealing hands upon his breast.

"O sir, at another time you shall know my name, and who my mother was, and who my father, and how I never knew their hard, hard history. But I cannot tell you at this time, and I cannot tell you here. All that I may tell you, here and now, is that I pray to you to touch me and to bless me. Kiss me, kiss me! O my dear, my dear!"

His cold, white head mingled with her radiant hair, which warmed and lighted it as though it were the light of freedom shining on him.

"If you hear in my voice—I don't know that it is so, but I hope it is— if you hear in my voice any resemblance to a voice that once was sweet music in your ears, weep for it, weep for it! If you touch, in touching my hair, anything that recalls a beloved head that lay on your breast when you were young and free, weep for it, weep for it! If, when I hint to you of a home there is before us, where I will be true to you with all my duty and with all my faithful service, I bring back the remembrance of a home long desolate, while your poor heart pined away, weep for it, weep for it!"

She held him closer round the neck, and rocked him on her breast like a child.

"If, when I tell you, dearest dear, that your agony is over, and that I have come here to take you from it, and that we go to England to be at peace and at rest, I cause you to think of your useful life laid waste, and of our native France so wicked to you, weep for it, weep for it! And if, when I shall tell you of my name, and of my father who is living, and of my mother who is dead, you learn that I have to kneel to my honoured father, and implore his pardon for having never for his sake striven all day and lain awake and wept all night, because the love of my poor mother hid his torture from me, weep for it, weep for it! Weep for her, then, and for me! Good gentlemen, thank God! I feel his sacred tears upon my face, and his sobs strike against my heart. Oh, see! Thank God for us, thank God!"

He had sunk in her arms, with his face dropped on her breast: a sight so touching, yet so terrible in the tremendous wrong and suffering which had gone before it, that the two beholders covered their faces.

When the quiet of the garret had been long undisturbed, and his heaving breast and shaken form had long yielded to the calm that must follow all storms—emblem to humanity, of the rest and silence into which the storm called life must hush at last—they came forward to raise the father and daughter from the ground. He had gradually drooped to the floor, and lay there in a lethargy, worn out. She had nestled down with him, that his head might lie upon her arm ; and her hair drooping over him curtained him from the light.

"If, without disturbing him," she said, raising her hand to Mr. Lorry as he stooped over them, after repeated blowings of his nose, "all could be arranged for our leaving Paris at once, so that, from the very door, he could be taken away——"

"But, consider. Is he fit for the journey?" asked Mr. Lorry.

"More fit for that, I think, than to remain in this city, so dreadful to him."

"It is true," said Defarge, who was kneeling to look on and hear. "More than that : Monsieur Manette, is, for all reasons, best out of France. Say, shall I hire a carriage and post-horses?"

"That's business," said Mr. Lorry, resuming on the shortest notice his methodical manners ; "and if business is to be done, I had better do it."

"Then be so kind," urged Miss Manette, "as to leave us here. You see how composed he has become, and you cannot be afraid to leave him with me now. Why should you be? If you will lock the door to secure us from interruption, I do not doubt that you will find him, when you come back, as quiet as you leave him. In any case, I will take care of him until you return, and then we will remove him straight."

Both Mr. Lorry and Defarge were rather disinclined to this course, and in favour of one of them remaining. But, as there were not only carriage and horses to be seen to, but travelling papers ; and as time pressed, for the day was drawing to an end, it came at last to their hastily dividing the business that was necessary to be done, and hurrying away to do it.

Then, as the darkness closed in, the daughter laid her head down on the

*His daughter fell upon her knees before him.*

hard ground close at the father's side, and watched him. The darkness deepened and deepened, and they both lay quiet, until a light gleamed through the chinks in the wall.

Mr. Lorry and Monsieur Defarge had made all ready for the journey, and had brought with them, besides travelling cloaks and wrappers, bread and meat, wine, and hot coffee. Monsieur Defarge put this provender, and the lamp he carried, on the shoemaker's bench (there was nothing else in the garret but a pallet bed), and he and Mr. Lorry roused the captive, and assisted him to his feet.

No human intelligence could have read the mysteries of his mind, in the scared, blank wonder of his face. Whether he knew what had happened, whether he recollected what they had said to him, whether he knew that he was free, were questions which no sagacity could have solved. They tried speaking to him ; but he was so confused, and so very slow to answer, that they took fright at his bewilderment, and agreed for the time to tamper with him no more. He had a wild, lost manner of occasionally clasping his head in his hands, that had not been seen in him before ; yet he had some pleasure in the mere sound of his daughter's voice, and invariably turned to it when she spoke.

In the submissive way of one long accustomed to obey under coercion, he ate and drank what they gave him to eat and drink, and put on the cloak and the other wrappings that they gave him to wear. He readily responded to his daughter's drawing her arm through his, and took—and kept—her hand in both of his own.

They began to descend ; Monsieur Defarge going first with the lamp, Mr. Lorry closing the little procession. They had not traversed many steps of the long main staircase when he stopped, and stared at the roof and round at the walls.

" You remember the place, my father ? You remember coming up here?"

" What did you say ? "

But, before she could repeat the question, he murmured an answer as if she had repeated it.

" Remember ? No, I don't remember. It was so very long ago."

That he had no recollection whatever of his having been brought from his prison to that house, was apparent to them. They heard him mutter, " One Hundred and Five, North Tower ; " and when he looked about him, it evidently was for the strong fortress walls which had long encompassed him. On their reaching the courtyard, he instinctively altered his tread, as being in expectation of a drawbridge ; and when there was no drawbridge, and he saw the carriage waiting in the open street, he dropped his daughter's hand and clasped his head again.

No crowd was about the door ; no people were discernible at any of the many windows ; not even a chance passer-by was in the street. An unnatural silence and desertion reigned there. Only one soul was to be seen and that was Madame Defarge—who leaned against the doorpost, knitting, and saw nothing.

The prisoner had got into the coach, and his daughter had followed him, when Mr. Lorry's feet were arrested on the step by his asking, miserably, for his shoemaking tools and the unfinished shoes. Madame Defarge immediately called to her husband that she would get them, and went, knitting, out of the lamplight, through the courtyard. She quickly brought them down and handed them in ; and immediately afterwards leaned against the doorpost, knitting, and saw nothing.

Defarge got upon the box, and gave the word " To the barrier ! " The postillion cracked his whip, and they clattered away under the feeble over-swinging lamps.

Under the over-swinging lamps—swinging ever brighter in the better streets, and ever dimmer in the worse—and by lighted shops, gay crowds, illuminated coffee-houses, and theatre-doors, to one of the city gates. Soldiers with lanterns, at the guard-house there. " Your papers, travellers ! " " See here then, monsieur the officer," said Defarge, getting down, and taking him gravely apart, " these are the papers of monsieur inside, with the white head. They were consigned to me, with him, at the——" He dropped his voice, there was a flutter among the military lanterns, and one of them being handed into the coach by an arm in uniform, the eyes connected with the arm looked, not an every day or an every night look, at monsieur with the white head " It is well. Forward ! " from the uniform. " Adieu ! " from Defarge. And so, under a short grove of feebler and feebler over-swinging lamps, out under the great grove of stars.

Beneath that arch of unmoved and eternal lights—some so remote from this little earth that the learned tell us it is doubtful whether their rays have even yet discovered it, as a point in space where anything is suffered or done —the shadows of the night were broad and black. All through the cold and restless interval, until dawn, they once more whispered in the ears of Mr. Jarvis Lorry—sitting opposite the buried man who had been dug out, and wondering what subtle powers were for ever lost to him, and what were capable of restoration—the old inquiry—

" I hope you care to be recalled to life ? "

And the old answer—

" I can't say."

# VALENTINE'S DAY

### *by* CHARLES KINGSLEY

OH ! I wish I were a tiny browny bird from out of the south,
    Settled among the alder-holts, and twittering by the stream ;
I would put my tiny tail down, and put up my tiny mouth,
    And sing my tiny life away in one melodious dream.

I would sing about the blossoms, and the sunshine and the sky,
    And the tiny wife I mean to have in such a cosy nest ;
And if some one came and shot me dead, why then I could but die,
    With my tiny life and tiny song just ended at their best.

# SANTA CLAUS

### ANON.

HE comes in the night! He comes in the night!
He softly, silently comes;
While the little brown heads on the pillows so white
  Are dreaming of bugles and drums.
He cuts through the snow like a ship through the foam,
  While the white flakes around him whirl;
Who tells him I know not, but he findeth the home
  Of each good little boy and girl.

His sleigh it is long, and deep, and wide;
  It will carry a host of things,
While dozens of drums hang over the side,
  With the sticks sticking under the strings.
And yet not the sound of a drum is heard,
  Not a bugle blast is blown,
As he mounts to the chimney-top like a bird,
  And drops to the hearth like a stone.

The little red stockings he silently fills,
  Till the stockings will hold no more;
The bright little sleds for the great snow hills
  Are quickly set down on the floor.
Then Santa Claus mounts to the roof like a bird,
  And glides to his seat in the sleigh;
Not the sound of a bugle or drum is heard
  As he noiselessly gallops away.

He rides to the East, and he rides to the West,
  Of his goodies he touches not one;
He eateth the crumbs of the Christmas feast
  When the dear little folks are done.
Old Santa Claus doeth all that he can;
  This beautiful mission is his;
Then, children, be good to the little old man
  When you find who the little man is.

# JOHNNY-SCAN-THE-DUST

### by STEPHEN SOUTHWOLD

JOHNNY TWEMMETT was the only son of Gaffer and Dame Twemmett. He lived with his mother and father in a small cottage in the village of Bucolia. Gaffer Twemmett was a hedger and ditcher; and Dame Twemmett kept ducks and hens, two nanny-goats, and a reckling-piglet that ran about the cottage like a dog. Johnny was a queer boy. With his red hair, blue eyes, freckled face and pleasant smile, he was very good to look upon; but he had so strange a habit that he was the butt for all the village wit; always as he walked along he stared hard at the ground.

Because of this strange habit of his, the parish priest called him " Johnny-Scan-the-Dust "; the schoolmaster called him " Mud-Gazer "; the blacksmith called him " Young-Look-Down," and the children called him by all three of these names and by many others beside.

One day Gaffer Twemmett said to him : " My son, why do you always stare at the ground ? 'Tis a bad habit, and you should break yourself of it before it is too late."

" Father," replied Johnny, " I'm not exactly staring at the ground; I'm just thinking."

" Then why not look at the sky for a change," said his father; " the sky with its blueness and its sun and clouds is worth looking at. Why, as you go about the village, you'll see most of us cocking an eye up at the sky. And I've seen Farmer Boyle standing at his gate and looking up at the sky for hours on end."

" Yes, father, I know," answered Johnny; " but perhaps they're not thinking."

"Not thinking, my son!" gasped Gaffer Twemmett, "why, what be you saying! 'Tis well known we're the most thoughtful village in the whole of the land."

But Johnny made no reply, and turning away, walked off slowly, staring harder than ever at the ground.

When Johnny was fourteen, he went to work. First he worked in the shop of Mr. Babchick, the grocer. But the grocer soon dismissed him saying :

"Boy, you'll frighten away all my customers ; they'll think you're staring at their boots to see if they're patched."

Then Johnny worked a while for Pumpey, the milkman. But the milkman very soon had enough of him, and told him to go, saying :

"Boy, don't look at the ground if you're a milkman ; watch the sky for rain and be prepared."

Johnny tried all things ; from place to place he went, one after another —to McDushty, the miller, to Bonke, the blacksmith, to Dinney, the haberdasher, and he even carried round pills for Quacker, the apothecary. But all, one after another, told him to be gone about his business.

At last when he was seventeen, his father sent for him and said gravely :

"My son, I fear you are a wastrel, a good-for-nothing, a ne'er-do-well, and a nincompoop into the bargain. It has been a bad year for hedging and ditching, and we cannot afford to keep you at home. You must go to seek your fortune, but if you continue to stare at the ground, you'll come to a bad end. Look at the sky for a change, and then there's no knowing what may happen."

So the next day Johnny, having kissed his mother and shaken hands with his father, set off to seek his fortune.

He soon passed through the village, and came out upon the dusty highroad that led over the hill and far away to distant villages, towns and countries.

As he went along, staring at the ground, and thinking deeply but a little sadly, he noticed a pin lying in the dust. He stooped, and picking it up, placed it in his coat.

Presently the sun came out, the birds began to chirrup from the hedges, two donkeys brayed joyously at one another in a field, and afar off a cuckoo called gaily. These pleasant sounds cheered Johnny's heart ; he stepped out more briskly, began to smile, and presently was singing softly a merry song.

He soon came into a strange village, and still singing gaily, went marching through the main street. A voice hailed him from the side of the road.

"You're a merry one," said the voice, "once I'd a son with blue eyes and freckles and a nice, red knob like yours." And there, smiling pleasantly at him from her cottage gate, was a white-haired, fresh-faced, little old woman.

Johnny stopped. "Good-morning," he said gaily, "what a jolly morning for lambs, ducklings, children, green peas and winkles."

"Why winkles?" asked the little old woman with a laugh.

"Why not?" chuckled Johnny.

"You're the daft one," laughed the little old woman ; "but I like daft ones. Now if only I'd a pin, I'd give you a flower for your buttonhole."

Johnny took the pin from his coat. "Here we are!" he cried.

Plucking a blue flower, the little old woman pinned it in his coat, kissed his freckled face, and giving him a gentle push, said :

" Now, go along with you, you gaby, and may the blessing of all the holy saints go with you."

Away went Johnny, the blue flower in his coat, a song upon his lips, and his eyes upon the ground. Soon he had left the village far behind him and had come into a town. As he walked through the narrow, dirty cobbled street, he heard a sigh, and looking up at the window of a little house, saw a pair of sad eyes watching him. The eyes stared sorrowfully from a pale face. Johnny stopped, and smiling waved his hand to the window. The window was pushed slowly up, and a little girl leaned out.

*Johnny took the flower from his coat.*

" Now then, lazy-legs," cried Johnny, " why aren't you up, eh ? Do you know what the time is ? "

" I'm sick," said the little girl ; " I cannot get up, and so I lie in bed and look out of the window to watch the folk go by. Some I like and some I don't."

" Do you like me ? " asked Johnny.

" I like you best of all," she said.

Johnny took the flower from his coat. " Catch ! " he cried ; and throwing it into the window upon the bed, kissed his hand to her, and went upon his way.

He had not gone ten paces when a voice called after him to stop. He turned quickly, and saw a woman leaning out of the sick girl's window, and beckoning to him.

Johnny went back. " You're a rascal ! " said the woman with a smile. Her eyes were wet.

"I am, ma'am," said Johnny, "and my father says I'm a good-for-nought and a nincompoop into the bargain."

"You're not hungry, I suppose?" asked the woman.

"I could eat an elephant, a billy-goat, a plate of shrimps, and a shepherd's pie," cried Johnny hungrily.

"Wait then, you sad scamp," said the woman, wiping her eyes upon her apron, yet smiling all the while.

And presently she came out of the cottage and gave him a packet of food with a piece of string round it.

She kissed his freckled nose. "The saints watch over you, nincompoop," she said softly; and turning quickly was gone.

On went Johnny, staring at the ground as ever, and thinking hard.

"As soon as I come to a nice piece of grass," he said to himself, "I'll sit and munch for a while."

Presently he had left the town behind him, and was once more upon a country road.

Suddenly he was struck a buffet in the chest and knee. Looking up he saw a dusty and ragged tramp standing so close to him that their noses touched.

"Look where you're going, carrots," said the tramp affably.

"I don't know *where* I'm going," answered Johnny pleasantly, "but why didn't *you* look?"

"I look on the ground as *I* walk," went on the tramp, "to see if I can find a diamond ring. What do *you* look for?"

"Dreams, perhaps," laughed Johnny; "have you found a ring yet?"

"Well, not yet," said the tramp; "but have you found your dreams?"

"No," answered Johnny, "but I've found this, in a way of speaking," and he showed the tramp his packet.

"Grub, eh?" asked the tramp, with eager, hungry eyes.

Johnny nodded. "Now," he went on slyly, "if only you were hungry——"

The tramp struck himself a blow in the stomach.

"Hungry, young carrots!" he cried. "Hungry! I could eat till Sunday and then start again."

And so they sat down upon the grass by the roadside, and there Johnny untied his parcel. It contained two thick slices of bread and butter, two hard-boiled eggs, two onions, two apples, two chunks of cheese and a piece of seed-cake.

As Johnny shared the food equally, the tramp said, between his bites: "You keep the cake, young carrots, for the seeds tickle my poor old gums."

And when the feast was over, and they stood up to go upon their different ways, the tramp said, as he loosened his belt a hole, "Young carrots, you're daft."

"That's what the little old woman said!" chuckled Johnny.

"You need some one to look after you," went on the tramp.

"Maybe, maybe," laughed Johnny.

"Here," said the tramp, "take my old stick, and may it be as good a friend to you as it has been to me." And thrusting his old gnarled stick into Johnny's hands, he went shuffling away along the dusty road.

On went Johnny, swinging his stick, humming a song, and as ever, staring at the ground.

Not many miles farther had he gone when he heard a cry for help coming from a clump of trees near the roadside. Hurrying to the spot, Johnny found an old grey-haired man struggling with two fierce, black-haired, hook-nosed, scowling rogues.

" Ah, ha ! " cried Johnny, and with his big stick he laid the first rogue low. " Oh, ho ! " cried Johnny ; but before he could smite the second scoundrel, the villain took to flight, crying :

" Murther ! murther ! help ! help ! "

" Oh, carroty one," said the old grey-haired man in a shaking voice, " you are indeed a thumper. Lead me, I beg, to my little cottage, for I am afraid and weary."

And when Johnny had taken the grey-haired old man to his cottage, put him to bed with a hot-water bottle, and made him a bowl of steaming gruel with six drops of Heart's-Delight stirred in, he was about to take his leave, when the old man whispered :

" Look in the top drawer over there."

Johnny walked over to the top drawer, and opening it, saw a telescope.

" Take it out," said the little old man ; " it's yours."

" It's too good for me," replied Johnny, putting it in his pocket.

" It's *no* good to me," went on the little old man, " for it's as much as I can do now to see a wasp on the end of my nose. I'm not sure it's there until I'm stung, and then it's too late. So take it and welcome. And now I'll sleep."

Away went Johnny, stick in hand, telescope poking out of his pocket, song upon his lips, and eyes, as ever, upon the ground.

Late that afternoon he came to a little seaside town. He walked down to the harbour and there saw a woman gazing out to sea. Tears were streaming down her face.

" Why do you cry ? " asked Johnny.

" My husband's ship should have been home from its long voyage this morning," replied the woman sadly. " He has been away ten months, and now I fear I'll never see him again."

Johnny clapped the telescope to his eye and looked out over the water.

" Black hull, red band, three masts, and brown sails ; is that your man's ship ? " he asked.

The woman cried aloud with joy. " Bless your blue eyes ! " she laughed tearfully ; " that's the ship—*The Blackbird.* Now you must stay and meet my husband at supper."

And when Captain Snookum of *The Blackbird* sat down to supper that night, opposite to him sat his loving wife, and upon his right hand sat Johnny.

And when supper was over, and they sat talking round the fire, the Captain said to Johnny.

" Why don't you come to sea and be a sailor ? I've room for an able-bodied, loose-limbed, knuckle-jointed, red-polled, jolly sort of joker like you. Now then ? "

And so, when next *The Blackbird* sailed to foreign parts, Johnny sailed with Captain Snookum as third mate.

Two years later, when the Captain and his wife both died from old age, Johnny became captain and owner of *The Blackbird.*

Before ten years had passed, Johnny owned a fleet of ships all named after birds, except the two biggest of them all : one of these was named *Johnny-Scan-the-Dust*, and the other *The Mud-Gazer*.

And then one day Johnny went to pay a visit to the little village of Bucolia where he was born. He was dressed as richly as a prince, and rode in a carriage drawn by ten cream horses.

As he passed Farmer Boyle's farm, the farmer was leaning on his gate staring at the sky.

" Bless my 'taties ! " muttered Farmer Boyle, turning his eyes from the clouds to stare after Johnny in his carriage, " must be the King."

Johnny found most of the other villagers mooning round gazing at the sky. They certainly stopped gazing at the sky to gaze at him. But they did not know him, and thought he must at least be a prince.

But when Johnny came at last to his father's cottage, Gaffer and Gammer Twemmett, now so very, very old and bent, cried out together in shrill, shaking voices :

" Ah, our boy Johnny. And so you learnt at last to look up, hey, lad ? We told you so."

And Johnny had not the heart to tell them the truth.

# THREE OLD LADIES

*by* RUTH M. ARTHUR

MISS DOLLY, Miss Sue, and Miss Agatha-May
Live in a house on the king's highway,
And sometimes I go there to bid them " Good-day,"
And sometimes to tea, if they ask me to stay.

Miss Dolly says, " Goodness, child ! Look at your feet !
You've brought in a cart-load of mud on your shoes ! "
Miss Susan says, " Are not her pigtails a treat !
And how is your mother, dear ? Tell us your news ! "
But Miss Agatha-May whispers, " Kiss me, my sweet.
Fruit-drop or peppermint, which will you choose ? "

In dresses of sable, and purple, and grey,
They wave their lace hankies when I go away,
And " Come back and see us again, child," they say,
Miss Dolly, Miss Sue, and Miss Agatha-May.

# THE NIX OF THE MILL-POND

## *by* THE BROTHERS GRIMM

AT the head of the valley was the pond where the Nix lived. It was a lovely little pond. Fresh young larch-trees circled it about, and dropped their scented needles on its breast. Its limpid waters reflected the blue of the sky and the fleecy clouds of summer, as well as the old mill that stood upon its banks. That, indeed, was a picture in itself. Artists came from a distance to paint it, and told each other how beautiful and picturesque it was.

Unhappily the old mill has fallen on evil days. Once the miller and his wife had been rich and prosperous, courted by their friends, pleasantly at ease among their own broad acres. Then, like hail upon a field of standing corn, misfortunes had rained on them. The crops failed; the cattle died; the mill fell into disrepair and the miller had no money to restore it with.

He did not in the least know how he was to mend his fortune. Careful and industrious he had always been—but that did not help him, or drive away the bad luck that was dogging his steps.

One morning he rose very early. Off he went before the sun was up to wander in the woods. His head ached, and he hoped that the cool air would clear his brain, and help him to think constructively.

Presently the sun awoke and cast a drowsy gleam over the pond. The miller heard a faint splash beside him, and turning quickly saw a fair maiden rising out of the water! Pond-weed twined with the wet strands of her hair. Her look was wild and sweet beyond that of mortal maid. He knew at once who she was—the Nix of the Pond!

"Now may Heaven aid me!" he muttered, as he thought of all he had heard of the Nix and her evil ways. He did not know whether to stay or to fly. While he debated the point she spoke to him.

275

" Tell me, poor fellow, why are you so sad ? "

Her voice was like the singing of the wind in the tops of the larch trees. It brought the poor miller a strange consolation. His fears vanished, and he found himself unburdening his heart to the lovely being who (even if she were a Nix and had no soul as mortals have) was so friendly and kind.

" And now," he said, concluding his tale, " I am likely to lose the very mill itself, that was my father's and my grandfather's before I was born."

" Let me help you," sighed the nix. " I think I can restore you all that you have lost, and more besides. All I ask in return is one small gift."

" What is that ? " asked the miller, anxiously, hoping it was something in his power to bestow.

The Nix looked up at him under her long lashes.

" The little creature that has just been born in your house ! "

" Why, then it is a bargain ! " cried the miller delightedly, thinking that, puppy or kitten or whatever the little creature might be, it was a small return for the restoration of his wealth.

He thanked the Nix and returned to the mill in excellent spirits. At the door a servant met him.

" Good news, master ! " she said, her face wreathed in smiles. " Your wife has just brought you a lovely little boy ! "

Instantly the miller's joy was changed to woe.

" Oh, fool, fool ! " he said to himself—" to trust the promise of a wicked Nix ! And all the time she knew that my son had been born—she was laughing at my simplicity in putting him into her power ! "

His wife was troubled that he looked so wan and woeful when she had expected joyful smiles. He had to tell her at last of his meeting with the Nix, and though she tried faithfully to comfort him she could not hide her dismay.

The neighbours, too, who came to rejoice with them, showed plainly their uneasiness when the tale was told. They looked at each other meaningly, without saying very much ; and when they came to cheer the poor miller they could only tell him to trust in Heaven and hope for the best.

Time passed. The baby grew to be a sturdy youngster—then a handsome youth, the delight of both his parents. The miller was richer than ever he had been before. All that he did prospered. Wealth and good fortune came to him as iron to a magnet. Yet he was never quite happy. For, though the Nix was neither seen nor heard of, his very prosperity warned him that she had not forgotten their bargain.

The boy was carefully instructed to avoid the pond. " If you so much as touch the water," his father told him, " a hand will come up and seize you and drag you to your doom ! " Quite scared at the prospect, he promised to heed the warning.

When he was old enough he was apprenticed to a huntsman. In due time he became a huntsman himself, and was taken into the service of the lord of the village.

His skill and courage made him quite a favourite. When by and by he fell in love with a charming girl and wished to marry her, his master gave them a pretty house to live in. They had a jolly wedding and every one was happy, even the old miller, who had at last begun to think that his fears were unfounded.

Not long afterwards the young man was hunting a roe in the forest. The chase was long and hard. When finally he killed his quarry he did not notice that it had led him to the neighbourhood of the mill-pond.

He cleaned the stag and went to wash his hands. Here was the Nix's chance. Before he had time to draw back she had wound her arms round his neck and pulled him under the water. Then all was quiet. Not even a ripple showed where they had been.

The day wore on. When it came to the hour of his usual homecoming his wife was alarmed. She knew the story of the Nix—the old miller had told it to her over and over again. Could it be that she had claimed the young huntsman after all ?

Distraught, his wife ran to the pond, and there, to confirm her worst fears, lay his hunter's pouch, close to the water's edge !

Here and there she went, calling on his name, praying him to return. When there was no response she made piteous appeals to the Nix, offering all that she had in exchange for her husband's release. Still there was no ripple on the quiet pond. Only the image of the young moon looked up at her and and seemed to mock her plight.

At last, worn out with grief and anguish, she sank down under a tree and fell asleep.

As she slept she dreamed that she was climbing a steep hill. Thorns and and tangled boscage held her back. A gale swept down on her between rocky walls. Still she pressed on, weary and footsore, and at last she won to the top.

What a change was there ! All was green and lovely. The air was soft and laden with the breath of flowers. The sun shone from an unclouded sky.

A pathway led her to the prettiest cottage she had ever seen—white and sparkling, with flowers growing over it and around the door. In the doorway sat an old woman with snowy hair and a sweet and kindly face.

"Come in," she said with a smile ; but just as the poor girl was about to enter she awoke and all her sorrows surged over her anew.

Now, however, it was light—and there, to her surprise, was the very hill she had climbed in her dream.

"Perhaps there is help there," she thought, and set herself to clamber up the steep slope. A bitter wind blew down upon her head. Thorns and briers delayed her progress. But at last she reached the top, and saw that everything was just as she had seen it in her dream. There was the pretty cottage, and there sat the white-haired old woman with her welcoming smile.

"What brings you here, my child ? Only those who are in trouble brave the dangers of the road to seek me out."

"I *am* in trouble," said the huntsman's wife ; and she told the whole story of the Nix's bargain, from the very morning that her husband was born. When she came to describe how she had found his hunter's pouch beside the pond, she burst into tears.

"Hush, my dear," said the old woman gently. "I think I can help you. See, now, here is a golden comb. When the next full moon appears, sit by the pond and comb your hair over the water. When you have done that lay the comb aside and wait to see what will happen."

Thanking the Wise Woman for her help, the girl took the comb and made her way down the mountainside.

Heavily the time passed until the next full moon ! When at last the silver orb rose from behind the trees—there was the hunter's wife, combing her long dark tresses with a golden comb. Presently she laid the comb by the waterside and waited as the Wise Woman had bidden her.

Then a strange thing happened. A little wave rolled softly to the bank and bore the comb away ! A moment later, the huntsman's head appeared above the water. He said no word but gazed with love and sorrow on his youthful bride. Almost at once the waters seemed to rise and engulf him. Again the moon shone silver on a calm untroubled surface.

The girl was more distraught than ever.

*This time he rose much farther out of the water, and even stretched out his arms to his wife.*

"Alas," she sobbed, "have I found you only to lose you in the same instant ? Oh, cruel Nix, let him come back to me ! "

Eagerly as she waited there was no response. Only the echoes sent back her plaintive cries—her passionate pleading with the Nix to let him go.

Still she could not bring herself to leave the pond, but roamed its banks until at last she sank to sleep on a mossy couch.

Again she seemed to be climbing the mountainside. Sharp thorns tore at her gown. The storm had risen, and stones and boulders flew past her down the slope. But again she reached the top.

In the morning she followed the same rough road—even rougher and more cruel than in her dream—and at last emerged in the summer land above. Balmy breezes blew as she approached the white cottage. The Wise Woman greeted her kindly.

"How fared you, my dear ? "

" Alas, mother, not at all well ! My husband rose but for a moment, looked on me sadly, then sank again in the pond."

" Dear, dear," said the old lady, " that is sad news. We must think of another plan." She went indoors and brought out a pretty golden flute.

" When the full moon comes again take this to the pond and play upon it. Then lay it aside and wait to see what will happen."

She taught her a lovely haunting air before she sent her home.

Again the full moon was a long, long time in coming ! But come it did, of course, in its proper season.

It found the young wife by the pond-side, playing on the golden flute. The mournful cadences throbbed through the woods and floated out on the silvery waters of the pond. When the last echo had died away she laid the flute beside her on the grass.

A bigger wave than before came and carried it away, and while she waited her husband appeared.

This time he rose much farther out of the water, and even stretched out his arms to his wife, but once more the rising wave engulfed him.

" Ah, cruel fate ! " sobbed the girl, " to be tortured by the sight of one who will never more return ! "

She wrung her hands, and wept, and called upon his name, but there was no response. The silver pond lay still and quiet among the shadowy trees.

Once more she sank down exhausted, and yet once more she dreamed of journeying to the Wise Woman's house.

In the morning she followed the pathway of her dream. The road seemed rougher than before—the storm more fierce, the thorns more cruel. In the land above, however, the summer bloomed and the flowers lifted their pretty faces to the sun. The Wise Woman sat by her cottage door.

" How fared you this time, my dear ? "

" Not so well, mother. My husband rose half-way out of the water and held out his arms to me. But almost at once he sank again."

" Well, well, we must think of a better way. Now dry your tears, my dear, and do as I bid you. Here is a fine gold spinning wheel. Take it to the edge of the pond at the next full moon, and spin until the spool is full. Then lay it aside and see how things will go."

Another month came and went. The moon rose full and round above the pond. It shone on the hunter's wife, sitting by her gold spinning wheel as the Wise Woman had bidden her. The hum of the wheel rose and fell softly as she plied the shuttle till the spool was full. Then she laid the wheel aside and gazed upon the pond.

Quite a large wave bore the gold spinning wheel to the Nix's abode. In a moment the huntsman appeared, jumped ashore and caught his wife in his arms.

" Come ! " he cried. " We are in deadly peril ! "

Hand in hand they raced through the woods and into the open country beyond. All at once there was a dreadful sound behind them. The little pond rose into the air and streamed after them down the valley.

" Oh, if only the Wise Woman were here ! " the wife cried in her terror.

Far off on the hill-top the Wise Woman heard her. It was little that she could do, but such as it was she did it, out of pity for the poor young lovers.

She turned the girl into a toad, and her husband into a frog. Now they were able to escape, for the angry pond could not destroy them. But it could and did tear them apart and bear them to widely separate spots.

When presently the waters fell the young couple regained their human shape but could find no trace of each other. They were among strangers, who had no interest whatever in their fate. In order to earn their living they became shepherds and drove the flocks to pasture, sometimes far away from where their masters lived. Neither could forget the tragedy that had blighted their lives and all their songs were lilts of sorrow and sadness.

So it was through many years. Once when spring appeared and sprinkled the earth with flowers it chanced that they both lighted on the same pasture. They did not recognise each other. Yet the herdsman felt strangely drawn to the lovely herdmaid, and she felt oddly comforted when he was by. Thus it came that they were often feeding their flocks in the same neighbourhood, though they seldom spoke to each other.

How long things might have continued in this wise no one knows, but on a summer evening, when the moon shone round and fair, the husband took out his shepherd's pipe and began to play.

The herdmaid drew near to listen to the haunting strains. It was the tune the Wise Woman had taught her—the tune she herself had played to the Nix of the Pond ! Her sorrows broke over her afresh and she burst into tears.

The shepherd was much distressed.

" Why, what ails thee, fair herdmaid ? "

" Alas," she wept, " 'tis the very air I played on the golden flute when my beloved rose from the mill-pond and opened his arms to me."

The moonlight shone on her face, beautiful still and full of love and faith. A blindness seemed to fall from the shepherd's eyes and he beheld his own dear wife !

At his cry of joy she looked up and saw that it was indeed her husband !

Peace and happiness was restored to them. Henceforth they fed their flocks together, and neither Nix nor pond troubled them any more.

# FABLES ~ ~
# FROM ÆSOP

## THE FOX AND THE MONKEY

A MONKEY once danced in an assembly of the beasts, and so greatly pleased all by his performance that they elected him their king.

A fox who envied him the honour, having discovered a piece of meat lying in a trap, led the monkey to the tit-bit and said :

" Look ! I have found this store, but have not used it. It is not for the subject to lay claim to treasure trove ; the king himself should take it."

The monkey approached carelessly and was caught in the trap, whereupon he accused the fox of purposely leading him into the snare.

The fox replied, " O monkey, and can it be that you, with so simple a mind, could rule as king over the beasts ? "

MORAL : The simple are easily deceived.

---

## THE DOG AND THE COCK

A DOG and a Cock decided to go on a journey together. They were travelling through a wood when night fell. The Dog went to sleep in a hollow at the foot of a tree, and the Cock roosted in the branches above.

It crowed at its usual hour to welcome the dawn, and its cry awoke a Fox who lived nearby and who hurried to the wood, thinking he would find a meal. When he saw the Cock he began to praise its voice and begged the bird to come down from the tree so that he could congratulate it properly.

" I will come down," said the Cock, who saw through the Fox's plan, " if you will first speak to the porter below to open the door."

The Fox, not suspecting the trick, did as he was told. When the Dog awoke he soon put an end to the Fox, and he and the Cock continued their journey in safety.

MORAL : Meet cunning with cunning.

# THE ASTROLOGER AND THE TRAVELLER

A CERTAIN Astrologer, who was so interested in gazing at the stars that he forgot to watch his way, had the misfortune to fall into a ditch one dark night. His fellow-traveller, who had been watching the road and not the heavens and was therefore unharmed, said, " Friend, take a lesson from your misfortune and let the stars go quietly on their course in future. It would serve you better if you kept your eye on the way you were going."

MORAL : Look where you're going.

# THE BEES, THE DRONES, AND THE WASPS

SOME bees built a comb in the hollow trunk of an oak-tree, but some drones claimed that they had built it, and that it belonged to them.

The case was brought into court before Judge Wasp, who, knowing something of the habits of both parties, addressed them thus :

" The plaintiffs and defendants are so much alike in shape and colour that it is difficult to say which are the rightful owners, and the case has very properly been brought before me. Now I think that justice will best be served by following out the plan which I propose. Let each party take a hive and build up a new comb, so that from the shape of the cells and the taste of the honey it will be quite clear to whom the comb in dispute belongs."

The bees readily agreed to the wasp's plan, but the drones, on the other hand, would not do so.

Whereupon the wasp gave judgment : " It is clear now who made the comb, and who cannot make it ; the court gives judgment in favour of the bees."

MORAL : We may know a tree by its fruit.

*The court gives judgment in favour of the bees.*

# THE HORSE AND THE STAG

A HORSE was pastured upon a wide meadow, which he had all to himself until a stag broke in and trod down the grass. This greatly annoyed the horse, which appealed to a man for help in punishing the intruder.

"Yes," said the man. " I will help you to be revenged upon the stag ; but first you must let me put a bit in your mouth and mount upon your back. I will provide weapons."

The horse readily agreed, and together they chased and overcame the stag. Very pleased with his revenge, the horse began to thank the man for his aid, but he received answer :

" No, do not thank me. I did not know until now how useful you could be to me. I should thank you, for henceforth I will keep you for my servant." Thus from that time the horse has been the slave of man.

MORAL : Revenge is dearly bought at the price of liberty.

---

# THE ARAB AND THE CAMEL

A N Arab, having loaded his camel, asked him whether he preferred to go uphill or downhill.

"Why do you ask, master ? " said the camel dryly. " Is the level way across the plain shut up ? "

MORAL : Of what use is it to pretend there is a choice when there is none ?

# THE HUSBANDMAN AND THE STORK

FINDING that cranes were destroying his newly-sown corn, a farmer one evening set a net in his field to catch the destructive birds. When he went to examine the net next morning he found a number of cranes in its meshes, also a stork.

"Release me, I beseech you," cried the stork, "for I have eaten none of your corn, nor have I done you any harm. I am a poor innocent stork, as you may see—a most dutiful bird. I honour my father and mother. I——"

But the farmer cut him short. "All this may be true enough, I dare say, but I have caught you with those who were destroying my crops, and you must suffer with the company in which you are found.

MORAL : People are judged by the company they keep.

# THE CROW AND THE MUSSEL

ONCE a hungry Crow discovered a Mussel and tried hard to break it open with his beak so that he could get at the fish. He was struggling without success when a Carrion-Crow came along and said, "I advise you to use a little strategy, my friend. Carry the Mussel into the air as high as you can fly, and then let it drop down on this rock and you will find it will break open."

The Crow thanked him heartily and, thinking it a good plan, flew off, but while he was on the wing the Carrion-Crow remained on the ground, and ate the Mussel himself when it dropped down.

MORAL : Most people are kind to their neighbours for their own sakes.

# THE TORTOISE AND THE EAGLE

A TORTOISE became dissatisfied with his lowly life when he saw so many birds enjoying themselves in the air.

" If I could only get up into the air, I could soar with the best of them," he thought.

One day an eagle came to rest on a rock beside him, and, seizing such a favourable opportunity, the tortoise offered all the treasures of the sea if only the monarch of the air would teach him to fly.

The eagle at first declined the task, for he considered it not only absurd but impossible, but, being further pressed by the entreaties and promises of the tortoise, he at length consented to do his best.

Taking him to a great height in the air, he loosed his hold, bidding the stupid creature to fly if he could.

Before the tortoise could express a word of thanks he fell upon a huge rock and was dashed to pieces.

MORAL : The over-ambitious often destroy themselves.

# THE TRAVELLERS AND THE BEAR

TWO friends were travelling on the same road together when they came face to face with a bear.

One in great fear, and without a thought of his companion, climbed into a tree and hid.

The other, seeing that, single-handed, he was no match for Bruin, threw himself on the ground and feigned death, for he heard that a bear will not touch a dead body.

The bear approached him, sniffing at his nose and ears, but the man, with great courage, held his breath and kept still, and at length the bear, supposing him to be dead, walked slowly away.

When Bruin was well out of sight the first traveller came down from his tree and asked his companion what it was that the bear had said to him. " For," said he, " I observed that he put his mouth very close to your ear."

" Why," replied the other, " it was no great secret. He only advised me not to keep company with those who, when they get into difficulty, leave their friends in the lurch."

MORAL : Misfortune tests the sincerity of friends.

# THE TWO KINGS' CHILDREN

## *by* THE BROTHERS GRIMM

HERE was once on a time a King who had a little boy of whom it had been foretold that he should be killed by a stag when he was sixteen years of age, and when he had reached that age the huntsmen once went hunting with him. In the forest, the King's son was separated from the others, and all at once he saw a great stag which he wanted to shoot, but could not hit. At length he chased the stag so far that they were quite out of the forest, and then suddenly a great tall man was standing there instead of the stag, and said, " It is well that I have thee, I have already ruined six pairs of glass skates with running after thee, and have not been able to get thee." Then he took the King's son with him, and dragged him through a great lake to a great palace, and then he had to sit down to table with him and eat something. When they had eaten something together the King said, " I have three daughters, thou must keep watch over the eldest for one night, from nine in the evening till six in the morning, and every time the clock strikes, I will come myself and call, and if thou then givest me no answer, to-morrow morning thou shalt be put to death, but if thou always givest me an answer, thou shalt have her to wife."

When the young folks went to the bedroom there stood a stone image of St. Christopher, and the King's daughter said to it, " My father will come at nine o'clock, and every hour till it strikes three ; when he calls, give him an answer instead of the King's son." Then the stone image of St. Christopher nodded its head quite quickly, and then more and more slowly till at last it stood still. The next morning the King said to him, " Thou hast done the business well, but I cannot give my daughter away, thou must now watch a night by my second daughter, and then I will consider with myself, whether thou canst have my eldest daughter to wife, but I shall come every hour myself, and when I call thee, answer me, and if I call thee and thou dost not reply, thy blood shall flow." Then they both went into the sleeping-room, and there stood a still larger stone image of St. Christopher, and the King's daughter said to it, " If my father calls, do you answer him." Then the great stone image of St. Christopher again nodded its head quite quickly and then more and more slowly, until at last it stood still again. And the King's son lay down on the threshold, put his hand under his head and slept. The next morning the King said to him, " Thou hast done the business really well, but I cannot give my daughter away : thou must now watch a night by the youngest princess, and then I will consider with myself whether thou canst have my second daughter to wife, but I shall come every hour myself, and when I call thee answer me, and if I call thee and thou answerest not, thy blood shall flow for me."

Then they once more went to the sleeping-room together, and there was a much greater and much taller image of St. Christopher than the two first had been. The King's daughter said to it, " When my father calls, do thou answer." Then the great tall stone image of St. Christopher nodded quite half an hour with its head, until at length the head stood still again. And the King's son laid himself down on the threshold of the door and slept. The next morning the King said, " Thou hast indeed watched well, but I cannot give thee my daughter now ; I have a great forest, if thou cuttest it down for me between six o'clock this morning and six at night, I will think about it." Then he gave him a glass axe, a glass wedge, and a glass mallet. When he got into the wood, he began at once to cut, but the axe broke in two, then he took the wedge, and struck it once with the mallet, and it became as short and as small as sand. Then he was much troubled and believed he would have to die, and sat down and wept.

Now when it was noon the King said, " One of you girls must take him something to eat." " No," said the two eldest, " We will not take it to him, the one by whom he last watched, can take him something." Then the youngest was forced to go and take him something to eat. When she got into the forest, she asked him how he was getting on. " Oh," said he, " I am getting on very badly." Then she said he was to come and just eat a little. " Nay," said he, " I cannot do that, I shall still have to die, so I will eat no more." Then she spoke so kindly to him and begged him just to try, that he came and ate something. When he had eaten something she said, " I will comb thy hair a while, and then thou wilt feel happier."

So she combed his hair, and he became weary and fell asleep, and then she took her handkerchief and made a knot in it, and struck it three times on the earth, and said, " Earth-workers, come forth." In a moment, numbers of little earth-men came forth, and asked what the King's daughter commanded ? Then said she, " In three hours' time the great forest must be cut down, and the whole of the wood laid in heaps." So the little earth-men went about and got together the whole of their kindred to help them with the work. They began at once, and when the three hours were over, all was done, and they came back to the King's daughter and told her so. Then she took her white handkerchief again and said, " Earth-workers, go home." On this they all disappeared.

When the King's son awoke, he was delighted, and she said, " Come home when it has struck six o'clock." He did as she told him, and then the King asked, "Hast thou made away with the forest?" "Yes," said the King's son. When they were sitting at table, the King said, "I cannot yet give thee my daughter to wife, thou must still do something more for her sake." So he asked what it was to be, then? "I have a great fish-pond," said the King, "Thou must go to it to-morrow morning and clear it of all mud until it is as bright as a mirror, and fill it with every kind of fish." The next morning the King gave him a glass shovel and said, "The fish-pond must be done by six o'clock." So he went away, and when he came to the fish-pond he stuck his shovel in the mud and it broke in two, then he stuck his hoe in the mud, and broke it also. Then he was much troubled.

*" In three hours' time the great forest must be cut down."*

At noon the youngest daughter brought him something to eat, and asked him how he was getting on? So the King's son said everything was going very ill with him, and he would certainly have to lose his head. "My tools have broken to pieces again." "Oh," said she, "thou must just come and eat something, and then thou wilt be in another frame of mind." "No," said he, "I cannot eat, I am far too unhappy for that!" Then she gave him many good words until at last he came and ate something. Then she combed his hair again, and he fell asleep, so once more she took her handkerchief, tied a knot in it, and struck the ground thrice with the knot, and said, "Earth-workers, come forth." In a moment a great many little earth-men came and asked what she desired, and she told them that, in three hours' time, they must have the fish-pond entirely cleaned out, and it must be so clear that people could see themselves reflected in it, and every kind of fish must be in it. The little earth-men went away and summoned all their kindred to help them, and in two hours it was done. Then they returned to her and said, " We have done as thou hast commanded." The King's daughter took the handkerchief and once more struck thrice on the ground with it, and said, " Earth-workers, go home again." Then they all went away.

When the King's son awoke the fish-pond was done. Then the King's daughter went away also, and told him that when it was six he was to come to the house. When he arrived at the house the King asked, " Hast thou got the fish-pond done ? " " Yes," said the King's son.

When they were again sitting at table the King said, " Thou hast certainly done the fish-pond, but I cannot give thee my daughter yet ; thou must just do one thing more." " What is that, then ? " asked the King's son. The King said he had a great mountain on which there was nothing but briars which must all be cut down, and at the top of it the youth must build up a great castle, which must be as strong as could be conceived, and all the furniture and fitting belonging to a castle must be inside it. And when he arose next morning the King gave him a glass axe and a glass gimlet with him, and he was to have all done by six o'clock. As he was cutting down the first briar with the axe, it broke off into pieces that flew all round about, and he could not use the gimlet either. Then he was quite miserable, and waited for his dearest to see if she would not come and help him in his need.

When it was midday she came and brought him something to eat. He went to meet her and told her all, and ate something, and let her comb his hair and fell asleep. Then she once more took the knot and struck the earth with it, and said, " Earth-workers, come forth ! " Then came once again numbers of earth-men, and asked what her desire was. Then said she, In the space of three hours they must cut down the whole of the briars, and a castle must be built on the top of the mountain that must be as strong as any one could conceive, and all the furniture that pertains to a castle must be inside it. They went away, and summoned their kindred to help them and when the time was come, all was ready. Then they came to the King's daughter and told her so, and the King's daughter took her handkerchief and struck thrice on the earth with it, and said, " Earth-workers, go home," on which they all disappeared. When therefore the King's son awoke and saw everything done, he was as happy as a bird in air.

When it had struck six, they went home together. Then said the King. " Is the castle ready ? " " Yes," said the King's son. When they sat down to table, the King said, " I cannot give away my youngest daughter until the two eldest are married." Then the King's son and the King's daughter were quite troubled, and the King's son had no idea what to do. But he went by night to the King's daughter and ran away with her. When they had got a little distance away, the King's daughter peeped round and saw her father behind her. " Oh," said she, " what are we to do ? My father is behind us, and will take us back with him. I will at once change thee into a briar, and myself into a rose, and I will shelter myself in the midst of the bush." When the father reached the place, there stood a briar with one rose on it, then he was about to gather the rose, when the thorn came and pricked his finger so that he was forced to go home again. His wife asked why he had not brought their daughter back with him ? So he said he had nearly got up to her, but that all at once he had lost sight of her, and a briar with one rose was growing on the spot.

Then said the Queen, "If thou hadst but gathered the rose, the briar would have been forced to come too." So he went back again to fetch the rose, but in the meantime the two were already far over the plain, and the King ran after them. Then the daughter once more looked round and saw her father coming, and said, "Oh, what shall we do now? I will instantly change thee into a church and myself into a priest, and I will stand up in the pulpit, and preach." When the King got to the place, there stood a church, and in the pulpit was a priest preaching. So he listened to the sermon, and then went home again.

Then the Queen asked why he had not brought their daughter with him, and he said, "Nay, I ran a long time after her, and just as I thought I should soon overtake her, a church was standing there and a priest was in the pulpit preaching." "Thou shouldst just have brought the priest," said his wife, "and then the church would soon have come. It is no use to send thee, I must go there myself." When she had walked for some time, and could see the two in the distance, the King's daughter peeped round and saw her mother coming, and said, "Now we are undone, for my mother is coming herself: I will immediately change thee into a fish-pond and myself into a fish."

When the mother came to the place, there was a large fish-pond, and in the midst of it a fish was leaping about and peeping out of the water, and it was quite merry. She wanted to catch the fish, but she could not. Then she was very angry, and drank up the whole pond in order to catch the fish, but it made her so ill that she was forced to vomit, and vomited the whole pond out again. Then she cried, "I see very well that nothing can be done now," and said that now they might come back to her. Then the King's daughter went back again, and the Queen gave her daughter three walnuts, and said, "With these thou canst help thyself when thou art in thy greatest need." So the young folks went once more away together. And when they had walked quite ten miles, they arrived at the castle from whence the King's son came, and close by it was a village. When they reached it, the King's son said, "Stay here, my dearest, I will just go to the castle, and then will I come with a carriage and with attendants to fetch thee."

When he got to the castle they all rejoiced greatly at having the King's son back again, and he told them he had a bride who was now in the village, and they must go with the carriage to fetch her. Then they harnessed the horses at once, and many attendants seated themselves outside the carriage. When the King's son was about to get in, his mother gave him a kiss, and he forgot everything which had happened. On this his mother ordered the horses to be taken out of the carriage again, and every one went back into the house. But the maiden sat in the village and watched and watched, and thought he would come and fetch her, but no one came.

Then the King's daughter took service in the mill which belonged to the castle, and was obliged to sit by the pond every afternoon and clean the tubs. And the Queen came one day on foot from the castle, and went walking by the pond, and saw the well-grown maiden sitting there, and said, "What a fine strong girl that is! She pleases me well!" Then she and all with her looked at the maid, but no one knew her. So a long time passed by during which the maiden served the miller honourably and faithfully.

In the meantime, the Queen had sought for her son a wife, who came from quite a distant part of the world. When the bride came, they were at once to be married. And many people hurried together, all of whom wanted to see everything. Then the girl said to the miller that he might be so good as to give her leave to go also. So the miller said, " Yes, do go there." When she was about to go, she opened one of the three walnuts, and a beautiful dress lay inside it. She put it on, and went into the church and stood by the altar. Suddenly came the bride and bridegroom, and seated themselves before the altar, and when the priest was just going to bless them, the bride peeped half-round and saw the maiden. Then she said she would not be given away until she had as beautiful a dress as that lady there.

*She would not be given away until she had as beautiful a dress.*

So they went back to the house again, and sent a messenger to ask the lady if she would sell that dress. The maiden replied that she would not sell it, but the bride might perhaps earn it. Then the bride asked her how she was to do this ? Then the maiden said if she might sleep one night outside the King's son's door, the bride might have what she wanted. So the bride said, " Yes, she was to do that." But the servants were ordered to give the King's son a sleeping drink, and then the maiden laid herself down on the threshold and lamented all night long. She had had the forest cut down for him, she had had the fish-pond cleaned out for him, she had had the castle built for him, she had changed him into a briar, and then into a church, and at last into a fish-pond and yet, he had forgotten her so quickly. The King's son did not hear one word of it, but the servants had been awakened, and had listened to it, and had not known what it could mean.

The next morning when they were all up, the bride put on the dress, and went away to the church with the bridegroom. In the meantime the maiden opened the second walnut, and a still more beautiful dress was inside it. She put it on, and went and stood by the altar in the church, and everything happened as it had happened the time before. And the maiden again lay all night on the threshold which led to the chamber of the King's son, and the servant was once more to give him a sleeping drink. The servant, however, went to him and gave him something to keep him awake, and then the King's son went to bed, and the miller's maiden bemoaned herself as before on the threshold of the door, and told of all that she had done. All this the King's son heard, and was sore troubled, and what was past came back to him. Then he wanted to go to her, but his mother had locked the door.

The next morning, however, he went to his beloved, and told her everything that had happened to him, and prayed her not to be angry with him for having forgotten her. Then the King's daughter opened the third walnut, and within it was a still more magnificent dress, which she put on, and went with her bridegroom to church, and numbers of children came who gave them flowers, and offered them gay ribbons to bind about their feet, and they were blessed by the priest, and had a merry wedding. But the false mother and the bride had to depart. And the mouth of the person who last told all this is still warm.

# AUTUMN
### *by* F. POLITZER

WHIRLING leaves, golden and brown,
   Twisting and turning,
Hurrying down.

Driving wind, gusty and strong,
   Whistling and sighing,
Rushing along.

Scudding clouds, grey-leaden sky,
   Laughing and playing,
Galloping by.

Roaming birds, gathered for flight
   Chirping and preening,
Seeking sun-light.

Curling smoke, mindful of fires,
   Blowing and puffing,
Hiding the spires.

Drooping rose, scattered to earth,
   Dying and fading,
Waiting new birth.

# BOFFIN'S BOWER

## by CHARLES DICKENS

VER against a London house, a corner house not far from Cavendish Square, a man with a wooden leg had sat for some years, with his remaining foot in a basket in cold weather, picking up a living in this wise :—Every morning at eight o'clock, he stumped to the corner, carrying a chair, a clothes-horse, a pair of trestles, a board, a basket, and an umbrella, all strapped together. Separating these, the board and trestles became a counter, the basket supplied the few small lots of fruit and sweets that he offered for sale upon it and became a foot-warmer, the unfolded clothes-horse displayed a choice collection of halfpenny ballads and became a screen, and the stool planted within it became his post for the rest of the day.

All weathers saw the man at the post. This is to be accepted in a double sense, for he contrived a back to his wooden stool by placing it against the lamp-post. When the weather was wet, he put up his umbrella over his stock-in-trade, not over himself ; when the weather was dry, he furled that faded article, tied it round with a piece of yarn, and laid it crosswise under the trestles : where it looked like an unwholesomely forced lettuce that had lost in colour and crispness what it had gained in size.

He had established his right to the corner by imperceptible prescription. He had never varied his ground an inch, but had in the beginning diffidently taken the corner upon which the side of the house gave. A howling corner in the winter time, a dusty corner in the summer time, an undesirable corner at the best of times. Shelterless fragments of straw and paper got up revolving storms there, when the main street was at peace ; and the water-cart, as if it were drunk or short-sighted, came blundering and jolting round it, making it muddy when all else was clean.

On the front of his sale-board hung a little placard, like a kettle-holder, bearing the inscription in his own small text :—

> *Errands gone*
> *On with fi*
> *Delity By*
> *Ladies and Gentlemen*
> *I remain*
> *Your humble Serv*.
> *Silas Wegg.*

He had not only settled it with himself in the course of time, that he was errand-goer by appointment to the house at the corner (though he received such commissions not half a dozen times in a year, and then only as some servant's deputy), but also that he was one of the house's retainers and owed vassalage to it and was bound to leal and loyal interest in it. For this reason, he always spoke of it as " Our House," and, though his knowledge of its affairs was mostly speculative and all wrong, claimed to be in its confidence. On similar grounds he never beheld an inmate at any one of its windows but he touched his hat. Yet, he knew so little about the inmates that he gave them names of his own invention, as—" Miss Elizabeth," " Master George," " Aunt Jane," " Uncle Parker "—having no authority whatever for any such designations, but particularly the last—to which, as a natural consequence, he stuck with great obstinacy.

Over the house itself he exercised the same imaginary power as over its inhabitants and their affairs. He had never been in it, the length of a piece of fat black waterpipe which trailed itself over the area door into a damp stone passage, and had rather the air of a leech on the house that had " taken " wonderfully ; but this was no impediment to his arranging it according to a plan of his own.

It was a great dingy house with a quantity of dim side window and blank back premises, and it cost his mind a world of trouble so to lay it out as to account for everything in its external appearance. But, this once done, was quite satisfactory, and he rested persuaded that he knew his way about the house blindfold, from the barred garrets in the high roof to the two iron extinguishers before the main door—which seemed to request all lively visitors to have the kindness to put themselves out, before entering.

Assuredly, this stall of Silas Wegg's was the hardest little stall of all the sterile little stalls in London. It gave you the face-ache to look at his apples, the stomach-ache to look at his oranges, the tooth-ache to look at his nuts. Of the latter commodity he had always a grim little heap, on which lay a little wooden measure which had no discernible inside, and was considered to represent the penn'orth appointed by Magna Charta. Whether from too much east wind or no—it was an easterly corner—the stall, the stock, and the keeper were all as dry as the Desert.

Wegg was a knotty man, and a close-grained, with a face carved out of very hard material, that had just as much play of expression as a watchman's rattle. When he laughed, certain jerks occurred in it, and the rattle sprung. Sooth to say, he was so wooden a man that he seemed to have taken his wooden leg naturally, and rather suggested to the fanciful observer, that he might be expected—if his development received no untimely check—to be completely set up with a pair of wooden legs in about six months.

Mr. Wegg was an observant person, or, as he himself said, " took a powerful sight of notice." He saluted all his regular passers-by every day, as he sat on his stool backed up by the lamp-post; and on the adaptable character of these salutes he greatly plumed himself. Thus, to the rector, he addressed a bow, compounded of lay deference, and a slight touch of the

*For Uncle Parker, who was in the army, he put his open hand to the side of his hat, in a military manner.*

shady preliminary meditation at church; to the doctor, a confidential bow, as to a gentleman whose acquaintance with his inside he begged respectfully to acknowledge; before the quality he delighted to abase himself; and for Uncle Parker, who was in the army (at least, so he had settled it), he put his open hand to the side of his hat, in a military manner, which that angry-eyed, buttoned-up, inflammatory-faced old gentleman appeared but imperfectly to appreciate.

The only article in which Silas dealt, that was not hard, was gingerbread. On a certain day, some wretched infant having purchased the damp ginger-bread-horse (fearfully out of condition), and the adhesive bird-cage, which had been exposed for the day's sale, he had taken a tin box from under his stool to produce a relay of those dreadful specimens, and was going to look in at the lid, when he said to himself, pausing, "Oh! Here you are again!"

The words referred to a broad, round-shouldered, one-sided old fellow in mourning, coming comically ambling towards the corner, dressed in a pea overcoat, and carrying a large stick. He wore thick shoes, and thick leather gaiters, and thick gloves like a hedger's. Both as to his dress and to himself, he was of an overlapping rhinoceros build, with folds in his cheeks, and his forehead, and his eyelids, and his lips, and his ears; but with bright, eager, childishly-inquiring grey eyes, under his ragged eyebrows, and broad-brimmed hat. A very odd-looking old fellow altogether.

"Here you are again," repeated Mr. Wegg, musing. "And what are you now? Are you in the Funns, or where are you? Have you lately come to settle in this neighbourhood, or do you own to another neighbourhood? Are you in independent circumstances, or is it wasting the motions of a bow on you? Come! I'll speculate! I'll invest a bow in you."

Which Mr. Wegg, having replaced his tin box, accordingly did, as he rose to bait his gingerbread-trap for some other devoted infant. The salute was acknowledged with :—

"Morning, sir! Morning! Morning!"

("Calls me Sir!" said Mr. Wegg to himself. "*He* won't answer. A bow gone!")

"Morning, morning, morning!"

"Appears to be rather a 'arty old cock, too," said Mr. Wegg, as before. "Good-morning to *you*, sir."

"Do you remember me, then?" asked his new acquaintance, stopping in his amble, one-sided, before the stall, and speaking in a pouncing way, though with great good-humour.

"I have noticed you go past our house, sir, several times in the course of the last week or so."

"Our house," repeated the other. "Meaning——?"

"Yes," said Mr. Wegg, nodding, as the other pointed the clumsy forefinger of his right glove at the corner house.

"Oh! Now, what," pursued the old fellow, in an inquisitive manner, carrying his knotted stick in his left arm as if it were a baby, "what do they allow you now?"

"It's job work that I do for our house," returned Silas dryly, and with reticence; "it's not yet brought to an exact allowance."

"Oh! It's not yet brought to an exact allowance? No! it's not yet brought to an exact allowance. Oh!—Morning, morning, morning!"

"Appears to be rather a cracked old cock," thought Silas, qualifying his former good opinion, as the other ambled off. But in a moment he was back again with the question :—

"How did you get your wooden leg?"

Mr. Wegg replied (tartly to this personal inquiry), "In an accident."

"Do you like it?"

"Well! I haven't got to keep it warm," Mr. Wegg made answer, in a sort of desperation occasioned by the singularity of the question.

"He hasn't," repeated the other to his knotted stick, as he gave it a hug, "he hasn't got—ha!—ha!—to keep it warm! Did you ever hear of the name of Boffin?"

"No," said Mr. Wegg, who was growing restive under this examination. "I never did hear of the name of Boffin."

" Do you like it ? "

" Why, no," retorted Mr. Wegg, again approaching desperation, " I can't say I do."

" Why don't you like it ? "

" I don't know why I don't," retorted Mr. Wegg, approaching frenzy, " but I don't at all."

" Now, I'll tell you something that'll make you sorry for that," said the stranger smiling. " My name's Boffin."

" I can't help it ! " returned Mr. Wegg. Implying in his manner the offensive addition, " and if I could, I wouldn't."

" But there's another chance for you," said Mr. Boffin, smiling still. " Do you like the name of Nicodemus ? Think it over. Nick, or Noddy."

" It is not, sir," Mr. Wegg rejoined, as he sat down on his stool, with an air of gentle resignation, combined with melancholy candour ; " it is not a name as I could wish any one that I had a respect for, to call *me* by ; but there may be persons that would not view it with the same objections.—I don't know why," Mr. Wegg added, anticipating another question.

" Noddy Boffin," said that gentleman. " Noddy. That's my name. Noddy—or Nick—Boffin. What's your name ? "

" Silas Wegg.—I don't," said Mr. Wegg, bestirring himself to take the same precaution as before, " I don't know why Silas, and I don't know why Wegg."

" Now, Wegg," said Mr. Boffin, hugging his stick closer, " I want to make a sort of offer to you. Do you remember when you first see me ? "

The wooden leg looked at him with a meditative eye, and also with a softened air as descrying possibility of profit. " Let me think. I ain't quite sure, and yet I generally take a powerful sight of notice, too. Was it on a Monday morning, when the butcher-boy had been to our house for orders, and bought a ballad off me, which, being unacquainted with the tune, I run it over to him ? "

" Right, Wegg, right ! But he bought more than one."

" Yes, to be sure, sir, he bought several ; and, wishing to lay out his money to the best, he took my opinion to guide his choice, and we went over the collection together. To be sure we did. Here was him as it might be, and here was myself as it might be, and there was you, Mr. Boffin, as you identically are, with your selfsame stick under your very same arm, and your very same back towards us. To—be—sure ! " added Mr. Wegg, looking a little round Mr. Boffin, to take him in the rear, and identify this last extraordinary coincidence, " your very selfsame back ! "

" What do you think I was doing, Wegg ? "

" I should judge, sir, that you might be glancing your eye down the street."

" No, Wegg. I was a-listening."

" Was you, indeed ? " said Mr. Wegg dubiously.

" Not in a dishonourable way, Wegg, because you was singing to the butcher ; and you wouldn't sing secrets to a butcher in the street, you know."

" It never happened that I did so yet, to the best of my remembrance," said Mr. Wegg cautiously. " But I might do it. A man can't say what he might wish to do some day or another." (This, not to release any little advantage he might derive from Mr. Boffin's avowal.)

"Well," repeated Boffin, "I was a-listening to you and to him. And what do you—you haven't got another stool, have you? I'm rather thick in my breath."

"I haven't got another, but you're welcome to this," said Wegg, resigning it. "It's a treat to me to stand."

"Lord!" exclaimed Mr. Boffin, in a tone of great enjoyment, as he settled himself down, still nursing his stick like a baby, "it's a pleasant place, this! And then to be shut in on each side with these ballads, like so many book-leaf blinkers! Why, it's delightful!"

"If I am not mistaken, sir," Mr. Wegg delicately hinted, resting a hand on his stall, and bending over the discursive Boffin, "you alluded to some offer or another that was in your mind?"

"I'm coming to it! All right. I'm coming to it! I was going to say that when I listened that morning, I listened with hadmiration amounting to haw. I thought to myself, 'Here's a man with a wooden leg—a literary man with——'"

"N—not exactly so, sir," said Mr. Wegg.

"Why, you know every one of these songs by name and by tune, and if you want to read or to sing any one on 'em off straight, you've only to whip on your spectacles and do it!" cried Mr. Boffin. "I see you at it!"

"Well, sir," returned Mr. Wegg, with a conscious inclination of the head, "we'll say literary, then."

"'A literary man—*with* a wooden leg—and all Print is open to him!' That's what I thought to myself that morning," pursued Mr. Boffin, leaning forward to describe, uncramped by the clothes-horse, as large an arc as his right arm could make, "'all Print is open to him!' And it is, ain't it?"

"Why, truly, sir," Mr. Wegg admitted with modesty, "I believe you couldn't show me the piece of English print, that I wouldn't be equal to collaring and throwing."

"On the spot?" said Mr. Boffin.

"On the spot."

"I know'd it. Then consider this. Here am I, a man without a wooden leg, and yet all Print is shut to me."

"Indeed, sir?" Mr. Wegg returned with increasing self-complacency. "Education neglected?"

"Neg—lected!" repeated Boffin with emphasis. "That ain't no word for it. I don't mean to say but what if you showed me a B, I could so far give you change for it, as to answer Boffin."

"Come, come, sir," said Mr. Wegg, throwing in a little encouragement, "that's something, too."

"It's something," answered Mr. Boffin, "but I'll take my oath it ain't much."

"Perhaps it's not as much as could be wished by an inquiring mind, sir," Mr. Wegg admitted.

"Now, look here. I'm retired from business. Me and Mrs. Boffin—Henerietty Boffin—which her father's name was Henery, and her mother's name was Hetty, and so you get it—we live on a compittance, under the will of a diseased governor."

"Gentleman dead, sir?"

"Man alive, don't I tell you? A diseased governor? Now, it's too late for me to begin shovelling and shifting at alphabeds and grammar-books. I'm getting to be an old bird, and I want to take it easy. But I want some reading—some fine bold reading, some splendid book in a gorging Lord-Mayor's-Show of wollumes (probably meaning gorgeous, but misled by association of ideas), as'll reach right down your pint of view, and take time to go by you. How can I get that reading, Wegg? By " (tapping him on the breast with the head of his thick stick) "paying a man truly qualified to do it, so much an hour (say twopence) to come and do it."

"Hem! Flattered, sir, I am sure," said Wegg, beginning to regard himself in quite a new light. "Hem! This is the offer you mentioned, sir?"

"Yes. Do you like it?"

"I am considering of it, Mr. Boffin."

"I don't," said Boffin in a free-handed manner, "want to tie a literary man—with a wooden leg—down too tight. A halfpenny an hour shan't part us. The hours are your own to choose, after you've done for the day with your house here. I live over Maiden Lane way—out Holloway direction—and you've only got to go East-and-by-North when you've finished here, and you're there. Twopence halfpenny an hour," said Boffin, taking a piece of chalk from his pocket and getting off the stool to work the sum on the top of it in his own way—" two long 'uns and a short 'un—twopence halfpenny; two short 'uns is a long 'un, and two two long 'uns is four long 'uns—making five long 'uns; six nights a week at five long 'uns a night,' scoring them all

*"Half a crown," said Wegg, meditating. "It ain't much, sir."*

down separately, "and you mount up to thirty long 'uns. A round 'un!
Half a crown!"

Pointing to this result as a large and satisfactory one, Mr. Boffin smeared
it out with his moistened glove, and sat down on the remains.

"Half a crown," said Wegg, meditating. "Yes. (It ain't much, sir.)
Half a crown."

"Per week, you know."

"Per week. Yes. As to the amount of strain upon the intellect now.
Was you thinking at all of poetry?" Mr. Wegg inquired, musing.

"Would it come dearer?" Mr. Boffin asked.

"It would come dearer," Mr. Wegg returned. "For when a person
comes to grind off poetry night after night, it is but right he should expect
to be paid for its weakening effect on his mind."

"To tell you the truth, Wegg," said Boffin, "I wasn't thinking of poetry,
except in so fur as this :—If you was to happen now and then to feel yourself
in the mind to tip me and Mrs. Boffin one of your ballads, why then we should
drop into poetry."

"I follow you, sir," said Wegg. "But not being a regular musical professional, I should be loath to engage myself for that ; and, therefore, when
I dropped into poetry, I should ask to be considered, so far in the light of a
friend."

At this, Mr. Boffin's eyes sparkled, and he shook Silas earnestly by the
hand, protesting that it was more than he could have asked, and that he took
it very kindly indeed.

"What do you think of the terms, Wegg?" Mr. Boffin then demanded,
with unconcealed anxiety.

Silas, who had stimulated this anxiety by his hard reserve of manner,
and who had begun to understand his man very well, replied with an air
as if he were saying something extraordinarily generous and great :—

"Mr. Boffin, I never bargain."

"So I should have thought of you!" said Mr. Boffin admiringly.

"No, sir. I never did 'aggle and I never will 'aggle. Consequently I
meet you at once, free and fair, with—Done, for double the money!"

Mr. Boffin seemed a little unprepared for this conclusion, but assented,
with the remark, "You know better what it ought to be than I do, Wegg,"
and again shook hands with him upon it.

"Could you begin to-night, Wegg?" he then demanded.

"Yes, sir," said Mr. Wegg, careful to leave all the eagerness to him,
"I see no difficulty if you wish it. You are provided with the needful implement—a book, sir?"

"Bought him at a sale," said Mr. Boffin. "Eight wollumes. Red and
gold. Purple ribbon in every wollume, to keep the place where you leave off.
Do you know him?"

"The book's name, sir?" inquired Silas.

"I thought you might have know'd him without it," said Mr. Boffin,
slightly disappointed. "His name is Decline-and-Fall-Off-The-Rooshan-
Empire." (Mr. Boffin went over these stones slowly and with much caution.)

"Ay, indeed!" said Mr. Wegg, nodding his head with an air of friendly
recognition.

" You know him, Wegg ? "

" I haven't been not to say right slap through him, very lately," Mr.
Wegg made answer, "having been otherways employed, Mr. Boffin. But
know him ? Old familiar declining and falling off the Rooshan ? Rather,
sir ! Ever since I was not so high as your stick. Ever since my eldest brother
left our cottage to enlist into the army. On which occasion, as the ballad
that was made about it describes :—

> " Beside that cottage door, Mr. Boffin,
>     A girl was on her knees ;
> She held aloft a snowy scarf, sir,
>     Which (my eldest brother noticed) fluttered in the breeze.
> She breathed a prayer for him, Mr. Boffin,
>     A prayer he could not hear ;
> And my eldest brother leaned upon his sword, Mr. Boffin,
>     And wiped away a tear."

Much impressed by this family circumstance, and also by the friendly
disposition of Mr. Wegg, as exemplified in his so soon dropping into poetry,
Mr. Boffin again shook hands with that ligneous sharper, and besought him
to name his hour. Mr. Wegg named eight.

" Where I live," said Mr. Boffin, " is called The Bower. Boffin's Bower
is the name Mrs. Boffin christened it when we come into it as a property.
If you should meet with anybody that don't know it by that name (which
hardly anybody does), when you've got nigh upon about a odd mile, or say,
and a quarter if you like, up Maiden Lane, Battle Bridge, ask for Harmony
Jail, and you'll be put right. I shall expect you, Wegg," said Mr. Boffin,
clapping him on the shoulder with the greatest enthusiasm, " most joyfully.
I shall have no peace or patience till you come. Print is now opening ahead
of me. This night, a literary man—*with* a wooden leg——" he bestowed an
admiring look upon that decoration, as if it greatly enhanced the relish of
Mr. Wegg's attainments—" will begin to lead me a new life ! My fist again,
Wegg. Morning, morning, morning ! "

Left alone at his stall as the other ambled off, Mr. Wegg subsided into
his screen, produced a small pocket-handkerchief of a penitentially-scrubbing
character, and took himself by the nose with a thoughtful aspect. Also,
while he still grasped that feature, he directed several thoughtful looks down
the street, after the retiring figure of Mr. Boffin. But, profound gravity sat
enthroned on Wegg's countenance. For, while he considered within himself
that this was an old fellow of rare simplicity, that this was an opportunity to
be improved, and that here might be money to be got beyond present calcula-
tion, still he compromised himself by no admission that his new engagement
was at all out of his way, or involved the least element of the ridiculous.

Mr. Wegg would even have picked a handsome quarrel with any one who
should have challenged his deep acquaintance with those aforesaid eight
volumes of Decline and Fall. His gravity was unusual, portentous, and
immeasurable, not because he admitted any doubt of it himself, but
because he perceived it necessary to forestall any doubt of himself in
others. And herein he ranged with that very numerous class of impostors,

who are quite as determined to keep up appearances to themselves, as to their neighbours.

A certain loftiness, likewise, took possession of Mr. Wegg; a condescending sense of being in request as an official expounder of mysteries. It did not move him to commercial greatness, but rather to littleness, insomuch that if it had been within the possibilities of things for the wooden measure to hold fewer nuts than usual, it would have done so that day. But, when night came, and with her veiled eyes beheld him stumping towards Boffin's Bower, he was elated too.

The Bower was as difficult to find, as Fair Rosamond's without the clue. Mr. Wegg, having reached the quarter indicated, inquired for the Bower

*"Eddard and me is a-goin' by* him! *Jump in."*

half a dozen times without the least success, until he remembered to ask for Harmony Jail. This occasioned a quick change in the spirits of a hoarse gentleman and a donkey, whom he had much perplexed.

"Why, yer mean Old Harmon's, do yer?" said the hoarse gentleman, who was driving his donkey in a truck, with a carrot for a whip. "Why didn't yer niver say so? Eddard and me is a-goin' by *him!* Jump in."

Mr. Wegg complied, and the hoarse gentleman invited his attention to the third person in company, thus:—

"Now, you look at Eddard's ears. What was it as you named, again? Whisper."

Mr. Wegg whispered, "Boffin's Bower."

"Eddard! (keep yer hi on his ears) cut away to Boffin's Bower!" Edward, with his ears lying back, remained immovable.

"Eddard! (keep yer hi on his ears) cut away to Old Harmon's."

Edward instantly pricked up his ears to their utmost, and rattled off at such a pace that Mr. Wegg's conversation was jolted out of him in a most dislocated state.

" Was-it-Ev-vera jail ? " asked Mr. Wegg, holding on.

" Not a proper jail, wot you and me would get committed to," returned his escort ; " they giv' it the name, on accounts of Old Harmon living solitary there."

" And-why-did-they-callitharm-Ony ? " asked Wegg.

" On accounts of his never agreeing with nobody. Like a speeches of chaff. Harmon' Jail ; Harmony Jail. Working it round like."

" Do you know Mist-Erboff-in ? " asked Wegg.

" I should think so ! Everybody do about here. Eddard knows him (keep yer hi on his ears). Noddy Boffin, Eddard ! "

The effect of the name was so very alarming, in respect of causing a temporary disappearance of Edward's head, casting his hind hoofs in the air, greatly accelerating the pace and increasing the jolting, that Mr. Wegg was fain to devote his attention exclusively to holding on, and to relinquish his desire of ascertaining whether his homage to Boffin was to be considered complimentary or the reverse.

Presently, Edward stopped at a gateway, and Wegg discreetly lost no time in slipping out at the back of the truck. The moment he was landed, his late driver with a wave of the carrot, said, " Supper, Eddard ! " and he, the hind hoofs, the truck, and Edward, all seemed to fly into the air together, in a kind of apotheosis.

Pushing the gate, which stood ajar, Wegg looked into an enclosed space where certain tall dark mounds rose high against the sky, and where the pathway to the Bower was indicated, as the moonlight showed, between two lines of broken crockery set in ashes. A white figure advancing along this path proved to be nothing more ghostly than Mr. Boffin, easily attired for the pursuit of knowledge, in an undress garment of short white smock-frock. Having received his literary friend with great cordiality, he conducted him to the interior of the Bower and there presented him to Mrs. Boffin—a stout lady of a rubicund and cheerful aspect, dressed (to Mr. Wegg's consternation) in a low evening dress of sable satin, and a large black velvet hat and feathers.

" Mrs. Boffin, Wegg," said Boffin, " is a high-flyer at Fashion. And her make is such, that she does it credit. As to myself, I ain't yet as Fash'nable as I may come to be. Henerietty, old lady, this is the gentleman that's a-going to decline and fall off the Rooshan Empire."

" And I am sure I hope it'll do you both good," said Mrs. Boffin.

It was the queerest of rooms, fitted and funished more like a luxurious amateur taproom than anything else within the ken of Silas Wegg. There were two wooden settles by the fire, one on either side of it, with a corresponding table before each. On one of these tables the eight volumes were ranged flat, in a row, like a galvanic battery ; on the other, certain squat case-bottles of inviting appearance seemed to stand on tiptoe to exchange glances with Mr. Wegg over a front row of tumblers and a basin of white sugar. On the hob a kettle steamed ; on the hearth a cat reposed. Facing the fire between the settles, a sofa, a footstool, and a little table, formed a centrepiece devoted to Mrs. Boffin. They were garish in taste and colour, but were expensive articles of drawing-room furniture that had a very odd look beside the settles and the flaring gaslight pendent from the ceiling. There was a flowery carpet on the floor ; but, instead of reaching to the fireside, its glowing vegetation stopped short at Mrs. Boffin's footstool, and gave place to sand and sawdust.

Mr. Wegg also noticed, with admiring eyes, that, while the flowery land displayed such hollow ornamentation as stuffed birds and waxen fruits under glass shades, there were, in the territory where vegetation ceased, compensatory shelves on which the best part of a large pie and likewise of a cold joint were plainly discernible among other solids. The room itself was large, though low ; and the heavy frames of its old-fashioned windows, and the heavy beams in its crooked ceiling, seemed to indicate that it had once been a house of some mark standing alone in the country.

" Do you like it, Wegg ? " asked Mr. Boffin, in his pouncing manner.

" I admire it greatly, sir," said Wegg. " Peculiar comfort at this fireside, sir."

" Do you understand it, Wegg ? "

" Why, in a general way, sir," Mr. Wegg was beginning slowly and know-ingly, with his head stuck on one side, as evasive people do begin, when the other cut him short :—

" You *don't* understand it, Wegg, and I'll explain it. These arrangements is made by mutual consent between Mrs. Boffin and me. Mrs. Boffin, as I've mentioned, is a high-flyer at Fashion ; at present I'm not. I don't go higher than comfort, and comfort of the sort that I'm equal to the enjoyment of. Well, then. Where would be the good of Mrs. Boffin and me quarrelling over it ? We never did quarrel, before we come into Boffin's Bower as a property ; why quarrel when we *have* come into Boffin's Bower as a property ? So Mrs. Boffin, she keeps up her part of the room, in her way ; I keep up my part of the room in mine. In consequence of which we have at once Sociability (I should go melancholy mad without Mrs. Boffin), Fashion and Comfort. If I get by degrees to a highflyer at Fashion, then Mrs. Boffin will by degrees come for'arder. If Mrs. Boffin should ever be less of a dab at Fashion than she is at the present time, then Mrs. Boffin's carpet would go back'arder. If we should both continny as we are, why then, *here* we are, and give us a kiss, old lady."

Mrs. Boffin, who, perpetually smiling, had approached and drawn her plump arm through her lord's, most willingly complied. Fashion, in the form of her black velvet hat and feathers, tried to prevent it, but got deservedly crushed in the endeavour.

" So now, Wegg," said Mr. Boffin, wiping his mouth with an air of much refreshment, " you begin to know us as we are. This is a charming spot, is the Bower, but you must get to appreciate it by degrees. It's a spot to find out the merits of, little by little, and a new 'un ever day. There's a serpentin-ing walk up each of the mounds, that gives you the yard and neighbourhood changing every moment. When you get to the top, there's a view of the neighbouring premises, not to be surpassed. The premises of Mrs. Boffin's late father (Canine Provision Trade), you look down into, as if they was your own. And the top of the High Mound is crowned with a lattice-work Arbour, in which, if you don't read out loud many a book in the summer, ay, and as a friend, drop many a time into poetry too, it shan't be my fault. Now, what'll you read on ? "

" Thank you, sir," returned Wegg, as if there were nothing new in his reading at all. " I generally do it on gin and water."

" Keeps the organ moist, does it, Wegg ? " asked Mr. Boffin with innocent eagerness.

" No—no, sir," replied Wegg coolly, " I should hardly describe it so, sir. I should say, mellers it. Mellers it, is the word I should employ."

His wooden conceit and craft kept exact pace with the delighted expectation of his victim. The visions rising before his mercenary mind, of the many ways in which this connection was to be turned to account, never obscured the foremost idea natural to a dull overreaching man, that he must not make himself too cheap.

Mrs. Boffin's Fashion, as a less inexorable deity than the idol usually worshipped under that name, did not forbid her mixing for her literary guest, or asking if he found the result to his liking. On his returning a gracious answer and taking his place at the literary settle, Mr. Boffin began to compose himself as a listener, at the opposite settle, with exultant eyes.

" Sorry to deprive you of a pipe, Wegg," he said, filling his own, " but you can't do both together. Oh ! and another thing I forgot to name ! When you come in here of an evening, and look round you, and notice anything on a shelf that happens to catch your fancy, mention it."

Wegg, who had been going to put on his spectacles, immediately laid them down, with the sprightly observation :—

" You read my thoughts, sir. *Do* my eyes deceive me, or is that object up there a—a pie ? It can't be a pie."

" *When you notice anything that happens to catch your fancy, mention it.*"

" Yes, it's a pie, Wegg," replied Mr. Boffin, with a glance of some little discomfiture at the Decline and Fall.

" *Have* I lost my smell for fruits, or is it a apple pie, sir ? " asked Wegg.

" It's a veal and ham pie," said Mr. Boffin.

" Is it, indeed, sir ? And it would be hard, sir, to name the pie that is a better pie than a weal and hammer," said Mr. Wegg, nodding his head emotionally.

" Have some, Wegg ? "

" Thank you, Mr. Boffin, I think I will, at your invitation. I wouldn't at any other party's, at the present juncture ; but at yours, sir !—And meaty jelly too, especially when a little salt, which is the case where there's ham, is mellering to the organ, is very mellering to the organ." Mr. Wegg did not say what organ, but spoke with a cheerful generality.

So the pie was brought down, and the worthy Mr. Boffin exercised his patience until Wegg, in the exercise of his knife and fork, had finished the dish, only profiting by the opportunity to inform Wegg that although it was not strictly Fashionable to keep the contents of a larder thus exposed to view, he (Mr. Boffin) considered it hospitable : for the reason, that instead of saying, in a comparatively unmeaning manner to a visitor, " There are such and such edibles downstairs ; will you have anything up ? " you took the bold practical course of saying, " Cast your eye along the shelves, and, if you see anything you like there, have it down."

And now, Mr. Wegg at length pushed away his plate and put on his spectacles, and Mr. Boffin lighted his pipe and looked with beaming eyes into the opening world before him, and Mrs. Boffin reclined in a fashionable manner on her sofa, as one who would be part of the audience if she found she could, and would go to sleep if she found she couldn't.

" Hem ! " began Wegg. " This, Mr. Boffin and Lady, is the first chapter of the first wollume of the Decline and Fall of——" here he looked hard at the book, and stopped.

" What is the matter, Wegg ? "

" Why, it comes into my mind, do you know, sir," said Wegg with an air of insinuating frankness (having first again looked hard at the book), " that you made a little mistake this morning, which I had meant to set you right in, only something put it out of my head. I think you said Rooshan Empire, sir ? "

" It is Rooshan ; ain't it, Wegg ? "

" No, sir. Roman. Roman."

" What's the difference, Wegg ? "

" The difference, sir ? " Mr. Wegg was faltering and in danger of breaking down, when a bright thought flashed upon him. " The difference, sir ? There you place me in a difficulty, Mr. Boffin. Suffice it to observe, that the difference is best postponed to some other occasion when Mrs. Boffin does not honour us with her company. In Mrs. Boffin's presence, sir, we had better drop it."

Mr. Wegg thus came out of his disadvantage with quite a chivalrous air, and not only that, but by dint of repeating with a manly delicacy, " In Mrs. Boffin's presence, sir, we had better drop it ! " turned the disadvantage on Boffin, who felt that he had committed himself in a very painful manner.

Then Mr. Wegg, in a dry unflinching way, entered on his task ; going straight across country at everything that came before him ; taking all the hard words, biographical and geographical ; getting rather shaken by Hadrian, Trajan, and the Antonines ; stumbling at Polybius (pronounced Polly Beeious, and supposed by Mr. Boffin to be a Roman virgin, and by Mrs. Boffin to be responsible for that necessity of dropping it) ; heavily unseated by Titus Antonius Pius ; up again and galloping smoothly with Augustus ; finally, getting over the ground well with Commodus ; who, under the appellation of Commodious, was held by Mr. Boffin to have been quite unworthy of his English origin, and " not to have acted up to his name " in his government of the Roman people.

With the death of this personage, Mr. Wegg terminated his first reading ; long before which consummation several total eclipses of Mrs. Boffin's candle behind her black velvet disc, would have been very alarming, but for being regularly accompanied by a potent smell of burnt pens when her feathers took fire, which acted as a restorative and woke her. Mr. Wegg having read on by rote and attached as few ideas as possible to the text, came out of the encounter fresh ; but Mr. Boffin, who had soon laid down his unfinished pipe, and had ever since sat intently staring with his eyes and mind at the confounding enormities of the Romans, was so severely punished that he could hardly wish his literary friend Good-night, and articulate " To-morrow."

" Commodious," gasped Mr. Boffin, staring at the moon, after letting Wegg out of the gate and fastening it, " Commodious fights in that wild-beast-show, seven hundred and thirty-five times, in one character only ! As if that wasn't stunning enough, a hundred lions is turned into the same wild-beast-show all at once ! As if that wasn't stunning enough, Commodious, in another character, kills 'em all off in a hundred goes ! As if that wasn't stunning enough, Vittleus (and well named too) eats six millions' worth, English money, in seven months ! Wegg takes it easy, but upon my soul to a old bird like myself these are scarers. And even now that Commodious is strangled, I don't see a way to our bettering ourselves." Mr. Boffin added as he turned his pensive steps towards the Bower and shook his head, " I didn't think this morning there was half so many Scarers in Print. But I'm in for it now ! "

# THE WIND

### by DOROTHY WORDSWORTH

WHAT way does the Wind come ? What way does he go ?
He rides over the water, and over the snow,
Through wood, and through vale ; and, o'er rocky height
Which the goat cannot climb, takes his sounding flight.

He tosses about in every bare tree,
As, if you look up, you plainly may see ;
But how he will come, and whither he goes,
There's never a scholar in England knows.

# THE HERD-BOY

## *by* H. A. E. ROBERTS

ONCE upon a time there was a poor herd-boy, who had a cruel stepmother. One day the stepmother had sent the boy up the hillside to tend the cattle, without having given him a morsel of food. The poor lad felt very unhappy. He was sitting on a fallen tree-stump and wondering what he could do, when suddenly he caught sight of something shining in the grass. He jumped to his feet and ran to the spot. To his surprise he found a pair of the tiniest glass slippers imaginable. The boy was delighted with them. They were so small and so pretty. He wondered who could have left them lying there.

At sunset, just as he was preparing to drive his cattle home, a tiny boy appeared before him.

"Have you found a pair of slippers, herd-boy? I left them here last night."

"Yes," said the herd-boy, "I did find some slippers. Here they are. Won't you let me keep them though? I want to show them to my stepmother. Then perhaps she will not beat me when I go home to-night."

But the little elf-boy said:

"No, no, I must have my slippers. I cannot do without them."

So the herd-boy gave them to him.

"Thank you," said the little boy. "I will do you a kindness some day, in return."

So saying, he ran away into the thicket. The herd-boy sighed and drove his cattle home, His stepmother was unkind to him as usual.

"Take this crust of bread for your supper, and be off to bed," she shouted.

The poor boy ate his crust, and crept upstairs to the attic where he slept. All night long he dreamed of the tiny boy and his pretty glass slippers.

Next morning he awoke early and again he drove his herds up the hill-side to graze. There at the same spot he noticed the tiniest red cap. It was sewn all round the edge with silver bells. The boy picked it up, greatly wondering.

Just then a tiny girl appeared before him. She was hardly bigger than his hand.

"Please, herd-boy, give me back my red cap," she begged. The herd-boy had never seen such a dainty creature before.

"Oh, do let me keep it, please!" he said. "I want to show it to my stepmother, and then perhaps she will not beat me to-night."

But the tiny girl pleaded so hard that the herd-boy gave her back the red cap.

Now on the third morning, when the boy took his cattle up the hillside to graze, what should he find but a tiny, silver bell!

He picked it up and rang it. It gave out a sweet, silvery tinkle, and at once all his cows came gallop-a-trot towards him.

"Aha!" thought the boy, "I will keep this bell. It will be very useful to me when my cows go astray."

He put the bell into his pocket, and away he went. But at sunset, just as he was preparing to go home, a tiny old man, with a long white beard, appeared before him and asked him for the bell.

"No," said the herd-boy. "I want to keep it for myself. Yesterday I gave back a little red cap to a fairy maiden, and the day before I gave back a pair of glass slippers to a fairy boy. This bell will be very useful to me when my cattle go astray. That is why I want to keep it."

But the little old man told him that he was the King of all the Fairies, and that if he would only give him back the bell he would grant him three wishes.

"Very well," said the boy. "Here is your little bell, and now for my three wishes. I wish to be made very rich: I wish to live in a fine palace: and I wish to have a beautiful princess for a bride."

"Those are three good wishes," said the little man. "Take this pipe with you and walk to the far north lands, until you come to a royal palace. If you are ever in trouble of any kind, blow upon the pipe. If you are ever in great danger break the pipe in two, and I will come to your aid."

Then the little man disappeared, and the herd-boy was left staring at the place where he had been. That night, when the herd-boy had taken his cattle home, his stepmother was more unkind than usual. She beat him soundly and sent him to bed without any supper.

"Never mind," thought the lad, "I will be off, and away before sunrise." And after he had slept for a little time, he got up, dressed himself, stole away from the house as quietly as he could.

He walked to the far north, and on the evening of the third day he came to the royal palace. He tapped at the kitchen-door and the cook answered his knock.

"Please have you any work that I could do?" he asked.

"What kind of work can you do?"

"Well, I can mind cattle or goats or sheep."

"It so happens," said the cook, "that the King is without a cow-herd at the present moment. I will go and ask him if he will hire you."

Away went the cook, and soon he came back with the news that the King was willing to give the lad a trial.

"But woe betide you!" said the cook. "For if you should lose one of the cattle, the King would be very angry indeed."

"The wolf shall steal no cow from me," said the boy.

He was taken into the King's service, and he did his work so well that he was respected by all the other servants.

Each day the King's daughter, who was a most beautiful Princess, gave the herd-boy her little pet lamb to take up the hillside with the other animals. Each night the herd-boy brought back the pet lamb safely, and gave it into the Princess's keeping.

*Whilst he stood looking at the castle a maiden came to one of the windows.*

But one day a dreadful thing happened. The King's daughter disappeared. She had been carried away by night, and all the court was troubled.

Princes and nobles came from far and near to join in the search for her. But it was all of no avail. The Princess could not be found.

Weeks passed by, and then one day, greatly daring, the herd-boy went to the King and asked if he might be allowed to join in the search.

The King laughed him to scorn. "How can you, a herd-boy, hope to do that which princes and nobles have failed to do?"

"A heart of gold often lies beneath the coarsest coat," said the youth. The King was pleased with this answer, and he allowed the boy to go.

So he journeyed to the far north. Soon he came to a castle set in the middle of a great lake. Whilst he stood on the shore of the lake looking at the castle, a maiden came to one of the upper windows. The herd-boy recognised, to his joy, the lost Princess!

He drew forth the pipe which the fairy man had given him, and he blew upon it.

Immediately the little boy whose glass slippers he had found, appeared before him, saying :

" What can I do for you ? "

" I wish to cross the water to yonder castle," said our hero. At once the fairy boy changed himself into a great hawk.

" Jump upon my back," he said.    " I will take you across."

The herd-boy jumped upon the hawk's back and wink, blink, nod three times ! There he was beneath the window at which the Princess was standing.

" Quick !  Hide yourself ! " called the Princess.

The herd-boy hid himself behind some bushes as the owner of the castle, a huge giant, passed by. The giant went into a boat and rowed away far out on to the lake.

Now was our hero's chance. He called to the Princess softly from below.

" How can I rescue you ?  I am here at your bidding."

The Princess whispered back :

" I cannot move.  I am bound with chains of gold.  Can you climb to my window ? "

But the youth could not climb so far. Each time he tried he slipped back. At last he thought of his magic pipe. He blew upon it, and the fairy girl, whose red cap he had found, appeared, saying :

" What can I do ? "

" I wish to climb up to yonder window."

The fairy girl changed herself into a great white eagle, and flew with the youth to the upper window. The youth then broke the chains of gold and set the Princess free.

" Get on my back," said the white eagle, and the youth and the Princess both found room between the wide wings.

Down, down, down, they flew, and when they came to the shore of the lake the eagle vanished.

" How can we cross to the other side ? " asked the Princess.

This time the youth broke his pipe in two.

Immediately the King of all the Fairies appeared. He changed himself into a great fish.

" Sit upon my back," said he, " and do not be afraid."

They sat upon his back and he began to swim. But when they were half-way across the lake, the giant saw them from his boat. He lashed the waters in his fury and started in pursuit of them.

" Quick !  Throw out your girdle ! " cried the fish.

The Princess let loose her girdle, and threw it out. Immediately the water rose into a huge wave. It delayed the giant until the Princess and her rescuer reached the other side.

As soon as they set foot upon the opposite shore, they began to make their way home. When the herd-boy at last delivered the Princess to her father, the King, there were great rejoicings throughout the land. The herd-boy married the Princess ; he was given half of her father's kingdom, and he lived in a fine palace of his own. Thus were his three wishes granted.

# THE ROYAL MAGICIAN

## *by* WINIFRED MULLEY

### CHAPTER I

#### THE SKY PRINCESS

ONCE upon a time, the King and the Queen and the Prince were riding home to their capital city after a long day's hunting. The King was feeling pleasantly tired and, on the whole, good-humoured. The Queen, however, was feeling unpleasantly tired, and therefore snappy—but then she often was like that. The Prince, who was young and handsome, and as yet untouched by love, was not tired at all, and was singing gaily as he rode. He had just started " Heigho, welcome to May "—of which he knew three lines and the chorus—for the fifth time, when suddenly, without any warning whatever, the sky fell down !

They were amazed ! There it lay around them, in great billowy heaps, almost as high as their saddle-bows. They had never seen anything like it before ; it wasn't wet and foaming like the sea ; it wasn't cold and thick like deep snow ; it wasn't foamed and frothy like beaten egg ; it wasn't like ice-cream. It was quite different, and the colours of it were lovely. Most of it was white and blue, but here and there, where the sun had touched it, pinky gold hues were faintly lingering, and all the colours seemed to live and dance like the diamond buckles on the Queen's shoes.

" My dear," said the King to the Queen, " this is most unprecedented ; I really don't quite know what to do about it."

" Then ask the Prime Minister," said the Queen snappily, for she was very tired. " He's sure to know—always does—a most tiresome man. Why you keep him I can't imagine. Only yesterday the creature said——"

" Oh, mother, oh, father," cried the Prince suddenly. " Look up, look up."

They looked—the Queen with her mouth open, ready to finish what she she had been saying the minute she'd seen all there was to see, for she was that kind of woman. . . . And they saw a wonderful sight.

Far up above them, above where the sky had been, lay a marvellous country. They saw a great blue river, winding through meadows bright with flowers, and on the river were gay barges. A bridge of gold spanned the river, and across it lay a wide white road leading to a great palace, the size and splendour of which made their own palace seem like a woodman's cot.

The Palace was turreted, and every turret had a roof of gold. The walls were of mother-of-pearl which caught the sun, and the great doors were studded with diamonds. Before the palace lay a lovely garden full of roses and lavender, delphiniums and golden rod, and as they looked the great doors opened and the Princess came out. She was more lovely than words could tell, and wherever she stepped a rose bloomed. She saw them far below and smiled, and her smile fell down into the heart of the Prince.

" Oh, father, oh, mother," he cried, " how lovely she is ; if I cannot marry her I shall surely die."

" Rubbish," said the Queen. " You cannot get up there, and people don't die for love nowadays." She had forgotten about the Prime Minister, but as her mouth was open ready, it seemed a pity not to contradict some one, for she was that kind of a woman.

" Mother, I cannot live without her," said the Prince.

" Eh, what ? " said the King. " Well, yes, very pretty, very pretty indeed, but most unprecedented. You were right, my dear ; I really must consult the Prime Minister about it."

" If you have quite finished," interrupted the Queen, rudely—for, remember, she was that kind of woman—" may I say that, firstly, I consider it all very showy, much too showy in fact for my taste, and secondly, that if you look up there much longer your neck will ache, and thirdly, that I am very tired. Indeed I only came out at all because you insisted, and if you will not ride home with me I must ride alone."

" No, no, my dear ; you must not do that ; it is most unsuitable," said the King.

" Then come with me," and she spurred on her horse.

The Prince followed slowly, gazing upward all the time, so that he very nearly ran over the Royal Stonemason. When he realised what he had nearly done, he apologised, for he was a polite young man, and not at all like his mother.

" Alas," he said, " Master Stonemason, my heart is as heavy as lead. If I cannot reach that wondrous kingdom and marry the Princess I shall surely die. Build me a stairway there at once."

" Nay, I cannot do that," said the Stonemason. " It is too far away. If I had all the stone in your father's kingdom I could not build so high."

" Alas, then I must die," said the Prince, and rode on.

But as he entered the Palace gates, he met the Royal Laddermaker. " Ah,

Master Laddermaker!" he cried. "Build me a ladder to yonder kingdom, for if I cannot reach it and marry the Princess I shall surely die."

"Nay," said the Laddermaker, "I cannot do that; had I all the wood in your father's kingdom I could not build a ladder so long."

"Alas, then," said the Prince, "I must die," and dismounted from his horse. But as he entered the great hall he met the Royal Ropemaker. "Ah, Master Ropemaker!" he cried. "Make me a rope so that I may climb to yonder kingdom, for if I do not marry the Princess I must die."

"Nay," said the Ropemaker, "had I all the hemp in your father's kingdom, I could not make a rope so long."

"Alas, then," said the Prince, "I must die." And he went to his room and lay down on his bed with his face to the wall.

*The Princess was more lovely than words could tell.*

For three days he neither ate, nor spoke, and he grew pale and thin. The King and Queen grew sadder and sadder, and they feared he would die. But they could do nothing: even the Prime Minister could do nothing, though they consulted him every hour, and for the first time in all his years of office, he felt the Queen really appreciated him. Horsemen rode through all the length and breadth of the land offering an immense reward to any one who would build a ladder to the Kingdom above the sky—which all this time lay around the Palace, so that those going in and out through it rode and marvelled.

But on the fourth day, at evening, a horseman rode into the courtyard with a stranger on his pillion. He brought the stranger into the Prince's room, and said to the King and the Queen who were there: "Your Majesties, this man says he can build a ladder to the Kingdom in the sky."

"What?" said the Prince, forgetting his manners, and leaping out of bed in his joy, "What?"

" It is true," said the stranger ; " but the ladder must be built of solid gold, and you must go up and back in half a day."

" Alas," said the Chancellor of the Exchequer, who was in the room, " it is impossible ; there is not enough gold in the Royal Treasury."

And the Prime Minister, who was also there, nodded his head sadly.

" Then get some more," said the Queen. " This nonsense has gone on long enough. Go and get enough gold, or your heads shall answer for it."

So they went, and the Prime Minister issued a proclamation in the King's name, and all the people brought their gold into the courtyard, for they loved their Prince, and piled it up in great glittering heaps. Then the stranger began to build, and the ladder rose, and rose. The Prince stood by watching and the Princess up above came from her Palace and watched too, smiling and singing. And as she sang, the golden notes of her song fell down into the courtyard below, so that it seemed as though the more gold the stranger used the greater grew the pile.

At last the ladder was finished, and the Prince sprang up and climbed with a speed no man had ever seen before. He reached the top, took the Princess in his arms, then carefully, for his burden was precious, climbed down again, and all the people cheered and threw up their hats. Even the King so far forgot his royal dignity as to throw up his Crown, and the Prime Minister threw up his umbrella. This the Queen said was not only undignified, but dangerous, as it might easily have fallen on some one's head, but that it was just like him.

Then just as the Prince reached the ground, the sky, which all this time had lain around the Palace, began to rise in clouds of beauty to its proper place, which was a good thing, for as the King said, it was most unprecedented, and could not possibly have been allowed to remain.

And so every one was happy.


## CHAPTER II

### THE SEA PRINCESS

IT happened one day that the Queen was so bored that she said so at breakfast ! Now you know just how bored she must have been, for no one ever speaks at breakfast except to say " More coffee ? " or " Pass the butter, please," unless they feel very deeply about something. Well, the Queen did ; she felt bored.

The Lord High Steward, who was standing, of course, behind the King's chair, shivered. The last time the Queen had been bored he had nearly been dismissed, although he had served the King for thirty years. And now she was bored again !

" Sir," she said to the King. " Sir, this Kingdom of yours gets more dull and dreary every day. When I married you, twenty-five years ago— though it feels like a hundred—you said we were setting out on a joyous adventure into realms of unknown beauty ; " she sniffed. " I have yet to find them. You neglect me shamefully and give all your time and confidence to low-born men and Prime Ministers ! "

At this point, the Prime Minister, who was just taking a drink of coffee, choked. It was nervousness that made him choke really, but the Queen thought it was bad manners and glared. She had never liked him, and he knew it.

"And," she went on, "you have even forgotten that to-day is the anniversary of our wedding."

Whereupon the Prime Minister choked again, for of course he ought to have remembered and reminded the King the night before. The King gave him one look of reproach. The Prime Minister had never let him down like that before. Then he tried to calm the angry Queen.

"My dear," he said. "My dear, I had not forgotten, how could I forget——?" and he smiled worriedly, for he always got rather worried when the Queen was in a temper. The Prime Minister was worried too, but, being a man of resource, he rose manfully to the occasion, to the King's great relief.

"No, indeed, madam," said the Prime Minister. "You wrong his Majesty, who has planned a great pleasure for you, but who meant it for a surprise and was not going to tell you until after breakfast. His Majesty has planned "—he went on quickly before the Queen had time to ask the King any questions—" a day's excursion to the island of Mauree to visit your lady mother, for he thought, madam, that on this most happy day, you might, by visiting your old home, recapture memories of the day he first met you there."

The Queen beamed. "The Royal Galley is even now awaiting your coming." And he rose hastily and went out, for of course he knew it wasn't, and he was anxious to make sure that it would be before the Queen found out that it hadn't been.

The King gasped and then recovered. What a man ! What would he do without him ? Then he rose, bowed gallantly and gave his arm to the Queen, and together they went to the Royal docks, the Queen still smiling happily. And there lay the Royal Galley, just as the Prime Minister had said, her crimson sails flapping idly in the breeze, her decks scrubbed whiter than snow, her brass shining like gold and twinkling in the sun like the sailormen's eyes. The Queen was charmed. Crimson had always been her favourite colour and the sails were obviously new. (My goodness, hadn't the Prime Minister worked !) And she loved to see everything looking scrubbed and clean.

They stepped on board, and as the King passed the Prime Minister, he winked once, and the Prime Minister winked once, and the Queen didn't see ! Then as the graceful ship drew slowly away from the quay, as the red sails filled and the people cheered, the Lord High Admiral, who, as you know, always takes command when the King and Queen go sailing, led their Majesties on to the high deck, and there they sat chatting pleasantly and admiring the view. With them was their second son, Prince Amiable, for one Prince always accompanied their Majesties, and their eldest son, Prince Charming, was, you will remember, on his honeymoon with the Sky Princess.

For about an hour they had been sailing in this pleasant fashion when suddenly, without any warning whatever, the sea dried up ! It rose into the air slowly and with great majesty and floated there above their heads, half-way up to the sky. The good ship settled slowly on to a rock as a bird settles on to its nest, and there it stayed.

" Good gracious," said the King. " Good gracious, what does this mean?" He looked at the Prime Minister, but the Prime Minister understood it as little as he.

" But this is most unprecedented; such a thing has never happened before, not in all the annals of my kingdom, and really——"

But at that point the Queen recovered her breath.

" Oh, yes, it has," she snapped, " you forget, but I don't, that a short time ago the sky fell. If you had any foresight at all, which you haven't, you would have realised that similar occurrences might take place in the future and you would have made plans to deal with them when they did take place."

All this, of course, was very awkward for the Admiral and the Prime Minister. The latter tried as usual to help the King.

" But, madam," he said, " who would have dreamed——"

" My good man," said the Queen. " your place is not to dream, but to act. Do something at once. Amiable, what are you gaping at ? "

" Oh, mother," said the Prince, enraptured. " Look! Do look, at the bottom of that rock valley! Isn't she beautiful ? "

" What, where," said the Queen. " Oh ! "

For at the bottom of the rock valley, far, far below, on a throne of mother-of-pearl, sat a Princess of the sea, and she was as beautiful as the dawn. Her eyes were blue like bits of sky, her cheeks were faintly pink, and her forehead white like clouds at dawn, that the sun has kissed, and her hair as golden as its early beams. She looked up and saw the Prince : she smiled, then shyly looked down again.

" Oh, mother ! Oh, father," said Prince Amiable, " how I love her. If I cannot marry her I shall surely die."

" That," said the Queen, " is what Charming said. You never yet had an idea that wasn't some one else's first. You had better put her out of your head at once for you will never get down there as Charming got up to the sky. For one thing you haven't the energy, and for another, it cost all the gold in the kingdom to get Charming a wife. Besides that, your father went and appointed that person who made the ladder, Court Magician, at a perfectly ridiculous salary, and much use he has been so far. So there is no money left to spend on you, and if there were, it isn't here." And she left them and went into her State cabin.

" Oh, father," said Prince Amiable, " you will help me."

" Well, my dear boy, I would if I could, but how? In spite of what your mother has just said, I maintain that it is unprecedented for the sea to dry up."

" Certainly, certainly," said the Prime Minister.

" But what concerns me most," the King went on, " is how to get your mother home again, for she will never consent to staying here."

" Sir," said the Prime Minister. " May I venture to suggest that as the sky returned to its usual place after His Royal Highness Prince Charming brought down his wife, that perhaps the sea would do likewise if only Prince Amiable could find a way to bring up the Sea Princess. Then we could return home as easily as we came."

*A huge fountain welled up from the bed of the sea.*

"A very sensible remark, 'pon my word," said the King. "Now, Amiable!"

"But, father, how?" said Amiable.

But just at that moment a black speck appeared in the distance which grew larger and larger, and came rapidly nearer. It looked like a cloud, but really it was the Royal Magician, who learning, in the way magicians do, that his Royal Master was in difficulties, was coming, in the way magicians can, to help.

"Sir," he said, bowing very low, "I can help you."

"Well, I never," said the King. "How did you get here?"

"That," said the Magician mysteriously, "is my secret. I am here and I can help."

"Then do so at once," said the Queen, who had come out of the cabin to see who had arrived. "That is, if it please you," she added hastily, for she remembered suddenly that the last person who had spoken rudely to him had been turned into a spider, and she hated spiders.

The Magician said nothing, but he smiled at the King and threw a crystal ball into the rock valley. At once there was a loud crash, a great flash of light and a huge fountain welled up from the bed of the sea, rose high above the ship and dropped down again. A moment later it rose once more and again sank down as before. Every one stood gaping in amazement.

"Now, sir," said the Magician, "His Highness must jump on to the fountain when it comes level with the ship, go down with it, jump off, seize the Princess, jump on again and so return with her. He must do so at once for the fountain will only rise once more after he has got down."

At this, Amiable, with a cry of delight, leapt on to the fountain and was carried far below. The Princess ran to meet him. He seized her in his arms and jumped for the fountain, only just in time, and back they came, laughing gaily.

It was all over in a moment. Even as the panting Prince placed his precious burden on the deck, the fountain sank down and suddenly as it had risen the sea fell back into its accustomed place, deluging them all with spray, and the good ship floated free of the rock.

So amid great rejoicings they came to Mauree, and there at the sight of her old home the Queen regained her good humour.

## CHAPTER III

### THE MAGICIAN'S TEMPER

A FEW days after Prince Amiable had returned home with his bride, the Royal Magician began to be rather objectionable. For, you may remember, every one had been so busy rejoicing over the Prince's new-found bride that no one had remembered to thank him, and as, in order to get there at all, he had had to change himself into a magic carpet, this was a very painful process, and so you can understand that he was feeling rather sore about the whole business. He went about sulking terribly and making mysterious remarks about ingratitude and spiders. No one quite understood, but every one was rather frightened.

The King asked the Prime Minister if he knew what was the matter, and he didn't.

The Prime Minister asked the Lord High Steward if he knew what was the matter, and he didn't.

The Lord High Steward asked the Butler, and the Butler asked the First Footman, and the First Footman asked the Second Footman, who asked the Third, who asked the Fourth, who asked the Fifth. There were only five, and none of them knew, but they were all frightened.

Then the Queen got tired of it all, and being a brave woman determined to ask the Royal Magician himself. For as she said to the King there would be no peace in the Palace until his temper improved. He already had changed one housemaid and two under-gardeners into ducks. They had not been able to have duck for dinner since, and she liked ducks for dinner, but dared not risk eating under-gardeners for fear it would not agree with her. So she turned to him one day at dinner, just as he had turned the Second Footman into a hen for giving him the wrong kind of wine, and said, " Now what *is* the matter with you ? "

He turned on her in a rage and cried, " Alacam-an-za, fitz, footz ! " No sooner had he said this than the Queen turned into a spider.

" Dear me, dear me, poor woman," said the King, for he was fond of his wife in spite of her sharp tongue. " What has distressed you so ? Why ever didn't you tell me at once, and the offender should have been punished. My poor wife ! How could you treat her so ? I pray you, restore her to her natural shape."

### THE ROYAL MAGICIAN
The Queen and her ladies-in-waiting, her page and sundry
gentlemen of the Court, were taking the air. (Page 326)

**THE ROYAL MAGICIAN**

Then the South wind, seeing that the Queen had lost her hat,
dived gracefully after it and brought it back to her. (Page 337)

" Never," said the Royal Magician. " And never have I been treated with such ingratitude. Did I not win the Prince his longed-for bride, and bring you all safely home ? Did I not change myself into a flying carpet— a very painful process—in order to do so ? And was I thanked for it ? No, not by any one ! And I thought I had found such a happy home here." And he laid his head upon the table and wept.

" Cheer up, old fellow," said Prince Compassionate, the youngest son of the King and Queen. " Father, did you really forget ? But you know, dear old Magician, we *were* all grateful and pleased, and their Majesties were both delighted."

" No, they weren't," sobbed the Magician, " and the Queen has never liked me."

" Tut, tut, nonsense, my dear man," said the King. " Her Majesty has a hasty tongue, that is all, and indeed I thought we had thanked you. I certainly meant to, but in the excitement of the moment I must have forgotten. Pray forgive me, it was a most regrettable oversight. Allow me to thank you now."

" Yes, yes," said Prince Compassionate eagerly. " We all thank you, old chap, and now," he said coaxingly, " come and find me a wife, the wife of my dreams. You are so clever, I am sure you can."

" Of course I can," said the Magician, cheering up a little. " I can do anything ; I can do everything."

The Prime Minister stared, and the King said, " But my dear Compassionate, isn't that just a little rash ? How do you know you will love her ? "

The Prince laughed. " I have loved her in my dreams for years, but," he sighed, " I shall never find her alone."

" Leave all that to me," said the Magician. " I can find her ! Come ! " And he seized the Prince by the arm, and ran him out of the room.

" But the Queen, the Queen," cried the King after them. " Compassionate, your mother." But they had gone, vanished. And no one could find them, not even the Prime Minister, though he looked everywhere.

For three months they were neither seen nor heard of, and the King got so worried that he became quite thin. The Palace was in a terrible state, for the King had given orders and the Prime Minister had proclaimed them, that any one treading upon, or otherwise slaying a spider, would be executed. The whole Palace was swarming with spiders. Cobwebs hung in festoons from the ceiling, across every corner, across every window, and no one dared to open a window that was shut, however hot it might be. Neither dared any one shut a window that was open, however cold it might be, for fear of squashing the Queen.

Cobwebs hung across the archway leading from the Banqueting Hall to the Kitchen so that the King's dinner had to be taken out of the back door, all the way round the courtyard, and in through the front door, and so it was always cold. If there was one thing the King hated, it was cold food. His temper grew rapidly worse, and every one longed for the day when the Prince and the Magician should return. As for the poor Queen, well, nobody knew what she suffered. Not yet !

Then suddenly one day there was a clatter of hoofs in the courtyard and a noise of shouting. In dashed Prince Compassionate.

" Oh, father, oh, father," he cried, " I have found her, and she is all that I dreamed and more. She is more beautiful than either of my elder brother's wives. You are sure to love her."

" Well, thank goodness you have come back," said the King. " Fetch the Royal Magician at once and ask him to change back your poor mother —if she still lives," he sighed.

" Mother," exclaimed the Prince. " Good gracious, I had forgotten all about mother." He laughed.

" You disgraceful boy," said the King.

" Oh, never mind, father," said Compassionate. " The Royal Magician is in a wonderfully good temper, he's sure to make it all right : only for goodness' sake don't forget to thank him this time. He expects it, you know."

" I will not forget," said the King ; " only fetch him."

The Prince dashed off and a minute later returned with the Magician.

" My dear sir," said the King, " how wonderful you are. What should we do without you. How happy you have made my dear son."

" Yes," replied the Magician. " As you say, I am rather wonderful." He beamed.

" Indeed, yes, marvellous," said the Prime Minister, backing up the King for all he was worth.

" But, er—er," began the King rather timidly, " there is—er—the—er— little matter of the—er—Queen ; you know, just before you went—er——"

" Oh, yes, of course," said the Magician. " How careless of me. My dreadful temper ! Please forgive me," and he clapped his hands. Out from behind the sideboard came the Queen, looking tired and very dusty.

" What a house," she said. " We must spring-clean at once." And they did.

## CHAPTER IV

### FROM THE HOUSE OF DREAMS

A WEEK after the return of Prince Compassionate and his bride, the Court met to hear the story of their adventures. The King had promised that the Royal Magician should tell the story himself, and he had been looking forward to it very much for he was sure it would give him a chance to show the Court how clever he was. It had had to be a week later because of the spring cleaning, and to the Prime Minister had been given the difficult task of explaining this to the Magician, who had, of course, wanted to show off at once. But he had done it very well and the Magician had said he quite understood. So you see he must have done it well, for the Magician was a very difficult man to manage.

So the Court met in a very good temper expecting to be highly entertained. The Queen was pleased because her house was once more clean and tidy. The King was pleased because the Queen was pleased, the Prime Minister was feeling proud of himself, and as for the Royal Magician, it would be impossible to say how full of importance *he* was.

When they were all quiet he began : " Sire, and Madam, we have been to strange places and seen strange things, so at least His Highness thought, for, of course, nothing can ever surprise a Magician." He smiled, then continued : "We rode all day far into the west, following the path of the setting sun, for beyond the sunset lies the House of Dreams, where we hoped to find the Princess whom His Highness loved. Into that house no mortal ever goes except in sleep and alone. His Highness could never have found it."

He paused and waited for applause. No one did. He looked annoyed and the King, seeing it, said hastily :

"True, true, pray continue, we are all ears."

"Well," went on the Magician, "we reached Earth's rim just as the sun was sinking below it. Taking His Highness by the hand, I leapt with him into its fiery heart."

He paused again. The Court gasped. The Queen recovered her breath first.

"Impossible," she exclaimed. "Ridiculous ! You would have been burnt to death."

The Magician frowned.

"Hush, my dear," said the King ; "remember last time."

The Queen remembered with a shudder and was silent. The Magician continued :

"As I have just said, we leapt into the heart of the sun—and it bore us down far below the earth to the portals of the House of Dreams. There we alighted."

"He talks as if it were a lift," said the Queen sarcastically, and her page Rudolf tittered. The Magician looked black.

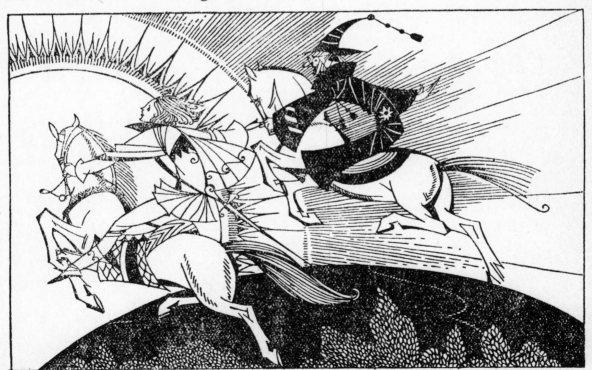

*" We reached Earth's rim just as the sun was sinking below it, and, taking His Highness by the hand, I leaped with him into its fiery heart."*

" To me, madam," he said angrily, " the sun is of no more consequence than a lift."

The page giggled again, he thought the Magician a silly fellow, but fortunately the Magician thought he was giggling because the Queen had been reproved. He went on :

" The door opened and we went in. His Highness was a little scared."

" Rather," put in the Prince.

" But, I assured him, with me no harm could have befallen him."

" Of course not," said the Queen, but her sarcasm was lost on the Magician.

" We crossed a wide hall——"

" Preceded by the butler, I suppose," said the Queen.

" Of course not—by a dream," said the Magician scornfully.

" Oh, what sort ? " asked the King, interested.

" Well, as a matter of fact he was a nightmare," said the Magician, " the nightmare that you are being chased by horrible monsters and can't run ; but, of course, he was off duty."

" I felt a bit queer though, all the same," said the Prince. " I get that one often. But he was a very decent fellow. He said he didn't like being a nightmare at all, but it was his month. They seemed to take it in turns being nightmares and dreams, a month at a time. Said too, that it was rather dangerous being that nightmare, because people got so frightened that they sometimes awoke, and then the nightmare got broken. Last time he had been in hospital for four days afterwards, because he had been broken almost to bits by the suddenness of the dreamer's awakening. Still, he said, the pay was double that for being a dream because of the risk."

" Really ! " said the Queen, interested at last, " did you meet that one I get sometimes about running up and down stairs without getting anywhere ? "

" Yes, we did," answered the Prince, " he was a cheeky chap. Said he roared with laughter every time he went on duty, especially at the fat ones who got so puffed."

The Prince laughed too, but the Queen looked offended. She was not fat, but she did not relish the idea of being laughed at by a mere dream.

At this point the Magician lost his temper. For at least five minutes some one else had been telling his story. He was furious.

" Sire," he burst out, " I cannot tell my story if all these people keep on interrupting me. After all, it is my story, I was asked to tell it, but if you don't want me to I shall go away."

He almost looked as if he were going to weep again.

" I say, I'm sorry," said the Prince. " Do go on, old chap ! "

" Well, it is my story. If I hadn't taken you, there would have been nothing for you to tell," said the Magician peevishly. " Still, I will go on. We were ushered into the presence of the King. He was most surprised to see us, but welcomed us most graciously. I told him of His Highness's love, and how His Highness wished to marry his daughter, and he graciously gave his consent to the match. Then he complimented me on my skill and cleverness, and said he thought Your Majesty was very fortunate in having so clever a Magician at your Court."

The Queen's page grinned, and the Magician saw him.

" Turn that boy out," he cried passionately. " I will not have him, he does nothing but laugh at me."

" How absurd," said the Queen. " Why shouldn't he laugh, if he wants to ? There is no law against laughing, is there ? "

" If he doesn't go, I shall," shrieked the Magician. " I will not stay here to be insulted. I should never have been so treated in the House of Dreams. I wish I had stayed there."

" It's a pity that you didn't," said the Queen angrily. " You have no manners at all."

" Oh, oh," screamed the Magician, and bursting into angry tears, he rushed from the hall.

The Queen's page burst into howls of laughter, but he was soon silenced.

" Boy," said the King severely, " leave us. You have offended one of my most valued servants."

" My dear," went on the King to the Queen. " I could wish that you would treat my Magician with more consideration. You know how easily he is upset, and I really do value him."

" This is too much," said the Queen. " I sometimes think you value your servants more than your wife," and she rose with dignity.

" No, my dear, my dear, I did not mean that," said the King. " But you surely must realise that——" But the Queen had gone.

The King looked at the Prime Minister.

" Dear, dear," he said, " this is very trying. What are we to do ? "

The Prime Minister shrugged his shoulders. He was annoyed with all three ; the Queen, the page and the Magician. He didn't approve of people who lost their tempers over trifles.

" I will do my best to calm the Magician, sir. I think I can," he said.

" Good," said the King. " For we cannot afford to lose him," he sighed. Then he said to the Court, who all this time had been trying to look as though nothing unusual had happened.

" Perhaps my son, Prince Compassionate, will tell us the rest of the story."

" Yes, yes," said the Court eagerly.

But the Prince was rather bashful about it.

" Oh, well," he said, " there isn't much more to tell. The King let me marry his daughter." Here he smiled at the Princess, who blushed prettily. " And then we came home again, same as we went. That's all, not very interesting. . . . I can't tell stories, you know."

" But what was it like in the sun ? " asked some one.

" Oh, I dunno ! Rather like a lift, don't you know. Not half so exciting as it sounds. I say, sir," he went on to the King, " hadn't I better go and see what's happened to the R.M. He's a decent chap really, and I don't like him being upset after all he's done for me."

" Perhaps you had," said the King.

And so the Court broke up and went to bed, all except the Prince, who stayed all night with the Royal Magician, for the Prime Minister had not been able to calm him, and his nerves were in an awful state. He was better by the morning though, and didn't leave them after all.

# CHAPTER V

### THE QUEEN'S PAGE HAS AN ADVENTURE

ONE day, as the Prime Minister was sitting at his desk writing letters, a young squire came dashing into the room from the gardens where the Queen and her ladies-in-waiting, her page and sundry gentlemen of the Court who had nothing else to do, were taking the air.

" Oh, sir, oh, sir," he cried.

" What's the matter now ? " asked the Prime Minister, without looking up, for he was very busy.

" Oh, sir, oh, sir, a terrible thing has just happened, and the Queen is distracted with grief."

" What about ? " said the Prime Minister, laying down his pen.

" Oh, sir, as we were walking in the garden, admiring the roses, suddenly the earth opened right at our feet."

" I was expecting that," said the Prime Minister. " First the sky falls, then the sea dries up, then the earth opens. Naturally. These things always go in threes, as you will know when you are older. In this Kingdom, however," he went on severely, " we do not lose our heads about such things. They always right themselves in the end—the Queen, of course, is an exception ! However, you are quite right to come to me at once about it, though I confess I am at a loss to explain why it should happen now. All the Princes are married. I had rather expected Prince Compassionate's bride to come from the earth. Still, doubtless, with a little thought I could find out——"

" Oh, but, sir, that is not all," broke in the squire. " When the earth opened the Queen's page went to look over, and he must have been standing too near the edge, for——"

" He would be," interrupted the Prime Minister. " If ever there was an edge, that boy would be standing too near it. What happened ? "

" Oh, sir, he fell in."

" And a good riddance," said the Prime Minister, and took up his pen. " Did the Queen fall in too ? "

" Oh, no, sir, but she is nearly distracted with grief, and she sent me to tell you to make arrangements to get him out at once."

" Eh, what ? Not likely ; a most impertinent boy—and anyhow, I couldn't."

" But, sir, the Queen says you must, and I am to inform the King, and ask him to go to her at once."

At this point the King came into the room. The squire ran to him.

" Oh, sire," he cried, " Her Majesty's page has fallen into the middle of the earth, and the Prime Minister says he cannot get him out, and what shall I say to Her Majesty ? "

" Fallen into the middle of the earth," exclaimed the King. " Dear, dear ! Why ? "

" Because, sire, a great yawning pit opened suddenly in the garden, and he was standing too near the edge and fell in, and the Queen is distracted and begs you to go to her at once."

"Dear, dear, dear," said the King worriedly. "Really I don't know what is coming to my kingdom these days. This last year has been full of a series of events for which there is no precedent in all our history—no precedent whatever. Really it is most trying. I must go to Her Majesty at once; she might fall in herself. She adored that boy; why, I can't imagine, but she did. You say you cannot get him out?"

"I see no hope of it, sir," said the Prime Minister.

"Then the Royal Magician must," said the King. "Thank heaven he is still with us. I feared last week that he would leave. Go and summon him at once." This was to the squire. "Her Majesty adores that boy; we shall have no peace until he is restored to her."

"*The page fell in and the Queen is nearly distracted with grief.*"

"And," added the Prime Minister as the squire was going, "say that His Majesty wants him himself—most urgently—that he is in grave difficulty and that no one else can help."

"That'll fetch him," he said to the King. "He loves to feel important."

"True," said the King; "now go."

"But whether he'll do anything when he comes," went on the Prime Minister, "remains to be seen, for the boy was impudent to him the night he told his story and the fellow hasn't forgiven him."

"I know, I know," said the King. "Really, it is all very trying. Still, if we flatter him—we must flatter him—he might. He is a most enterprising fellow, and I am sure he can. In spite of his tempers and his airs I have the highest regard for his skill. After all, it must be a trying profession to follow—almost as trying, I should imagine, as being a King."

"True, sir, true," replied the Prime Minister. "Shall I see him, or will you stay?"

" I really don't know. I summoned him, and I ought to stay, but I ought to go to the Queen, poor woman. What do you advise ? "

" Well, sir, if I may say so——" He paused.

" Of course, say what you like, my dear fellow. I have the greatest confidence in your judgment and ability. I have not forgotten the anniversary of our wedding." He smiled, and the Prime Minister went on :

" Well, sir, I should suggest that you stay. I doubt if he will do it for me, but he has a very great respect for Your Majesty, as indeed we all have." He bowed. " And if Her Majesty's page is restored to her I am sure she would understand why you did not go to her at once, and that you were more truly—er—serving her by remaining here."

" Yes, I think so, too," said the King. " Her Majesty is a trifle hasty at times, but at heart an understanding woman."

" Indeed, yes, sir, but here he comes." For at that moment the squire returned with the Magician.

" Your Majesty sent for me ? I was busy, very busy. But, of course, when I heard that your Majesty needed me urgently, I came at once. Nothing is too difficult for me to perform. I can do anything, everything." He waved his arms widely as if to embrace the world, and then went on grandly :

" Sir, I await your request," and bowed very low to the King.

" Thank you, my dear fellow, thank you," said the King. " I have good servants, and faith, to-day I need 'em. The fact is, my dear Magician, there has been a little accident in the garden—Her Majesty's page has—er—well, it sounds rather absurd, I know—but he's fallen into the middle of the earth and we need your help to get him out. You see, the Queen——"

" Oh, is that all," said the Magician. " I know all about that."

" But, how ? " said the King, amazed.

" Because I arranged it myself." They gasped. " I have known for some time," he went on, " that the boy was a nuisance to every one at Court, and so I took the liberty of removing him. Now may I go back to my work ? Since I put him there deliberately, I cannot be expected to get him out. I thought you would thank me." And he turned to go.

" Come back at once," commanded the King. " Why, Her Majesty adores him—if it were known that you were responsible for this, neither you nor I would ever hear the last of it. Much as I sympathise with you, I must beg you—nay, command you—to restore him to Her Majesty at once. I myself will see that he does not offend again, but restore him you must. And Her Majesty must think it an accident. Follow me at once."

And strangely enough the Royal Magician did.

In the garden they found the Queen and her ladies on the edge of a great pit seven yards wide and seven miles deep, that stretched right across the garden. The Queen had recovered from her grief, for Rudolf had called to her that he was not hurt. But she had lost her temper, for none of her gentlemen, though they made themselves very hot and dirty with ropes and ladders and things, had been able to get down.

" At last," she said, when she saw the King and the Royal Magician, " at last ! He might have been dead by now."

The King drew her aside and tried to calm her, while the Magician, disguising his disgust rather badly, went to the edge of the pit and looked over. The Queen came back.

" What are you going to do ? " she said snappily. " Looking is no use. We have all looked several times. Change yourself into a magic carpet, fly down to him at once, and bring him up again."

" Certainly not," said the Magician. " I only do that for Royalty, not for pages. It is too painful."

" Well, do something ! What is the use of being a Magician if you can only stand and look ? "

" I am going to, Madam. Stand back every one, please. Now if you watch carefully, you will see how great and powerful I am, and that even the earth is subject to me and obeys my slightest wish."

Then he leaped seven times into the air, landing first on his left foot and then on his right. At the seventh leap the earth began to roll back and fold itself into steps until there was a broad staircase from the edge of the pit to the bottom.

" Now you can come up," he shouted to the page.

" What ! climb all that way after such a fall ! " exclaimed the Queen. " How very inconsiderate of you ; it will take him all the afternoon."

" Until nightfall, Madam," replied the Magician.

" And do him good," said the Prime Minister, who had just come up. " Very sound idea of yours, Magician."

" My ideas are always sound," smiled the Royal Magician, as he walked away.

" Oh," said the Queen. " Sir, I must beg you to escort me to my room. I can bear no more." The King escorted her, but there was a twinkle in his eye, and when he came back and found the Prime Minister alone, he said :

" Yes, I quite agree, a very sound idea ! We will come back at nightfall, and explain the soundness of it to him."

This they did, and for some time after that the page behaved much better.


## CHAPTER VI

### THE QUEEN VISITS THE MOON

ONE fine day the Queen flew away to the Moon. It happened quite simply, just like this. She was walking in the garden on a windy day in her new lilac brocade gown, which had a very wide full skirt, and somehow the wind got underneath it and she rose into the air like a balloon. Before her startled courtiers could even gasp, she was half-way up to the Moon. They shrieked all together and one or two ladies fainted.

The King, hearing the commotion, came running out, closely followed by the Prime Minister. As a matter of fact the Prime Minister was the better runner of the two, but of course no one ever gets in front of the King. But by the time they arrived, the Queen was but a speck in the distance, and in less than a moment she was not to be seen at all.

Where had she gone ? And where, oh where, would she drop ? Would they ever see her alive again, and if they did would she ever forgive them ?

Not that it was their fault, but she would be sure to say it was. She was that kind of woman, as doubtless you have already learned.

The King was terribly upset. This time it really was unprecedented; even the Prime Minister admitted that it was. But what could they do? The Royal Magician had gone away for his summer holidays the day before, and in his usual thoughtless way had forgotten to leave his address, so they had no idea where to look for him.

As the King said, if only he had been there it would have been the easiest thing in the world to send him flying after her. But he wasn't, and though the Prime Minister was a very good fellow and all that sort of thing, and would do his best, still he couldn't fly, could he? And the Prime Minister

*The Royal Army was on the land, the Royal Navy on the sea and the fishermen on the coast, all ready with landing nets.*

admitted sadly that he could not. The only thing he could suggest at the moment was to send out messengers to warn all the people of what had happened, and to tell them to be on the look-out, and ready to catch Her Majesty as she descended.

This, the King agreed, was the only thing to do, so the Prime Minister did it. The Royal Army was scattered at intervals across the country with landing nets. The Royal Navy was sent to patrol the sea, also with landing nets, and the fishermen were lined up along the coast, with their fishing nets, so that if Her Majesty had not yet fallen she might be caught safely. Balloons were sent up to look for her. And when by the middle of the afternoon the messengers returned, after having ridden over all the length and breadth of the land, and reported that Her Majesty had not fallen yet, the King grew more hopeful that she would be caught unhurt when she did fall.

But when the evening came and it began to grow dark and yet there was no news, his fears came back. How would they see her in the dark? Then the Prime Minister ordered all the beacons to be lighted, and that every one should carry a torch, and that no one but the children should go to bed. But though the King was grateful to him for his thought, he hadn't much hope left.

All night long he paced restlessly up and down the terrace and watched the lights of the beacons and torches twinkling far across the country. But there were terrible dark patches between, and though Prince Compassionate walked with his father and tried to comfort him, and the Princess his wife made tempting little meals for him at intervals, he would neither eat nor be comforted. When the dawn broke at last, after what had seemed the longest and most terrible night of his life, the King looked haggard and grey and ten years older. For he loved his wife in spite of her tempers and sharp tongue.

The Prime Minister looked weary too; he had been in the saddle all night, but had heard no news of the Queen. The Lord High Admiral reported to the King at seven o'clock, but he had no news. The General-in-Chief of the Army reported at eight o'clock, but he had no news. The Mayor of the Fishing Village reported at nine o'clock, but he had no news. Then when the whole day passed and still there was no news, the King feared that she had floated far beyond the limits of the Known World into the grey and fearsome Unknown that lies outside, and that they would never see or hear of her again.

He told the Prime Minister to tell the people to go to bed, and recall the Army and Navy and the balloons, and tell the fishermen to go on with their work. But they didn't, for they were loyal and loving people, and for two days and two nights more they kept watch, and the King was touched to his heart. He rode through the land with his son and his court, and with tears in his eyes he thanked his people for their devotion. But though their love warmed his heart, it could not give him back his Queen.

His eldest son, Prince Charming, and his second son, Prince Amiable, came hurrying back from their honeymoons in the south. But they had no help to offer him save the comfort of their presence, and no one had heard a word of the Royal Magician.

The King was secretly very hurt by this, for he had thought that, in some magic way, the Magician would have heard of his trouble, and would have come to help him. He could not believe that the Magician had really deserted him, and yet it seemed that he had. Secretly, too, the Prime Minister was thinking the same. He had looked everywhere for his address, thinking he might have left it in the laboratory, but he could not find it.

"If only the fellow had said where he was going," he said to Prince Compassionate, who knew the Magician best. "But there, he always *was* mysterious."

And Compassionate agreed that if only they had known they could have sent for him. "For," he said, "I am sure he would have come. I know he is a decent fellow at heart and admires my father immensely. His queerness, you know, is only one of the tricks of the trade; he almost confessed as much to me once. I wonder where he is." He got up and began to pace restlessly up and down the room. "I don't really believe my mother is gone for ever, but I fear my father will be ill. Wish I knew where that Magician has got to——"

He stopped suddenly, then swung round and pointed his finger at the Prime Minister. " I've got it—he's gone to my father-in-law's court—the House of Dreams, you know. I'll swear he has ! You know what a fuss they made of him." He came excitedly up to the Prime Minister, took him by the arm and dragged him from his chair and across the room.

" Come on," he said. " Let's look for my wife and see if she doesn't agree." And he hauled the astonished Prime Minister off to his wife's boudoir.

" Why, of course," she said, when they got there with the news. " How clever you are, Compassionate."

The Prince looked modestly at his feet.

" Yes," said the Prime Minister. " Maybe you're right, but how to get there and get him back is quite another matter. For he said, you remember, that no mortal could ever go there alone."

" So he did," said the Prince, unhappily. " Then we can't do anything."

" Silly, of course we can," said the Princess. " I am not a mortal, I can go. I often go ; at night when you are all asleep I go in my dreams to visit my dear father and mother. I will go this very day, and if he is there I will tell him. I expect he will be there, for I seem to remember my father inviting him when he said good-bye to us."

" Hooray ! Oh, you darling ! " shouted the Prince. " Off you go," he said to the Prime Minister, " and tell my father," and shoved him out of the room.

The King was overjoyed. He rushed into the room and the years seemed to fall off him as he ran. He was almost his old happy self again, and the words came tumbling over themselves as he tried to thank the Princess. She kissed him and made him go to rest. Then she lay down on her couch, and the Prince Compassionate, who had rather a pleasant voice, sang to her until she fell asleep. He watched her sleeping and thought how beautiful she looked, and after a time he saw her smile happily. A little while later she smiled again, and she looked so lovely that he stooped and kissed her. As he kissed her she waked and smiled again sleepily.

" Well ? " said the Prince eagerly.

" Oh, Compassionate," she said, " he was there and he is coming. He didn't know."

At that moment the curtains streamed suddenly inwards and the Royal Magician rode into the room on the back of the breeze. The Prince gave a shout of mingled surprise and welcome that roused the whole palace. The King came hurrying in and the Magician bowed to the very ground.

" Sire," he said, " I offer you my most humble and sincere apologies for any hurt or inconvenience I may have caused you. The news of your trouble has but this moment reached me. Into the House of Dreams no news of the outside world ever comes. That, indeed, is why I went, for I felt I needed a complete rest and holiday."

" My dear Magician," said the King. " I could not believe that you had really deserted me, yet you seemed to have vanished utterly."

" You might have left your address," said the Prime Minister.

" But I thought I had."

"Well, you didn't; not where it could be found anyway, for I looked everywhere myself."

"Nearly blew ourselves up in your beastly laboratory, too," put in the Prince.

"In my laboratory! I hope you have not disturbed any of my experiments; they are most important and——"

"Oh, what does that matter?" interrupted the King. "What matters is that you are here now and can help us to find the Queen—if she still lives, poor woman."

"I have," said the Royal Magician calmly.

"What!" exclaimed every one at once. "Where, when?"

"Well," said the Magician. "The breeze who brought me here happened to be the same breeze who carried her off. He is a servant of the King of the Moon, and the Moon Queen admired our Queen's new lilac gown and wanted to see it more closely. So the Moon King sent this breeze to fetch her." The breeze rustled agreement. "That's all. Quite simple."

"Quite simple—yes," exclaimed Prince Compassionate. "But what cheek!"

"It was a lovely gown," said the Princess. "I admired it myself."

"I think it was most inconsiderate of His Moon Majesty," said the King. "Most inconsiderate, and most undiplomatic too. Wars have been made for less."

"But one cannot make war on the Moon," said the Prime Minister.

The Magician smiled tolerantly at him.

"With my aid you could," he remarked. "But there will be no need. His Moon Majesty cannot really be blamed. He is old and the slave of his young wife, and when she asks anything he gives it to her at once. And, sire, he did indeed try to let you know that Her Majesty was safe. He sent a message by a breeze which he expected I should be here to interpret. But as I was away the breeze could not give his message."

"Hum," said the King. "Not a very useful sort of messenger. Still, I suppose he did his best. Well, well, we will not do anything hasty. Is the Queen happy there?"

"Perfectly, sire. She thinks you know she is safe, and has fallen in love with the Moon Queen's new baby. A strange taste—for it is very ugly—but she has."

The King smiled.

"She always loved babies," he said, "and if she is happy, the best thing we can do is to pretend we knew she was safe and didn't worry. Otherwise, she might be upset about it when she returns. Don't you think so?" he said to the Prime Minister.

"I do, sir," replied the Prime Minister fervently. He knew what the Queen was like when she was upset. "We must not upset Her Majesty. Shall I give orders for a banquet and an entertainment to be held on the night of Her Majesty's return?"

"A very fine idea," said the King. "She would be charmed. You think of everything."

The Prime Minister bowed. Then he went away and prepared a magnificent banquet, and sent for all the finest musicians and dancers in the country.

The Lord Chamberlain decorated the whole palace with flowers, and the Palace Guard turned out to receive the Queen.

She was delighted. She had thought the manner of her going most original. She had enjoyed herself immensely in the Moon. The Royal Magician had changed himself into a flying carpet to bring her back—an attention that had pleased her mightily—and now there was this excellent banquet and entertainment, and both her sons to welcome her. No wonder she was delighted. But it was a long time before she was told all that had happened while she had been away.

## CHAPTER VII

### THEY ALL VISIT THE MOON

IT was the King's birthday and so he wanted every one to have a good time, for he was a kind-hearted man. He ordered the Prime Minister to proclaim a national holiday, and the Prime Minister had done so. With the aid of the Royal Magician he had planned three delightful little homes for his three sons : the Royal Magician had built them in a night, and the Princes were delighted with their father's birthday gifts to them. He had invented a new order of nobility and made the Royal Magician the first member of it, and the Magician was as proud as seven peacocks as a result.

Then he had promoted his three sons, the Admiral, and the General-in-Chief to the same order. He had wanted to promote the Prime Minister too, but the Prime Minister had gracefully declined the honour, saying that he was too old (he was quite young really, but the cares of state made him seem older than he was) and that honours did not sit lightly on his shoulders. Really he refused because he knew the Royal Magician would be jealous, and he didn't want to cause any bother of that sort on the King's birthday. The King must have guessed his real reason, for he allowed the Prime Minister to have his own way and accepted his lame excuses without a word.

So every one was delighted. They all said to each other that though they had had many good Kings, there had never been one with so kind a heart as this King. And as the Prime Minister with his usual tact had managed to convey this to the King without seeming to flatter him, for you remember he hated flattery, the King was delighted too. So at breakfast he had said to the Queen :

" After the public business of the day is over, my dear, you shall choose for us how we shall spend the rest of the day."

And the Royal Magician was so far moved by the genial spirit of the day —or perhaps by his new honour—to say :

" Whatever you choose to do, madam, I will make possible, even if it means changing myself into a flying carpet."

The Queen was charmed and said so. The King was charmed and said so, and the three Princes and their three wives were charmed and said so, and the Royal Magician basked in the warmth of their approval as a cat basks in the sun. Indeed, as the Prime Minister whispered to the Admiral, he almost purred. The Prime Minister had said, " How charming," with the rest, but secretly wondered how long it would last.

*The Ambassador at once sent off a breeze with the news.*

Well, the Queen chose to visit the Moon again, for the last envoy from the Moon Court had brought a private letter to the Queen saying that the new baby had got a tooth, and the Queen was longing to see it. So she said that if the Royal Magician could arrange it that was where she would like to go. The Magician, delighted that she had chosen something that gave him a chance of showing off, said :

"Of course I can arrange it. We will start at once."

But the King reminded him of the morning's public business, and added that they must send word first ; it would not do for the whole Court to arrive unheralded. To this the Magician agreed, but rather reluctantly.

So they went for the Ambassador from the Court of the Moon, and told him, and he at once sent off a breeze with the news. In the meantime the Magician had hurried away to his laboratory, from which after a time there arose much smoke and many smells, which told the Court that he was preparing great magics.

By lunch time they were all pleasantly excited, for they knew the King had given him a free hand and he had sent word that he would be ready by lunch time to take them to the Moon. He had not said how, neither did he come in to lunch. That was always his way, to be mysterious. All they knew was that the stables had been emptied of their horses, which had been taken across to the laboratory. This they knew, because the Head Groom had been in to ask the Prime Minister if it was all right, and the Prime Minister had said he supposed so, as the King had given the Royal Magician a free hand.

A little later he had sent for all the grooms, but that was all they knew. So when after lunch they put on their coats and wraps—for the Queen had said it grew chilly as you got high up—and went outside, they were amazed by the sight that met their eyes. For a moment they could only gasp and gaze, while the Royal Magician bowed and beamed and smirked, waved his arms about and waited for the praise he knew must come when they got their breath back.

It really was rather wonderful. It really did almost take their breath away. There were all the King's horses and there were all the King's grooms, but how changed. Every horse had been turned to gold. Pure gold they were, yet they were still living horses. Every horse had a pair of sapphire wings. The grooms had been changed into gleaming alabaster and their tunics were of sapphire and their wings of gold. (As a matter of fact, some of them had rather objected to this transformation, but the Royal Magician had promised to turn them back afterwards, so they had agreed, though not very willingly, and one or two still looked rather sulky.)

It was the Magician's hour of hours. "How wonderful!" "How marvellous!" "How beautiful!" "How exquisite!" said every one. They crowded round the horses, touching them to see if they were real, and they crowded round the Royal Magician, and chorused their praise and wonder. They would probably have been doing it yet had not the Queen, growing impatient, said that if they wished to be there in time for tea they had better start.

At this, of course, the Royal Magician became a little annoyed. They were not, he said, going to travel by breeze as the Queen had, but by flying horses, invented by himself, and the time it would take depended on him alone, and that if he wished, the journey could be over in a flash. The Prime Minister began to wonder if his fears of the morning were going to be justified, for the Queen was looking offended and irritable, and the Royal Magician very black.

Luckily, at that moment the King came up, and asked the Magician to ride with him at the head of the procession, and his anger vanished as he walked importantly to the front. Then they all mounted blissfully. It is true the Queen refused the Prime Minister's assistance, but then Prince Charming, with a pleasant smile, asked her if he might ride beside her, and this put her in a better temper, for he was her favourite son. Then the Magician waved his whip, and off they went, each groom holding the bridle of the horse nearest to him. They rose gracefully into the air and flew away up and up towards the Moon.

Some of the ladies-in-waiting were a little frightened when they saw the palace, trees and houses grow smaller and smaller beneath them, but they forgot it when they began to race through the sunlit clouds. Even the Queen remarked on the loveliness of the clouds, and Prince Charming said it reminded him of the day the sky fell, and he first saw his dear wife.

Soon they were in sight of the gates of the Moon. But then they began to get into difficulties. For to honour them the King of the Moon had sent out the Four Winds of Heaven to meet them. On the winds came, abreast, blowing full strength. The horses began to falter and stumble, for the Royal Magician, not expecting this, had not given the horses strength to struggle against such a torrent of wind, and they were almost held up.

Then to make matters worse, the Queen's hat blew off. She was very

## LONDON CAB HORSE
To be petted again and talked to in a gentle voice was
a great treat. (Page 361)

**MR BROCKLEHURST'S VISIT**

"This child, the native of a Christian land, worse than many a
little heathen . . . – this girl is – a liar." (Page 382)

angry, and blamed the Royal Magician for it, and said that it might just as easily have been herself as her hat in that wind. But luckily, just as she was getting really angry, the winds drew level, wheeled and flew with them, so that the horses hadn't to struggle any longer. So that made matters a little easier.

Then the South Wind, seeing that the Queen had lost her hat, dived gracefully after it and brought it back to her. So that by the time they drew up at the gates of the Moon they were all good-tempered again. All, that is, except the Royal Magician, who was sulking because he had not thought of everything, and because the Queen had blamed him.

The gates of the Moon, which were made of gleaming silver moonlight, streaked with the blackness of night and very lovely, were flung wide to receive them. The Royal Guards of the Moon were drawn up in their black and silver uniforms, with their swords at the salute. It was an imposing sight.

The grooms and horses folded their wings as they alighted on the threshold. Then they stepped forward on to the road to the palace. Now this sounds a very ordinary thing to do, but the result of it was most extraordinary. For at every step they took they rose high into the air in a most annoying manner. They thought they were just lifting their feet an inch or two, as they always did, but actually they went up yards, and however hard they tried they couldn't prevent it. The Moon people thought they were mad. They gasped, and gaped, and stared, and pointed, and then they began to laugh and laugh. The more the Court struggled to walk in an ordinary manner the more the Moon people laughed and jeered and pointed.

" My dear, my dear," gasped the King, struggling to keep his feet down. " Why ever didn't you warn us."

" Warn you ? " snapped the Queen. " This didn't happen to me. I was carried in by the Breeze, and the same Breeze wafted me wherever I went. I didn't walk a step all the time I was here. So how could I warn you ? "

So the King turned to the Prime Minister and said :

" My dear sir, surely this is most unprecedented."

" Most indeed," gasped the Prime Minister, bouncing up and down. " Can you explain it ? "

" No, I can't explain. Magician, can you ? "

" Yes, it's the air."

" Then stop it at once," panted the Queen. " All this is your fault."

" No, it isn't," snapped the Royal Magician. " You say everything is my fault, and I shall go home," and with that he vanished. Then the Queen turned to the King.

" This," she said, " is what comes of honouring and trusting a man like that. Just when we need him he goes."

But the King was too shaken to reply.

All this time the Moon people were staring and pointing and laughing. They thought them quite mad, and the Court became more and more angry. When at last they did get to the Palace where the Moon King and his wife were waiting to greet them, the King was too breathless to reply. But the Prime Minister managed to gasp out something in the King's name, and the King thanked him with a look, which was all he was capable of at the moment.

Then they went in, but the same thing happened again. They bounced along the corridor in the same absurd manner, banging their heads on the ceiling at every step. When at last they reached the banqueting hall and sat down, every one was most thankful. The Earth people were shaken and their heads sore, and the Moon King had a black eye where the Queen had kicked him when he tried to catch her heels and pull her down, the first time he saw her rise into the air. She had kicked him quite accidentally, but it had upset his temper just the same, and it was not improved by the King's first remark, though made quite innocently.

"My dear sir," said the King, "what an extraordinary climate."

"Extraordinary climate indeed, extraordinary way of walking."

*They fell down over the edge of the moon and into the sea.*

At that the young Moon Queen, who all this time had been holding her breath trying not to laugh, suddenly began to giggle. It was very rude of her, but really she couldn't help it, they had looked so funny.

"Well," said the Queen, "if this is the way we are received, I do not wish to stay, much as I enjoyed my last visit," and she jumped angrily out of her chair. The result was astounding. She had jumped up with such vigour that when her feet touched the floor she rebounded with immense force, and soared right up and through the ceiling. The whole Court leaped to its feet in consternation. First rose the King, then the Prime Minister, then the three Princes and Princesses, and one by one they too rebounded, crashed through the roof and fell down, down, down over the edge of the Moon and into the sea with a great splash, right in the middle of the fishing fleet.

They might have been drowned but that the fishermen, with great presence of mind, flung out their nets and hauled them all safely into their boats. But imagine the Queen's feelings, to be trawled for like a common fish!

Oh, it was terrible ! And it was all the King's fault for trusting that knave of a Magician, she said, and he must dismiss him at once, when they got home.

But when they did get home they found that the Royal Magician had wisely disappeared. So they all went to bed, the King and the Queen, and the Prime Minister, Prince Charming and his wife, Prince Amiable and his wife, and Prince Compassionate and his wife, and all the rest of the Court, with hot-water bottles, and there they stayed for several days. It was a sad ending to the King's birthday.

## CHAPTER VIII

### TROUBLE WITH THE MOON

FOUR days after their Majesties' sudden return from the Moon, a message was brought to the Prime Minister's bedroom, that ambassadors had arrived from the Court of the Moon King, and that they were asking for an audience. The Prime Minister got up and dressed, although he was still very shaky, and his head was still very sore. Then he went down to the Ambassadors who were waiting in the Great Hall.

He bowed to them and asked them courteously to be seated and explain their business, thinking they had come to inquire after the King and Queen and express regret at what had happened in the Moon four days before. Imagine his astonishment when they curtly announced that they had come to demand payment for the damage caused to the Moon King's palace roof !

The Prime Minister was so shocked and astonished for a moment that he could hardly speak. Then he rose and answered them stiffly, but with great dignity.

" I can hardly believe, your Excellencies, that I have heard aright. The damage done was quite accidental, and I can assure you that it was far from being equal to the damage done to their Majesties, who are still suffering from injuries and shock received while guests of your Court. It is we, rather than you, should demand satisfaction. However, I will convey your message to His Majesty, and give you a formal answer later. In the meantime I will order all that is necessary for your comfort and refreshment."

With that he rose and went out. He went to the King and told him, and the King was deeply hurt and angered by the attitude of the Moon King and his Ambassadors. He wanted to get up and go down to them, but the Prime Minister persuaded him that it was unnecessary, so as the King was still feeling bruised and annoyed, he sent a written answer instead, saying to the Moon King what the Prime Minister had said to the Ambassadors.

They returned to the Moon, but were soon back again, and this time demanded an audience with the King himself. This the King granted. They said that the Moon King denied their claim entirely, said the damage to their Earth Majesties was their own fault for not walking properly, and demanded the sum of one million pounds, to pay for the mending of the roof.

This made both the King and the Prime Minister very angry. The King replied that the way they had walked was due to the extraordinary climate of the Moon, and that it was inconsiderate of His Moon Majesty to have allowed them to return home the way they did. He ought to have sent a Breeze to catch them, or several Breezes if necessary, for he had plenty. Finally, he said, the amount of reparation due to us from you is being worked out by our Court Mathematician, by algebra, and when he reports the result we will give you another audience. In the meantime you may tell your Court what we have said.

The Ambassadors were furious, but they could do nothing. The next day the negotiations were reopened. The Court Mathematician had reported that he had compared the amount claimed by the Moon with the amount due to the Earth, and that the answer to his sum was that $x=0$. As the King had never been very good at algebra, he asked him to explain in greater detail. So the Court Mathematician explained that the meaning to his answer, in plain words, was that both amounts were equal, and that therefore neither side should pay anything. The King was quite satisfied with the answer, thought it quite fair and sufficient to end the matter, so he sent it to the Moon King.

But the Ambassadors came back yet again, and said that the Moon King was not satisfied with the answer of the Court Mathematician. His Mathematician, he said, had worked it out by arithmetic, a much safer way, and that the two amounts were not equal. He therefore demanded the difference, namely, half a million pounds, plus a hundred pounds for feeding the King's horses and grooms, which had been left in the Moon. The King was aghast at such an answer, said so forcibly, and broke off the negotiations. " This will mean war," threatened the Ambassadors. The King laughed.

" Do you know," he said, " that I have a powerful Magician at my Court, and that you have none. Do you think, then, that I fear war ? "

" True," said the Ambassadors, " but we rule the air, so beware." And they rose and went away, laughing too, rather unpleasantly.

" Now," said the King when they had gone, " where is that Magician. I've not heard anything of him since we got home. We must find him."

" Leave that to me, sir," said the Prime Minister. " I'll find him." And he did and brought him along to the King.

" An awkward corner you have got us into," said the King. " If you want to be forgiven you must get us out again. They are going to make war."

The Magician had got over his temper by this time, and said he was ready to help, only the Queen mustn't make rude remarks about what he did when he was doing his best. The King said she wouldn't, and when next day war was declared by the King of the Moon, he summoned the Royal Magician to his Council.

When the Council, consisting of the King, the Prime Minister, the Admiral, the General and the Royal Magician met, the King said :

" Now what did they mean by that reference to the air ? How can the air hurt us ? "

" I don't quite know," said the Prime Minister, " but I am worried."

" So am I," said the King. " What do you think, Magician ? "

" I am not quite sure yet. But whatever they do, you may trust me to beat them. I rather think that they imagine that because I did not control the air the day we visited them, that I cannot do so. As a matter of fact I could have done easily, but I was so upset by what the Queen said that I——"

" Quite, quite," interrupted the King. " So we need not worry."

" Not in the very least," said the Magician. " There is nothing I cannot do. Leave all to me and all will be well."

" Yes, yes," said the General impatiently, " that sounds very fine, but what exactly are you going to do. I am not at all sure that it is in accordance with the rules of war to use magic. There is no mention of it in the Rules for Land Warfare."

" Nor for Sea Warfare, either," added the Admiral.

" But there is no express rule against it, is there ? " asked the Prime Minister.

" No," they said. " But it would be unprecedented."

" We should not do anything unprecedented," said the King reluctantly. " But how else are we to fight the Moon ? We cannot send ships and men in the ordinary way. The whole idea of a war with the Moon is unprecedented, and I am very bothered." He shook his head sadly, and so did the Admiral and the General. But the Prime Minister was a practical man and saw no other way out. So he said so, and the Royal Magician beamed.

" Create a precedent, sir," said the Prime Minister, " and smash the Moon. They are too insolent and need a lesson."

Just at that very moment all the air in the room began to go swiftly out of the window, leaving them choking and gasping for breath.

The Prime Minister leapt for the window, and shut it just in time to save a little air. All the rest went flying across the country and buried itself at the bottom of the sea.

" Good Heavens," gasped the King. " So that is what they meant. It is abominable. My people will die."

" I can save them," cried the Royal Magician, and he dashed out. He could exist without breath.

He found all the people choking and panting. There was a great hole in the sea, and all the air in the world was vanishing rapidly down it. Swiftly he flung pipes down the hole, called the Fire Brigade to help him, dressed them in divers' clothes—the new kind with extra-large air tanks—and together they pumped air from the bottom of the sea and ran with it, in milk cans, to the people's houses. They flung it through the windows, then shut and barred them so that it couldn't get out again. So the people did not die, but they could not leave their houses.

By this time all the air had gone, and the world was absolutely still. Not a leaf moved. The silence was awful. Only down by the sea was there any life at all. There the firemen and the divers who were helping them worked without ceasing, pumping up air. Twice a day they delivered it at the houses, in the milk cans, and the people took it in through the windows.

In the meantime the Magician had returned to the palace, where he found the Council sitting in candlelight, for the closing of the shutters had made it dark inside. It was terribly stuffy too, for though the divers and firemen were doing their best, the air supply was not good, and the King refused to have more air than his people got. Even the candles were dim and flickering because they need air, too.

" This is awful," said the General, mopping his forehead, for he was a fat man and the room was very hot. " It is inhuman. What can we do, shut up here ? "

" Do ? " said the Prime Minister. " Nothing, except try to keep cool. Only the Magician here can do anything now. We can't use precedented methods against this sort of thing, sir."

" We can't," said the King sadly. " What a barbarous people they must be. This is worse than cutting off the water supply, and that, we all know, is against the rules of war."

" It is indeed," said the Admiral and General both together. " We might all have been dead by now."

The King went on : " Magician, I give you a free hand, only fight fair. This sort of thing appals me."

" I shall lift the sea and flood the Moon," said the Royal Magician. " Flooding is fair, isn't it ? "

" Yes," said the General.

" But my ships ! " cried the Admiral.

" I will put them in dry-dock," replied the Magician.

So the Magician went out, and a little later, if they had been able to look out of the window—but, of course, they weren't—they would have seen the sea rising up in a mighty fountain, and pouring down upon the Moon. Soon the streets and crops and houses were flooded. Haystacks went floating across the land, and all the people had to sit in their attics. And still the water went on rising.

Terrified, the Moon King sent Ambassadors to ask for an armistice. They were the same men who had come before, but how different their attitude. They were most humble and meek. The King received them with dignity. The Council was no longer hot and gasping, for, of course, when the sea rose there was nothing to hold the air down, so it was floating in its usual place. They could then open the windows and breathe freely.

All this time the water kept on rising in the Moon, and the people were now sitting on their roofs. Even the attics were flooded, and frenzied messages kept coming from the Moon King begging for the sea to be ordered back and promising anything—everything ! So the King told the Royal Magician to stop the water rising, but to leave it where it was and keep the Moon people sitting on their roofs till peace was signed, for he did not trust them.

The peace meetings were very short, for, of course, the Moon people were absolutely beaten. They had to pay a very heavy fine, and to apologise for the things that had happened on the Moon, and for the things that had been said afterwards. They had to return the horses and grooms and give up their claim for damages to the palace roof. All this they did. They had to, or they would all have been drowned, and they didn't want to be drowned.

Then the Royal Magician put back the sea, but it was years before the Moon recovered its prosperity, for all the crops had been destroyed and the cattle drowned. They never made war on the Earth again.

## CHAPTER IX

### THE COMET'S TAIL

THE Queen was angry; very angry. She often was, but this time she was specially angry. The reason was that there was to be a Court Ball that night in honour of the coming out of the eldest Princess, and the Queen had no jewels to wear. All her jewels except her crown had been sold to pay the expenses of the war. For, you see, though they hadn't had to pay for soldiers and munitions, still the wages of the divers and firemen had been enormous, and the reward the King had given to the Royal Magician had taken all the indemnity. That, the Queen had said, was unnecessary, but the King said it wasn't; they would all have been dead but for the Royal Magician, so he had paid it gladly. But the Queen was frightfully angry, and that was her reason.

The Prime Minister said to the Keeper of the Royal Jewels that they had much to be thankful for in that she had a reason at all, for often she was angry without reason, just because she felt like it. The Keeper of the Royal Jewels was just about to agree when a page summoned them to the King's presence. They found him looking very worried, naturally. He was worried for the Queen had said she would not appear at the ball without jewels; at least she must have necklace and tiara. She would feel disgraced otherwise. But what were they to do? There was no money and the Keeper of the Royal Jewels had nothing in his room but the two crowns, and it was evening already.

*They stood wondering and shaking their heads and talking.*

The Prime Minister suggested asking the Royal Magician to do something about it, but the King said :

" That is no use. The Queen refuses to allow him to help. She says it's all his fault, that if he'd had any decency at all he would have refused to take more than half the money I gave him. I do not agree with her, but she got most annoyed when I just mentioned his name, so I dropped the subject at once." He sighed. Secretly, the Prime Minister agreed with the Queen, but as the King seemed quite satisfied he could not say anything. And he could not think of anything else. He had already lent his spare money to the King to pay the firemen.

So they stood wondering and shaking their heads and talking without getting any further, until the sun set and the stars came out. But just as the dressing-bell rang they heard a shout and the sound of people running to the door. They rushed to the window and looked out, and there they saw a strange sight.

A Comet with a great fiery tail came swooping from the sky and tore swiftly round the palace. Round and round it swept, flashing a thousand glorious colours from its streaming tail. Every one's head was out of the windows, and every one's eyes were starting from their heads in surprise and wonder. It was a lovely sight ; never had they seen anything more beautiful.

While they were watching, it rose over the roof, but it cannot have noticed the weathercock on the highest tower, for it caught its tail on the cock's beak and tore it off. Down it fell, flashing and sparkling right under the King's window, and there it lay. The Comet soared away far into the sky not noticing that its tail had come off. It must have been a careless comet !

" Well," said the King. " How extraordinary. I didn't know they came off like that ! What on earth are we to do with it ? "

Then the Prime Minister had a brain-wave. He jumped out of the window, picked it up, and brought it in.

" It's the very thing," he said, " the very thing."

" What for ? " asked the King.

" Why, for the Queen, of course. Here is her tiara and necklace, perfect ! "

The King gasped at the audacity of the idea.

" But can we ? " he cried.

" We can, indeed," exclaimed the Keeper of the Royal jewels. " I will make it into a tiara and necklace within half an hour." And off he went to do it.

The King went joyfully to tell the Queen that in half an hour he would bring her the most wonderful tiara and necklace ever seen, fashioned out of the jewelled beauty of a Comet's tail. She was delighted, said she would wear her black gown to show it off, and went to her room to dress for the Ball.

When she appeared in the ballroom wearing the wonderful jewels, every one said that they had never seen the Queen look so magnificent, or the eldest Princess so beautiful, or the King so happy. Even the Royal Magician said he could not have made more beautiful jewels, and the Queen was so gratified that she forgave him. So it was a most successful Ball, and everything went well.

But at midnight there was an interruption. Some one must have told the Comet that he had lost his tail. Anyway he came back to look for it, and, of course, for a long time he couldn't find it. He sped anxiously round and round the palace, looking everywhere, on the roof, in the trees, on the ground, but it was not there. So he looked inside and there he saw it. He was furious. He dashed through the open window and tore round and round the Queen's head, trying to pull it off, and making more noise than seventeen swarms of angry bees.

The Queen screamed. The King shouted to the Royal Magician, who ran to the rescue.

"Take it off, take it off," moaned the Queen. "This is driving me crazy." And then she fainted in the King's arms. Hastily the Royal Magician took it off and fastened it on to the Comet again with nails and a hammer that the Prime Minister had run to fetch. Then the Comet flew out again by the same window as he came in.

The Queen revived, but she felt so shaky that she had to be carried to her room. But the Prime Minister with great presence of mind ordered the band to play a fox-trot, and soon the Court was dancing again just as if nothing had happened. The King was very upset by the incident, but he didn't want the Princess's first Ball to be spoilt, so he was pleased by the Prime Minister's action. The Ball went on, though the Queen did not come back. But towards two o'clock there was another interruption. A footman came running in terrified.

" All the stars in the Heavens," he gasped, " are lined up on the lawn."

The King ran to the door, followed by the Magician, the Princes, and the eldest Princess, who wanted to see what would happen. The Prime Minister followed, too, after he had emptied one of the fire-buckets over the footman, who had fainted. There on the lawn they saw millions of stars lined up in rows, blazing with anger, carrying great flashing spears, sharp-pointed and terrible. At their head was the Comet. The Royal Magician had fastened his tail on back to front, and he was furious.

" You have fastened on my tail back to front," he shouted. " Alter it at once or we advance and slay."

" Aye, slay, slay, with the flaming spear," shouted all the stars at once, and they shook their spears angrily, while sparks flew, and all the grass was scorched.

The King was nearly blinded by the glare, and did not know what to do. But the eldest Princess stepped bravely forward.

" Peace," she said. " It shall be done."

She waved the Royal Magician forward. She looked so brave and beautiful that the stars stopped shouting and the Comet even bowed to her. Then the Magician stepped out and undid the tail, fastening it on again properly and securely.

The Princess smiled, and the Comet bowed to her again. Then he turned to the stars and said :

" Let us now return. By the grace of this most lovely lady, I am now restored to honour and dignity."

So they returned again to the sky, singing as they rose the most wonderful harmonies in honour of the Princess's courage and beauty.

# CHAPTER X

## THE PRINCE OF THE NORTH POLE STAR

It was breakfast-time, the morning after the Ball, and the Court was discussing the events of that exciting night. The discussion had begun because the Queen, who, you remember, had not seen the second arrival of the Comet, wished to hear about it. So they had been telling her. But when they said that all the stars had come she said that that was impossible.

" I remember being distinctly told in my childhood that there was one star that could not move," she said. " The North Pole Star, they told me, remained fixed always as a guide to all good sailors." And the Admiral looked up and said. " That is true, madam, we always steer by the North Pole Star, for it never moves, and so is a safe guide. There is no trusting the others, they are always on the move. We should be lost if the North Pole Star did the same."

So as the Queen had been able to correct the whole Court, she was in a good temper all day.

Her pleasure was greatly increased by the fact that no less than three Princes of neighbouring lands had fallen in love with the eldest Princess at the Ball, and had asked leave to marry her.

The King had agreed to decide between them within three days, and though he loved his daughter and did not wish to lose her, yet it was a great triumph to have had three requests for her hand on the very first day of her " coming-out."

But when the King and Queen told the eldest Princess about it she was rather tiresome. She was excited by her adventure of the night before, and rather rebellious. She said that her three brothers had married for love, and had married Princesses from strange lands after wonderful adventures, and she didn't see why, after that, she should get married tamely to a Prince from next door whom she didn't even love.

One she said was too fat, another too thin and the third too ugly. All her brothers were handsome, and their wives beautiful, and so she pouted her lovely lips and sulked.

In vain the King urged and the Queen persuaded. She would not give in. Her three brothers backed her up, so in despair the King said he would give her another week to decide, but that at the end of that time she must decide.

During that week three more Princes rode in to ask for her hand. She would have none of them either, charming and handsome though they were. They had come tamely on horseback, she said. Her eldest brother's wife had come on a golden ladder from the sky, her second brother's wife had come on a fountain from the sea, and her third brother's wife had come in the sun from the land of dreams, and she wasn't going to marry any one less exciting than they had.

At last the Queen lost her temper. All six Princes were living at the Court, each with a retinue of a hundred men, waiting for the King's decision, and the amount of food those six hundred and six men ate was enormous. She refused

*One by one, the Princes were presented.*

to feed them any longer. Also the retinues quarrelled, and the Prime Minister's hair was going grey with the worry of settling their disputes. So to pacify them all, the King announced that he would hold a Court that evening (it was seven days after the Ball) and that there the Princess should choose her bridegroom. The Princess wept, and wept, and wept, but it was no use. She had to give in. When the King did put his foot down he had to be obeyed.

So the evening came. One by one, the Princes were presented, each followed by his glittering train. It was a gorgeous sight. There was the Prince of the Lands of the West and his retinue in liveries of Sunset Red. There was the Prince of the Eastern Plains and his retinue in liveries of Pink of the Dawn. There was the Prince of the Southern Deserts and his retinue in liveries of Sand-in-Flame. There was the Prince of the Icebound Seas and his retinue in liveries of White of the Snows bordered with Green of the Berg. There was the Prince of the Mountain Forests and his retinue in liveries of Sable and Purple Gloom. There was the Prince of the Isles of the Sea and his retinue in liveries of Mother-of-Pearl and Blue.

Such a blaze of colour had seldom been seen at Court, and the eyes of all were dazzled. The Princess's eyes were not dazzled, they were clear and cold ; she felt that she hated them all. Yet by the time the clock struck twelve she had got to decide, for such had been the King's decree.

They crowded around her, each one praising the riches and glory of his own land, and the greatness of his love for her. She smiled at them all, but her heart was full of wretchedness. She clung tight to Prince Compassionate's hand. He was her favourite brother, and he was doing his best to cheer her by staying beside her, so that she should not feel quite so alone. But as the hands of the clock drew round to midnight her wretchedness grew greater.

The clock struck twelve : a hush fell upon the Court : the Princess turned white. As the last echoes of the hour died away the King arose from his throne. The Princess gasped, her hands fluttered to her throat, she tried to speak, but couldn't.

"Steady," whispered Prince Compassionate, and she remembered that she was a King's daughter, and tried to smile.

"The Princess will now choose her bridegroom," said the King. She rose still trying to smile, but her eyes were aching with tears unshed.

"I will choose," she said. "Let the Princes advance."

But at that moment the doors were flung open with a mighty crash. A blaze of unearthly light swept into the hall.

"Hold," cried a voice. Every one stared. It was that wretched Comet again. "The Prince of the North Pole Star would urge his suit," cried the Comet, and in through the open doors came a Prince alone. He was tall, but not too tall ; he was dressed in Black of the Night, his only decoration a gleaming star upon his forehead. Holding his head high, and quite at ease amid all those staring eyes, he walked slowly down the length of the hall, a striking solitary figure in that blaze of colour. The courtiers made a lane for him to pass through, but he seemed not to see them at all, for his eyes were fixed on the Princess. When he reached her he knelt at her feet.

"Gracious lady," he began, and his voice was deep and musical. "Enraptured by the tale of your beauty and courage, which this Comet has told me, I have come with a heart full of love to lay it at your feet. Never before has the North Pole Star bowed before maid or woman. Calm and immovable I have gazed down upon the ages with a heart aloof. But now I come, to you. Come with me and be my bride, that the Heavens may be graced by a new star of surpassing loveliness, and I will place my everlasting devotion as a crown upon your brow. Refuse me, and the light of the North Pole Star will be dimmed for ever."

He rose, and holding out his arms to the Princess he smiled, and his smile drove the tears from her eyes and brought laughter to her lips, for seeing him, she loved him.

"I have chosen," she said. "I will be the bride of the Prince of the North Pole Star." She then gave him her hand, and led him up on to the dais to the King and Queen.

"Whee-ew," said Prince Compassionate. "Well, I'm blest !"

Then what a hubbub broke out in the Court. Each of the six Princes began to storm and protest, and the retinues began to quarrel. "The fellow is an impostor," they cried. "He cannot be the North Pole Star ; the North Pole Star cannot move. He has to remain fixed for ever as a guide to all good sailors. The Queen and the Admiral have both said so. Throw him out !" And the clamour rose higher and higher.

The King signalled to the Prime Minister and he rose. "Silence," he roared. "His Majesty will speak." When the noise had died away the King began. "My daughter has decided," he announced, "and her decision holds." Then he turned to the Prince of the North Pole Star.

"Sir," he said courteously, "you have come alone and we have not met you before. We have heard that the North Pole Star cannot move, and we have always believed that it was true. Therefore it seems that we should not be discourteous in asking you for proof that you are indeed he whom you claim to be. Our daughter is very dear to us, and her happiness is our wish. She has chosen you, but we should be glad to know more of you before we give her to you for ever."

" A just request," replied the Prince. " I come alone for fear of alarming my subjects the stars, for as you may know, I rule the Heavens, with the exception of the Sun and the Moon. For indeed I should not move. But I have left my younger brother in charge of my star, so its light still shines as a beacon for all good sailors. With your gracious permission I will take you there to-morrow to prove to you my truth, honour and wealth and substance."

With this reply the King said he was satisfied, and so the rest of them had to be satisfied too. Then he dismissed the Court and they all went to bed.

But at three o'clock in the morning the King was wakened. The Lord High Admiral was below, he was told ; he apologised for his early arrival, but his business was most urgent, a dreadful thing had happened. So the King rose hastily and went down to him.

" Sir," began the Admiral, " I implore you command the Prince of the North Pole Star to return home at once. For the light of his star has gone out, and we have been without guidance all night. My captains in despair have been trying to steer by the Southern Cross with the result that the whole fleet has turned upside down."

" What ! " exclaimed the King.

" Yes, sir, upside down, every one of them. Everything has fallen out of them into the bottom of the sea, and as fast as the divers bring things up and replace them, they fall out again.

" All night long my divers have been working, and now they have gone on strike. All our valuables, furnishings and guns are at the bottom of the sea ; the very pots and pans out of the cook's galley have gone, and my sailors are hungry and dispirited. Sir, I beg you, if you would not disgrace me and lose your navy, command the Prince to return.

" The fishing fleet is in an equal plight. Their whole night's work has been undone. Sir, help us, and send him back." He paused for breath.

" Dear, dear," said the King. " Upside down, you say ? Really this is most unprecedented. The fellow was the North Pole Star then—this proves it. I will send for him at once. I cannot have my navy in this plight, indeed, no ! "

So he sent for the Prince of the North Pole Star, and told him of the Admiral's complaint.

" It is that young brother of mine," exclaimed the Prince. " I thought I could rely on him. I must return at once."

" Thank goodness," said the Admiral.

" Sir," said the Prince to the King, " this proves who I am. Let me marry the Princess at once, and take her back with me, for I shall never dare to come back again. You will be able to visit us later on in our home in the sky."

After a little consideration the King agreed, largely because the Admiral urged him. For the Admiral was afraid the Prince would refuse to go without his bride, and was in despair over the state of his navy. So the Princess was wakened and they were hastily married.

She was delighted with the excitement of it all, and when they rode away together on the Comet's tail you might have searched the wide world over and not found a happier Princess.

Soon the light of the North Pole Star shone out again, the ships righted themselves and all was well once more. That is to say, all was well until the Queen got up next morning, and discovered that her daughter had gone away with the stranger Prince without even saying good-bye. There was trouble over that, you may be sure, and it went on for some time.

But since the navy was right side up again, the King didn't worry much about the Queen's annoyance. He was sure that before long he could make her realise the soundness of his action. Besides, there was plenty of precedent for bad temper on the part of the Queen, and none for upside-downness on the part of the navy. Unprecedented occurrences were always a worry to him, and there had been far too many during the last year.

## CHAPTER XI

### THE QUEEN MIS-GOVERNS

BUT the King was not able to make the Queen realise the soundness of his action as easily as he had hoped. She was very angry for several days. For one thing she had favoured the suit of the Prince of the Isles of the Sea, for he was overlord of her mother's island, which would some day be hers, and then her eldest daughter's, and she had wanted the alliance badly. Also, no news had come of her daughter since the night she had gone away, and that worried her too.

So to calm her the King said he would go, if the Royal Magician would take him, and see for himself that all was well. The Royal Magician said he would be very pleased to take the King. He changed himself into a Flying Carpet and away they went one fine evening, leaving the Queen to govern the land.

Now the Queen's method of governing was very different from the King's. She was not so tactful, she was not so wise, and she would have her own way in spite of all the Prime Minister said. She would take advice from no one, and she was very independent. So she very soon turned the Kingdom upside down.

She offended the Lord High Admiral so deeply by ordering the navy to use sails of cloth of gold and red instead of plain sailcloth, which she said looked dingy, that only his regard for the King prevented him from resigning. For, as he said to the Prime Minister, the idea was ridiculous, the sunlight would flash from the golden sails and show them for miles, and in time of war would be positively dangerous.

When the Prime Minister said he agreed with the Admiral and told the Queen so, she dismissed him.

Then the people grew angry, for they had known and trusted the Prime Minister for years. And when she began to interfere with them too, passing a silly law saying they must have their windows open when they liked them shut, because it was healthier with them open, they became almost rebellious.

Then the new Prime Minister, whom the Queen had appointed, began to dabble in magic, and the Queen encouraged him, hoping to be able to persuade the King, when he came back, to dismiss the old Royal Magician, and have the new man as Magician and Minister, and so save money by paying one salary instead of two.

But his magic soon began to have queer results. The real Royal Magician had been able to rule Nature and the elements. This man only thought he could.

One evening the new Magician told the Queen he would turn her garden into a perfect fairyland. So he went to the Royal Magician's laboratory, which he had carelessly forgotten to lock up when he went away, and began to play about with the magics there.

After a time, he was satisfied that he had done as he wished, for he heard sounds of movement and change in the garden. He went to the Queen and asked her to come out and see. The Queen went out, but it was so dark that she could hardly see anything. She thought the lawn felt very lumpy, and she wondered why the Magician hadn't lighted her fairyland, but she thought he would do it in a moment, suddenly, to surprise her. The surprise she got, however, was of a very different kind.

Something began to drop on her head. It was harder than rain and softer than hail, and when she put her hand up to her head she felt something squashy. Then a minute later something icy-cold, wet, and wriggly dropped down her neck. She gave a little squeal of horror, and ran inside to the light. The squashy stuff was soil, and the wet wriggly thing was a worm! It was horrible! Hastily she sent men with torches to see what had happened in the garden, and what a sight met their eyes.

*The wet wriggly thing was a worm!*

Nature had revenged herself on the meddler. All the trees were growing upside down, their roots in the air, scattering soil and slugs and worms, their leaves buried in the earth. All the grass and flowers were upside down too. No wonder the lawn had felt lumpy !

Horrified, they told the Queen, and some of the courtiers began to mutter among themselves that it was her fault. But they dared not say it aloud. The Queen sent for her Magician.

" You have done this," she said. " You must have said the magic words wrong. Put it right at once."

But try as he would the wretched man could not put matters right. In fact, the more he said the more things went wrong. First, all the rivers started to flow backwards, and the boats could not get down to the sea. Then the mountains went upside down, and all the sheep fell off, and their snow-clad tops froze all the land for miles around. Then the tides went wrong, and the empty fishing boats were driven back into harbour, while those that were full of fish were driven out to sea again. Now all the birds began to dive into the sea, and swim about there, while the fishes flew across the land, and made nests in the trees.

The whole Kingdom was upside down, and it was all the Queen's fault. There was no pasture for the cattle and sheep : the corn crops had vanished into the earth, and when the farmers tried to pull them up and plant them again right side up, they broke off.

Ruin and starvation were facing the nation, and all within four days of the King's departure. They had never realised before what a good King he had been, and how they longed for his return ! But he had said a week, and so they could not hope to see him until three more days had passed. The Prime Minister did his best to calm the people, saying that all would be well when the King returned, and in the meantime every one had to go about with their umbrellas up, to prevent things dropping down their necks.

In vain the Queen stormed at her Magician.

" Say it all backwards," she commanded him, " then things will go right." But the poor man had said so many things in his efforts to undo his first mistake that he couldn't remember more than a quarter of them, and the Queen was sick of the things that dropped on her every time she went out.

She had broken her umbrella, and no one would lend her one. She was sure the horrid worms and things waited to drop until they saw her coming, and if she had but known it, she was right. It is not wise to offend Dame Nature, unless you are a very powerful Magician.

Then the King came back, and what a reception he got ! He couldn't understand it at all. First he asked where the Prime Minister was : and who had sent him away. Then he asked who the upstart in his place was, and who had put him there : then he asked why his Kingdom, which he had left so peaceful and happy, was now upside down, and who had turned it upside down. And the answer to all his questions was, " The Queen."

He turned to the Royal Magician in despair.

" What are we to do ? " he asked.

And the Royal Magician, although he was tired and aching from having just turned himself back from being a Magic Carpet, felt sorry for the King and with one move of his hand put everything right.

There was a crash as the mountains fell back into their places. There was a roar and a hiss as the tides turned and the rivers swept back their proper courses, and the whirring of thousands of wings as the birds came back from the sea, and a great splash as the fishes dived in. The earth trembled and shook as the trees righted themselves, but the smell of the earth and worms went away, and once more the scent of flowers sweetened the garden.

The Queen came running to the door, thinking that at last her man had got things right.

" Have you done it ? " she cried.

" No, madam, I have done it," replied the Royal Magician. " Now I suppose I must go and tidy my laboratory. I expect everything is upside down there too."

" Never mind," said the King. " Order anything new that you want. I will see that it is paid for, and a thousand thanks, my dear Magician, for all you have done for me to-day."

So the Magician was appeased and happy again.

Then the King turned to the Queen.

" Perhaps you will explain," he said, and the more he heard the angrier he got. At the end he rebuked the Queen severely.

Then he recalled the Prime Minister, and settled down to the business of governing his Kingdom as it ought to be governed, and every one was very glad.

## CHAPTER XII

### THE SUN GOES OUT

THE Queen had not forgotten that the King had rebuked her, and being the sort of woman she was, she determined to get her own back. She was convinced that in time she could have straightened things out herself, and that therefore his rebuke was undeserved. She was determined, too, to do something to the Prime Minister, for since he had returned to office she had hated him more than ever. She was convinced that he was laughing at her behind her back, but he wasn't. What had made her think so was that he had given her an umbrella, hearing that her old one was broken. She took it as a reminder of the mistake she had made, but he had meant it as an offering of peace. He was always unlucky in his dealings with the Queen.

Just now it was specially unfortunate, because he had fallen in love with the youngest Princess, who had sympathised with him on his fall from office. He had spoken to the King about it, and the King had been delighted, but he said :

" There will be some difficulty in getting the Queen to agree, because it is not usual for the youngest Princess to marry until after the second Princess."

The King would have been ready to forget about his love of " precedent " on this occasion, because he thought a lot of the Prime Minister, who had been a Prince in his own land before the Revolution. But he doubted whether the Queen would agree with him. They both knew that this would not be the real reason why the Queen would not agree, but they both pretended it was. Such are the ways of Court.

That difficulty could have been overcome, for the Prince of the Isles of the Sea had transferred his affections to the second Princess, and they could have been married any time, because every one approved of the match. The second Princess, too, was quite ready to marry the Prince of the Isles of the Sea, for she had loved him since the night of the Ball, and though the youngest Princess had said that she wouldn't have married a Prince who had loved some one else first, the second Princess didn't seem to mind. She was a very placid person, not adventure-loving like the eldest Princess.

So you see that difficulty might have been overcome. However, the King and the Prime Minister kept up the pretence that it couldn't, because neither wished to discuss the Queen's temper, which temper daily grew worse, because

*" What has happened ? " the Queen cried.*

she couldn't think how to get her own back, and prove to the King that she could get good magic done as well as he could. If she could prove that, she thought she would win back his respect again, and so regain her old power over him.

Then one day a Magician arrived at Court from Goodness-Knows-Where, which is the place where all Magicians come from. She got hold of him before the King knew he had arrived, and bribed him to keep his arrival secret, and help her. He advised her to let him do something that had never happened before, and suggested using the Sun. He would make it, he said, travel in a zigzag line across the sky instead of straight. Then when every one was worried and wondering what it meant, the Queen would be able to say that she knew all about it and had arranged it. Every one would be amazed, and she would arouse the awe and admiration of the whole Court. The Queen smiled. At last, she thought, she would show them ! So she began.

The King, who was in Council, was hastily summoned by the news that the sun was travelling in a wild zigzag line across the sky. The people were terrified. The King ran to look. At first he thought it was some of the Royal Magician's work, and hastily sent to ask him. The Royal Magician knew nothing about it. Then the Prime Minister came running out.

" What can it mean," said the King. " The Royal Magician knows nothing about it."

The Prime Minister thought a moment, then he grinned.

" I think, sir, that it must be the Queen's doing ! "

" What do you mean ? " exclaimed the King, a little startled. " How can it be ? "

" Well, sir, I saw a stranger arrive yesterday evening, and he was shown straight to the Queen's Chambers. So naturally I made inquiries."

" Quite right," said the King. " But what has that to do with this ? "

" He is a Magician, sir, from Goodness-Knows-Where."

The King chuckled.

" Oh, I see ! Oh, the silly woman. Send for the Royal Magician. We'll see if he can't stop this fellow."

The Royal Magician came.

" Look," said the King. " We have a new Magician at Court. It would give us great pleasure if you could blot him out."

" Of course I can," said the Royal Magician. " Am I not the greatest Magician in the world ? "

So he did.

But it was the Sun he blotted out, which was not quite what the King had meant. Still the effect was very gratifying to His Majesty. The Queen was terrified ; she thought the second Magician had made a mistake like the first. And when he vanished in a puff of smoke (that also was the Royal Magician's doing) she came running to the door. In the hall she found the Prime Minister lighting candles.

" What has happened ? " she cried.

" Happened ! " said the Prime Minister. " Oh ! nothing much. His Majesty did not care for the way the Sun was behaving, so he asked the Royal Magician to put it out. That's all. When it has learned how to behave sensibly then His Majesty may allow it to shine again. In the meantime, madam, we are to use candles. I trust it will not inconvenience your Majesty in any way."

The Queen was relieved and much impressed. The King, who was standing in a dark corner listening, smiled to himself. Then he came out.

" Silly little woman," he said. " Do you really think your twopenny-ha'penny Magician is the equal of mine ! Why, *my* Magician is the finest Magician in the world, and would be just as ready to please you as me if you would be nice to him. He admires you very much really, and is always most upset because you do not like him. Come and make friends with him now."

The Queen realised at last that the Royal Magician really could beat all other Magicians, and, being a sensible woman at heart, decided to make friends with him.

" My dear," she said to the King, " we are very foolish to quarrel."

" Indeed, yes," he replied, and kissed her hand.

After that things went smoothly. The Queen even consented to the marriage of the Prime Minister and the youngest Princess. For having admitted that the King was wiser than herself on the subject of Magicians, she began to wonder whether he wasn't wiser on the subject of Prime Ministers too.

So there was a double wedding at Court between the Prime Minister and the youngest Princess, and the Prince of the Isles of the Sea and the second Princess. The Sun shone on both brides, for, of course, the Royal Magician had unblotted it for the occasion, and everything was gay.

The Queen smiled graciously on every one, and the King beamed all over his face. The Royal Magician, delighted as a child with a new toy because he had at last won the Queen's approval, gave the wedding guests the most wonderful exhibition of magic that had ever been seen.

So after a year of trials and upheavals that had been quite unprecedented, peace and happiness reigned once more throughout the land, and the King was very glad.

# SOLDIER, REST !

*by* SIR WALTER SCOTT

" SOLDIER, rest ! thy warfare o'er,
    Sleep the sleep that knows not breaking ;
Dream of battled fields no more,
    Days of danger, nights of waking.
In our isle's enchanted hall,
    Hands unseen thy couch are strewing,
Fairy strains of music fall,
    Every sense in slumber dewing.
Soldier, rest ! thy warfare o'er,
Dream of fighting fields no more :
Sleep the sleep that knows not breaking,
Morn of toil, nor night of waking.

" No rude sound shall reach thine ear,
    Armour's clang, or war-steed champing,
Trump nor pibroch summon here
    Mustering clan, or squadron tramping.
Yet the lark's shrill fife may come
    At the daybreak from the fallow,
And the bittern sound his drum,
    Booming from the sedgy shallow.
Ruder sounds shall none be near
Guards nor warders challenge here,
Here's no war-steed's neigh and champing,
Shouting clans, or squadrons stamping."

# THE ELVES

## *by* THE BROTHERS GRIMM

HERE was once on a time a rich King who had three daughters, who daily went to walk in the palace garden, and the King was a great lover of all kinds of fine trees, but there was one for which he had such an affection, that if any one gathered an apple from it he wished him a hundred fathoms under ground. And when harvest time came, the apples on this tree were all as red as blood.

The three daughters went every day beneath the tree, and looked to see if the wind had not blown down an apple, but they never by any chance found one, and the tree was so loaded with them that it was almost breaking, and the branches hung down to the ground. Then the King's youngest child had a great desire for an apple, and said to her sisters, " Our father loves us far too much to wish us underground, it is my belief that he would only do that to people who were strangers." And while she was speaking, the child plucked off quite a large apple, and ran to her sisters, saying, " Just taste, my dear little sisters, for never in my life have I tasted anything so delightful." Then the two other sisters also ate some of the apple, whereupon all three sank deep down into the earth, where they could hear no cock crow.

When midday came, the King wished to call them to come to dinner, but they were nowhere to be found. He sought them everywhere in the palace and garden, but could not find them. Then he was much troubled, and made known to the whole land that whosoever brought his daughters back again should have one of them to wife. Hereupon so many young man went about the country in search, that there was no counting them, for every one loved the three children because they were so kind to all, and so fair of face.

Three young huntsmen also went out, and when they had travelled about for eight days, they arrived at a great castle, in which were beautiful apartments, and in one room a table was laid on which were delicate dishes which were still so warm that they were smoking, but in the whole of the castle no human being was either to be seen or heard. They waited there for half a day, and the food still remained warm and smoking, and at length they were so hungry that they sat down and ate, and agreed with each other that they would stay and live in that castle, and that one of them, who should be chosen by casting lots, should remain in the house, and the two others seek the King's daughters. They cast lots, and the lot fell on the eldest; so next day the two younger went out to seek, and the eldest had to stay at home.

At midday came a small, small mannikin and begged for a piece of bread, then the huntsman took the bread which he had found there, and cut a round off the loaf and was about to give it to him, but whilst he was giving it to the mannikin, the latter let it fall, and asked the hunstman to be so good as to give him that piece again. The huntsman was about to do so and stooped, on which the mannikin took a stick, seized him by the hair, and gave him a good beating. Next day, the second stayed at home, and he fared no better. When the two others returned in the evening, the eldest said, " Well, how have you got on ? "

" Oh, very badly," said he, and then they lamented their misfortune together, but they said nothing about it to the youngest, for they did not like him at all, and always called him Stupid Hans, because he did not exactly belong to the forest. On the third day, the youngest stayed at home, and again the little mannikin came and begged for a piece of bread. When the youth gave it to him, the elf let it fall as before, and asked him to be so good as to give him that piece again. Then said Hans to the little mannikin, " What ! canst thou not pick up that piece thyself ? If thou wilt not take as much trouble as that for thy daily bread, thou dost not deserve to have it."

Then the mannikin grew very angry and said he was to do it, but the huntsman would not, and took the mannikin, and gave him a thorough beating. Then the mannikin screamed terribly, and cried, " Stop, stop, and let me go, and I will tell thee where the King's daughters are." When Hans heard that, he left off beating him and the mannikin told him that he was an earth-mannikin, and that there were more than a thousand like him, and that if he would go with him he would show him where the King's daughters were.

He showed him a deep well, but there was no water in it. And the elf said that he knew that the companions Hans had with him did not intend to deal honourably with him, therefore if he wished to deliver the King's children, he must do it alone. The two other brothers would also be very glad to recover the King's daughters, but they did not want to have any trouble or danger. Hans was therefore to take a large basket, and he must seat himself in it with his hanger and a bell, and be let down. Below were three rooms, and in each of them was a princess, with a many-headed dragon, whose heads she was to comb and trim, but he must cut them off. And having said all this, the elf vanished.

When it was evening the two brothers came and asked how he had got on, and he said, " Pretty well so far," and that he had seen no one except

at midday when a little mannikin had come who had begged for a piece
of bread, that he had given some to him, but that the mannikin had let it
fall and had asked him to pick it up again ; but as he did not choose to
do that, the elf had begun to lose his temper, and that he had done what
he ought not, and had given the elf a beating, on which he had told him
where the King's daughters were. Then the two were so angry at this that
they grew green and yellow.

Next morning they went to the well together, and drew lots who should
first seat himself in the basket, and again the lot fell on the eldest, and he
was to seat himself in it. Then he said, " If I ring, you must draw me up
immediately." When he had gone down for a short distance, he rang, and

*One of the princesses was sitting there, combing the dragon's heads.*

they at once drew him up again. Then the second seated himself in the basket,
but he did just the same as the first, and then it was the turn of the youngest,
but he let himself be lowered quite to the bottom. When he had got out of
the basket, he took his hanger, and went and stood outside the first door
and listened, and heard the dragon snoring quite loudly. He opened the door
slowly, and one of the princesses was sitting there, and had nine dragon's
heads lying upon her lap, and was combing them. Then he took his hanger
and hewed at them, and the nine fell off. The princess sprang up, threw
her arms round his neck, embraced and kissed him repeatedly, and took her
stomacher, which was made of red gold, and hung it round his neck. Then
he went to the second princess, who had a dragon with five heads to comb,
and delivered her also, and to the youngest, who had a dragon with four
heads, he went likewise. And they all rejoiced, and embraced him and kissed
him without stopping.

Then he rang very loud, so that those above heard him, and he placed the princesses one after the other in the basket, and had them all drawn up, but when it came to his own turn he remembered the words of the elf, who had told him that his comrades did not mean well by him. So he took a great stone which was lying there, and placed it in the basket, and when it was about half-way up, his false brothers above cut the rope, so that the basket with the stone fell to the ground, and they thought that he was dead, and ran away with the three princesses, making them promise to tell their father that it was they who had delivered them, and then they went to the King, and each demanded a princess in marriage.

In the meantime the youngest huntsman was wandering about the three chambers in great trouble, fully expecting to have to end his days there, when he saw, hanging on the wall, a flute; then said he, "Why dost thou hang there, no one can be merry here?" He looked at the dragon's heads likewise and said, "You too, cannot help me now." He walked backwards and forwards for such a long time that he made the surface of the ground quite smooth. But at last other thoughts came to his mind, and he took the flute from the wall, and played a few notes on it, and suddenly a number of elves appeared, and with every note that he sounded one more came. Then he played until the room was entirely filled. They all asked what he desired, so he said he wished to get above ground back to daylight, on which they seized him by every hair that grew on his head, and thus they flew with him on to the earth again.

When he was above ground, he at once went to the King's palace, just as the wedding of one princess was about to be celebrated, and he went to the room where the King and his three daughters were. When the princesses saw him they fainted. Hereupon the King was angry, and ordered him to be put in prison at once, because he thought he must have done some injury to the children. When the princesses came to themselves, however, they entreated the King to set him free again. The King asked why, and they said that they were not allowed to tell that, but their father said that they were to tell it to the stove. And he went out, listened at the door, and heard everything. Then he caused the two brothers to be banished from the land, and to the third he gave his youngest daughter, and on that occasion I wore a pair of glass shoes, and I struck them against a stone, and they said, "Klink," and were broken.

# LONDON CAB HORSE

## by ANNA SEWELL

MY new master's name was Jeremiah Barker, but as every one called him Jerry, I shall do the same. Polly, his wife, was just as good a match as a man could have. She was a plump, trim, tidy little woman, with smooth, dark hair, dark eyes, and a merry little mouth. The boy was nearly twelve years old—a tall, frank, good-tempered lad; and little Dorothy (Dolly they called her) was her mother over again at eight years old. They were all wonderfully fond of each other; I never, before or since, knew such a happy, merry family.

Jerry had a cab of his own and two horses, which he drove and attended to himself. His other horse was a tall, white, rather large-boned animal, called Captain. He was old now, but when he was young he must have been splendid; there was still the proud way of holding his head and arching his neck; in fact, he was a high-bred, fine-mannered, noble old horse, every inch of him.

He told me that in his early youth he went to the Crimean War, for he belonged to an officer in the cavalry, and used to lead the regiment: I will tell more of that hereafter.

The next morning, when I was well groomed, Polly and Dolly came into the yard to see me and to make friends. Harry had been helping his father since the early morning, and had stated his opinion that I should turn out "a regular brick." Polly brought me a slice of apple, and Dolly a piece of bread, and they made as much of me as if I had been the "Black Beauty" of olden time. To be petted again and talked to in a gentle voice was a great treat; and I let them see as well as I could that I wished to be friendly. Polly thought I was very handsome and a great deal too good for a cab, if it was not for the broken knees.

"Of course, there's no one to tell us whose fault that was," said Jerry, " and as long as I don't know, I shall give him the benefit of the doubt ; for a firmer, neater stepper I never rode. We'll call him ' Jack,' after the old one —shall we, Polly ? "

"Do," she said, " for I like to keep a good name going."

Captain went out in the cab all the morning. Harry came in after school to feed me and give me water. In the afternoon I was put into the cab. Jerry took as much pains to see if the collar and bridle fitted comfortably as if he had been John Manly over again. When the crupper was let out a hole or two, it all fitted well. There was no bearing rein or curb, nothing but a plain ring snaffle. What a blessing that was !

After driving through the side-street we came to the large cab-stand where Jerry had said " Good-night." On one side of this wide street were high houses with wonderful shop fronts, and on the other was an old church, and churchyard surrounded by iron palisades. Alongside these iron rails a number of cabs were drawn up, waiting for passengers. Bits of hay were lying about on the ground. Some of the men were standing together talking ; others were sitting on their boxes, reading the newspapers ; and one or two were feeding their horses with bits of hay and a drink of water. We pulled up in the rank at the back of the last cab. Two or three men came round and began to look at me and to pass their remarks.

" Very good for a funeral," said one.

" Too smart-looking," said another, shaking his head in a very wise way ; " you'll find out something wrong one of these fine mornings, or my name isn't Jones."

" Well," said Jerry pleasantly, " I suppose I need not find it out till it finds me out, eh ? and, if so, I'll keep up my spirits a little longer."

Then came up a broad-faced man dressed in a great grey coat with great grey capes and great white buttons, a grey hat, and a blue comforter loosely tied round his neck. His hair was grey too, but he was a jolly-looking fellow, and the other men made way for him. He looked me all over, as if he had been going to buy me ; and then straightening himself up, he said with a grunt, " He's the right sort for you, Jerry ; I don't care what you gave for him, he'll be worth it." Thus my character was established on the stand.

This man's name was Grant, but he was called " Grey Grant," or " Governor Grant." He had been the longest of any of the men on that stand, and he took it upon himself to settle matters and stop disputes. He was generally a good-humoured, sensible man ; but if his temper was a little out, as it was sometimes when he had drunk too much, nobody liked to come too near his fist, for he could deal a very hard blow.

The first week of my life as a cab horse was very trying ; I had never been used to London, and the noise, the hurry, the crowds of horses, carts, and carriages through which I had to make my way, made me feel anxious and harassed ; but I soon found that I could perfectly trust my driver, and then I made myself easy and got used to it.

Jerry was as good a driver as I had ever known ; and, what was better, he took as much thought for his horses as he did for himself. He soon found out that I was willing to work and to do my best ; and he never laid the whip on me, unless it was to draw the end of it gently over my back when I was to go on. Generally I knew this quite well by the way in which he took up the reins ; and I believe his whip was more frequently stuck up by his side than in his hand.

In a short time my master and I understood each other as well as horse and man could do. In the stable, too, he did all that he could for our comfort. The stalls were of the old-fashioned style—too much on the slope ; but he had two movable bars fixed across the back of our stalls, so that at night and when we were resting he just took off our halters and put up the bars, and thus we could turn about and stand whichever way we pleased ; this is a great comfort.

Jerry kept us very clean, and gave us as much change of food as he could, and always plenty of it ; and not only that, but he always gave us plenty of

*In the stable he did all he could for our comfort.*

clean fresh water, which he allowed to stand by us both night and day, except of course when we came in warm.

Some people say that a horse ought not to drink as much as he wishes ; but I know if we are allowed to drink when we want it, we drink only a little at a time, and it does us a great deal more good than swallowing it down half a bucketful at a time, as we do if we have been left without water till we are thirsty and miserable.

Some grooms will go home to their beer and leave us for hours with our dry hay and oats, with nothing to moisten them ; then, of course, we gulp down too much water at once, which helps to spoil our breathing and sometimes chills our stomachs.

But the best thing that we had here was our Sundays for rest. We worked so hard during the week that I do not think we could have kept up to it but for that day's rest ; besides, we then had time to enjoy each other's company. It was on these days that I learned my companion's history.

## AN OLD WAR HORSE

Captain had been broken in and trained for an army horse, his first owner being an officer of cavalry going out to the Crimean War. He said he quite enjoyed the training with all the other horses—trotting together, turning together to the right hand or the left, halting at the word of command, or dashing forward at full speed at the sound of the trumpet, or signal of the officer. When young, he was a dark, dappled iron grey, and was considered very handsome. His master, a young, high-spirited gentleman, was very fond of him and from the first treated him with the greatest care and kindness. He told me he thought the life of an army horse was very pleasant ; but when it came to being sent abroad in a great ship over the sea, he almost changed his mind.

"That part of it," he said, " was dreadful ! Of course we could not walk off the land into the ship ; so they were obliged to put strong straps under our bodies, and then we were lifted off our legs in spite of our struggles, and were swung through the air, over the water, to the deck of the great vessel. There we were placed in small, close stalls, and never for a long time saw the sky, or were able to stretch our legs. The ship sometimes rolled about in high winds, and we were knocked about, and felt very ill. However, at last it came to an end, and we were hauled up, and swung over again to the land. We were very glad, and snorted and neighed for joy when we once more felt firm ground under our feet.

" We soon found that the country to which we had come was very different from our own, and that we had many hardships to endure besides the fighting ; but many of the men were so fond of us that they did everything they could to make us comfortable, in spite of snow, wet and the fact that all things were out of order."

" But what about that fighting ? " said I ; " was not that worse than anything else ? "

" Well," said he, " I hardly know. We always liked to hear the trumpet sound, and to be called out, and were impatient to start off, though sometimes we had to stand for hours, waiting for the word of command. But when the word was given we used to spring forward as gaily and eagerly as if there were no cannon-balls, bayonets, or bullets. I believe so long as we felt our rider firm in the saddle, and his hand steady on the bridle, not one of us gave way to fear, not even when the terrible bombshells whirled through the air and burst into a thousand pieces.

" With my noble master, I went into many actions without a wound ; and though I saw horses shot down with bullets, others pierced through with lances or gashed with fearful sabre-cuts, though I left them dead on the field, or dying in the agony of their wounds, I don't think I feared for myself. My master's cheery voice as he encouraged his men made me feel as if he and I could not be killed. I had such perfect trust in him, that whilst he was guiding me I was ready to charge up to the very cannon's mouth.

" I saw many brave men cut down, and many fall from their saddles mortally wounded. I have heard the cries and groans of the dying, cantered over ground slippery with blood, and frequently had to turn aside to avoid trampling on a wounded man or horse; but, until one dreadful day, I had never felt terror : that day I shall never forget.

Here old Captain paused for a while and drew a long breath ; I waited, and he went on.

" It was one autumn morning, and, as usual, an hour before daybreak our cavalry had turned out ready caparisoned for the day's work, whether fighting or waiting. The men stood waiting by their horses, ready for orders. As the light increased there seemed to be some excitement among the officers ; and before the day was well begun we heard the firing of the enemy's guns.

" Then one of the officers rode up and gave the word for the men to mount, and in a second every man was in his saddle, and every horse stood expecting the touch of the rein, or the pressure of his rider's heels—all animated, all eager. But still we had been trained so well, that, except by the champing of our bits, and by the restive tossing of our heads from time to time, it could not be said that we stirred.

" My dear master and I were at the head of the line, and as all sat motionless and watchful, he took a little stray lock of my mane which had turned over the wrong side, laid it over on the right and smoothed it down with his hand ; then, patting my neck, he said : ' We shall have a day of it to-day, Bayard, my beauty ; but we'll do our duty as we always have done.'

" That morning he stroked my neck more, I think, than he had ever done before ; quietly on and on, as if he were thinking of something else. I loved to feel his hand on my neck, and arched my crest proudly and happily ; but I stood very still, for I knew all his moods, and when he liked me to be quiet, and when gay.

" I cannot tell all that happened that day, but I will tell of the last charge that we made together ; it was across a valley right in front of the enemy's cannon. By this time we were well used to the roar of heavy guns, the rattle of musket fire, and the firing of shot near us ; but never had I been under such a fire as we rode through that day. From right, left and front, shot and shell poured in upon us. Many a brave man went down, many a horse fell, flinging his rider to the earth ; many a horse without a rider ran wildly out of the ranks ; then, terrified at being alone with no hand to guide him, came pressing in amongst his old companions, to gallop with them to the charge.

" Fearful as it was, no one stopped, no one turned back. Every moment the ranks were thinned, but as our comrades fell we closed in to keep the others together ; and instead of being shaken or staggered in our pace, our gallop became faster and faster as we neared the cannon, all clouded in white smoke, while the red fire flashed through it.

" My master, my dear master, was cheering on his comrades, with his right arm raised on high, when one of the balls, whizzing close to my head, struck him. I felt him stagger with the shock, though he uttered no cry. I tried to check my speed, but the sword dropped from his right hand, the rein fell loose from the left, and sinking backward from the saddle, he fell to the earth ; the other riders swept past us, and by the force of their charge I was driven from the spot where he fell.

" I wanted to keep my place at his side, and not to leave him under that rush of horses' feet, but it was in vain. And now, without a master or a friend, I was alone on that great slaughter-ground. Then fear took hold of me, and I trembled as I had never trembled before. Then I, too, as I had seen other horses do, tried to join in the ranks and to gallop with them ; but I was beaten off by the swords of the soldiers.

"Just then, a soldier whose horse had been killed under him caught at my bridle and mounted me, and with this new master I was again going forward. But our gallant company was cruelly overpowered, and those who remained alive after the fierce fight for the guns came galloping back over the same ground.

"Some of the horses had been so badly wounded that they could scarcely move from loss of blood ; other noble creatures were trying on three legs to drag themselves along ; and others were struggling to rise on their fore feet when their hind legs had been shattered by shot. Their groans were piteous to hear, and the beseeching look in their eyes as those who escaped passed by and left them to their fate I shall never forget. After the battle, the wounded men were brought in, and the dead were buried."

"And what about the wounded horses ? " I said ; " were they left to die ? "

"No, the army farriers went over the field with their pistols, and shot all that were ruined. Some that had only slight wounds were brought back and attended to, but the greater part of the noble, willing creatures that went out that morning never came back ! In our stables there was only about one in four that returned.

"I never saw my dear master again. I believe he fell dead from the saddle. Never did I love any other master so well. I went into many other engagements, but was only once wounded, and then not seriously ; and when the

*A soldier whose horse had been killed under him caught at my bridle.*

war was over I came back again to England, as sound and strong as when I went out."

I said, " I have heard people talk about war as if it was a very fine thing."

" Ah ! " said he, " I should think they have never seen it. No doubt it is very fine when there is no enemy, only just exercise, parade, and sham-fights. Yes, it is very fine then ; but when thousands of good, brave men and horses are killed or crippled for life, then it has a very different look."

" Do you know what they fought about ? " said I.

" No," he said, " that is more than a horse can understand ; but the enemy must have been awfully wicked people if it was right to go all that way over the sea on purpose to kill them."

## JERRY BARKER

I never knew a better man than my new master—kind and good, as strong for the right as John Manly, and so good-tempered and merry that very few people could pick a quarrel with him. He was very fond of making little songs, which he would sing to himself. His favourite was this :—

> " Come, father and mother,
> And sister and brother,
> Come, all of you, turn to
> And help one another."

And so they did ; Harry was as clever at stablework as a much older boy, and always wanted to do what he could. Then Polly and Dolly used to come in the morning to help with the cab—to brush and beat the cushions and rub the glass, while Jerry was giving us a cleaning in the yard and Harry was cleaning the harness. There used to be a great deal of laughing and fun between them, and it put Captain and me in much better spirits than if we had heard scolding and hard words. They were always early in the morning, for Jerry would say :—

> " If you in the morning
> Throw minutes away,
> You can't pick them up
> In the course of the day.
> You may hurry and skurry,
> And flurry and worry,
> You've lost them for ever,
> For ever and aye."

He could not bear any careless loitering and waste of time ; and nothing was so near making him angry as to find people who were always late wanting a cab horse to be driven hard to make up for their idleness.

One day two wild-looking young men came out of a tavern close by the stand, and called Jerry.

" Here, cabby ! look sharp, we are rather late ; put on the steam, will you, and take us to Victoria in time for the one o'clock. You shall have a shilling extra."

" I will take you at the regular pace, gentlemen ; shillings don't pay for putting on the steam like that."

Larry's cab was standing next to ours. He flung open the door and said, " I'm your man, gentlemen ! Take my cab, my horse will get you there all right " ; and as he shut them in, with a wink towards Jerry, he said, " It's against his conscience to go beyond a jog-trot." Then, slashing his jaded horse, he set off as hard as he could. Jerry patted me on the neck—" No, Jack, a shilling would not pay for that sort of thing, would it, old boy ? "

Although Jerry was steadfastly set against hard driving to please careless people, he always went at a good fair pace, and was not against putting on the steam, as he said, if only he knew *why*.

I well remember one morning, as we were on the stand waiting for a fare, that a young man carrying a heavy portmanteau trod on a piece of orange-peel which lay on the pavement and fell down with great force.

Jerry was the first to run and lift him up. He seemed much stunned, and as they led him into a shop, he walked as if he were in great pain. Jerry, of course, came back to the stand, but in about ten minutes one of the shopmen called him, so he drew up to the pavement.

" Can you take me to the South-Eastern Railway ? " said the young man. " This unlucky fall has made me late, I fear ; but it is of great importance that I should not lose the twelve o'clock train. I should be most thankful if you could get me there in time, and will gladly pay you an extra fare."

" I'll do my very best," said Jerry heartily, " if you think you are well enough, sir," for he looked dreadfully white and ill.

" I *must* go," he said earnestly. " Please open the door, and let us lose no time."

The next minute Jerry was on the box. He gave a cheery chirrup to me, and a twitch to the rein, that I well understood.

" Now then, Jack, my boy," said he, " spin along ; we'll show them how we can get over the ground if we only know why."

It is always difficult to drive fast in the city in the middle of the day, when the streets are full of traffic, but we did what could be done ; and when a good driver and a good horse, who understand each other, are of one mind, it is wonderful what they can do. I had a very good mouth—that is, I could be guided by the slightest touch of the rein, and that is a great thing in London, amongst carriages, omnibuses, carts, vans, trucks, cabs, and great wagons creeping along at a walking pace ; some going one way, some another, some going slowly, others wanting to pass them, omnibuses stopping short every few minutes to take up a passenger, obliging the horse that is coming behind to pull up too, or to pass and get before them ; perhaps you try to pass, but just then something else comes dashing in through the narrow opening, and you have to keep in behind the omnibus again ; presently you think you see a chance, and manage to get to the front, going so near the wheels on each side that half an inch nearer and they would scrape.

Well, you get along for a bit, but soon find yourself in a long train of carts and carriages all obliged to go at a walk ; perhaps you come to a regular block-up and have to stand still for minutes together, till something clears out into a side street, or the policeman interferes. You have to be ready for any chance—to dash forward if there be an opening, and be quick as a rat dog to see if there be room, and if there be time, lest you get your own wheels locked, or smashed, or the shaft of some other vehicle run into your chest or shoulder. All this is what you have to be ready for. If you want to get through London fast in the middle of the day, it wants a deal of practice.

Jerry and I were used to the thickest traffic, and no one could beat us at getting through when we were set on it. I was quick and bold, and could always trust my driver ; Jerry was quick and patient at the same time, and could trust his horse, which was a great thing too. He very seldom used the whip ; I knew by his voice and his click, click, when he wanted to get on fast, and the rein told me where I was to go, so there was no need for whipping.

*A young man carrying a heavy portmanteau fell down on the pavement.*

The streets were very full that day, but we got on pretty well as far as the bottom of Cheapside where there was a block for three or four minutes. The young man put his head out and said anxiously : " I think I had better get out and walk ; I shall never get there if this goes on."

" I'll do all that can be done, sir," said Jerry. " I think we shall be in time ; this block-up cannot last much longer, and your luggage is very heavy for you to carry, sir."

Just then the cart in front of us began to move on, and then we had a good turn. In and out, in and out we went, as fast as horseflesh could do it, and for a wonder, we had a good clear time on London Bridge, for there was a whole train of cabs and carriages all going our way at a quick trot —perhaps wanting to catch that very train. At any rate, with many others, we whirled into the station just as the great clock pointed to eight minutes to twelve.

" Thank God ! we are in time," said the young man ; " and thank you, too, my friend, and your good horse. You have saved me more than money can ever pay for ; take this extra half-crown."

" No, sir, no, sir, thank you all the same. So glad we hit the time, sir ; but don't stay now, sir, the bell is ringing. Here, porter ! take this gentleman's luggage—Dover line—twelve o'clock train—that's it ; " and without waiting for another word, Jerry wheeled me round to make room for other cabs that were dashing up at the last minute, and drew up on one side till the crush was past.

" So glad ! " he said, " so glad ! poor young fellow ! I wonder what it was that made him so anxious."

Jerry often talked to himself quite loud enough for me to hear when we were not moving.

On Jerry's return to the rank there was a good deal of laughing and chaffing at him for driving hard to the train for an extra fare, as they said, all against his principles ; and they wanted to know how much he had pocketed.

" A good deal more than I generally get," said he, nodding slyly ; " what he gave me will keep me in little comforts for several days."

" Gammon ! " said one.

" He's a humbug," said another, " preaching to us, and then doing the same himself."

" Look here, mates," said Jerry. " The gentleman offered me half a crown extra, but I didn't take it ; 'twas quite pay enough for me to see how glad he was to catch that train ; and if Jack and I choose to have a quick run now and then to please ourselves, that's our business and not yours."

" Well," said Larry, " *you'll* never be a rich man."

" Most likely not," said Jerry, " but I don't know that I shall be the less happy for that. I have heard the commandments read a great many times, and I never noticed that any of them said, ' Thou shalt be rich ' ; and there are a good many curious things said in the New Testament about rich men that, I think, would make me feel rather queer if I was one of them."

" If you ever do get rich," said Governor Grant, looking over his shoulder across the top of his cab, " you'll deserve it, Jerry, and you won't find a curse come with your wealth. As for you, Larry, you'll die poor, you spend too much in whipcord."

" Well," said Larry, " what is a fellow to do if his horse won't go without it ? "

" You never take the trouble to see if he will go without it ; your whip is always going as if you had the St. Vitus's dance in your arm ; and if it does not wear you out, it wears your horse out. You know you are always changing your horses, and why ? because you never give them any peace or encouragement."

" Well, I have not had good luck," said Larry, " that's where it is."

" And you never will," said the Governor. " Good Luck is rather particular with whom she rides, and mostly prefers those who have common sense and a good heart ; at least, that is my experience."

Governor Grant turned round again to his newspaper, and the other men went to their cabs.

# THE WATERFALL

## by M. G. DRURY

AT the edge of a wood below the sheep pastures on the hills there was a waterfall. The river, after flowing quietly along a lonely valley, here dropped to a lower level between huge boulders set every way in the river. And in some places the river came down between the boulders with a rush and a roar, but in other places it only trickled, murmuring gently to itself.

Here and there among the boulders lay still pools where many eels lived, staying generally motionless in the water, but sometimes wriggling gently to and fro.

Along the river banks grew stately trees with moss and ferns growing at their feet and singing birds in their branches.

In one place above the waterfall the bank jutted into the river and on this little bit of land which was almost an island grew thick furze bushes and brambles. In the middle of one of the thickest bushes lived a wren and his wife and family of nine. All day the wren and his wife were busy hunting along the ground and in the bushes for insects to feed their hungry children. But occasionally, when he felt specially happy, the wren would hop on to a bramble that hung right over the water and, with his tail cocked right in the air, would sing and sing for pure joy. Often it seemed as if even the waterfall kept silence for an instant that it might hear the song.

In summer time when the river was low it would have been possible to cross it in a zigzag way by jumping from rock to rock, and once long ago a hunter had done this. But usually no human being ever came to that valley, except perhaps once or twice in a lifetime a shepherd from the hill pastures might wander that way.

In the centre of the waterfall was one enormous boulder which stood so high above the water that grass grew on the top of it, and in its side was a cavern whose entrance was hidden by falling water and jutting rock; so that no man had ever been aware that it was there.

Now in this cavern lived a water nymph who was the spirit of the waterfall.

She was young and joyous and beautiful, and she would sing to the waters, and her voice would mingle with them. And sometimes she would lie on the grassy crest of the great rock and sing a sweet duet with the little brown wren on the bramble ; and then the wren would fly on to her hand and look at her with bright, friendly eyes.

At other times the nymph would dance and play on the greensward near the waterfall with the dryads who are the spirits of the trees. Merrily the hours slipped by as they danced light as shadows and flitted among the tree trunks on their slim, bare feet.

One great oak tree of immense age grew near the water at the foot of the waterfall. In it lived a gentle and graceful dryad, and she was the friend of the nymph of the waterfall. Many hours of every day they spent together by the river-side.

One day when the cuckoo was calling merrily and the wild hyacinths were making a misty blue carpet under the trees, the nymph and the dryad were lying together under the oak tree, their talk and laughter making a low accompaniment to the sound of the waterfall. At their feet sat an old rabbit watching them placidly.

Then far away from the sheep pastures they heard music, and gradually it became clearer and clearer, and it was the music of a fiddle. The player played many tunes ; some were jigs that would almost set your feet a-dancing whether you would or no, and some were laments that brought a pang to your heart and made you think of the sadness that is in all loveliness, but the sweetness of the spring was in all the tunes that he played.

The nymph, the dryad, and the rabbit listened enthralled, so that they almost forgot to slip out of sight when the sound of footsteps warned them that the player was drawing near. Soon he appeared among the trees, still playing away to himself and to the woods around him. He came and sat down at the foot of the dryad's oak tree, and the day being now at its height and the sun hot, he soon put the fiddle aside and lay down and fell asleep.

Then the nymph, the dryad, and the rabbit crept nearer and nearer to the fiddler, and peeped at him from behind the oak tree. They saw a youth of twenty or so, slight and small. He wore a rough brown suit, and his hair, which he rumpled in his sleep, was dark red. His face was thin, and even with his eyes closed had an inquiring look about it. It was a fine and sensitive face. Many days of exposure to sun and air had bronzed him, but where the sleeve of his jacket had slipped up the skin showed very white. He smiled as he lay there, and moved restlessly now and then, rumpling his hair still more.

At last when the evening sun was shining sideways on the tree trunks, the fiddler sat up and rubbed his eyes, and then he rubbed them again for he looked upon a sight that few mortal eyes had ever seen before. All around him, standing amongst the trees, were dryads who whispered and laughed together while they watched him.

While he gazed around him in wonder, the nymph of the waterfall came up to him and said, " Mortal, who hast intruded upon us, stay for a while and play to us sweet music, that we may dance to it and be mirthful here together."

And the fiddler looked upon the nymph, who was very fair, and he looked around him at the dryads, and then at the wild hyacinths and the glades of the wood, and at some rabbits who sat at a safe distance, and at the wren on a branch of the oak tree, and at the waterfall. Then he looked again at the nymph, and he smiled and his brown eyes danced, and he said, " Fair lady, I will stay and play to you the sweetest music that I know." All the dryads whispered in excitement, and it was as if a sudden breeze had rustled in the leaves of the trees.

So the fiddler played merry tunes, and for many hours the nymph and the dryads danced tirelessly, swaying to and fro as gracefully as tall flowers when the wind sweeps them. The fiddler watched them, absorbed and quite contented, forgetting time and place and everything but the beauty of the dance.

But at length after the moon had risen and was shining softly through the trees, the fiddler's music ceased and the dancers paused. Then the fiddler rose to his feet and walked slowly up to the nymph with his eyes fixed upon her, and without a word spoken they began to dance together. The nymph was tall and willowy and dark was her hair and her eyes, and it seemed to the fiddler as if he danced with a shadow, and he danced as a man inspired.

Upon the greensward they flitted backwards and forwards and among the trees, and the dryads stayed still to watch them. But at last they fell exhausted on to the mossy roots of the oak tree. There, with the dryads beside them, they stayed laughing and talking for a long time till the fiddler fell into a deep sleep. Then like a dream the nymph and the dryads vanished.

When he awoke in the morning he thought that he had had a vision, and soon he began to feel lonely and very sad. But as he looked up at the branches of the oak tree above him, he saw the dryad looking down. She smiled and pointed to the waterfall, and there on the great boulder he saw the nymph lying on the grass in the sun and singing to the waters.

*The wild things of the wood became his friends.*

So he arose and went down to the river-side, and he leapt and climbed and scrambled till at length he reached the top of the great boulder and sat down beside the nymph. But before she would speak with him she went to her cavern and fetched him milk to drink and bread and wild honey, and sweet herbs to eat, and never did food taste so pleasant to him.

Then he listened to the nymph singing and to the singing of the waters, and from the two he made music which he played on his fiddle. But the music had no words, for with the gift of music he had not been granted also the gift of words.

And after a time the nymph ceased singing and listened to his music, and it pleased her. So she taught him to put word to word, and to choose this word and to reject that. Day by day she taught him to the sound of the waterfall, and it was not long before he became a poet as well as a musician; for he knew already how to look deep into the heart of things, and how to catch the music of the softest sound, and to understand the meaning of the thought that is but half-spoken.

The days sped swiftly by and the fiddler took no count of them, and he forgot the thing that is called time. He wandered about in the wood and the valley, and frolicked with the dryads, and he made sweet songs and sang them as he played on the fiddle. The wild things of the wood became his friends, forgetting that he was a mortal. The wren and the other birds would sing to him and perch on his shoulder, and the rabbits and squirrels and little wild creatures would run near him, heedless of his presence.

So the fiddler, out of his love and understanding of the wild creatures, made songs about them. He made the song of the fledgeling breaking from his egg, and the song of the young rabbits when they play together on a dewy summer morning, and the song of the squirrel who collects his winter store. He made too the song of the misty blue of the wild hyacinths, and the song the leaves sing to the passing wind, and also the song of sweet-smelling things, from the good smell of earth to the sweet mingled smell of primroses and young ferns. But the best of all the songs he made was the song of the waterfall, and the different voices of its waters, and of the nymph who is its spirit, and of her beauty and her grace.

He made a merry tune of dancing for the dryads, and every evening as the sun set the nymph and the dryads danced to the sound of his fiddle. At the end he always danced with the nymph, and it would be long before they were wearied. So the summer days sped on.

The chilly nights of autumn came, and for warmth the fiddler slept in the cavern of the nymph upon a thick soft couch of moss. And he built himself a bridge of stones from boulder to boulder that he might walk dry above the swelling river.

One night a great storm raged in the valley. The wind howled and moaned and swept through the trees making them groan in agony, and sometimes a great branch came crashing to the ground. The swollen river roared angrily as the rain came swirling down.

Though he was used to the sound of the waterfall, the fiddler lay awake for a long while for his thoughts would not let him sleep. Then, suddenly, above the roar of the water, he heard a terrible crashing sound, and there was a pause, and then came a mournful cry.

He sprang to his feet and clambered out of the cavern. In the pale light of a wild dawn he saw that the great oak tree had fallen, and half-lay in the river with the water rushing over its branches. Then suddenly he saw something white in the water and he strained his eyes to see what it might be ; with a feeling of horror it came to him that it was the body of the dryad of the oak tree.

As he began to stumble towards the river bank, the white figure was dislodged from the branches by the furious waters, and was carried, twisting and turning and tossing, swift as an arrow down the river. Then he went back, for he knew that it was vain for him to follow.

Hearing a sound of wailing coming from the top of the boulder, he clambered up and found the water nymph lying on the grass. Her dark hair streamed round her and her face was pale and distraught. She wept and wailed bitterly, and paid no heed to him when he would have comforted her.

Then something within him warned the fiddler that the time had come when he must leave this place. So he fetched his fiddle from the cavern and stumbled to the river bank, drenched to the skin. Wretched and miserable, he wandered through the wood like a blind man, not caring where he went.

So he walked over hills and through valleys and crossed rivers, and plunged into woods, and he heeded not where he was going ; but at last he came into the world of men.

He wandered from town to town, and from village to village, playing on his fiddle and singing his own sweet song, and men and women would pause at their work to listen to him.

As the years grew his fame spread, and the cities opened their gates to him when they heard that he was drawing near. But he cared not for fame and heeded not their praise. He would escape away from the cities to some quiet country place where he would beg for a night's shelter from a humble cottage, too remote to have heard his name. And there he would love to play his sweetest music, and he would sing to these simple people of the wild creatures he loved.

So he grew old, and all the world loved his music and his poetry, and held him in reverence. But all his days he was a wanderer in lonely places, and to his dying day he was for ever haunted by the music of the Waterfall.

# MR. BROCKLEHURST'S VISIT

## *by* CHARLOTTE BRONTË

MY first quarter at Lowood seemed an age, and not the golden age either ; it comprised an irksome struggle with difficulties in habituating myself to new rules and unwonted tasks. The fear of failure in these points harassed me worse than the physical hardships of my lot, though these were no trifles.

During January, February, and part of March, the deep snows, and after their melting, the almost impassable roads, prevented our stirring beyond the garden walls, except to go to church, but within these limits we had to pass an hour every day in the open air. Our clothing was insufficient to protect us from the severe cold ; we had no boots, the snow got into our shoes, and melted there ; our ungloved hands became numbed and covered with chilblains, as were our feet. I remember well the distracting irritation I endured from this cause every evening, when my feet inflamed; and the torture of thrusting the swelled, raw, and stiff toes into my shoes in the morning. Then the scanty supply of food was distressing : with the keen appetites of growing children, we had scarcely sufficient to keep alive a delicate invalid. From this deficiency of nourishment resulted an abuse which pressed hardly on the younger pupils : whenever the famished great girls had an opportunity they would coax or menace the little ones out of their portion. Many a time I have shared between two claimants the precious morsel of brown bread distributed at tea-time, and after relinquishing to a third half the contents of my mug of coffee, I have swallowed the remainder with an accompaniment of secret tears, forced from me by the exigency of hunger.

Sunday were dreary days in that wintry season. We had to walk two miles to Brocklebridge Church, where our patron officiated. We set out cold, we arrived at church colder ; during the morning service we became almost paralysed. It was too far to return to dinner, and an allowance of cold meat and bread, in the same penurious proportion observed in our ordinary meals, was served round between the services.

At the close of the afternoon service we returned by an exposed and hilly road, where the bitter winter wind, blowing over a range of snowy summits to the north, almost flayed the skin from our faces.

I can remember Miss Temple walking lightly and rapidly along our drooping line, her plaid cloak, which the frosty wind fluttered, gathered close about her, and encouraging us, by precept and example, to keep up our spirits, and march forward, as she said, " like stalwart soldiers." The other teachers, poor things, were generally themselves too much dejected to attempt the task of cheering others.

How we longed for the light and heat of a blazing fire when we got back ! But, to the little ones at least, this was denied ; each hearth in the school-room was immediately surrounded by a double row of great girls, and behind them the younger children crouched in groups, wrapping their starved arms in their pinafores.

A little solace came at tea-time, in the shape of a double ration of bread —a whole, instead of a half, slice—with the delicious addition of a thin scrape of butter ; it was the hebdomadal treat to which we all looked forward from Sabbath to Sabbath. I generally contrived to reserve a moiety of this bounteous repast for myself : but the remainder I was invariably obliged to part with.

The Sunday evening was spent in repeating, by heart, the Church Catechism, and the fifth, sixth, and seventh chapters of St. Matthew ; and in listening to a long sermon read by Miss Miller, whose irrepressible yawns attested her weariness. A frequent interlude of these performances was the enactment of the part of Eutychus by some half-dozen of little girls : who, overpowered with sleep, would fall down, if not out of the third loft, yet off the fourth form, and be taken up half-dead. The remedy was, to thrust them forward into the centre of the schoolroom, and oblige them to stand there till the sermon was finished. Sometimes their feet failed them, and they sank together in a heap ; they were then propped up with the monitors' high stools.

I have not yet alluded to the visits of Mr. Brocklehurst ; and indeed that gentleman was from home during the greater part of the first month after my arrival, perhaps prolonging his stay with his friend the archdeacon : his absence was a relief to me. I need not say that I had my own reasons for dreading his coming : but come he did at last.

One afternoon (I had then been three weeks at Lowood), as I was sitting with a slate in my hand, puzzling over a sum in long division, my eyes, raised in abstraction to the window, caught sight of a figure just passing : I recognised almost instinctively that gaunt outline ; and when, two minutes after, all the school, teachers included, rose *en masse*, it was not necessary for me to look up in order to ascertain whose entrance they thus greeted. A long stride measured the schoolroom, and presently beside Miss Temple, who herself had risen, stood the same black column which had frowned on me so ominously from the hearthrug of Gateshead. I now glanced sideways at this piece of architecture. Yes, I was right : it was Mr. Brocklehurst buttoned up in a surtout, and looking longer, narrower, and more rigid than ever.

I had my own reasons for being dismayed at this apparition : too well I remembered the perfidious hints given by Mrs. Reed, about my disposition, etc. ; the promise pledged by Mr. Brocklehurst to apprise Miss Temple and the teachers of my vicious nature. All along I had been dreading the fulfilment of this promise—I had been looking out daily for the " Coming Man," whose information respecting my past life and conversation was to brand me as a bad child for ever : now there he was. He stood at Miss Temple's side ; he was speaking low in her ear ; I did not doubt he was making disclosures of my villainy ; and I watched her eye with painful anxiety, expecting every moment to see its dark orb turn on me a glance of repugnance and contempt. I listened too ; and as I happened to be seated quite at the top of the room, I caught most of what he said ; its import relieved me from immediate apprehension.

" I suppose, Miss Temple, the thread I bought at Lowton will do : it struck me that it would be just of the quality for the calico chemises, and I sorted the needles to match. You may tell Miss Smith that I forgot to make a memorandum of the darning needles, but she shall have some papers sent in next week ; and she is not, on any account, to give out more than one at a time to each pupil—if they have more, they are apt to be careless and lose them. And oh, ma'am ! I wish the woollen stockings were better looked to ! When I was here last, I went into the kitchen-garden and examined the clothes drying on the line ; there was a quantity of black hose in a very bad state of repair ; from the size of the holes in them I was sure they had not been well mended from time to time."

He paused.

" Your directions shall be attended to, sir," said Miss Temple.

" And, ma'am," he continued, " the laundress tells me some of the girls have two clean tuckers in a week : it is too much ; the rules limit them to one."

" I think I can explain that circumstance, sir. Agnes and Catherine Johnstone were invited to tea with some friends at Lowton last Thursday, and I gave them leave to put on clean tuckers for the occasion."

Mr. Brocklehurst nodded.

" Well, for once it may pass ; but please not to let the circumstance occur too often. And there is another thing which surprised me : I find, in settling accounts with the housekeeper, that a lunch, consisting of bread and cheese, has twice been served out to the girls during the past fortnight. How is this ? I look over the regulations, and I find no such meal as lunch mentioned. Who introduced this innovation ? and by what authority ? "

" I must be responsible for the circumstance, sir," replied Miss Temple : " the breakfast was so ill-prepared that the pupils could not possibly eat it ; and I dared not allow them to remain fasting till dinner-time."

" Madam, allow me an instant. You are aware that my plan in bringing up these girls is, not to accustom them to habits of luxury and indulgence, but to render them hardy, patient, self-denying. Should any little accidental disappointment of the appetite occur, such as the spoiling of a meal, the under or the over dressing of a dish, the incident ought not to be neutralised by replacing with something more delicate the comfort lost, thus pampering the body and obviating the aim of this institution ; it ought to be improved to the spiritual edification of the pupils, by encouraging them to evince fortitude under the temporary privation. A brief address on those occasions would not be mistimed, wherein a judicious instructor would take the opportunity of referring to the sufferings of the primitive Christians : to the torments of martyrs : to the exhortations of our Blessed Lord Himself, calling upon His disciples to take up their cross and follow him : to His warnings that man shall not live by bread alone, but by every word that proceedeth out of the mouth of God : to His divine consolations, ' If ye suffer hunger

*"What is that girl with curled hair ? Red hair, ma'am, curled all over ?"*

or thirst for my sake, happy are ye.' Oh, madam, when you put bread and cheese, instead of burnt porridge, into these children's mouths, you may indeed feed their vile bodies, but you little think how you starve their immortal souls ! "

Mr. Brocklehurst again paused—perhaps overcome by his feelings. Miss Temple had looked down when he first began to speak to her ; but she now gazed straight before her, and her face, naturally pale as marble, appeared to be assuming also the coldness and fixity of that material ; especially her mouth, closed as if it would have required a sculptor's chisel to open it, and her brow settled gradually into petrified severity.

Meantime, Mr. Brocklehurst, standing on the hearth with his hands behind his back, majestically surveyed the whole school. Suddenly his eye gave a blink, as if it had met something that either dazzled or shocked its pupil ; turning, he said in more rapid accents than he had hitherto used.

"Miss Temple, Miss Temple, what—*what* is that girl with curled hair? Red hair, ma'am, curled—curled all over?" And extending his cane he pointed to the awful object, his hand shaking as he did so.

"It is Julia Severn," replied Miss Temple very quietly.

"Julia Severn, ma'am! And why has she, or any other, curled hair? Why, in defiance of every precept and principle of this house, does she conform to the world so openly—here in an evangelical, charitable establishment—as to wear her hair one mass of curls?"

"Julia's hair curls naturally," returned Miss Temple still more quietly.

"Naturally! Yes, but we are not to conform to nature. I wish these girls to be the children of Grace: and why that abundance? I have again and again intimated that I desire the hair to be arranged closely, modestly, plainly. Miss Temple, that girl's hair must be cut off entirely; I will send a barber to-morrow: and I see others who have far too much of the excrescence —that tall girl, tell her to turn round. Tell all the first form to rise up and direct their faces to the wall."

Miss Temple passed her handkerchief over her lips, as if to smooth away the involuntary smile that curled them; she gave the order, however, and when the first class could take in what was required of them, they obeyed. Leaning a little back on my bench, I could see the looks and grimaces with which they commented on this manœuvre: it was a pity Mr. Brocklehurst could not see them too; he would perhaps have felt that, whatever he might do with the outside of the cup and platter, the inside was farther beyond his interference than he imagined.

He scrutinised the reverse of these living models some five minutes, then pronounced sentence. These words fell like the knell of doom :—

"All those top-knots must be cut off."

Miss Temple seemed to remonstrate.

"Madam," he pursued, "I have a Master to serve whose kingdom is not of this world: my mission is to mortify in these girls the lusts of the flesh, to teach them to clothe themselves with shamefacedness and sobriety, not with braided hair and costly apparel; and each of the young persons before us has a string of hair twisted in plaits which vanity itself might have woven: these, I repeat, must be cut off; think of the time wasted, of——"

Mr. Brocklehurst was here interrupted: three other visitors, ladies, now entered the room. They ought to have come a little sooner to have heard his lecture on dress, for they were splendidly attired in velvet, silk, and furs. The two younger of the trio (fine girls of sixteen and seventeen) had grey beaver hats, then in fashion, shaded with ostrich plumes, and from under the brim of this graceful head-dress fell a profusion of light tresses, elaborately curled; the elder lady was enveloped in a costly velvet shawl, trimmed with ermine, and she wore a false front of French curls.

These ladies were deferentially received by Miss Temple, as Mrs. and the Misses Brocklehurst, and conducted to seats of honour at the top of the room. It seems they had come in the carriage with their reverend relative, and had been conducting a rummaging scrutiny of the rooms upstairs, while he transacted business with the housekeeper, questioned the laundress, and lectured the superintendent. They now proceeded to address divers remarks and reproofs to Miss Smith, who was charged with the care of the linen and the inspection of the dormitories; but I had no time to listen to what they said, other matters called off and enchained my attention.

Hitherto, while gathering up the discourse of Mr. Brocklehurst and Miss Temple, I had not, at the same time, neglected precautions to secure my personal safety; which I thought would be effected, if I only could elude observation. To this end, I had sat well back on the form, and while seeming to be busy with my sum, had held my slate in such a manner as to conceal my face. I might have escaped notice, had not my treacherous slate somehow happened to slip from my hand, and falling with an obtrusive crash, directly drawn every eye upon me; I knew it was all over now, and, as I stooped to pick up the two fragments of slate, I rallied my forces for the worst. It came.

"A careless girl!" said Mr. Brocklehurst, and immediately after—"it is the new pupil, I perceive." And before I could draw breath, "I must not forget I have a word to say respecting her." Then aloud—how loud it seemed to me! "Let the child who broke her slate come forward!"

Of my own accord, I could not have stirred; I was paralysed: but the two great girls who sat on each side of me set me on my legs and pushed me towards the dread judge, and then Miss Temple gently assisted me to his very feet, and I caught her whispered counsel:—

"Don't be afraid, Jane, I saw it was an accident; you shall not be punished."

The kind whisper went to my heart like a dagger.

"Another minute and she will despise me for a hypocrite," thought I; and an impulse of fury against Reed, Brocklehurst, and Co. bounded in my pulses at the conviction. I was no Helen Burns.

"Fetch that stool," said Mr. Brocklehurst, pointing to a very high one from which a monitor had just risen: it was brought.

"Place the child upon it."

And I was placed there, by whom I don't know. I was in no condition to note particulars. I was only aware that they had hoisted me up to the height of Mr. Brocklehurst's nose, that he was within a yard of me, and that a spread of shot orange and purple silk pelisses, and a cloud of silvery plumage extended and waved below me.

Mr. Brocklehurst hemmed.

"Ladies," said he, turning to his family: "Miss Temple, teachers, and children, you all see this girl?"

Of course they did; for I felt their eyes directed like burning-glasses against my scorched skin.

"You see she is yet young; you observe she possesses the ordinary form of childhood; God has graciously given her the shape that He has given to all of us; no single deformity points her out as a marked character. Who would think that the Evil One had already found a servant and agent in her? Yet such, I grieve to say, is the case."

A pause—in which I began to steady the palsy of my nerves, and to feel that the Rubicon was passed, and that the trial, no longer to be shirked, must be firmly sustained.

"My dear children," pursued the black marble clergyman with pathos, "this is a sad, a melancholy occasion; for it becomes my duty to warn you that this girl, who might be one of God's own lambs, is a little castaway—not a member of the true flock, but evidently an interloper and an alien. You must be on your guard against her ; and you must shun her example—if necessary, avoid her company, exclude her from your sports, and shut her out from your converse. Teachers, you must watch her : keep your eyes on her movements, weigh well her words, scrutinise her actions, punish her body to save her soul—if, indeed, such salvation be possible, for (my tongue falters while I tell it) this girl, this child, the native of a Christian land, worse than many a little heathen who says its prayers to Brahma and kneels before Juggernaut—this girl is—a liar ! "

Now came a pause of ten minutes, during which I—by this time in perfect possession of my wits—observed all the female Brocklehursts produce their pocket-handkerchiefs and apply them to their optics, while the elderly lady swayed herself to and fro, and the two younger ones whispered, " How shocking ! "

Mr. Brocklehurst resumed.

" This I learned from her benefactress—from the pious and charitable lady who adopted her in her orphan state, reared her as her own daughter, and whose kindness, whose generosity the unhappy girl repaid by an ingratitude so bad, so dreadful, that at last her excellent patroness was obliged to separate her from her own young ones, fearful lest her vicious example should contaminate their purity. She has sent her here to be healed, even as the Jews of old sent their diseased to the troubled pool of Bethesda ; and, teachers, superintendent, I beg of you not to allow the waters to stagnate round her."

With this sublime conclusion, Mr. Brocklehurst adjusted the top button of his surtout, muttered something to his family, who rose, bowed to Miss Temple, and then all the great people sailed in state from the room. Turning at the door, my judge said :—

" Let her stand half an hour longer on that stool, and let no one speak to her during the remainder of the day."

There was I, then, mounted aloft : I, who had said I could not bear the shame of standing on my natural feet in the middle of the room, was now exposed to general view on a pedestal of infamy. What my sensations were, no language can describe ; but, just as they all rose, stifling my breath and constricting my throat, a girl came up and passed me : in passing, she lifted her eyes. What a strange light inspired them ! What an extraordinary sensation that ray sent through me ! How the new feeling bore me up ! It was as if a martyr, a hero, had passed a slave or victim, and imparted strength in the transit. I mastered the rising hysteria, lifted up my head, and took a firm stand on the stool. Helen Burns asked some slight question about her work of Miss Smith, was chidden for the triviality of the inquiry, returned to her place, and smiled at me as she again went by. What a smile ! I remember it now, and I know that it was the effluence of fine intellect, of true courage ; it lit up her marked lineaments, her thin face, her sunken grey eye, like a reflection from the aspect of an angel. Yet at that moment Helen Burns wore on her arm " the untidy badge " ; scarcely an hour ago I had heard her condemned by Miss Scatcherd to a dinner of bread and water on the morrow, because she had blotted an exercise in copying it out. Such is the imperfect nature of man ! Such spots are there on the disc of the clearest planet ; and eyes like Miss Scatcherd's can only see these minute defects, and are blind to the full brightness of the orb.

Ere the half-hour ended, five o'clock struck ; school was dismissed, and all were gone into the refectory to tea. I now ventured to descend ; it was deep dusk ; I retired into a corner and sat down on the floor. The spell by which I had been so far supported began to dissolve ; reaction took place, and soon, so overwhelming was the grief that seized me, I sank prostrate with my face to the ground. Now I wept : Helen Burns was not there ; nothing sustained me ; left to myself I abandoned myself, and my tears watered the boards. I had meant to be so good, and to do so much at Lowood : to make so many friends, to earn respect, and win affection. Already I had made visible progress : that very morning I had reached the head of my class ; Miss Miller had praised me warmly ; Miss Temple had smiled approbation ; she had promised to teach me drawing, and to let me learn French, if I continued to make similar improvement two months longer ; and then I was well received by my fellow-pupils ; treated as an equal by those of my own age, and not molested by any ; now, here I lay again crushed and trodden on ; and could I ever rise more ?

"Never," I thought ; and ardently I wished to die. While sobbing out this wish in broken accents, some one approached : I started up—again Helen Burns was near me ; the fading fires just showed her coming up the long, vacant room ; she brought my coffee and bread.

"Come, eat something," she said ; but I put both away from me, feeling as if a drop or a crumb would have choked me in my present condition. Helen regarded me, probably, with surprise : I could not now abate my agitation, though I tried hard ; I continued to weep aloud. She sat down on the ground near me, embraced her knees with her arms, and rested her head upon them ; in that attitude she remained silent as an Indian. I was the first who spoke :—

"Helen, why do you stay with a girl whom everybody believes to be a liar ? "

"Everybody, Jane ? Why, there are only eighty people who have heard you called so, and the world contains hundreds of millions."

"But what have I to do with millions ? The eighty I know despise me."

"Jane, you are mistaken : probably not one in the school either despises or dislikes you ; many, I am sure, pity you much."

"How can they pity me after what Mr. Brocklehurst said ? "

"Mr. Brocklehurst is not a god : nor is he even a great and admired man : he is little liked here ; he never took steps to make himself liked. Had he treated you as an especial favourite, you would have found enemies, declared or covert, all around you ; as it is, the greater number would offer you sympathy if they dared. Teachers and pupils may look coldly on you for a day or two, but friendly feelings are concealed in their hearts ; and if you persevere in doing well, these feelings will ere long appear so much the more evidently for their temporary suppression. Besides Jane——" She paused.

"Well, Helen ? " said I, putting my hand into hers, she chafed my fingers gently to warm them, and went on :—

"If all the world hated you, and believed you wicked, while your own conscience absolved you from guilt, you would not be without friends."

"No; I know I should think well of myself; but that is not enough; if others don't love me, I would rather die than live—I cannot bear to be solitary and hated, Helen. Look here; to gain some real affection from you, or Miss Temple, or any other whom I truly love, I would willingly submit to have the bone of my arm broken, or to let a bull toss me, or to stand behind a kicking horse, and let it dash its hoof at my chest——"

"Hush, Jane! you think too much of the love of human beings; you are too impulsive, too vehement: the sovereign Hand that created your frame, and put life into it, has provided you with other resources than your feeble self, or than creatures feeble as you. Besides this earth, and besides the race of men, there is an invisible world and a kingdom of spirits: that world is round us, for it is everywhere; and those spirits watch us, for they are commissioned to guard us; and if we were dying in pain and shame, if scorn smote us on all sides, and hatred crushed us, angels see our tortures, recognise our innocence (if innocent we be; as I know you are of this charge which Mr. Brocklehurst has weakly and pompously repeated at second-hand from Mrs. Reed; for I read a sincere nature in your ardent eyes and on your clear front), and God waits only the separation of spirit from flesh to crown us with a full reward. Why, then, should we ever sink overwhelmed with distress, when life is so soon over, and death is so certain an entrance to happiness—to glory?"

I was silent: Helen had calmed me; but in the tranquillity she imparted there was an alloy of inexpressible sadness. I felt the impression of woe as she spoke, but I could not tell whence it came; and when, having done speaking, she breathed a little fast, and coughed a short cough, I momentarily forgot my own sorrows to yield to a vague concern for her.

Resting my head on Helen's shoulder, I put my arms round her waist; she drew me to her, and we reposed in silence. We had not sat long thus, when another person came in. Some heavy clouds, swept from the sky by a rising wind, had left the moon bare; and her light, streaming in through a window near, shone full both on us and on the approaching figure, which we at once recognised as Miss Temple.

"I came on purpose to find you, Jane Eyre," said she; "I want you in my room; and as Helen Burns is with you, she may come too."

We went: following the superintendent's guidance, we had to thread some intricate passages, and mount a staircase before we reached her apartment; it contained a good fire, and looked cheerful. Miss Temple told Helen Burns to be seated in a low arm-chair on one side of the hearth, and herself taking another, she called me to her side.

"Is it all over?" she asked, looking down at my face. "Have you cried your grief away?"

"I am afraid I never shall do that."

"Why?"

"Because I have been wrongly accused; and you, ma'am, and everybody else will now think me wicked."

"We shall think you what you prove yourself to be, my child. Continue to act as a good girl, and you will satisfy us."

" Shall I, Miss Temple ? "

" You will," said she, passing her arm round me. " And now tell me who is the lady whom Mr. Brocklehurst called your benefactress ? "

" Mrs. Reed, my uncle's wife. My uncle is dead, and he left me to her care."

" Did she not, then, adopt you of her own accord ? "

" No, ma'am ; she was sorry to have to do it : but my uncle, as I have often heard the servants say, got her to promise before he died, that she would always keep me."

" Well, now, Jane, you know, or at least I will tell you, that when a criminal is accused, he is always allowed to speak in his own defence. You have been charged with falsehood ; defend yourself to me as well as you can. Say whatever your memory suggests as true ; but add nothing and exaggerate nothing."

I resolved in the depth of my heart, that I would be most moderate—most correct ; and, having reflected a few minutes in order to arrange coherently what I had to say, I told her all the story of my sad childhood. Exhausted by emotion, my language was more subdued than it generally was when it developed that sad theme ; and mindful of Helen's warnings against the indulgence of resentment, I infused into the narrative far less of gall and wormwood than ordinary. Thus restrained and simplified, it sounded more credible : I felt as I went on that Miss Temple fully believed me.

In the course of the tale I had mentioned Mr. Lloyd as having come to see me after the fit : for I never forgot the, to me, frightful episode of the red-room ; in detailing which, my excitement was sure, in some degree, to break bounds ; for nothing could soften in my recollection the spasm of agony which clutched my heart when Mrs. Reed spurned my wild supplication for pardon, and locked me a second time in the dark and haunted chamber.

I had finished : Miss Temple regarded me a few minutes in silence ; she then said :—

" I know something of Mr. Lloyd ; I shall write to him ; if his reply agrees with your statement, you shall be publicly cleared from every imputation : to me, Jane, you are clear now."

She kissed me, and still keeping me at her side (where I was well contented to stand, for I derived a child's pleasure from the contemplation of her face, her dress, her one or two ornaments, her white forehead, her clustered and shining curls, and beaming dark eyes), she proceeded to address Helen Burns.

" How are you to-night, Helen ? Have you coughed much to-day ? "

" Not quite so much, I think, ma'am."

" And the pain in your chest ? "

" It is a little better."

Miss Temple got up, took her hand and examined her pulse ; then she returned to her own seat ; as she resumed it, I heard her sigh low. She was pensive a few minutes, then rousing herself, she said cheerfully :—

" But you two are my visitors to-night ; I must treat you as such." She rang her bell.

" Barbara," she said to the servant who answered it, " I have not yet had tea ; bring the tray, and place cups for these two young ladies."

*Presently Miss Temple disclosed to our eyes a good-sized seed-cake.*

And a tray was soon brought. How pretty, to my eyes, did the china cups and bright teapot look, placed on the little round table near the fire ! How fragrant was the steam of the beverage, and the scent of the toast ! of which, however, I, to my dismay (for I was beginning to be hungry), discerned only a very small portion : Miss Temple discerned it too.

"Barbara," said she, "can you not bring a little more bread and butter ? There is not enough for three."

Barbara went out. She returned soon.

"Madam, Mrs. Harden says she has sent up the usual quantity."

Mrs. Harden, be it observed, was the housekeeper, a woman after Mr. Brocklehurst's own heart, made up of equal parts of whalebone and iron.

"Oh, very well !" returned Miss Temple ; "we must make it do, Barbara, I suppose." And as the girl withdrew, she added, smiling, "Fortunately, I have it in my power to supply deficiences for this once."

Having invited Helen and me to approach the table, and placed before each of us a cup of tea with one delicious but thin morsel of toast, she got up, unlocked a drawer, and taking from it a parcel wrapped in paper, disclosed presently to our eyes a good-sized seed-cake.

"I meant to give each of you some of this to take with you," said she ; "but as there is so little toast, you must have it now." And she proceeded to cut slices with a generous hand.

We feasted that evening as on nectar and ambrosia ; and not the least delight of the entertainment was the smile of gratification with which our hostess regarded us, as we satisfied our famished appetites on the delicate fare she liberally supplied. Tea over and the tray removed, she again summoned us to the fire ; we sat one on each side of her, and now a conversation followed between her and Helen, which it was indeed a privilege to be admitted to hear.

Miss Temple had always something of serenity in her air, of state in her mein, of refined propriety in her language, which precluded deviation into the ardent, the excited, the eager : something which chastened the pleasure of those who looked on her, and listened to her, by a controlling sense of awe ; and such was my feeling now : but as to Helen Burns, I was struck with wonder.

The refreshing meal, the brilliant fire, the presence and kindness of her beloved instructress, or, perhaps, more than all these, something in her own unique mind, had roused her powers within her. They woke, they kindled : first, they glowed in the bright tint of her cheek, which till this hour I had never seen but pale and bloodless ; then they shone in the liquid lustre of her eyes, which had suddenly acquired a beauty more singular than that of Miss Temple's—a beauty neither of fine colour nor long eyelash, nor pencilled brow, but of meaning, of movement, of radiance. Then her soul sat on her lips, and language flowed, from what source I cannot tell ; has a girl of fourteen a heart large enough, vigorous enough to hold the swelling spring of pure, full, fervid eloquence ? Such was the characteristic of Helen's discourse on that, to me, memorable evening ; her spirit seemed hastening to live within a very brief span as much as many live during a protracted existence.

They conversed of things I had never heard of ; of nations and times past ; of countries far away ; of secrets of nature discovered or guessed at : they spoke of books : how many they had read ! What stores of knowledge they possessed ! Then they seemed so familiar with French names and French authors ; but my amazement reached its climax when Miss Temple asked Helen if she sometimes snatched a moment to recall the Latin her father had taught her, and, taking a book from a shelf, bade her read and construe a page of Virgil ; and Helen obeyed, my organ of veneration expanding at every sounding line. She had scarcely finished ere the bell announced bedtime ; no delay could be admitted ; Miss Temple embraced us both, saying, as she drew us to her heart :—

" God bless you, my children ! "

Helen she held a little longer than me ; she let her go more reluctantly. It was Helen her eye followed to the door ; it was for her she a second time breathed a sad sigh ; for her she wiped a tear from her cheek.

On reaching the bedroom we heard the voice of Miss Scatcherd : she was examining drawers, she had just pulled out Helen Burns's, and when we entered Helen was greeted with a sharp reprimand, and told that tomorrow she should have half a dozen of untidily folded articles pinned to her shoulder.

" My things were indeed a shameful disorder," murmured Helen to me, in a low voice. " I intended to have arranged them, but I forgot."

Next morning Miss Scatcherd wrote in conspicuous characters on a piece of pasteboard the word " Slattern," and bound it like a phylactery round Helen's large, mild, intelligent, and benign-looking forehead. She wore it till evening, patient, unresentful, regarding it as a deserved punishment. The moment Miss Scatcherd withdrew, after afternoon school, I ran to Helen, tore it off, and thrust it into the fire. The fury of which she was incapable had been burning in my soul all day, and tears, hot and large, had continually been scalding my cheek ; for the spectacle of her sad resignation gave me an intolerable pain at the heart.

About a week subsequently to the incidents above narrated, Miss Temple, who had written to Mr. Lloyd, received his answer : it appeared that what he said went to corroborate my account. Miss Temple, having assembled the whole school, announced that inquiry had been made into the charges alleged against Jane Eyre, and that she was most happy to be able to pronounce her completely cleared from every imputation. The teachers then shook hands with me and kissed me, and a murmur of pleasure ran through the ranks of my companions.

Thus relieved of a grievous load, I from that hour set to work afresh, resolved to pioneer my way through every difficulty. I toiled hard, and my success was proportionate to my efforts ; my memory, not naturally tenacious, improved with practice ; exercise sharpened my wits. In a few weeks I was promoted to a higher class ; in less than two months I was allowed to commence French and drawing. I learned the first two tenses of the verb *Etre*, and sketched my first cottage (whose walls, by the way, outrivalled in slope those of the leaning tower of Pisa) on the same day. That night, on going to bed, I forgot to prepare in imagination the Barmecide supper, of hot roast potatoes, or white bread and new milk, with which I was wont to amuse my inward cravings. I feasted instead on the spectacle of ideal drawings, which I saw in the dark—all the work of my own hands ; freely pencilled houses and trees, picturesque rocks and ruins, Cuyp-like groups of cattle, sweet paintings of butterflies hovering over unblown roses, of birds picking at ripe cherries, of wrens' nests enclosing pearl-like eggs, wreathed about with young ivy sprays. I examined, too, in thought, the possibility of my ever being able to translate currently a certain little French story-book which Madame Pierrot had that day shown me ; nor was that problem solved to my satisfaction ere I fell sweetly asleep.

Well has Solomon said, " Better is a dinner of herbs where love is, than a stalled ox and hatred therewith."

I would not now have exchanged Lowood with all its privations for Gateshead and its daily luxuries.

# THE MISSES BROWN

## *by* KATHERINE L. OLDMEADOW

VERYBODY knows that it is a nuisance to have a neighbour with the same name as one's own ; a nuisance which causes all sorts of inconveniences through letters, parcels and callers going to the wrong houses ; but all one can do is to go on being polite by returning the things that belong to our neighbour and assuring them that it is really quite *too* annoying of us to be born with the same name as themselves.

At least, this is what Mrs. Brown always did ; but *Miss* Brown took quite a different view of the situation, and nobody could say that *she* was polite when mistakes occurred and her door bell was rung by tiresome people wanting the other Browns.

Mrs. Brown was a charming widow with three children, and they lived at Number 36 River Street, and were newcomers to the town.

Miss Brown lived at Number 26—so much more tiresome that both numbers should contain a 6—and she was a cantankerous spinster.

She kept one maid named Alice, as old as herself, whose chief joy in life was to keep the doorstep as white as driven snow and the door bell as brightly gold as the bell on the door of Paradise. The very sight of an errand boy with dirty boots upset her for the day; and she was a household treasure that needed so much consideration that sometimes Miss Brown wondered if perhaps she wouldn't be happier without Alice, even if it meant having a spotty doorstep, and a bell with metal polish in its cracks like the one belonging to " those dreadful Browns " at 36.

When six letters, a parcel of groceries, a leg of mutton and a telegram (the boy had muddy boots and rang so loudly he gave Miss Brown palpitation)

389

had all been delivered at 26, though ordered by the other Browns, Alice gave notice and Miss Brown in a rage sat down and wrote Mrs. Brown a scathing letter of protest.

" Did you ever hear anything so tiresome ? " Mrs. Brown was really upset, for nobody likes to be a nuisance, and Miss Brown had already written to complain of their dog, Pepper, barking, and about Romeo, the cat, though all poor Romeo had done was to pay a friendly call at 26, leaving four muddy footprints on the sacred doorstep instead of a visiting card. These complaints had caused the young Browns to call their neighbour, " That horrid old animal hater at 26."

" Old witch ! She ought to be jolly glad to have some rings on the bell. I bet nobody ever calls on her," was all the comfort Mrs. Brown received from Dick.

" Nonsense ; nobody wants to be bothered with other people's parcels, and yet what *can* I do ? "

Bobby's suggestion that they should change their name to " Jones," and live in peace, and Elizabeth's brilliant idea of calling the house " The Brownies," instead of number 36, was greeted with, " Don't be silly, children, you don't help me at all." And Mrs. Brown once again sat down and wrote a most humble apology to her neighbour, who replied with four circulars, a post card, and a curt message to the effect that if anything else came to her house wrongly addressed she would keep them, as her maid was too busy to run after other people's business, and if Mrs. Brown received anything belonging to number 26, she was at liberty to do the same.

" Pretty safe to say we can keep her letters and parcels, considering she never has any ! "

With such indignant comments the young Browns greeted this un-neighbourly decree, which was really the result of another hysterical outburst from the tyrannical Alice.

As luck would have it, the very next day Elizabeth's godmother sent her godchild a birthday cake decorated with lucky sugar horseshoes, and addressed it to *Miss E. Brown, River Street*, and though the other Elizabeth Brown at 26 had not got a godmother and had left off acknowledging she ever had a birthday, she and Alice not only kept it, but ate it, both possessing what is most unpleasantly known as " a sweet tooth."

When Elizabeth's godmother wrote and asked why her godchild had not acknowledged her gift, there was such an indignant uproar at 36 that Mrs. Brown bravely wrote a charming little note to their neighbour, inquiring if a parcel intended for her daughter had been left at 26.

Miss Brown replied that she regretted the mistake, " but unfortunately was unable to rectify it."

" Which jolly well means she's wolfed it ! " cried Dick, and Elizabeth felt inclined to shed tears because the six school friends who had come to her birthday party had been feasted on a very ordinary cake bought at the baker's at the last moment.

The plums in the birthday cake did not choke the old lady as Bobby so wickedly hoped ; but neither did the sugar horseshoes bring her luck. In fact, one of those extraordinary coincidences occurred which make people say that truth is stranger than fiction ; for Miss Elizabeth Brown at Number

26, and Miss Elizabeth Brown at Number 36, both entered for a cross-word competition and the elder lady, for the first time in her whole life, actually won a prize of ten shillings, which by mistake was delivered to Miss Elizabeth Brown, the younger !

The excitement at Number 36 was intense. Not only because ten-shilling notes were extremely scarce, but because it was felt to be an honour to have a prize-winner in the family. Elizabeth—usually a little snubbed by her brothers—became a respected sister, and the respect increased when she announced that she was going to spend her prize money in a display of fireworks that very night, which happened to be the 5th of November.

*Elizabeth stood absolutely paralysed with horror. Then she gasped out,*
*" But I'm Elizabeth Brown, too."*

It was the first time in the memory of the elder Miss Brown that vulgar explosions had ever been heard in the exclusive River Street, and egged on by Alice, who had found an expiring rocket on the sacred doorstep, she wrote another note to Mrs. Brown in which she called her young namesakes " public nuisances."

This caused hilarity amongst the young people at 36, and acute distress to their peace-loving mother.

But a shock far greater than a fireworks explosion came to poor Miss Brown a few days later, when she read her name among the cross-word prize winners and guessed that the only prize she had ever won had been undoubtedly appropriated by those " scheming Browns."

She put on her toque with trembling hands and hurried to 36, to accuse her neighbours of fraudulent behaviour.

It was Saturday morning and Mrs. Brown was out and the little maid so busy that Elizabeth opened the door. It was a shock to see Miss Brown, but she received her so charmingly that the angry old lady found it hard to explain her errand.

"Please come into the dining-room—it's rather untidy, but it's nice and warm."

Elizabeth led the guest into a room in such comfortable disorder that she gasped, for in her own house Alice never allowed a thing out of place. In this room a cat and a dog sprawled before a roaring fire, snoring loudly, and a bowl of water with DOG written on it under the table.

"Is your Mamma in?" Miss Brown tried to speak haughtily.

"I'm so sorry, mother's gone out shopping. Can I give her any message?"

"Certainly. Perhaps she can tell me why a money order sent to me by the *Day Star* as a prize for giving a correct solution of a cross-word puzzle has been retained here though addressed to Miss Elizabeth Brown."

Elizabeth stood absolutely paralysed with horror. Then she gasped out, "But *I'm* Elizabeth Brown too—and I tried for the *Day Star* competition."

"Indeed! And may I ask if you have seen the result in to-day's paper?"

Blushing, Elizabeth acknowledged she had not, and fetching the paper from the hall and glancing over the correct solution, she was forced to admit that she was guilty of getting money under false pretences.

"It's terrible—oh, Miss Brown, I am so dreadfully sorry. I'll give you back the prize money at once if you'll please wait."

Elizabeth flew upstairs into the playroom and announced the awful news to the boys.

"Gosh! Do you mean to say she's downstairs waiting for the ten bob?"

Dick didn't quite know which was the greater blow; the spent money, or the news that "the old witch" at Number 26 had turned out to be cleverer than Elizabeth.

"Yes, and mother's out and I've only got five shillings in my savings box! You must turn out yours instantly, or I shall faint with shame!"

The young Browns turned out their pockets and their money-boxes, borrowed from the obliging little maid, Susan, and at last Elizabeth returned to the visitor and gave her the money with more apologies.

But if she had wished—and she didn't—to pay out Miss Brown for all those unneighbourly complaints she had now done so; for never had that lady felt so utterly small and mean as when she received this money, and yet she was determined to have her rights.

A worse moment was to come; for Bobby, who had followed Elizabeth, fixed his eyes on the visitor, and said, "I do hope, Miss Brown, that you enjoyed Elizabeth's birthday cake—frightfully sickening for us all having the same name—isn't it?"

He received a deadly look from both Elizabeths, and the elder departed with dignity, but no sooner was she outside than she realised the awful fact that her recovered prize was all in small, silver coins. She guessed it had been hastily collected, and determined to have no debt on her own conscience, she marched into a confectioner's and ordered an iced cake to be sent to Miss Elizabeth Brown with her card.

After the disaster of the morning this came as a pleasant surprise, and when Elizabeth discovered it was decorated with a sugar dove (unnoticed by the unpoetical Miss Brown) she said it was a sign that their neighbour wanted to make peace, and without a word to any one she put on her best hat and actually called on Miss Brown to thank her.

She found the old lady busy with the latest cross-word, and having made herself popular by helping to solve a knotty problem, Elizabeth became bolder and asked Miss Brown to come back to tea, and share the cake.

After that peace was permanently established and the whole affair turned out to be a blessing in disguise, because Miss Brown, urged on by her new friends, actually stood up to Alice and told her plainly that she didn't care a button about owning the whitest doorstep and the shiniest door bell in the street.

Being neighbourly with young people quite seemed to cure her touchiness too, for when she said one day how much pleasanter her life had been since getting to know her neighbours, and Bobby said, " Well, you can't swallow a whole cakeful of lucky horseshoes without getting some luck ! " she actually laughed at the joke.

# THE WAYSIDE INN

*From the German*

I HALTED at a pleasant inn,
  As I my way was wending ;
A golden apple was the sign
  From knotty bough depending.

Mine host—it was an apple-tree—
  He smilingly received me,
And spread his choicest, sweetest fruit,
  To strengthen and relieve me.

Full many a little feathered guest
  Came through his branches springing ;
They hopped and flew from spray to spray,
  Their notes of gladness singing.

Beneath his shade I laid me down,
  And slumber sweet possessed me ;
The soft wind blowing through the leaves
  With whispers low caressed me.

And when I rose, and would have paid
  My host, so open-hearted,
He only shook his lofty head ;
  I blessed him and departed.

# A MERRY CHRISTMAS

## *by* LOUISA M. ALCOTT

JO was the first to wake in the grey dawn of Christmas morning. No stockings hung at the fireplace, and for a moment she felt as much disappointed as she did long ago, when her little sock fell down because it was so crammed with goodies. Then she remembered her mother's promise, and slipping her hand under her pillow, drew out a little crimson-covered book. She knew it very well, for it was that beautiful old story of the best life ever lived, and Jo felt that it was a true guide-book for any pilgrim going the long journey. She woke Meg with a " Merry Christmas," and bade her see what was under her pillow. A green-covered book appeared with the same picture inside, and a few words written by their mother, which made their one present very precious in their eyes. Presently Beth and Amy woke, to rummage and find their little books also—one dove-coloured, the other blue ; and all sat looking at and talking about them, while the east grew rosy with the coming day.

In spite of her small vanities, Margaret had a sweet and pious nature, which unconsciously influenced her sisters, especially Jo, who loved her very tenderly, and obeyed her because her advice was so gently given.

" Girls," said Meg seriously, looking from the tumbled head beside her to the two little night-capped ones in the room beyond, " mother wants us to read and love and mind these books, and we must begin at once. We used to be faithful about it ; but since father went away, and all this war trouble unsettled us, we have neglected many things. You can do as you please ; but *I* shall keep my book on the table here, and read a little every morning as soon as I wake, for I know it will do me good, and help me through the day."

Then she opened her new book and began to read. Jo put her arm round her, and leaning cheek to cheek, read also, with the quiet expression so seldom seen on her restless face.

" How good Meg is ! Come, Amy, let's do as they do. I'll help you with the hard words, and they'll explain things if we don't understand," whispered Beth, very much impressed by the pretty books and her sisters' example.

" I'm glad mine is blue," said Amy ; and then the rooms were very still while the pages were softly turned, and the winter sunshine crept in to touch the bright heads and serious faces with a Christmas greeting.

" Where is mother ? " asked Meg, as she and Jo ran down to thank her for their gifts, half an hour later.

" Goodness only knows. Some poor creeter come a-beggin', and your ma went straight off to see what was needed. There never *was* such a woman for givin' away vittles and drink, clothes and firin'," replied Hannah, who had lived with the family since Meg was born, and was considered by them all more as a friend than a servant.

" She'll be back soon, I guess ; so do your cakes, and have everything ready," said Meg, looking over the presents, which were collected in a basket and kept under the sofa, ready to be produced at the proper time. " Why, where is Amy's bottle of Cologne ? " she added, as the little flask did not appear.

" She took it out a minute ago, and went off with it to put a ribbon on it, or some such notion," replied Jo, dancing about the room to take the stiffness off the new army-slippers.

" How nice my handkerchiefs look, don't they ? Hannah washed and ironed them for me, and I marked them all myself," said Beth, looking proudly at the somewhat uneven letters which had cost her such labour.

" Bless the child, she's gone and put ' Mother ' on them, instead of ' M. March ' ; how funny ! " cried Jo, taking up one.

" Isn't it right ? I thought it was better to do so, because Meg's initials are ' M.M.,' and I don't want any one to use these but Marmee," said Beth, looking troubled.

" It's all right, dear, and a very pretty idea ; quite sensible, too, for no one can ever mistake now. It will please her very much, I know," said Meg, with a frown for Jo, and a smile for Beth.

" There's mother, hide the basket, quick," cried Jo, as a door slammed, and steps sounded in the hall.

Amy came in hastily, and looked rather abashed when she saw her sisters waiting for her.

" Where have you been, and what are you hiding behind you ? " asked Meg, surprised to see, by her hood and cloak, that lazy Amy had been out so early.

" Don't laugh at me, Jo ; I didn't mean any one should know till the time came. I only meant to change the little bottle for a big one, and I gave *all* my money to get it, and I'm not going to be selfish any more."

As she spoke, Amy showed the handsome flask which replaced the cheap one ; and looked so earnest in her little effort to forget herself that Meg hugged her on the spot, and Jo pronounced her " a trump," while Beth ran to the window and picked her finest rose to ornament the stately bottle.

" You see, I felt ashamed of my present after reading and talking about being good this morning, so I ran round the corner and changed it the minute I was up ; and I am *so* glad, for mine is the handsomest now."

Another bang of the street door sent the basket under the sofa, and the girls to the table, eager for breakfast.

" Merry Christmas, Marmee ! Lots of them ! Thank you for our books ; we read some, and mean to every day," they cried in chorus.

" Merry Christmas, little daughters ! I'm glad you began at once, and hope you will keep on. But I want to say one word before we sit down. Not far away from here lies a poor woman with a little new-born baby. Six children are huddled into one bed to keep from freezing, for they had no fire.

*Amy came in hastily, looking rather abashed.*

There is nothing to eat over there ; and the oldest boy came to tell me they were suffering hunger and cold. My girls, will you give them your breakfast as a Christmas present ? "

They were all unusually hungry, having waited nearly an hour, and for a minute no one spoke, only a minute, for Jo exclaimed impetuously :—

" I'm so glad you came before we began ! "

" May I go and help carry the things to the poor little children ? " asked Beth eagerly.

" *I* shall take the cream and the muffins," added Amy, heroically giving up the articles she most liked.

Meg was already covering the buckwheats, and piling the bread into one big plate.

" I thought you'd do it," said Mrs. March, smiling, as if satisfied. " You shall all go and help me, and when we come back we will have bread and milk for breakfast, and make it up at dinner-time."

They were soon ready, and the procession set out. Fortunately it was early, and they went through back streets : so few people saw them, and no one laughed at the funny party.

A poor, bare, miserable room it was, with broken windows, no fire, ragged bed-clothes, a sick mother, wailing baby, and a group of pale, hungry children cuddled under one old quilt, trying to keep warm. How the big eyes stared, and the blue lips smiled, as the girls went in ! "

" Ach, mein Gott ! it is good angels come to us ! " cried the poor woman, crying for joy.

" Funny angels in hoods and mittens," said Jo, and set them laughing.

In a few minutes it really did seem as if kind spirits had been at work there. Hannah, who had carried wood, made a fire, and stopped up the broken panes with old hats and her own shawl. Mrs. March gave the mother tea and gruel, and comforted her with promises of help, while she dressed the little baby as tenderly as if it had been her own. The girls, meantime, spread the table, set the children round the fire, and fed them like so many hungry birds ; laughing, talking, and trying to understand the funny broken English.

" Das ist gute ! " " Der angel-kinder ! " cried the poor things, as they ate, and warmed their purple hands at the comfortable blaze. The girls had never been called angel-children before, and thought it very agreeable, especially Jo, who had been considered " a Sancho " ever since she was born. That was a very happy breakfast, though they didn't get any of it ; and when they went away, leaving comfort behind, I think there were not in all the city four merrier people than the hungry little girls who gave away their breakfast and contented themselves with bread and milk on Christmas morning.

" That's loving our neighbour better than ourselves, and I like it," said Meg, as they set out their presents, while their mother was upstairs collecting clothes for the poor Hummels.

Not a very splendid show, but there was a great deal of love done up in the few little bundles ; and the tall vase of red roses, white chrysanthemums, and trailing vines, which stood in the middle, gave quite an elegant air to the table.

" She's coming ! Strike up, Beth ! Open the door, Amy. Three cheers for Marmee ! " cried Jo, prancing about, while Meg went to conduct mother to the seat of honour.

Beth played her gayest march, Amy threw open the door, and Meg enacted escort with great dignity. Mrs. March was both surprised and touched ; and smiled with her eyes full as she examined her presents, and read the little notes which accompanied them. The slippers went on at once, a new handkerchief was slipped into her pocket, well scented with Amy's Cologne, the rose was fastened in her bosom, and the nice gloves were pronounced " a perfect fit."

There was a good deal of laughing, and kissing, and explaining, in the simple, loving fashion which makes these home-festivals so pleasant at the time, so sweet to remember long afterwards, and then all fell to work.

The morning charities and ceremonies took so much time that the rest of the day was devoted to preparations for the evening festivities. Being still too young to go often to the theatre, and not rich enough to afford any great outlay for private performances, the girls put their wits to work, and, necessity being the mother of invention, made whatever they needed. Very clever were some of their productions : pasteboard guitars, antique lamps made of old-fashioned butter-boats covered with silver paper, gorgeous robes of old cotton, glittering with tin spangles from a pickle factory, and armour covered with the same useful diamond-shaped bits, left in sheets when the lids of tin preserve-pots were cut out. The furniture was used to being turned topsy-turvy, and the big chamber was the scene of many innocent revels.

No gentlemen were admitted ; so Jo played male parts to her heart's content, and took immense satisfaction in a pair of russet-leather boots given her by a friend, who knew a lady who knew an actor. These boots, an old foil and a slashed doublet once used by an artist for some picture, were Jo's chief treasures, and appeared on all occasions.

The smallness of the company made it necessary for the two principal actors to take several parts apiece ; and they certainly deserved some credit for the hard work they did in learning three or four different parts, whisking in and out of various costumes, and managing the stage, besides. It was excellent drill for their memories, a harmless amusement, and employed many hours which otherwise would have been idle, lonely, or spent in less profitable society.

On Christmas night, a dozen girls piled on to the bed, which was the dress circle, and sat before the blue and yellow chintz curtains, in a most flattering state of expectancy. There was a good deal of rustling and whispering behind the curtain, a trifle of lamp-smoke, and an occasional giggle from Amy, who was apt to get hysterical in the excitement of the moment. Presently a bell sounded, the curtains flew apart, and the operatic tragedy began.

"A gloomy wood," according to the one play-bill, was represented by a few shrubs in pots, a green baize on the floor, and a cave in the distance. This cave was made with a clothes-horse for a roof, bureaus for walls ; and in it was a small furnace in full blast, with a black pot on it, and an old witch bending over it. The stage was dark, and the glow of the furnace had a fine effect, especially as real steam issued from the kettle when the witch took off the cover. A moment was allowed for the first thrill to subside ; then Hugo, the villain, stalked in with a clanking sword at his side, a slouched hat, black beard, mysterious cloak, and the boots. After pacing to and fro in much agitation, he struck his forehead, and burst out in a wild strain, singing of his hatred to Roderigo, his love for Zara, and his pleasing resolution to kill the one and win the other. The gruff tones of Hugo's voice, with an occasional shout when his feelings overcame him, were very impressive, and the audience applauded the moment he paused for breath. Bowing with the air of one accustomed to public praise, he stole to the cavern, and ordered Hagar to come forth with a commanding, "What ho ! minion ! I need thee ! "

Out came Meg, with grey horsehair hanging about her face, a red and black robe, a staff, and cabalistic signs upon her cloak. Hugo demanded a potion to make Zara adore him and one to destroy Roderigo. Hagar, in a fine dramatic melody, promised both, and proceeded to call up the spirit who would bring the love philter :—

" Hither, hither, from thy home,
   Airy sprite, I bid thee come !
Born of roses, fed on dew,
Charms and potions canst thou brew !
Bring me here, with elfin speed,
The fragrant philter which I need ;
Make it sweet, and swift and strong ;
Spirit, answer now my song ! "

A soft strain of music sounded, and then at the back of the cave appeared a little figure in cloudy white, with glittering wings, golden hair, and a garland of roses on its head. Waving a wand, it sang :—

" Hither I come,
   From my airy home,
Afar in the silver moon ;
   Take the magic spell,
   Oh, use it well !
Or its power will vanish soon——"

and dropping a small gilded bottle at the witch's feet, the spirit vanished. Another chant from Hagar produced another apparition—not a lovely one, for, with a bang, an ugly black imp appeared, and having croaked a reply, tossed a dark bottle at Hugo, and disappeared with a mocking laugh. Having warbled his thanks, and put the potions in his boots, Hugo departed ; and Hagar informed the audience that, as he had killed a few of her friends in times past, she has cursed him, and intends to thwart his plans, and be revenged on him. Then the curtain fell, and the audience reposed and ate candy while discussing the merits of the play.

A good deal of hammering went on before the curtain rose again ; but when it became evident what a masterpiece of stage carpentering had been got up, no one murmured at the delay. It was truly superb ! A tower rose to the ceiling ; half-way up appeared a window with a lamp burning at it, and behind the white curtain appeared Zara in a lovely blue and silver dress, waiting for Roderigo. He came, in gorgeous array, with plumed cap, red cloak, chestnut lovelocks, a guitar, and the boots, of course. Kneeling at the foot of the tower, he sang a serenade in melting tones. Zara replied, and after a musical dialogue, consented to fly. Then came the grand effect of the play. Roderigo produced a rope-ladder with five steps to it, threw up one end, and invited Zara to descend. Timidly she crept from her lattice, put her hand on Roderigo's shoulder, and was about to leap gracefully down, when, " alas ! alas for Zara ! " she forgot her train—it caught in the window ; the tower tottered, leaned forward, fell with a crash, and buried the unhappy lovers in the ruins !

A universal shriek arose as the russet boots waved wildly from the wreck, and a golden head emerged exclaiming, " I told you so ! I told you so ! " With wonderful presence of mind Don Pedro, the cruel sire, rushed in, dragged out his daughter with a hasty aside :—

" Don't laugh ; act as if it was all right ! " and ordering Roderigo up, banished him from the kingdom with wrath and scorn. Though decidedly shaken by the fall of the tower upon him, Roderigo defied the old gentleman, and refused to stir. This dauntless example fired Zara; she also defied her sire, and he ordered them both to the deepest dungeons of the castle. A stout little retainer came in with chains, and led them away, looking very much frightened, and evidently forgetting the speech he ought to have made.

Act Third was the castle hall; and here Hagar appeared, having come to free the lovers and finish Hugo. She hears him coming, and hides; sees him put the potions into two cups of wine, and bid the timid little servant " Bear them to the captives in their cells, and tell them I shall come anon." The servant takes Hugo aside to tell him something, and Hagar changes the cups for two others which are harmless. Ferdinando, the " minion," carries them away, and Hagar puts back the cup which holds the poison meant for Roderigo. Hugo, getting thirsty after a long warble, drinks it, loses his wits, and after a good deal of clutching and stamping falls flat and dies; while Hagar informs him what she has done, in a song of exquisite power and melody.

This was a truly thrilling scene; though some persons might have thought that the sudden tumbling down of a quantity of long hair rather marred the effect of the villain's death. He was called before the curtain, and with great propriety appeared leading Hagar, whose singing was considered more wonderful than all the rest of the performance put together.

Act Fourth displayed the despairing Roderigo on the point of stabbing himself, because he had been told that Zara has deserted him. Just as the dagger is at his heart, a lovely song is sung under his window, informing

*This was a truly thrilling scene.*

**HOP O' MY THUMB**

So they walked on and on, hoping to find some path they
knew, but all in vain. (Page 421)

**THE BELLS OF OLD LONDON**
Oranges and lemons,
Say the bells of St Clement's. (Page 426)

him that Zara is true, but in danger, and he can save her if he will. A key is thrown in, which unlocks the door, and in a spasm of rapture he tears off his chains, and rushes away to find and rescue his ladylove.

Act Fifth opened with a stormy scene between Zara and Don Pedro. He wishes her to go into a convent, but she won't hear of it; and, after a touching appeal is about to faint, when Roderigo dashes in, and demands her hand. Don Pedro refuses, because he is not rich. They shout and gesticulate tremendously, but cannot agree, and Roderigo is about to bear away the exhausted Zara, when the timid servant enters with a letter and a bag from Hagar, who has mysteriously disappeared. The letter informs the party that she bequeaths untold wealth to the young pair, and an awful doom to Don Pedro if he doesn't make them happy. The bag is opened, and several quarts of tin money shower down upon the stage, till it is quite glorified with the glitter. This entirely softens the " stern sire "; he consents without a murmur, all join in a joyful chorus, and the curtain falls upon the lovers kneeling to receive Don Pedro's blessing, in attitudes of the most romantic grace.

Tumultuous applause followed, but received an unexpected check; for the cot-bed on which the " dress circle " was built suddenly shut up, and extinguished the enthusiastic audience. Roderigo and Don Pedro flew to the rescue, and all were taken out unhurt, though many were speechless with laughter. The excitement had hardly subsided when Hannah appeared, with " Mrs. March's compliments, and would the ladies walk down to supper."

This was a surprise, even to the actors; and when they saw the table they looked at one another in rapturous amazement. It was like " Marmee " to get up a little treat for them, but anything so fine as this was unheard of since the departed days of plenty. There was ice-cream, actually two dishes of it—pink and white—and cake, and fruit, and distracting French bonbons, and in the middle of the table four great bouquets of hot-house flowers !

It quite took their breath away; and they stared first at the table and then at their mother, who looked as if she enjoyed it immensely.

" Is it fairies ? " asked Amy.

" It's Santa Claus," said Beth.

" Mother did it; " and Meg smiled her sweetest, in spite of her grey beard and white eyebrows.

" Aunt March had a good fit, and sent the supper," cried Jo, with a sudden inspiration.

" All wrong; old Mr. Laurence sent it," replied Mrs. March.

" The Laurence boy's grandfather ! What in the world put such a thing into his head? We don't know him," exclaimed Meg.

" Hannah told one of his servants about your breakfast party; he is an odd old gentleman, but that pleased him. He knew my father years ago, and he sent me a polite note this afternoon, saying he hoped I would allow him to express his friendly feeling toward my children by sending them a few trifles in honour of the day. I could not refuse, and so you have a little feast at night to make up for the bread and milk breakfast."

" That boy put it into his head, I know he did ! He's a capital fellow, and I wish we could get acquainted. He looks as if he'd like to know us; but he's bashful, and Meg is so prim she won't let me speak to him when we pass," said Jo, as the plates went round, and the ice began to melt out of sight, with ohs ! and ahs ! of satisfaction.

" You mean the people who live in the big house next door, don't you ? " asked one of the girls. " My mother knows old Mr. Laurence, but says he's very proud, and don't like to mix with his neighbours. He keeps his grandson shut up when he isn't riding or walking with his tutor, and makes him study dreadfully hard. We invited him to our party but he didn't come. Mother says he's very nice, though he never speaks to us girls."

" Our cat ran away once, and he brought her back, and we talked over the fence, and were getting on capitally, all about cricket and so on, when he saw Meg coming and walked off. I mean to know him some day, for he needs fun, I'm sure he does," said Jo decidedly.

" I like his manners, and he looks like a little gentleman ; so I've no objection to your knowing him if a proper opportunity comes. He brought the flowers himself, and I should have asked him in if I had been sure what was going on upstairs. He looked so wistful as he went away, hearing the frolic, and evidently having none of his own.

" It's a mercy you didn't, mother," laughed Jo, looking at her boots. " But we'll have another play sometimes, that he *can* see. Maybe he'll help act ; wouldn't that be jolly ! "

" I never had a bouquet before ; how pretty it is," and Meg examined her flowers with great interest.

" They *are* lovely, but Beth's roses are sweeter to me," said Mrs. March, sniffing at the half-dead posy in her belt.

Beth nestled up to her, and whispered softly, " I wish I could send my bunch to father. I'm afraid he isn't having such a Merry Christmas as we are."

---

# THE LITTLE WAVES OF BREFFNY

### by Eva Gore-Booth

THE grand road from the mountain goes shining to the sea,
  And there is traffic on it and many a horse and cart,
But the little roads of Cloonagh are dearer far to me,
  And the little roads of Cloonagh go rambling through my heart.

A great storm from the ocean goes shouting o'er the hill,
  And there is glory in it and terror on the wind,
But the haunted air of twilight is very strange and still,
  And the little winds of twilight are dearer to my mind.

The great waves of the Atlantic sweep storming on their way,
  Shining green and silver with the hidden herring shoal,
But the Little Waves of Breffny have drenched my heart in spray,
  And the Little Waves of Breffny go stumbling through my soul.

# THE THREE GIFTS

## *by* H. A. E. ROBERTS

ONCE upon a time there lived a poor weaver and his wife. They let lodgings to three rich students. Now when the time came for the three students to leave, they collected amongst themselves a hundred crowns, which they gave to the old weaver as a parting gift. The weaver was overjoyed. Never before had he even seen so much money, and he made up his mind that he would save it up for a " rainy day."

His wife happened to be away from home at the time, so he hid the money carefully, as he thought, beneath a bundle of rags in a cupboard.

His wife returned home, but the weaver thought, " Perhaps I had better not tell her anything about the money. She might want to spend it."

So he held his peace, and said nothing at all about it.

One day the ragman happened to pass by, calling out : " Rags-ho ! Rags-ho ! " The good woman ran at once to the cupboard, and brought out the bundle of rags, which she gave to the ragman. He gave her a few pence for them, and carried them away, silver crowns and all !

When her husband returned home, you may imagine how he scolded his wife for having given away his little fortune. He wrote to the three young students and told them what had happened. They felt very sorry for him, and sent him another gift of fifty crowns.

This time the man hid the money under a dustbin, thinking that it would be quite safe there !

One day, when he had gone out to work, his wife, little knowing what she was doing, called out to a dustman, who happened to be passing by : " Come and empty my dustbin, please. It has not been emptied for days."

403

So the dustman emptied the dustbin, taking with him, of course, the fifty silver crowns. This time, when the man heard what had happened, he scolded his wife so soundly that she began to cry.

Just at that moment who should happen to be passing by but the three students who had given them the money.

" Let us call upon old Wilhelm," said one.

So they tapped at the door, and they overheard the story of the sad fate of their second gift. Then one of the young men threw a lump of lead upon the table.

" That is all you shall have this time, Wilhelm. You are too stupid to have any money. You cannot take care of it when you do have it."

So saying, the young man and his two friends left the weaver's house. The wife picked up the lump of lead and placed it on the window-sill. A few days later their neighbour, who was a fisherman, came to the door.

" Friends ! Have you, by any chance, such a thing as a lump of lead ? I want some to weigh down my nets, and I cannot find a bit anywhere."

" Take this," said the woman, and she gave him the piece of lead from the window-sill.

The fisherman thanked her and promised to give her in return the first large fish from his catch that day.

In the evening he brought her the fish, and the woman prepared it for cooking. Inside the fish she found a round, shining stone. It glowed with many colours, and the darker the night grew, the more brightly did it seem to shine.

" It will make a nice lamp," said the woman, and she put the lovely thing on the window-sill.

Soon a rich merchant passed by, and seeing the shining stone, he knocked at the cottage door.

" How much money will you take for that stone, my good woman ? " he asked.

" I was not thinking of selling it."

" But I am thinking of buying it. Tell me, will you take a thousand crowns ? "

The good woman fairly gasped.

" A—thousand—crowns ! Yes, I will."

The bargain was made, and the merchant rode off with the diamond, for such indeed it was !

When the weaver came home that night his joy knew no bounds. But his wife, like the woman that she was, insisted on having the last word.

" All the credit is due to me. If I had not thrown away the other gifts, we should never have had this one ! " Which, after all, was perfectly true !

# HOW A SCULLION WON HONOUR

## *by* STUART CAMPBELL

SOON after Sir Lancelot had returned to the court, to be joyfully welcomed by King Arthur and Queen Guinevere, the king gave a banquet to the Knights of the Round Table. When the feast was nearly ended, two tall and well-dressed men entered the hall, supporting between them a young man. This youth was taller than his companions by at least a foot and a half, although they were big men themselves, and he was handsome and broad of shoulder. Yet he walked as if he could not keep himself upright, until he stood before the king, when he stood up straight without help.

" Sire," he said to King Arthur, " I have come to beg you to grant me three favours. They are not unreasonable things that I shall ask, or things that it would be dishonourable to grant, and it will cost you little if you consent. The first favour I will ask now, but the other two I will ask in a year's time from to-day."

" Ask," said King Arthur, " and you shall have your wish."

" My first request," replied the stranger, " is that you will grant me food and drink for twelve months, at the end of which time I shall ask my other two favours."

" Your first wish is easily granted," said the king, " for I am ever ready to give food and drink to either friend or foe. But tell me, what is your name? "

" That I cannot tell you now," the stranger replied, " for I am under a vow to keep it secret."

King Arthur marvelled at his answer, but he called to him Sir Kay, who was his steward. He bade Sir Kay give the youth the best of fare to eat and drink, and to treat him as if he were the son of a great nobleman.

" That would be unnecessary waste," declared Sir Kay, " for I believe he is of lowly birth and will never make a worthy man. Had he been well born, he would have asked for horse and armour instead of food. And now, since he has no name, I will call him Fair-hands. He shall be lodged in the kitchen, where he can feed to the full on what is left from the tables of the court."

Sir Lancelot and Sir Gawaine heard Sir Kay mocking the youth, and rebuked him for doing so.

"One day," said Sir Lancelot, "this youth shall prove himself a man of great honour."

But Sir Kay was not to be turned from his purpose, and he found a place for Fair-hands in the lower part of the hall, among the menials and scullions, where he had to eat the leavings from the tables of the gentlefolk.

Sir Lancelot and Sir Gawaine saw him there, and would have had him come to their own apartments, where he might have dainty food and drink, but Fair-hands refused their kindness.

For a full twelve months Fair-hands dwelt in the royal kitchen, performing lowly duties and being at the call of every one. Yet never a word of complaint did he utter.

Whenever possible he attended to watch the jousting between the knights of the court, and at any feats of strength he soon proved himself able to beat the rest of King Arthur's servants. Even Sir Kay grew proud of the youth's prowess, and would bring knights to witness what Fair-hands could do.

When the year had passed since Fair-hands first came to the court, King Arthur once more called his barons and knights together to feast.

While the feast was in progress, a maiden entered the great hall, and advanced to kneel before the king.

"I come to beg for aid, sire," she said.

"For whom, and in what way?" asked King Arthur.

"Sire," she answered, "I serve a noble lady, who is besieged in her castle by an enemy. And I have come to beseech the help of your Knights of the Round Table, whose chivalry is known all over the world."

"Tell me the name of your lady," said the king. "Also, who is the enemy assailing her?"

"Sire," the maiden replied, "I am under a pledge not to reveal my lady's name, but she is of high birth and possessed of wide lands. As for her enemy, he is called the Red Knight of the Red Fields."

"I have never before heard of him," said King Arthur.

But Sir Gawaine was sitting close to the king, and he now spoke.

"I know this Red Knight well," he declared. "He is reputed to be one of the most powerful warriors in the world, having the strength of seven men. Once I fought him, and only narrowly escaped with my life."

The king thought for a moment before he replied to the maiden.

"There are knights here who would gladly ride to serve your lady," he said, "but since you will not tell me her name, I will not ask them to go."

Now Fair-hands had been listening to what was said, and at this moment he approached the king, bowing low before him.

"Sire," he said, "it is now a year since you granted me my first wish. To-day I come to ask the other two favours that you promised me."

"Name them, and my pledge shall be fulfilled," replied King Arthur.

"First, then," Fair-hands said, "I ask that you will permit me to accept the adventure which this fair maiden offers, and to ride forth as champion of her lady. Secondly, I ask you to bid Sir Lancelot make me knight, for I wish to be knighted by him and him alone. Please grant that he may set out with me, to make me knight when I shall ask him to."

"It shall be done as you desire," promised the king.

But the maiden was displeased, and stamped her foot in rage.

"Shame to you, King Arthur," she cried. "If you will appoint only a scullion from your kitchen to help me, then I refuse your aid."

And she ran from the hall, to mount her horse and ride away in a temper.

A servant unknown to the court now came to Fair-hands and told him that his horse and his armour were waiting him.

When Fair-hands had armed himself and mounted his horse, everybody marvelled. For his sword and armour were of rich quality, and his steed was a noble one, so that he looked as splendid a knight as any at the court as he took leave of the king. Yet, unlike other knights, he carried neither lance nor shield.

*Fair-hands struck a blow which cleaved through Sir Kay's armour.*

Fair-hands rode off to overtake the maiden, but he begged Sir Lancelot to follow so that King Arthur's promise should be kept.

Ever since he first saw him, Sir Kay had shown his dislike for the youth, and now he was more than ever jealous of Fair-hands.

"I will ride after my kitchen-boy," he cried, so that all should hear him, "and we will see if he is so gallant a knight as he would appear."

Sir Lancelot and Sir Gawaine advised him to let the youth alone, but the headstrong Sir Kay took his lance and went in pursuit. He caught up to Fair-hands just as the youth overtook the maiden.

"Fair-hands," cried Sir Kay, "do you know me?"

"Indeed I do," replied the youth, recalling all the insults which Sir Kay had heaped upon him. "I know you for an unworthy knight, and warn you not to interfere with me."

But the angry knight took no heed of the warning. Instead, he couched his lance and charged at Fair-hands, who in turn spurred his horse to meet him. Putting aside the point of the lance with his sword, Fair-hands then struck a shrewd blow which cleaved through Sir Kay's armour, and stretched him wounded on the ground.

Sir Lancelot had drawn near in time to witness Sir Kay's downfall, and Fair-hands now asked if they might joust together, to test each other's skill at arms. Sir Lancelot willingly agreed, and for fully an hour they fought without either gaining an advantage.

" Fair-hands," said Sir Lancelot at last, " let us fight no longer. There is no quarrel between us that we must do each other hurt."

" True enough," agreed Fair-hands. " Yet I found joy in combating with so able a knight as yourself, and would have fought on had you not spoken the word. For I had not exerted myself to my uttermost."

" Then I am glad you did not do so," laughed Sir Lancelot, " for I had a hard task to stand against you. I truly think that you have little to fear from any knight in fair battle."

Fair-hands flushed with pleasure at receiving such praise from so renowed a warrior as Sir Lancelot.

" If you think me worthy," he said, " I beg that you will give me the order of knighthood."

" Gladly will I do so," answered Sir Lancelot, " but first you must tell me your name, and inform me to what noble family you belong."

" Sir," replied the youth, " if you will keep my identity secret for the present, I will tell you who I am."

Sir Lancelot promised that he would keep the secret until the time when Fair-hands should give him permission to make it known. Then the youth told him that his name was Gareth, and that he was actually the brother of Sir Gawaine. It was so long since Sir Gawaine left his home that he had failed to recognise Gareth when he had appeared at court, for the youth had been only an infant when last the elder brother saw him.

" Ah," declared Sir Lancelot, " I knew that you must be of noble blood when first I saw you, which was why I felt regret when Sir Kay vented his ill-will by banishing you to the kitchen."

After Sir Lancelot had knighted him, Sir Gareth rode on with the maiden. while Sir Kay was carried home to be healed of his wound.

The maiden had witnessed Fair-hands' defeat of Sir Kay, and she had also seen him joust with Sir Lancelot. But she had not heard him announce his name, nor did she know that he had been knighted.

As they rode, the maiden kept her horse away from Sir Gareth's, and tilted her nose disdainfully into the air.

"Do not come too near to me, I beg," she said haughtily. "You smell of the kitchen that you have come from. You are only a scullion, and I will have you follow me no farther. Turn back and leave me, I bid you."

" Maiden," replied Sir Gareth patiently, " you may say to me what you please, but I will not leave you. In King Arthur's presence I undertook this adventure on your behalf, and I shall finish it or die."

Soon afterwards they were passing through a dark wood, when a man ran towards them who was evidently fleeing in panic.

" Why do you fly so wildly ? " asked Sir Gareth as the man reached them.

" Lord," cried the man, " six robbers attacked my master in a dell back yonder, and have bound him captive. I fear that they intend to kill him."

"Lead me to the place," commanded Sir Gareth.

Directly the robbers saw Sir Gareth they gathered to meet him, but the knight charged down upon them. Three he struck down with as many strokes of his sword, upon which the others fled.

Sir Gareth pursued the thieves so hotly that they were forced to turn and defend themselves, but he made speedy work of them.

When he had returned and released the knight whom the robbers had made prisoner, the rescued man thanked him with deep gratitude, and invited him to ride to his castle for rest and food.

"Sir, I must not linger," replied Sir Gareth. "I must follow this maiden on an adventure to which I am pledged."

Once more the maiden bade him go back as he joined her.

"I wish neither your company nor your help," she said. "And do not glory in these small deeds which you have done, for good luck has been on your side. If you persist in accompanying me, you shall see sights which will frighten you, and then you will be glad enough to turn back in haste."

But Sir Gareth took no notice of her taunts.

Leaving the wood, they came to a wide river, across which there was only one ford. On the far side awaited two knights, ready to dispute the passage with all who came.

Sir Gareth would not have turned back had a dozen knights been there to challenge him, and galloped his horse into the water. He had been given lance and shield by the knight he had saved, and he met his first opponent in midstream.

At the first onslaught both lances were broken, and the two knights smote at each other with their swords. Soon Sir Gareth struck his foe such a blow on his helmet that he was stunned, and fell into the river to be drowned.

Spurring on to the far shore, Sir Gareth met the second knight, whom he vanquished after a hard struggle. Then he rode back to conduct the maiden across the river.

"Alas," she said, "how sad it is that two such doughty knights should be laid low by a mere scullion. You think that you have performed a great deed again, but once more it was luck that aided you. For the horse slipped of the first knight, so that he fell in the river and drowned. While with the second knight, you came upon him from behind in unfair advantage, and thus overcame him."

"Maiden," answered Sir Gareth, "you may say what you will to me. My task is to serve you, lady, as I promised, and I shall gladly meet all perils that stand in my way."

"Fire low scullion!" she retorted, "you will change your tune when you see some of the knights who will bar your path."

They rode on until evening was near, and all the time her tongue was busy heaping scorn and insult upon Sir Gareth, to which he made no reply.

Then they came to a field wherein earth and grass were black. There was also a black hawthorn tree, upon which hung a black banner and a black shield, with a long, black lance leaning against it. Close by, a knight in black armour sat on a black rock, with a black horse standing near.

"This," said the maiden, "is the Knight of the Black Field. If you do not wish to die, Fair-hands, you had better return whence you came."

"Why do you always think me a coward?" asked Sir Gareth, as he advanced beside her.

"Have you brought this knight of King Arthur's to be your champion?" demanded the Black Knight of the maiden.

"He is no knight," laughed the maiden scornfully, "but only a knave from the royal kitchen. I have told him many times to leave me, but he accompanies me against my will. You would do me a service if you rid me of him."

"Willingly will I do so," returned the Black Knight. "I will teach him a lesson and send him back to his master afoot, leaving his armour and horse with me."

"Sir," said Sir Gareth, "you are unwise to decide what you will do with my horse and armour before you have dealt with me. To get them, you must win them with your hands. And I must tell you that I am no scullion as this maiden has said, but I am of nobler birth than you, as I will prove in combat."

The two knights drew apart, then rushed at each other as hard as their horses could thunder. The Black Knight's spear splintered on Sir Gareth's shield, but the latter's lance sped true and hurled the Black Knight dead from his steed.

Thinking the Black Knight's armour better than his own, Sir Gareth dismounted and donned it instead. He also took the dead man's horse, his own being weary with travel.

Again the young knight prepared to ride on his way with the maiden, who still had only scornful words to reward him for his victory.

"So once more a mischance has caused a valiant knight to fall before you," she said, "and I must still be burdened with your company. But never mind, there is one close at hand who will teach you a lesson, unless you are wise enough to turn back now."

*"Is that my brother, the Black Knight, whom you bring with you?"*

" You have told me that many times," answered Sir Gareth, " yet on each occasion I have vanquished my enemy. Let us waste no time, but ride on that I may come to your lady's help."

It was not long before they met a knight who was all in green, while his horse was caparisoned with green silk. The maiden was riding in front, and the Green Knight stopped to speak with her.

" Is that my brother, the Black Knight, whom you bring with you ? " he inquired.

" No," she replied. " It is a kitchen knave who slew your brother by mischance, and who then took his horse and armour."

" Alas," cried the Green Knight, " my brother was a noble knight, and it was an evil thing that a mere scullion should kill him. Look to yourself, knave, for I will avenge him ! "

He levelled his green spear and charged at Sir Gareth, who spurred to meet him. Both lances were splintered, and the Green Knight's horse was sent to the ground as they crashed together.

The Green Knight jumped clear of his horse as it fell, and Sir Gareth likewise dismounted in order to make the fight a fair one.

For some time they fought with their swords, without either gaining an advantage over the other. Then the maiden began to taunt the Green Knight.

" Shame upon you, Sir Green Knight," she cried. " Why do you take so long to overcome this kitchen knave ? It puzzles me to think how you earned your knighthood, when a mere youth can withstand you."

In his anger the Green Knight dealt a mighty blow, which split Sir Gareth's shield in two. But in return Sir Gareth struck so hard that he brought his foe helpless to his knees.

" I yield ! " cried the Green Knight. " Do not slay me."

" You shall die," answered Sir Gareth, " unless this maiden begs for you life."

" Let him live, foul scullion," said the maiden, " for if you kill him you shall regret it."

" Very well, Sir Green Knight," Sir Gareth said, " I will spare you as she wishes."

In his gratitude the Green Knight offered Sir Gareth his sword in homage and promised to place himself and thirty other knights at the service of his conqueror.

" I grieve at your hurts, Sir Green Knight," said the maiden, " and also at the death of your brother, the Black Knight. For I had great need of your help, fearing to pass through the forest before me."

" Fear not," replied the Green Knight. " You shall lodge with me to-night and in the morning I will escort you through the forest."

He conducted Sir Gareth and the maiden to his manor, which was situated quite near. Food was put before them, but the maiden would not allow Sir Gareth to sit at the same table as herself, saying that a scullion should eat with the servants.

But the Green Knight recognised that his guest must be of noble birth and sat with him at another table. He also commanded thirty knights to guard Sir Gareth during the night, that no danger should befall him.

Next morning the Green Knight and his followers escorted Sir Gareth and the maiden safely through the forest, bidding them farewell upon reaching the other side.

" Sir Fair-hands," he said, for he did not know Sir Gareth by his real name, " if ever you need help, I and my thirty knights will be ever at your command."

" I thank you," replied Sir Gareth. " When I call upon you, then, you must go to King Arthur with your following."

Sir Gareth rode on with the maiden, who still bade him leave her and return to his kitchen.

That day Sir Gareth fought and vanquished a third brother of those he had already encountered, this time called the Yellow Knight. Again he spared his enemy at the maiden's request, and that night they stayed in the castle of the Yellow Knight, who had pledged himself and his fifty followers to be ever at Sir Gareth's command.

When they had left the castle of the Yellow Knight the maiden began anew to taunt Sir Gareth, and as before the young knight gave only gentle answers in reply. Then, suddenly, the maiden's manner changed.

" Fair-hands," she said in a kindly voice, " I marvel at your good-nature. Surely no woman ever insulted her champion as I have you, yet never have you become angry with me. Such chivalry could only belong to a true knight."

" Lady," he answered, " I bear you no ill-will for the things you have said of me. Indeed, your taunts have helped me to overcome my enemies, for I have tried to prove myself a worthy champion in your eyes. Now, since you treat me so differently, I may tell you that I am no scullion pretending to be a knight. I dwelt for a year in King Arthur's kitchen only that I might be the better able to judge my friends."

" Alas, good Fair-hands," she cried, " forgive me all the cruel things I have said and done."

" With all my heart I do so," he told her, " and there is no knight living whom I will not face on your behalf."

It was not long before Sir Gareth's courage was tested again, this time by Sir Persant of Inde, who was the fourth brother to the three knights already encountered.

Sir Persant was the most formidable of the brethren, and his armour, spear and shield were of a deep blue colour, as were the trappings of his horse.

The combat between Sir Gareth and the Blue Knight lasted fully two hours, but in the end the young knight was again victorious. He granted the Blue Knight his life on condition that he did him homage, and also received a pledge that Sir Persant and a hundred knights would ever hold themselves ready to serve him.

Sir Gareth and the maiden remained the night as guests of Sir Persant, and in the morning made ready to continue their journey.

" Maiden," said Sir Persant, " whither are you leading this young knight?"

" Sir," she answered, " he is riding with me to the aid of my sister, who is besieged in her castle by the Red Knight of the Red Fields."

" Then I wish you success in your adventure," said the Blue Knight to Sir Gareth. " Yet must you beware, for the Red Knight is a powerful enemy, having the strength of seven men. Many knights have lost their lives through trying to aid the lady he besieges, who is one of the most beautiful women in the world. If I mistake not, this maiden is her sister, Linet."

"That is my name," the maiden answered, "and my sister is the Lady Liones. And now, Sir Persant, before this noble youth goes to meet the Red Knight on my sister's behalf, I beg that you will give him the order of knighthood."

"Gladly I will," said Sir Persant heartily, "if he will accept the honour from so humble a knight as myself."

At this, however, Sir Gareth revealed that he had already been knighted by Sir Lancelot. He also disclosed the secret of his birth, telling Sir Persant and Linet that he was the youngest son of the King of Orkney, and brother to Sir Gawaine and two other knights of King Arthur's court.

*The Blue Knight wished him God-speed.*

"As yet," he concluded, "neither King Arthur nor my brothers know my true name."

Once again the Blue Knight wished him God-speed, then Sir Gareth and Linet rode on.

At last they came to the plain where stood the castle of the Lady Liones, with the tents of the Red Knight's army all around it.

Passing a grove of trees, Sir Gareth saw the bodies of many knights hanging from the branches, each with his shield about his neck. All of them were men who had come to do battle for Lady Liones, and after conquering them the Red Knight had put them to a shameful death. But Sir Gareth was undaunted by what he saw, and rode boldly onwards.

Presently he came to a sycamore tree standing alone, and from one of its boughs hung a great horn, fashioned from the tusk of an elephant. This the Red Knight had placed there, so that any knight who wished to challenge him might blow it.

Sir Gareth seized the horn, and sounded such a blast that every one heard it among besiegers and besieged.

The Red Knight of the Red Fields heard the challenge and bade his attendants prepare him for combat. Two lords who owed him homage assisted him to don his armour, and an earl buckled the straps of his helmet. His weapons and all that he wore were blood-red in colour, and his grooms led forth a red steed for him to mount.

The place where the two were to fight was on an open space just in front of the castle, and looking up, Sir Gareth saw the Lady Liones watching him from a window. She was so beautiful that Sir Gareth loved her as soon as her saw her, and vowed to conquer or die in her cause.

"Gaze at her no longer, Sir Knight," cried the Red Knight mockingly, "but make ready for the conflict."

They rode together at top speed, and each lance struck the other shield with such force that both riders were hurled from their saddles. For so long did they both lie stunned that the onlookers thought they had broken their necks in the fall, but both recovered at the same moment and ran at each other like lions.

Both were wounded in many places, and both had their armour dented and battered. But they fought on until both were exhausted, and they had to draw apart and sit to rest awhile. As he sat there, Sir Gareth glanced up at Lady Liones, upon which she waved encouragement to him.

Directly they had regained their breath the two knights renewed their battle.

Almost at once a cunning stroke knocked the sword from Sir Gareth's hand, and a blow on his helmet stretched him on the ground. The Red Knight sprang forward to complete his victory.

But Linet stood near, and seeing Sir Gareth's peril she shouted to him : "Up, Fair-hands! My sister weeps to think you conquered."

Sir Gareth heard, and the words awakened him to fresh efforts. He rolled aside to avoid the Red Knight's thrust, then picked up his own sword and attacked with redoubled strength.

Soon he had struck his enemy down and the Red Knight begged for mercy at his feet.

Remembering the knights whom he had seen hanging in the grove, Sir Gareth was reluctant to spare their slayer, but all the crowd prayed that he would grant the Red Knight his life, and Sir Gareth at last consented. As a condition, he said that the Red Knight must recompense Lady Liones for all the injuries that he had done to her, and afterwards he and his followers must all pay homage to King Arthur at his court.

The Red Knight gratefully promised to do these things, and then Sir Gareth entered the wide-opened gates of the castle to receive the thanks he had so richly earned.

When she saw her champion without his helmet, Lady Liones fell in love with him as deeply as Sir Gareth had with her. When her brother, who was her guardian, learned that Sir Gareth was a king's son, he readily agreed to their betrothal.

# THE BLUE LIGHT

## *by* THE BROTHERS GRIMM

A SOLDIER had served a king his master many years, till at last
he was turned off without pay or reward. How he should get his
living he did not know : so he set out and journeyed homeward
all day in a very downcast mood until in the evening he came to
the edge of a deep wood. The road leading that way, he pushed
forward, but had not gone far before he saw a light glimmering
through the trees, towards which he bent his weary steps ; and soon came
to a hut where no one lived but an old witch. The poor fellow begged for
a night's lodging and something to eat and drink ; but she would listen to
nothing : however, he was not easily got rid of ; and at last she said, " I
think I will take pity on you this once : but if I do you must dig over all
my garden for me in the morning." The soldier agreed very willingly to
anything she asked, and he became her guest.

The next day he kept his word and dug the garden very neatly. The job
lasted all day ; and in the evening, when his mistress would have sent him
away, he said, " I am so tired of my work that I must beg you to let me stay
over the night." The old lady vowed at first she would not do any such thing :
but after a great deal of talk he carried his point, agreeing to chop up a whole
cart-load of wood for her the next day.

This task too was duly ended ; but not till towards night ; and then he
found himself so tired, that he begged a third night's rest : and this too was
given, but only on his pledging his word that he next day would fetch the
witch the blue light that burnt at the bottom of the well.

When morning came she led him to the well's mouth, tied him to a long
rope, and let him down. At the bottom sure enough he found the blue light
as the witch had said, and at once made the signal for her to draw him up

again. But when she had pulled him up so near to the top that she could reach him with her hands, she said " Give me the light, I will take care of it," —meaning to play him a trick, by taking it for herself and letting him fall again to the bottom of the well. But the soldier saw through her wicked thoughts, and said, " No, I shall not give you the light till I find myself safe and sound out of the well." At this she became very angry, and dashed him, with the light she had longed for many a year, down to the bottom. And there lay the poor soldier for a while in despair, on the damp mud below, and feared that his end was nigh. But his pipe happened to be in his pocket still half-full, and he thought to himself, " I may as well make an end of smoking you out ; it is the last pleasure I shall have in this world." So he lit it at the blue light, and began to smoke.

Up rose a cloud of smoke, and on a sudden a little black dwarf was seen making his way through the midst of it. " What do you want with me, soldier ? " said he. " I have no business with you," answered he. But the dwarf said, " I am bound to serve you in every thing, as lord and master of the blue light." " Then first of all be so good as to help me out of this well." No sooner said than done : the dwarf took him by the hand and drew him up, and the blue light of course with him. " Now do me another piece of kindness," said the soldier : " Pray let that old lady take my place in the well." When the dwarf had done this, and lodged the witch safely at the bottom, they began to ransack her treasures ; and the soldier made bold to carry off as much of her gold and silver as he well could. Then the dwarf said, " If you should chance at any time to want me, you have nothing to do but to light your pipe at the blue light, and I will soon be with you."

The soldier was not a little pleased at his good luck, and went into the best inn in the first town he came to, and ordered some fine clothes to be made and a handsome room to be got ready for him. When all was ready, he called his little man to him, and said, " The king sent me away penniless, and left me to hunger and want : I have a mind to show him that it is my turn to be master now ; so bring me his daughter here this evening, that she may wait upon me, and do what I bid her." " That is rather a dangerous task," said the dwarf. But away he went, took the princess out of her bed, fast asleep as she was, and brought her to the soldier.

Very early in the morning he carried her back : and as soon as she saw her father, she said, " I had a strange dream last night : I thought I was carried away through the air to a soldier's house, and there I waited upon him as his servant." Then the king wondered greatly at such a story ; but told her to make a hole in her pocket and fill it with peas, so that if it were really as she said, and the whole was not a dream, the peas might fall out in the streets as she passed through, and leave a clue to tell whither she had been taken. She did so ; but the dwarf had heard the king's plot ; and when evening came, and the soldier said he must bring him the princess again, he strewed peas over several of the streets, so that the few that fell from her pocket were not known from the others ; and the people amused themselves all the next day picking up peas, and wondering where so many came from.

When the princess told her father what had happened to her the second time, he said, " Take one of your shoes with you, and hide it in the room you are taken to." The dwarf heard this also ; and when the soldier told him to

RING O' ROSES

Ring a ring o' roses round the rose-red world. (Page 435)

THE CHRISTMAS TREE

With spangles gay and candle light.
And many toys, our tree is bright. (Page 440)

bring the king's daughter again he said, "I cannot save you this time; it will be an unlucky thing for you if you are found out—as I think you will." But the soldier would have his own way. "Then you must take care and make the best of your way out of the city gate very early in the morning," said the dwarf. The princess kept one shoe on her as her father bid her, and hid it in the soldier's room: and when she got back to her father, he ordered it to be sought for all over the town; and at last it was found where she had hid it. The soldier had run away, it is true! but he had been too slow, and was soon caught and thrown into a strong prison:—what was worse, in the hurry of his flight, he had left behind him his great treasure the blue light and all his gold, and had nothing left in his pocket but one poor ducat.

*"Do not fear, master,—only mind to take the blue light with you."*

As he was standing very sorrowful at the prison grating, he saw one of his comrades, and calling out to him said, "If you will bring me a little bundle I left in the inn, I will give you a ducat." His comrade thought this very good pay for such a job: so he went away, and soon came back bringing the blue light and the gold. Then the soldier soon lit his pipe: up rose the smoke, and with it came his old friend the little dwarf. "Do not fear, master," said he: "keep up your heart at your trial and leave everything to take its course; —only mind to take the blue light with you." The trial soon came on; the prisoner found guilty, and was ordered to be hung forthwith on the gallows tree.

But as he was let out, he said he had one favour to beg of the king. "What is it?" said His Majesty. "That you will deign to let me smoke one pipe on the road." "Two, if you like," said the king. Then he lit his pipe at the blue light, and the black dwarf was before him in a moment. "Be so good as to kill, slay, or put to flight all these people," said the soldier: "and as for the king, you may cut him into three pieces." Then the dwarf began to lay about him, and soon got rid of the crowd around: but the king begged hard for mercy; and to save his life, agreed to let the soldier have the princess for his wife, and to leave the kingdom to him when he died.

# THE MOUSE AND THE CAKE

*by* ELIZA COOK

A MOUSE found a beautiful piece of plum-cake,
The richest and sweetest that mortal could make ;
'Twas heavy with citron and fragrant with spice,
And covered with sugar all sparkling as ice.

" My stars ! " cried the mouse, while his eye beamed with glee,
" Here's a treasure I've found ;  what a feast it will be :
But hark !  There's a noise, 'tis my brothers at play ;
So I'll hide with the cake, lest they wander this way.

" Not a bit shall they have, for I know I can eat
Every morsel myself, and I'll have such a treat ; "
So off went the mouse, as he held the cake fast,
While his hungry young brothers went scampering past.

He nibbled, and nibbled, and panted, but still
He kept gulping it down till he made himself ill ;
Yet he swallowed it all, and 'tis easy to guess,
He was soon so unwell that he groaned with distress.

His family heard him, and as he grew worse,
They sent for the doctor, who made him rehearse
How he'd eaten the cake to the very last crumb,
Without giving his playmates and relatives some.

" Ah me ! " cried the doctor, " advice is too late,
You must die before long, so prepare for your fate ;
If you had but divided the cake with your brothers,
'Twould have done you no harm, and been good for the others.

" Had you shared it, the treat had been wholesome enough ;
But eaten by one it was dangerous stuff ;
So prepare for the worst ; " and the word had scarce fled,
When the doctor turned round, and the patient was dead.

Now all little people the lesson may take,
And some large ones may learn from the mouse and the cake,
Not to be over-selfish with what we may gain ;
Or the best of our pleasures may turn into pain.

# HOP O' MY THUMB

## (*An Old Fairy Tale*)

LONG, long ago, in a land far, far away, there lived a poor man, who earned only a very little money by cutting down trees.

He had a wife and seven boys, and he found it very hard to get food enough for them all.

One of the boys was such a tiny little fellow that he was called Hop o' my Thumb. But, though he was small, he had a very wise head, and was more clever than any of his brothers.

Then, too, when he saw his parents looking very sad, he would frisk about, do such droll things, and make such funny jokes, that they quite forgot their troubles for the time.

At play it was always Hop o' my Thumb who thought of the nicest games. In fact, Hop o' my Thumb was the joy of the whole family, whose home was a poor little cottage close to a great forest.

One night, after the weather had been very bad and little work could be done, the poor wood-cutter sat with his wife, talking about the hard life they had to live. Their money was all gone, there seemed no chance of getting more for a long time, and there was left only enough food for breakfast next day.

The boys had been put to bed, and all were fast asleep but Hop o' my Thumb. Seeing his parents so sad, he lay awake, thinking how he could help them.

Presently he heard his father say, " Well, goodwife, if our boys are to die for want of food, I will take them right away into the forest. There I shall lose them, as I could not bear to see them suffer."

The poor woman begged, with tears in her eyes, that he would wait a few days longer, to see if things would change for the better.

Hop o' my Thumb knew how much she loved them all, and felt sure she would try her best to save them.

But the father, who was very hard to turn, only said, in answer to his wife's pleading, " It is of no use for you to try to make me alter my mind. To-morrow I will take them into the forest, and there leave them. If you will only think a little, you will agree that this is the best thing to do.

" Would you like to see the boys dying day by day, and know that we could do nothing to save them ? No, I am sure you would not ; and so, as they must die, let it be as I say."

With a sore heart the poor mother lay down to sleep. But Hop o' my Thumb lay very still, and kept awake till the first light of day peeped in at the cottage window.

Then, quietly dressing, he slipped out of the house, ran quickly to a little stream near by, gathered some nice white little stones, and went back to his bed without having wakened any one.

Having roused the boys, the poor mother gave them the last of the food. Then they all went to help their father with his work.

419

The wood-cutter took them very much farther into the forest than usual, into a part which was quite strange to them. As they went, Hop o' my Thumb dropped the white stones to show them the way back.

Their father cut a lot of small branches, and set the boys to work to tie them into bundles.

When he had cut a great many, he said to the boys, "Now, my children, work away as well as you can, and when you have done, come home quickly, or your mother and I will be afraid you have lost yourselves."

So saying, he left them, feeling sure they would never find their way out of the thick forest.

Having tied up all the wood, the boys set off for home. After they had gone a little way, one of them said, "I say, Hop o', where are we? I don't know this part of the wood at all!"

"It's all right, Franz. I know the way; come along."

And as they knew their tiny brother was nearly always right, they followed him without a word.

Their mother could not bear to sit in the lonely cottage, so she went out to the edge of the forest. She was thinking of the merry little Hop o' my Thumb and his brothers, and longing ever so much to clasp them all in her arms again.

All at once they heard the sound of happy voices. Very soon the seven boys were running and dancing about her, glad that they had got safely out of the thick wood.

She was happy at having her boys again with her, but she wondered what their father would say. On getting near the cottage, however, she saw a man talking to her husband at the door.

She at once knew that this was a serving-man from the big hall a long way off, and wondered what he wanted with her husband.

When the man had gone, she took the boys to the cottage, fearing that their father would be angry at their return. What was her surprise, therefore, when he came forward, saying, "Welcome home, my boys. Your father is happy to see you all again. Come, wife, the good baron has sent us enough food to last for some days. Let us at once sit down to supper."

So down to the table they sat, and never were folk more happy than they.

But, alas! when the food was done they were merry no longer. The father told his wife he must again take the boys away and lose them, and this time he would make sure they should not find their way back.

Therefore, when the morning came, he told them all to follow him into the forest, and took them quite a long way, into a part they knew nothing about.

But Hop o' my Thumb guessed what his father meant to do, and so, being unable that morning to get stones as before, he had saved the bread given him for his breakfast.

This he broke up on the way, dropping the crumbs, as he had dropped the stones, to guide them out of the forest again.

Having set the boys to work, their father left as before. They made the best use of their time, and, when their task was done, started for home.

They were quite happy about finding their way, for had they not Hop o' with them? This time, however, their little brother was not able to help them, for the birds had eaten all the crumbs!

So they walked on and on, hoping to find some path they knew, but all in vain. At last they sat down at the foot of a big tree to rest and think what was best to be done.

Hop o' my Thumb, being a nimble little fellow, instead of sitting down with the rest, climbed up the tree and took a good look round. He caught sight of a bright light some way off.

Down he went to tell his brothers, and away they ran towards the light, which shone out from a large house. They thumped with all their might on the big door. After a time, a woman with a sad, yet kind face, came and asked them what they wanted.

*She lifted the boys into the drawer.*

"Oh, if you please, kind lady," said Hop o' my Thumb, for the brothers thought he could speak more politely than they, "we have lost our way in the wood. Will you very kindly allow us to sleep in your house, for we are afraid the wolves will eat us up. And, oh, if you please, we are so hungry!"

The woman threw up her hands in wonder.

"Sleep here, my boys?" said she. "Do you know whose house this is? You would all be much safer in the wood, for the wolves might not find you, while my husband would be sure to do so if I let you in here.

"He is a dreadful big ogre, and he likes eating little children better than anything."

Now, just at that moment, a great thump! thump! was heard. The woman, telling the boys quietly to follow her, went quickly into the house, and shut the door behind them.

She took them down a long passage and into a huge kitchen. Walking straight to a great dresser in which were some very deep drawers, she lifted the boys into these drawers and shut them up tight. Just then the great ogre tramped into the room.

"What's this smell of fresh meat? Ho, ho! ha, ha! he, he! Bring it out quickly!" roared the monster.

"Fresh meat, my lord!" answered his wife, in a fright. "Oh, no, it's only the sucking pigs I am cooking for your supper that you smell."

Now, at the thought of supper the huge fellow smacked his thick lips.

Ordering it to be served at once, he sat down to the table and stretched his great feet toward the fire.

Having eaten till he could swallow no more, the greedy ogre again fancied that he could smell flesh.

"Wife!" roared he, "I am sure there is flesh quite near, and raw flesh, too!"

"Oh, no, there is not, my lord," again said his wife, "unless you can smell the sheep that I have saved for your dinner to-morrow!"

But the giant got up and walked round the kitchen till he came to the dresser. Then, all at once, he opened the drawers and pulled out the poor, frightened boys.

"Aha!" shouted he, "what have we here? Did I not say I could smell raw meat? Woman, what means this?"

The goodwife was almost dead with fear, but she meant to save the children if she could. So, going quite close to her husband, she said quietly, "I am sorry you have found these boys, as I meant to truss and roast them, and place them before you as a pleasant surprise."

At this the ogre seemed pleased, but, after looking at them for some little time, he said, "That *would* have been nice, but now I know that they are here, I cannot rest till I have eaten them. Come, cook them at once, as I long to pick their bones."

Again the woman tried to save them.

"See, my lord," said she, bringing Hop o' my Thumb forward, "they are not fit for killing. They must be fattened, and then you will have a great treat!"

Picking the little fellow up in his great hand, the ogre said, "True, goodwife, there is not much flesh on this fellow. Give them plenty to eat, and make them fat quickly, for I long to eat them."

So the ogre's wife took them away, gave them a good supper, and told them to sleep in the passage till the morning, when she would try to set them free.

After a time all in the house was still, save for the loud snoring of the sleeping giant. Up got Hop o' my Thumb. Going softly upstairs, he found a tiny window left open on a landing.

Then he went downstairs again, and called his brothers. On looking out, they saw that the side of the house was covered with thick ivy. One after another they climbed down the ivy to the ground.

They hurried off as fast as they could, in case the giant should waken, and, finding them gone, follow and catch them.

Now, not long after the escape of the boys, the giant, waking up, thought he would take a peep at them. Very angry was he when he could find them nowhere.

Getting his seven-league boots, he put them on and set out to follow the seven little boys. On trying to put his right foot forward, he found it would only go backward, while the left foot was quite willing to go in the way it was wanted.

Again and again the giant tried to follow the boys, but in vain; the boots would not both go the same way. At last he sat down to look at them, and found that he had them on the wrong feet!

Having put them on properly, he again started, and this time, at every stride, he went over seven leagues of ground. In this way he soon overtook the children. But he did not see them, for they had hidden in a thick bush.

All at once they heard a noise like thunder, and fancied the earth shook beneath them. They felt sure this was the ogre coming, and soon saw his huge figure stride through the air above them.

They crept together, very much afraid, when suddenly they heard a sweet voice say, " Do not fear, dear children. I am the Fairy Good-Heart, and will help you."

To the great surprise of the boys, the giant came to the earth all at once, and, sitting down on the side of a high hill, began to rub his legs very quickly.

"See!" said the Fairy Good-Heart, "some of my elves are sticking

*One after another they climbed to the ground.*

needles into his legs. When he has rubbed them enough, he will not be able to rise from the hill, for others of my people are tying him to the earth with very fine strong bands.

"He will, in a short time, take off his boots to rub his feet. You, Hop o' my Thumb, must then go softly behind, and gently draw the boots away. I will make them to fit you, and once you have them on your feet, all your troubles will be over."

So Hop o' my Thumb, bidding his brothers hurry home, did as the fairy told him.

The boots fitted him as the Fairy Good-Heart had said, and away he strode right before the giant. Then the ogre, breaking the bands by a great effort, rose from the hill and followed the little fellow, hoping soon to catch him. But he did not remember that he had taken off his magic boots.

Over hill and dale he chased Hop o' my Thumb, never heeding where he stepped, till all at once, he found himself falling heels over head over a cliff.

Down, down he fell, till his head struck on the edge of a sharp rock. A long time afterwards he was found quite dead at the bottom of the cliff, and every one was glad because he would never trouble them again.

Hop o' my Thumb knew that the ogre had started to follow him, but he never once looked back till he got home, when no sign of the huge monster was to be seen.

Into the cottage he danced with delight, and found that his brothers had not yet come back. So he told his parents all that had happened to them.

Just as they were hugging and kissing him, and telling him how glad they were to see him safely home again, in walked the six brothers. They were all very tired, but all very pleased to be at home once more.

That night, as they lay asleep, the Fairy Good-Heart came and said to him, " Waken, Hop o' my Thumb, waken ! Heed what I now tell you, for to no one else has this news been given.

" Far away, across the black forest, and the high hills, and the blue waters of a big, big sea, there is a land which never yet mortal has trod. Thither you must go, having on your feet the magic boots.

" In a spot which I will show you, you must dig deep into the earth, where you will find more gold than you can carry. Bring as much back with you as you can, and your family will never be in want again."

Before Hop o' my Thumb could even say " Thank you ! " the kind fairy was gone. He hardly knew how to lie quiet till the morning. As soon as it was light, he called to his father and mother and all his brothers to rise at once.

As they sat at breakfast, he told them he was going a long way off ; but of the Fairy Good-Heart and the gold he said nothing.

His mother begged him with tears in her eyes to be careful, and come home safely. But he wiped away her tears, danced about in his magic boots, and said so many droll things, that soon she was laughing quite happily as she bade him good-bye.

The weather had now settled fair, and the poor wood-cutter went day after day to work with his boys in the forest, while the mother worked in the home and in the garden.

So the time passed, and one evening when they sat at their supper, in came little Hop o' my Thumb, all smiles and laughter.

Oh, how glad they were to see him !

" Dear little Hop o'," said his mother, " you must never leave us again ! "

" Indeed, mother mine,

*" Here is gold enough to make us all rich ! "*  I shall not need to, for see,

here is gold enough to make us all rich for the rest of our lives!" Then he placed on the floor a sack full of yellow shining gold. The surprise of Hop o' my Thumb's parents was more than one can tell.

They had a fine palace built, and put in it the loveliest of things. They had servants, and horses, and carriages, and the fame of their riches soon reached the king. Hearing that all these fine things were obtained by means of the seven-league boots, he said he should like to see them.

So Hop o' my Thumb brought them before the king, who was at once filled with a great desire to have them, but did not care to say so.

Wise little Hop o' my Thumb, however, knew what was passing through the king's mind. Feeling sure that the Fairy Good-Heart would agree, he said, " O king, listen to the prayer of your most humble servant.

" I here and now do beg that you do me the honour of taking, as a free gift, these wonderful boots, that your majesty may thus be able to visit the faraway land of gold."

This was just what the king wished to do, so he was not long in making up his mind. And no visitors, however noble they might be, were more welcome at the palace of the king than the once poor wood-cutter and his wife.

# FIRE FAIRIES

*by* EDITH E. MILLARD

SOMETIMES when I have gone to bed
And blown my candle out,
Fire fairies dressed in gold and red
Dance round and round about.

I see them best on nights so dark
That not one wee star shows,
Each is at first a little spark
That to a fairy grows.

They dance upon the polished floor
Just where the hearthrug ends,
Right to the shadows near the door
The blazing pine-log sends.

I keep as quiet as a mouse
And watch the pretty sight:
I wonder, now, if in *your* house
Fire fairies dance at night?

# THE BELLS OF OLD LONDON

### ANON.

GAY go up and gay go down,
To ring the bells of London Town.

Bulls'-eyes and targets,
Say the bells of St. Marg'ret's.

Brickbats and tiles,
Say the bells of St. Giles.

Halfpence and farthings,
Say the bells of St. Martin's.

Oranges and lemons,
Say the bells of St. Clement's.

Pancakes and fritters,
Say the bells at St. Peter's.

Two sticks and an apple,
Say the bells at Whitechapel.

Old Father Baldpate,
Say the slow bells at Aldgate.

You owe me ten shillings,
Say the bells at St. Helen's.

When will you pay me?
Say the bells at Old Bailey

When I shall grow rich,
Say the bells at Shoreditch.

Pray, when will that be?
Say the bells at Stepney.

I am sure I don't know,
Says the great bell at Bow.

# MR. MINNS AND HIS COUSIN

## by CHARLES DICKENS

MR. AUGUSTUS MINNS was a bachelor, of about forty as he said—of about eight-and-forty as his friends said. He was always exceedingly clean, precise, and tidy ; perhaps somewhat priggish, and the most retiring man in the world. He usually wore a brown frock-coat without a wrinkle, light inexplicables without a spot, a neat neckerchief with a remarkably neat tie, and boots without a fault ; moreover, he always carried a brown silk umbrella with an ivory handle. He was a clerk in Somerset House, or, as he said himself, he held " a responsible situation under Government." He had a good and increasing salary, in addition to some £10,000 of his own (invested in the funds), and he occupied a first floor in Tavistock Street, Covent Garden, where he had resided for twenty years, having been in the habit of quarrelling with his landlord the whole time ; regularly giving notice of his intention to quit on the first day of every quarter, and as regularly countermanding it on the second. There were two classes of created objects which he held in the deepest and most unmingled horror—these were dogs and children. He was not unamiable, but he could, at any time, have viewed the execution of a dog, or the assassination of an infant, with the liveliest satisfaction. Their habits were at variance with his love of order ; and his love of order was as powerful as his love of life.

Mr. Augustus Minns had no relations, in or near London, with the exception of his cousin, Mr. Octavius Budden, to whose son, whom he had never seen (for he disliked the father), he had consented to become god-father by proxy. Mr. Budden having realised a moderate fortune by exercising the trade or calling of a corn-chandler, and having a great predilection for the country, had purchased a cottage in the vicinity of Stamford Hill, whither he retired with the wife of his bosom, and his only son, Master Alexander Augustus Budden.  One evening as Mr. and Mrs. B. were admiring their son, discussing his various merits, talking over his education, and disputing whether the classics should be made an essential part thereof, the lady pressed so strongly upon her husband the propriety of cultivating the friendship of Mr. Minns in behalf of their son, that Mr. Budden at last made up his mind that it should not be his fault if he and his cousin were not in future more intimate.

"I'll break the ice, my love," said Mr. Budden, stirring up the sugar at the bottom of his glass of brandy-and-water, and casting a sidelong look at his spouse to see the effect of the announcement of his determination, "by asking Minns down to dine with us on Sunday."

"Then pray, Budden, write to your cousin at once," replied Mrs. Budden. "Who knows, if we could only get him down here, but he might take a fancy to our Alexander, and leave him his property?  Alick, my dear, take your legs off the rail of the chair!"

"Very true," said Mr. Budden, musing, "very true, indeed, my love!"

On the following morning, as Mr. Minns was sitting at his breakfast-table, alternately biting his dry toast, and casting a look upon the columns of his morning paper, which he always read from the title to the printer's name, he heard a loud knock at the street door; which was shortly afterwards followed by the entrance of a servant, who put into his hand a particularly small card, on which was engraven, in immense letters, "Mr. Octavius Budden, Amelia Cottage (Mrs. B.'s name was Amelia), Poplar Walk, Stamford Hill."

"Budden!" ejaculated Minns; "what can bring that vulgar man here! Say I'm asleep—say I'm out, and shall never be home again—anything to keep him downstairs."

"But please, sir, the gentleman's coming up," replied the servant; and the fact was made evident by an appalling creaking of boots on the staircase, accompanied by a pattering noise, the cause of which Minns could not, for the life of him, divine.

"Hem!—show the gentleman in," said the unfortunate bachelor.  Exit servant, and enter Octavius, preceded by a large white dog, dressed in a suit of fleecy hosiery, with pink eyes, large ears, and no perceptible tail.

The cause of the pattering on the stairs was but too plain.  Mr. Augustus Minns staggered beneath the shock of the dog's appearance.

"My dear fellow, how are you?" said Budden, as he entered.

He always spoke at the top of his voice, and always said the same thing half a dozen times.

"How are you, my hearty?"

"How do you do, Mr. Budden?  Pray take a chair!" politely stammered the discomfited Minns.

"Thank you—thank you—well—how are you, eh?"

"Uncommonly well, thank you," said Minns, casting a diabolical look at the dog, who, with his hindlegs on the floor, and his forepaws resting on the table, was dragging a bit of bread-and-butter out of a plate preparatory to devouring it, with the buttered side next the carpet.

"Ah, you rogue!" said Budden to his dog; "you see, Minns, he's like me, always at home, eh, my boy?—Egad, I'm precious hot and hungry! I've walked all the way from Stamford Hill this morning."

"Have you breakfasted?" inquired Minns.

"Oh, no!—came to breakfast with you; so ring the bell, my dear fellow, will you? and let's have another cup and saucer, and the cold ham. Make myself at home, you see!" continued Budden, dusting his boots with a table-napkin. "Ha!—ha!—ha!—'pon my life, I'm hungry."

Minns rang the bell, and tried to smile.

"I decidedly never was so hot in my life," continued Octavius, wiping his forehead. "Well, but how are you, Minns? 'Pon my soul, you wear capitally."

*My dear fellow, how are you?" said Budden as he entered.*

"D'ye think so?" said Minns; and he tried another smile.

"'Pon my life, I do!"

"Mrs. B. and—what's his name—quite well?"

"Alick—my son, you mean; never better—never better. But at such a place as we've got at Poplar Walk, you know, he couldn't be ill if he tried. When I first saw it, by Jove! it looked so knowing, with the front garden, and the green railings, and the brass knocker, and all that—I really thought it was a cut above me."

"Don't you think you'd like the ham better," interrupted Minns, "if you cut it the other way?" He saw, with feelings which it is impossible to describe, that his visitor was cutting, or rather maiming, the ham in utter violation of all established rules.

"No, thank ye," returned Budden with the most barbarous indifference to crime. "I prefer it this way—it eats short. But I say, Minns, when will you come down and see us? You will be delighted with the place; I know you will. Amelia and I were talking about you the other night, and Amelia said—another lump of sugar, please ; thank ye—she said, don't you think you could contrive, my dear, to say to Mr. Minns, in a friendly way—come down, sir—damn the dog ! he's spoiling your curtains, Minns—ha !—ha ! ha ! " Minns leaped from his seat as though he had received the discharge from a galvanic battery.

" Come out, sir !—go out, hoo ! " cried poor Augustus, keeping, nevertheless, at a very respectful distance from the dog ; having read of a case of hydrophobia in the paper of that morning. By dint of great exertion, much shouting, and a marvellous deal of poking under the tables with a stick and umbrella, the dog was at last dislodged, and placed on the landing outside the door, where he immediately commenced a most appalling howling ; at the same time vehemently scratching the paint off the two nicely-varnished bottom panels, until they resembled the interior of a backgammon board.

" A good dog for the country that ! " coolly observed Budden to the distracted Minns, " but he's not much used to confinement. But now, Minns, when will you come down ? I'll take no denial, positively. Let's see, to-day's Thursday. Will you come on Sunday ? We dine at five—don't say no—do."

After a great deal of pressing, Mr. Augustus Minns, driven to despair, accepted the invitation, and promised to be at Poplar Walk on the ensuing Sunday at a quarter before five to the minute.

" Now mind the direction," said Budden ; " the coach goes from the Flower-pot, in Bishopgate Street, every half-hour. When the coach stops at the Swan, you'll see, immediately opposite you, a white house."

" Which is your house—I understand," said Minns, wishing to cut short the visit, and the story, at the same time,

" No, no, that's not mine ; that's Grogus's, the great ironmonger's. I was going to say—you turn down by the side of the white house till you can't go another step further—mind that !—and then you turn to your right, by some stables—well, close to you, you'll see a wall with ' Beware of the Dog ' written on it in large letters—(Minns shuddered)—go along by the side of that wall for about a quarter of a mile—and anybody will show you which is my place."

" Very well—thank ye—good-bye."

" Be punctual."

" Certainly ; good morning."

" I say, Minns, you've got a card."

" Yes, I have ; thank ye." And Mr. Octavius Budden departed, leaving his cousin looking forward to his visit of the following Sunday with the feelings of a penniless poet to the weekly visit of his Scotch landlady.

Sunday arrived ; the sky was bright and clear ; crowds of people were hurrying along the streets, intent on their different schemes of pleasure for the day ; everything and everybody looked cheerful and happy except Mr. Augustus Minns.

The day was fine, but the heat was considerable. When Mr. Minns had fagged up the shady side of Fleet Street, Cheapside, and Threadneedle Street, he had become pretty warm, tolerably dusty, and it was getting late into the bargain. By the most extraordinary good fortune, however, a coach was waiting at the Flower-pot, into which Mr. Augustus Minns got, on the solemn assurance of the cad that the vehicle would start in three minutes—that being the very utmost extremity of time it was allowed to wait by Act of Parliament. A quarter of an hour elapsed, and there were no signs of moving. Minns looked at his watch for the sixth time.

" Coachman, are you going or not ? " bawled Mr. Minns, with his head and half his body out of the coach window.

" Di—rectly, sir," said the coachman, with his hands in his pockets, looking as much unlike a man in a hurry as possible.

" Bill, take them clothes off." Five minutes more elapsed ; at the end of which time the coachman mounted the box, from whence he looked down the street, and up the street, and hailed all the pedestrians for another five minutes.

" Coachman ! if you don't go this moment, I shall get out," said Mr. Minns, rendered desperate by the lateness of the hour, and the impossibility of being in Poplar Walk at the appointed time.

" Going this minute, sir," was the reply ; and, accordingly, the machine trundled on for a couple of hundred yards, and then stopped again. Minns doubled himself up in a corner of the coach, and abandoned himself to his fate, as a child, a mother, a bandbox, and a parasol became his fellow-passengers.

The child was an affectionate and an amiable infant ; the little dear mistook Minns for his other parent, and screamed to embrace him.

" Be quiet, dear," said the mamma, restraining the impetuosity of the darling, whose little fat legs were kicking and stamping, and twining themselves into the most complicated forms in an ecstasy of impatience. " Be quiet, dear, that's not your papa."

" Thank Heaven I am not ! " thought Minns, as the first gleam of pleasure he had experienced that morning shone like a meteor through his wretchedness.

Playfulness was agreeably mingled with affection in the disposition of the boy. When satisfied that Mr. Minns was not his parent, he endeavoured to attract his notice by scraping his drab trousers with his dirty shoes, poking his chest with his mamma's parasol, and other nameless endearments peculiar to infancy, with which he beguiled the tediousness of the ride, apparently very much to his own satisfaction.

When the unfortunate gentleman arrived at the Swan, he found, to his great dismay, that it was a quarter-past five. The white house, the stables, the " Beware of the Dog " —every landmark was passed with a rapidity not unusual to a gentleman of a certain age when too late for dinner. After the lapse of a few minutes, Mr. Minns found himself opposite a yellow brick house with a green door, brass knocker and doorplate, green window frames and ditto railings, with " a garden " in front—that is to say, a small loose bit of gravelled ground, with one round and two scalene triangular beds, containing a fir tree, twenty or thirty bulbs, and an unlimited number of marigolds. The taste of Mr. and Mrs. Budden was further displayed by the appearance of a Cupid on each side of the door, perched upon a heap of large chalk flints, variegated with pink conch-shells. His knock at the door was answered by a stumpy boy in drab livery, cotton stockings, and high-lows, who, after hanging his hat on one of the dozen brass pegs which ornamented the passage, denominated by courtesy, The Hall, ushered him into a front drawing-room, commanding a very extensive view of the backs of the neighbouring houses. The usual ceremony of introduction, and so forth, over, Mr. Minns took his seat—not a little agitated at finding that he was the last comer, and, somehow or other, the Lion of about a dozen people, sitting together in a small drawing-room, getting rid of that most tedious of all time, the time preceding dinner.

" Well, Brogson," said Budden, addressing an elderly gentleman in a black coat, drab knee breeches, and long gaiters, who, under pretence of inspecting the prints in an Annual, had been engaged in satisfying himself on the subject of Mr. Minn's general appearance, by looking at him over the tops of the leaves—" well, Brogson, what do Ministers mean to do ? Will they go out, or what ? "

" Oh !—why—really, you know, I'm the last person in the world to ask for news. Your cousin, from his situation is the most likely person to answer the question."

Mr. Minns assured the last speaker that, although he was in Somerset House, he possessed no official communication relative to the project of His Majesty's Ministers. But his remark was evidently received incredulously ; and no further conjectures being hazarded on the subject, a long pause ensued, during which the company occupied themselves in coughing and blowing their noses, until the entrance of Mrs. Budden caused a general rise.

The ceremony of introduction being over, dinner was announced, and downstairs the party proceeded accordingly—Mr. Minns escorting Mrs. Budden as far as the drawing-room door, but being prevented, by the narrowness of the staircase, from extending his gallantry any farther. The dinner passed off as such dinners usually do. Ever and anon, amidst the clatter of knives and forks, and the hum of conversation, Mr. B.'s voice might be heard, asking a friend to take wine, and assuring him he was glad to see him ; and a great deal of by-play took place between Mrs. B. and the servants, respecting the removal of the dishes, during which her countenance assumed all the variations of a weather-glass, from " stormy " to " set fair."

Upon the dessert and wine being placed on the table, the servant, in compliance with a significant look from Mrs. B., brought down " Master Alexander," habited in a sky-blue suit with silver buttons ; and possessing hair of nearly the same colour as the metal. After sundry praises from his mother, and various admonitions as to his behaviour from his father, he was introduced to his godfather.

" Well, my little fellow—you are a fine boy, ain't you ? " said Mr. Minns, as happy as a tomtit on birdlime.

" Yes."

" How old are you ? "

" Eight, next We'nsday. How old are *you* ? "

" Alexander," interrupted his mother, " how dare you ask Mr. Minns how old he is ? "

" He asked me how old *I* was," said the precocious child, to whom Minns had from that moment internally resolved that he never would bequeath one shilling. As soon as the titter occasioned by the observation had subsided, a little smirking man with red whiskers, sitting at the bottom of the table,

*" I'm eight next Wednesday. How old are you ? "*

who during the whole of dinner had been endeavouring to obtain a listener to some stories about Sheridan, called out, with a very patronising air, " Alick, what part of speech is *be ? *"

" A verb."

" That's a good boy," said Mrs. Budden, with all a mother's pride. " Now, you know what a verb is ? "

" A verb is a word which signifies to be, to do, or to suffer ; as, I am—I rule—I am ruled. Give me an apple, ma."

" I'll give you an apple," replied the man with the red whiskers, who was an established friend of the family, or, in other words, was always invited by Mrs. Budden, whether Mr. Budden liked it or not, " if you'll tell me what is the meaning of *be*."

" Be ? " said the prodigy, after a little hesitation. " An insect that gathers honey."

" No, dear," frowned Mrs. Budden ; " B double E is the substantive."

" I don't think he knows much yet about *common* substantives," said the smirking gentleman, who thought this an admirable opportunity for letting off a joke. " It's clear he's not very well acquainted with *proper names*. He ! he ! he ! "

" Gentlemen," called out Mr. Budden, from the end of the table, in a stentorian voice, and with a very important air, " will you have the goodness to charge your glasses ? I have a toast to propose."

" Hear ! hear ! " cried the gentlemen, passing the decanters. After they had made the round of the table, Mr. Budden proceeded—" Gentlemen, there is an individual present——"

" Hear ! hear ! " said the little man with red whiskers.

"*Pray* be quiet, Jones," remonstrated Budden.

"I say, gentlemen, there is an individual present," resumed the host, "in whose society I am sure we must take great delight—and—and—the conversation of that individual must have afforded to every one present the utmost pleasure." ("Thank Heaven, he does not mean me!" thought Minns, conscious that his diffidence and exclusiveness had prevented his saying above a dozen words since he entered the house.) "Gentlemen, I am but a humble individual myself, and I perhaps ought to apologise for allowing any individual feelings of friendship and affection for the person I allude to, to induce me to venture to rise, to propose the health of that person—a person that I am sure—that is to say, a person whose virtues must endear him to those who know him—and those who have not the pleasure of knowing him cannot dislike him."

"Hear! hear!" said the company, in a tone of encouragement and approval.

"Gentlemen," continued Budden, "my cousin is a man who—who is a relation of my own." (Hear! hear!) Minns groaned audibly. "Who I am most happy to see here, and who, if he were not here, would certainly have deprived us of the great pleasure we all feel in seeing him. (Loud cries of hear!) Gentlemen, I feel that I have already trespassed on your attention for too long a time. With every feeling—of—with every sentiment of—of——"

"Gratification," suggested a friend of the family.

"—Of gratification, I beg to propose the health of Mr. Minns."

"Standing, gentlemen!" shouted the indefatigable little man with the whiskers—"and with the honours. Take your time from me, if you please. Hip! hip! hip!—Za!—Hip! hip! hip!—Za!—Hip! hip!—Za—a—a!"

All eyes were now fixed on the subject of the toast, who, by gulping down port wine at the imminent hazard of suffocation, endeavoured to conceal his confusion. After as long a pause as decency would admit, he rose, but, as the newspapers sometimes say in their reports, "we regret that we were quite unable to give even the substance of the honourable gentleman's observations." The words "present company—honour—present occasion," and "great happiness"—heard occasionally, and repeated at intervals, with a countenance expressive of the utmost confusion and misery, convinced the company that he was making an excellent speech; and, accordingly, on his resuming his seat, they cried "Bravo!" and manifested tumultuous applause. Jones, who had been long watching his opportunity, then darted up.

"Budden," said he, "will you allow *me* to propose a toast?"

"Certainly," replied Budden, adding, in an undertone to Minns right across the table, "Devilish sharp fellow that; you'll be very much pleased with his speech. He talks equally well on any subject." Minns bowed, and Mr. Jones proceeded :—

"It has on several occasions, in various instances, under many circumstances, and in different companies, fallen to my lot to propose a toast to those by whom, at the time, I have had the honour to be surrounded. I have sometimes, I will cheerfully own—for why should I deny it?—felt the overwhelming nature of the task I have undertaken, and my own utter incapability to do justice to the subject. If such have been my feelings, however, on former occasions, what must they be now—now—under the extraordinary circumstances in which I am placed ! (Hear ! hear !) To describe my feelings accurately would be impossible ; but I cannot give you a better idea of them, gentlemen, than by referring to a circumstance which happens, oddly enough, to occur to my mind at the moment. On one occasion, when that truly great and illustrious man, Sheridan, was——"

Now, there is no knowing what new villainy in the form of a joke would have been heaped on the grave of that very ill-used man, Mr. Sheridan, if the boy in drab had not at that moment entered the room in a breathless state, to report that, as it was a very wet night, the nine o'clock stage had come round, to know whether there was anybody going to town, as, in that case, he (the nine o'clock) had room for one inside.

Mr. Minns started up ; and, despite countless exclamations of surprise and entreaties to stay, persisted in his determination to accept the vacant place. But the brown silk umbrella was nowhere to be found; and as the coachman couldn't wait, he drove back to the Swan, leaving word for Mr. Minns to " run round " and catch him. However, as it did not occur to Mr. Minns, for some ten minutes or so, that he had left the brown silk umbrella with the ivory handle in the other coach, coming down ; and, moreover, as he was by no means remarkable for speed, it is no matter of surprise that, when he accomplished the feat of " running round " to the Swan, the coach—the last coach—had gone without him.

It was somewhere about three o'clock in the morning when Mr. Augustus Minns knocked feebly at the street door of his lodgings in Tavistock Street, cold, wet, cross, and miserable. He made his will next morning, and his professional man informs us, in that strict confidence in which we inform the public, that neither the name of Mr. Octavius Budden, nor of Mrs. Amelia Budden, nor of Master Alexander Augustus Budden, appears therein.

---

# RING O' ROSES

### *by* W. GRAHAM ROBERTSON

HUSH a while, my darling, for the long day closes,
   Nodding into slumber on the blue hill's crest ;
See the little clouds play " Ring a ring o' roses,"
   Planting fairy gardens in the red-rose west.

Greet him for us cloudlets, say we're not forgetting
   Golden gifts of sunshine, merry hours of play ;
Ring a ring o' roses round the sweet sun's setting,
   Spread a bed of roses for the dear dead day.

Hush-a-bye, my little one, the dear day dozes,
   Doffed his crown of kingship and his fair flag furled ;
While the earth and sky play ring a ring o' roses,
   Ring a ring o' roses round the rose-red world.

# FORTUNE TELLING

## *by* MARY RUSSELL MITFORD

E have few gipsies in our neighbourhood. In spite of our tempting green lanes, our woody dells and healthy commons, the rogues don't take to us. I am afraid that we are too civilised, too cautious ; that our sheepfolds are too close watched ; our barnyards too well guarded ; our game and ducks too fastly penned ; our chickens too securely locked up ; our little pigs too safe in their sty ; our game too scarce ; our laundresses too careful. In short, we are too little primitive : we have a snug brood of vagabonds and poachers of our own, to say nothing of their regular followers, constables and justices of the peace : we have stocks in the village, and a treadmill in the next town ; and therefore we go gipsyless—a misfortune of which every landscape painter, and every lover of that living landscape, the country, can appreciate the extent. There is nothing under the sun that harmonises so well with nature, especially in her woodland recesses, as that picturesque people, who are, so to say, the wild genus—the pheasants and roebucks of the human race.

Sometimes, indeed, we used to see a gipsy procession passing along the common, like an eastern caravan, men, women, and children, donkeys and dogs ; and sometimes a patch of bare earth, strewed with ashes and surrounded with scathed turf, on the broad green margin of some cross-road, would give token of a gipsy halt ; but a regular gipsy encampment has always been so rare an event, that I was equally surprised and delighted to meet with one in the course of my walks last autumn, particularly as the party was of the most innocent description, quite free from those tall, dark, lean, Spanish-looking men, who it must be confessed, with all my predilection for the caste, are rather startling to meet when alone in an unfrequented path : and a path more solitary than that into which the beauty of a bright October morning had tempted me could not well be imagined. . . .

In this lonely place (for the mansion to which the park belongs has long been uninhabited) I first saw our gipsies. They had pitched their tent under one of the oak trees, perhaps from a certain dim sense of natural beauty, which those who live with nature in the fields are seldom totally without ; perhaps because the neighbourhood of the coppices, and of the deserted hall, was favourable to the acquisition of game, and of the little fuel which their hardy habits required. The party consisted only of four—an old crone, in a tattered red cloak and black bonnet, who was stooping over a kettle, of which the contents were probably as savoury as that of Meg Merrilies, renowned in story ; a pretty black-eyed girl, at work under the trees ; a sunburnt urchin of eight or nine, collecting sticks and dead leaves to feed their out-of-door fire, and a slender lad two or three years older, who lay basking in the sun, with a couple of shabby dogs, of the sort called mongrel, in all the joy of idleness, whilst a grave, patient donkey stood grazing hardby. It was a pretty picture, with its soft autumnal sky, its rich woodiness, its sunshine, its verdure, the light smoke curling from the fire, and the group disposed around it so harmless, poor outcasts ! and so happy—a beautiful picture ! I stood gazing on it till I was half-ashamed to look longer, and came away half-afraid that they should depart before I could see them again.

This fear I soon found to be groundless. The old gipsy was a celebrated fortune-teller, and the post having been so long vacant, she could not have brought her talents to a better market. The whole village rang with the predictions of this modern Cassandra—unlike her Trojan predecessor, inasmuch as her prophecies were never of evil. I myself could not help admiring the real cleverness, the genuine gipsy tact with which she adapted her foretellings to the age, the habits, and the known desires and circumstances of her clients.

To our little pet, Lizzy, for instance, a damsel of seven, she predicted a fairing ; to Ben Kirby, a youth of thirteen, head batter of the boys, a new cricket-ball ; to Ben's sister Lucy, a girl some three years his senior, and just promoted to that ensign of womanhood, a cap, she promised a pink top-knot ; whilst for Miss Sophia Matthews, our old-maidish schoolmistress, who would be heartily glad to be a girl again, she foresaw one handsome husband, and for the smart widow Simmons, two. These were the least of her triumphs. George Davis, the dashing young farmer of the hill-house, a gay sportsman, who scoffed at fortune-tellers and matrimony, consulted her as to whose greyhound would win the courser's cup at the beacon meeting : to which she replied, that she did not know to whom the dog would belong, but that the winner of the cup would be a white greyhound, with one blue ear, and a spot on its side, being an exact description of Mr. George Davis's favourite Helen, who followed her master's steps like his shadow, and was standing behind him at this very instant. This prediction gained our gipsy half a crown. . . .

No wonder that all the world—that is to say, all our world—were crazy to have their fortunes told—to enjoy the pleasure of hearing from such un-doubted authority that what they wished to be should be. Amongst the most eager to take a peep into futurity was our pretty maid Harriet, although her desire took the not unusual form of disclaimer—" Nothing should induce her to have her fortune told, nothing upon earth ! She never thought of the gipsy, not she ! " and, to prove the fact, she said so at least twenty times a day. Now Harriet's fortune seemed told already ; her destiny was fixed. She, the belle of the village, was engaged, as everybody knows, to our village beau, Joel Brent ; they were only waiting for a little more money to marry ; and as Joel was already head carter to our head farmer, and had some prospect of a bailiff's place, their union did not appear very distant. But Harriet, besides being a beauty, was a coquette, and her affecton for her betrothed

*There stood the gipsy, in the very act of palmistry.*

did not interfere with certain flirtations which came in like Isabella, " by the by," and occasionally cast a shadow of coolness between the lovers, which, however, Joel's cleverness and good humour generally contrived to chase away. There had probably been a little fracas in the present instance, for at the end of one of her daily professions of unfaith in gipsies and their predictions, she added, " that none but fools did believe them ; that Joel had had his fortune told, and wanted to treat her to a prophecy—but she was not such a simpleton."

About an hour after the delivery of this speech, I happened, in tying up a chrysanthemum, to go to our woodyard for a stick of proper dimensions, and there, enclosed between the faggot pile and the coal shed, stood the gipsy, in the very act of palmistry, conning the lines of fate in Harriet's hand. Never was a stronger contrast than that between the old withered sibyl, dark as an Egyptian, with bright laughing eyes, and an expression of keen humour under all her affected solemnity, and our village beauty, tall and plump and fair, blooming as a rose, and simple as a dove. She was listening too intently to see me, but the fortune-teller did, and stopped so suddenly that her attention was awakened, and the intruder discovered.

Harriet at first meditated a denial. She called up a pretty innocent unconcerned look; answered my silence (for I never spoke a word) by muttering something about "coals for the parlour"; and catching up my new-painted green watering-pot, instead of the coal-scuttle, began filling it with all her might, to the unspeakable discomfiture of that useful utensil, on which the dingy dust stuck like birdlime—and of her own clean apron, which exhibited a curious interchange of black and green on a white ground. During the process of filling the watering-pot, Harriet made divers signs to the gipsy to decamp. The old sibyl, however, budged not a foot, influenced probably by two reasons—one, the hope of securing a customer in the new-comer, whose appearance is generally, I am afraid, the very reverse of dignified, rather merry than wise; the other, a genuine fear of passing through the yard-gate, on the outside of which a much more imposing person, my greyhound Mayflower, who has a sort of beadle instinct anent drunkards and pilferers, and disorderly persons of all sorts, stood barking most furiously. . . .

Of course, Harriet was exposed to some raillery, and a good deal of questioning about her future fate, as to which she preserved an obstinate but evidently satisfied silence. At the end of three days, however—my readers are, I hope, learned enough in gipsy lore to know, that unless kept secret for three entire days, no prediction can come true—at the end of three days, when all the family except herself had forgotten the story, our pretty soubrette, half-bursting with the long retention, took the opportunity of lacing on my new half-boots to reveal the prophecy. "She was to see within the week, and this was Saturday, the young man, the real young man, whom she was to marry."—" Why, Harriet, you know poor Joel."—" Joel, indeed! the gipsy said that the young man, the real young man, was to ride up to the house dressed in a dark greatcoat (and Joel never wore a greatcoat in his life—all the world knew that he wore smock-frocks and jackets), and mounted on a white horse—and where should Joel get a white horse?"—" Had this real young man made his appearance yet?"—" No; there had not been a white horse past the place since Tuesday; so it must certainly be to-day."

A good look-out did Harriet keep for white horses during this fateful Saturday, and plenty did she see. It was the market-day at B., and team after team came by with one, two, and three white horses; cart after cart, and gig after gig, each with a white steed: Colonel M.'s carriage, with its prancing pair—but still no horseman. At length one appeared; but he had a greatcoat whiter than the animal he rode; another, but he was old farmer Lewington, a married man; a third, but he was little Lord L., a schoolboy, on his Arabian pony. Besides, they all passed the house; and as the day wore on, Harriet began, alternately, to possess her old infidelity on the score of fortune-telling, and to let out certain apprehensions that, if the gipsy did really possess the power of foreseeing events, and no such horseman arrived, she might possibly be unlucky enough to die an old maid—a fate for which, although the proper destiny of a coquette, our village beauty seemed to entertain a very decided aversion.

At last, at dusk, just as Harriet, making believe to close our casement shutters, was taking her last peep up the road, something white appeared in the distance coming leisurely down the hill. Was it really a horse? Was it not rather Titus Strong's cow driving home to milking? A minute or two dissipated that fear; it certainly was a horse, and as certainly it had a dark rider. Very slowly he descended the hill, pausing most provokingly at the end of the village, as if about to turn up the Vicarage lane. He came on, however, and after another short stop at the Rose, rode up full to our little gate, and catching Harriet's hand as she was opening the wicket, displayed to the half-pleased, half-angry damsel, the smiling triumphant face of her own Joel Brent, equipped in a new greatcoat, and mounted on his master's newly-purchased market nag. Oh, Joel! Joel! The gipsy! The gipsy!

# THE CHRISTMAS TREE

*by* ISABEL DE SAVITZKY

WITH spangles gay and candle light
And many toys, our tree is bright.
And gold and silver birds there are:
While over all there hangs a star.

The toys are given first of all.
For me a doll, for Hugh a ball.
The spangle stuff is pulled about.
The candles are then all put out.

The tree now strip't is dark and bare,
But still the star is shining there
As shone the star the shepherds saw,
Who heard the angels song of yore.

The star that was a guiding light,
To kings and shepherds, through the night
Where patient oxen calm and mild,
Shared their bed with Mary's Child.

Christmas night is our Saviour's birth.
Joy in Heaven, and Peace on earth.
This was the story Mummy told me,
As she hung the star on our Christmas Tree.

# LORD GARLING'S WIG

*by*

## H. G. PROCTOR

### I

OM MERRIMAN leapt to his feet, surprise and guilt in his eyes. His hands dropped the apples he had been stuffing into his pockets and he turned to face his captor. There was no one to be seen. "Yo ho, you villain, I have you!" He had heard the words distinctly enough and the voice had been that of the squire himself. He was more afraid of Sir George Manson than of all his gardeners and other servants put together. Sir George was no man to be trifled with.

"Now through your gizzard! Guard yourself, fool."

The boy heaved a sigh of relief. The squire was the other side of the high wall which bounded the orchard. By the sound of things, he was fighting a duel in the stableyard. Tom ran towards the wall.

It was a mad thing to do; for by all the rules of caution he should have been running in the opposite direction, the way he had come. Unlike his father, the new squire seemed to resent even the presence of any but his own servants within a hundred yards of the house, and it was not nice to think what he might do to an orchard robber. Yet none of the tenants had any cause to complain of the way the young squire treated them in the way of business.

Who Sir George could be fighting was not to be guessed. Curiosity and a desire to watch the duel sent Tom up a large old tree which threw a branch over the wall. Here was a chance of excitement not to be missed.

The lad, one of the village youngsters and not yet fourteen years old, crawled out along the branch. He got a shock with his first glimpse over the wall. There was nobody in the yard but Sir George alone, and he was dancing about in front of a stable door, every now and again jabbing his sword into the wood. Leaves, however, still interfered with a clear view and some more edging along the branch was necessary.

Tom gasped. Chalked on the stable door was the rough outline of a man, and it was this that the squire was punishing so severely. But it was not merely the sight of a respectable gentleman amusing himself with sword practice which was startling. The chalked figure had been provided with a full-bottomed wig after the fashion of those times, a long pipe and an eyeglass. There could be no possible doubt that it was meant to represent Lord Garling of Anster, whose house and estate were three miles away over the hill.

Once more the sword bit into the stable door, dead in the centre of his lordship's wig. Sir George gave an audible sigh of satisfaction, withdrew his weapon and turned round. His eye met Tom's.

Which of the two was the more embarrassed it would be difficult to say. The apples were forgotten. The squire of Shepfield, who had a reputation for being cold, aloof, austere, had been caught in his shirt-sleeves, dancing about like a youngster and wreaking vengeance on a figure of his neighbour. What on earth he would do, Tom could not imagine. He felt acutely miserable.

*Sir George was dancing about in front of a stable door.*

Retreat was useless. The squire, little though he appeared among them, knew all the villagers by name and had already recognised him.

"Tom Merriman, come here." The command was quiet but like ice on the back, and the speaker's grey eyes were glinting hardly.

Miserably Tom edged himself a bit farther along the branch till he could transfer his weight to the wall; then, swinging his legs over and turning on his stomach, he held on to the top for a second with his fingers and let himself drop. He half-expected to feel a point of steel pierce him as he descended, but his fate was postponed. He picked himself up and turned to see the squire standing with his right foot on a mounting-block, his sword hand resting on his knee.

He felt scared but knew it was no use showing it. Besides, the reputation for reckless courage which he held among his cronies was at stake. He faced Sir George boldly.

Sir George raised an eyebrow and quizzed him, but there was little sign of mercy about his mouth.

"At least you seem to possess a certain courage," he said at last, "even if you haven't honesty." And lifting his sword he prodded it into the top of a bulging pocket and drew it out with an apple spitted on the point. A flick of the wrist sent the apple flying over the wall.

"Now, since what you were doing is plain, young man, will you kindly say what you think I was doing when you had the misfortune to look over the wall."

Tom gulped awkwardly and then with a sudden astounding boldness spoke his mind so that the squire dropped his foot and stood bolt upright, looking at the boy with amazement.

"Practising to kill the Queen's friends and put the Pretender on the throne, like all the rest in these parts, if I make no mistake, Sir George."

Once spoken, all his courage seemed to ebb immediately, and he dropped his eyes and had to bite his lip to stop it trembling. Utterly wretched but for the thought that he had spoken like a loyal subject, he waited for the avalanche that was surely about to fall on his head.

Slowly Tom looked up again. Sir George was standing right over him, but his expression was less forbidding than it had been a few moments before. " Did I hear you aright ? " He spoke slowly. " Are you for Queen Anne and the Settlement, Tom Merriman ? "

Tom nodded, wondering what was coming.

" Methinks, then, I have a use for you. Come back again to-night and come secretly. You shall learn who is the Queen's friend, and why my sword must learn to strike accurately. Now get away quickly and tell nobody what you have seen me doing."

## II

At ten minutes to six that evening Tom Merriman was crouched in some bushes near the boundary wall of the hall grounds. Since Sir George had bidden him come secretly, he had avoided the iron gates on the road. The sun was just setting as he looked over the neighbouring fields to make sure he was unobserved. Then, with an agility which would have made the builder of the wall lose hope, he was over and in the orchard where he had been before.

He saw the pile of apples he had emptied from his pockets after leaving the squire a few hours ago. Although nothing else had been said about them, he had felt no wish to take them away after their brief but thrilling conversation.

Sir George Manson was for the Queen, even as he was himself, in this countryside hotbed of traitors ! There had been no doubt about it ; the sudden softening in those cold eyes and the look of relief on that thin, rather long face.

Almost the whole village was for Prince James and his foreign friends, blind to all that would follow from his rise to the English throne. It was said openly that the new squire was also one of his supporters ; indeed this was given as a reason why he kept himself so much to himself. Tom, on the other hand, had always flaunted his loyalty and had had many a fight and hard knock for it. It seemed too good to be true that the stern young squire was really one of his friends, also for the established rule.

Making his way round the house, he eventually came out through a shrubbery on the open gravel space near the front door. His hand took hold of the bell-rope of Shepfield Hall with far more misgivings than he had ever felt when grabbing at its apples. But the door opened before he could ring and a cracked voice bade him enter.

He stepped round the half-opened door and confronted the old, bent manservant who had served with Sir George's father for more years than most men could remember. This person led the way down the hall, and opening a door at the far end, ushered Tom inside.

At a table in a long, low, half-panelled room sat Sir George and another man whom Tom did not recognise. The stranger was strikingly handsome, a circumstance which made the boy quite forget his nervousness. They both jumped up as Tom entered, and it was the stranger who spoke.

"So this is your assistant for to-night's escapade, eh, Manson? He looks young for the work."

Sir George laughed. Here at home he seemed a much jollier man than outside, Tom thought.

"A boy is less likely to be noticed, your Grace. Besides, he is well practised at trespassing. You should see him get over walls." And turning to Tom he finished : "You may find your accomplishment useful to-night, my lad, if you are not afraid to do as I tell you."

"If it is for the Queen, Sir George, I'll promise you to do my best in any way you ask," said Tom.

"Spoken like a man," laughed the stranger. "By jove, Manson, I believe you've chosen your companion well."

"There are, alas, few enough in these parts to choose from," was the bitter reply. "The whole countryside is a hotbed of revolution. But to business," and he turned to Tom.

"Young Merriman, I shall ask you to take no oath of loyalty, though your defection from our cause to-night might have disastrous results for England. I believe I can trust you implicitly ? "

"You can, sir, indeed. I got this cut over my eye for not loving Prince James," he added proudly.

Both men smiled but the stranger was listening intently. "So he is bearing out what you have said about this district, Sir George. I begin to think you have more reasons for your actions and your expedition of to-night than I had supposed."

"That we shall yet see, your Grace," the squire answered. "And now, Tom. You recognised, I expect, whom my poor art had attempted to portray on my stable door this morning ? "

"If I mistake not, Sir George "—Tom suppressed a grin at the memory —"it was the Viscount Garling."

"Yes. I would like to ask you, seeing that you are so well acquainted with the feeling of the countryside, have you ever heard his lordship's name mentioned in connection with any plot on behalf of Prince James ? "

Tom saw that both his companions were watching him narrowly. "Never, sir. I have always understood that Lord Garling speaks loudly for the Queen and that it is unwise so much as to mention the Prince and his Frenchmen in his presence."

"H'm ! Now I feel not so sure you are right in your suspicions, Manson," intervened the stranger. "Still, this may be only his cunning. I will stay here till the boy returns. If you are wrong in your strange idea, I cannot promise to wait for you yourself." He got up and walked to the window. "You may not return alive. His lordship is one of the finest swordsmen in the country."

Sir George also jumped to his feet and banged the table with his fist. "Garling will undo himself in his cups. A man who can remain sober must surely get the better of one who cannot. But if I am wrong, it will seem no more than a fool's prank such as he often plays himself. Come on, lad, we must be going. The horses are waiting for us. I suspect our neighbour of treason and we are going to pay him a visit. Your part will be to wait outside a window I will show you. Whatever I send through that window seize and with all the speed you can summon bring it back here to his Grace of Marlborough, who will await you."

## III

IT was nearly dark when the two horsemen rode down the hill towards Anster Castle, but the early autumn night was warm and still. Merriman tethered his horse in a small copse just outside the park and slipped unobserved over the wall and across to the garden. Sir George rode boldly in at the main gates and up to the front door of the house. Tom saw the door opened and watched him step inside.

Lord Garling was, according to his nightly custom when at home, entertaining several congenial spirits in his large dining-room, which, situated at a corner of the house, was lighted by four mullioned windows. Two of these were open to cool the heads which were already growing heated within. Tom, acting on his instructions, went cautiously to one which was approached by some ornamental bushes, and having settled down as well as he could, found himself with a better view of the interior than he had hoped.

The arrival of the neighbouring squire from Shepfield had been hailed boisterously. Sir George Manson had already visited Anster several times since he had come into his inheritance, and indeed before, though he had no love for the florid, burly, hard-drinking viscount.

Lord Garling, for all his red face and broad shoulders, was renowned as a dandy. Tom could see him now, sitting not far from the window where he was waiting, dressed in a coat of royal blue, magnificently embroidered down its open front. On his head was the wig which was his special pride, a glossy black, cunningly flecked with silver.

Dinner had been cleared away and the company sat round a mahogany table, apparently intent on starting a carouse.

"Make room for another," roared the host, though without rising to greet his guest. "You come well, Sir George; the bigger the company, the louder the laughter." But some of those present, Tom noticed, looked askance at the newcomer and one whispered behind his hand to the man who sat next to him.

For over an hour, however, it seemed Sir George was as bent on enjoying himself as all the rest. His grey eyes gleamed and laughed in a way that would have surprised his own tenants had they seen him. Glasses were filled and emptied; though the observant watcher did not fail to notice that the latest arrival was in reality drinking hardly anything at all. For all that, he was making as much noise as any of them.

An hour and a half passed and Tom was feeling stiff and numb. Moreover, the night was getting cooler and he was afraid some one inside might notice the change and shut the windows; though he knew his fellow-patriot would loudly demand air if such a contingency befell. But at last things began to happen.

His lordship, by now in an expansive frame of mind, rose to make a speech. There was no trace of unsteadiness about his redoubtable figure and his voice came harsh and strong. It would have been a dangerous speech for a man to make who felt less sure of his company.

At first circumspectly, then more and more openly as he heard his hearers laughing and applauding, he began to belittle the Queen and her advisers. A reference to the Duke of Marlborough drew forth jeering and merriment; while allusions to friends across the sea were signals for glasses to be raised and healths drunk. Sir George was raising his glass with the others but no wine was passing his lips. Yet still he did nothing. Plainly by now, if any had had doubts, all thought him to be of their own way of thinking.

*Back went his chair with a crash.*

After a while the speaker sat down and the conversation turned to people nearer home. Insults and gibes could be heard, and it was one of these which the squire of Shepfield seized for his opportunity, some ill-timed jest about his own kinsmen which might naturally have brought any man to his feet. Back went his chair with a crash and with blazing eyes he demanded an apology from the flushed, ill-mannered dandy who was still laughing at his own sally.

Lord Garling remained seated but his face sobered and his eyes hardened dangerously. "How now, you fool; can you not take a joke?" he rasped.

"I can take a joke as well as any man," replied the other, still apparently in hot blood, "but I will not sit quietly under an insult to my house." And with this he drew his sword from its sheath.

There was a hubbub on the instant. But the company was not in a state of quick understanding, and in spite of their cries, a moment or two had elapsed before any one else was on his feet, and in these few seconds Sir George had done his business. It was apparently no more than a return insult of challenge and contempt.

His sword gleamed in the light of the candles, leapt forward and neatly speared his lordship's magnificent wig above the forehead. Up it came from its owner's half-bald cranium and then with a swirl of the weapon went flying towards the open window where Tom Merriman waited. For a moment it spread over the sill and then slipped down into the laurels.

## IV

Tom waited to see no more. He heard the uproar which immediately broke out within the house and the sound of a door hastily opened. He grabbed the wig and hared off with it, avoiding the open lawn and keeping in the shelter of bushes and shrubberies till he was far enough from the house not to be seen in the darkness.

He found his horse, a little brown mare, where he had left her, and with a tug on his highwayman's hitch and a leap into the saddle, he had her out of the sheltering copse and on to the rough road to Shepfield.

The cries of bewilderment and exasperation from those who were searching the laurels for the precious wig came faintly to him as he rode away, and turning in his saddle he could see the flare of their torches across the park. No one had guessed the existence of an accomplice to Sir George, and he laughed aloud as he thought how more and more angry they would get as their search proved fruitless.

His brow clouded, however, as he thought of Sir George. The squire might find it difficult to escape from his furious host and his cronies. He would much have liked to have turned back and gone to his help. But he had his orders and knew that he was playing a part in a game much bigger than the lives of the players.

He touched the mare with his heels; for a light was beginning to come into the sky and the road showed like three narrow ribbons on the ground— two ruts and the centre path. After a mile the moon appeared and the game little animal increased her speed as she saw her way more clearly.

This was the life for a man, thought Tom. Riding alone and at night on the Queen's business, with no less a personage than the great Duke of Marlborough waiting his coming. He had not yet got over the shock of hearing the name of the handsome, pleasant-mannered stranger. It must be matter of the highest importance.

After a while he left the road, jumping the hedge where it was low, and in one last gallop covered the short cut across the fields and came to the rear of Shepfield Hall.

He found grooms waiting ready to lead his horse to the stables. The old manservant who had opened the front door to him a few hours before appeared again silently as if from nowhere and conducted him into the house. He was taken at once to the long, half-panelled room.

The duke was there and rose as he entered. Tom swept him a bow that might have made a lesser man smile. The duke returned it courteously and advanced to meet him.

"You have been successful?" he exclaimed; and then, seeing the wig in Tom's hand, "Ah, yes! You have brought the trophy. You shall assist me at the skinning."

If Tom had been in the dark up to now over the precise significance of Lord Garling's wig, his mystification was fully resolved during the next few minutes.

"For the sake of his reputation as a gentleman it is to be hoped our friend George Manson has made no mistake," said the duke, drawing a plain but very useful knife from beneath his coat.

Then, sitting down, he began to perform the most careful surgical operations on that expensive creation of a fashionable foreign wig-maker in London on whom his lordship frequently called.

First he felt the lining with his fingers and Tom heard him draw in his breath sharply as he did so. Then very carefully he began to rip the lining away round its edges. Lifting it, several sheets of paper, closely written upon, were exposed to view. They were none too flat, as was to be expected from their hiding-place, but the duke smoothed them out.

"Bring the candle closer, boy. Ha! Methinks your young squire is by no means such a fool as I was at one time inclined to think. By Jupiter, no! Look at this."

Tom bent forward and looked at the papers the duke was scanning with an intense, almost fierce expression. His lips were tight-set and his eyebrows drawn down.

"The traitor!" he exploded. "Full, and what is more, accurate descriptions of this country's affairs both civil and military. All of the utmost value to the French in their war with our country. What's this?" His finger followed the writing and he read aloud: "'I can vouch for the loyalty of many of the common folk of this country to Prince James should he choose to essay a landing.'"

His Grace stood upright and looked down at his young companion. "Tom Merriman, you have done your Queen and country a great service to-night. Let us hope the master of this house will come home safely to attend to your future."

Even as he spoke the door of the room opened and Sir George Manson strode in looking somewhat dishevelled.

"Were my suspicions well founded, your Grace?" He asked the question in obvious excitement, oblivious to all else but the answer.

"They were; only too well." The duke handed him the papers. "You managed to get away then?"

"There was a bit of an upset but they had more thought for the wig than for me. I managed to get out in the hubbub and to my horse." The squire turned to the boy who had helped him and held out his hand. "You shall hear more of this, Tom Merriman."

"So shall Lord Garling," observed the duke grimly.